The Lakota raced to their chief's aid

The steady blasterfire from Ryan's friends converged on the warriors, and he glimpsed a bare-chested man jerk and stagger backward, a crimson arterial spray jetting from a severed carotid.

Behind him, over the thunderous noise, Ryan heard Krysty cry out in pain and surprise. Instinctively his head turned in that direction.

He saw Krysty, her back against the curving cavern wall, slowly sliding toward the floor of the walkway. Her hand was pressed against her chest, just below her left breast. A feathered shaft jutted between splayed fingers. She kept her hand there as she eased into a sitting position, as though she were trying to catch the blood.

For an instant their eyes met, hers showing a dull green in the throbbing bright green glow of the cave.

Ryan saw death in them.

JAMES AXLER

DEATH LANDS.

Demons of Eden

A GOLD EAGLE BOOK FROM
WORLDWIDE.

TORONTO • NEW YORK • LONDON
AMSTERDAM • PARIS • SYDNEY • HAMBURG
STOCKHOLM • ATHENS • TOKYO • MILAN
MADRID • WARSAW • BUDAPEST • AUCKLAND

For Melissa and Jim Mooney—
Artists and sacred warriors of the circle

First edition May 1997

ISBN 0-373-62537-5

DEMONS OF EDEN

Printed in U.S.A.

Nothing lives long,
Only the earth and the mountains.
                        —Death song of White Antelope,
                        Cheyenne war chief

THE DEATHLANDS SAGA

This world is their legacy, a world born in the violent nuclear spasm of 2001 that was the bitter outcome of a struggle for global dominance.

There is no real escape from this shockscape where life always hangs in the balance, vulnerable to newly demonic nature, barbarism, lawlessness.

But they are the warrior survivalists, and they endure—in the way of the lion, the hawk and the tiger, true to nature's heart despite its ruination.

Ryan Cawdor: The privileged son of an East Coast baron. Acquainted with betrayal from a tender age, he is a master of the hard realities.

Krysty Wroth: Harmony ville's own Titian-haired beauty, a woman with the strength of tempered steel. Her premonitions and Gaia powers have been fostered by her Mother Sonja.

J. B. Dix, the Armorer: Weapons master and Ryan's close ally, he, too, honed his skills traversing the Deathlands with the legendary Trader.

Doctor Theophilus Tanner: Torn from his family and a gentler life in 1896, Doc has been thrown into a future he couldn't have imagined.

Dr. Mildred Wyeth: Her father was killed by the Ku Klux Klan, but her fate is not much lighter. Restored from predark cryogenic suspension, she brings twentieth-century healing skills to a nightmare.

Jak Lauren: A true child of the wastelands, reared on adversity, loss and danger, the albino teenager is a fierce fighter and loyal friend.

Dean Cawdor: Ryan's young son by Sharona accepts the only world he knows, and yet he is the seedling bearing the promise of tomorrow.

In a world where all was lost, they are humanity's last hope....

Chapter One

Ryan Cawdor withdrew his head from the crest of the ridge and mouthed, "Trouble."

Krysty Wroth slowly raised her head over the edge of the ridge, catching only a brief glimpse of a strange, wheeled vehicle outfitted with a white broadcloth sail before Ryan pushed her head down.

"Your hair might as well be a signal flare," he whispered.

"Sorry, lover."

Mildred Wyeth, J. B. Dix, Doc Tanner and Jak Lauren looked up at them tensely, holding the reins of their horses. They didn't voice any questions. The companions were so in tune with one another's moods from their time of traveling through Deathlands together that they instantly assessed from Krysty's and Ryan's body language that a triple-red situation was in progress.

Ryan tapped her shoulder. "Take a look if you have to, but keep your head down."

Krysty cautiously poked her head up over the crest of the bluff. She stared at the scene below, barely able to suppress the utterance of horror rising to her lips.

The prairie schooner—or "wind wagon" as they were sometimes called—matched the configurations of a longboat. It was about twelve feet long from bow to stern, and a tall mast with a furled sail was set amidships, stretching upward twenty feet. A pair of maneuvering sails was folded like wings against the sides of the craft. Four spoked wooden wheels lifted the keel several feet above the ground. Mounted astern was a huge, wire-encased, four-bladed fan and a diesel engine.

Flapping from the rigging attached to the mast were clumps of human hair, finger bones and shriveled ears. A black pennant fluttered from the masthead, bearing the outline of a scarlet skull. Pirates.

Krysty recognized that emblem, if not from sight, then from tales she had heard in small western outposts, including her Colorado ville of Harmony. It was the insignia of the Red Cadre, a loosely knit group of scalphunters and marauders who preyed primarily on the Indian tribes in Montana, the Dakotas and Wyoming.

According to rumor, the Red Cadre set forth on its raids of pillage and murder in a fleet of wind wagons. The leader of the Cadre called himself Hatchet Jack, and as far as she knew, he could be one of the four freebooters below.

As if picking up on her thoughts, Ryan whispered, "Don't think Hatchet Jack is with them, but he'll be close by. This little raiding party wouldn't wander far from the fleet, not in that small craft."

The schooner stood in the center of a small cup formed by three sloping bluffs and a dry creek bed. To the left was a grove of poplar trees running raggedly between the farthermost hills. Three ponies were hobbled nearby, grazing on the tough saw grass. Two of the animals bore saddles made of wood and blankets. The third was apparently a packhorse.

A dark mound, like a huge, humped cigar, lay at the rear of the schooner. It was a buffalo carcass, waiting to be skinned. Its wooly hide was still intact, which was more than could be said for the Cheyenne man tied spread-eagled to the wooden spokes of the schooner's rear wheel.

Krysty had heard stories of "peeling," a torture certain marauder bands reserved exclusively for Indians. The pirates had practiced the ritual with great enthusiasm on the man. Entire strips of flesh had been flayed from his torso and upper arms. Great red, raw patches were exposed to flies and the late-afternoon sunlight.

Though she felt acidic bile climbing up her throat in a burning column, Krysty studied the victim for any sign of movement. She saw none. His swarthy face was a livid mask of dried blood that had flowed from the crimson patch atop his skull where his scalp had been torn away.

She squeezed her eyes shut as the bluff beneath her seemed to spin like a cork caught in a whirlpool. She had seen many monstrous deeds during her life in Deathlands, and had narrowly escaped similar fates more than once. Still, she had never grown accustomed to the horrors people inflicted on others simply for the sake of seeing them suffer.

It took a great effort for her to open her eyes again. She sensed Ryan watching her, gauging her reaction. Krysty gritted her teeth and focused her gaze on the woman tied to the front wheel. She wasn't spread-eagled—rather, she sat on the ground, her back against the hub, her wrists tied to the spokes level with her ears. She was totally naked, and her knees were drawn up to her chest and pressed tightly together. Krysty couldn't see what her face was like, but her skin was white, though dabbed red in places. Her head was bowed, and her hair, though hayrick tangled, was cut short and dark blond in color.

A pirate strutted past her, carrying an earthenware jug. He ignored her and she did the same. Another marauder walked over to the Indian, pushed his coat aside, fumbled briefly and urinated on the man's blood-drenched pant leg.

Hoots of laughing approval came from the man's three companions. Krysty squinted her eyes and studied the pirates. The man with the jug was huge and ugly. His swart, flat-nosed face was embraced by a square-cut beard of an unidentifiable color. Gray threads were interspersed with tobacco-stained streaks. He looked to be about fifty years old.

The other three were undistinguished in attitude and appearance. None was tall; in fact the one who was emptying his bladder looked shorter than even Jak Lauren's five feet five inches. One of the pirates was beefy, and a potbelly swelled over the waistband of his trousers. All of them had long, wild-looking hair.

The only firearms Krysty spied among them were a battered Winchester repeating carbine cradled carelessly in the crook of the tall man's arm and a single-shot muzzle loader propped against the stern of the schooner. The stock and barrel of the Winchester were patched and bound in two places with shrunken and stitched deer hide. The other weapons were a variety of knives, nail-studded clubs and a short-handled ax.

The tall man handed the jug to the beefy, swag-bellied man and wiped his beard with bloodstained fingers.

Ryan tugged on her sleeve, and she eased back down beside the big, dark-haired man. She dabbed at the film of sweat on her upper lip. "What are we going to do?"

Adjusting the black patch covering his left eye, Ryan replied quietly, "We ride in and kill them."

He and Krysty slid down the hillside on the seats of their pants. The expressions on the faces of the four people below were tense and watchful. J.B. took off his eyeglasses and stowed them in one of the many capacious pockets of his coat. The brim of his battered and bullet-holed fedora was pulled down over his forehead. With his left hand he held the reins of a roan mare, and his right hand rested lightly on the trigger guard of the Uzi hanging from a lanyard around his neck.

Though Jak's white, scarred face was as impassive as ever, his ruby eyes glittered at the sense of danger. The young albino's stance reminded Krysty of a vicious snow leopard, straining at its leash.

The other two people tending the horses were the only ones who hadn't been born into the war-ravaged remnants of the United States of America. Dr. Mildred Wyeth and Dr. Theophilus Tanner had been thrust into Deathlands due to prenukecaust technology.

A stocky black woman with beaded, plaited hair, Mildred Wyeth looked as though she were in her midthirties, but chronologically she was well over a century old. A medical doctor and former specialist in cryogenic sciences, Mildred had entered a hospital in late 2000 for minor surgery, but an allergic reaction to the anesthetic had necessitated her body being placed in cryonic stasis until a treatment could be found.

It never was. The world was blown apart before she was revived, and she slept, like a fly trapped in amber, for nearly a hundred years. Ryan and his companions had found and freed her. They had brought her back to life, into a world she had never dreamed existed. By her perspective, she had gone to sleep as a thirty-six-year old professional woman and awakened a moment later to the devastating realization her hundredth birthday had come and was long gone. Amazingly the ill effects of the anesthetic had disappeared.

Other than her skills as a medic, Mildred had also proved herself invaluable as a tenacious survivalist. She had won a silver medal for free pistol shooting in the last-ever Olympic Games, and she was the best shootist that any of the companions had ever seen.

Doc Tanner, unlike Mildred—who had bobbed unknowingly down the temporal stream—was the subject of a cold-hearted scientific practice known in pre-dark days as trawling. Since the 1940s, American military scientists, and their counterparts in other countries, had tried to reconcile relativistic physics with quantum mechanics. By the late 1990s, the reconciliation attempts had spawned the supersecret experiment known as the Totality Concept. There were several subdivisions of the experiment, such as Overproject Whisper, Project Cerberus and finally Operation Chronos.

With the use of a complex matter-transfer device called a gateway, the project scientists had tried time and again to snatch subjects from a past temporal line and trawl them to the present.

Their only success was a man from 1895. Theophilus Algernon Tanner, Ph.D., scientist and scholar, was plucked from the bosom of his beloved family and deposited in a sterile subterranean chamber a century down the timeline.

Though he learned all he could about the twentieth century, Doc never abandoned the hope of returning to his wife and two children. His constant attempts to return to his own era so angered the whitecoats of Operation Chronos that they eventually used him as a trawling subject again. Rather than send him back, they opted to transfer him to a year nearly a century in the future. The wrenching changes left their marks on Doc. In his worn frock coat, his skinny frame looked gaunt, and his face old beyond his actual years.

Sixteen-year-old Jak Lauren had all the hard, bitter experience of a man twice his age. He had whiter than white skin, with fearsome ruby eyes and a shock of blindingly white hair. He possessed incredible hand and eye coordination and favored bladed weapons over blasters. Scars from several near-fatal encounters marked his body, the least of which curved up from the corner of his mouth and across his high-planed face. Though Jak had buried two sets of families during his young life, he hid the tragedies behind a taciturn mask and an eerily calm, detached manner.

Ryan Cawdor and J. B. Dix had been companions for many years, since they traveled the Deathlands in a pair of war wags with the legendary Trader. Tall and hard muscled, with a scar running down his face from the edge of the patch over his left eye, Ryan was a natural-born leader.

J.B. was an armorer, and he had served Trader's war wags as a weapon smith. His wiry, short frame and unmemorable face disguised a devious mind and a facility with weapons that approached the artistic.

By contrast, Krysty Wroth was tall and slim. Because she possessed the empathic ability to sense danger in the offing, she was, by Deathlands definition, a mutie. Her fiery mane of thick red hair was the outward manifestation of her mutation, stirring, curling, moving as if it were a separate, sentient organism.

Krysty was also gifted with a power that had been passed down the female line of her family. The women were in tune with the electromagnetic energies of Gaia, the great Earth Mother. By tapping into these energies, the geopower field of the planet itself, Krysty could gain superhuman strength for a limited time.

Though Ryan was the group's undisputed leader, he and Krysty were equal partners in their relationship. Though he rarely spoke of it openly, Ryan loved her fiercely. The other great love of his life was his eleven-year-old son, Dean. The issue of a brief encounter between Ryan and a young woman named Sharona, Dean had been united with his father for only a short time. Recently Ryan had enrolled the lad in the Brody School in Colorado, and he missed the boy far more than he had thought he would. He found himself thinking of his son often, concerned for his safety. But travel was hazardous, and the locational jumps unpredictable. So he bided his time to give Dean a chance for independent growth, to let him cope on his own.

Ryan and his companions used the gateway chambers to make mat-trans jumps. Though gateways were hidden in subterranean redoubts all over the continent, the vast majority were concentrated in the Southwest. There was always an element of danger when using the gateways, since the destinations were random. As Doc had frequently pointed out, it was like deliberately jumping from a warm yet familiar frying pan into a potentially raging fire of unknown temperature.

The last jump had deposited them in a redoubt on a Montana mountain plateau. It was, ironically enough, the first of the subterranean installations they had ever found. The century-old garish painting of Cerberus, the three-headed black hound, was still on the wall, though faded and peeling.

Doc was adamant about not making another jump so soon, so the band of travelers decided to strike out overland to explore the area. Though the last time they had visited the region they had been pursued by a warlike band of Sioux, they saw no trace of any tribesmen.

They reached a small settlement nestled in the foot-hills of the mountain and, after staying there a day and a night, they purchased mounts and provisions and rode off cross-country. It wasn't as dangerous an undertaking as it seemed, since both J.B. and Ryan had skirted the fringes of the region years before with the Trader. Recalling rumors of a "free ville" near Yellowstone, Ryan had made that their destination.

At the base of the hill, the six companions quietly engaged in a war conference. Ryan quickly outlined the situation to his friends.

"We've got nine blasters between us," he said. "As far as I could tell, they've only got two."

Mildred shifted uneasily. "You want to stage an ambush?"

"Welcome to the Deathlands," J.B. drawled, checking out the firing mechanism of his Uzi.

Mildred cast him an irritated glance. "I don't need to be reminded of where I am, John."

Walking over to his horse, a big-chested sorrel, Ryan withdrew his Steyr SSG-70 rifle from its saddle scabbard.

Doc spoke for the first time, his tone flat yet touched by anxiety. "You have a plan in mind, my dear Ryan?"

Ryan nodded, carefully cycling a 7.62 mm round into the chamber. "Mildred, you're our best shot. Climb to the top of the hill and choose a target with this. When you pick it off, I'll ride out and engage them."

"Why just you?" Jak asked.

"I'm the best horseman, and this maneuver will call for some fast and fancy riding."

Krysty fastened her eyes onto Ryan's face. "You may be the best horseman, but I'm the best horse-*woman*. I'm going with you."

Ryan didn't object. "Fine. Shoot to kill."

"What about rest of us?" Jak asked.

"Mop-up," Ryan answered. "Move in on foot after our charge." He handed the rifle to Mildred and swung into the saddle.

"'Half a league, half a league, half a league onward,'" Doc muttered. No one bothered to ask him the meaning of his recitation. One of his most endearing—and sometimes most annoying—habits was his fondness for quoting predark poetry and proverbs.

Krysty mounted her bay as Mildred, with the rifle cradled in her arms, scaled the hillside. Seating her denim-encased buttocks firmly in the saddle, she drew her .38-caliber Smith & Wesson 640 revolver. Glancing over at Ryan, she saw that he had already pulled his SIG-Sauer P-226 blaster from his holster. He directed his horse to the right-hand foot of the bluff, and Krysty cantered over to the left-hand side.

She sat immobile in the saddle, holding the pistol skyward in her right hand, reins held loosely in her left. She waited. The sound of the rifle shot was an unbelievably loud crack. The vibration knocked against Krysty's eardrums.

Almost without conscious thought, Krysty dug her

boot heels into her mount's flanks, and the horse lunged forward. Hoofbeats hammered in a thundering rhythm, and she saw Ryan galloping furiously toward the wind wag. He had a good hundred-foot lead on her.

The pirates didn't freeze. One of their number lay facedown in the dust, the earthenware jug still gripped in his hand. Thick red fluid leaking from a bullet-blasted skull mingled with the liquor dripping from the jug. The other three men scrambled for their lives, and Krysty tried to track them with her Smith & Wesson. The range was still too great for accurate shooting with a handblaster, but she squeezed the trigger anyway.

She focused on the running pirates. They were dashing for the line of poplar trees that bordered the far side of the creek bed. One had snatched the hemp halter of a grazing pony and was hauling the animal behind him.

Krysty passed the prairie schooner and continued to gallop toward the poplar break, determined not to allow the pirate to get astride a horse. The bearded freebooter with the Winchester paused in his running, turned and drew the rifle to his shoulder. He fired directly at her, flame and smoke spouting from the barrel.

She thought she felt the wind of displaced air as the bullet spun past the right side of her head. She extended her arm and fired the Smith & Wesson, double-actioning the trigger so fast her hand and wrist began twinging with the strain. The pirate whirled and dashed into the trees, bullets kicking up clods of earth all around him. A dark spot appeared in his lower back, black against the tan of his coat. The man's momentum carried him several yards farther before his legs folded and he fell.

A shape entered Krysty's line of vision from her left, and she reined in her horse, swinging her pistol in a short arc in that direction, squeezing the trigger. As the hammer fell, she realized it was Ryan, riding up abreast of her. Krysty cried out in panic and jerked down her gun hand. It was too late. The firing pin fell on an empty chamber.

Ryan galloped past her without a word, as if Krysty had done nothing more life threatening than point a finger. Her overwhelming wave of relief was swallowed up by an equally overwhelming wave of embarrassment and anger.

Then, yelping a wolflike cry, a pirate cut in front of Krysty. He was astride the pony, leaning over its neck. She recognized him as the coldheart who had pissed on the Cheyenne man.

Krysty kicked the bay down into the creek bed, fumbling with her empty blaster, not daring to holster the weapon for fear of dropping it. For a minute it was a wild race, with her horse's long-legged stride overtaking the pony. Chunks of gravel and dirt flew in a shower in the wake of both galloping animals.

The bay was gaining, and the woman felt a growing surge of triumph, which abated quickly when she remembered she was pursuing a murderous savage with a blaster that couldn't be fired. She reined in her horse.

The pirate, as though sensing his pursuer's predicament, slowed his mount, then cast a fierce, dark-eyed glance over a shoulder. Barking, *"Yee-haw,"* he sharply yanked the pony's head up and around. The animal neighed in protest, reared, then was bearing down on Krysty. The pirate placed the blade of a knife between the decayed stumps of his teeth and thumped the pony's sides, urging it on.

Krysty snapped the bay's head around and heeled it in the opposite direction. The horse floundered for a moment, trying to set its hooves firmly to lunge into another gallop. But before it could move, a heavy weight slammed into the woman's body from behind and a little to her right. She glimpsed and felt a stained sleeve encircling her neck. The fading sunlight glinted from steel, and Krysty took the first course of action that occurred to her. She threw herself to the left, releasing the reins, grabbing the sleeve and kicking free of the stirrups.

The fall raised a small explosion of dust as Krysty and the pirate, locked in a straining, belly-to-back embrace, slammed into the creek bed. The red-haired woman released the sinewy arm and tried to roll away, flinging herself painfully across sharp-edged rocks. She levered herself onto her back, kicking out with her right leg, the chiseled silver point on the toe of her boot smashing full into the man's open mouth. His rotted teeth caved in, and blood spurted in liquid tendrils onto his chin.

Her attacker made a gargling sound as he coughed up splinters of bone, crimson froth bubbling on his pulped lips. Face a mask of rage, he scrambled toward her, knife held for a downward thrust. He reached out to grasp her by an ankle.

Suddenly the pirate leaped to his feet, eyes wide and filled with astonishment. The knife fell from his suddenly slack fingers, and as he turned slightly, Krysty saw a blue-rimmed hole in his temple. He swayed, sighed, sat down carefully, then fell facedown in the rocks. A red-edged, fist-sized cavity occupied the back of his head.

Weak-limbed and trembling, Krysty tried to rise. She made it to one knee and slowly turned her head in the direction of the pounding hoofbeats coming down the creek bed. Ryan cantered toward her, SIG-Sauer in hand.

He reined to a stop and swung out of the saddle. Standing over Krysty, he extended his left hand. "Why do you look so surprised, lover? You're still alive."

Relieved laughter rolled from Krysty's throat. "I appreciate you telling me that."

"Thought you might."

Taking his hand, Krysty allowed herself to be pulled to her feet. Then Ryan caught her up in a crushing embrace, and pressed his lips to her face.

Chapter Two

By the time Ryan and Krysty caught her horse and returned to the wind wag, Mildred had freed the woman and Jak had cut loose the skinned Indian and covered him with a tarp. Doc and J.B. were standing a watchful guard, blasters in hand. Doc's weapon of choice was an old, ornately engraved Le Mat. The commemorative Civil War–era blaster had two barrels and an adjustable hammer. Like a shotgun, it fired a single .63-caliber round and, like a revolver, it had a chambered cylinder holding nine .44-caliber bullets.

A blanket was draped about the woman's shoulders, and Mildred kneeled before her, offering her a tin cup. The contents had been poured from the earthenware jug. "This might help to steady you some."

From what Ryan could see of the woman, she didn't need steadying. She stared straight ahead, her blue eyes unblinking, her face expressionless. She took the cup, sipped it, then gulped the liquor in a single swallow.

Ryan gauged her age at twenty-something, though she could have been younger.

The pair of pirates lay where Ryan's and Mildred's shots had hammered them. Mildred had delivered a fatal head wound to one, and the other, lying on his side, had two holes in his torso. The ground around him was clotted with blood, bone fragments and bits of pink tissue Ryan identified as his lungs.

Krysty gestured to the poplar break. "One got away from me."

Ryan clicked his horse toward the line of trees. "Let's make sure he won't be getting up."

Krysty turned her bay to follow. Ryan noticed how she rubbed her rib cage and grimaced. She had taken a hard fall, perhaps even cracked a bone or two, but she wasn't complaining. At the edge of the trees they dismounted and walked among them carefully. Krysty had reloaded her blaster and held it in a two-handed grip.

Ryan pointed the barrel of the SIG-Sauer at a narrow spattering of blood on the ground. The Winchester rifle lay nearby. "The one you back-shot."

"His back was to me," Krysty replied.

The trail of blood extended a few yards, then terminated at the bole of a tree. The bearded pirate sat against it, his face wet with sweat but locked in a mask of defiance and hate. He had his hands clasped over a hole in his midsection, where the .38-caliber slug had exited, and blood dribbled between his fingers. Ryan and Krysty stood and stared at the man for a long moment.

"Well?" the man challenged. "The day's not gettin' any younger."

Ryan's lips quirked in a cold half smile. He raised his blaster, finger crooking around the trigger. "Neither are you, stupe."

The freebooter snorted contemptuously. "Once Jack and the rest of the Cadre starts howlin' along your track, you ain't got much to look forward to, either. You or that hell-haired gaudy slut."

Krysty's blaster came up in reflexive anger, and the pirate grinned at the hollow bore with red-filmed teeth.

"Where's Hatchet Jack now?" Ryan demanded.

"Think I'd tell you?" The man's grin twisted into a grimace. He coughed, and blood spilled out of his mouth and clung in gummy strands to his beard. "Chill me and be fucked, One-eye."

Ryan lowered the SIG-Sauer. "Think I'd rather leave you here for the wolves to find. Won't be long, and you can spend the last few minutes of your life watching them unwind your guts."

Fear replaced the defiance in the pirate's eyes. A gut-shot man could live for a long time, consumed with agony, provided the scent of blood and ruptured internal organs didn't draw predators. A death inflicted by razor-keen fangs and rending talons might be quick, but it was by no means painless.

The freebooter coughed again, this time deliberately, hawking up from deep in his lungs. He spit a jet of blood directly into Krysty's face. She cried out and recoiled in disgust. Ryan lifted his blaster, stepped forward and fired once. The pirate's broad forehead sprouted a neat blue-ringed hole. The back of his head broke apart, sending skull shards, blood and grayish pink brain matter splattering against the bark of the tree.

Ryan shoved the blaster back into its holster. The scar on his face glowed lividly, like a bolt of angry lightning. Krysty wiped away the blood from her face, repressed a shudder and whirled away. "Let's get back while we still have some daylight."

They led their horses through the trees, neither of them speaking. Krysty moved quickly, as if she didn't want to walk beside him, and Ryan knew the reason why.

More than once she had cautioned him about allowing a quick flare of rage to consume him, to control him. Ryan had agreed with her that surrendering to murderous fury was contrasurvival, and he had gone to great effort to bring those surges of berserk anger under control.

However, he couldn't and wouldn't tolerate the kind of swaggering scorn displayed by the likes of the pirate. In the past, especially during his years with the Trader, men had died under his gun or knife, and sometimes his bare hands, for far less. He knew his rare bursts of homicidal rage frightened Krysty, and sometimes even himself, and he also knew his swift execution of the pirate bothered her. Though Ryan and Krysty shared more similarities than differences, she would never commit murder unless her life, or the lives of those she loved, was directly threatened.

When Ryan and Krysty emerged from the grove, they saw that all the corpses had been moved to the far side of the little valley. Mildred was doing her best to make the woman comfortable, though she was still unresponsive.

J.B. looked up from examining the fuel tank of the wind wag's ancient diesel motor. "It's about a quarter full," he said. "It holds twenty or so gallons, and it probably gets about that many miles to the gallon, so they haven't strayed too far from the fleet and their supply boats."

Ryan nodded as he walked toward Mildred and her patient. "Is she hurt?"

Mildred shrugged. "A few bruises and abrasions, nothing serious. She's in shock, though."

"We need to know where she came from and if she lives with one of the Indian tribes in the area."

Without looking at him, the woman spoke in a clear, toneless voice. "Amicus. We came from Amicus."

Easing to a kneeling position in front of her, Ryan put a friendly smile on his face. "That's where we're headed. We weren't sure if it really existed."

The woman said nothing.

"What's your name?" he asked.

The woman's eyes were blank. Ryan recognized the symptoms of a person who had undergone such terror and witnessed such horror that all emotions were frozen, locked deep within the soul. He could see the pain in her eyes, the memory of it fresh and frightful. She held her body in the stiff posture that came as a result of pain, and of a fear that it would return.

"Look," he said, "we need our questions answered. You need to guide us to Amicus and to tell us how and when the Red Cadre jumped you. That'll give us an idea of how close the rest of them are."

The woman didn't react to his words or his tone, so he slapped her openhanded across her right cheek. Her head jerked back, and Mildred hissed in anger.

Lifting a hand to her stinging, reddening face, the woman fluttered her eyelids, her eyes darting wildly back and forth. They suddenly brimmed with tears. Bowing her head, she began to weep in a racking, dry-heave sob.

Mildred murmured to her, and Krysty kneeled beside her, massaging her neck and shoulders, trying to knead the tension out of them. She had been trained long ago in massage therapy, of how to use subtle pressures to block pain and allow rigid muscles to relax.

Ryan rose and left the woman to the gentle ministrations of Mildred and Krysty. Doc joined him, commenting quietly, "I do not believe your bedside manner met with Dr. Wyeth's approval."

"Got no time to coddle someone who can walk and talk."

Jak was gazing out over the valley. His exceptionally keen sight picked out details of the ruts dug by the wind wag's wheels.

"Came from southeast," he declared. "Could backtrack them."

"No time for a recce before sundown," Ryan replied. "The Cadre might miss these four and send out a search party. I don't much like the idea of meeting them in the dark."

He returned to the three women. "She found her tongue yet?"

"Says her name is Felicity," Krysty answered.

"Did she tell you how far it is to Amicus?"

The woman looked up. She was no longer sobbing, but tears glistened on her face. "No need to treat me like a jolt-brain. I can talk."

"Then do it," Ryan replied. "We don't have much time."

Felicity tried to stand, then groaned and allowed Mildred to help her to her feet. She looked at Ryan with a half sneer on her lips. She was still very close to hysteria, but she was successfully controlling it.

Gesturing with one hand, holding the blanket closed with the other, she said, "Amicus is about twenty miles that way. My husband—" she hesitated, almost gagging on the word "—and me came out here to hunt buffalo. We were attacked before we could start the butchering. About two hours ago, I reckon."

"Your husband was the Indian?" Ryan asked.

"Spotted Hawk. A lot of the Cheyenne and the Lakota Sioux live in Amicus."

"Will you guide us there?"

The woman nodded once, her lips tight.

Jak approached him, handing over a small packet bound by oilcloth and twine. "One had this on him."

Ryan untied the twine and withdrew a square of paper. He opened it, careful not to tear it along the creases. The sheet of parchment seemed ready to fall apart with age and use. He looked over the drawings it bore and realized it was some kind of map. The written words were unpronounceable.

Lips unconsciously moving as he struggled to read the words, he studied a dotted line leading north from a squiggly area labeled *Jaune-roc* to a jagged region labeled *Mystère Montagneux.*

"French," Jak announced, looking over his shoulder.

Having been raised in Louisiana Cajun country, Jak was familiar with the language.

"What's it say?"

Touching the wavy lines with a skinny forefinger, the teenager said, "Yellowstone. Must mean river. Other words mean Mystery Mountains or Mountains of Mystery."

Ryan refolded the paper and slid it into a shirt pocket. "Probably a map of prime hunting grounds Let's move out. We're wasting daylight."

Doc and Ryan unsaddled the horses and piled the tack in the stern of the wind wag. The bridles were left on, but Mildred insisted the bits be removed from their mouths. Jak fashioned a long lead from the reins and a length of rawhide he found in the wag, securing one end to a cleat at the rear of the craft. The body of Spotted Hawk was placed in the bow. The corpses of the pirates were left to the scavengers.

After everyone was aboard, J.B. manned the engine block. He jerked the starting cord, but nothing happened. Grimacing, he made a couple of adjustments and yanked again. And again.

After the third failure, he went back to tinkering, checking the plugs, the coil wires and the oil level. Then he grasped the cord, took and held a deep breath, obviously steeling himself for another failure. Despite his impatience to get moving, Ryan couldn't help but smile.

J.B. pulled the cord violently, stumbling over the saddles and almost falling. With a series of stuttering pops, the engine roared to life, filling the air with noxious fumes. Everyone nearly sprang overboard. Birds rushed up from the trees in a squawking flock, taking panic-stricken flight. The fan blades whirled, stirring hair and clothing.

"Spread the sail!" J.B. shouted.

Krysty and Doc struggled to open the heavy sheet of broadcloth. The wind caught it, billowing it out, and with a squeak and creak of wheels, the schooner slowly rolled forward.

The next few minutes were controlled chaos as J.B. yelled orders and instructions, and everyone concentrated on bringing the craft under control.

Ryan managed to figure out how to steer the ungainly craft with a crude wheel, and Doc, who had more boating experience than any of them, dealt with the sail, making sure it didn't swell up with the artificially generated wind and rip loose from the rigging. As it was, he nearly brained Mildred by swinging the boom to and fro.

By the time the craft gained speed and rolled out of the little valley, everyone was at ease within it. The wind wag entered a broad, nearly treeless vista of high plains. Felicity gave directions, and Doc struggled to align the sail properly. The engine noise was too loud to have a conversation unless it was shouted, so to spare their throats, talk was kept to a minimum.

The wag sailed on, bouncing over ruts and rocks, the terrain changing very little. The area was filled with the ruins of old farms. Every mile or so they spotted a barn, leaning red and rickety on itself, its roof cocked sideways, tarred shingles flapping in the breeze.

As the sky began to darken with approaching twilight, Ryan became concerned. He didn't fancy camping out on the plains, especially in one of the ruined barns or farmhouses. But there was very little other cover available.

Turning over the steerage controls to Krysty, he scanned the horizon in all directions for a collection of trees or even a good-sized boulder. What he saw instead was a faint smudge of wispy gray against the deep azure of the sky. Though it was too distant to make an accurate judgment, he guessed the smudge wasn't smoke. It was trail dust.

Withdrawing a battered set of compact binoculars from his saddlebag, he went portside and squinted through the lenses. A little less than half a mile off, he saw four prairie schooners rolling in a fast, tight formation. They were several times larger than their own wag, and Ryan supposed theirs was a scout craft of some type. The bows of the approaching vessels were pointed on intercept course. He was able to make out a man standing at the bow of the center craft, a set of binoculars lifted to his eyes.

Though he was too far away to pick out details beyond a mane of blond hair, Ryan was positive the man lowered the binoculars for a second and flashed him a gap-toothed grin.

Sweeping the lenses across the four wags, Ryan made a quick head count. At least fifty figures appeared to be aboard the quartet of schooners. They were all long-haired and armed with knives, swords and muskets. From the top of each mast fluttered the crimson skull standard.

Ryan lowered the binoculars and hissed, "Fireblast."

Chapter Three

The wind wag had skimmed across the plains for thirty minutes, and now the fuel tank was nearly drained.

Ryan's hands tightened on the steerage, hoping his grip alone would coax at least one more mile out of the craft. He didn't look behind him, focusing instead on the dark bulk of two hills a mile or so ahead. According to Felicity, the ville of Amicus lay on the other side of the hills, through a narrow gorge running between them.

The roar of the diesel engine faltered, broke its steady rhythm, coughed and died altogether. The fan blades slowly stopped spinning, but the sail didn't drop. A steady breeze blew from behind them. It wasn't very strong, but the current was powerful enough to keep the sail half-filled and the wind wag moving. Still, it slowed.

Ryan glanced over his shoulder. Strung out across the darkening horizon were four white shapes, the full sails of the Red Cadre's prairie schooners. The wind carried the snarl of their engines. They were gaining fast.

"We need to get rid of some weight," J.B. announced.

Felicity's eyes flashed in sudden fear. Ryan knew that she realized the most obvious weight to jettison was the body of her husband.

"Cut the horses loose," he said to Jak. "They're ready to drop anyway."

Felicity said nothing, but she directed a look of silent thanks toward him.

Producing one of his leaf-bladed throwing knives, Jak moved aft and sliced through the rawhide leads attaching the animals to the wag. They instantly stopped galloping, cantering in tandem into the gathering gloom.

Doc came to Ryan's side, eyeing the hills ahead. "If the wind does not drop or change direction, we may make it, even at this speed."

The light of a quarter moon peeped over the rim of the world, staining the dark sky with a silver halo. The thudding growl of the diesels seemed to rise in volume. Inexorably the pursuing prairie schooners drew closer.

Ryan called Krysty over and had her replace him at the controls. He made his way aft and peered through the binoculars again, hoping to pick out more details of their pursuers, since the lead craft was only a hundred or so yards behind them.

Tightening the focus on the center wag, he saw a black-bearded man shouldering a short, blunt-barreled object. Though it had a rifle stock, it was far too bulky and spike nosed to be a rifle. When the deep, hollow bore aligned itself with the rear of their craft, recognition rushed through Ryan like a flow of icy water.

The pirate was aiming an old M-79 grenade launcher. The maximum range of the 40 mm high explosive round was three hundred and fifty yards, and they were well within its field of effect. Though the M-79 and its ammunition were probably a hundred and twenty years old, they couldn't rely on a misfire.

"Krysty!" he bellowed. "Hard to port!"

Before the final word had passed his lips, the dark bore of the grenade launcher spouted a puff of white smoke, followed immediately by a mushy pop.

Responding to Ryan's order, Krysty wrenched the steering handles. The wag drifted sideways, the maneuver seeming to be maddeningly slow and clumsy.

A few yards ahead and to the right of the bow, the night lit up with a hot orange flash, a fireball ballooning up and outward. Shrapnel and chunks of sod rattled against the hull.

"Son of a bitch!" J.B. snarled, unlimbering his Uzi. He checked the selector switch and flicked it to full-auto, firing a long, stuttering burst in a left-to-right pattern. Spent cartridges spewed from the ejector port and clattered across the deck.

Then the wind died.

The sail drooped, flapping slack and flaccid.

Carried on by its momentum, the wag kept rolling, wheels and chassis creaking, but by degrees it slowed to a crawl, then to a complete stop. From behind echoed a strident cry of malicious triumph.

No one needed to be told what to do. They all snatched up their possessions, jumped overboard and began to run, feet churning up the dry soil. The blanket dropped from Felicity's shoulders, and she ran naked toward the hills with a steady lightness and sureness of stride that came of long practice.

Ryan hazarded one quick backward glance. Unsurprisingly the wags of the Red Cadre were still on course, bearing down on them. He estimated he and his friends would reach the base of the hills with only a handful of seconds to spare. The skin between his shoulder blades itched in anticipation of a musket bullet drilling into his flesh.

Felicity, in the lead, altered direction, heading for the tumble of rocks at the foot of the nearest hill. They followed her, running across stone-strewed ground. Ryan heard Doc gasping, wheezing and cursing as he tried to keep his footing.

They dodged among larger rocks, banging knees and scraping elbows. The pain of a stitch stabbed along Ryan's left side, the muscles of his legs felt as if they were caught in a tightening vise and his vision was shot through with gray specks. Nevertheless, he kept running, stumbling and lurching from boulder to boulder.

Suddenly Felicity cried out sharply, a confusing jumble of words. *"Okiya nitakola!"*

From ahead and above them came the unmistakable sound of thrumming bowstrings vibrating through the air, as well as the solid chocking of arrowheads finding hard and soft targets.

Behind them the night erupted in an animal roar of outraged frustration. Ryan looked over his shoulder, catching a brief glimpse of the wind wags sluggishly changing course, one barely avoiding a collision with another. The wooden hulls of all four craft bristled with feathered shafts. The wags of the Red Cadre were barely twenty yards away. A discordant noise bleated from the center craft, the notes of a frantically blown bugle, sounding a retreat.

"Come on!" Felicity gasped.

They followed her flashing nude figure as she picked a path between low rock tumbles and emerged into a narrow pass, the sides of the two hills rising on either side.

There were men in the pass, and when Felicity stopped running, so did everyone else. Ryan and his people stood and swayed, panting, trying to regain their breath and slow the rapid hammering of their hearts.

Though the light was uncertain, Ryan saw a half-dozen men, and an odd collection they were. Some of them were Amerindians, their long dark hair bedecked with feathers. They wore a combination of deerskin tunics, breechclouts and jeans. The other men, though white, were similarly dressed. All of them were armed with bows and quivers of arrows. The only blaster was a long-barreled muzzle loader, and it was in the hands of a stocky, black-bearded white man who wore boot moccasins and a long-billed cap bearing the faded insignia of some predark sports team.

Felicity rushed up to this man and spoke quickly to him. Ryan couldn't catch much of what she said, since his blood pounded in his ears and his lungs were noisily laboring to suck in oxygen.

The man kept watchful eyes on Ryan and his friends as the woman spoke. When she was done, he gave her a quick hug and strode toward Ryan, extending a hand. "My name is Mose Autry. Welcome to Amicus."

Ryan shook the hand and between deep breaths made introductions all around. Autry nodded politely to each person in turn.

"Thank you for bringing Felicity back to us. She and Spotted Hawk were valuable members of our community. His loss will be mourned."

Jerking a thumb behind him, J.B. coughed and asked, "What about those sons of bitches? They may take his body."

Autry smiled sadly. "They may. Unfortunately all forms of banditry are endemic to this region, including defilement of the dead. However, the Cadre won't dare the pass at night. Now, if you all will follow me..."

The man turned and said a few words to the other men in the same language Felicity had spoken. Ryan recognized it as Lakota, a dialect of the Sioux language. Arm around Felicity's shoulders, Autry started walking down the dark gorge.

Ryan hesitated, exchanging quizzical glances with his friends, then they fell into step behind the man. The pass sliced through the narrow hills. It curved this way and that, and all of them had trouble with its navigation. They were feeling weary and wanted to rest.

The hair at Ryan's nape suddenly tingled and lifted. He looked quickly at Krysty and saw that her sentient hair was lying loose and relaxed across her shoulders. Then he scanned the perpendicular sides of the gorge. They reared only a hundred feet above the pass, and the sky was clear and dark beyond them.

Something shifted soundlessly atop the crest of the right-hand ridge. Ryan's hand made a reflexive move to his blaster.

Limned by the moonlight, the shifting shape resolved into a shaggy, four-legged figure. Though it was only in his field of vision for a fraction of a second, Ryan realized it was a coyote or a wolf.

When it vanished, Ryan didn't relax. An eerie aura hung over the pass, as if the lupine shadow had been a symbol of savage events yet to come.

The pass turned west, then opened up. Amicus lay before them in the moonlight. At first glance, even on the second, Amicus looked typical of thousands of frontier pesthole villes he had passed through. A big lake spread like a rain cloud in the center of the ville. On its shores was a jumble of tarpaper shacks and tepees, as well as a couple of old predark structures, probably outbuildings of a long-ago farm. Three or four huge fires sputtered redly.

A narrow main street was choked with mud, the boardwalk rotted through and lined by canting houses. A row of outhouses occupied the city square. Even the big vegetable garden at the far end of the settlement looked untidy, what with its straggly bean and tomato poles and mounds of rotting compost rearing from the ground.

A herd of perhaps fifty horses and mules jostled one another in a wide, cockeyed corral. Dogs of all shapes, sizes and breeds ambled along the streets. The air smelled richly of pig and cattle manure.

Doc sniffed and murmured, "Ah, the very best of domestic cologne."

As they followed Autry and Felicity into the settlement, a few of the dogs winded their unfamiliar scents and set up a ferocious racket. A couple of them trotted forward, stiff legged and growling, to sniff at the companions. Everyone kept on walking.

When they neared one of the tepees, a flap opened and a toothless old woman with yellow braids and a buckskin shirt looked out anxiously. Felicity saw her and ran into her arms. She murmured into the old woman's ear, then both of them burst into tears, hugging each other in shared grief.

"Her mother," Autry explained. "Spotted Hawk was their sole support."

He gestured to a low-roofed, ramshackle building up the street. Light shone from the windows, and violin music floated in the air. "Our local public house. If we tell your story in there, it'll be all over Amicus within the hour. Save you from having to say the same thing over and over again."

Autry opened the leather-hinged door and stepped aside, allowing the others to enter. Only a few people were inside, but the big room smelled of sweat, tobacco and potent homemade whiskey. Two men stood on either side of the rough-hewn slab of pine that served as the bar.

One, a scrawny fellow with a luxuriant waxed mustache, was obviously the tavern keeper. The other man had his back to the door, and all they could see of him was a massive, leather-clad torso and the rear of a black-haired head.

A small middle-aged man with a balding pate and a parsimonious face was sawing vigorously at a fiddle. Judging by the musician's vacant stare, the patrons of the establishment could have started hacking away at one another with tomahawks and he would have gone on playing, perhaps shifting a little to avoid bloodying his shoes.

Autry spoke to both men at the bar. The big man turned, giving Ryan and his people a cool, appraising stare. He was an Amerindian, wearing a beaded-diamond-and-triangle design on his shirt. It was the ancient symbol of the Sioux. His black hair hung in two braids halfway to his waist.

The tavern keeper filled seven mugs from a jug of amber liquid. With a word of thanks, Ryan took a long, satisfying swallow, as did Doc and Jak. As the corn liquor burned its way into their stomachs, Autry silenced the musician with a wave of his hands.

"I've heard some of the story from Felicity," he told them. "Let's hear the rest of it from you."

In simple, unadorned language, Ryan told how they had come across the scene of torture and murder. At the mention of the Red Cadre, the barkeeper sputtered, the ends of his mustache fluttering.

"Oh, shit," he choked out. "Chillin' four and stealin' one of their boats—Hatchet Jack will slit you from crotch to eyeball with a dull deer antler. He'll burn this place to the ground to get you!"

Autry cast him an angry glare. "Shut up, Micah. The Cadre knows better than to molest us."

"Why is that?" Krysty asked. Though she held a mug of liquor, she had yet to taste it.

"Amicus does too much trade with the local Cheyenne and Lakota," Autry replied. "Too many of the tribes live here, at least part of the year." He nodded toward the big man. "Like Little Mountain."

Little Mountain was staring hard at them, in a way most Indians would have considered impolite. Ryan met that stare.

The man blinked, then touched his left eye. "Ochi-nee," he rumbled.

"One-eye," Autry translated. "Little Mountain isn't fluent in English."

The big man turned to Autry and spoke quickly in Lakota. Autry's face registered surprise. "Says he knows of all of you," he told them. "Claims his chief met you, and that you're mighty warriors."

Ryan and J.B. had met a number of tribesmen during their years with Trader. "Who's his chief?" J.B. asked.

Autry asked Little Mountain the question. After the Sioux had replied, he translated, "Yutan-kin-Mahipiya. Never heard of him."

Little Mountain's eyes shone with agitation. He spun on one deerskin-shod heel and made for the door. Autry called after him in Lakota, but the man either didn't hear him or didn't care to respond.

"I told him to watch out for the Cadre," Autry explained. "Guess he's not worried."

"Maybe he's not," Mildred said, "but I am. Wil the Cadre bottle up the pass? Are they that venge ful?"

Autry shrugged. "Hatchet Jack has that reputation All of you are free to enjoy our hospitality for as long as you care to do so. I'll find you comfortable quar ters."

Ryan wasn't sure if the calm the man exhibited in the face of the Cadre's presence was admirable, fool ish or forced. "What's the population of Amicus?" he asked.

"It shifts with the seasons. We're at our mos crowded when the buffalo hunters follow the herds but it's too early for that. Right at the moment, we probably have a hundred permanent residents."

"Out of that number, how many are of fighting age?"

Autry frowned. "Hard to say. My best guess would be around thirty, maybe forty."

"And blasters," J.B. put in. "How many in town and what type?"

"What's the point of these questions?" Autry de manded impatiently.

"The point," Ryan answered, "is that a pack o blood-drunk coldhearts is camping outside your burg I'm not sure of their arsenal, but they have at leas one gren launcher. If it comes down to a face-off, we need to know what you can throw against them."

"Muzzle loaders, primarily," Autry admitted "Old man Hasslich is our gunsmith, makes gunpow der, bullets and so forth. He may know if there are more advanced blasters in town. Personally I wa: never interested enough to make an inventory."

"If I were you," J.B. said grimly, "I'd get inter ested quick."

Autry paused for a moment, then asked, "Do you think they'll attack us to get at you?"

Micah snorted out a derisive laugh. "Hell, yes, if Hatchet Jack has a mind that these folks owe him a blood debt!"

Jak's eyes narrowed to suspicious slits. "How come you know about him?"

Micah looked over at Autry, who cleared his throat uncomfortably. He said, "For a few years, the Cadre used Amicus as a sort of winter camp. They behaved pretty well while they were here, but one day they raided the wrong Cheyenne village. The warriors tracked them down, waited in ambush outside the pass and chilled damn near half of them. Hatchet Jack blamed me for not warning him, for setting him up."

"And were you innocent of blame?" Doc inquired.

Autry sighed and shook his head. "No. It was poltics, you see. Amicus relies too heavily on the goodwill of the Cheyenne. If we alienated them, we would have alienated the Sioux, the Arapaho and the Crow, as well. Not only would the trade with them have ended, they would've razed the town to make it useless to the Cadre as a base. I had no choice but to cooperate with the ambush."

J.B. smiled without mirth. "Sounds like the Red Cadre owes Amicus more of a blood debt than us."

"Too true. And Hatchet Jack may use you six as the reason he needs to finally collect. Two debts collected for the price of one."

"Unless," Krysty said, "you made a preemptive strike, as long as they're so handy."

Autry wagged his head in a vehement, vigorous negative. "That's not our way. Not our way at all. Amicus came together ten years ago as an experiment in communal, cooperative living. If we start chilling

people we disagree with, we'll be no different tha
any other frontier ville.''

"Admirable ideals, Mr. Autry," Doc said. "How
ever, judging by what you just told us, more honore
in the breach. You allowed the local Indian tribes t
solve your pirate problem."

Autry waved Doc's words away with a dismissiv
gesture. "Enough of this for tonight. I'm certai
you're hungry and tired. Let me show you to you
quarters, and I'll arrange for food to be brought t
you."

They went with Autry back out onto the muddy
rutted strip that passed as Amicus's main street. Face
filled all the doorways as they walked by—mainl
children's faces and women's faces, some of then
young and pretty, most of them seamed and smok
colored.

From far off came a faint, howling call that wa
answered by another and then another. Ryan saw tha
the moon had risen higher. "The hills must be crawl
ing with wolves," he said.

Autry grinned at him. "They're talking to us."

"What do you mean?"

"Wolves are highly respected by most of the tribes
They're regarded as allies, talking to people, tellin
them what's going to happen."

Doc lifted an eyebrow. "And if you do not happer
to speak wolfese, I suppose you are out of luck."

"Not necessarily," Autry replied. "I understand
them—sometimes. Right now they're talking abou
you."

Autry led them to a dilapidated building with a
stone facade. "Amicus doesn't have an inn as such
but this place serves as a visitors' hostel."

The interior of the building was warm and smoky

with a floor of hand-hewn planks and walls shored up
with heavy, smoke-blackened beams. A cast-iron
stove glowed in one corner of the common room, its
pipe disappearing into the adobe ceiling.

"Three bedrooms," Autry said. "Afraid you'll
have to double up. I'll arrange for supper and break-
ast. We'll talk more tomorrow. Good night."

All of the rooms were furnished identically with
medium-sized beds holding mattresses that exuded a
faint sour odor. Krysty and Ryan chose one room at
random, dropped their gear in a corner and stretched
out on the bed.

Chapter Four

Ryan was in Front Royal, riding across his father'
green meadows. He was twelve years old an
mounted on Witch, his favorite pony. He had both o
his eyes, and he saw that Baron Cawdor was still aliv
and waving to him from the top of a gently rollin
hill. Ryan shouted in happiness and urged Witch to
ward him.

Then the pony stopped, and Ryan kicked her im
patiently. Her equine shape melted beneath him, shif
ing and transmogrifying. And then he was riding o
a giant, dark gray wolf. He was afraid and he starte
to cry. The wolf shushed him.

You've been here before, manling, the wolf sai
kindly. The voice had no gender, and he sensed i
rather than heard it. *Time to take you to a new place*

The wolf turned and loped away from the hil
Ryan looked behind him and saw his father sti
standing there, receding swiftly in the distance. Whe
he turned, he was a grown man again, but he still ha
both of his eyes. He knew the wolf was responsibl
for this gift, and gratitude welled up within him.

"How can I ever thank you? You've restored m
sight. "

You never lost it, the wolf replied. *You do not nee
eyes to see.*

The wolf leaped from the meadow and ran throug
a nightmare landscape. All around them were mon

trous mushroom clouds, rising in roaring columns oward heaven, flashing and flickering with hellish ight. They loped past ruined cities overgrown with vegetation, and bounded over fetid swamps. Overhead boiling, glowing belt of radioactive dust scorched cross the sky.

And everywhere there was death, corpses and animated cadavers with their flesh peeled and blistered, heir internal organs hanging out boiled and burst, heir empty eye sockets weeping gelatinous tears. They reached out with skeletal fingers and gurgled nd moaned, and Ryan recognized some of them.

They screamed his name, and there was Lori and)'Mara, Hunaker and Okie and all the crew from War Vag One and Two and all the people he had chilled. And there were the billions who had died in the nukeaust, and they were all equally dead, but it was worse because they hadn't been meant to die. Deathlands vasn't supposed to have happened.

"They're dead," Ryan said. "Everything, everybody is dead. Dead."

The dead, the wolf replied, *will live forever if they lie inside the circle.*

Ryan didn't understand, and didn't the wolf understand that they lived in a land of death, and death vould be with him as it always had been and always vould be?

Four circles of life, the wolf said. *We are passing through the fourth and last circle. We will go to the beginnings of the first circle.*

"Why?"

So you may see what you have never seen.

The wolf began to sing, in a lilting voice full of primal power and pride and happiness so heart-deep nd vast that Ryan felt a pain at the roots of his soul.

Grandfather, Great Spirit, you have been always
and before you no one has been. There is no othe
one to pray to but you. Everything has been made b
you. The star nations all over the universe you hav
finished. Grandfather, Great Spirit, lean close to th
earth that you may hear the voice I send.

On the far horizon Ryan saw a glimmering of ligh
breaking through the black curtain of the Deathlands

You toward where the sun goes down, behold me
You where the White Giant lives in power, behold me
You in the depths of the heavens, an eagle of power
behold! And you Grandmother Earth, the onl
mother, you who have shown mercy to your childre
who have ripped and burned and poisoned you,
shall heal you!

Lifting his voice, Ryan sang, "I shall heal you!"

Hear me, four quarters of the world—a relative
am! Give me the eyes to see and the strength to un
derstand, that I may heal you!

The light spread out over the horizon, like a warn
wave, so bright, so brilliant, so blinding, Ryan had n
choice but to close his eyes. He could still see th
light—green and orange, yellow and red—spreadin
out, sweeping across Deathlands, changing it, trans
forming it.

RYAN OPENED HIS EYE, shutting it again as sunligh
shafted through the window. He heard the murmur o
voices and smelled a sweetish odor. His wrist chro
told him it was half-past eight, and he sat up. His ey
patch still covered his left eye, and he had slept i
his clothes, except for his boots. Krysty had to hav
pulled them off after he had fallen asleep.

He pushed the residue of the dream into the bacl
of his mind—except it hadn't felt like a dream, no

even like the hallucinatory, almost-real illusions he occasionally experienced after a particularly rough gateway transfer.

Smelling bacon from the common room, Ryan stuffed his feet into his boots and quickly laced them up. He felt hungry and thirsty.

The others were sitting around a table laden with platters of food. J.B. sipped at a cup of steaming liquid and grimaced.

Ryan sat in a chair, and Mildred handed him a cup of dark green-black fluid that exuded a strange aroma. "It's some kind of tea," she offered.

Tentatively sipping at it, Ryan found it was strong, bitter and pungent. The platters contained loaves of bread, fatty, blistered strips of bacon and crumbling wedges of cheese. He hacked off a hunk with a knife and chewed it slowly, the cheese so sharp it made his sinuses ache.

Jak spit a half-chewed piece of bacon rind onto his plate. "If plan to kill us, this food simplest way."

Krysty and Doc were silent, nibbling on crusts of bread and nursing cups of tea, their eyes downcast.

"What's with you two?" Ryan asked.

"We took a walking tour of Amicus this morning," Krysty replied.

"And?"

"And," Doc answered, "this is not salubrious ground. As his honor the mayor indicated, the populace is now aware of the circumstances that brought us here. They are displeased about our being encamped on their front doorstep."

"They hold us responsible," Krysty added. "They want us to leave."

"Someone told you that?" Mildred asked.

"They did not need to voice it," Doc stated.

"Their desire is evident in the backs turned to us, the fish-eyed stares and the all-around frigid temperatures of their shoulders."

"Fuck 'em," Jak snapped. "We leave."

"That may not be easy," Krysty told him. "The Red Cadre has bottled up the main way in and out."

Ryan sipped at the tea, shuddered and said "There's got to be a back door."

"There is," said a voice from the doorway. "But it won't solve the immediate problem."

Mose Autry leaned against the door frame. His face was drawn and pale with worry. "The Cadre hasn't made any overtures yet, but the guards at the pass tell me the fleet is tied up a quarter mile away."

"So why can't we go out the rear exit?" Mildred asked.

"If it's you Hatchet Jack is after, he'll take vengeance on Amicus for providing you sanctuary. Whether you're here or not, he'll expect blood to be paid in blood."

"I thought you said he was afraid of pissing off the local Indians," J.B. said.

"He's more afraid of losing face with his crew," Autry responded dolefully. "As it is, even our resident tribesmen are afraid to leave town and go hunting. He might decide to sit tight and try to starve us out."

Ryan nodded. "A typical tactic. But let's hear what he has to say before scaring ourselves with 'what-ifs.'"

"Yes, but what if he wants you six in exchange for leaving us alone?"

Ryan favored Autry with a slit-eyed stare, and steel slipped into his voice. "Let's hear what he has to say."

Standing, Ryan said, "Show me around so I can get an idea of how defensible this place is."

"That will not take long," Doc remarked.

After visiting the outhouse behind the hostel, Ryan went with Autry through the ville. Amicus lay in fairly open country, in a swale between several broad, low hills. There were no walls, and the only barrier to an incursion from the rear was a great, tangled heap of mottled bones, the remains of all kinds of animals, from trout to muck-sucker to buffalo.

The people they encountered gave Ryan sullen, up-from-under stares. There were many Amerindians in the settlement, but most of them appeared to be old women and children.

They completed the circuit at a low, squat adobe building. Inside was a forge, a crude smelter, work-tables and a clean, ruddy-faced old man Autry introduced as Hasslich. His alert face shone with sincerity, only to be betrayed by the avarice in his eyes when he spied the SIG-Sauer at Ryan's hip.

His English was broken, his voice thick and raspy. "Make you gun and give you powder and ball, ho-kay? Make you trade for your blaster, hokay?"

"No hokay," Ryan said. He examined one of Hasslich's rifles from a stack propped up in a corner. It was a home-built, single-shot flintlock, made of cold-rolled steel, a few brass-alloy fittings and a walnut stock. On a table lay several flintlock pistols. The workmanship wasn't spectacular, but it was adequate. Ryan had seen better and far worse, though J.B. might disagree.

"What other kinds of blasters are in town?," he asked.

Hasslich screwed up his forehead in thought. "I t'ink Bobby Mayhew has old AK-47, no ammo for it, though. Mrs. Red Bear used to have a Ruger Blackhawk revolver, an' a HK VP-70. No, dat's right, she sold it.''

Ryan returned the rifle to the stack and surveyed the rest of the stock in the workroom. Three casks of charcoal and sulfur and a few sealed kegs of processed gunpowder were aligned against the north wall.

"Make you trade," Hasslich said again.

"You ever trade with the Red Cadre?" Ryan asked.

Hasslich shrugged. "Sometimes. Sometimes de Hatchet Jack don' wanna trade, wanna take."

"You let him?"

The old man ran his finger across his throat. "I let 'um take hokay.''

As Ryan and Autry returned to the street, Hasslich called after him, "You wan' make trade, you come back, hokay?"

Autry was silent for moment, then commented quietly, "Not much to work with, is it?"

"Not much, no."

"Then you can understand why we never made a stand against the Cadre."

"It's never a bad idea to have an idea of your available arsenal." Ryan paused, then said, "Not too long ago a gang of marauding stickies took over a ville in Colorado, a placed named Harmony. The folks there knew the gang was coming, but they didn't prepare. I guess they figured if they didn't prepare, the gang would leave them alone. An old friend of mine used to say, 'Ain't no virtue in hoping for the best when the worst is on its way.'"

Autry swallowed hard before asking, "What happened?"

"Pretty much what you'd expect to happen. The muties chilled a lot of innocent people and took over the ville, used it as a base to launch their raids. Sound familiar?"

"What happened to the gang?"

Ryan waved a casual hand through the air. "Me and my friends chilled the whole lot of them. Didn't take long."

"Why not?"

"Because we were prepared."

Autry blinked at the end of the story, not having realized there could be any connection. "Interesting analogy, Mr. Cawdor."

Ryan didn't respond. He was watching a young man on horseback gallop toward them from the direction of the pass.

"Mose!" he yelled as he reined his horse to an unsteady halt. "Got news!"

"What is it, William?" Autry inquired calmly, in deliberate counterpoint to the youth's excitement.

"Hatchet Jack sent word! He wants to parley at noon!"

Autry's face went the color of old ashes, but he showed no emotion otherwise. "Where?"

"In the pass. Said he'll come under a flag of truce."

Autry turned to Ryan. "Under the circumstances you'll forgive me if I leave you to your own—"

"Not with you," William interrupted. His forefinger jabbed toward Ryan. "With *him*."

Autry exhaled a surprised, startled breath. "With you, Mr. Cawdor. There's no reason to meet with him, though perhaps you may be able to defuse any hostilities. I can't force you, but I can ask. Will you meet with him?"

Ryan had plenty of experience of this sort of situation, and he needed the opportunity to size up the opposition.

"I'll do it," he said. "But the hostilities are already out in the open. I doubt a face-to-face palaver will close them up. Could make things worse."

Autry combed nervous fingers through his beard. "I doubt that's possible."

Ryan turned back toward the hostel. "Believe me, Mr. Autry, it is."

Inside the common room, Ryan told his five friends about Hatchet Jack's request for a conference. None of them was pleased by the notion.

"Parley for what?" J.B. demanded. "He won't let us leave."

"Ryan, dear fellow, though your judgment is sound in most matters, meeting this man might be tantamount to pouring gasoline on a fire," Doc stated.

"I agree," Krysty said. "It's probably a trap."

"Gotta be," Jak added.

Ryan nodded. "More than likely. That's why you're going with me. He might want to talk to me alone, but that doesn't mean I can't arrange for my own cover."

The six companions spent the next two hours cleaning and loading their weapons. A few minutes shy of noon, Autry came to the door and beckoned to Ryan. When the others arose, his gaze narrowed.

"I'm certain Hatchet Jack meant for you to go alone, Mr. Cawdor."

"I'll talk to him alone," Ryan replied, "but I want my back covered."

"There are guards at the pass."

"With bows and arrows and maybe a muzzle loader," Mildred said, hefting her Czech-made ZKR target revolver. "I think our firepower will more than complement your own."

Autry opened his mouth to voice an objection, then shut it and smiled in resignation. "As you wish."

Most of the population of Amicus seemed to be lining the street as they marched toward the pass. None of them spoke or so much as smiled.

"They're scared," Krysty said quietly, her hair shifting.

"I don't blame them," Mildred replied.

"Not of the Cadre, of us, of what we might bring down on them."

A blond woman shouldered her way out of the row of onlookers. She was wearing a long, fringed dress of soft doeskin. It took Ryan a moment to recognize Felicity, with her hair combed, face clean and wearing clothes. She fell into step beside him.

"You're going to talk to Hatchet Jack?" she asked.

"Yeah."

Fingers tugging nervously at her skirt, she said, "Mebbe you can ask him to return my husband's body."

Ryan knew that most Plains tribes performed ceremonies for their honored dead, believing the rituals allowed their journey to the spirit world to be speedy and uneventful. Felicity evidently shared those beliefs.

"I'll do what I can," Ryan told her.

Felicity ducked her head and dropped back.

A pair of men stood at the mouth of the cleft cut between the hills. One, leaning on a flintlock rifle, was a white man with a seamed, scarred face. The other was a very young Amerindian, an arrow already nocked into the string of his bow.

Autry stopped at the pass, and the others entered,

Ryan in the lead. The noonday sun filtered its rays through the clouds, playing with the colors of the gorge walls. Rock streaks of green melted into pale blues, which lightened into sandstone yellows. Ryan was reminded of the light he had seen in his dream.

At the curve in the gorge, Ryan halted and slowly poked his head around. A lone man stood on the sandy ground, holding a rifle. Attached to the barrel was a scrap of dirty white linen. No one else was in sight.

"Stay here," Ryan whispered, then stepped around the bend in the gorge wall.

Hatchet Jack didn't move. He watched his enemy's confident approach with no expression on his face. Ryan's gaze swept him up and down in a swift appraisal.

He appeared to be about the same age and height as Ryan, but built along heavier, massive lines. Dark blond hair flowed from beneath a feather-decorated slouch hat. A matted beard of the same hue clothed his face. His buckskin tunic and leggings were fringed and beaded with Indian finery. A polished powder horn hung by a strap from his right shoulder, and a long-handled tomahawk had been thrust in at his wide belt, beside a fourteen-inch bowie knife. A metal ring was attached to the belt, and from it dangled what looked, at first glance, to be a thatch of coarse black threads. Then Ryan saw the faint pink of a human scalp shining through the hairs.

Ryan strode to within six feet of the man and halted.

Impaling him with frosty gray eyes, the man demanded, "You who I think you are, beauty?"

"Depends," Ryan said.

"On what?"

"On who *you* are."

"Name's Hatcher, John Jacob Hatcher. Though them that speaks of me at all calls me Hatchet Jack."

"I'm Ryan Cawdor."

Hatcher nodded brusquely. "Seems like I've heard that name before."

"Mebbe. I get around. Speak your piece, Hatcher."

"You have my property in your paws. I want it back."

Ryan hadn't expected that, and it took a great deal of effort to keep the surprise from showing on his face. "Property? You mean your wind wag?"

"No, you one-eyed piece of shit," Hatcher barked. "I mean the map you stole off one of my men."

Ryan realized the twine-and-oilcloth-bound packet was still resting in his shirt pocket. "Assuming I have it, why is it so important to you?"

"My business," Hatcher rumbled.

"Not the way I see it," Ryan replied with a mocking smile. "If I do have it, it's spoils of war. Law of Deathlands."

"I say it's mine, Cawdor." Hatcher hooked his thumbs into his belt and rocked lightly on his moccasined feet. He smiled. "This don't have to be a medley, you know."

Instantly Ryan's instincts flashed a triple red. "If it's so important to you, why did one of your piss-breathed underlings have it?"

"He weren't an underling. He was my cousin. Did you chill him?"

"Is it important?"

Hatcher snorted a laugh. "Not particularly. He never were worth much more than a catfish choked to death on a sandbar." He grinned broadly. "A man like you is different. I could let you in on the deal.

Might be you'd be real helpful in this here undertaking I got in mind."

"What undertaking is that?"

"Hand over the map," Hatcher said reasonably, "and we'll talk about it."

"We'll talk about it now," Ryan said stolidly, "or not at all. Mebbe we can arrange a trade."

"What kind of trade?"

"The body of the man your men murdered yesterday. Turn it over to me, and I might just consider giving you the map."

Hatcher stared at him incredulously. "We dragged that maggot bait away. Fucking coyotes have probably already got it."

"Then," Ryan said coldly, "I guess we don't have anything more to discuss."

Hatcher bared his teeth, then took a careful step backward. "I tried, by God," he snarled. "You can't say I didn't."

Then men rose from the sand-covered floor of the gorge.

Chapter Five

In a thinly shaved fraction of a second, Ryan realized the mechanics of the trap—the pirates of the Cadre had lain in shallow ditches dug in the ground, covering themselves with neutral-colored blankets. Someone else, Hatcher probably, had sprinkled sand over them.

There were three men, about ten feet behind Hatcher, all armed with oversize flintlock hand-blasters. Before any of the pistols could spit fire and lead, Ryan took the first course of action that occurred to him. He lunged forward, kicking himself off the ground and slamming hard into Hatcher. It was like body-blocking a tree.

Hatcher didn't go down. Snarling out a stream of profanity, he grappled with Ryan, trying to swing him into a direct line of fire with the flintlocks. The one-eyed man set his feet and resisted. There hadn't been time to draw the SIG-Sauer when the men had risen from the ground and drawn beads on him, and now both his hands were filled with fistfuls of deerskin tunic.

Close locked, the two men wrestled and struggled, staggering on wide-braced legs. Hatcher's arms encircled Ryan's body, and they tightened across his spine. The pirate then jacked up a knee, seeking to crush his testicles, but Ryan managed to shift a few inches so the blow landed against his upper thigh. Still, it hurt.

Mildred's ZKR banged like a door slamming, and though Ryan didn't see her target, he heard a man shrill in pain and surprise.

"Cocksucker!" Hatcher hissed, and tried to knee him in the groin again.

Instead of fighting his way out of the hug, Ryan drove the top of his head into Hatcher's face. The pirate's head snapped up and back, blood springing from his lips. He staggered and Ryan was able to wrench himself from his adversary's grip. He drew the SIG-Sauer and triggered it all in the same whip-lash motion.

One of the pirates fell backward, his chest caved in by the bone-shattering impact of the 9 mm round. Ryan hadn't wasted time on Hatcher. Though the man was certainly dangerous, he had dropped his musket when Ryan jumped him.

The third pirate, his face flushed with fury, eyes shining in outrage, aimed his blaster and pulled the trigger. The lock fell, the flint igniting the powder trail in the pan with a little puff of smoke and a flash of sparks. The main charge fired, noise, flame and black-powder smoke blooming from the bore. The ball spun over Ryan's right shoulder, making a faint swishing sound.

The one-eyed man squeezed off a second shot. The bullet struck the pirate in the throat, smashing through his larynx and pulverizing his neck vertebrae. He flailed over on his back, blood fountaining from his open mouth.

Hatcher flung out his hands. "I'm unarmed, Cawdor!"

Ryan centered the bore of the blaster on the man's forehead. "What makes you think I give a shit?"

Hatchet Jack gaped at him. When he saw the promise of his death in that single blue eye, his shoulders sagged. As they did so, the strap of his powder horn slipped off. As it fell to the ground, Hatcher closed his hand around the loop of leather, and he swung it in an eye-blurring, thrumming circle.

Ryan squeezed the trigger, but the shot went wild as the tip of the horn caught the baffle silencer and slapped the SIG-Sauer out of his hand.

Backing away, Ryan shook his stinging fingers. If the horn had struck his hand, all the delicate bones would have probably been broken. The horn was full of more than just powder.

Hatcher swung the horn in a whistling arc that passed over Ryan's head. He began a backswing, but a fusillade of shots cracked and bullets blasted chips from the rock wall. He ducked his head and swore.

Return fire came from the opening in the gorge behind Hatcher, the reports softer than modern blasters. More of the Cadre pirates were firing muzzle loaders at Ryan's people to keep them pinned down. They couldn't shoot without risking their leader's life, and the companions couldn't shoot at Hatcher without taking the same gamble.

Ryan leaped forward, throwing a fist at Hatcher's face. The pirate evaded the driving fist with a side-step, and he swung the horn viciously in return. The container struck Ryan across the ribs, and the impact numbed his left side. In an instant he was fighting for air and trying to keep from falling.

Whooping, Hatcher whipped the powder horn toward him again. Ryan ducked, the horn struck the rock wall and the lid popped off. No powder poured out, only thick, dully gleaming chunks of metal. They caught the sun and sparkled.

Screaming wordlessly in fury, Hatcher sprang forward and looped the leather strap around Ryan's throat. His wind was immediately cut off, and within seconds he heard nothing but his own blood pounding in his ears.

Gagging, he tore at the garrote with his hands, but the pressure on his windpipe only increased. A knee was thrust brutally into the small of his back. Blindly Ryan fumbled for the handle of his eighteen-inch panga sheathed at his hip. After two groping motions, his hand closed over the handle, and he managed to drag it free. He struck behind him and felt the blade sink into yielding flesh.

Through the hammering in his temples, he heard a scream, and the agonizing pressure around his throat lessened. Ryan lunged forward, yanking the strap from Hatcher's grasp. He pulled the strip of leather from his neck and unsteadily scrambled to his feet. Blood streamed from a stab wound high on Hatcher's left thigh, and the man's face was contorted in a mask of rage and pain.

The pirate started to draw his own knife, then he froze, his eyes on something behind Ryan. He backpedaled, limping slightly. Ryan turned and saw Jak, J.B. and Krysty racing down the gorge, blasters in hand.

Hatcher began to run, expertly keeping Ryan between him and the blasters of his friends. As he ran unsteadily, he roared, "You're dead, Cawdor! You are so fuckin' *dead!*"

Ryan thought again of his dream, then his friends were all around him. J.B. and Jak started to run farther down the pass, but Ryan called them back. He retrieved his SIG-Sauer and checked it for damage.

"Damn close," Jak said tightly. "Couldn't get clear shot at him."

"He had it planned that way," Krysty said. "What did he want, besides to chill you?"

Ryan didn't answer immediately. He bent and picked up the chunks of metal from the gorge floor. There were three of them, each about the size and thickness of a big man's thumb, and they felt as heavy as lead. All had fairly smooth surfaces. He turned the largest one over. The side was far brighter, rough textured, the marks of a saw still upon it.

Gold. They were pieces of gold, measuring perhaps three inches long and less than a quarter of an inch thick.

He pulled the oilcloth-wrapped packet from his shirt and said, "Now I think I'm getting it."

Krysty frowned, taking the packet from him and opening it. Mildred and Doc joined them, looking over her shoulder.

"A map," she said. "To what and where?"

Ryan clicked the pieces of gold together in his closed fist. "I would imagine this is the what. To where I have no idea. Mebbe Mr. Autry will have an opinion or two."

They met Autry and the pair of guards before they reached the end of the pass. Their faces didn't register relief when they caught sight of the six people, alive and unharmed, but they didn't look disappointed, either.

"We heard shots," Autry said breathlessly.

"Took long enough to make recce," Jak said.

Autry ignored the observation. "Hatchet Jack, is he—?"

"No," Ryan replied, "but three of his crew are."

"Did he want you to give yourselves up to him?"

"That subject wasn't raised." Ryan opened his hand, showing the slices of gold. With the other hand he gave Autry the map. "He wanted me to give this up instead. Jak found it on one of Spotted Hawk's killers."

Autry's gaze flicked from the gold to the map, then back again. He was silent for so long, Ryan wondered if he was stunned into speechlessness. Then his face displayed an odd, unidentifiable emotion.

"This map is probably two hundred and fifty, mebbe three hundred years old," he said flatly. "It was the cause of a lot of ugly history a few centuries ago."

"Why?"

Autry sighed, handing it back. "Golden dreams and ugly realities. Let's get back to town, and I'll tell you what I know."

People were still milling about the street, and when they saw the party of outlanders alive and ambulatory, they shuffled away, muttering and mumbling.

"Hell of a chamber of commerce you've got here," Mildred commented.

Autry led them to the tavern, fetched a jug of a concoction he called White Mule and sat at the largest table in the room. When everyone was seated, holding brimming mugs, he asked, "Have any of you ever heard of Coronado?"

Only Doc and Mildred nodded.

"Francisco Vasquez Coronado," Doc said, "provincial governor of Mexico and Texas, explorer, plunderer and, some would say, genocidal monster."

Autry stared wide-eyed at Doc. "You know more about him than I do. All I know are the legends, the campfire tales that have been passed down from generation to generation.''

"Let's hear them," Krysty suggested.

"Over six hundred years ago, during one of Coronado's expeditions, he heard about the Seven Cities of Cibola. These were supposed to be Native American treasure cities, scattered all over the West and Southwest. According to legend, they were so full of gold, silver and precious gems that sunlight was reflected off them for miles around. Coronado and a company of conquistadores set out to find these cities.''

"There's a similar legend in Central America," Mildred said. Since she had minored in American Indian history at her university, she knew quite a few obscure facts about aboriginal cultures. "Tales of the city of El Dorado have circulated for centuries."

"At any rate," Autry continued, "months passed and the conquistadores were decimated by Indian attacks, disease and exposure. Some believed Coronado traveled beyond the Yellowstone, deep into Utah. He found nothing and returned to Mexico, a defeated man.

"However, the legend of the Seven Cities persisted, due mainly to one of Coronado's soldiers who'd committed their route to paper. According to the soldier, they had indeed found the location of one of the cities, but they were driven back by an army of Indians before they laid eyes on it. During the early days of colonization of this territory, the map and the story wouldn't have been given any credence whatsoever if some of the Sioux groups hadn't enjoyed visiting the Franciscan missions, flaunting ornaments fashioned from gold and silver.

"In the mid-1700s, French explorer de Varennes

chanced upon the map while staying at the mission near the Sweetwater River. He made a copy of the map—in French, of course—and went to Norleans intent on gathering men and materials to mount a major expedition. As the story goes, the man died and the map was thought to be lost.''

"What happened to the original copy, the one in the mission?'' J.B. asked.

"Crazy Horse burned down the mission in the 1870s,'' Autry answered. "It was probably destroyed.''

Ryan flicked the gold pieces on the table with a fingertip. "Like you said, campfire stories.''

"Perhaps,'' Autry replied. "But your map is obviously very old. It may be a copy of de Varennes's copy, but it definitely shows the route from the Yellowstone, across the Washakie Basin where we are, toward mountains that can only be the Wind River Range.''

"If you've identified the landmarks,'' Mildred said, "then why are the mountains labeled 'mountains of mystery'?''

Reluctantly Autry said, "Aside from the stories about the Seven Cities of Cibola, there are old Indian legends about hidden places in the Wind River and Medicine Bow Range. Medicine spots, they're called, doorways to the other side. If these power points, these doorways, are sealed off, Indians believe their souls will wander for eternity. In these hidden places, in valleys and mountain peaks, dwell the ghosts of the First People, the prehuman ancestors of the Indian.''

Pausing long enough to swallow a mouthful of liquor, Autry added, "And rich veins of gold are also supposed to be there. To this day some of the Lakota and Cheyenne wear gold ornaments and trade them here for goods. What you have there doesn't look like raw, stream-panned ore. Looks to me like it was hacked from a molded ingot.''

Revolving a piece of the gold between thumb and forefinger, Ryan realized he was right. The chunk of metal had been melted, worked and formed some time in the past. Though gold wasn't sought after as a rare commodity in some regions of Deathlands, in most of the baronies of the West, it was still prized and valuable enough to kill for.

''You figure Hatchet Jack thinks one of these Seven Cities is in the Wind River Range?'' J.B. asked.

''Seems likely,'' Ryan replied. ''If he could find it, he could set up the most powerful barony in this part of the country.''

''Is that not a delightful prospect?'' Doc commented sourly.

''Wonder where he got that gold?'' J.B. said. ''He probably traded or stole or chilled to get the map, but where'd he find the gold?''

''Probably tortured or chilled some poor Indian,'' Krysty said.

To Ryan, she said, ''This Red Cadre is a bad bunch, about as bad as we've ever seen.''

Ryan tapped the gold pieces and the map. ''And we've got four things he wants.''

''Five,'' Krysty corrected. ''Your scalp.''

Chapter Six

By late afternoon the guards at the pass had reported no suspicious activity among the Red Cadre, but no one in Amicus seemed relieved. The settlement was unusually quiet. Every door, tepee flap and shutter was closed, and there wasn't a sign or sound of movement from the interiors.

Jak and Doc, walking down the street, were made uneasy by the hush. Though neither was familiar with habits of Amicans, they were fairly well versed in villes, and the absence of children, men and women stirred their hackles.

As the only single members of the group of travelers, Doc and Jak were accustomed to giving Krysty and Ryan, and Mildred and J.B. some privacy whenever they sensed it was necessary. It sometimes was inconvenient to make themselves scarce, but they understood the need for couples to be alone from time to time.

As they walked through the town, Jak asked, unconsciously lowering his voice, "Think people moved out?"

Doc considered the possibility then shook his head. "According to Mr. Autry, the rear exit is really no exit from danger, since it simply leads to the plains."

Sounds from the tavern attracted their attention. They heard voices, male and female, and quite a few judging by the near-constant murmur.

They pushed open the door and stepped inside. There were about twenty people, fairly evenly divided between men and women. The few who noticed Jak and Doc's entrance shot them cold glances and went back to their discussions.

Everyone was talking, arguing, debating, deliberating: the Red Cadre, Hatchet Jack, mountain passes, Spotted Hawk, pack animals. Their words were interspersed with noisy slurps as they downed mug after mug of liquor.

One burly, soot-faced, stump-legged and stump-toothed man talked the loudest. He held court at a corner table, gripping a mug in one hand and a jug in the other.

"Shit, me and John Hatcher go way back," he announced, his aggressive voice punching against Jak's sensitive eardrums. "Used to hunt buffalo with him on the Washakie Divide. Saved his life when a chem storm came up."

"Is he as bloodthirsty as his rep makes him out to be, Eli?" one of the men at the table asked. "Can he be reasoned with?"

The man addressed as Eli looked thoughtful for a moment. "He's a lusty infant, no denyin' that," he admitted. "But he ain't unreasonable. Just don't cross him."

Eli's gaze settled on Jak and Doc. "Nope, just don't cross him, like some donkey-shit dumb outlanders I recently heard about."

Though Jak's body tensed, Doc whispered, "Ignore him, lad. He's simply passing wind the frontier fashion."

They walked to the bar. Micah was perspiring heavily, and sweat dripped from the ends of his mustache. "White Mule?"

"If that is all you have on the list," Doc answered.

"It is." The bartender poured a three-fingered amount of liquid into a chipped ceramic mug and pushed it across the wet pine to him. "You and your group stayin' or goin'?"

"We have yet to decide," Doc replied, sipping at the rancid, fiery liquor.

The man tried to grin, exposing brown-speckled teeth. "Like the rest of these souls. Don't know if they want to light out for points east or stay and see what the Cadre is gonna do. Right now they're lettin' the corn make up their minds."

Jak looked around him, and his nostrils detected an odor he hadn't noticed upon entering. Mixed in with the other aromas of the tavern was a faint but pungent smell. Jak had scented it many times before—the smell of desperation, of fear. Of confusion. The eyes of the people mirrored it, and it shone there brightly, not in the least dimmed by the liquor they poured down their throats.

Jak understood and sympathized with their confusion. The Amicans were faced with making a decision that could alter, even end their lives. The citizens knew, without really knowing, that if they threw themselves into a fray against the Red Cadre, it would be a far more serious scrape than a backstreet brawl. And they also knew that even if they drank themselves into oblivion, they would still be there when the jugs ran dry—to run and live or fight and die.

It was a choice Jak had faced more than once during his short life.

Doc leaned over and said quietly, "My lad, this is not a saloon. It is a waiting room in Hell."

A young man shouldered in between Doc and Jak. He was dressed rather dapperly in a snakeskin vest over a coarse cotton shirt. His breath was redolent with whiskey fumes. He wasn't much older than Jak, and he introduced himself as Allen.

Facing Doc, swaying a bit, he said, "So, tell me, sir, will you and your party oppose the tyrant?"

"Do you mean Mr. Autry?" Doc asked, smiling a bit.

Allen shook his head, and his body lurched unsteadily. "Of course not. I mean—" he swallowed a belch "—John Hatcher."

"I believe we already have, sir."

The youth nodded. "I, too, wish to oppose him."

"Ah. And do you think that can be accomplished from here?"

Allen started to reply, then favored the older man with a knife-eyed glare. "Are you questioning my courage, sir?"

"Certainly not," Doc said smoothly. His hands tightened around the lion's-head pommel of his cane, silently loosening the sheath encasing the blade of Toledo steel. "I'm only requesting information."

The young man grunted. "Lucky for you that you were not casting aspersions on the fierce fighting men of Amicus. For if you were—"

"Oh, shut your pan, boy," came Eli's weary voice from the corner table.

Allen looked around unfocusedly for the man who had given him the order, then he complied with it. He lifted the cup to his lips, and the rim clinked against his teeth. For a moment his face was that of an embarrassed little boy.

Doc clapped him on the shoulder and said cheerfully, "Never mind, Master Allen. You are all sand, by the Three Kennedys, else you would not be here. I admire your fortitude."

The youth's face flushed, with either pride or drink, and he shuffled away. Jak met Doc's eye and smirked, shaking his white-maned head. "Stupe," he muttered.

A gentle hand touched Doc's shoulder from behind. He turned to see Felicity standing there, her hair pulled back severely from her face.

"Excuse me, Dr. Tanner, but I never heard. Did Mr. Cawdor ask Hatchet Jack about my husband?"

A little jolt of pain went through Doc's heart when he looked into those blue eyes. For a moment he wrestled with his conscience. He had overheard Hatcher's response to Ryan's question about Spotted Hawk, and he knew relaying it might devastate the young woman.

Still, telling her the truth was preferable to allowing her to spend another day wondering and aching.

"I am truly sorry, madam," Doc said quietly. "Mr. Hatcher was unmoved by the plight of your husband's remains."

Felicity blinked, then she nodded. "I expected him to be."

With a swirl of her doeskin skirt, she spun and left the tavern.

Staring after her, Doc felt the pain within him transform into anger. It was the same anger he felt toward the scientists of Operation Chronos who had wrenched him from his wife, Emily, and two children, Rachel and Jolyon.

His constant pleas to be returned to his own era, to his family, had fallen on uncaring ears. To the scientists he was only a test subject, and his emotional agony meant less than a sparrow's tears to the success of the time-trawling experiments.

The scientists had justified their cold-hearted practices by claiming patriotism as a motive, since they were ensuring the safety of the United States against all aggressors. They had told Doc that, as an American citizen—albeit one from 1895—he should share their motivations.

The old proverb "Patriotism is the last refuge of the scoundrel" was never more descriptive of anybody in history than the overseers of Operation Chronos.

Doc wasn't the least ashamed of the satisfaction he felt whenever he remembered how all of the scientists had perished in the nukecaust. Appeals to patriotism and advanced technology had not saved them, but the latter, misused as it was, had saved him.

He took a long, burning swallow of the liquor. A moral was in there someplace, he reflected.

There was a faint and distant popping sound, as if a faraway balloon had burst. Jak glanced quickly around. "Hear that?"

"Hear what?" Doc asked.

Then the tavern moved, as though a giant boot had given the foundation a ferocious kick. Mugs fell over, sloshing liquor on the tables, laps and the floor. The ceiling cracked, showering the room with sawdust and wood particles.

The sound of the explosion wasn't painfully loud, but it was loud enough for Jak to realize a grenade had detonated either against or just outside the tavern.

Acrid smoke rolled into the one window, and as the Amicans coughed, wheezed and fought one another to get outside, Doc and Jak joined Micah beneath the bar, just in case the ceiling collapsed altogether. The bartender was shaking in fright, but both Jak and Doc had been under fire too many times to allow fear to control them.

When the tavern had cleared of people, Jak, Doc

and Micah went outside. The wall facing the pass was blackened and chewed up by shrapnel, and a pumpkin-sized crater smoldered a scant five feet from the clapboard siding.

"Close," Jak said, shading his eyes and gazing toward the hills.

The people milled in the street, shouting in fear and anger. Ryan, Krysty, Mildred and J.B. jogged from the hostel. When they spied Doc and Jak, they slowed their pace.

"Gren," Jak said when they came abreast of him. "Almost direct hit."

Ryan and J.B. eyed the hills but saw no one.

"About four hundred yards," J.B. stated with grudging admiration in his voice. "Whoever aimed the launcher had a decent eye."

"Half the fuckin' town was in there!" Micah shrilled.

"A direct hit would have gone a long way to clearing Hatcher's path," Ryan commented. "How was he able to put men on top of the hill without raising an alarm?"

"Interesting question," Krysty said. "Let's take a recce."

The six companions, followed by a dozen townspeople, ran down the muddy street toward the pass. Mose Autry met them at the opening, waving at them to halt.

"I called for the guards. Nobody answered."

"How many on duty?" Ryan asked.

"The same as before. Two."

"Two?" echoed Mildred incredulously. "With those scumbags creeping around outside of town, you posted two guards?"

"The Cadre has made no direct threats against us,

have they?'' Autry responded with some heat. "Their quarrel isn't with us.''

"It goddamn well is now!'' a female voice shouted from the rear of the crowd.

Ryan pushed past Autry and indicated with sign language that he, Krysty and Jak would climb the left-hand slope, while the other three scaled the one on the right.

As was customary, Ryan took the point. Clouds, low and heavy, scudded across the afternoon sky. They were too thin to bring rain, but they cast shifting shadows over the rocky hillside.

When Ryan cautiously topped the crest and looked out on the plain below, the first thing he saw was the bodies of the two guards. They lay about a hundred yards beyond the mouth of the pass. Naked, they were staked to the ground in spread-eagled positions. Their faces, or what could be seen of them, were livid with blood. Ryan figured their tongues had been cut out or their throats cut. Perhaps both.

John Hatcher and four of his pirates stood a hundred yards beyond the mutilated bodies. He cradled the gren launcher in his arms and when he saw Ryan top the rise, he lifted the weapon over his head and gave voice to a fierce, victorious howl.

The pirates were just outside of blaster range. To fire at them would be a waste of ammunition. Ryan fixed his eye on the giant form of Hatchet Jack, and a fury swelled within him, the homicidal rage that made his heart and temples pound.

Up until that moment, Hatchet Jack and the Red Cadre were problems of a tactical nature, not personal. Now they became enemies to be destroyed.

Hatcher bellowed something. Because of the distance, the word was faint, but Ryan understood the meaning nonetheless.

The word was "Soon."

Chapter Seven

The westward horizon swallowed the sun, the dying rays turning the sky variegated shades of magenta and purple.

Fires flared in the street of Amicus. The faces of the people were bathed in flickering light, and red pinpoints gleamed from the many pairs of frightened eyes fixed upon Autry and Ryan. The crowd set up a clamor, wanting to know what was happening, and more importantly, how they should react.

Autry managed to quiet them with a few words and announced, "We're in a predicament, but Amicus has been in a number of them during its short history."

"Nothin' like this!" a man croaked. "Not even when the Sioux had hairs up their asses did they bottle up the town this way."

Autry ignored the outburst. "Inasmuch as we're a democracy, I'm soliciting your opinions on our best course of action."

That was the cue for a general bickering session to commence.

"What can we do against the Cadre?"

"They hold a grudge against us, remember?"

"Let's absquatulate at first light!"

"First light, hell! Let's get over the back hills now!"

Autry lifted calming hands. "Even if we could skulk out of here, and if the Cadre indeed harbors inimical feelings toward us, they could easily track us and catch us out in the open.''

''And if we stay here,'' cried a man sounding half-crazed by fear, ''we'll die penned up like ground-hogs!''

People shouted their agreement with that sentiment, voices clamoring at once, trying be heard over their neighbors. The Amicans went into criticisms of personal habits and snared themselves in their own arguments. They would switch sides or even forget on whose behalf they were speaking. Finally, when hands clutched at weapons, Ryan realized Autry had lost control of the democratic process, so he stood up beside him.

''Listen to me, *listen to me!*'' Ryan had to yell in order to be heard over the frightened babblings. ''This place is defensible. If the Cadre mounts a siege, we'll be able to hit them hard every time they stage an attack.''

''And then what?'' roared the man Doc had identified as Eli. ''Our food supplies won't last more than a week.''

''And the Cadre's provender probably can't be stretched out more than two days,'' Ryan retorted.

''They can at least hunt,'' a woman said. ''We'll be eating our dogs for breakfast if the Cadre decides to wait us out.''

Eli stabbed a grimy finger at Ryan. ''It's your scalp Hatchet Jack wants, outlander. I think we oughta just turn you over to him, all dressed out and gift wrapped.''

There was a muttering of agreement, and a segment of the crowd surged forward. Instantly Jak, Krysty, Doc, J.B. and Mildred materialized around Ryan, hands on blaster butts.

Autry lost his temper, shaking clenched fists. "You goddamn fools! Hatcher wouldn't spare us now, no matter what we do to appease him. It's a matter of principle, of pride. His ego won't allow us to live!"

"What do you want us to do?" Micah asked, his voice quavering.

"All I want," Autry snapped, "is for you to do something that might save your skins and the ville. God knows you've been leaving that responsibility up to others long enough."

His declaration was countered by a few derisive hoots and sarcastic comments.

"I ain't gonna die because of some outlanders," Eli snarled. "There ain't no need to."

"Who's asking you to die?" Ryan asked sharply. "If you can't see the real threat, you'll die with us outlanders, not because of us. That's the godawful bastard truth."

Felicity suddenly stepped into the firelight. Her face was an emotionless mask, and she spoke hesitantly. "My husband—you all knew him—was murdered by the Cadre for no other reason than they wanted to murder someone and Spotted Hawk was close at hand. And it's funny, since we came to Amicus three years ago so we wouldn't always have to be looking backward to see who was going to shove a blade into us."

Her chin trembled, but her eyes swept boldly over the crowd. "A lot us came here to get away from enforced slavery to some fat-assed baron, to live free. Freedom from jack grubbing, from chilling another poor bastard so you could take what he had. Freedom from stinking buzzard turds who live only so they can inflict pain on others. You pay for freedom, I guess. Mebbe our lives are the price. But Spotted Hawk used to say, 'The dead will live forever if they die inside a circle.'"

Ryan swiveled his head toward her, having a difficult time keeping the astonishment he felt from showing on his face.

"I never knew what he meant," Felicity continued. "Now I do. Amicus, our community, the place we built, is a circle. I hope you know that before it's too late to do you any good. But I'd rather die than live and eat the shit Hatchet Jack wants to shove down our throats. And unless all of you have acquired a taste for it, you'll stand with me and the outlanders."

Felicity took another step and stood shoulder to shoulder between Krysty and Ryan. The assembled Amicans said nothing for a very long time. The hush was broken by Eli's harsh voice.

"Ain't that inspirin'? Well, I ain't joinin' up with no shirttail army. I know Hatcher, and I know he's a reasonable man."

Turning to him, Autry said wearily, "You're free to ride out and strike your own deal if you've a mind to, Eli."

"Think I won't?" the burly man said with a sneer. "You're wrong. I'll go for a gab, and if I can't talk Jack into leavin' us alone in exchange for cyclops here, I'll kiss ol' Hasslich's ass."

Facing the crowd, Eli demanded, "Who'll go with me and prove this outland blowhard wrong?"

Eli received many a doubtful stare and a shuffling of feet, but no one elected to accompany him. Snorting out a scornful laugh, he stomped toward the corral.

"I'll be back afore the moon sets. Or mebbe I won't. Mebbe I'll come to my senses and join up with the Cadre. I can do without you mush-minded fools."

Watching him stride away, Hasslich edged out of the crowd and over to Ryan. "No offense, Mr. Cawdor," he whispered, "but I sorta hopes my ass ends up gettin' kissed."

The people who heard the comment laughed. It was a bit forced, but some of the pall of tension hovering over the Amicans lifted.

"As much as I hate to take anything Eli says seriously," Autry said, "perhaps we should wait and find out if his talk with the Cadre bears any fruit."

"Don't be stupe," Mildred said. "Would you believe anything either one of them might say?"

Autry shrugged. "If nothing else, Eli might be able to give us an idea of the Cadre's firepower and actual numbers. If he doesn't return by the time he set, we'll begin making definite preparations."

"Preparations for what?" Felicity asked. "For a siege, a surrender, a flight or a fight?"

Autry dry washed his face with his hands. "I don't know."

As the crowd drifted away, Ryan and Doc decided to visit the pass to see what would be required to barricade it and to check on the six guards Autry had posted. Hasslich and Felicity volunteered to go with them.

As they walked toward the hills, Ryan asked Felicity, "That stuff about dying in a circle—that a common Cheyenne saying?"

"I don't know. It was something Spotted Hawk used to say. He said there is a life circle, and that it must not be broken. That there are some things worth dying for, and more importantly, worth living for. Why do you ask?"

"No reason."

Hasslich had provided the arms to the guards.

When they reached the pass, he inspected each one, making sure the weapons were being given the proper care and attention.

The guards reported no movement within a hundred-yard perimeter of the entrance to the gorge. They were edgy, anxious to be relieved. Though the bodies of the murdered guards had been retrieved, they feared the Cadre would creep up on them in the dark. Since their predecessors had been chilled in broad daylight, their fears weren't entirely without justification.

At the narrow mouth of the gorge, Ryan eyed the dark plain. In the distance, at least half a mile away, was a flickering spear point of firelight. It was the camp of the Red Cadre.

"T'ain't gettin' it, Mr. Cawdor," Hasslich said, looking up at the overhanging ledges. "I don' fancy bein' hemmed up in here by prairie pirates."

Ryan didn't respond, and Hasslich said no more. He moved away to rejoin the guards. The only sounds were the faint hum of a breeze and the infrequent chirp of a night bird. Very distantly, almost at the edge of Ryan's hearing, a wolf's howl wafted through the darkness and a chill crawled up his backbone.

Doc sidled up to him and said in a low voice, "Has it occurred to you that we six could easily appropriate mounts from the corral and ride into the night? The Crimson Fraternity may follow us and leave Amicus unmolested."

"It's occurred to me," Ryan admitted. "But I doubt Hatcher would bypass Amicus to get on our trail. He'd suspect they helped us to escape. He owes Amicus a serious bloodletting, anyway."

"Then I submit a variation to that same scenario—

we simply ride into the night, leaving Amicus and Hatcher to settle their scores their own way.''

Ryan leaned against an outcropping and ran a hand through his dark hair. ''I remember one time Trader found a stockpile of nerve gas on an old military base. Nasty stuff, still potent. A whole lot of it, too, since it didn't get used during the nuking. Trader had customers for it, serious jack, but he disguised the site so no one, not even him, could make a profit from it.''

''The point being?'' Doc inquired.

''Trader accepted the responsibility. He took the responsibility for uncovering it and he took the responsibility for covering it up again. There were some things that even he felt were too fucking foul to set loose on the world again, no matter how much jack he could put in his pockets.''

''And you feel we should take responsibility for leading the Cadre to Amicus.''

''You don't agree?''

''Oh, no. I entirely agree. I was just interested in hearing you say it, since you are normally so taciturn when your emotions are involved.''

From the gloom came music, rising and falling notes, mournful and angry at the same time. The bugler of the Red Cadre played a tune that carried a relentless savagery in it, stirring, repetitious and a little nerve-racking.

''What're they doing?'' Ryan asked. ''Serenading us?''

Doc's lean body tensed. ''No, they're sending us a message. That's the 'Deguello.'''

''The what?''

''The 'Deguello,' the throat-cutting song,'' Doc replied, ''a perennial of Mexican army regimental bands a few hundred years ago. Very old, dating back to the bloody wars between Spain and the Moors. When Generalissimo Santa Anna had the Texans boxed up within the Alamo, his bands played it on the night and morning preceding the final assault.''

Ryan nodded in comprehension. ''No quarter. No mercy for the loser.''

Suddenly Felicity ran swiftly toward them. ''Rider coming in. Looks like Eli.''

Hasslich and the guards joined them at the edge of the pass. A rider was coming across the plain, but the horse was walking.

''What's wrong with the fool?'' one of the guards demanded. ''Why's he meanderin' like that?''

The guards raised their voices in irritated mutterings at the horseman's leisurely pace. As he drew nearer, they could see it was indeed Eli.

''Perhaps he's hurt,'' Doc ventured.

''Or drunk,'' Hasslich growled.

Ryan drew his blaster and, bidding a guard and Hasslich to follow him, sprinted out of the gorge. All of them stopped dead in their tracks when they came to within twenty feet of the mounted man. They walked the remaining distance. There was no need to hurry.

Eli was bound to his saddle by a wooden A-frame that held him upright. His face, drained of all color, save for a smear of blood, was twisted in a rictus of terror and pain. The blood had streamed from the top of his head where his scalp had been before it had been shorn away. His chest bore a narrow, gaping wound that had obviously been made by the blade of a broad-headed hatchet.

Pinned to the front of his coat with a sharpened bone needle was a square of paper. Scrawled on the paper, no doubt in Eli's own blood, was a single word: "Soon."

Ryan turned away from the corpse, his face expressionless. In a flat voice he said, "Well, Mr. Hasslich, I hope your ass isn't too disappointed."

Chapter Eight

Ryan's plan was simple. There was no need to fancy it up, at least not at first.

Leaving the guards at their posts, despite their terror, he, Doc, Felicity and Hasslich ran back to Amicus to rouse the citizens. They had freed Eli's corpse from the framework, and Hasslich led his horse, the man's body draped over the saddle. The animal wasn't very tall, and Eli's fingers and toes dragged the ground, the blood from his raw scalp leaving a sticky crimson trail in the dust.

Ryan fetched Mose Autry from his shack at the shores of the lake. He was pale and reluctant to go.

"The Cadre will strike at first light," said Ryan. "We've got to be ready."

Autry wagged his head repeatedly from side to side. "Why would Hatcher warn us like this?"

"Ego, like you said. Also to shake us up, scare us so we can't think clearly. Right now we'll concentrate on defense. When that's done, we'll map out an offensive strategy."

"You think either one will do us any good against all of them?"

"Mebbe it will, mebbe it won't, but we can't sit here all night waiting to die at dawn."

When Autry didn't respond, Ryan growled, "You're the leader here."

"They blame me for this. By offering you and your people refuge, I dragged them into this predicament."

"You can let them think you can drag them out of it."

Autry massaged his eyes with the heels of both hands. "I'm tired, Cawdor. Tired of fighting for lost causes. That's all Amicus is, you know—another lost, empty dream. And Deathlands won't suffer dreams to live. I should have known."

Ryan grasped the man's arm, squeezing so tightly Autry grimaced in pain. "I know about lost dreams, believe me. I also know it's not always possible or even desirable to fight on the winning side. Maybe the buzzards'll end up making dinner out of our carcasses, but we can make sure we won't be the only courses."

Autry dropped his hands and stared unblinkingly at Ryan. Slowly a smile spread across his face. He clapped him on the shoulder, saying, "You've the gift of finding hope in hopeless situations, Mr. Cawdor. Mebbe some of that gift will rub off on me, and I can pass it on to my people."

Within twenty minutes most of the Amican population was assembled at the main bonfire. Autry told them of Eli's fate and the message he carried, which drew a collective moan of dismay.

"No, don't let that bastard scare you," Autry shouted. "Brothers and sisters, we can give Hatcher a fight yet. We'll send the Red Cadre back to the Yellowstone to die on its banks. They'll be coming about breakfast time, so by God, let's give them *snakes* to eat!"

None of the people cheered at the words, but they listened and they accepted the reality there was no other option than to make a fight of it. They weren't determined or inspired; they were simply resigned. Nevertheless, they hustled off in all directions to prepare.

All of the weapons in town were brought to the tavern. Most of them were Hasslich's muzzle loaders, rifles and pistols. Everyone had knives, many of the them homemade replicas of Bowie's famous blade. A few possessed tomahawks, and there were plenty of bows and arrows. Hasslich had powder and shot in his workshop, but it was barely enough for a protracted battle.

As Hasslich had indicated, there was an AK-47 in town. J.B. inspected it, opening the breech and snorting in disgust. "The firing pin's busted. Might make someone a piss-poor club, though."

Autry took a group of men and women to the mouth of the pass and set them to work building a barricade of rock, linking the largest boulders by chest high walls of sandstone and shale that would serve as adequate battlements for the defenders.

The defenders themselves consisted of thirty-six people, nineteen men and seventeen women, none under the age of fifteen or over the age of fifty. All of them had lived many years on the frontier, and Ryan saw no need to drill them. The rest of the citizens were either too old, too young, too infirm or not inclined to take part. They were confined to hastily erected shelters near the boneyard.

The night wore on, with Autry and Ryan supervising the Amicans' appointed tasks. The hills on either side of the pass worried him more than he let on. Barricade or no barricade, he knew that the Red Cadre would split its force, some sweeping through the gorge and others scaling the hills. There weren't enough people to defend both hills and the pass.

Krysty, who had been helping to build the barricade, called to Ryan. In a voice low enough so the others couldn't hear, she said, "With that gren launcher of his, Hatcher could stand out on the plain and pepper the town to pieces."

"I know, but he'll be firing blind. We'll have blasters on the hilltops to keep them from climbing. They'll have to come through the pass."

Glancing at the gorge, she said, "If there was only some way to bring the walls down when they're jammed in there—"

"Mr. Cawdor!"

Felicity jogged up to them, rifle cradled in her arms. She wore a brace of flintlock blasters in a sash at her waist, as well as a long-bladed knife. "I need to ask you something."

"What?"

"No matter what happens, Hatchet Jack will be coming after you, right?"

"I'm counting on it."

Felicity took a deep breath. "If you can, will you spare his life?"

Ryan's eye narrowed. "Why?"

"So I can have it."

"Revenge for your husband?" Krysty asked.

Felicity shook her head. "Not revenge. A reckoning of the spirits. It has to be done, or Spotted Hawk's spirit will never rest."

"I can't promise anything. I'll do what is necessary, even if that includes sparing his life for you."

Felicity's lips compressed, and she turned and walked away.

Ryan shook his head in bewilderment. "I never heard of that spirit-balancing belief before."

"It's not too different from balancing Gaia's earth

energies," Krysty commented. "They've got to be maintained on a certain level, or one side will tip and cause a negative- or positive-power avalanche."

"Avalanche," he echoed.

Taking Krysty by the arm, he rushed back into the ville, fetching Doc, J.B., Mildred and Jak along the way. Ryan sent Jak and Mildred to the tavern to collect every jug—empty, full or otherwise—they could find. Micah was out building fortifications and wasn' able to object when they poured the acrid contents of some of the jugs onto the ground. They joined the others in Hasslich's workshop and examined the ten one-gallon jugs for punctures or cracks. All of them were whole.

Prying up the lids of two kegs of gunpowder standing against the wall, Ryan explained his plan. If it failed, the supply of powder would either be inaccessible to the defenders or literally up in smoke.

"If we fill these jugs with gunpowder, drill holes in the corks and if a fuse can be run from each of these jugs and braided and linked to make one long fuse," Ryan said, "do you think the bang will be big enough to drop the sides of the gorge down on the heads of the Cadre?"

Eyeing the kegs, J.B. replied uneasily, "If the powder is of halfway decent burn quality, yeah. If it isn't we'll just have a fizzle and no way to retrieve the powder—unless Hatcher finds it and uses it himself against us."

"That's a chance we'll have to take."

Hasslich had the proper material for a fuse in the workshop, and Jak and Doc set to work puncturing the corks of the jugs with knives. Mildred and J.B. with the use of a funnel, carefully poured the gunpowder into the jugs. Ryan and Krysty busied themselves partially unbraiding the long loop of fuse, sprinkling powder along its length, then entwining it again.

When the jugs were filled and the corks punctured, Ryan bound the containers together with rope so if one detonated prematurely, the others wouldn't be hurled away by the explosion. Putting them all in a big burlap bag, he and Krysty made their way back to the pass. According to his wrist chron, it was nearly five o'clock.

The climb to the top of the right-hand hill was rugged, with Ryan weighed down by the jugs of gunpowder. He was panting with exertion when they reached their destination. There were a few tangled mesquite bushes at the crest, as well as patches of wildflowers with drooping petals.

Not stopping to rest, Ryan examined the lip of the ridge overhanging the gorge for cracks or faults. He found a deep split in the strata, seven steps from the edge. It was three feet deep and fifteen feet long. He and Krysty inserted the loose tendrils of fuse into the holes in the corks.

When the job was finished, Ryan stood and ran out the fuse, tossing it down the face of the hill. The powder-impregnated line was not long enough to reach the barricades, so when the time came, someone—probably him—was going to have to expose himself and climb fifty-odd feet to light it.

Chapter Nine

The sun was a bare finger's width above the horizon when they began to arrive. The wind wags of the Red Cadre swept across the plain. They rolled in a compact, orderly formation, from two different directions. A few hundred yards from the pass, the pirates disembarked. Ryan had expected a disorganized mass, like spooked cattle, but the men marched in ordered ranks.

Ryan stood atop the right-hand hill with Krysty and Jak. Six men stood behind them. On the left-hand hill were six men, all identically armed with long blasters. Mose Autry stood with them. Mildred, Doc and J.B. were at the fortifications below.

"There's more of them than I thought," Krysty breathed. "Must be two hundred."

Ryan scanned the approaching pirates and said, "More like fifty. The manner they march in is an old Indian trick, to make the enemy think he's hopelessly outnumbered." He peered through the binoculars and saw well-built men with faces devoid of warmth or humor. Most of them carried muzzle loaders, but he spotted a few multishot blasters here and there among them.

John Hatcher brought up the rear. On his belt was a new scalp, the color of Eli's hair. He cradled the M-79 gren launcher, and a bag hung from one shoulder. It looked heavy, and Ryan figured it contained the explosive rounds. A man walked beside him holding a battered, verdigris-eaten green bugle.

Turning to the men assembled behind him, Ryan said, ''Remember what we planned. Pick your targets and fire. While you reload, me and my people will blaze away.''

Ryan glanced at Krysty. She had her Smith & Wesson in both hands, and she gave him a reassuring smile. He propped the cushioned stock of the Steyr against his right hip.

The bugler sounded a brassy, bleating note. At the same moment the pirates thundered across the plain, moving as though they were being pushed forward by a wind from death's kingdom. They uttered strident, wordless cries. Blaster stocks slapped against shoulders, and puffs of smoke bloomed amid a staccato popping sound.

A few musket balls rattled on the stones around the defenders. The men aiming their long blasters murmured prayers and muttered curses. But most of them were veterans of frontier battles, and they waited until the first wave of pirates was clearly framed in their weapons' sights. When they fired, it was without haste and without mistake.

At each shot, one of the Cadre either tumbled to the ground or slapped at a wound. As the men fell back to reload, Ryan shouldered the Steyr, squinted through the Starlite nightscope and squeezed the trigger. Within the crosshairs of the telescopic sight, he saw a pirate pitch over backward as though struck by lightning. Working the bolt action smoothly, Ryan fired twice more, picking his targets with care. A clear view of Hatcher was obscured by running, milling men.

Jak fired his .357 Magnum Colt Python and cursed

when he missed his target. Even with a six-inch barrel, the range was too great for a handblaster.

The pirates wavered, turned, then raced back toward their wind wags. Seven of them would never sail the prairie again, and as they fled Autry drilled one of the rearmost marauders in the center of the back.

A ragged cheer erupted along the ranks of the men arrayed on both sides of the pass. Ryan didn't join in, nor did Jak or Krysty.

"Were testing us," Jak said. "Won't turn them back easy next time."

A raspy voice shouted across the plain. Hatcher was exhorting his brigands to do better next time. The defenders heard him, too, and they feverishly finished reloading their weapons. None of them had been so much as scratched, but Ryan knew such good fortune couldn't last.

Ryan watched the activity through the binoculars. The Cadre milled around their wags, and several clambered aboard each one, Hatcher included. The low growl of the diesel engines turning over and catching wafted through the early-morning air. With a series of lurches, the fleet rolled forward. The wags were maneuvered closely together until a gap of only six or seven feet separated the hulls.

The pirates were crouched between the curving sides of the craft snug on the inside of the formation. The remainder marched behind. Almost every man was protected by mobile cover.

It was a strategy Ryan had expected and feared. The first sortie had been experimental, testing their defenses and the quality of their marksmanship. Hatcher hadn't wanted to risk damage to his craft unless it was absolutely necessary. Apparently he now considered the risk necessary.

The engines that powered the fan blades, which in turn filled the sails, were protected by sheet-metal cowlings. The balls fired by the muzzle loaders didn't have the velocity to penetrate the sheathing. Even shooting the sails full of holes would only slow the advance, not halt it.

The fleet picked up speed, and bullets began to pound into the hillsides. A man on the right hilltop screamed and fell backward, hands over a pulsing throat wound. A disconcerted shout went up from the defenders. They gazed in shock at the wounded, bleeding man.

"Eyes on your targets!" Ryan yelled. Across from him, Mose Autry repeated that command.

Bullets bounced from stone and hard-packed dirt, sending up sprays of soil and ricocheting away. Ryan raised the Steyr to his shoulder, fixing one of the pirates in the scope's crosshairs. He waited until the man's head, shoulders and torso filled the sight. Though the light was growing stronger, the Starlite scope's laser image enhancer was still useful.

"Fire!" he shouted.

The men on both hilltops squeezed the triggers of their long blasters. A hail of bullets smote the wind wags, splintering handrails, tearing gouges in the woodwork and puncturing sails.

Ryan kept his eye glued to the sight. He squeezed the trigger. A man standing on the deck of the second wag to his left jerked as the 7.62 mm round walloped him in the belly, bending him double and slapping him overboard.

Shifting the sights of the Steyr to a center wag, he saw Hatcher appear on the deck. A ferocious grin split the man's bearded face, and Ryan's finger tightened on the trigger. At the same instant, Hatcher brought up the M-79, a plume of smoke spurting from its bore.

Ryan had barely enough time to shout "Down!" before the hill trembled beneath his boots. The gren had fallen short, impacting explosively against the face of the hillside. Still, the concussion shook the ground and gouted dirt, turf and gravel in all directions.

A cloud of smoke, dust and pulverized rock particles hung in the air like a veil of soiled chiffon. A couple of the defenders, unnerved by the explosion, fired blindly through the haze.

Ryan retreated across the crest, yelling, "Fall back! Everybody fall back!"

Just as the defenders began to comply, a gren landed no more than three feet away. Ryan turned, and a giant fist punched him the small of the back, a blizzard of dirt and pebbles swirled around him and a battering ram of hot, almost solid air slammed him off the top of the hill.

He cartwheeled down the slope, hearing rocks pattering all around him. He tried to maintain his grip on the Steyr, but he struck a projecting finger of earth, and the body-numbing jolt jarred the long blaster from his hands. His thrashing descent came to a breath-robbing, spine-compressing halt against the stone barricade at the foot of the hill.

Dizzy, his ears ringing, Ryan clawed at the rocks, fighting his way to his feet. Then Mildred and Doc were on either side of him, pulling him erect, helping to steady him.

A column of smoke twisted up from the top of the hill, and he saw the sparse grass was covered with a glistening crimson dew.

"Krysty," he croaked, and started a shambling, stumbling run to the base of the slope. He tried to shake free of Doc and Mildred, but their grips were tight and he dragged both of them along with him.

"No!" Mildred said sharply. "Ryan, stop fighting us!"

Krysty, Jak and two of the riflemen appeared on the crest of the hill. All four people were daubed and streaked with blood, but they appeared uninjured, though Jak was favoring his right leg.

Ryan waited until they had half climbed and half fallen to the bottom before running out to meet them.

"Blood isn't mine," Krysty said unsteadily. "I was standing behind the man it belonged to."

Mildred ran exploratory fingers up and down Jak's leg. "Chunk rock hit me," he said in a voice tight with repressed pain.

"I don't think any bones are broken," Mildred observed. "But I imagine you'll have a hell of a bruise."

At that moment a gren arced down out of the sky and landed on the hilltop to their left. The blast sent bodies as limp as rag dolls flailing into the air, rending them apart with shrapnel and shock waves. The detonation bit a sizable portion out of the hill and spit it skyward.

From the far side of the hills, from the plain, rose laughing catcalls of vicious delight and victory.

A body came tumbling down the face of the hill, and J.B. broke from the cover of the barricade and ran toward it. Before the corpse rolled all the way to the bottom, it reached out a bloody hand and grasped a handful of tough grass to stop the tumble.

J.B. ran up the slope and grabbed Mose Autry. The man's eyes were unfocused and glassy, and he breathed heavily through his open mouth. Blood trickled from lacerations on his arms and legs, and from his ears.

Recognizing the symptoms of concussion-induced hemorrhage, J.B. grasped Autry's wrists, stooped and wrestled him over his shoulder in a fireman's carry. As he sprinted back toward the fortifications, a few bullets rattled on the rocks. The Cadre was pushing through the gorge and climbing the hills.

Retrieving the Steyr, Ryan joined his friends behind the makeshift battlements just as a pack of pirates appeared at the mouth of the pass. No one gave the defenders at the walls an order. Half of them shouted in fear and anger and squeezed the triggers of their muzzle loaders. At that range every ball found a target, but the men of the Red Cadre managed to return fire.

The defenders of Amicus sheltered themselves behind their barricade as the bullets hammered into it. A man cried out and fell, hands over his belly, crimson squirting between the fingers.

The bugle sounded a discordant retreat. The men and women with fully loaded weapons straightened and fired a volley, raking the marauders who were backing into the gorge and running back over the hills. There was sporadic return fire from the Cadre, and two more Amicans went down, writhing and crying out.

Then the six outlanders were the only ones firing. Their blasters kept the pirates cowering in the pass while the defenders reloaded. Everyone continued to glance toward the hilltops for any sign of Hatchet Jack or a gren.

The stretch of ground between the battlements and the pass was carpeted with bodies, some moaning and trying to move, most motionless and leaking fluids. A pirate whimpered, shot through the head but somehow still alive. Smoke drifted in flat planes over them.

The companions quickly reloaded their weapons. Ryan glanced around, and J.B., Mildred, Jak, Doc and Krysty all met his gaze with self-assured nods.

A small dark object rocketed out of the cleft between the hills and struck the barricade broadside, with a shuddering shock and rolling boom of thunder and a ball of flame. The gren tore a ragged hole in the stonework. None of the people standing at the detonation point had the time to scream.

Fragments of rock blew in a horizontal column inside the perimeter. A chunk the size of a hen's egg hit Ryan on the right side of his rib cage, bringing a sharp dart of pain. A few gobs of torn, blood-slick flesh thudded to the ground, and a red mist mingled with the dust and smoke. A shout of rage, terror and despair rang out among the defenders.

The air was still shivering with the vibrations of the explosion when the Red Cadre boiled out of the gorge in a shouting, shooting mass.

The wall hadn't collapsed under the concussive force of the gren as Hatcher had evidently hoped. The men leading the charge hesitated, slowing their pace. The marauders behind them kept coming, throwing the first wave headlong against the rock barricades.

Men fell, were dashed against the jagged bulwark, and screams of pain replaced the war yells.

In an instant the Amican defenses were a writhing welter of shrieks, kicks and thrashing bodies. The men in the rear had to pick their way over their fallen and broken-limbed comrades as they swept forward. The defenders fired, the blended gunshots giving rise to a loud thunderclap.

The bullet-slashed pirates dropped atop their dead or crippled brothers, but more appeared to clamber over the red shambles of flesh and bone. Like a tide, the howling horde flooded over the half-toppled battlements.

The Amicans met the Cadre with knives, tomahawks and clubbing blaster stocks. Along the line of stone was screaming, bloody chaos. Hatchets chopped, knives broke on rock, skulls were split with blaster butts.

The Amicans fought with the fury of desperation. They hacked, slashed, bludgeoned and died.

Ryan, half-blinded by dust and black-powder smoke, glimpsed Micah go down with a tomahawk buried in the crown of his head. He saw one of the Cadre rush toward Mildred, who had her back turned, and he fired his blaster point-blank. The marauder flopped facedown, a geyser of scarlet pumping from a cavity in the side of his head.

A rush of bodies knocked Ryan sprawling, and a knife blade thrust for his throat. He wrenched himself aside and heard the blade break against the rocky ground. He fired the SIG-Sauer into the bearded face snarling over him, and the eyes and nose dissolved in a bloody smear. Elbowing aside the corpse, he leaped to his feet, working the trigger, the blaster bucking in his fist.

It was J.B.'s Uzi that tipped the scales. The diminutive Armorer squeezed off 3-round burst after 3-round burst, and at that range he didn't miss a single target, nor did any of the targets survive the pounding hail of 9 mm stingers.

Responding to a bleating note from the bugle, the Cadre engaged in a slow, stubborn retreat, climbing over the barricade and backing away toward the gorge. Their covering fire was ragged and sporadic.

No one cheered the rout. There were too many dead and too many wounded inside the fortifications. Ryan went to Krysty, who was bleeding from a wound in her right arm. He didn't have the opportunity to check on the rest of his friends—Mose Autry forced himself through the dust and smoke and came to his side. His lower torso was sodden with blood, and he held a scarf over the knife slash across his belly.

His upper lip was split, and through clenched, red-filmed teeth, he said, "We're done. It's over. Almost no ammunition left, dead and wounded everywhere. All Hatcher has to do is fire one more gren."

Ryan looked toward the cleft. He saw no movement, but he knew the narrow gorge was clogged with the survivors of the last assault and the walking wounded.

Then Hatcher's voice rolled out from within the pass. "Listen to me, you dumb shits. Listen to reason! There's no escape. I have more men than you can ever kill!"

"Bullshit," J.B. muttered, his face streaked with soot and dirt. "I bet he's out of grens, or down to his last one."

"I can blow you out of there, but let's end this now!"

No one responded to Hatcher's words.

"The outlander, Cawdor, knows what I want! All he has to do is give it to me, and this is over. You have my word!

"Do you all want to die," he went on, "all your women, your children? You want your houses burned, your animals slaughtered, your crops stomped flat? Is that what you want?"

Hatcher barely waited for a response. His hoarse, maddened voice roared, "If that's what you fuckers want, we'll give it to you!"

A volley of shots ripped out of the gorge mouth. Everyone ducked, and the bullets flattened themselves against rock. Then the bugle sounded, playing a familiar series of melancholy rising and falling notes.

"No quarter," Doc said with a bleak smile.

"Good," Ryan replied. "That's just the way I want it."

Chapter Ten

Wincing in pain, Autry said, "Even if he's out of grens, he still holds the pass. We're still boxed in."

Ryan laughed, a low, harsh chuckle without humor. "Not as boxed in as he's about to be."

Rising, he and his friends conducted a quick inspection of the fortifications, Autry shuffling along behind them. Of the thirty-six defenders, only eleven remained on their feet. More than a dozen were injured so severely that they could only lie on the ground, bleeding and groaning.

Making a quick head count, Ryan counted at least nineteen Cadre casualties, both in and outside the perimeter. He could only guess at how many wounded were within the pass.

The young man named Allen sat upright against the rock wall, his legs stretched in front of him. Both hands were clasped over a hole in his stomach, and pink-gray entrails showed between bloody fingers. When Doc knelt beside him, he stared up at him through unfocused eyes reflecting the sure awareness of imminent death.

Face white beneath its coating of soot, Doc patted him on the shoulder and murmured a few words to him. As he did so, Allen expired quietly, his body relaxing and slowly sliding to one side.

With gentle fingers Doc closed the lids over the

young man's staring eyes and rose, turning away from the others.

After completing the circuit, Ryan said to Autry, "When I get over the wall, I want you to pin down the Cadre inside the pass. Shoot at them, throw rocks, anything to stop them from coming through it again."

"Get over the wall?" Autry asked. "Where are you going?"

Ryan holstered his blaster and didn't reply. He handed the Steyr to Krysty and vaulted over the barricade and sprinted toward the foot of the right-side hill. He had run only a few yards when musket balls began to strike around him. He saw the winks of several muzzle flashes in the shadows of the gorge's mouth.

Heavier fire answered from the barricades behind him: a triple burst from the Uzi, the door-slamming bang of Mildred's ZKR, then deeper reports from Krysty's and Jak's handblasters, as well as a few softer pops from flintlocks.

A couple of musket balls plucked at his clothes, but he kept running. His eye was fixed on the powder-impregnated fuse that stretched down from the top of the hill.

But even as he looked at it, the length of line suddenly quivered, was drawn upward in a jerky fashion, then came flying back down, looping and coiling.

Ryan snarled and scrambled up the slope, grabbing at rocks and tufts of grass. When he reached the crest, he flung himself to where the jugs of gunpowder were cached. Then he rocked to such a sudden halt, his feet nearly went out from under him.

Standing spraddle legged over the containers of powder, slapping the blade of his hatchet into an open palm, was John Hatcher. As Ryan's hand darted for he butt of his blaster, Hatcher brought the hatchet up and over his head. The SIG-Sauer cleared leather at the same time the hatchet spun toward Ryan. It rotated through the air, on a direct line with his head.

Ryan didn't aim, squeezed the trigger from the hip. The bullet struck the blade of the hatchet and deflected it from its course. It spun crazily to one side.

Hatcher didn't gape at the incredible accuracy of he hip shot. Roaring in anger, he bounded forward n a flying leap, feet first. The soles of his moccasins hudded solidly into Ryan's stomach. The one-eyed man stumbled, his nervous system momentarily overwhelmed by the force of the unexpected kick.

A moment was all Hatcher needed. One hand wrested the blaster from Ryan's suddenly slack fingers, and the other, clenched in a fist, sent him staggering half a score of feet away. His foot caught in a issure, and he fell on his right side.

Hatcher aimed the SIG-Sauer at him. "I want the nap and my gold, you one-eyed thief," he said hoarsely.

From below rose the sound of strife—gunshots, houts and the blaring notes of the "Deguello."

Hatcher smiled. "Hear that, Cawdor? It's just about over, but me and you ain't done yet. Before we're hrough, you'll give me exactly what I want."

Ryan's hand made a motion toward the panga knife it his hip. Hatcher stepped in and delivered a kick to he side of his head, flipping him over on his back.

Grunting with exertion and pleasure, Hatcher kicked him three more times, once in the belly and wice in the head.

"Try it again, Cawdor," Hatcher said, affecting a wheedling note. "I ain't had much fun today, but then he day's still young."

Ryan tried to rise, but his strength was gone, as if his muscles had been drained through a sieve. Blood streamed over his good eye from a laceration in his forehead, and a ringing pain echoed within the walls of his skull.

Raising his head, he blinked back blood and tried to collect enough saliva in his mouth so he could spit at the coldheart chief of the Red Cadre. A light breeze whispered across the hilltop. Its touch was soft, a caress on Ryan's throbbing face. The breeze helped his senses return to him.

"You cost me, Cawdor," Hatcher grated. "Cost me more than I can ever get back, and I mean to cost you plenty."

Suddenly Hatcher's body twitched, as if he had received a blow in the back. His deerskin shirtfront acquired a ragged hole, and a splash of crimson spread across it in an artless pattern. He grunted in pain and surprise.

Neither man heard the shot, but both of them saw Felicity struggling over the lip of the hill, a blaster in her right hand, a tendril of pale smoke curling from the barrel. The left side of her face was completely covered with a sliding flow of blood, gushing from a bullet wound in her scalp.

Hatcher swayed, gasping out a curse. He fired the SIG-Sauer, and the 9 mm round caught her in the chest, between her breasts, smashing her sternum and ripping her lungs asunder.

The woman didn't cry out, but her body was jolted backward and to one side. The shock waves of the bullet's impact traveled down her arm and sent the blaster twirling from her fingers. In one sweeping, red-tinted glance, Ryan saw the blaster lying only

hree feet from his right hand, the cache of gunpowder
nd the two-foot length of fuse that ran from it.

His weakness and pain gave a great surge and
aded. He shot out one arm for the blaster, but as his
ingers closed over it, Hatcher spun toward him and
unged. He cursed, but only a crimson spray came
rom his lips.

Ryan fell onto his back, and, unable to check his
lummet, Hatcher met his adversary's uplifted boots
vith his stomach. As those legs straightened, the pi-
ate stumbled backward, his arms windmilling. He
rabbed at the mesquite bush to regain his balance
nd dropped the SIG-Sauer. But one foot slipped into
he crack where the jugs of gunpowder were placed.
Ie sat down atop them with a grunt of forcefully
xpelled air.

Ryan dived forward, thumbing back the blaster's
ock. Hitting the ground, he aimed the weapon toward
he fuse. Hatcher struggled to his feet at the same time
Ryan squeezed the trigger. The lock fell, striking the
lint, and a spark jumped and touched the powder-
reated fuse. Sizzling, the spark smoked its way along
he fuse.

Ryan had just enough time to roll away from the
dge before the spark flashed its way along the fuse
o the jugs of powder.

The explosion dazzled him, deafened him, coated
im with a fine layer of dust, and the concussion
olled him over and over. Through the tongues of
lame, the upflung clouds of smoke and grit, he
limpsed a dark shape flying overhead, limbs flailing.

The echoes of the explosion were swallowed up by
a grinding roar that grew louder with every passing
eartbeat. Peering through the shifting planes of

smoke, he saw the entire edge of the ridge sliding from view. The "Deguello" ceased trumpeting.

Rock cracked and split, then the entire wall of the gorge was in motion, flowing down in a grinding, crashing torrent. Ryan got to his feet and peered down. He had only the briefest of glimpses of buckskin-clad men jamming the narrow passage below, then they were blocked from sight by the down-rushing tons of dirt, shale and sandstone.

The few of the Cadre still out on the plain stared at the bouncing storm of stones in wide-eyed shock. Their upturned faces blanched, and they began to race toward the wind wags. There was less than a dozen, and they all clambered aboard the largest craft, fighting one another to align the sail and to start the engine. There was no strategy, no order, only the half-mad desire to flee.

Turning away, Ryan looked down over the Amican defenses. Everyone was looking up at him. He waved, and the people below waved in return, voicing a wordless victory cry. The few who were able began to dance. He picked up his SIG-Sauer and absently brushed away the grit.

Halfway down the hill lay Felicity's body, arms outflung, face turned to the sky. Far above her, with wings outstretched, a hawk glided gracefully on the air currents.

The sickening odor of scorched human hair and flesh was more overpowering than the acrid reek of burned powder. Sprawled facedown at the far end of the hilltop was John Hatcher. Smoke curled from the seat and legs of the man's pants, but moans of agony bubbled from the loose-limbed, fire-blackened shape. John Jacob Hatcher was still alive.

Ryan limped over and toed him over onto his back.

His long hair was crisped black, only a stinking, smoking fuzz covering his head. His beard was a smoldering patch of charred bristles, and his face was covered by red, raw patches and huge, leaking blisters. He gazed down at him and Hatcher gazed back, trying to bite back the groans. He breathed in whistling gasps, his lungs and sinuses cooked.

Staring into his eyes, Ryan removed the map from his pocket, unfolded it and waved it before Hatcher's eyes. Then he touched one corner of the parchment to a tiny flame on the man's pant leg, and the map went up in a flash of fire and cinders.

Ryan blew the handful of ashes directly into Hatcher's face. The ashes scattered, dancing on the breeze. The wind shredded the gray scraps to bits, leaving only a thin residue adhering to Hatcher's peeled, sticky flesh.

Hatcher's chest rose and fell, then rose no more.

"I gave you exactly what you wanted," Ryan whispered. "No quarter."

Chapter Eleven

The voice spoke in Ryan's mind as he slept, penetrating his dreams. There was a nonhuman quality to its vibration that set even his slumbering mind bristling with suspicion. It was a voice he had heard before.

Grandfather, Great Spirit, you have been always, and before you no one has been.

Ryan knew he was dreaming, knew he was stretched out on a cot in Amicus, sleeping the sleep of the utterly exhausted. His mind crawled at the inhuman, relentless tone of the voice as it spoke again.

Grandmother Earth, you who have shown mercy to your children who have ripped and burned and poisoned you, I shall heal you!

"I shall heal you," Ryan heard himself say.

Then his eye snapped open, and he lunged up from the cot, reaching for his blaster and panga, staring wildly around the dim room. A shadow slid past the open window and was gone before his blurred eye could focus. He scrambled to the window, shoving aside the blanket serving as a curtain. He heard the padding of feet out in the gray, oyster-hued light just after sunrise, but he could see nothing.

He stood at the window, confused and a little angry, his mind still fogged by fatigue. The tension of nerves eased. There was nothing out there in the dark but a few lights and bodies that had yet to be recovred. Scraps of pink and orange glowed in the eastern sky. The cool air still retained a faint odor of blood, gunpowder and seared human flesh.

Turning away from the window, he saw that Krysty was gone, but he heard her voice from the other room. Making a deliberate effort to push away the strangeness of his dream and the voice in his mind, he holstered the SIG-Sauer, sat on the edge of the narrow bed and tugged on his boots.

He checked his chron, noting it was nearly twenty-four hours to the minute since the Red Cadre had arrived. During the day and most of the night following the battle, he and his friends had patched up their wounds as best they could and helped the survivors of the battle collect and tidy the dead. The thought of remaining in Amicus another day suddenly revolted him.

Ryan went through the door into the common room of the little hostel. Jak and Krysty sat at the table with a pot of the pungent tea before them. Doc stood shaving in front of a tiny trade mirror, carefully scraping the straight razor across his face. Mildred and J.B. were evidently still asleep, since he heard snores from an adjoining room.

"Did you call out in there?" Krysty asked.

"Mebbe," Ryan replied. He pulled out the chair next to her and sat.

"Bad dream?"

Ryan hesitated. "I don't know. Thought I heard someone outside the window."

Jak narrowed his eyes. "Who?"

"Mebbe I just dreamed it," Ryan answered with a shake of his head.

"I'm not surprised," Krysty said, placing her hand over his. "The past few days have been a nightmare.

And if what's left of the Red Cadre manages to re-group—''

"We'll be long gone before that happens," Ryan interrupted a bit more harshly than he intended. "Let's be out of here after breakfast."

A voice spoke from the doorway. "I'd hoped you might stay until at least lunch."

Ryan turned, facing Autry who leaned against the door frame. He was wearing a wooly buffalo robe that was far too big for him. His gentle, bearded face sagged with pain and grief.

"We'd rather get on the move as soon as possible."

Autry nodded. "We'll be sorry to see you go. Amicus owes you great debt." He didn't need to add, what's left of it.

Ryan smiled slightly. He knew the survivors of the battle still blamed the outlanders for bringing such a flood tide of blood and pain to their community. If they stayed, he and his friends would be resented almost as much as the Cadre.

"Give us some food and some mounts, and we'll call it even."

"Where will you go?" Autry asked.

"Does it matter?"

Autry shrugged. "I suppose not. I'll have some food brought to you."

He turned and left the hostel.

"Where we go?" Jak asked. "Mountain ranges all around. Can't sail wags on them."

"We can go back to Colorado, mebbe, so we can see how Dean is doing at school."

"And after that," Doc added, toweling the lather from his face, "I daresay we shall make another jump."

Autry returned, bearing platters of food. It was the same mixture of cheese, bread and bacon they had eaten on their first morning in Amicus, and it was even less appetizing this time around.

After Autry put down the platters on the table, he said, "If you're looking for a guide, there's a Lakota tribesman who arrived late last night. He wants to talk to you."

"Who is he?" J.B. asked.

"Little Mountain—remember him?—says he's a highly placed war chief."

"You mean this Yutan-kin-Mahipiya?" Krysty asked, stumbling over the pronunciation.

Autry nodded. "Says he knows you."

Jak's eyes narrowed. "Knows who?"

"All of you. Wait a minute, I'll fetch him."

Through the open door they watched Autry cross the muddy street toward a tepee. A man sat there, wearing a hooded deerskin cape. He rose with the lithe, coiled movements of a panther when Autry approached. There was something vaguely familiar about his smooth, quick motions. He cradled a Gewehr automatic assault rifle in his arms.

Autry and the stranger marched across the street. As they entered the room, the man pulled back the hood of his cape. His face was lean and sharply planed. His black-haired head was alertly erect, and a pair of red hawk feathers were pinned at the back. He was no wild tribesman. His face and dark eyes had fire and pride and a haughty intelligence. Mildred recognized him first.

"Touch-the-Sky," she blurted.

"Call me Joe," the Lakota replied in uninflected English. "I'm pleased you remember me."

Ryan wasn't sure if he was pleased; the summer

before they had met Touch-the-Sky in the Black Hills. Though they hadn't been allies, the Lakota and his band of warriors had saved Krysty, Mildred, J.B., Jak and Doc from the guns of Helskel's sec men. From what he had been told, the rescue had been unintentional, more of a by-product of the Lakotas' attack on Lars Hellstrom and his squad of sec men.

Touch-the-Sky himself, who preferred to be called "Joe" by the whites, prowled the ancient tribal lands of his people, seeking out and punishing interlopers and desecrators. He had warned them about the chill-crazy citizens of the settlement of Helskel, and a few days later Ryan had spared the man's life when he could have just as easily ended it. Under the circumstances he supposed they owed each other nothing and had to renew their relationship on fresh terms.

At a loss for something say, Ryan ventured, "Autry told us your name was Yutan-kin-something-or-other."

"That's the Lakota pronunciation," Joe replied with a thin smile. "The English translation is, of course, Touch-the-Sky."

"Care to join us for breakfast?" Krysty asked.

Joe shook his head. "Thank you, no. This isn't a social call. When Little Mountain told me that Ochinee—that's you, Mr. Cawdor—and his friends were here in Amicus, threatened by the Red Cadre, I came straightaway. I arrived too late to help rout them, I see."

"That blaster of yours would have been a big help to us. As it is, some got away," J.B. told him.

"The survivors, the stragglers, have already been dealt with." Joe's tone was cold, firm and decisive.

Ryan leaned back in his chair. "You said this isn't a social call. What do you want with us?"

Joe pointed through the open door toward the gray-green mountains on the horizon. "My people dwell there, in the mountains you call the Wind River Range, in a valley called Ti-Ra'-Wa. We have enemies there, and they are too powerful for us to conquer on our own. We have few weapons. I came to Amicus when I heard you were here because you left Helskel aflame and drove their evil from my people's ancestral land. You can help us in our struggle."

Ryan suddenly felt certain Joe wasn't seeking aid to win a petty intertribal conflict. The stakes were far larger than property or hunting rights.

"Not mercies," Jak said.

Joe shrugged. "You are warriors, and that is enough. I'd hoped to reach Amicus in time to aid you in your battle with the Cadre, and you would subsequently discharge the debt by helping me. Therefore, we must bargain. Though I won't pay you, I will reward you."

Doc's face suddenly showed interest. "Reward us with what?"

Joe reached beneath his deerskin cloak and brought forth a dully gleaming object that he laid carefully, almost reverently on the tabletop.

It was a flat wafer of dull yellow metal, several inches long. Inset on either side of the wafer were two small hexagons of crystal. Though they looked like quartz, there was something odd about their structure. Each was only an inch in diameter, but bore an interlocking pattern of facets that blurred the vision, made it difficult to focus directly on them.

"More shiny metal," Jak snorted scornfully.

"Not again," J.B. muttered.

Joe started. "What do you mean?"

Ryan dug around in his pocket and brought out the

pieces of gold he had taken from John Hatcher. "Got this off Hatchet Jack."

Joe's eyes widened, and his nostrils flared. "That is from Ti-Ra'-Wa! It is the Mazaska Waken—Sacred Gold. How did he get it?"

"He never said," Doc replied, picking up the slice of metal. "He was more concerned about accruing more."

Gingerly Doc nipped at one corner of the wafer. He examined it closely, saw the faint indentations of his teeth and exclaimed, "By the Three Kennedys! Pure gold!"

Ryan looked up at Joe. "Where did this come from?"

"From Ti-Ra'-Wa," the Lakota answered. "There is more. All you can carry away. If you help me."

"The map Hatcher had on him," Autry said in surprise. "It must have been legitimate after all."

J.B. turned to Ryan. "This could be big. All the years you and me traveled with Trader, we never had an opportunity like this."

Jak merely gazed impassively at the metal wafer. Doc looked interested, but not particularly excited. Krysty and Mildred eyed him, waiting for his reaction.

Taking the slice of gold from Doc, Ryan fingered it. "It looks almost like it was machined, more like some kind of instrument, not an ornament."

Joe hesitated before replying. When he spoke, his tone was evasive. "It came from a cavern in Ti-Ra'-Wa."

"Did your people mine it?" Krysty asked.

"There is much more like it there," Joe responded.

"That's no answer," J.B. said. "Is there a gold mine in this Ti-Ra'-Wa of yours?"

"Ti-Ra'-Wa," Mildred repeated slowly, musingly. "That seems familiar, from my Native American studies."

Joe stiffened. "Your answer, Ochinee. Will you come?"

Ryan exchanged a quick glance with Krysty. Her hair wasn't stirring, and she shrugged, indicating she sensed no danger, or at least not an immediate threat. Still, there was too much about Joe's proposal that was in the dark. But the promise of a definite destination was a strong inducement.

Fixing his gaze on Joe's angular face, Ryan said, "I won't commit us to anything without a discussion. We've just fought one battle for others. That might be enough for a while. I'll let you know by sundown."

Joe nodded. "Until then."

With that he picked up the gold wafer and stepped out of the room and into the street.

When the Lakota was well out of earshot, Mose Autry smiled sourly. "He doesn't seem like a fool, but doesn't he realize with your blasters and skill you can just take his gold and walk off with it?"

Krysty turned on the man, her eyes flashing emerald sparks. "No matter what we agree to do, we'd never do that. If we were that sort, we'd have sold out your pesthole ville to Hatchet Jack."

Autry cast his eyes downward, shame spreading across his face in a red flush. "Of course. I'm sorry. I'm just tired. I'll leave you now."

He shuffled out of the door.

Addressing Ryan, Doc inquired, "What is your initial reaction to our noble savage's invitation?"

"To tell him thanks but no thanks," Ryan replied.

"Gold is still the best grease in most of Death-lands," J.B. reminded him.

"Could buy anything we want," Jak offered.

"Except safety," Mildred said. "We'd draw packs of two-legged coyotes to our trail."

"If the setup is how he said it is, we'd be fighting someone else's battle—for solid jack this time," J.B. stated.

"We could have fought this last one for gold if we'd had a mind to," Krysty said. "We could have followed Hatcher's map. It probably would have led us right to this Ti-Ra'-Wa."

"Mildred, didn't you say there was something familiar about this place?" Ryan asked.

"Vaguely. Though my studies revolved around tribal linkages and genotyping, I touched on creation myths from time to time."

"And?"

Mildred shook her head, the beads in her plaited hair clicking faintly. "It's been a long time, and my recollection is foggy. Anyway, there's a legend among some Plains tribes that says the source of creation came from a cave in a valley. Ti-Ra'-Wa means, roughly, Sacred or Mystery Valley."

"Is this place anything like the villes of Cibola and El Dorado you told us about?" J.B. asked.

"No, not really. It's more of a Garden of Eden type of myth. I remember a bit of poetry about it. 'Magic Ti-Ra'-Wa/Life, death, good, evil, joy and sorrow/All born in the Cavern of Creation.'"

"A myth, mebbe," Krysty said. "But Joe said he came from Ti-Ra'-Wa."

Ryan shrugged. "The tribe in the mountains probably named their valley after the legend."

Doc chuckled. "'Nature imitates art,' Wilde said."

He turned to Mildred. "Are you suggesting Joe wants us to fight a war in the Native American equivalent of Eden?"

"I'm suggesting nothing of the sort," Mildred answered a bit sharply. "I'm not even sure if I'm remembering the legend correctly, since all cultures share similar creation myths. I may be confusing Ti-Ra'-Wa with Tir na-Nog, the ancient Celtic land of promise. The two words are similar linguistically. It's been a very long time, and my memory is faulty. You should be able to relate to that, Doc."

At the acid reminder of his own unreliable and occasionally severely fogged thought processes, Doc lapsed into an abashed silence.

"I'll leave this decision to a vote," Ryan announced, "since nobody but me was anxious to leave this place. On the one hand, we can turn Joe down and stay, mebbe help Amicus rebuild. On the other hand, we can accept Joe's offer, have a destination in mind and, at least, be on our way to somewhere again."

Krysty tapped her fingers on the tabletop. "This really all boils down to whether we trust Joe."

"Only one way find out," Jak said.

No one could argue, or even cared to, with the statement. After an hour of discussion, it was agreed to accompany Joe and at least find out if he was telling the truth.

Chapter Twelve

Around midmorning Ryan sought out Joe and told him they would accept his offer. Joe said they would embark at dawn the next day, and he offered to buy the mounts and pack animals. He added that the march to the valley would take three to four days. It was agreed they would meet at the hostel at sunrise.

Taking a tour of Amicus with his friends, Ryan regretted ever raising the possibility of staying to help the citizens rebuild.

The population had been reduced by one-third, and the elderly and children had been pressed into service as medical aides and undertakers. The tavern served as a hospital, and the boneyard contained the unburied dead. The Amican defenders were covered with blankets and hides; the corpses of the Red Cadre had been stripped and dumped unceremoniously on the heap of animal bones and left to rot. The few able-bodied people in the ville were working at clearing the pass sufficiently so it could be used again as an egress.

As they passed them by, the Amicans eyed the companions distrustfully, even angrily. Ryan wasn't pleased that his assessment of their prevailing attitude had been so accurate.

Rebuilding the open ville of Amicus seemed like far more effort than it was worth.

They returned to their quarters in the afternoon to rest. Ryan and Krysty lay together in the narrow bunk, but she was unresponsive to his caresses; she was troubled, haunted by what had happened the day before.

She was also exhausted, as all of them were, since they had gone for nearly forty tension-drenched hours without sleep. Their rest the night following the battle had been fitful.

As aching and as tired as he was, Ryan found he was a little afraid of falling asleep. He tried to repress the memories of the ghostly, inhuman voices echoing through his dream, but he still felt uneasy.

He had experienced nightmares before, many of the most vivid and terrifying after a long mat-trans jump. He couldn't understand why he was so disturbed by his dreams of the wolf and the voice except he harbored a flicker of suspicion that they hadn't been dreams at all.

But exhaustion drove him into a deep slumber, and it was dreamless.

He awakened at close to sunset and he found he was alone, not only in the room, but the entire hostel. After getting dressed and splashing water on his face, he went out onto the twilight streets of Amicus. He walked toward the big corral to find out how Joe's preparations for the journey were coming along.

He didn't trust the Lakota any more than any other stranger he had met in his many years of trekking across Deathlands.

He drew in a deep breath. The air was still musky with the odor of violence and death. Usually after a victory the air smelled new, sweet and sharp. It was becoming apparent that he had seen too much death in his years, played too much a part in adding to the world's store of it. To cheat death, he had to deal death. He wondered what would happen when his killer's reflexes no longer obeyed his killer's instincts.

Ryan skidded to a sudden stop on the uneven ground. Tawny, greenish gold eyes blazed at him from directly ahead in the gloom.

A dark, shaggy, silver-shot shape crouched in the shadows, staring at him. For an instant Ryan thought it was a dog, then his hand went to the SIG-Sauer at his hip.

The creature was too big for a dog, its head a trifle too wide, the tail too bushy, the posture too feral. It was a wolf, watching his every move with a hypnotic intensity. Though very large, probably tipping the scales at close to one hundred sixty pounds, the wolf wasn't one of the mutie strains that prowled the Rockies.

Ryan carefully unleathered his blaster. Then a soft voice spoke from the darkness behind the animal.

"He will not harm you. He is a...friend," a soft woman's voice said.

She came toward him out of the dusk, past the crouching wolf. Her movements were light and lithe, with a grace that reminded him somehow of Joe. She wore the combination of homespun and buckskin clothing of the Amicans, and at first he took her for a Cheyenne. Her waist-length hair was sleek and black enough, but the face it framed wasn't ruddy and her eyes were a brown so light they were almost tan— or a shade of gold. She didn't look more than eighteen years old.

There was a pride and a touch of arrogance in those eyes, though there was something oddly childlike in them, too, almost an innocence.

"I am Sisoka," she said softly, her glance tilting to meet his. She was only a few inches over five feet tall. "It means Robin's Wing. His name is We'-mna. It means Blood-sniffer."

"I'm Ryan Cawdor," he replied.

"I have seen you here in Amicus, before the battle."

"I don't recall seeing you," he said. "Or your friend. I think I'd remember you both."

The instant he said it, he regretted it. With a chilly sensation at the base of his spine, he realized the wolf did indeed look familiar.

Sisoka stepped closer. "You fought well. You saved Amicus."

Ryan only grunted.

"You look tired," she murmured, "and a little sad. Is it because you are leaving us?"

Ryan glanced again at the wolf. It was still watching him with that fixed, faintly luminous green-gold gaze.

"If you'll pardon me," he said, making a move to step around her and the beast.

"You look," Sisoka continued as though she hadn't heard the dismissal, "as if you've had some bad dreams."

Ryan stopped. "What did you say?"

"Touch-the-Sky offers you only another bad dream, Ryan Cawdor."

Something in her tone, even the sound of her voice, set off a warning vibration in his brain. The caution and instinctive suspicion that had kept him alive for two decades in the Deathland hellzones came up to triple red. The SIG-Sauer fairly leaped into his hand.

Towering over Sisoka, he asked, "What do you know of Ti-Ra'-Wa?"

Sisoka barely glanced at the bore of the blaster. Her

eyes flicked to Ryan's glaring blue eye, and she said softly, almost sadly, *"Kte."*

It was a Lakota word Ryan understood. It meant "kill."

The wolf was a dark thunderbolt that sprang from the ground, and it struck Ryan full in the chest, knocking him sprawling. He felt razor-keen fangs on his right forearm, keeping his blaster hand immobilized.

Ryan knew that before he could switch the weapon to his left hand or even draw his panga, his throat would be ripped out. He squeezed off a shot, hoping the blaster's familiar cracking report would draw Krysty or one of the others.

Blood-sniffer's paws tore rents in his shirt as he struggled, and the jaws increased their pressure around his arm. Cursing, Ryan gathered a handful of furry hide at the beast's ruff and tried to wrench it backward and off balance. He wrapped his legs around the wolf's body and rolled to the left in an effort to outmuscle the animal long enough to unscabbard his blade.

The wolf resisted his maneuver, shifting its weight without voicing a growl or a snarl. As he strained and wrestled, Ryan received the strange impression that despite the young woman's command, the wolf had no intention of killing him, as though it were acting on its own agenda.

"Ryan!" Krysty shouted.

"We'-mna, inankni yo!" Sisoka called.

The wolf released its grip on the arm and bounded away, its hind feet springboarding from Ryan's chest and slamming him to the ground, the back of his head striking hard. He rolled to his feet, dazed and bleeding.

He began a shambling run, but he had no idea in which direction Sisoka or Blood-sniffer had gone. He bumped into Krysty. The titian-haired beauty had her Smith & Wesson revolver in hand and wore an anxious expression on her face.

"Are you all right?" she asked. "What the hell is going on?" She grasped his arm to examine the lacerations.

"The girl!" Ryan snarled, his daze dissolving in his anger. "Where is she?"

Krysty gestured to the northeast. Ryan got a shadowy glimpse of a horse and rider and a loping wolf racing past the boneyard and toward the bluffs beyond in the uncertain starlight.

"Who was she?" Krysty demanded, trying to get a better look at his fang-slashed forearm, but he wrenched it away.

"I don't know. She spoke to that wolf and it attacked me. I think she told it to kill me."

"Why?"

Ryan moved rapidly up the street of Amicus. "Mebbe Joe can make an educated guess."

They found Joe at the corral, overseeing the selection and hobbling of their mounts. He stood tensely, his figure telegraphing impatience. Jak and Doc were watching the procedure from the split-rail fence.

Ryan strode up to him, his question direct and flat. "Who is Sisoka?"

Joe wheeled like a bee-stung panther, his eyes narrowed. "How do you know her?"

"She introduced herself to me right before she sicced her pet wolf on my ass. She comes from Ti-Ra'-Wa, too, doesn't she?"

Joe, staring past Krysty and Ryan, spoke quietly

between gritted teeth. "Sisoka here. And We'-mna. They followed me, spied on me."

Doc and Jak moved closer to hear the exchange.

"Who the fuck is she?" Ryan rasped. His arm was throbbing and burning, blood streaming from the cuts to splatter on the ground.

Joe answered with a brooding reluctance. "She is the niece of Pizi, chief of the Akicita Sunkamitu Tanka."

"I never heard of that tribe," Ryan snapped.

"It is not a tribe, it is a warrior society. It means the Wolf Soldiers. They are enemies of my people."

"And who are your people, exactly?"

"Kiciyuha Makoholoka."

Ryan stared at him unblinkingly, waiting.

Joe said tightly, "Loosely translated, it means the Cavern Keepers. The Wolf Soldiers are striking at us here. They intend to prevent us from reaching Ti-Ra-'Wa. We must go swiftly if you are to help me and win your gold."

"Gold is seeming less alluring at this juncture," Doc said, "especially if we must contend with a witch-woman and her animal familiar."

Ryan was angry, mainly because he was a little frightened of the girl and the wolf.

And the dream.

As if sensing his emotions, Joe said softly, "You are Ochinee, the one-eyed warrior who brought much sorrow to the half men in the Black Hills. Surely you are not afraid? Surely you will not renege on your word?"

Ryan resisted the urge to barrel stroke the Lakota across the face with his blaster. Instead, he made a deliberately careful show of leathering it.

"All will become clear to you in time," Joe murmured. "Until then, know this—you will be fighting to heal the wounds of Grandmother Earth."

Ryan's body twitched, as if someone had tapped him hard on the shoulder. He quickly tried to compose himself, but he knew Krysty had noted his reaction.

Joe continued talking smoothly. "I may sound a bit melodramatic, but this is not the time or the place to explain further. Sisoka may have other spies here."

Jak pointed to a nearby dog who sat licking its privates. "Him?"

Ignoring the sarcastic query, Joe said, "You have my word, Ochinee."

"All right," Ryan replied. "That'll have to do— at least for right now."

Ryan, Krysty, Doc and Jak returned to the hostel and found Mildred and J.B. waiting for them in the common room. At the sight of blood on Ryan's arm, Mildred bustled about treating the wounds with the only materials at hand. As she cleaned and disinfected the lacerations with a dash of White Mule, Ryan told them the story and what Sisoka had said.

"There's something else," Krysty said. "Something Joe said bothered you."

Ryan sighed and nodded. He took a swig of the corn liquor, propping the jug on his forearm and tipping the neck toward his mouth. He shuddered. "Something Sisoka said bothered me more."

He told them about his dreams, about riding the singing wolf and the voice that had intruded on his slumber.

"If I didn't know better," Mildred said, tying a bandage around Ryan's forearm, "I'd be of the opinion you experienced a vision, or the beginnings of one."

Ryan knew Plains tribes attached a crowning importance to visions, but he also knew the normal procedure for obtaining one was a period of solitude, fasting and suffering.

"I don't want a vision," he said wryly. "I see just fine as it is."

Mildred smiled. "From what I've read, spirit guides and animal totems occasionally come unsolicited to befriend mortals. Maybe that's one interpretation."

"A wolf," Doc mused. "I can't think of any animal more appropriate to serve as your totem, my boy."

Mildred's words had brought an incredulous stare from J.B. "We don't need to get tangled up in Native religions."

"Mebbe not," Krysty said quietly. The sparkle of her emerald eyes was slightly dimmed by worry. "Can't help but wonder if we won't be."

Ryan took another swallow of White Mule. A long one.

Chapter Thirteen

If Ryan had felt worse the morning after indulging in corn liquor, he couldn't recall the occasion. When he was shaken awake by Krysty, he saw the sky was still dark, with no sign of the sun. Everyone else was up and in the common room, getting their possessions together.

Massaging his temples, he croaked, "I've changed my mind. Let's stay here and help rebuild Amicus."

"No," she said unsympathetically. "You should have known better than to drink that rotgut on the night before a journey."

"You didn't say anything."

"I'm not your mother, Ryan. You go on and on about folks taking responsibility for their actions. Well, you'd better take responsibility for this hangover or you'll be left behind."

Ryan felt too fragile to argue with her. At least he hadn't had another strange and disturbingly vivid dream. If he had dreamed at all, he couldn't recollect it.

He got up, managed to dress himself and stumbled over to the washbowl. After dunking his head four times into the water, the pain in his skull had abated enough for him to talk.

"Where's Joe?"

"Outside. He has our horses ready. Do you want breakfast?"

The very thought of the green-black tea, cheese and fatty, blistered bacon made him want to heave. He swallowed the column of burning bile working its way up his throat and shook his head, but not too vigorously.

Joe was waiting for them at the corner of the hostel, holding the lead ropes of seven horses and two mules. The mules had supplies packed onto their backs.

Everyone was pleased with Joe's ability to judge horseflesh, except for Doc. He had expressly asked for a small animal so he would have less distance to fall when he was inevitably thrown, and Joe had chosen a dun-colored mustang.

Doc walked around the animal, studying its legs and withers. It was a little bigger in the chest than Joe's pinto, and it gazed at him with an alert suspicion in its brown eyes. He took the reins from Joe and put one foot in the stirrup. The pony immediately shied, and he went down in the street.

"The reincarnation of Judas," he said tonelessly, referring to the tricky, recalcitrant, skew-backed mule that had served as his transportation at Jak's ranch in New Mexico.

With the help of J.B. and Joe, Doc managed to corner the little animal against the side of the hostel, and he climbed aboard the saddle. Everyone laughed at the ludicrous picture he made. He squatted on the pony's back, feet in the stirrups, his knees sticking outward like a grasshopper's.

"Just like Judas," Mildred said with a laugh.

Doc patted the mustang's neck and said, "Then that is what I shall christen him, Judas Redux."

At a walk the mounted party made for the pass. Though there were people up and about in Amicus, none spoke to them or bade them goodbye. Not even Mose Autry turned out to wish them good luck.

Ryan wasn't surprised. The Amicans were probably just as relieved to see them go as the Red Cadre.

They rode single file through the gorge, which had been cleared enough to make navigating it an extremely tight squeeze. They rode past the abandoned wind wags, or what was left of them. Vengeful Amicans had dismantled them piece by piece. Only the skeletal, wheelless frameworks lay on the plain. By the time they reached the open prairie, the sun had risen above the horizon, drenching the landscape with a yellow-red glow.

The seven people, their horses and two mules walked across the open grasslands of the Washakie Basin. Shallow coulees broke up the monotonous flatness of the plain, and here and there were cottonwood groves. They kept on a straight course for the Wind River Mountain Range far in the distance, so far in fact, it seemed they couldn't possibly reach them in three years, much less three days.

The stretch between the basin and the mountains was probably one of the least-known regions of Deathlands. Even before the nukecaust it hadn't been heavily populated. Even Trader and his old partner, Marsh Folsom, who had boasted a vast library of maps and predark aerial surveys, knew little about the area.

They rode through the morning, speaking very little. Joe was a cooperative, if somewhat taciturn, traveling companion. Doc complained about the low comfort level of his saddle, but not vociferously enough to get on anyone's nerves.

At midmorning they saw the black shapes of vultures wheeling and circling ahead of them. Their route

brought them within a few hundred feet of one of the
Red Cadre's wind wags. It hadn't been touched, but
bodies were strewed over the ground. The air buzzed
with flies, and several vultures feasted on the banquet
of rotting flesh, blood and excrement.

The body of a pirate dangled from the main mast
of the wag, lashed upside down by the ankles. His
cranium had been exposed by a scalping knife, revealing blue-white bone with a few clinging strips of
red tissue.

The stench made Ryan's mouth fill with sour saliva, and he cast a questioning look at Joe.

The Lakota shrugged and said, "I mentioned the
stragglers had been dealt with, didn't I?"

At noon they stopped to eat, but rather than building a fire, they ate beef jerky, washing it down with
swigs of water from their canteens. After an hour they
got under way again, this time walking to spare the
horses. The company was in a better mood, and Ryan
was almost completely recovered from his hangover.
Joe didn't speak of their destination or what they
might find when they reached it.

Gradually the plains gave way to hilly terrain. Toward midafternoon, as they were climbing the slope
of a rock-strewn bluff, Ryan felt the earth trembling,
every so slightly, beneath his boots. At the same time,
he detected a musky, wooly odor in the air. The others
became aware of the faint ground quake and smell at
the same time.

"Come on," Joe said, quickening his pace as he
urged his pinto up the face of the slope.

The seven people assembled on the crest of the
ridge and looked across the plains below. On the opposite side of a fast-running ribbon of water, a heavy
plume of dust shook with a sound like a continuous

rumble of distant thunder. Beneath the dust cloud, a sea of brown, moving bodies blotted out the prairie floor. It was a large herd of buffalo moving across the plains like a rolling, never-ending wave. The ground shivered under the impact of at least two thousand hooves.

"Ever hunted buffalo, Ochinee?" Joe asked with a smile.

"No, but they've hunted me," he replied. He glanced over at J.B., and both of them smiled at the memory of the time they'd been caught in a stampede of mutie buffalo in Colorado. These animals, however, didn't appear to be of the genetically altered variety. They were still very big, however.

Joe explained how buffalo had been hunted by his people several hundred years before. "The soldier band went first, riding twenty abreast, and anyone who dared to go ahead of them would be knocked off his horse. After them came the hunters, riding five abreast. The butchers came up in the rear. The hunters would circle around the herd and the cry went up— *'Hoka hey!'* as if in battle. All the hunters went in to kill—every man for himself. A bow's length away was the distance the hunters had to try for, and the preferred targets were the intestinal cavity just behind the last rib, and just back of the left shoulder and into the heart. Unless the buffalo was hit in a vital spot, he died slowly, which was a disgrace, or raced away and was lost to the tribe, which was an even greater disgrace."

Joe gazed down at the herd, his eyes viewing the distant past. "To the best hunters belonged the buffalo's liver, and when the chase had run its course, they would jump from their horses, cut it out and eat it raw—seasoned with gall and still steaming with body heat and dripping blood.''

Mildred shuddered. "I think I'll stick with the beef jerky, thanks.''

Joe consulted the position of the sun and heaved a sigh. "Time we get through the canebrakes and ford the river, it'll be too close to dark for a hunt.''

The party remounted their horses and made for the river. Ryan tried to keep the buffalo herd in view during the ride down the hill and across a wide, grassy swale that led to the river. The banks of the river were enclosed on both sides by huge brakes of cane.

The canebrakes were of a sort Ryan had never seen or even imagined. From the hilltop he had figured the stuff to be the same height and thickness as cane he had seen growing elsewhere, maybe ten feet high, an inch around at the base.

But these stalks of cane were thicker, and the shortest grew to a height of at least twenty-five feet. The bases were the diameter of his wrist. The growth was so densely packed that upon entering it, he was under the impression that a great cloud had passed over the face of the sun.

The ground was marshy and soft, and snakes, frogs and things less identifiable wriggled out of his horse's path. Insects whirled in abundance around everyone's faces and the eyes of their steeds. J.B. pulled off his fedora and tried to wave the buzzing, stinging horde away. What little sunlight that pierced the foliage arching overhead was of a pale greenish hue. The odor of rotting vegetation and sulfurous marsh gas became so strong that they all breathed through their mouths, though they ran the risk of inhaling a handful of bugs.

No one spoke as the horses forced their way through the heavy growth.

Finally a new sound replaced the steady tramp of hooves and the swish of brush: the sound of flowing water and chirping birds. Then there was a draft of clean, untainted air. Sunlight, strong and warm, fell upon them. Ryan tried to suppress a heartfelt sigh of relief at leaving the canebrakes, and he saw that the others were doing so, as well.

The river was a shallow one, with clear, frigid blue, mountain-fed water. It showed white foam in places and small wavelets on the surface. The place where they were to ford was perhaps sixty or seventy feet wide.

Joe leaned back on his saddle blanket and cut himself a strip of jerky with a knife. Popping it into his mouth, he said, ''River is only six, seven feet deep here, but it's running faster than usual. Be careful, gentlemen—'' he nodded toward Krysty and Mildred ''—and ladies.''

J.B. moved his horse close to Mildred's, and Ryan stood shoulder to shoulder with Krysty. The animals were fearful of the crossing, and many of them balked and whinnied. Only the mules displayed no nervousness. Ryan and Krysty hung back until most of the others had gained the opposite shore, then they urged their mounts into the water.

The water lapped at Ryan's shins, his thighs, then his waist, and to the base of his horse's neck. The animal was forced to walk across holding its head almost straight up. He took the SIG-Sauer from its holster and held it free of the river. Krysty did the same with her Smith & Wesson. There was nothing he could do about the Steyr scabbarded to the saddle but thoroughly dry, clean and oil it at the first opportunity.

The current was very strong, and Ryan could feel it tugging at his body. He and Krysty were at the halfway point of the ford, with Joe only a few feet ahead of them, when a flicker of furtive movement caught the corner of his eye.

Ryan turned his head, looking toward the shore behind him. He saw nothing, only the muddy tracks of their horses. Joe called his name, and he turned back.

The Lakota was leaning forward, gazing at the surface of the river. He asked, "Do you like trout? As I recollect, the first time we met, you were preparing a muck-sucker stew. I can assure you trout is preferable, easier on the palate and the digestion."

A feathered shaft miraculously appeared, quivering, in the meat of Joe's left shoulder blade. His body jerked convulsively, a cry of surprised pain bursting from his lips. Only then did Ryan hear the faint twang of a bowstring.

Twisting in his saddle, Ryan glimpsed a blur of a bestial face before it faded into the shadows of the cane. Though he caught only a flickering fragment of motion, the impression he received was of a lupine, wolfish head.

Spinning back, he saw Joe sliding from his pinto's back into, and under, the foaming blue water. Both he and Krysty forced their horses forward and flailed with their free hands at the surface. Ryan caught what felt like the fringes on the hem of the deerskin cape. Though his face was almost under the water, he held on. On the shore, attracted by a shout from Krysty, his friends stared uncomprehendingly for a moment.

Ryan urged his horse forward, clinging to Joe's

cape. Through a water-blurred eye, he saw J.B. riding his mount into the river, unslinging his Uzi.

Backbone crawling in anticipation of catching an arrow, Ryan continued to kick his horse toward the riverbank. Krysty rode to the other side of him, reaching down and pulling Joe's head out of the water by his long hair. Splashing out to them, J.B. grabbed the rope bridle of the pinto and dragged it toward the bank, water erupting in the wake of their passage.

Ryan and Krysty maintained their grips on Joe until they had crossed the river. Mildred waded out and grabbed the coughing man, helping him to the bank and sitting him down.

"Who shot?" Jak demanded. "Didn't see person."

"I thought I did," Ryan said, swinging out of the saddle and yanking the Steyr free of the scabbard. "And it wasn't a who. More like a what."

Joe, his face tight against the pain, asked, "What did you see?"

"I thought it was a wolf."

"What?" J.B. demanded. "A wolf that shoots a bow and arrow?"

Joe bit back a groan. "You saw a man dressed as a wolf. One of the Wolf Soldiers. I should've known they would lie in wait for me."

Everyone dismounted and, with blasters drawn, scanned the opposite shore. Mildred knelt behind Joe, took hold of the arrow and broke the shaft. She threw back the wet deerskin cape. Joe wasn't wearing a shirt, and the jagged stump of the shaft rose from the muscles of his shoulder, moving with the labor of his breathing. There was very little blood. Quickly she examined the wound.

The arrow, fired at fairly long range, had penetrated his cloak easily enough, but hadn't sunk deeply into the muscles. The angle was such that if the bow had been stronger and the shaft had more velocity, it would have punctured his heart. That obviously had been the idea.

"Whoever shot you must have thought you were a buffalo," she said. "If you know who it was, maybe you know if they use barbed points on their arrows."

Joe shook his head. "No. Leastways it doesn't feel like it."

"Good. The arrowhead has to be withdrawn, and there might be some blood loss. If it's heavy, then we're in trouble, because I don't have the materials to stop a serious flow."

Joe nodded, his breathing labored and harsh. "And if it is not withdrawn, then I run the risk of bleeding internally. It has to be removed. At once."

He gestured to his pony. "In that parfleche, the one made of badger skin, is my medicine pouch. "

Doc searched through the bundles tied to the pinto and found the furry pouch. It was decorated with wrapped quill bands and beadwork done in Sioux colors and patterns. He handed it to Mildred.

Inside she found seven small hide packets of herbs, the entire foot of an eagle, a small piece of elk horn and a bear claw. On the inner edge of each packet was a small insignia, each different, each in a different color.

Following Joe's instructions, Mildred removed two of the packets and emptied half their contents into her left hand. They looked like chopped-up herbs, diced so fine they were almost a powder.

"Yarrow plant," Krysty said after a glance. "And something else."

"Buffalo tallow," Joe told her. "Dried and ground up."

"Okay," Mildred said. "What do you want me to do?"

"Rub the herb and the tallow in your hand," Joe directed. "Mix them up."

With both hands Mildred rubbed the material between them. "Done. Now what?"

"Put the mixture in your mouth. When your saliva has softened it, pull out the arrow and spit the stuff into the puncture, then smooth it out with your fingers, making sure the hole is plugged."

Mildred's eyes flicked at the crushed-up substance in her hand and then back to Krysty. "Mother Sonja ever hear of a remedy like this?"

With a wan smile Krysty shook her head.

Impatiently Joe said, "Are you going to do it or not? I thought you were a healer."

"I'll do it," Mildred muttered. "But it's not my field. If you wanted me to freeze some part of you— like your tongue—I'd feel more at home."

Jak and Doc knelt in front of Joe and took grips on both of his arms. Mildred popped the mixture in her mouth, then she sat behind Joe, planted a foot at the small of his back, grasped the broken shaft and yanked. The arrowhead came free, blood trailing from the sharp iron point.

Joe didn't cry out, but he bit his lip and squeezed his eyes shut. Blood began to flow heavily from the wound, down his back, the top of his breechclout soaking it up. Leaning forward, Mildred spit the semiliquid gob of yarrow plant and tallow at the puncture. She scored a direct hit, and quickly her fingers kneaded the substance, pressing it into the wound, spreading it evenly around the edges. Almost immediately the bleeding stopped.

"I'll be damned," she said in a pleased voice. "A

natural coagulating agent.'' Then she frowned and rushed to the edge of the river, where she dipped handful after handful of water into her mouth, rinsing and spitting repeatedly.

Joe slowly stood, careful not to place too much strain on his back. ''Under the circumstances,'' he said, ''I think we'd better find a suitable campsite for the night.''

Chapter Fourteen

After Mildred rigged a makeshift bandage and arm sling for Joe, they pressed on for another hour. By the time they reached an animal-forged trail in the high grass, the sun was setting. Following a barely defined path, they walked through a thicket and into a small clearing.

They set up camp there, unsaddling the horses and mules, picketing them so they could graze nearby. J.B. dug a foot-deep hole and encircled the edge with piled stones. He kindled a blaze in the hole, and no firelight was visible from the "owlhoot's oven."

Doc made a stew from chunks of the jerky, seasoning it with carrots and slices of some unidentifable root vegetables he had raided from the larder of the hostel in Amicus.

All of them ate slowly, since the meat was tough and had to be chewed carefully. Later they sipped cups of coffee sub. It wasn't particularly delectable, but it was a definite improvement over the bark tea favored by the Amicans.

By the time they'd finished eating, stars burned in the blue-black sky. Jak and Krysty volunteered to stand the first watch, patrolling the perimeter. Though the firelight was poor illumination, Ryan field-stripped the Steyr and meticulously cleaned and oiled all its moving parts. After reassembling it, he did the same to Joe's weapon. The man watched him silently but intently.

"How are you feeling?" Ryan asked him.

"Much better. By tomorrow I'll be much better still."

"Good. Then mebbe you feel good enough to explain about the Wolf Soldiers, and why they're so anxious to keep you from reaching Ti-Ra'-Wa."

Joe shook his head. "I doubt you would believe everything I told you."

"Try us," Mildred suggested.

Joe tried to shrug, winced, then sighed. "Though we are of the same tribe, there are two factions in the valley, the Wolf Soldiers and the Cavern Keepers, of which I am a chief. We believe in keeping the high laws, strengthening our spirit bodies and strengthening the energies of Ah-badt-dadt-deah."

"What?" Jak asked.

"The Grandfather, the One Above."

J.B. rolled his eyes. "Religion. I was afraid of this."

Joe ignored him. "When you strengthen your spirit body, you exercise these high laws against low laws that the material world obeys. The Wolf Soldiers have abandoned the high laws and practice the low."

"You may have to define the practice of low law," Doc said. "I presume you do not mean divorce proceedings."

"Low law is the lust for material power," Joe said. "Power over everything, even the methods of healing Grandmother Earth."

"Healing?" Ryan inquired, looking up from the pieces of the blaster scattered on a blanket before him. "Explain."

"I cannot. It is something you will not believe or even understand until we reach the valley."

Joe drew a blanket around him with such a flourish it ended the discussion. Ryan put the weapon back together, then went to relieve Krysty. He told her what Joe had said. She pursed her lips but said nothing.

"What do you think?" he asked. "Tribal superstitions?"

"Who knows?" Krysty shrugged, then patted back a yawn with her hand. "Want me to stay out here for a while?"

"No," Ryan said. "I'll be okay. Send J.B. out to take over for Jak in a little while, though."

Krysty kissed his cheek, then returned to the campsite.

Leaning against a tree, Ryan looked toward the distant mountain range. Clouds squatted on the snowy peaks. Before the nukecaust and the earth-shaker bombs, the Continental Divide had followed the crest line of the Wind River Range. God only knew what it was like now, but it was possible it had been unaffected. This was still good, strong country and it had always been.

A couple of hundred years earlier, a government Indian reservation at the base of the Wind River Range had confined the Crow, the Ute, the Bannock, the Sioux and the Cheyenne. He couldn't help but wonder how they'd felt to look up at those tree-lined hills, carpeted with high, sweet grass, and know they could never roam among them again.

The nukecaust had been a blessing to most Indian peoples, the "purification" of ancient prophecy. The white man's government had dissolved in a twinkling, and though the world wasn't as rich and beautiful as it had been when the tribes had raced wild and free across the plains and the mountains, this part of the country was still rich and beautiful enough.

SETTING OUT at first light, the company of travelers followed an old, overgrown paved road that traced its way across high-plains country, flat acres and plateaus of good pasture. In the far distance was the burned-out ruin of an old ranch house.

The day dawned overcast, with thick clouds, but rain didn't come. The color of the day fit the moods of the travels. Everyone seemed absorbed in his or her own somber reflections.

The longer they traveled, the rougher the terrain became, slashed with narrow ravines and steep drop-offs, reminders of the quakes that had shaken the West Coast more than a century earlier.

At midmorning the rumble of countless hooves reached them. The party reined in and studied a dust cloud hanging in the distance.

"There's your buffalo again," Mildred said to Joe, standing in her stirrups and staring at the cloud beneath a shading hand.

"About a mile away," Joe replied. "Cost us a couple of hours if we wanted some fresh meat."

"After last night's stew," J.B. said. "I wouldn't mind."

"Nor would I," Doc added.

The consensus was in favor of going after the game. Mildred was the only dissenter.

The animals picked their way carefully over the uneven ground, following the crest of a ridge that dipped down into an open meadow. As they continued along the stony slant to the prairie, Jak saw a one-story log cabin set back a quarter of a mile from their path. It squatted in a barren clearing, surrounded by upthrusts of shale and scraggly thornbush.

The cabin displayed no sign of human habitation except for a trickle of smoke that rose from the crude chimney. Also from the chimney fluttered a tattered red flag.

When Ryan pointed this out to Joe, the Lakota replied rather uneasily, "An old woman lives there. A seer, what you would call a doom-sniffer. Everyone thinks she is touched, so even the tribes leave her alone."

Doomseers, "doomies," were human mutants, possessed or cursed with the psychic ability to foresee death. Krysty's ability was somewhat similar, but she couldn't visualize exact details, though she often sensed danger in the offing.

"What's the flag for?" Jak asked.

"Means she wants company, or help for a chore. She always pays off in provisions."

"The flour got wet at the river crossing," J.B. said. "Might be good idea to mosey down there and trade for some."

"What about the buffalo?" Ryan asked, frowning.

"We'll keep them in sight," Joe replied. "Won't take but a few minutes for someone to go down there and get back to us."

"I'll go," Mildred volunteered, "if someone comes with me."

"I'll accompany you," Doc said. "My mouth is already primed for biscuits."

"We'll wait for you here," Ryan told them.

Doc and Mildred guided their horses down the rock-ribbed slant. A chill wind sprang up and plucked at their hair and clothing. Their pants were still slightly damp from the river crossing the day before, and they shivered.

They cantered into the cabin's compound. Reining Judas Redux to a halt, Doc glanced around, feeling an invisible, strange *something* emanating from the structure's interior, like radiation. The hairs at his nape tingled, and he looked quickly at Mildred. If she sensed the same thing, she showed no sign of it.

Dismounting, they then started walking toward the cabin, but froze in their tracks when a low animal growl reached their ears. Rigid with fear and astonishment, they saw, tethered to a post at a corner of the log building, a tawny cougar, only it was gigantic, a breed spawned by radiation-induced polyploidism, the doubling of all or part of the chromosome complement.

Though this monster wasn't as large as the twenty-five-foot puma that had nearly bitten Doc's head off months earlier, it still stretched fifteen feet from nose to tail tip, and probably weighed nine hundred pounds.

The mouth was open, saliva dripping from the long yellow fangs. The creature didn't snarl or hiss. It growled, very low, very menacing, and regarded them with calculating brown-green eyes. Looking at the rust-eaten chain that attached the beast to the post, both Doc and Mildred went for their blasters.

"He will not molest you, strangers," a clear voice stated.

An old black woman stood in the doorway of the cabin, wearing a collection of colorful rags and scraps of fur. "You saw my flag?" Her voice was strong despite her advanced age.

After exchanging a glance with Doc, Mildred said, "Yes, ma'am. We'd like to trade for some flour."

"Trade with what?"

"Chores or jack."

The old woman smiled a speculative smile, and for a moment the expression on her face seemed a mirror image of the panther's. "What are your names?"

"Dr. Mildred Wyeth and—" Mildred hesitated, then nodded toward Doc "—Dr. T. A. Tanner."

The wrinkled face collapsed in a network of lines and creases, and they realized the woman was laughing silently. "An embarrassment of doctors today. Enter, both of you, and be welcome."

They tied their mounts to a post at the opposite corner from the cougar and, drawn by a gesture from a black-nailed hand, they ducked under the low doorway and entered the cabin. Something about the crone's secret smile and easy manner made Doc's hand itch for the comforting weight of his Le Mat. Surreptitiously he loosened the ebony case sheathing the blade of Toledo steel.

The old woman stoked the fire of buffalo chips in the shallow hearth, and the flames leaped higher. Mildred and Doc quickly studied the single-room dwelling. The wooden walls were covered by stretched animal hides and grinning skulls, bears with great fangs, long-horned steers and immense buffalo skulls. Dried herbs, desiccated birds and mummified reptiles dangled from the rafters. Doc was reminded of an apothecary's shop.

The woman bade them to sit on a splintery wooden bench, and she busied herself stirring the contents of the pot in the hearth. "You are strangers to this land, you doctors?" she asked.

"Yes, ma'am," Mildred replied.

"Why do you ask?" Doc inquired.

"Everyone else fears to enter the abode of the

doomie woman. I sniff deaths, you see. That is how I have lived here for so many years, unharmed by the tribes, the beasts, the brigands. I can foretell deaths, and no one wants to know about it. They are afraid that if they learn the time and manner of their death, it will arrive before they are ready.''

She turned and gave both of them searching stares. ''You come from far, far away. Far beyond my range of sight. But I do not concern myself with where you have been. You look only ahead, dreaming golden dreams.''

Doc stirred uneasily. ''Madam—''

The crone laughed, but there was little mirth in the sound, only a smug, cackling mockery. ''It is a poor gift, this doom sight. But it keeps me safe from harm.''

Mildred shifted on the bench. ''Our companions are waiting for us. We can't stay long.''

As if she hadn't heard, the woman went on. ''My sight does not work on command. I see only when my mind is clear and untroubled. Then, I may glimpse the deaths of others. Of late I have seen colors—red for blood, gold for greed, black for doom.''

She gazed at Doc and Mildred with a steady, penetrating gaze. ''For instance I have known for some time that your company of travelers would be passing this way. More, I knew that you two would be the only ones foolish—or ignorant—enough to come here.''

Doc and Mildred said nothing.

''Unfortunately,'' she continued quietly, ''my sight is frequently dimmed. And then others must arrange the dooms I cannot see.''

Some soft sound or some scent goaded Doc to bound to his feet and reach for his holstered Le Mat.

Behind him a narrow portal covered with an animal pelt was swinging open. Before he could draw his blaster or Mildred could get to her feet, the razor-keen point of an arrow was thrust into the room. It was followed half a heartbeat later by a crossbow. Two men stepped inside quietly, rail-thin Indians wearing wolf skins, the hollowed-out, furry skullcaps resting on their heads like hoods.

"They see your dooms," the crone went on. "Whether it is a true vision or merely a wish that will never be fulfilled is too soon know."

Doc opened his mouth and the warrior with the crossbow growled, *"Inila!"*

"He wants you to be silent," the crone said helpfully.

"What else does he want?" Mildred murmured.

The unarmed Wolf Soldier spoke rapidly, quietly.

"He wants the old one to go to the door and beckon your comrades," the old woman translated.

"Madam," Doc said firmly, "our comrades are very well armed. This pair would not stand a chance against them."

"They want only Yutan-kin-Mahipiya. Do not make it difficult for yourself and your fellow physician."

Doc didn't move. The warrior with the crossbow mumbled something to his companion, and the Indian approached Mildred. Drawing a knife from his belt, he placed the edge against the side of her neck.

"They can kill you," the old woman said calmly. "Your people would hear nothing and only much later find your corpses."

The Indian pressed the edge of his knife into Mildred's flesh. She didn't cry out, but she bit her lower lip.

Doc held up a hand. "Very well," he said wearily, his voice thin and reedy. "I shall do as they ask."

Shoulders slumped, he shuffled painfully toward the open door, leaning heavily on his cane. When he reached the opening, he ducked his head as if to go through it, then he paused and half turned, a questioning look in his eyes. He opened his mouth.

The warrior with the crossbow snarled, *"Hoppo!"*

Sighing, Doc lifted the cane as if to administer an admonishing wag, then he snapped his wrist and whipped the black sheath from the blade of gleaming Toledo steel. In the same motion he hurled the sword point first at the Wolf Soldier.

The blade traveled only three feet before the point struck into the warrior's open mouth and became fixed in his brain stem. With the sword hanging out like a ghastly metal tongue, the Wolf Soldier's eyes bugged, his knees buckled and his fingers closed convulsively on the crossbow's trigger. The string hummed as the tension was released, and the long shaft drove past Doc's head, close enough to feather-whip his right ear.

The reaction of the other warrior was almost comical. He gave a great leap backward, dragging the edge of the knife along the side of Mildred's neck and drawing a thread of blood.

She spit out a curse and rolled off the bench. When she came out of the roll, the ZKR was in her fist and seeking a target.

The Wolf Soldier's extravagant back-leap had carried him against the hidden door panel. His back struck it, knocking it open, but his heels caught on the raised lip of the narrow portal, and he fell just as Mildred squeezed the revolver's trigger.

The bullet sped toward the shaggy wolf's head, but

it dropped down and the slug missed one of the pointed ears by less than a finger's width. The warrior struggled to his feet and raced away from the cabin, across the rear of the compound. Mildred rushed to the opening, aligning the frantically sprinting figure within the sights of her blaster. Her finger had just begun to squeeze the trigger when a huge tawny shape bounded in from her left.

The monster mutie cougar, trailing the length of rusty, clanking chain, caught up with the fleeing human with two spring-steel-legged bounds. A swipe of curving, unsheathed claws flayed the wolf skin and almost all the flesh from the warrior's back. He went down amid flying liquid ribbons of crimson.

As Mildred watched with a horrid fascination the giant cat gutted the man with a single slash of a hind paw. Loops of blue-pink intestines spilled onto the ground. Huge jaws closed over the warrior's head with a sickening crunch, and the cougar's neck jerked back and forth. Arms and legs flopped, like those of a disjointed marionette's.

The cat gathered itself and bounded from sight, the flesh-stripped, eviscerated body dangling from its blood-flecked jaws.

Doc came to her side, Le Mat in hand. He scanned the compound over her shoulder, demanding, "Where is he? Did he get— Oh."

When he saw the thick whorls of blood and coils of viscera glistening on the barren ground, he swallowed noisily and stepped back with haste.

"It happened so fast," Mildred said huskily. "Like it had been waiting for him."

"He had," the old woman said. "He has sharp teeth and a keen nose. He had already sniffed out who was fated to die."

Mildred and Doc released their pent-up breath in loud exhalations, but the woman's was punctuated by a loud curse. Holding one hand to the blood-oozing line on her neck, she advanced on the crone, blaster cocked.

"You old bitch! How about if I show you your doom?"

Doc restrained her with a hand. "She's old enough to be your grandmother."

Grunting, the old woman turned back to stirring the contents of the pot hanging over the fire in the hearth. She ignored the dead, sword-transfixed man sprawled on the floor.

"When the cat came this morning," she said cheerfully, "I knew you were in no danger."

"How?" Mildred asked angrily.

The crone touched one of her eyes. "I see through his eyes. He knew who would die, and so did I."

"So..." Doc hesitated. "You mean that vicious predator was never chained up?"

"Oh, no. That would be cruel."

Closing her eyes, shaking her head, Mildred pinched the bridge of her nose. "I don't understand any of this."

The woman gestured to a five-pound burlap sack in a corner. "There is your flour, Dr. Wyeth. You'd better get it back to your friends. They have heard the shot and are already on their way down."

Doc worked the blade of the sword loose from the Indian's open mouth. "What do we owe you?"

"I've been paid."

Doc frowned. "At least allow us to remove this carcass from your home."

The old woman straightened and tapped the spoon against the rim of the pot. "You don't understand," she said gently, as if trying to explain a complex equation to a child.

She gestured with the spoon toward the corpse and repeated, "I've been paid."

Chapter Fifteen

"What I can't figure," Mildred said, "is if that old lady meant to trap us or the Indians."

Doc shrugged. "Since we're still alive, I presume she meant the Indians." He tapped the five-pound sack on his saddle. "Besides, we acquired the flour, didn't we?"

Doc and Mildred had rejoined the rest of their companions and told them the story of the Wolf Soldiers and their grisly fates. Only Joe didn't appear overly disconcerted by the tale of the doomie, her cannibalistic diet and her partnership with a mutie cougar. His only comment was "Life is strange and cheap out here on the basin."

They rode away from the ridges and rock slants and emerged onto the prairie again. Multicolored wildflowers grew among the high grasses. The sound of muted thunder reached them, yet the sky overhead was clear.

"Coming up on the buffalo soon," J.B. said with an eager smile.

Urging their horses to the top of a gentle bluff, they gazed awestruck at the violently undulating sea of buffalo. They were less than a quarter of a mile from the herd's right flank. The ground quaked at the pounding of their hooves, and the air was choked with the dust of their passing. Their massive tufted humps and domed, horned heads bobbed as they thundered by, the farthest reaches of the herd shrouded by dust-clogged distance.

Tersely, his body taut with anticipation, Joe explained how they would hunt the great animals. They would travel in pairs, pick out a buffalo from the herd and while one hunter tried to drop it with a single, killing shot, the partner would keep a loaded blaster at the ready.

"Buffalo are unpredictable," he added. "Sometimes what seems to be a mortal wound won't kill it. It will be angered enough to charge as its last act of life. That's why standby blasters are needed."

"We only have a couple of long blasters," Ryan argued. "Will our handblasters do?"

Joe eyed the weapons critically, then nodded. "They have plenty of stopping power, at least. Just don't get too close."

Doc waved a hand grandly. "I, for one, do not intend to do so. I shall be more than happy to participate in a feast of fresh meat, but I have no desire to risk my life to put it on my plate. Judas Redux, the flour and myself will sit this one out."

Joe glanced at Jak. "Partner up with me."

Jak nodded his agreement and unholstered his Colt Python. "Let's do it."

The six people directed their horses down the bluff toward the westward-rumbling herd. Joe's face was alight with excitement. He howled a hunting cry, raised his rifle and heeled his pony into a gallop.

Jak followed him, wondering briefly what would happen if his, or someone else's, horse slipped beneath the hooves of the herd. It wasn't a mental picture he wanted to dwell on.

They shouted encouragement to one another as they rode along the flank of the herd, but the rumble of the buffalo's passage was so loud, their voices were overwhelmed.

Jak had yet to test his mount's speed and gait, so he kicked it hard in the ribs. The next moment he was clinging to the reins for his life. It was as though his horse had exploded forward. The steed rushed at a nightmare pace beside the outer edge of the herd. Rather than reining in the horse, Jak enjoyed the wild ride. The teenager had, more than his companions, the capacity for taking things as they came.

Whether outrunning an acid rainstorm, wading through toxic swamps in the bayou or swapping strangleholds with muties, Jak didn't usually bother to look far ahead.

He had done so only once in his life, when he settled down on a spread in New Mexico with his wife, Christina, and their daughter, Jenny. After they had been murdered by marauders, Jak had steadfastly refused to look very far into the future. There was no percentage in it.

Joe caught Jak's attention by waving and shouting. He pointed out a huge bull that snorted and eyed the approaching mounted men with something akin to anger. From hoof to hump, it stood half a head taller than Jak and it was perhaps ten feet long from nose to the brushy end of its tail. The coarse, curly hair was a muddy brown, with black streaks blended into it. It looked as if it would weigh out at close to a ton. The bull shook its massive horned head, a challenging bellow rising above the cacophony of hoofbeats and bawls.

Nodding in wordless agreement, Joe and Jak picked out the big bull as their common target. They rode closer. The never-ending roar, the choking dust and the cloying odor of the great beasts exhilarated Jak.

He galloped alongside the shaggy herd, watching their humps heaving up and down like the prows of ships breasting rough seas.

Joe shouted at the bull, trying to cut it out of the herd. Both men started up a raucous hooting. Foam was wind whipped from the beast's open mouth, and its red-shot eyes bored in on them.

Suddenly, so suddenly that the dodging maneuver of Jak's horse nearly unseated him, the buffalo lunged away from the herd and charged. The mammoth humpback came directly for its tormentors, hooves tearing up clods of earth, horns questing for enemies to rend.

Both Joe and Jak managed to swerve their steeds out of the bull's path, and it kept going. Unhindered by the press of the herd, the big animal's speed was astonishing. It galloped away from them, heading south. Howling with the joy of the hunt, Joe and Jak gave chase, exhorting their mounts to give everything they had.

The horses managed to maintain a long-legged, full-out pace for a mile, yet the buffalo continued to elude them. Glancing over his shoulder, Jak barely discerned the distant figures of Doc and Judas Redux on the bluff. He also noticed that the herd and his friends were almost out of sight, but he didn't worry about either.

The chase after the bull continued, the land gradually sloping into a marsh. Stunted trees stood in tight groups, and the grasses of the rolling plains were replaced by reedy strands of cane and cattails, which formed borders around a narrow creek.

The buffalo splashed through a shallow pond, sending a sheet of muddy water cascading into the air. Both Jak and Joe were soaked, and by the time they wiped the water out their eyes, the buffalo had run into a copse of cottonwood trees. It didn't reappear on the opposite side. The two men approached the copse from either side. Jak was too excited to be cautious.

With a bellow that seemed to make the air shiver, the buffalo thundered out of the stand of trees, crashing through saplings, snapping off branches like matchwood. Jak's horse neighed in a mad panic, and as he tried to align the sights of his blaster with the shaggy skull, his mount reared, its forelegs slashing the air wildly.

The buffalo's curved horns missed the horse's belly by a hairbreadth. Jak felt himself slipping from the saddle, and he kicked himself free of the stirrups, trying to land on his feet. He managed to hit the turf upright, but he stumbled and went to one knee.

The buffalo came to a sudden, dirt-flinging halt, whirled and charged. He raised his blaster, sighted coolly and calmly and squeezed the trigger. The Colt Python boomed with its characteristically full, deep-throated sound.

Nothing happened. The buffalo didn't falter. It lowered its head and charged on. Even as the echoes of the shot rang in the air, a wedge of a huge, woolly shoulder clipped Jak as he tried to leap aside.

The impact jarred the breath out of him, and he slammed down on his left side, rolling over and over. When he came to a stop, he was gasping for air, utterly astounded he was still alive. He hurt too much to be dead.

He had kept his grip on the Colt, and he tried to push himself to his feet. The buffalo veered, turned and began another charge. Jak could see a splash of blood on the beast's shaggy skull where the dense bone had partially deflected the first round. He aimed his blaster at it.

Joe galloped around the stand of trees and placed his pony squarely in the maddened bull's path. He placed the stock of the Gewehr against his shoulder and cheek and fired, then he kneed his horse out of the way.

A new splotch of blood had appeared on the skull. The bull thundered on for another second, then its forelegs folded and it skidded forward, sledding along the marshy ground like a down-sliding boulder. It left a wide, scoured path in its wake, turf rolling up before it like a strip of carpet. The buffalo came to a grinding stop less than six feet from Jak's position.

Throwing one leg up and over his pony's head, Joe dismounted and approached the buffalo. Its dark, humped form was slumped over, looking like a shaggy, debilitated volcano.

Examining the wound, Joe remarked, "A head shot is something of a break with tradition, but at least only one bullet brought him down."

Walking over to the dead bull, Jak said, "Two."

Joe glanced up at him. "What?"

Extending a pair of fingers, Jak repeated, "Two." He pointed to himself, then to Joe. "One. Two."

"Your bullet did not bring it down, therefore it cannot be counted." Joe's tone brooked no debate.

"You keeping score?" Jak demanded. "Like contest?"

"All life is a contest, young man. Past time you learned that."

Jak glared at the Lakota, then he quickly raised his blaster. Joe recoiled, fumbling to bring up his weapon, eyes wide with sudden fear. Jak's blaster continued to rise, over his head, and he fired two shots into the air.

"Signal," he said. "Two bullets. You lose two points for flinching."

Joe's lips tightened, then he muttered something in his own tongue and turned his attention to the buffalo. Stripping down to his breechclout, Joe removed his pack of possessions from his pony and withdrew a very long skinning knife from a fur-lined sheath. It had no hilt, and the steel blade widened and curved slightly toward the tip.

After recovering his horse, Jak watched the butchering process with an expressionless face but an interested eye. The difficulty with butchering the buffalo was that it could neither be hanged and dressed like a deer nor turned onto its back. Lashing ropes to the buffalo's legs and knotting them around his pony's neck, Joe then backed up his steed until the legs were pulled and braced outward.

By the time Jak saw his friends riding toward them across the plain, Joe had already made the first cut crosswise at the nape and the second cut along the length of the spine. Lateral cuts were made along the insides of all four legs. Tugging, wrestling and grunting, Joe peeled the skin away from the body, revealing the thick layer of fat and tallow beneath. The hump looked like a small hill covered in glistening fat of surprising whiteness. Joe continued to pull the hide back in jerks of several feet at a time. It was hard, bloody work, and since Jak wasn't asked to help, he wasn't about to offer it.

When Ryan and the others cantered up, Joe was spreading the hide around the flayed beast like a picnic cloth. He was covered with gore, his near-naked body plastered with grease, hair, fat and blood. It was clotted thickly between his fingers.

"You had better luck than we did," J.B. said, swinging out of the saddle. "Stampeded on us. Lucky we weren't all stomped and squashed right into the basin."

Joe didn't respond. He plunged the knife into the buffalo, almost at ground level, and slit it open. Then his drove his hand inside the carcass and ripped out the liver, dripping blood and seemingly palpitating. He rose and carried it over to Jak, holding it up in front of his face. He said nothing.

Jak stared at him over the dark, crimson-smeared organ, then leaned forward and sank his teeth into one dangling end. He gnawed off a hunk of the raw, hot liver, keeping his eyes on Joe's face all the while. It was tough, and he chewed through a few stringy vessels before he was able to tear it free and swallow it.

Once he swallowed the mouthful, he felt his muscles begin to tense and quiver, relax, then tense again. For a moment he felt as if he could have caught the breeze and flown to the Wind River Mountain Range. Despite himself, he felt a smile crossing his face, his teeth red filmed, blood streaking his white chin.

He knew Joe's offer of the first bite of the liver was the closest thing he could expect by way of an acknowledgment of his shot or an apology, and Jak decided not to push it further.

Joe bit off a morsel of liver himself, then went back to butchering the buffalo, taking the cuts he claimed were the most desirable. While he worked, he asked the others to set up camp and collect firewood. An owlhoot's oven wouldn't suffice for the feast he had in mind.

"At least we won't want for food," Mildred commented.

J.B. and Doc walked near the creek in search of wood dry enough to burn, and Ryan, Krysty and Jak collected armloads of twigs and branches from the copse of trees.

Once the fuel was collected and piled, Doc built a ring of stones and jammed a pair of Y-notched sticks into the ground over the tinder. He started a fire and, using his steel sword as a spit, cuts of hump meat were slowly roasted over the flames.

Joe was a true Amerindian gourmet when it came to ways of preparing buffalo dishes. He handed them saucers full of what looked like watery custard, but were in reality bone marrow mixed with melted fat. He dumped the buffalo's tongue in a metal cooking pot and placed it directly on the flaming wood to bake. The aroma of wood smoke and roasting and baking meat slowly filled the campsite, and appetites grew.

Joe carried a grease-sheened coil of intestines over the fire, flipped them over the far side of the ring of stones, then dragged them slowly through the flames, searing them and blistering the blue-gray tissue. Looping the guts meticulously at his feet, he sat cross-legged in front of them.

He held up one sliced end and asked, "Anyone care to join me?"

The question received polite "No, thank yous" and headshakes all around, though at one time or another, most of the companions had been forced to eat viands far less appetizing.

Joe shove the end of the gut into his mouth and began to gobble it down, not using his hands or even chewing. He swallowed yard after yard of the buffalo intestines, the entire length gliding easily down his throat, like a snake entering its burrow.

Ryan and J.B. watched the process in fascination. Mildred turned her face away.

In an astonishingly short span of time, Joe managed to bolt the entire length of intestine. Wiping his mouth with the back of one hand, he reached over with his knife and stabbed the hump meat roasting on the spit. Fat and blood dripped sizzling onto the fire.

"Done," he announced, "to a turn."

He sliced off large portions of the rich, gamey meat. Ryan and the others dug in without hesitation. Though the meat was rare, it was tender and easy to digest. He knew the Plains tribes often subsisted on almost nothing else but buffalo meat for long periods of time. It was common knowledge that illnesses endemic to settlements, such as scurvy, were unknown to Indians.

After everyone had eaten their fill, Joe dug out the tongue from where it had been baking in the glowing embers. It was the last delicacy and it was so soft, its flavor so sweet, that even Mildred had to admit she had rarely tasted anything quite as savory.

As the moon climbed over the horizon, Doc loosened his belt and patted his belly. He sighed, tried to swallow a belch and said, "A time like this is when I truly miss my pipe, my slippers and my armchair."

Ryan looked up at the night sky, the sprawling constellations glinting like powdered diamonds on a black velvet backdrop, and murmured, "Shining times."

For a moment he wondered where that thought had come from. Then fireflies danced around the campsite, winking like stars. A night breeze stirred the grass and the cottonwoods, their leafy boughs rustling and sighing softly.

Krysty moved closer to him and leaned her head against his shoulder. "Shining times," she whispered.

Chapter Sixteen

Ryan looked back down the shoulder of the gray-green mountain. The little line of people and animals crawled up the trail after him. The fourth day of their journey gathered toward the climax of a spectacular western sunset.

The treeless slope ahead of them went up to a hog-back ridge. Against the blazing glory of fusing colors that fired the sky, Joe and his pony loomed like statues graven from granite.

Ryan was in a good mood, the best he had been in for longer than he cared to remember. He found keen pleasure in exploring new lands, and he found trekking through the wilderness very congenial. Other than his friends, he hadn't seen another human being in two days, and the animals crossing his field of vision appeared normal, not mutated. Their provisions had held out, and the grass growing in the valleys was thick and rich enough to provide proper graze for the horses and mules. Even the injuries he had suffered in Amicus, from the laceration on his forehead to the wolf bite on his arm, were almost completely healed.

As Ryan rode toward the ridge, he saw Joe suddenly stiffen, point and shout. He gestured to Ryan and the people below to increase their pace.

"Now what?" J.B. demanded, riding up beside Ryan. "Has he sighted his valley yet? He should have. This is the fourth day."

"No, something's wrong," Ryan replied, kneeing his horse forward.

They reached Joe at the very crest of the ridge. From there they looked northward toward another and parallel mountain range. Its highest, most northern peaks were snowcapped, and beyond them was a stupendous vista of other, smaller ranges, probably extending into Canada.

A deep, thickly wooded gully yawned between the crest on which they stood and another rocky rampart. The tall trees were fir and pine and poplar, and the ground was carpeted with high grass.

"Your rifle!" Joe shouted as Ryan and J.B. rode up. "Shoot them quickly!"

Ryan followed Joe's pointing finger to the gully below. At first he saw nothing, but then he spotted two dark shapes skulking through a glade.

"You mean the wolves?" he asked.

"Yes. You must kill them or our danger is great!" Joe was in deadly earnest, his jet black eyes gleaming with fear.

Ryan drew the Steyr from its saddle scabbard and shouldered it, peering through the scope. Despite the dimming light, the laser image enhancer brought the animals into sharp focus.

The nearer wolf was close to the six-hundred-yard range. He centered the crosshairs on the furry skull, wondering about Lakota superstitions. From what Mose Autry had said about Amerindian beliefs, wolves were respected to the point of reverence. Joe's fearful demand that they be killed made no sense, regardless of his enmity with the Wolf Soldier society.

"Why do you want them chilled?" J.B. asked. "They're too far away to bother us."

"They'll take word of our coming to Ti-Ra'-Wa," Joe answered grimly. "Hurry, Ochinee."

Ryan's finger tensed on the Steyr's trigger. The wolf's skull was framed perfectly for a lethal head shot. Suddenly the animal glanced up. There was a swift flash of intelligence, of understanding in the green-gold eyes. In those eyes Ryan saw no malice, and moreover, he recognized them.

On impulse Ryan shifted the rifle's position a fraction of an inch and squeezed the trigger. The Steyr cracked, and a plume of dirt spouted between the wolf's forepaws. Both animals sprang backward and raced into the dappled shadows between the trees.

Joe clenched his fists and glared at Ryan. "You deliberately missed! Now they'll—"

His lips clamped tight over his next words, and he made a visible effort to repress his anger.

"Now they'll what?" Ryan demanded. "What can wolves do but act like wolves?"

He didn't add that he suspected the wolf named Blood-sniffer had spared his life in Amicus, a decidedly unlupine act.

Joe didn't answer. His fierce obsidian eyes swept over the figures of Jak, Doc, Mildred and Krysty and the two pack mules as they topped the crest of the ridge.

"We can't camp anywhere near here now," he said quickly. "We must keep moving through the night and moving fast. The soldiers will be out to cut us off now their scouts have taken back word of our arrival."

Ryan slid the rifle back into its scabbard. "We're not moving at all until we hear some explanations."

"All will be made clear when we reach Ti-Ra'-Wa."

Ryan shook his head. "You've been saying that for days. You'll fucking well make it clear here and now. It seems like you want us to get involved in something more than an intertribal conflict about high laws and low laws. Straight tongue, or we'll backtrack out of here."

Joe smiled humorlessly. "You're forgetting about the gold, aren't you?"

"Don't think we're so greedy you have us where you want us. Curiosity drove us most of the way. You need us worse than we need you. Talk, or we ride out."

Joe eyed the six people, his mind obviously gauging and weighing Ryan's threat. Then he shrugged.

"There is no time to tell you everything. We must move fast or we die."

"Then talk fast," Jak said.

Joe opened his mouth, closed it, shook his head and sighed. "I've told you about the two factions, the Wolf Soldiers and the Cavern Keepers. My faction believes in healing the Grandmother Earth so that all men and women may benefit from the restored earth energies. But Pizi, Sisoka and the Wolf Soldiers aspire to keep the planet the way it is, so the entire world will always be a Deathlands. The earth will never recover from the nuking, and it will continue to be a rad-blasted nightmare."

There was a stunned silence for a moment. Then Jak laughed scornfully. "Man is jolt-brain."

"Mebbe so, mebbe not so," J.B. said. "The gold is real enough."

"So it is," Doc agreed. "But what has it to do with tribal superstitions?"

Joe made a fierce, impatient gesture. "I knew you

would doubt me, that was why I dared not tell you the truth.''

'''Magic Ti-Ra'-Wa,''' Mildred intoned softly. '''Life, death, good, evil, joy and sorrow/All born in the Cavern of Creation.'''

Ryan spit on the ground, breaking the spell of the fantastic Joe and Mildred's words had woven. ''This is all bullshit, but we can spread it out thin later. Right now I want to know what kind of danger we're talking about. How far are we now from Ti-Ra'-Wa?''

Joe gestured to the craggy cliffs on the far side of the wooded gully. ''The valley lies on the other side of those cliffs. But reaching it will be extremely tricky now.''

''Why?'' Krysty asked.

''There is only one entrance into the valley. It leads near the lair of the Wolf Soldiers, yet we must pass through it to reach my people. Now, if the wolves get back word of us, they'll block us at the pass.''

''Wolves?'' Jak echoed incredulously, his crimson eyes glowing with suspicion. ''Wolves tell on us?''

''The beasts of Ti-Ra'-Wa are not the beasts of the white man's world,'' Joe declared. ''They are intelligent, some as intelligent as men. That is why we must hurry.''

Ryan and his five friends grasped at least the urgency of the situation. They had, all of them, fought too many battles and made too many forced marches through dangerous territory not to understand the need for stealth and strategy.

''Let's do as he says,'' Ryan told his friends. ''He's either a liar, a lunatic or a superstitious stupe. We'll find out later. Right now I smell trouble.''

Joe's face was tight with anger at Ryan's words,

but he said nothing as he jerked his pony's head toward the path to the gully below.

The sun continued to sink, and darkness came with an unwelcome rush as Joe led the little caravan down into the heavily treed gorge. They made their way through the tangle of fir, pine and poplar. A stream rushed noisily somewhere nearby.

Joe knew the trails. He turned southward, and the companions turned after him, their horses stumbling on loose turf and stones. J.B. swore beneath his breath each time his steed's footing faltered. Only Judas Redux tramped on without mistake.

A cold breeze sighed down from the mountains, stirring tree limbs. Ryan had a sudden and claustrophobic awareness of the huge mountain ranges that boxed them into this wild pocket of the world, and he thought of how the Red Cadre had been trapped in a gorge.

A wolf howled, a long, mournful cry that floated from somewhere up in the wooded slopes on the west side of the gully.

Joe turned on his pony's back. "Faster!"

The wolf cry came again, echoing thinly through the night.

Joe abruptly reined in his pinto and dismounted. "They've pinpointed our position."

Drawing his SIG-Sauer, Ryan turned to his friends. "Blasters primed and loaded. Triple red."

Joe reached beneath his fringed deerskin cape. Ryan assumed he was pulling out a weapon, but in his hand was the wafer of gold with the two crystal disks mounted on either side of it.

"What are you doing?" Ryan demanded in a harsh whisper.

"Quiet," Joe commanded. "I need to concentrate."

He pressed the wafer of metal to his forehead. The crystals caught the glow of the rising moon and the frosty starlight, and the facets seemed to sparkle.

Ryan felt stunned wonder and a swelling fear that the Lakota had suddenly and completely lost his mind.

"What is it? What's he doing?" came Mildred's anxious whisper from behind. There was the rattle of hooves on stones.

"More jolt-brain shit," Jak said angrily. "Can't stand here all night."

The wolf howled again, and this time it was answered by another yelping cry, then a third.

And a fourth.

And a fifth.

"Go," Jak declared. "Leave him."

"Wait, Jak," Krysty said softly. "Joe seems to know what's he doing."

The wolves howled in unison, a quintet wail full of menace.

J.B. scanned the darkness, holding his Uzi in both hands. "Getting closer, sounds like. Surrounding us."

Joe suddenly wheeled toward Ryan, lowering the golden slice of metal from his forehead. He spoke in a brisk whisper. "A force of Wolf Soldiers is on its way to cut us off inside the pass. My warriors can't reach us in time to help."

"How did you come by that tidbit of knowledge?" Doc asked.

Joe didn't answer him. He continued urgently, "We must get through the pass and into Ti-Ra'-Wa before we're encircled."

Ryan exchanged baffled glances with his companions, then faced Joe again. "What kind of opposition can we expect? How many men?"

"Perhaps not so many men, but they have many warriors."

"More crazy talk," Jak said disgustedly. "Means animals come against us."

"They may use trained wolves as fighters, like the one that was set on me in Amicus," Ryan said. "Not too crazy, but damn messy if they catch us in a narrow pass."

He made a snap decision. "Let's get moving. Whatever's waiting for us, we'll be better off meeting it in the valley than down here or in the pass."

Joe remounted and led them up a trail that twisted among giant boulders and gaunt fir trees. As they climbed out of the gully, the moonlight allowed them a glimpse of a crack splitting the stone rampart towering above and ahead of them.

A pulse-quickening sense of danger filled Ryan as he urged his horse upward along the rock-littered trail. They came up clear of the last trees and onto naked granite shelves and ledges. The lofty rampart loomed before them. The pass was a narrow crack, barely twenty feet wide, shaped like a lopsided, upside-down triangle.

The seven people, their horses and two mules moved into it in single file. It was a place of deep, cold shadows and heavy silences. Only the sound of hooves clattering and clinking on loose pebbles broke the brooding quiet.

The pass wasn't long, barely an eighth of a mile, and ran a fairly straight course. They emerged onto a wide, shelflike ledge splashed with moonlight. Joe reined his pony to a stop and gestured with a sweeping wave of one arm.

"Ti-Ra'-Wa."

A gasp was torn from six throats.

Chapter Seventeen

Ryan found himself looking down on a place he had never visited, yet had always known in his dreams. He sat in the saddle and stared, not moving, not thinking, not blinking, not even breathing. He looked upon a land magically silvered by the moon and the shining, wheeling constellations overhead.

It was a bowl-shaped valley at least twenty miles in diameter, completely and protectively enclosed by towering ranges that rose up toward stupendous, snow-crowned peaks. The valley was a breathtaking vista of green pastures, forests, ponds, lakes and a river. It smelled clean and fresh, untainted by blood or greed or anger. For a moment he felt dizzy. His skin tingled; his heart raced.

J.B. reined in his horse beside Joe's. "Where's the encampment of your people?"

Joe pointed in a southwesterly direction, toward the forest. "That way."

Straining his eye, Ryan discerned shapes and light, a collection of dimly glimmering structures, strangely interconnected with the surrounding tree line. Though he could pick out no details, it looked like no Indian village he had ever seen.

Joe gestured to the northwest. "The lair of the Wolf Soldiers is there."

Ryan followed his pointing hand. The river that flowed across the valley, the loops reflecting the moon, bent toward a little cluster of flickering lights on the far side. Beyond those dancing pinpoints of fire, seemingly against the foothills of the upthrusting ramparts, was another light. It shimmered, seemed to vibrate, a vague, unreal, green-yellow glow.

The blood-freezing call of hunting wolves echoed through the pass behind them. The horses shifted nervously as the howl was answered faintly from the great moonlit valley below.

Joe jerked his pony's head to the left. "They're signaling to the other warriors. We must ride like the wind."

"The pack mules can't go like the wind," Mildred objected.

"Leave them!" Joe snapped, heeling his mount's ribs.

Following Joe, the six companions rode pell-mell down the rocky slopes, the horse's hooves triggering miniature avalanches of loose shale. The forest came up to meet them, and they galloped between tree trunks, ducking limbs and slapping branches aside. The horse beneath Ryan ran with all its strength in a stretch-legged, thundering stride. An undulating howl drifted from somewhere to their right. It didn't sound like any of the other wolf cries, but the screech was full of anger. Ryan glimpsed dark blurs sliding among the trees, only momentarily visible through the tangle of foliage and underbrush.

Suddenly they emerged from the forest and galloped across a rolling, grassy sward. Far ahead were a few closely grouped flickering lights. Joe directed his pony toward them, then they were lost from view as the party raced down into a declivity of the plain.

The wolves hailed one another with their eerie call as they loped and bounded across the valley to encircle the fleeing humans and horses. Ryan leaned over his animal's neck, its mane smacking his face.

The seven riders topped a rise in the plain, and at the same moment the distant firelight came again into view, Doc uttered a strangled yell, "Damn hellhounds!"

Ryan turned in his saddle and saw a dark shape snapping at the legs of Judas Redux. The mustang screamed in fear and reared, then began to buck frantically.

Doc lost his seat, his silver hair flying out like a sunburst, and he went up and then down on the shadow-splotched plain.

Shaggy forms leaped all about them, eyes gleaming and teeth snapping. There were too many moving too fast to be counted, so Ryan didn't try. Dragging back on the reins, he shouted, "Off saddle before they pull us down! Make a stand here!"

Even as he yelled the order, he was sliding from his saddle, kicking free of the stirrups, trying to hold the reins of his terrified horse. A black, hairy bulk rushed soundlessly from the murk, and he triggered his SIG-Sauer three times. The staccato crack of the blaster seemed to startle the bounding, snarling forms. The wolf howled in pain, yelped and loped away on three legs.

Krysty, Jak, J.B. and Mildred formed a rough circle around Ryan, standing back to back, blasters at the ready.

"Where's Doc?" Mildred asked, her voice tight with tension and worry.

At that moment he staggered up to them, grass stained and groaning. He had the Le Mat in his right hand and his unsheathed sword in the left. Through gritted teeth he said, "Just when I was reconsidering rechristening that monster, he has to live up to his name.''

Joe dismounted with a feline grace, drawing the blaster from its beaded scabbard with one smooth motion. ''Shoot to kill!''

''Look!'' Krysty cried. ''It's not just wolves!''

The shaggy beasts charging them were apparently the advance guard. Painted men upon horseback, wearing wolf-skin cloaks and hoods, wielding feathered lances and tomahawks, pounded across the plain like a wave. They voiced high-pitched ''Yi-yi-yi!'' screams.

Ryan, Krysty and Joe fired more or less simultaneously at the anthropomorphic forms surging toward them through the moonlight. The horses neighed and reared, then turned and galloped away, and three writhing figures were left behind on the grass.

''Chill men!'' Jak shouted, triggering his blaster. ''Wolves run away if we shoot masters!''

Ryan knew, without really knowing how he knew, that Jak was mistaken. The wolves displayed independent tactical thinking. They showed it by the way they came on in irregular zigzag bounds to minimize the chances of falling victim to weapons that were obviously new and fearsome to them.

For a long moment it was all crazy confusion with everyone firing in random patterns, the air full of gunshots, animal and human howling and pounding hooves.

Then, as always, the veterans of hundreds of fights for survival tightened into a well-oiled gestalt of destruction. Ryan and his friends chose their targets coolly and squeezed off careful shots, oblivious to the racket their attackers were deliberately making.

Though flights of arrows and the occasional lance

zipped their way, the steady storm of lead exploding from handblasters broke full on their human and beast enemies. The blood-chilling war cries and predatory howls became screams of pain and surprise.

Horses reared, dumping their riders, wolves twisted and fell, painted warriors catapulted from wooden saddles. The hail of blasterfire continued, a torrent of death spraying in all directions. A bullet fired from Jak's Colt Python struck a pony in the chest.

The beast lurched to a thundering fall, throwing its rider, and Jak managed to jump clear. Another shot from the heavy .357 blaster took the wolf-rider in the right eye, punching a fist-sized, scarlet-squirting crater in the back of his head. More lances arced their way, sticking quivering in the earth.

The charge of wolves and horsemen wavered, then broke. Wolf howl and war cry rose and fell as the attackers retreated in the face of the deadly and accurate fire. Departing hooves drummed on the grassy sward. A comparative silence followed, and Ryan called a cease-fire.

At least a dozen bodies, man and animal, dotted the plain. Joe shouted a cry of victory and held his long blaster over his head. Then something in the shadows attracted his attention, and he moved toward it quickly.

Ryan followed him and saw the Lakota approaching a crouching wolf. The fur of its right haunch was matted with blood, and its leg was obviously injured. The beast turned its face toward them. It didn't snarl. It continued to crouch, glaring from Joe to Ryan, as if trying to decide which human presented the greater threat.

With a start Ryan recognized the wolf as Sisoka's "friend," the one she had called Blood-sniffer, and

NO RISK, NO OBLIGATION TO BUY... NOW OR EVER!

CASINO JUBILEE

"Scratch 'n Match" Game

Here's how to play:

1. Peel off label from front cover. Place it in space provided at right. With a coin, carefully scratch off the silver box. Then check the claim chart to s what we have for you — FREE BOOKS and a gift — ALL YOURS! ALL FR

2. Send back this card and you'll receive hot-off-the-press Gold Eagle book never before published. These books have a total cover price of $18.50, they are yours to keep absolutely free.

3. There's no catch. You're under no obligation to buy anything. We charge nothing — ZERO — for your first shipment. And you don't have to make minimum number of purchases — not even one!

4. The fact is thousands of readers enjoy receiving books by mail from the Gold Eagle Reader Service.™ They like the convenience of home delive they like getting the best new novels before they're available in stores... they think our discount prices are dynamite!

5. We hope that after receiving your free books you'll want to remain a subscriber. But the choice is yours — to continue or cancel, any time at So why not take us up on our invitation, with no risk of any kind. You'll glad you did!

YOURS FREE!

SURPRISE MYSTERY GIFT COULD BE YOURS FREE WHEN YOU PLAY

CASINO JUBILEE

CASINO JUBILEE
"Scratch 'n Match" Game

CHECK CLAIM CHART BELOW
FOR YOUR FREE GIFTS!

YES! I have placed my label from the front cover in the space provided above and scratched off the silver box. Please send me all the gifts for which I qualify. I understand that I am under no obligation to purchase any books, as explained on the back and on the opposite page.

164 CIM A7YW (U-M-B-05/97)

Name: _____

Address: _____ Apt.: _____

City: _____ State: _____ Zip: _____

CASINO JUBILEE CLAIM CHART

🍒🍒🍒	**WORTH 4 FREE BOOKS AND A FREE MYSTERY GIFT**
🔔🔔🍒	**WORTH 4 FREE BOOKS**
🔔🔔🍒	**WORTH 3 FREE BOOKS** CLAIM Nº **1528**

Offer limited to one per household and not valid to current subscribers.
All orders subject to approval.

BUSINESS REPLY MAIL

FIRST-CLASS MAIL   PERMIT NO. 717   BUFFALO, NY

POSTAGE WILL BE PAID BY ADDRESSEE

GOLD EAGLE READER SERVICE
3010 WALDEN AVE
PO BOX 1867
BUFFALO NY 14240-9952

NO POSTAGE
NECESSARY
IF MAILED
IN THE
UNITED STATES

automatically he raised his blaster. The gold-green eyes flamed into his, and Ryan hesitated before squeezing the trigger.

Then, despite an injured leg and with eye-blurring speed, the wolf sprang directly for Ryan's throat.

Involuntarily stepping back, Ryan stumbled on an uneven patch of ground. He barely saw the motion of Joe's weapon as the Lakota swung it at the plunging wolf.

Ryan heard the thud of metal against bone, felt the wolf's massive weight slam into him and knock him sprawling. He elbowed the limp body of Blood-sniffer off him and scrambled to his feet.

He heard running footfalls and J.B.'s angry voice demand, "Why didn't you just shoot the fucking thing?"

Joe smiled, a thin slash of triumph across his high-planed face. Nudging the motionless animal with a toe, he said, "He's far more valuable to us alive."

Ryan and his friends looked around at the carnage of corpses in silence. Somehow all the bullet-blasted bodies seemed blasphemous in this valley.

Joe lifted his rifle over his head, turned his face to the moon and uttered another shrill, fierce scream of victory.

"We have a prisoner!" he exclaimed in a voice full of exultation. "And we have given our enemies their first taste of our new weapons and warriors!"

Krysty came to Ryan's side. The Smith & Wesson trembled in her hand. She looked more shaken than he had ever seen her. She stared at the dead animals lying on the moon-washed sward, her sentient hair coiled tight against her nape.

"Ryan, Joe was right. These wolves are intelligent," she whispered. "This is wrong."

Rather than agreeing or arguing with her, he announced, "Everyone reload."

As he rammed a fresh clip into the SIG-Sauer, he glanced down at the senseless wolf, completely at a loss as to why Joe would want to make an animal, no matter how well-trained or intelligent, a hostage.

Krysty was right—this was wrong, in an intangible fashion he couldn't easily identify. The battle wasn't like the conflict with the Red Cadre or so many others over the years. He couldn't shake the shameful sensation that he and his friends had invaded the promised land, a new Eden, their weapons enacting the role of serpents.

"We must go on and quickly," Joe declared, "or more of the Wolf Soldiers will be here."

Kneeling, he lashed rawhide thongs around the fore and hind paws of the unconscious wolf. With a wide strip of leather, he muzzled the beast, securing its jaws tightly.

As he tightened the knot, the wolf stirred slowly, its eyes opening. It didn't move, but a low whine escaped its black-rimmed lips. Its eyes blazed with fear, then with such a potent rage that Ryan felt his belly turn a cold flip-flop.

The ground suddenly trembled under the impact of many hooves.

"Riders," Jak declared.

Ryan and the others raised their weapons as the dull thudding grew in volume.

"Wait," Joe said. "They are my people."

Illumined by the white disk of the moon, a band of horsemen galloped toward them from the distant, flickering firelight. The half-dozen men wore buckskin leggings, and, like the Wolf Soldiers, were armed with lances, bows and arrows.

They pulled up their horses sharply, and a burly man slid from his steed and strode toward Joe. They clasped forearms and spoke in rapid-fire Lakota. Ryan recognized him as Little Mountain. Joe gestured for the others to step forward.

"This is Little Mountain, who brought me word of your arrival in Amicus. He will escort us to the village. We must hurry. The Wolf Soldiers are massing for another attack."

The warriors exchanged fierce, gloating words, nodding toward the bound and muzzled Blood-sniffer. Twice, Ryan heard them say "Sisoka."

Before he and his friends remounted, they ran quick examinations on their wounds. J.B. had taken a cut on his left arm, but it was superficial. Doc was bruised from his fall, though not really injured. However, his eyes were disconcerted as he gazed at the bound wolf.

"Loup-garou," he whispered.

Jak, who knew the legends of the Cajun people, was startled. "Men that change to wolves? Old story for old stupes, Doc. Surprised at you."

Overhearing the exchange, Joe said sharply, "Mount up!"

Everyone swung onto horseback. Blood-sniffer was slung across Little Mountain's pony and tied to the saddle with thongs.

As they trotted across the rolling sward, Ryan knew there was no way he could reconcile the valley of Ti-Ra'-Wa with the rest of Deathlands. This hidden pocket of Earth had existed long before the nuking and skydark, its people living an ancient way of life, unaffected by the outside world. Or perhaps not—the old ways seemed to be moving toward a climax of conflict as a direct result of the presence of him and his friends. They had brought Deathlands to the valley.

He doubted the intelligent animals were the mutated spawns of radiation. Biochemical warfare and fallout had created a host of genetically twisted monsters across the devastated face of America, Europe and the eastern republics, but the beasts of Ti-Ra'-Wa appeared to be throwbacks, survivors of a dim time in prehistory when humanity and animals had coexisted as equals.

He didn't really believe that, and he hoped the uncanny community of beasts and men had another explanation than that the animals were as intelligent as humans.

The party rode down a gentle slope toward a collection of structures near the banks of the valley's timber-bordered river. Ryan had expected tepees or bark lodges, but what he saw was so dumbfounding, he suspected hallucination.

The village was built into the forest, in some ways a part of the forest. Massive hollow tree trunks served as lodgings, giant boughs were like arboreal footpaths and low-hanging branches were so intertwined they formed roofs and shelters. Light shone from within many of the trees, through windows that didn't look cut, but formed out of the living wood.

Here and there, supported by frameworks and lattices of branches and limbs, were crystal disks, giant duplicates of the ones on Joe's golden wafer. They shimmered and glittered, reflecting the firelight. The interlocking facets gleamed with multicolored sparks, like prismatic pieces of a rainbow cut from the sky.

"My God," Mildred breathed in wonder. "This place—it's like it doesn't belong on Earth at all."

Mildred had voiced Ryan's own thoughts, or his

fears. He felt a rising sensation of xenophobia, as if he had stumbled into a city so alien it very well could have fallen from another planet. The air was aromatic with the scent of unfamiliar resins and oils.

Following Joe's lead, they reined their horses to a walk and rode through the crystal-and-forest-entwined village. There was little underbrush. The great trunks loomed like the pillars of ancient temples he had seen pix of in books. The moonlight, what little of it pierced the multilevel overhead tangle of branch, limb and leaves, was tinted green, as if they were underwater.

Ryan suspected that the tree city was inestimably old, far older than recorded human history. It looked as if the forest had grown around the crystal disks. The settlement didn't appear to have been built solely for human use. As it was, few people were in the forestways. The community seemed too big for the number of people he saw.

Yet men, women and a few children, clad alike in buckskin, ran toward the troop of riders. Joe gave them a proud wave of his hand, like a returning hero who had conquered fearsome enemies.

The people gaped in excited avarice at the blasters in the companions' possession. More than once the whisper of "Maza Wakan!" rippled through the crowd. Both Ryan and J.B. recognized the Lakota word for "blaster." In lower, almost frightened tones they heard *"kaga"* repeated over and over.

"I don't get it," J.B. said lowly. "A big place like this, yet they're crazy over a few blasters."

Joe led the way toward a complex of structures made of a wide belt of gigantically trunked trees. The huge limbs were intertwined, like wooden fingers, connecting one tree to the other. A canopy of leaves and branches formed a vast roof that blotted out the star- and moonlit sky.

Little Mountain, with the captive wolf, went around the center tree. Joe reined in and dismounted. The other warriors followed suit.

"We need not talk to the other chiefs until morning," he announced. "All of you must be tired."

Ryan hadn't realized the full depth of his weariness until he dismounted.

"Where do we sleep?" he asked.

Joe gestured to the central tree. "I will show you. Your weapons must remain with me."

Ryan sensed his friends stiffening with sudden tension. "No need."

Joe's response was unruffled and smooth. "I can assure you they will be well guarded."

"They will," Ryan replied stolidly. "By us."

Joe and Ryan locked stares for a long moment. The warriors looked back and forth from their chief to the one-eyed outlander.

Not caring to participate in a second firefight in less than half an hour, Ryan said, "It's for the best, Joe. In unskilled hands our weapons would be dangerous to the people they're supposed to defend."

Joe considered the response for a second, then shrugged and walked through the archway into the tree.

The door was like that of a cathedral, and the interior was broad and empty. Light flickered from torches of resinous wood flaming in crude sockets that looked like knotholes. Joe led them through an empty expanse into a small suite furnished with wooden chairs and bed frames piled high with soft furs. The workmanship was passable, utilitarian and not fancy.

he room had only one window, covered by the pelt
f some small animal.

"Food will be brought to you shortly," Joe said.
"Tomorrow, after you're rested, we will talk."

"Yes," Ryan agreed. "About many things."

Joe's eyes narrowed, but he nodded. "Many things,
ndeed."

Chapter Eighteen

As Joe left the room, J.B. stared after him, suspicion hardening his sallow face. "He's too goddamn cagey. He's got a joker in his pack."

Ryan sank onto one of the beds. The fur robes were soft and almost sensually comfortable. "Then we've got to find an ace on the line to play against him."

Krysty sat beside him, brushing a few strands of flame red hair away from her face. "I've never received impressions like this before."

Doc sat gingerly in a chair, wincing as his backside met the hard wood. "Unfortunately I have. Like the one I'm receiving from my gluteus maximus."

"What kind of impressions are you receiving?" Mildred asked.

Krysty frowned. "It's a jumbled mixture of human and animal emotions."

"Animal?" Jak questioned, eyebrows raised.

"I've picked up animal emotional impressions before," Krysty explained. "The higher animals, anyway. Generally their feelings are simple—fear, hunger, curiosity. What I detected from the wolves was stronger, very pure and clean. The animals here might not be as intelligent as humans, but their emotional reactions are similar in intensity."

Grunting, J.B. stretched out on a bunk, pillowing his head with his arms. "What was that business Joe pulled with the gold piece?"

"Some sort of psionic accelerator, mebbe," Krysty said. "Crystals and precious metals, particularly heavy ones like silver, gold and platinum, are believed to be conductors of psychic energy."

"Yeah," Mildred commented wryly. "I remember that vogue. Used to be called the New Age. Crystals and certain metals supposedly enhanced your spiritual awareness, purified your auras, drained off negative energy...and a fortune from the gullible."

Doc nodded in agreement. "In my day it was called spiritism. Some learned men, like Sir Arthur Conan Doyle, maintained telepathy was a transmission of electric thought waves. Some exponents of this theory believed the right instrument could serve as the transmitter. Maybe that is what these primitives are using. Not very sophisticated, however."

Krysty shrugged. "If that's what the gold-and-crystal pieces are, they don't have to be sophisticated. Quartz crystals have inbuilt electromagnetic properties."

"It sounds like 'far out, man' mumbo jumbo to me," Mildred said.

Krysty smiled tolerantly. "Mebbe it does to you, and mebbe it truly was in your day, but the fact remains that some Indian tribes discovered long ago how to interchange energy with certain kinds of crystals, thought-pattern energy included. Mother Sonja once told me crystals were used for sending and receiving telepathic messages, but because people lost the art, the discipline, the majority of the communications degenerated into three-dimensional visions, in a manner that became known as fortune-telling. In fact my mother could 'far-see' with a crystal. She called it scrying."

"Also called crapping," Jak stated. He was testing

the edge of one of his throwing knives against the ball of his thumb.

Ryan almost envied the young man's single-mindedness. The mystery of the valley and even of the strange forest city hadn't disturbed Jak at all. Lack of fear served him well.

A young, slim woman entered. Not even the shapeless doeskin smock and fringed mantle she wore disguised the full-breasted figure swelling beneath it. Ryan had always thought Indian women were supposed to be shy, but she gave Jak a speculative stare with dark, bold eyes. She placed a wicker tray of food platters on the table, and as she left, she strode by Jak, her hips swinging in an inviting fashion. Jak chose to ignore her, reaching for one of the plates of food.

The bowls were filled with a boiled stew of venison and vegetables and a jar of some kind of fermented fruit juice. It tasted something like cider, but it possessed a mild alcoholic kick. The stew was rich, thick and delicious, though the meat had a faint grassy undertaste.

"Are we dealing with a lost tribe of Indians here?" Mildred asked between bites.

Ryan shook his head and took a long drink of cider. "A lost band, mebbe, but not a tribe. They're Sioux, and they speak Lakota."

Doc cleared his throat. "Shortly before I was trawled, I read newspaper reports about a band of 'wild' Indians rumored to be living in the mountains of Montana and Wyoming."

"So?" Jak inquired. "Thought there still was wild Indians in your day."

"A misconception," Doc retorted. "All the Plains tribes had been pacified and restricted to reservations by the early 1880s. I remember hearing rumors of a band of Sioux vanishing from a reservation, disappearing from the face of the earth. Perhaps this is the valley to which they vanished, and the Sioux here are their descendants.''

Jak suddenly stiffened, his spoon poised before his open mouth. His head tilted slightly to one side. ''Hear something.''

Everyone fell silent, listening intently. Then they heard the sound Jak's exceptionally keen ears had detected. It was a distant, deep throbbing that came from outside. It seemed to roll through the giant tree like breakers on a beach in a steady heavy rhythm.

''Drums,'' J.B. stated.

''They're signaling, mebbe,'' Ryan suggested.

Mildred, head cocked, replied, ''No. It's a ceremony of some sort. Let's go and take a look.''

''Last Native ceremony nearly was end of me,'' Jak muttered.

Mildred laughed. ''Those were Central American Indians. North American tribes didn't practice human sacrifice. Well, hardly ever.''

The companions left the room and followed the drumming through the arched entranceway of the massive tree. A big, blazing fire had been built in the center of a clearing, its smoke rising unwaveringly straight in the breezeless night air. Two small boys tended the fire, placing more logs on it.

A crowd was assembled at the far edge of the clearing, and several men were beating big, hide-covered drums with wooden mallets. The throbbing vibrations were like the steady beat of the invisible wings of a giant bird.

A man strode from the crowd, wearing a headdress made of bird feathers and buffalo horns, and began a

high-pitched nasal chant. The chant didn't end but
trailed off, as if the man had forgotten the words. The
drum thumping continued for several more beats, then
it, too, ceased. Wordlessly the man in the headdress
stepped back into the crowd.

In the distance came the sound of small, tinkling
bells. The onlookers on the edge of the clearing
parted, and a man leaped nearly into the fire. Around
his hips was a loincloth bearing a green disk design,
and on his feet were boot moccasins. A white cloth
mask covered his head and face. It, too, bore the green
disk. His otherwise naked body was painted bright
yellow with bands of green on the chest, back and
arms. Bells were strapped to his wrists. In his right
hand he held what seemed to be a long piece of cord
with a gourd attached to its end.

The man danced around the fire, then around the
perimeter. He whirled the gourd over his head, and it
gave off a low, ominous humming sound.

Four girls in white doeskin detached themselves
from the spectators and arranged themselves into a
circle around the fire. The drumming began again, and
the girls began to move their feet in time to the drum-
beats. Ryan recognized one as the girl who had
brought them their dinner.

The hooded man continued to dance vigorously,
the bells jingling and tinkling. The girls danced
slowly, almost as if their ankles were tied together.

The ceremony progressed, and the six friends
watched it, trying to fathom as much of its meaning
as they could. The man threaded his way around and
between the girls, now and then taking one of them
by the hand and leading her in a sort of promenade
around the fire. The steady throb of the drums, the
incessant jingling, the occasional humming from the

man's bull-roarer, added to the confusing quality of the performance.

To one who had grown up with such ceremonies, the meaning was probably instantly clear, but to Ryan and his friends, it could only be puzzling, or perhaps disturbing.

The dancing, the drumming, the bell-jingling, all ended with an unnerving abruptness. As the girls returned to the edge of the clearing, the male dancer pulled off his hood, revealing Joe's sweat-pebbled face. He began to talk, and since he was speaking in Lakota, his speech was more or less incomprehensible. Only Ryan and J.B. were able to recognize one word out of every twenty.

Joe mentioned "Maza Wakan," "*wasicun,* Akicita Sunkamitu Tanka" and more than once, "Wokiconze Wakan," which Ryan finally realized meant Sacred Land.

Joe waved his arms in an elaborate gesture, and the crowd began to disperse. He glanced over, sighted the six travelers and nodded. He walked over to them.

"How did you like the ceremony?" he asked.

"Very edifying," Doc replied. "It would have been more so had we known what it meant."

"It was the Thanking Dance, acknowledging the help of the Four Old Men who brought us here safely."

Sudden understanding made Mildred nod. "The Four Old Men—the ones who direct the winds, the rains, the seasons."

"And who give my people the breath of life," Joe said. "Which is the wisdom necessary for an existence within the circle. You are the first outlanders to see the dance. You should feel honored."

No one said anything.

Joe looked them over warily and said, "A ceremony like this is a very emotional experience, at least for some people. It takes a lot out of me. I bid you a good night and urge you not to leave your quarters again until I send for you."

Before they could reply, he had turned away and strode back across the clearing.

Krysty tugged at Ryan's arm. "We should do as he says. It's been a long day."

They returned to their room and took bunks. Ryan intended to stand the first guard, but he had imbibed more of the cider than he should have. Its alcoholic content combined with his fatigue and pushed him onto the bed beside Krysty.

Jak volunteered to stand watch.

Ryan couldn't summon up the strength or the inclination to respond, and he didn't awaken until Krysty shook him. The others were all waking, sitting up, rubbing bleared eyes, looking around.

The same girl as before brought them food, placed it on the table and silently left. Breakfast was the same simple fare as supper, but instead of fruit juice, the jar contained a strong yet stimulating tea, probably boiled from bark. It was more palatable than the similar tea in Amicus.

As they finished eating, the burly Little Mountain came in and gestured curtly. *"Okihe."*

"Where's Joe?" Ryan demanded.

Little Mountain shrugged and gestured again, repeating impatiently, *"Okihe.* Follow."

Obviously Joe had taught him only that one English word to speak to the outlanders.

The six people made sure their weapons were primed and loaded and walked out of the room after the big-shouldered warrior. They went through a curving wooden corridor that opened up on a small room.

The chamber's walls were lined with clusters of crystal formations. Light swirled, sparkled and danced from the countless points and facets. The shades of color were variegated, shifting from light blue to a deeper amethyst to purplish tints.

Ryan was impressed by the chamber's beauty, but he was surprised to see that the mineral clusters conformed perfectly to the circular dimensions of the room, as if they had been grown by design.

In the center of the chamber, secured by a heavy, braided length of rawhide affixed to a wooden staple in the floor, crouched Blood-sniffer. Joe stood in front of the wolf, glaring down at the imprisoned beast. In one hand he held the wafer of gold, pressing it to his forehead.

"Guess he's talking wolf," Jak said, an edge of doubt in his voice.

Joe heard, lowered the wafer and strode toward them, his expression impatient and irritated. "That is exactly what I'm doing. You outlanders have much to learn about the ways of Ti-Ra'-Wa."

"That is quite the understatement," Doc said, jauntily angling his cane over a shoulder. "Perhaps you'll be so good as to educate us."

"During the early epochs of my culture," Joe replied stiffly, "the vast caverns wherein crystals grew were adapted as healing and communication chambers. Our forefathers knew how to tap the energy within them."

Lifting the wafer of gold, he continued, "When combined with gold or silver, my people learned the art of sending telepathic messages, using the Inyan Wakan, the Holy Stones, as receivers. Last night you all saw me call to Little Mountain for help. He stood in this room and was able to receive my thoughts at a distance.''

"You can read minds with your little doodads?'' J.B. asked, cocking a doubtful eyebrow.

"No. These 'senders' were created by the First People, who taught our forefathers to use them to communicate, one mind to another, not to use them to invade another's mind. Individual thoughts cannot be detected unless the mind is consciously prepared to receive or to send.''

Looking at the disbelieving faces, Joe waved at the shimmering facets and points on the walls of the room. "Come into this room, then you will understand.''

No one moved.

Smiling sardonically, Joe said, "It won't hurt you.''

A little hesitantly they entered the mineral-lined chamber. Joe directed each of them to find a crystal point and to stand before it, touching it with a hand. Tentatively they followed his instructions, hands pressed to the crystals.

The mineral structure was warm, not cool as Ryan had expected it. He experienced a not-unpleasant pins-and-needles tingling that spread up his fingers, along his arm and then flowed all over his body.

Can you hear me?

Ryan began to answer Joe's question, then he uttered a startled exclamation when he realized the Lakota hadn't spoken the question.

"Dark night,'' J.B. whispered in shock, jerking his hand from the wall as though he had been scalded.

All of them reacted with various degrees of surprise to the words in their minds. Only Krysty appeared unmoved, as if she had expected something of the sort. Joe was pressing the metal rectangle against his forehead and smiling a cold, superior smile.

"You got those things from your forefathers?" Ryan asked.

Aloud, Joe replied, "We shall talk later of it. Now, I want you to speak to our prisoner."

Ryan glanced at the wolf. It met his gaze with a quizzical tilt of the head. "Nice doggy," he said.

Ignoring the nervous laughter from Ryan's friends, Joe said acidly, "Not like that. Touch the crystal point as before."

Ryan did so, mentally focusing on the wolf. The image of a fanged, pointy-eared face materialized in his mind.

Tell him about your blasters, about their power to slay.

It took Ryan an uneasy moment to accept that Joe had addressed him telepathically, not audibly.

In his mind the image of the wolf's eyes flashed a blazing, green-gold fire, bright and beautiful, but almost painful to look upon. Involuntarily Ryan closed his eye.

I know about your weapons, outlander. They are the reason Sisoka bade me to slay you.

The thought-voice was strange, oddly filtered and husky, yet familiar. Underlying it, however, was a note of wisdom, a sadness combined with a guileless innocence.

Why didn't you? Ryan asked, a bit surprised at the ease with which he formed the thought-words.

Instincts. I trust them. So should you.

Why are you a prisoner?

To make a bargain, such as the bargain Touch-the-Sky made with you and your ignorant outland friends.

Ryan's skin crawled, not so much at the concept of a wolf brain communicating with a human brain, but at the ambient tone of sadness tinting the beast's reply.

What do you mean? Ryan asked.

You have been promised a reward Touch-the-Sky cannot give.

Silence! The thought-word flared with such passion that Ryan nearly stumbled backward.

"What?" J.B. snapped aloud, releasing his grip on the crystal point. If he had been amazed by the telepathic conversation between Ryan and the beast, it was submerged beneath a flood of angry suspicion.

Wheeling on Joe, he demanded, "What's it mean you can't give what you promised?"

Joe lowered the wafer and stared venomously at the wolf. The creature's tongue lolled from between open jaws, as if it were enjoying the punchline to a joke.

"He lies. I'll have him removed."

"Like hell," Ryan said sharply. He tightened his hand on the crystal point.

What do you mean?

A soundless burst of snarling lupine laughter filled Ryan's mind.

Touch-the-Sky promised you the yellow metal.

Yes. Is there none?

There is much of it. Ti-Ra'-Wa has gold in abundance, but you cannot reach it.

Why?

It is in the sacred-power place.

And where is that? Ryan demanded.

Enough! came Joe's enraged thought-shout.

Ryan ignored the man's command. *Explain.*

You will not understand.

Explain!

You are only a shadow of the real world, Blood-
iffer said reasonably, *and your life here means lit-
. But the places and things of power must be pre-
rved, for the sake of Grandmother Earth. Many
edicine spots were defiled during the purification.
u do not understand that if these things and places
power are destroyed, the life circle will be broken
d thus destroy the process of life itself.*

What are you talking about? Ryan demanded.

*The Cavern of Creation, which nurtures a spark of
e first circle. It is the place whence all life sprang,
ng, long ago.*

Why can't we reach it?

The wolf's answer was like a snap of its jaws—
ick, decisive and painful. *It is death for any human
10 has not been purified. You, with your blasters
d your greed, believe you can invade that holy
ace and steal away its wealth?*

We didn't come here to steal, Ryan responded an-
ily.

*The cavern is guarded by my brotherhood. Their
es are sworn to our Grandmother. You cannot hope
slay them all before you are slain.*

We didn't come here to steal, Ryan repeated.

There was a silence for an instant. *I know why you
me. You have been deceived, outlander. I am sorry
r you.*

Chapter Nineteen

Swinging away from the wall, eye blazing with cobal
fury, Ryan advanced on Joe. "Is that true?"

Joe shrugged. "It is true the gold is in the caver
at the far end of the valley."

"You said it was here," J.B. said harshly.

"I said it was in the valley. That is the truth. Whe
the Wolf Soldiers are conquered and we control th
cavern, you will have your weight in it."

"Double cross," Jak hissed, drawing a knife fro
inside his jacket.

The Lakota eyed Jak fearlessly. "How is it a dou
ble cross? Unless you planned to deceive me and tak
your reward before fulfilling your end of the ba
gain."

Ryan felt a grudging admiration for Joe's cleve
ness. Obviously mistrusting their motives, he had s
up a method to fight his fight before they could eve
glimpse the gold.

Jak didn't put his knife away. "Bullshit. We hea
only bullshit since we come with you."

"Take it easy, Jak," J.B. said curtly. "If the stu
is here, we can get it after the job is done."

The wolf whined plaintively, lifting a paw towar
Ryan.

"Ignore him," Joe said.

Ryan ignored Joe instead. He pressed his han
against the crystal point and opened his mind.

Touch-the-Sky lies, One-eye. Not only does my brotherhood bar the way to the cavern, but inside dwell the ghosts of the First People, which not even your weapons can harm.

What do you mean?

Do not listen! Joe's thoughts roared. Aloud, he spoke in the rapid-fire Lakota tongue.

Little Mountain stepped into the chamber and looped another braided-leather leash around Blood-sniffer's throat. He cinched it tight until the wolf gagged for air. Then, with the warrior pricking its wounded leg with a lance point, the creature allowed itself to be led limping from the room. It cast one backward glance toward Ryan.

Resting one hand on the butt of the SIG-Sauer, Ryan said to Joe, "Time for straight tongue between us. You got us here, and now we need all the facts before we do anything else."

"You shall have the facts," Joe responded. "But I had to prove some of them first and open your minds to other possibilities."

With a wry chuckle, Doc said, "You've certainly accomplished that, my lad."

"How can these animals be so intelligent?" Mildred demanded. "It makes no scientific sense."

"There is more to existence than white man's science," Joe said coldly. "It was science that destroyed your world. The laws your people imposed on the world are gone, and the old ones have returned."

He motioned them out of the crystal chamber, and they followed him back to their quarters. Joe remained standing as the others seated themselves.

"I'll start from the beginning, the very beginning," he said, "the story of this valley's origins and, in some ways, the origins of my people."

Ryan repressed a wry smile. If he was certain of one fact about Indians, it was they loved to talk as much, if not more, than the most long-winded, full-of-himself baron.

IN THE BEGINNING the First People lived in a world without light or substance. They were a queer folk, part animal, part human, part air, part mineral.

They fought so much among themselves in their dark, formless world that Ah-badt-dadt-deah, He Who Made All Things, took pity upon them. He decided to create a new world for them, one with light and warmth and sensation and substance. So Ah-badt-dadt-deah formed this planet from celestial mud, imbued it with the essence of His sister, Grandmother Earth, and reshaped the First People so they could live upon it. Some of them became rocks, some became trees, some became bears and wolves and buffalo and some He sculpted into the form such as present man, though they were gigantic in stature. Then He released them from their dark world, and they emerged into this one from a cavern, here in the valley of Ti-Ra'-Wa.

In gratitude for their freedom and their great gift, the reshaped First People swore to Ah-badt-dadt-deah that they would always protect His sister. To always remind them of their vow, He placed a tiny piece of the stuff of creation in the cavern, the womb of Grandmother Earth, and charged the First People with keeping it safe, throughout the four circles of existence until the time of purification.

The First People kept this vow and evolved further and learned to live gracefully within the circles. Though they eventually diverged from one another and spread out across the face of Grandmother Earth nd formed separate tribes, they were all of the same natter spawned in the Cavern of Creation.

But always a small group remained here in Ti-Ra'-Wa, living the ancient ways, in accordance with the igh laws, fulfilling the promise to Ah-badt-dadt-leah. All the many and diverse manifestations of nature lived in harmony here, the beasts and the humans, the rocks and the trees, the earth and the water.

The First People built this forest city, and their houghts became audible through the crystals taken rom the cavern. They channeled the power of Grandmother Earth to create, to heal, to communicate. It vas truly a paradise, a land of happiness.

The greatest warrior of the First People was the ounder of the holy Cavern Keepers society. His name vas Nanabozho, and when wounded in battle, he retreated deep into the Cavern of Creation to watch over he heart of the Grandmother in a kind of waking leath. It was believed his spirit still dwelt there.

Over the course of the centuries, tales of the valley eeped into the outer world. It was known as Quivira, Cibola, El Dorado. The greedy conquistadores and the vhite prospectors envisioned Ti-Ra'-Wa as having ilver spires, gold-paved streets, jade chairs, diamond lrinking vessels.

Many were the attempts to locate and invade the valley, and none was successful. Of all who had lived here, all were descendants of the First People, those vho were spawned there. They kept the ancient vow o protect the valley and the Cavern of Creation with heir lives.

Ti-Ra'-Wa was timeless. It existed unchanged and inchanging to that very day, perhaps to the very end of time.

"AND THAT," said Joe, "is Ti-Ra'-Wa's virtue and its curse."

"Were you born here?" Krysty asked.

"No. But the legend of its existence figured prominently in the lore of my people. When I came of age I wandered the length and breadth of my ancestral lands in search of clues to its whereabouts. I spent many years and suffered much. A few years ago I found this valley. I also found that the reality fell somewhat short of the legend, but in some instances exceeded it."

"Give us an instance," Mildred said.

Gesturing to the room, to the huge hollow tree around them, Joe replied, "Our forefathers apparently lived here with a great and vast knowledge of how to manipulate natural earth energies. This city is the most obvious example. Most of that knowledge was lost over the centuries, except for a few relics like this."

He hefted the crystal-encrusted wafer of gold. "The ability to communicate with the higher animals in this valley still exists, but now it is limited to the wolves. Somehow the animals here developed a human-level intelligence."

"Maybe due to a long-forgotten technique of bioengineering," Mildred muttered. "As fantastic as it seems, it's the only possible explanation. It may also serve as the basis for the belief in animism shared by most Native American tribes."

Seeing Jak and J.B. glance at her in puzzlement, she added, by way of an explanation, "Animism is the belief that every living thing is connected on a spiritual level, that even animals and trees have souls. It's generally regarded as a primitive religious belief mainly because it maintains that people, objects and even the heavens are imbued with a consciousness, self-aware and interactive with the larger material reality. If what Joe says has any foundation in truth, it's probable that his forefathers took the tenets of animism to their highest possible expression and developed a way, possibly due to deliberately inducing mutations, to raise the intelligence level of animals.''

Joe nodded thoughtfully. "Interesting theory. Whatever the explanation, the fact remains that in this valley, wolves are in many ways the equals of humans. At one time bears, cougars and even horses shared those traits. For some reason only the intelligent wolves remain. At any rate the prevailing belief in Ti-Ra'-Wa is that all life-forms were created at the dawn of time, spawned as equals from the Cavern of Creation. Animals were put on earth to teach men valuable lessons, and since all living things have a common creator, all animals are our relatives, our brothers.''

"And this cavern," Ryan said, "is the storehouse for the gold.''

"Side tunnels contain metal relics, but the primary cave has never been entered, at least not in recent historical times. There are supposedly great dangers, not just to the body but to the soul. Only the hereditary Guardian of the Cavern Keepers knows how to enter it safely. For many centuries it was a rite of passage for new Guardians to enter the cave and give Nanabozho gifts, articles taken from those who tried to invade the valley and defile the Grandmother. That practice ended a very long time ago.''

"Nanabozho," Mildred echoed. "Isn't that the name of the Algonquian trickster and cultural hero?''

Joe shrugged. "I believe so. Myth is woven so tightly around the cavern, it's almost impossible to untangle truth from legend. The primal energy of creation is believed to still pulse deep within the heart of the cavern, and the Guardian is the warden of the vast powers."

"Who is the current holder of that title?" Ryan asked.

Joe's face darkened a bit with anger and sorrow. "That is the cause of this conflict, Ochinee. The last Guardian was a shaman named Towasi. I was his student. He had no son, so I proved myself worthy of his mantle by going out into the world and destroying all the remains of the predark evil. I was on that path when you met me. When I returned to Ti-Ra'-Wa, I learned that Towasi had died, without officially passing on his knowledge or title."

"You said he had no son," Krysty said. "He had no other children?"

"One. You met her, Ochinee, that night in Amicus."

"Sisoka?"

Joe nodded grimly. "She has no more knowledge of how to enter the cavern safely and manipulate the energies there than I, but she claims the title. Over a period of months the people of Ti-Ra'-Wa broke into factions. The brotherhood of Cavern Keepers, of which I am a ranking chief, seized this, the main village. Sisoka organized our military, the Wolf Soldiers, and settled some miles from here, around the entrance to the cave."

Ryan sighed, shook his head. The story of Ti-Ra'-Wa seemed too incredible to believe, almost like stories he had read in books as a child, back at Front Royal. A long-hidden valley, holding the relics of an ancient civilization in North America, a valley from which all Native peoples, all life itself, had sprung, a valley where wild beasts were on the same footing as humankind.

"Surely," Doc said, "there is more to this conflict than a mere disagreement over who is the rightful heir to a largely meaningless title."

"Meaningless?" Joe repeated scornfully. "Perhaps it seems so to you, but whoever holds the title of Guardian holds the future of the world."

Mildred blinked in surprise. "I don't understand."

With an almost fanatical intensity, Joe whispered, "The energies pent up in the cavern are the same as that which were released at the moment of creation, when this planet, perhaps the entire universe exploded into existence. My ancestors tended to these energies, worshiped them, knew how to manipulate them to various degrees. You've seen evidence of that, and the use of these energies helped Ti-Ra'-Wa stay hidden for so many centuries. I and my brotherhood wish to manipulate those same energies again, to use them as they were used aeons ago—to reshape, to remold, to heal the Earth."

Everyone stared at Joe in shock. He was evidently accustomed to such incredulous reactions to his pronouncement, because he continued speaking quickly, giving no one time to interpose a question about his sanity or lack thereof.

"The world is an abomination," he said, "populated with unnatural monsters and spiritually dark people. The waters are poisoned, the sky full of deadly gases and radiation. All that can be reversed. Sisoka and her faction say my dream is only a power-mad ambition, that I am tampering with the natural order. I say the natural order has already been tampered with. It's been turned upside down, and it must be set right. The future of Grandmother Earth is at stake here, the future of humanity itself. Can we turn our backs on our Grandmother without turning our backs on the high laws themselves?''

Shaking his head vehemently, black tresses flying, Joe answered his own question. "No, we cannot. Not when we have the means and power to transform Deathlands into a mirror image of Ti-Ra'-Wa!''

Despite his growing doubt and suspicion, Ryan couldn't help but feel sympathy for Joe's burning passion. It was a wonderful dream, to turn the clock back, to transform the horror of this world into an Eden and vanquish all the demons spawned by the skydark. He also realized the magnetic power of the man, the innate leadership that had enabled him to overcome his followers' fears of breaking tribal tradition.

"Sisoka and the Wolf Soldiers do not agree with your ambition?'' Doc asked.

"Not in practice. We used to talk about it, she and I, at night—'' Joe broke off, and his eyes reflected a painful memory. "Sisoka believes that the energies are holy, the life source, the heart of Grandmother Earth. To manipulate them, even for a good cause, is arrogance, blasphemy. She fears that mortals cannot hope to command such power without incurring devastating results.''

"The cure might be worse than the disease?'' Mildred commented with a rueful smile.

"Such is her fear. I maintain that this valley is living evidence the energies can be manipulated successfully, beneficially.''

Jak shuddered. "Crazy talk gives me creeps.''

Seating his spectacles more comfortably on his nose, J.B. asked, "So what do you want us to do, Joe? Go over to the lair of the Wolf Soldiers and chill them all, the ones on two and four legs both?''

Joe looked dismayed and even a little shocked. "I don't want to exterminate them. It's simply that they must allow the Cavern Keepers to fulfill our purpose and duties and the ancient vow to Ah-badt-dadt-deah. However, I'm not ruling out any course of action."

J.B.'s practical mind zeroed in on tactics. "How much of this valley do you Cavern Keepers hold?"

"Only this southern quarter, and a few other places near the river."

"How long have you been at war?" Krysty asked.

"We've been observing an armed truce, at least until last night. But now blood has been spilled, and that means they're willing to kill to prevent us from entering the cavern. That means we must do the same. Sisoka must have followed me to Amicus to block my attempt to recruit you. She failed when she failed to kill you, Ochinee, and they failed last night. Now, though I regret it, open warfare begins."

"How many people live in this valley?" J.B. asked.

"A little over a thousand. My faction is in the minority. Only my blaster tipped the scales and allowed us to drive away the Wolf Soldiers and occupy the city. However, we can't put more than three hundred warriors into the field. The Wolf Soldiers not only outnumber us in manpower, but they have an equal number of wolves as allies."

"Pretty stiff odds," said J.B. "But if you drove them away with one blaster, we could really raise hell with ours."

Ryan nodded. "If the Wolf Soldiers have only bows and arrows and knives and spears—"

"And fangs and claws," interjected Jak.

"Then we should be able to adjust their advantage in numbers. No one has blasters at all?"

"No. Except for my rifle, Ti-Ra'-Wa is firearm free."

Ryan pursed his lips. "The best tactic is a frontal assault, under the cover of night. Hose our firepower around, make a lot of noise, mebbe scare them off without a great loss of life."

Joe grunted doubtfully. "Our warriors might not follow you if you stage a direct attack so near to the cavern. They're afraid of Sisoka."

"Why?" Jak demanded.

"As the daughter of a Guardian, even one who hasn't been initiated, she is suspected of being a warden of the power in the cavern. That's a superstition, of course."

J.B. looked exasperated, "How can we lead a campaign for you when your own people are controlled by superstition?"

Jak suddenly stood. "Let's leave triple-stupe place. Fuck gold. Fuck cave."

"The best strategy is to capture Sisoka," Joe said hastily.

"You don't want her chilled?" Ryan asked.

"You're warriors, not assassins. If that's what I wanted, I could have done it long ago. Besides, killing her would so infuriate the Wolf Soldiers they would never recognize my claim, even if they were defeated in fair battle. No, I think a few of us should penetrate their lair by night and seize Sisoka. Her wolf would lead us secretly and safely to her."

Doc chuckled. "Putting our trust in a wolf flies in the face of the lessons of folklore. What would be the creature's inducement to cooperate?"

Joe smiled mirthlessly. "Freeing him from bondage, of course. The wolves prefer death to captivity."

"We empathize," Krysty remarked. "But it sounds like a complicated plan. Dangerous as hell, too."

"If it's successful," Ryan said, "it would clear the way to returning peace to the valley and mebbe restoring a planet, turning Deathlands into Lifelands. It seems impossible, but it's worth a shot."

Chapter Twenty

Sunlight mottled through the canopy of the tree branches overhead. Ryan and Krysty strolled hand in hand between the gargantuan columns of the forest city. The diffused sunshine was a pale, cool, comforting green.

After a long while Ryan asked, "Do you believe Joe's story?"

Krysty stopped and gestured around them. "Some sort of power made all of this. In all of Mildred's and Doc's stories of predark marvels, I never heard of anything that could compare to this…artistry."

They began to walk again, both of them thinking the same thoughts. Though the bloodshed in Amicus was still fresh in their memories, it was difficult to believe that a similar slaughter might happen here.

Under other circumstances, Ryan would have had no misgivings, no hesitation, about smashing hard at the heart of their enemies with every bit of firepower they could muster.

But here, in the valley of Ti-Ra'-Wa, spilling blood and taking lives seemed so blasphemous as to be evil. The valley wasn't a dream, and everything about it had been created to offer a world without want, without need.

Ryan slipped his arm around Krysty, and she leaned her head on his shoulder, reaching down to unfasten the top button of her shirt, then to the second. She was intoxicating, and his arms encircled her, bringing his lips down to hers. Her hands stroked his back, the pressure of those fingers arousing. Then she reached for the belt of his pants.

Part of Ryan knew he should be planning, scheming, preparing for a recce. But here, in Eden with Krysty, time had no meaning. They could follow their hearts, their desires, whenever they wanted, and there would be no consequences.

Hastily they peeled each other's clothes off. It had been a long time since they had had the privacy to make love, an even longer time since Ryan had felt so clean, so young and so full of hope.

They embraced, devouring each other, trails of fire on their bodies from hands roving and fondling. Krysty pushed her full breasts against Ryan's chest, desire-hard nipples pressing against the muscular hardness.

Slowly she slipped beneath his encircling arms, dropping down before him. With her avid mouth, soft lips and warm tongue, she worshiped his rock-hard length.

Ryan groaned, resting his hands atop her head, and flaming tendrils of hair curled and coiled around his fingers.

Ryan gently disengaged himself from her, stepping back and lowering himself to the ground. Krysty stretched out on the grass, arms upflung, and opened her ivory legs. His lips moved over her, touching and exploring with his tongue.

Krysty moaned deeply, bit her lip, then didn't bother suppressing her orgasmic cries of passion. She reached her peak, shuddering, writhing, hands tangled in Ryan's thick dark hair.

Her limbs were still trembling when Ryan shifted

his weight above her, supported by his arms. He carefully thrust down and Krysty arched her back and hips eagerly to meet him. Both of them moaned at the sensation of steel hardness sinking into velvety soft, liquid heat.

Eyes locked, they undulated against each other. Krysty's long legs hugged Ryan's hips to keep him firmly seated within her as they rocked toward a fast, almost frantic rhythm.

The green-hued sunlight cast shifting bars of shadow across Krysty's face. It was a face Ryan loved, not simply because it was beautiful, but because it mirrored a beautiful spirit.

Grabbing his shoulders, fingernails biting into his flesh, Krysty raised her head and gasped into his ear, "Shining times, lover."

Ryan moved harder, faster, and panted, "Shining times."

Then he gritted his teeth as Krysty writhed and bucked beneath him, crying out. He cried out, too, erupting, spilling his seed deep within her.

Both of them breathed hard and unsteadily. Ryan lay atop her, their heartbeats racing. It was a moment to savor, in this perfect place. One that might not be repeated.

WHEN THEY RETURNED to their quarters, they found an argument raging between Doc and Mildred. That in itself wasn't unusual, but the topic certainly was. Jak and J.B. sat nearby, studiously paying no attention whatsoever.

"Bunkum and bosh!" Doc declared, rapping the ferrule of his sword stick on the floor for emphasis. "Fairy tales in modern dress."

"If anybody in this room has doubts about quantum physics, it shouldn't be you,'' Mildred said hotly. ''Quantum physics dragged your scrawny ass across two centuries!''

''What's this about?'' Krysty asked.

J.B. looked up from cleaning his shotgun. ''Millie's trying to make scientific sense out of Joe's bushwa. Her techno-bullshit got on Doc's nerves. Can't say as I blame him.''

''Techno-bullshit?'' she echoed hotly. ''Don't hold me responsible for your poverty of comprehension, John!''

''Or mine,'' Doc said.

Turning to Ryan and Krysty, he said, ''Dr. Wyeth is spinning an entirely theoretical fable regarding the scientific foundation for Joe's mythography about the so-called Cavern of Creation.''

Mildred's face was locked in a stubborn mask. ''Was the Totality Concept, which spun off Overproject Whisper, Project Cerberus and Operation Chronos and the mat-trans gateways, just theoretical? If we apply the insights of quantum mechanics to the mystery of this valley, then we can reach a sound hypothesis of how it was formed and created.''

Ryan repressed a smile. Mildred's intellect was like an anteater's tongue, always probing and poking into dark corners to find out what was there. Because of her scientific background, she continually tried to make some sort of sense out of the warped world in which she had awakened. Most of the time her theorizing made absolutely no difference about anything, especially her dissertations about genetics to explain the various human and animal mutie strains roaming Deathlands.

Still, there was no denying that her expertise in

medicine and cryonics had saved all their lives at one time or another.

Ryan sat at the table. "What's your hypothesis, Mildred?"

"The universe was formed from an explosion of gases, plasma and matter. It was known as the Big Bang theory. For the sake of discussion, let's assume a collection of those energies exists on Earth, in a temporal pocket or packet, fueled by the beginnings of the universe when it was still a primal monobloc."

Doc's eyebrows knitted tightly together. "What?"

"The essential building blocks of the universe are no more than ripples in the quantum field. Everything, even hard matter, is stable patterns of these ripples. On a subatomic scale, what appears to be a vacuum is really vibrating and shifting with particle- and wavicle-energy fluctuations. For example a single cubic centimeter of space can, theoretically, contain the hard matter energy equivalent of a thirty-megaton nuclear bomb."

Ryan resisted the impulse to massage his temples.

Mildred continued, and judging by the timbre of her voice and the expression on her face, she was enthralled with her own words. "This is the quantum stream, which exists on a different plane of reality than our own reality. The scientists of the Totality Concept knew this and, with the aid of technology, managed to tap into it. All the spin-off researches of the Totality Concept used the stream as a transit network between the physical *here* and *there*. That's basically how the gateways work—up to and including time trawling."

The irritated impatience on Doc's face was slowly giving way to interest. "What does all that have to do with what Joe said?"

"It stands to reason that if the quantum stream can be tapped into, there should be any number of arteries branching off from the primary flow. If whatever is in the cavern is a naturally occurring artery of the quantum stream, then perhaps it contains the energies released in the first picoseconds following the Big Bang, channeling the matrix of protoparticles that swirled through the universe before physical laws fully stabilized."

"You've lost me again," Doc said with a head-shake.

"Me, too," Ryan added. "Though this theory never really found me."

Mildred sighed. "If Joe is speaking the truth as he knows it, this energy packet may exist slightly out of phase with this dimension, with our space-time, just like many subatomic particles. The cavern may be an interphase and an interface point between our reality and another."

"Granting that all you say may possess a sub-atomic particle of truth," Doc said with a devilish smile, "how does all of that account for the tree city and the crystalline structures?"

"That's the easy part," Mildred declared. "Thousands of years ago the first humans who lived here, Joe's ancestors, learned how to manipulate the energies to build all of this, maybe not on a truly conscious level but through what was known as a 'probability wave function,' a theorem that states that any two particles that have once been in contact continue to influence each other. In other words Joe's ancestors, the observers of this energy packet, created their own branching probability, their own reality."

Tapping her forehead, Mildred continued, "I wouldn't be a bit surprised to learn that close contact with the energy packet enhanced the latent psychic powers of the mind. That may explain the intelligent animals, too.''

''As one of my scientist warders at Project Chronos was wont to implore,'' Doc said, '' 'bottom-line' it for me.''

''If my hypothesis has any foundation, then we may be able to manipulate the energies in the cavern to help ourselves. Maybe even return you to your own time period.''

J.B. looked up from his oiling and cleaning. His eyes blinked behind the lenses of his spectacles.

Doc sat up straight in his chair, eyes widening. ''Impossible!''

''No,'' Mildred replied firmly. ''Utilizing and manipulating quantum energies brought you here, Doc, with the use of technological interfaces to tap into the stream. If the same kind of energy interface exists in the cavern, a natural packet, then the possibilities are endless.''

''And Joe's plan to reshape the planet?'' Ryan asked. ''Is that possible, too?''

''I don't see why not. Of course, the downside, which this Sisoka woman fears, may be just as valid.''

''In what way?'' Krysty asked.

''If these energies are as potent as Joe claims, and if their effects can be influenced, even determined by force of will, then they may run wild. An apocalypse could be triggered that would make the nukecaust and the skydark look a Fourth of July celebration.''

''That,'' Joe said, ''is a risk I'm willing to take.''

The lithe Lakota stood leaning against the doorway, his arms folded across his chest. ''I've brought Bloodsniffer back to the crystal chamber. Come with me, Ochinee. There is no need for the rest of you.''

Ryan exchanged searching looks with his friends. Doc's eyes were clouded as he thought about the past, and now a possible way to return to it, to his family. That was his dream.

When Ryan and Joe reached the crystal-encrusted room, Little Mountain brought in the wolf, the leash taut around its neck. The animal swept Ryan with its gaze. Once again he felt an uncanny chill upon looking into those bright, cold eyes.

Joe gave Ryan a golden, disk-studded wafer, a twin to the one in his right hand. "Use this."

When both men had pressed the wafers to their foreheads, Joe thought, *You must choose now to help end this conflict between our people.*

The wolf's black lips writhed back from gleaming fangs in a soundless snarl. *You want nothing more than to rule our people,* came the fierce reply. *I will not help you. Kill me now.*

I do not wish to kill you. I wish to speak to Sisoka.

Speak to her, then, the wolf retorted contemptuously.

On my terms, Joe thought. *Not hers. You can guide a few of us into the camp of the Wolf Soldiers. Do so, and you will go free.*

Blood-sniffer's telepathic reply came after a long pause. *If I do that, I would be in direct disobedience to the Guardian's orders.*

Sisoka is not the Guardian. She does not have the support of all of Ti-Ra'-Wa.

Nor do you, the wolf coolly countered.

True, Joe agreed. *Therefore you will not be disobeying a Guardian's orders. There is no treachery in this act.*

The animal's eyes widened. The simple logic

seemed unshakable. It glanced back and forth between Joe and Ryan.

You promise not to kill any of my people?

You have my word.

The wolf's eyes flicked back to Ryan's face. *Do I have your word also, outlander?*

If my life is not directly threatened, nor those of my friends, Ryan replied mentally, *you also have my word.*

That is well, Blood-sniffer responded. *I give you my promise to guide you safely and secretly to my lair.*

Joe grunted and gestured to Little Mountain, who led the great wolf away.

"Good. Now we have a chance," Ryan said.

Joe looked at him with a sardonic smile. "Don't underestimate Blood-sniffer's cunning and resolution, nor his devotion to Sisoka. He intends to lead us inside the borders of his encampment, then turn on us and give the alarm."

Ryan scowled. "Then why the fuck are we dealing with him?"

Joe's eyes and smile hardened. "An intelligent animal he may be, but he's still only an animal. We can outguess him before he betrays us. However, we need to develop a contingency plan in case we're captured. It's tactically foolish for all of your people to accompany us, since their weapons are required to either stage an assault or a rescue. Choose only one of your companions to come with you."

"I don't command an army," Ryan told him coldly. "I'll ask for a volunteer."

Joe nodded. "Have it your way, Ochinee."

Chapter Twenty-One

The velvety night brooded over Ti-Ra'-Wa. The crystal disks entwined in the tree limbs of the forest city caught and reflected a thousandfold the stars burning the blue-black sky.

Ryan turned from the window and looked across the torchlit room at his friends. "The moon won't be full tonight. With luck we can get in and out before sunrise."

"I wish you weren't going. It feels wrong," Krysty murmured. Her beautiful face was troubled, her sentient hair curling and coiling.

"It does to me, too," Mildred added, glancing worriedly at J.B.

The Armorer had elected to accompany Ryan on the mission. He sat at the table, checking his Uzi. Jak sat beside him, watching with his crimson, expressionless eyes. He had volunteered to go on the mission, but Doc had pointed out that his albino coloring wasn't suitable for a stealthy night approach. The scar-faced teenager hadn't agreed, but he hadn't argued, either.

"It's risky," Ryan said, "but no more than a lot of deals me and J.B. pulled for Trader. And if we can capture Sisoka, we have a chance to clean up this trouble without a lot of bloodletting."

Jak nodded. "Watch wolf. It have your heart in belly if gets chance."

"What happens if you're the ones who are captured?" Doc inquired.

Ryan mulled that possibility over for a second. "Mebbe Joe has more of those sender gadgets. We'll leave one with you, Krysty, since you're the most sensitive."

"You don't know the range on those things," J.B. argued.

"They're not radios," Krysty replied. "Thought transmissions don't have range limitations like radio waves."

Joe and Little Mountain entered in warrior regalia, with beaded buckskins and faces painted black. Little Mountain carried a tomahawk, a knife, a bow and a full quiver of arrows. The Gewehr automatic rifle was cradled in Joe's arms. He held a pair of the golden wafers in one hand.

"You're ready?" he asked Ryan. "Then we'll fetch Blood-sniffer. Take these senders. You two must have them on you constantly."

"Can you spare one for me?" Krysty asked.

Joe hesitated. "I have only three—one for me, the others for Ochinee and Mr. Dix. The closer we come to the Wolf Soldiers' lair, the more silence is essential."

"Give mine to Krysty," J.B. said laconically. "I usually know what Ryan's thinking anyway."

Joe handed the wafer to Krysty, saying, "We must go now."

"I'll try contacting you at midnight," Ryan told her.

"I'll be waiting."

After quick embraces between Mildred and J.B., and Ryan and Krysty, the two men followed the Lakota into the corridor.

They walked outside, where the tethered Blood-sniffer stood between a pair of guards. It glanced up at them with its inscrutable eyes. At a word from Joe, a guard handed the leash to him and the animal limped cooperatively into a compound where warriors waited with five horses.

"We're taking an extra mount for Sisoka," Joe said.

The horses tossed their heads when they caught the wolf scent, but they calmed quickly. Ryan swung into the saddle of a bay mare. All of the horses were dark in color, except for Joe's pinto. Ryan had left behind the Steyr, since this was to be a close-in, stealth operation with a minimum of blaster play.

Little Mountain, Ryan, J.B. and Joe rode out of the compound, on through the silent, shadowed windings of the forest city. The wolf trotted at the end of the leash beside Joe's steed.

When they were out of the city and on the rolling sward, Joe put the wafer of metal to his head. He spoke aloud, in English, for the benefit of Ryan and J.B.

"Lead the way, Blood-sniffer, and remember if you break your word and play us wrongly, you will die."

Reaching down, he slipped the leash over the animal's neck. The wolf slid ahead, still favoring his hind leg, trotting almost due north.

Wind, chilled from the distant, snow-covered peaks, buffeted Ryan and stung his eye as the mare cantered steadily across the grassy plain. J.B. rode just behind him, and Little Mountain brought up the rear, leading the spare horse.

The wolf veered constantly to keep always as near as possible to the stands and groves of trees that dotted the plain. It occurred to Ryan that the beast might be leading them into an ambush, but he learned the reason for Blood-sniffer's strange route was exactly the opposite.

Just ahead of them the wolf spun, its eyes flashed a warning, and Joe whispered urgently, "Into the trees! Quickly!"

There was a stand of birch close ahead. They heeled their mounts into the little copse. The wolf hunkered down in front of Joe's pony, staring intently through the curtain of underbrush. Ryan followed its gaze and glimpsed three gray shadows gliding low over the plain. They were wolves, creeping toward the forest city.

After a minute Blood-sniffer stood. Joe whispered to Ryan, "They go to spy on us."

They left the grove of trees and rode on, continually changing course to keep near the infrequent wooded clumps and rises in the valley's floor. They topped one rise and saw a solid forest wall looming before them. The trees were tall, the spaces between them dark and quiet. It looked like the haunted forests he had read about as a child, full of mystery, gloom, witches and trolls.

Ryan didn't want to ride into that black wood, and neither did J.B. The Armorer's voice whispered from the dimness behind him. "If that goddamn wolf has his brotherhood waiting for us in there..."

He didn't finish the sentence. There was no need. Ryan's imagination was fully capable of completing the image of a pack of vicious wolves tearing out their livers and chewing their intestines.

When Blood-sniffer padded into the forest, everyone followed. At first it seemed pitch-dark beneath the towering trees, then Ryan's eye became adjusted o the gloom and he was able to pick out more and more details.

The ground was very dry. Rainless weeks had parched it so that each twig, each leaf the horses stepped on snapped or crackled, the sounds seeming as loud as gunshots. From their right came the faint rushing of the river.

Their animal guide was a deeper shadow in the murk, leading the way carefully between the trees by occasional backward glances and low whines.

Joe turned on his pad saddle and whispered, "No more talk unless I speak first. Use your sender from now on."

The horses were jumpy as they traversed the woods, climbing ridges and down into brush-clogged dells. The mare quivered beneath Ryan as if in fear. Wind gusts rustled the leaves of the trees, and at each faint rattle, the horse would snort and Ryan's hand would reach for his blaster. Now and then he heard the crunch of distant brush as something fled from their approaching party.

They had traveled a little less than an hour when a yelping wolf call from the west was answered by another in the direction of the river. Blood-sniffer stopped and looked up at Joe. The Lakota pressed the metal wafer to his forehead, glared down at the animal for a moment, then gestured to Ryan.

When Ryan had placed the slice of gold to his head, Joe's thoughts said, *We must leave the horses here. Too many of the Wolf Soldiers are about and will catch their scent.*

Ryan, J.B. and Joe dismounted. Using sign language, Joe ordered Little Mountain to remain behind with their mounts.

Blood-sniffer led them up the crest of a sparsely

treed slope, then northward along it, pausing often to sniff the wind. Again they heard howls, but there was no answer this time. The wolf stopped, nose turning back and forth, then it spun and stared at Joe.

Joe gestured sharply, and following his example, Ryan and J.B. crouched in the high shrubbery. Both of them drew their handblasters. Blood-sniffer bounded again, and peering through the screen of foliage, Ryan saw the beast stop between two trees and utter a low bark. He leveled his weapon toward it.

Instantly another bark answered, and a big, shaggy wolf padded out of the gloom. It was equal in size and weight to Blood-sniffer, but it seemed older.

The two animals sniffed each other's anus, both growling theatrically. Then the older wolf fell on its back, exposing its belly. Blood-sniffer obligingly closed its jaws around the submissive wolf's throat for the briefest of seconds.

The older wolf got to its feet, and the two animals exchanged whines and half-barking grunts for a few seconds. The newcomer slunk away into the night, heading southward down the wooded slope.

Ryan lowered the SIG-Sauer as their wolf guide loped back to them. Its eyes shone brilliantly, and the one-eyed man realized the animal had sent its brother off on the wrong trail. Blood-sniffer had obviously lied so it could keep its promise to the humans.

They rose and followed the beast nearly a mile along the crest of the ridge. Blood-sniffer led them down the face of the slope to a fire-scarred break in the trees and stopped, muzzle pointing downward. Below the slope was a curve in the river, and beside the waterway on the opposite side of it glimmered the lights of the Wolf Soldier encampment. A massive log, embedded deeply in the soft banks of the river,

stretched across the water course. The bark had long
been worn away by human and animal feet.

Bonfires burned brightly between the conical tepees. The camp sprawled before and below them like
rows upon rows of hide-covered church steeples. The
tepees were arranged in two loose concentric circles,
one surrounding the other. The smell of cooking meat
was carried to them by the breeze. To one side of the
village Ryan saw a herd of hobbled horses, and on
the other were racks that bore stretching hides.

Figures came and went past the fires, into the shelters and out of them. Not all the figures were human.
Men, women, children and wolves walked together
across the encampment, mingling, jostling, trotting.
At a quick count Ryan estimated there were an equal
number of animals and people.

Surveying the terrain, he saw a slight incline that
rose about an eighth of a mile beyond the outer circle
of tepees. The incline butted up against the base of a
rocky mountain rampart. Tumbles of stones, some
bigger than the tepees, reared out of the earth. Torch-
light flared at the outer border of the outcropping, and
men in wolf skins patrolled the perimeter.

Between the gargantuan boulders, Ryan glimpsed
an opening. He could see it easily because light shimmered from it—a vague, unreal, quivering glow.

The glow throbbed, a ghostly light, pulsing with an
eerie phosphorescence. Ryan discovered that if he focused his vision directly on it, the light seemed to
fade, becoming like a faintly luminous mist. He could
see it clearly only if he cast his eye away from it
slightly.

Joe followed his gaze, put the sender to his head
and indicated that Ryan should do the same.

Yes, that is the entrance to the cavern. The light is

only the feeble outer glow from the cavern core, deep within. It was never guarded until recently. Sisoka's doing.

Ryan felt a sharp wonder. The pulsing light indicated a powerful energy, maybe exactly of the type Mildred had theorized. And even if it wasn't, it was still powerful enough to have inspired awe and fear for countless generations. He was reminded of an old predark metaphor: "lightning in a bottle." If Joe's tale was only partially true, then he was actually looking at "creation in a bottle."

Joe's thoughts intruded. *I see Sisoka's lodge, but we cannot enter the camp openly.*

So I see, responded Ryan. *What other way is there?*

At the base of the hill there are a series of tunnels and passages, running adjacent, but not connected to the cavern. I have never been in them, but—

Ryan interrupted. *Then how will we keep from becoming lost?*

We must rely on Blood-sniffer to guide us.

Ryan glanced over at the wolf. It cocked its head at him. He didn't care for the prospect, but unless they took the wolf's way in, they might as well give up the whole attempt to seize Sisoka.

We'll try it.

Aloud, in a whisper, Ryan explained the plan to J.B., concluding by saying, "You can stay here if you want. Wouldn't blame you."

"I'm going."

The wolf slunk down the forested slope on a circuitous route away from the encampment and led them into a gully that opened up on a shallow ford at the river. The water was barely hip deep, and the pebble-spotted hump of a sandbar thrust up from the surface at the midway point.

The opposite bank was cut by a small streambed debouching from the river. It was almost dry at that time of year, the high banks hiding the encampment from them as they approached it at an oblique angle.

They moved down the streambed in close single file, treading on the muddy, rocky ground as carefully and as quietly as they could. Their path ended at a dark cleft, wide and tall enough for a human to enter.

The wolf paused before the mawlike opening, then it crept into the darkness. Joe, Ryan and J.B., weapons in hand, followed. After a few feet they were in absolute, impenetrable blackness. J.B. turned on his hand torch, startling everyone, including the wolf, with the bright white rod of light.

"What is this place?" J.B. demanded softly.

The flashlight beam glinted off mineral deposits embedded in the rough walls—silvery granite, brilliant quartz and green-speckled limestone. By the light they saw the walls were decorated with faded, crude paintings and carvings, representations of bizarre figures and shapes. J.B. paused to examine one of the paintings, which depicted some kind of horse-like, squat-bodied animal with two horns on its nose.

The tunnel was obviously very old. The brooding, unbroken silence bore down on it like the pressure of vast, invisible hands.

The wolf trotted deliberately forward, the tunnel gaining a slight incline. The three men followed, occasionally confused by their own writhing shadows. The passageway forked, and the wolf unhesitatingly took the left-hand path.

They moved after Blood-sniffer, wincing at the clink and crunch of stones beneath their feet. They hadn't gone far when Joe lurched to a halt, biting back a startled exclamation. Resting atop a shelf of

rock, at eye level, was a yellow-brown skull. Lookin
over his shoulder, Ryan saw it wasn't a human skul'
but that of an animal, one he had never seen. Felin
in shape, it was twice the size of a normal panther'
and two great fangs, six inches in length, curve
down from the upper jaw. Word-pictures were painte
across the brow. The sight of the skull raised Ryan'
nape hairs and stirred to life old stories and even pe
sonal experiences with cave-dwelling monsters.

The tense, silent progress through the tunnel con
tinued. Ryan tried to keep other thoughts, other wor
ries and fears, from intruding into his single-minde
march, but a few penetrated his guard. He couldn'
shake the feeling that he, J.B. and Joe were blithel
striding through a death trap.

He sneered at his growing dread, but when he haz
arded a swift backward glance, he glimpsed—o
thought he did—a shadow shifting in the gloom. The
he heard the faint sound of a stealthy footfall.

Aloud he said, "We're being followed—"

Even as the words left his lips, Blood-sniffer acted
The wolf whirled and bounded back in the directio
they had come in an explosion of hair-trigger reflexe
and steel-spring speed. Its heavy body was a shagg
battering ram that knocked Joe down, slammed Rya
to one side and sent the flashlight flying from J.B.'
hand.

"*Knew* it!" J.B. said as the hand torch clattere
and smashed out against the rocky tunnel floor.

A woman's voice shouted from the darkness be
hind them. The language was Lakota, but the ton
was unmistakably triumphant.

"Sisoka!" Joe raged. "Blood-sniffer somehov
managed to betray us without our knowledge!"

There was another rapidly spoken stream of Lakot

from behind them, the words "Maza Wakan" figuring prominently.

"We're ordered to lay down our blasters," Joe translated bitterly.

J.B. silently mouthed a curse and squeezed off a triple burst into the blackness. The rounds bounced in whining shrieks off the curved walls of the tunnel.

"They're back around the fork where our shots can't reach them," Ryan said.

Joe nodded tersely. "We can't go back, so we must go forward."

"Go forward to where?" J.B. asked.

"To wherever we end up."

The three men trotted through the black tunnel. Chunks of rock, feeling like malformed human skulls, clattered at their feet. They caromed off outcroppings and bumped their heads on stalactites.

Testing the air currents with a wetted forefinger, Ryan felt a fairly strong movement to their right. By groping and feeling, he found a narrow side passage branching off from the tunnel. Since they were in a dead end, they had no choice but to crawl into the rough-edged passageway.

All three men squeezed into it. It crept upward at a forty-five-degree angle, and the passage narrowed very quickly, the walls catching at Ryan's broad shoulders. He was forced to turn sideways and scrabble onward and upward. Sweat slid from his forehead and stung his eye. As he was blinking it back, he realized the darkness was no longer so absolute. He was able to pick out dim, dark gray shapes. Ahead and a little above them was a faint circle of starlight.

"There's our exit," he panted.

They clawed their way up the cramped tunnel toward the little opening. They climbed out in starlight, and J.B. staggered. They were standing on a sma hill, and about half a mile away were the cyclopea boulders around the cavern entrance. Below and t their right was the outer ring of tepees.

"One of us should wait here," J.B. panted. "Pic them off as they come out."

"I think they expected us to come out in th place," Ryan said. "They're probably running to ou flank us."

"Mebbe so," J.B. barked. "But I want to get tha double-crossin' wolf—"

Joe was looking around, his blaster held at wai level. "Listen."

At that moment a chorus of wolf howls echoed a around. It was a heart-stopping sound. Four-legge shapes raced swiftly toward them from all points of the compass.

Ryan shifted his SIG-Sauer to a double-handed gri and said, "Here's your chance, J.B."

The dark, leaping shadows of the wolf pac plunged over the ground. The three blasters poured stream of fire at the bounding, snarling shapes. Mo of them dodged the bullets with supernatural swif ness, but two twisted in midair and screamed in pai The hill became a bedlam of fire, noise and move ment. J.B. had the Uzi on full-auto and he swung in a left-to-right pattern, the muzzle-flash smearin the night with streaks of orange flame.

Ryan squeezed the trigger of the SIG-Sauer fou times in rapid succession and one of the loping bounding shapes leaped and fell.

Joe fired his weapon from the hip, holding dow the trigger, hosing the rounds in a semicircle. Bulle skittered over the ground, striking sparks from rock

There was a momentary lull in the attack. Rya

pulled the crystal-studded gold wafer from a pocket and slapped it against his forehead. He didn't have time to couch a telepathic call in words. His mind focused on a wordless message that was a plea, a pledge of love and a promise at the same time. If performed vocally, it would have been a yowl of anguish. The wolves came again in a circling rush, and he dropped the wafer.

Ryan, doing his best to pick his targets carefully, heard the Uzi's firing pin click dryly against the empty chamber. J.B. cursed, letting the blaster dangle from the lanyard around his neck and went to unsling the M-4000 scattergun from his shoulder. Then a wolf was at the Armorer's throat.

At the sound of J.B.'s half curse, half scream of pain and anger, Ryan wheeled, triggering his blaster at the dark gray shape ripping at the body of his friend.

He didn't have the opportunity to gauge the accuracy of his shot; a heavy weight slammed into his back with lung-emptying, bone-jarring, teeth-loosening force. Ryan was bowled over on his face, the wind crushed from his body.

Gasping, he levered himself onto his back and looked directly into the blazing gold-green eyes of a beast snarling in murderous fury. Ryan tried to swing his blaster up and around, but a wide, claw-tipped paw eclipsed everything else in his line of sight.

Then he knew what oblivion felt and looked like.

Chapter Twenty-Two

Krysty reeled. She staggered several paces back from the table, dropping the drinking gourd on the floor.

Alarmed, Doc rose from his chair and reached out to steady her.

She waved off his hand, her eyes wide and full of fear. In a thin, aspirated voice, she cried, "Ryan!"

Jak, Doc, Mildred and Sunlata stared at her in bewilderment. During the past hour or so, they had been playing *arcahey,* the Sioux game of bone-casting. Sunlata, the girl who had acted as their food server, had elected herself their one-person entertainment committee, as well.

Krysty had kept the golden wafer by her elbow and, as the night wore on, she consulted her wrist chron every few minutes. An hour shy of midnight, a chaotic explosion of emotions, sensations and colors bulled its way into her mind. There were so many, so fast, she was unable to sort them out. The mental-emotional cacophony lasted but a split second, but she knew, more by the texture of the thoughts than anything else, who had transmitted them.

Ignoring the questions from her friends, she snatched up the wafer and pressed it against her forehead. She didn't concentrate. She lowered her mental barriers, taking deep, relaxing breaths, waiting for a pattern to emerge.

Mother Sonja had taught her the technique of activating her "brow chakra," the seat of the sixth sense, the third eye of mystic legend. Through the opening of this chakra, this biological power-point, she possessed the capacity to "read" emotional communications.

Nothing came to her but flashes of color, psychic spillover from her friends' anxiety and worry. She saw-felt only a void, a lightless tunnel stretching past eternity and through infinity.

Krysty lowered the wafer. It was slick from the perspiration beading her forehead. She opened her eyes and realized she was lying on one of the beds. Mildred sat beside her, holding her left wrist and timing her pulse, her face etched in lines of worry.

"Krysty! Goddammit, girl, I thought you were dying. Your pulse and respiration rates slowed to a crawl!"

"How long?" Krysty's throat was dirt dry, and her tongue felt like old shoe leather.

"At least twenty minutes. Your entire body locked up, like you were having an epileptic seizure. Sunlata and the others went to fetch the medicine man or shaman."

"No need." Krysty sat up, and a wave of pain surged through her head, then faded. She knew what had happened, what her subconscious had done. She had only rarely entered a "far-seeing" trance, primarily because her mother hadn't fully trained her in protecting herself while in such a state. When her mind had expanded its awareness, her hind-brain took over, slowing her metabolism and reducing her need for oxygen. Leaving the trance state was more difficult than entering into it.

Jak, Doc, Sunlata and a skinny man wearing headgear made of feathers and buffalo horns rushed through the door. It was the same man who had participated in the Thanking Dance the night before.

Before Krysty could stand, the shaman began to skip in front of her, singing unintelligible words in a discordant voice. He shook a set of feathered diamondback's rattles over her head.

Impatiently Krysty elbowed him aside and got to her feet. Speaking loudly to be heard over the crack-voiced chanting, she said, "Ryan is in trouble, and more than likely, so is J.B."

Mildred sighed and muttered something.

"What?"

"I said I was afraid you'd say that!"

"He tried to contact me through the sender," Krysty went on. "Since I didn't have mine working, I couldn't pick up any details. I tried transmitting to him. Nothing."

"That doesn't necessarily mean anything dire," Doc replied, casting an irritated glance at the shaman. The skinny man was now hopping up and down on one foot, chanting louder.

Angrily Krysty shouted one of the few Lakota words she knew. "Leave!"

The shaman affected not to have heard. She grabbed him by one arm and, with rather more force than she intended, dragged him toward the door. "Leave," she repeated.

The man stopped hopping and shouting. He gave her a lingering look of reproach, then spit a mouthful of chewed-up flower petals in her face. Sunlata moved aside respectfully as the shaman exited the room in a huff.

Doc gazed after him, remarking, "He provides bed-side service, and this is the thanks he gets."

Krysty fingered the flower petals from her cheeks.

"I can't worry about hurt feelings now. We've got to go after Ryan and J.B."

"Don't know where are," Jak said. "Wolf lead them."

Mildred bit her lower lip, ran a hand through her plaited hair and said, "Jak's right. We'd be tearing off into the dark, both literally and figuratively."

Doc nodded in agreement. "Under the circumstances we should wait for word or for one of them to return. Or at least until daybreak."

He glanced sideways at Sunlata, adding quietly, "Besides, I suspect our hosts wouldn't allow us to depart without an armed guard. They're relying on us, remember."

"On our weapons, you mean," Krysty snapped. She glared at Sunlata, who blinked back at her uncomprehending.

She sighed. "All right. Let's wait until dawn. Then we go after them."

"And if our hosts would rather we did not?" Doc inquired.

"Then get demonstration of weapons," Jak growled.

Though she earnestly tried, Sunlata couldn't revive their interest in the game. Nor could she arouse Jak's interest in leaving the room with her. Around two o'clock she left quietly.

Jak and Doc sat around the table, sharpening and honing their blades with a whetstone the teenager always carried. Mildred and Krysty took turns, every half-hour or so, pacing to the window and peering into the darkness, looking for a sign of the sun. All of them knew they should catch some sleep, especially if they intended to undertake a rescue or investigative mission in a few hours. Adrenaline kept them alert.

According to Krysty's chron, it was half-past four when Jak's head swiveled toward the door. "Riders coming in," he whispered.

As one, all four people got to their feet and rushed out, none of them wanting to surrender to either the hope or dread battling for dominance in their hearts and minds.

Outside they circled the great tree, heading for the horse compound. They had taken only a few steps when Joe emerged from the darkness. The right sleeve of his buckskin tunic was ripped, and his hand showed a speckling of blood. The barrel of his blaster drooped toward the ground. In his left hand he held a small, blocky object.

When he saw the four friends, he stopped in his tracks. None of them spoke. With eyes clouded with fatigue and the bitterness of defeat, he swept his gaze across their faces, pausing at Krysty's, then finally settling upon Mildred's.

Joe stepped forward and extended his left hand. Gripped within it was J.B.'s fedora. The crown was battered, the brim notched and stained with a squiggly pattern of dried blood.

"I'm sorry" was all he said.

Chapter Twenty-Three

J.B. had slept for a time, but he had dreamed and the dreams were full of anthropomorphic shapes, obscene blendings of beast and man. He awakened suddenly, and his surroundings reminded him that his nightmares weren't all that removed from his reality.

He lay alone in the depths of the nighted forest and suffered. He had lost a fair amount of blood from the fang-inflicted gash across the base of his throat. The back of his head was swollen, and it throbbed in cadence with his pulse. He figured he was suffering from a mild concussion.

J.B. knew he had gotten off lucky, though. When the wolf had slashed his throat with razored teeth, missing his jugular by a fractional margin, he had fallen and struck his head against a stone. The animal had apparently believed him dead and left him.

The Armorer had awakened alone in the shadows, and his wrist chron told him that only a few minutes had elapsed. He had also awakened weaponless, his Uzi, his scattergun and all the spare ammo missing. He heard voices approaching from the direction of the village and so had climbed back into the cramped passageway.

Stumbling, dripping blood, feeling his way, he had backtracked through the tunnel, hoping to return to Little Mountain and the horses. He had no idea of the fates of Ryan or Joe, and his thinking was so clouded and fragmented, all he could do was stagger through the tunnel, flail across the river and stumble up the wooded slopes.

The effort exhausted him, and he crept into a hollow between two large, gnarled roots and lay down.

Now J.B.'s thinking was sharper, and he saw by his chron that only three hours remained until dawn. He doubted Little Mountain was still waiting. A rugged trek on foot stretched before him, a march he wouldn't have enjoyed even if he wasn't weak and racked with pain.

But J.B. had lived most of his life in the wild places of Deathlands. He had spent years on the ragged edge of death, and his inner fiber had been forged into an iron toughness. It was a point of pride with him. He wouldn't break, would not give in to pain and let himself be whipped by anything or anyone.

He stood slowly, wincing and grunting, and examined the wound on his throat by touch. The bleeding had stopped, but his shirtfront was caked and sticky with blood. Though his throat hurt, he realized it wasn't much more than superficial, more unsightly than critical. The swelling on the back of his head was more worrisome.

Mildred would diagnose it as a closed-skull injury, and he knew from his years on Trader's war wags that head traumas were tricky. He could have sustained a skull fracture and be suffering from a cranial leakage of blood for all he knew.

Grim determination steeled his mind. He was going back to his friends in the forest city and would return with them to rescue Ryan or recover his body. His brains could start to ooze from his ears, but he was going back.

It was difficult to move at first, but as his stiff body

warmed and loosened, the pain receded. He crept along the crest of the ridge, then down into the dell. He came across a little family of deer feeding there. For a minute he stood in the foliage and watched them, graceful, lovely things with their moist, black noses and great, innocent eyes: a proud buck, two does and a small, spotted fawn.

J.B. walked toward them. The deer lifted their heads and froze. The buck took a step forward, lowering its antlered head in a warning. Then it snorted at the unfamiliar man-scent and the pungent tang of blood. As one, they whirled fleetly and bounded away.

When he reached the outermost edge of the forest, he paused, scanning the open plains before him. The stars burned overhead like millions of tiny matchheads, but he saw nothing but grass. He started forward, walking in a long-legged, ground-eating stride.

J.B. didn't walk far before he wished he had a pair of moccasins. He'd probably end up cutting his combat boots off his swollen feet. The temperature had dropped, not enough to be dangerous, just enough to make him extremely uncomfortable. His breath plumed out in front of him with every exhalation.

He remembered a conversation he'd had with Hunaker, a fellow gunner on War Wag One. They had been hiding from a horde of stickies in a bug-infested swamp, and she had told him, "When the times get tough, just concentrate on a time that was worse."

"Does it help?" J.B. had asked.

The green-haired woman had shrugged. "Nah. Generally the other time seems like a quilting bee in comparison."

Hunaker was dead, chilled by crazy old Quint and his crazier wife. J.B. increased his pace, not wanting to think about her or any of Trader's old crew. A gust of wind slapped at him, setting off a spasm of shivering and numbing his ears. He pulled up his long coat over the top and sides of his head, cursing whoever had stolen his hat.

The terrain dropped into a narrow declivity, which sheltered him from the chill wind for a little while. He was tempted to remain there, but he forced himself to keep moving. He could only become more tired, so it was best to tramp on before he dropped in his tracks from exhaustion.

He managed to keep up a fairly brisk pace for the next few miles, but as the horizon began to glow with the approach of sunrise, exertion, blood loss and pain were taking their toll. He tottered on his throbbing feet like a horse with the blind staggers, and his breath was a constant cloud before his eyes. Though he raged at his lack of stamina, the walk didn't get any easier.

He stumbled up the side of a low bluff, fell and crawled up the rest of the way on his hands and knees. He crouched at the top, panting. In the distance he could make out the high stand of trees and the crystal glintings between and among them. He whooped with joy, but it was a pretty poor whoop. It sounded like the death caw of an elderly crow. He rolled rather than climbed down the opposite side.

"Hang on," he muttered between lips that were dry and cracked from the chafing wind.

The eastern sky was gray with false dawn. When the first flooding of red sunlight touched the distant, surrounding peaks, J.B. was entering the forest city. The few Indians he saw were bundled against the chill, and at a distance they assumed he was one of them, wrapped in a blanket.

He walked determinedly through the outer perimeter and into the silently brooding avenues between the gigantic trees. Dry leaves blew lonely on the wind, and not even the birds sang. The crystal disks glistened from the rising sun, but torches still burned inside the tree tower that served as their temporary home.

There were no guards at the arched entrance, and he shuffled along the corridor to the room where he and his friends were quartered. Before he walked in, he sensed somehow that only Mildred was there. One dim torch guttered in a wall bracket.

Mildred lay on their bunk. Her face wasn't relaxed in sleep. Dried tears shone dully on her cheeks, and his fedora was crumpled between her hands.

He moved stiffly toward her, slipped, stumbled and nearly fell atop her. Her upper body jackknifed up at the waist, her face contorted in anger and fear, reaching beneath the furry pillow. The ZKR was in Mildred's hands before she was able to recognize him.

He half crouched on the floor beside the bed, his limbs shaking as if caught in a spasm. "So, *you* have my hat," he croaked.

Mildred gaped at him. She couldn't speak, and for a moment she couldn't even breathe. What she could do and did was jump out of the bunk and catch him in her strong arms and hug him so hard he half groaned, half laughed.

She kissed his face, his lips, even his nose, and while she still held him tight to her body, she shouted, "Krysty! Jak! Doc!"

She repeated the call and released him when they hurried into the room. Their faces in the weak sunlight were masks of grief. Then, when they saw J.B. standing beside Mildred, their jaws dropped.

They crowded around him, pumping his hands, slapping his shoulders, shouting questions. Only when Mildred saw him wincing under their enthusiasm did she say, "Give him room, he's hurt."

Sitting at the table, J.B. allowed Mildred to clean and probe the ugly cut on his neck. Rapidly he told them what had happened at the Wolf Soldier encampment.

"This might need stitches," Mildred grunted, gently sponging the dried blood away.

"Perhaps I should fetch our singing shaman," Doc said.

In a voice tight with fear, eyes clouded by unshed tears, Krysty asked, "Ryan? Is he dead, like Joe said?"

"I don't know. Did he tell you *I* was dead?"

"Thoroughly," Mildred said, planting a careful kiss on the swelling at the back of his head.

"I honestly don't know," J.B. continued. "I don't think Joe knows, either. I guess he left me for dead, and here I am."

"A miscalculation," Joe said from the doorway. "I apologize, Mr. Dix."

The lithe Lakota came into the room, followed closely by Little Mountain.

"Wasn't only thing miscalculated," Jak said disgustedly. "Triple-stupe fuckup."

Joe shrugged, then winced in pain. "The fortunes of war. I admit I was a fool not to realize that when Blood-sniffer sent his pack brother back along our trail, he'd strike our scent and thus know something was wrong. He brought the Wolf Soldiers down on us."

"Outfoxed by a wolf," Doc commented dryly.

"Something of a first, I imagine, even in Ti-Ra'-Va."

"And a last," Krysty snapped. "I'm heading out to the Wolf Soldiers under a flag of truce. I'll find Ryan or his body."

"Or your death," Joe told her. "Too much blood has now been spilled to call a truce between our factions."

"We're not members of any factions," Krysty said angrily. "We're bowing out of this intertribal conflict right now."

Joe sighed, shook his head, then said in a harsh, grim tone, "You came here for gold and you can get it. Tomorrow we'll start our drive to the Wolf Soldiers' camp and the cavern. After we're victorious, you can do whatever you like."

"Are you deaf?" Mildred demanded. "We're through with it, through with you."

"And you're through, too," J.B. said, glaring at the Lakota men. "You can never take the camp or the cavern without us. The wolf packs will pull your asses down and tear them to bite-sized pieces."

Joe straightened his shoulders. "You're right. But we can do it without you."

"What do you mean?" Doc asked. "You brought us here to do what you could not."

"I don't need you," Joe answered. "All I need are your weapons."

With that, Joe reached behind him and brought out J.B.'s Uzi. Little Mountain stepped forward, the Smith & Wesson M-4000 scattergun held at waist level.

Krysty and Jak reached for their holstered blasters. Mildred, still ministering to J.B., was caught flat-footed, having left her revolver on the bunk. Doc's

Le Mat was snug inside the sheath strapped to his le
but the blaster wasn't designed for quick-draw artist
anyway.

Little Mountain thumbed back the hammer of th
scattergun. At the mechanical click, everyone froz
hands on gun butts.

"No," Joe said. "Go ahead and draw them. P
them on the table and step back. Your cane, too, D
Tanner."

Slowly, faces grim and sick, everyone obeyed an
moved against the far wall.

"You five are in a fix," Joe said curtly. "You hav
no choice but to live up to your end of our bargain."

"We're not helping you," Krysty replied. "Th
bargain was we would aid you for gold. We no longe
want it."

Joe chuckled. "You're forgetting something. I'
your only way of leaving this valley alive. Like M
Dix said, the wolf packs guarding the pass will te:
you to pieces."

"What do you propose to do about it?" Doc aske

"Simple. The prevailing wind blows north towar
the cavern, and in this dry season, the woods an
prairie grass are like tinder. All we need are a fe
torches."

"Fire?" Mildred asked incredulously. "If it ge
out of control, the damage to the valley's ecology wi
be—"

"Shut up!" Joe snapped. "It won't get out of co
trol, and even if it did, it wouldn't harm the cavern
Naturally there will be suffering, but that's the pric
of any victory."

Eyes narrowing, he added, "Besides, once I hav
mastery of the forces within the cavern, I'll easil
restore Ti-Ra'-Wa."

"Sounds like this thought out," Jak said. "May work."

Joe glanced toward him. "I'm glad you approve," he said sarcastically.

"Didn't say that."

Jak gave his right wrist a little shake, and his hand whipped up, a thin, flat, razor-edged knife gripped between thumb and forefinger.

"New contest, Joe," he said tonelessly. "See how fast you drop blaster before I put this in eye."

Chapter Twenty-Four

Ryan was dreaming dreams somebody else wante
him to dream. He thought he was asleep until a clum
of thick liquid appeared in his mouth, and he felt, i
his sleep, half the lump drip down his chin and th
other half slide down his throat.

Whatever the liquid lump was, it had no taste an
glided easily into his stomach. Then he dreamed
song that sang itself repeatedly to him, the words i
a language he didn't know but understood.

*You toward where the sun goes down, behold me
You where the White Giant lives in power, behold me
You in the depths of the heavens, an eagle of powe.
behold! And you, Grandmother Earth, the onl
Mother, you who have shown mercy to your childre
who have ripped and burned and poisoned you,
shall heal you!*

When the dream was over, he was propelled some
where new—or somewhere old, he wasn't sure which
He saw the whole valley of Ti-Ra'-Wa spread ou
below him, so far below that the great trees of th
forest city appeared as a mere ripple of texture, lik
a shawl thrown over the laps of the mountains. H
saw the high crags of the barrier peaks, thrusting u
into the sky, tossing the cold winds from their shou
ders in flying clouds of snow.

Colorful patterns and figures writhed, weaving int
complex geometric shapes. There were colors he ha

ever before seen, let alone imagined. The light, the
figures, the shapes and colors, melded and spiraled
themselves into a vision, a panorama of black man-
apes shambling out of a dark gray gloom.

The man-shapes were human but not truly human,
only reflections in a broken mirror, great, huge-
shouldered, deep-chested brutes of men, with powerfully knotted thews and heavy brows thrusting over
tiny eyes.

The brutes melted, became skin-clad red men bat-
ting huge, shaggy elephants, dying to gain their precious bounty of meat.

As Ryan dreamed, he could not watch the progression of visions quickly enough. The images seemed
to tumble over one another in their haste to enter and
exit his mind. He felt they had to slow down, to stop
moving, to stand still. They didn't.

He saw council fires of the great tribes bursting into
flame for the first time, the red men kneeling in awe
of Ah-badt-dadt-deah's mighty works and in gratitude
of the Grandmother's many gifts.

He saw a man, much like the Sioux or the Cheyenne, staring in wonder at a shimmering, dancing,
shifting column of light. Ryan stared at the light, trying to determine its color, but it blurred, and he
couldn't will it back into focus.

Slowly, reverently, the red man touched the light,
bowing his head before it.

The images swam faster now, flashing only a fraction of a split second in Ryan's mind. He saw armlets
of frozen gold and shimmering silver, and disks of
glinting crystal; homes made of living trees; armored,
helmeted men tramping uphill toward a mountain
pass; arrows whistling, spears flying, matchlocks
belching flame.

And over it all danced the unliving, undying light shining and glowing forever inside the womb of the Grandmother, inside the Cavern of Creation.

Then the light faded, and all Ryan knew was black, a black so deep he knew he was dying. But he also knew he had a choice, not of when to die, but of whether to die. He wasn't sure if he should live or die or dream.

He felt a throbbing pain, and a moment later he became aware of his body, and he knew he had decided to live, not to die or to dream.

Fear and memory exploded simultaneously in Ryan's mind. He made a convulsive effort and opened his eye. Brilliant sunshine shafting down from above blasted into it, and he squeezed the lid shut. He tried to touch his face and discovered he couldn't move either hand. Or his feet.

Carefully he opened his eye again, and this time he wasn't blinded. He focused slowly on the details of his surroundings.

He was in a room shaped like a cone. The sunlight poured in from an opening above him, where the cone narrowed to a point. Dust motes danced magically all around him.

He turned his head, first to the right, then the left, and finally down. He was hardly surprised that he was bound tightly—he was more surprised that he was alive.

Ryan's wrists, legs and ankles were tied securely by knotted leather thongs to a wood-framed, skin-covered latticework, like a hide-drying rack. He was in half-reclining position and his hands were bound to the frame at ear level. He also saw he was naked. He blinked. He didn't go away, so he was certain he wasn't dreaming.

"A precaution only," a woman's voice said from he shadows. "Not an attempt to humiliate you."

Sisoka moved toward him, cutting through the sparkling dust motes. She was clothed in soft, white-fringed doeskin and high moccasins. Her raven black hair cascaded down her back like an ebony waterfall.

Blood-sniffer moved forward at her side, and Ryan couldn't keep the anger that flowed through him from registering on his face.

Sisoka caught his expression and said, "You actually owe him a great debt. He saved your life from his pack brothers. Saved all your lives, actually."

"He betrayed us, deceived us," Ryan growled.

"It is no sin to betray a betrayer or to deceive a deceiver." Sisoka's tone was calm, neutral. "Touch-the-Sky is both, Ryan Cawdor."

It sounded strange, the way she said his name, as though she took pleasure in the sound and taste of it.

"Is Joe—Touch-the-Sky—here?"

Sisoka said nothing, but her long, sweeping lashes veiled her eyes for a moment.

"He escaped, didn't he?" Ryan said. "What about my friend?"

"No."

"No, what?"

"Neither of them escaped."

Ryan didn't reply, but he strained against his bonds.

"We allowed them to leave," Sisoka said quietly.

"What?"

"You were unconscious and so was your friend. There was no way to capture Touch-the-Sky alive without more loss of life. We allowed him to leave, allowed him to think he had escaped. Between the time we brought you here, to our camp, and returned

for your friend, he was gone. We could find no trac
of him, nor did we care to track him down.''

Ryan began to question her again about J.B., bu
bit off the words. He had no choice but to accept he
words. "Why didn't you chill me?"

"Are you afraid of death?" Sisoka countered.

"I don't want to die," he answered levelly, "but
can manage it if I have to."

Sisoka smiled faintly. "An honest answer, Rya
Cawdor." Then her smooth, girlish face sobered
"However, it is not death you fear."

Ryan forced a derisive smile. "How would yo
know, hiding in this valley, isolated from the rest o
the world since the time of the caveman?"

Sisoka's eyes narrowed in a way that reminde
Ryan of Joe. "How do you know that?" she asked.

He started to retort, then shut his mouth. He ha
no answer.

"How do you know that, Ryan Cawdor?" Sisok
demanded.

He groped for a response. "I don't know," he fal
tered. "I must have dreamed it."

"You dreamed it because *I* wished you to drean
it."

"I don't understand."

"I gave you a taste of the dew of Ah-badt-dadt
deah so you would understand."

Ryan ransacked his memory, recalled the liqui
slime being forced down his throat, and he snarled
"You drugged me. Made me high, made me hallu
cinate, tried to turn me into a jolt-brain so I'd believ
any bullshit you spouted."

Authority and arrogance were suddenly stampe
over her face like an ivory mask. "You are here t
be judged, outlander," she said coldly. "Not I."

Sisoka half turned away, stopped and spun to face him. "The visions you saw were true ones, plucked from the ancestral memories of all who dwell in Ti-Ra'-Wa."

Her voice was strong with resolve and conviction. "For centuries beyond counting, our valley has been threatened by the outside world, by invaders. The Spanish conquistadores, the white explorers and, more recently, the group you called the Red Cadre. We must protect the valley and the cavern as it has protected us, the lives and traditions of its children. Now it is threatened from within."

"How?" Ryan demanded. "Touch-the-Sky wants to use the power of your cavern to heal the Earth, the Grandmother, she who has shown mercy to the children who have ripped and burned and poisoned her."

Ryan broke off, mind reeling at the words he had spoken. He glared at Sisoka. "You conditioned me to say that while I was doped up, didn't you?"

"Don't be a fool, Ryan Cawdor," Sisoka responded impatiently. "The spirit of the Grandmother has touched you, using Blood-sniffer and myself as channels. I admit we entered and influenced your dreams a time or two—"

"With one of those sender gadgets," Ryan interrupted.

Sisoka acknowledged the correctness of his guess with a nod. "But," she continued, "if your innermost self, your spirit, had not been open to the contact, you would have never remembered the dreams, let alone been influenced by them."

Ryan nodded. "All right, I can't say I believe or disbelieve you. But I can say that I don't disagree with Touch-the-Sky's dream of healing the earth, setting right what the nukecaust did to it."

Sisoka sighed heavily. "He has the mind of a visionary, but it is still a human mind, filled with petty dreams of greed and power. He has no idea how easily he could be overwhelmed by the invisible forces in the cavern, powers beyond his control or comprehension."

"How can you be so sure?"

Sisoka stepped up close to him, her eyes shining with an almost fanatic fervor, again much like Joe's. "There is a tradition, in every religious culture, that holds that anyone who looks upon the face of God will certainly die. For a mere human to entertain the arrogant notion of commanding the forces of creation is the same thing. Only in this instance the entire world may die."

Ryan met her gaze, and his belly went cold. She wasn't being melodramatic. She was speaking the truth, at least as she understood it.

"Why should I believe you?" he rasped. "You might want to keep Touch-the-Sky from reaching the cavern simply because you're afraid of losing your position in the tribe."

"And how do I know," Sisoka asked, "that you are not the *wawihangya un kin oy'ate* Pizi claims you are?"

"I don't even know what that is."

Sisoka smiled slightly. "The destroyer of the world."

"Pretty big order for one man."

"I realize that." She moved closer, and her breath was warm on his naked throat. "Perhaps you're just a *kaga.*"

"I think I know that word. It means 'devil,' right?"

"Close. 'Demon.'" Her cool fingers came up and

tentatively touched his face. "Yes, I think you are more demon than destroyer, Ryan Cawdor."

Ryan tried to keep his body's reactions under control. He flicked his gaze to one side and saw Bloodsniffer staring up at him curiously. The heat of those blazing eyes cooled his heated, automatic responses quickly.

"You are very brave, outlander," she said in a breathy whisper. "But courage is a good quality only when one is wise enough to know when to use it."

On the far side of the tepee, the flap was thrown back with a rude, peremptory rustle. A man stepped inside. He was old enough to have iron gray hair, but he stood as straight as the feather-bedecked ceremonial lance he gripped in one hand. He wore a loose buckskin tunic and fringed leggings. A necklace of wolf's fangs hung about his throat.

Sisoka stepped away from Ryan. The man's eyes flicked from Ryan to her, then back to Ryan. He spoke to Sisoka in flawless English.

"So, the outlander has regained his senses. That is well. The pack leaders may now begin the judgment."

"Judgment?" Ryan echoed.

Sisoka nodded. "I said you were here to be judged. This is Pizi, my father's brother, chief of the Wolf Soldiers. He demands justice for the lives you took."

With a clicking of claws, three great gray wolves stalked into the tepee, their eyes glaring at him, hating him. Ryan felt icy fingers tracing down his spine. The concept of facing an inhuman panel of judges awoke in him a loathing he had never experienced.

"When does the judgment begin?" Ryan whispered to Sisoka.

Without looking at him, she replied, "It began the moment you entered this valley, Ryan Cawdor."

Chapter Twenty-Five

Sisoka gestured to Ryan and said clearly, "Before you judge, brothers, remember that this outlander may be the last thread by which we may draw Ti-Ra'-Wa out of danger."

Pizi looked solemnly at her. "The outlanders and their weapons are our greatest danger. This man and all those who came with him should die. He seeks to help Touch-the-Sky make Ti-Ra'-Wa like the outside world, a place of horror, bloodshed and suffering."

He shook the lance, the feathers rustled and his voice rose in an impassioned shout. "Blood of our dead calls out for justice! The outlanders have brought death and corruption into our sacred land. They have sinned against Ah-badt-dadt-deah and the Grandmother!"

The wolves growled and snarled, lips peeling back from saliva-slick fangs.

"This man sinned in ignorance," Sisoka said heatedly. "He knew nothing of us until he came to this valley. He was deceived, duped into killing without realizing his crime."

"He blundered here through greed," Pizi said with a sneer, "driven mad by the lust to possess the Grandmother's bounty. There can be only one penalty. What is the verdict of the pack?"

As from one throat, a skin-crawling howl burst from the wolves. Ryan saw that Blood-sniffer was the only animal abstaining from the bloodthirsty vocalization.

Pizi dipped the lance, and the point pressed lightly into the soft hollow at the base of Ryan's throat. He kept his expression impassive and fixed his eye on Pizi's face.

"Do the Wolf Soldiers so fear the power of the outlanders that you will murder me while I'm bound and helpless?" Ryan's words were heavy with contempt. "If so, then end this farce and chill me now. I'm sick of all this Wolf Soldier bullshit."

Anger flashed briefly in Pizi's eyes, and the pressure of the spear point increased.

"Enough!" Sisoka snapped. "The outlander, no matter what he has done, no matter what else he might be, is a warrior and deserving of a warrior's chance."

"He had his chance," Pizi said grimly.

"Henakeca!" Sisoka cried angrily.

The pressure of the sharp point lessened on Ryan's throat, but Pizi didn't lower the lance.

"You swore to recognize me as the one true Guardian," Sisoka said sternly. "The pack has rendered its verdict, but it is *my* duty, my right, to impose the final sentence."

Sisoka paused. Her face and tone were imperious as she announced, "He must face a soldier in equal combat. If he survives, he will be a member of the pack, and if he betrays the pack, then the pack's justice prevails."

In an angry motion Pizi pulled back the lance and slammed it butt-first to the floor. "One soldier must volunteer to face the outlander. If one does not, then he dies."

Without hesitation Blood-sniffer stepped forward

and nosed Sisoka's hand. She looked down on the wolf with a fond, sad smile. "We have the volunteer."

Ryan stared at the big, muscular animal, trying to convince himself that, armed with his panga, he could make short work of Blood-sniffer. After all, he had battled other beasts, giant mutie wolves included, and emerged alive, if not exactly victorious or unscathed.

As if sensing his thoughts, Blood-sniffer looked over at him. Something in that intense, inhuman gaze shook him.

Pizi stalked out of the tepee. The wolves remained, watching Ryan. Sisoka moved toward him, drawing a bone-handled knife with an obsidian blade from a voluminous sleeve. She began cutting the rawhide bindings around his arms and legs.

"What kind of weapon can I use?" he asked.

"The same as Blood-sniffer—your teeth and nails."

"What?"

She sawed through the last of the thongs holding him to the framework. "Equal combat. Nor may you stand erect."

As soon as she said it, Ryan fell down, his legs like dead fish, as numb as if they had never been alive. Sisoka helped him to kneel, massaging his deadened muscles to restore the circulation of blood in his arms and legs.

Ryan touched his head, his fingers brushing a crusted lump on his right temple. He felt scabbed-over claw marks. He glanced at the knife Sisoka had laid on the ground while she kneaded the stiffness from his shoulders, then to the four wolves scarcely an arm's length away from him.

Pizi returned, his arms full of a furry bundle. For

a moment, Ryan couldn't identify the dark, shaggy mass, then he recognized it as the skin of a huge black wolf. The fore- and hindlegs still retained their shape, as did the head and the thick, bushy tail.

Ryan painfully climbed to his feet, and Pizi shoved the bundle into his arms. "These are the remains of Deathmaul, one of our most respected soldiers. Do not dishonor them."

Ryan looked blankly at Sisoka, who said, "It is the custom of the Wolf Soldiers to retain the mortal coverings of their greatest warriors. The two-legged soldiers wear the skins of their departed four-legged brothers to give them strength and courage in battle."

"And," Pizi interjected sourly, "it is the only protection you will have."

Ryan slowly put on the wolf skin, slipping his hands through leather straps sewn on the underside of the forepaws, attaching the main trunk to his chest and waist with a harness. Pizi pulled the skullcap over Ryan's head and secured it there with a thong knotted under his chin. The muzzle covered his forehead like a cowl.

Outwardly Ryan remained very calm, determined not to allow the flummery of superstitions and ritual to shake his nerve.

"I am half-blind," he said to Pizi, indicating his eye patch. "Hardly an equal contest unless you put out one of Blood-sniffer's eyes."

"Blood-sniffer is lame in one leg," Pizi retorted. "Due to you, I am told. It is as equal a contest as you deserve. Follow."

Pizi marched out of the tepee, Ryan in step behind him. Sisoka and Blood-sniffer dogged his heels. The sun was fairly high, and Ryan estimated it was close to midmorning. He had at least had a rest, of sorts.

Only a few people were about in the encampment, men mostly, and he could feel the hostility of their stares as he passed by.

Pizi led the way through the ring of tepees and down a gently rolling incline to where the bases of four bluffs formed a natural bowl, like an amphitheater—or, as Ryan reminded himself, an arena.

Obeying Pizi's imperious gesture, Ryan went down into the bowl, Blood-sniffer following. Taking position in the center, he made a 360-degree visual circuit. Men, women and many wolves lined the base of the bluffs. All were staring at him unemotionally.

Anger grew within Ryan. No matter what ancient tradition lay behind this trial by ordeal, it was still bread and circuses for the masses, nothing but entertainment of the type he and his friends had been forced to participate in when they were captives of Baron Mandeville. He had survived those gladiatorial games, and he would survive this one.

Pizi raised his lance over his head, and Ryan prepared himself for a long ceremonial speech. But the chief of the Wolf Soldiers said nothing at all. He jerked down the head of the lance, and Blood-sniffer sprang in a beautiful, arching leap, straight for Ryan's throat.

The wolf's great forepaws struck his breast with a jarring shock, bowling him over. Even as he fell, Ryan seized Blood-sniffer by the throat and kicked him up and over. The wolf landed on its feet, though its balance was off due to its injured leg.

It spun and jumped. Ryan rolled facedown to keep his exposed torso and genitals away from the slashing teeth and rending claws. Blood-sniffer's weight landed on his shoulders, and its huge jaws closed on

he back of Ryan's fur-covered neck. The wolf shook
him as a terrier would shake a rat.

The animal's strength was enormous, and for what
seemed like an eternity, Ryan felt as if his head were
being torn from his neck. The world tipped and tilted
around him, and the ground rushed up to smash his
face.

With a final contemptuous shake, Blood-sniffer
flung Ryan to one side, rolling him over and over to
the very edge of the arena. Dizzy, spitting out grit,
Ryan fought his way to his hands and knees. Peering
from beneath the wolf snout canted over his forehead,
he saw Blood-sniffer strutting in a lordly fashion a
few feet away. The wolf was playing to the crowd,
red tongue run out between open, laughing jaws.

Around him Ryan heard human laughter and yip-
ping noises of wolf appreciation. He realized the beast
was toying with him, intending to humiliate him before ripping out his heart. The anger that had been
growing within Ryan suddenly burst in a wild flame
of rage.

But this rage was unlike the red fury that sometimes possessed him. He was dimly aware of a strange
linking of his familiar human anger to an emotion far
darker, more deep and primal. It was a man-rage co-
alescing with beast-rage, an atavistic fury fountaining
up from the buried wells of savagery lurking within
all human hearts.

Ryan's muscles coiled tightly as he crouched and
faced his enemy. He bared his fangs and snarled. He
sprang at Blood-sniffer, his powerful leg muscles cat-
pulting him in graceful bounds.

The wolf leaped to met him, and the pair of shaggy
bodies collided in midair. They clinched and rolled

together across the rough floor of the arena, snarling
clawing and biting.

Ryan closed a leg-scissors lock around Blood
sniffer's lean body and gripped a handful of ruff. He
kept his own throat covered and sank his teeth into
the side of his enemy's neck. He felt hair and hide
tear under his teeth, tasted sharp, salty wolf blood on
his tongue.

Blood-sniffer's body, all muscle and sinew
twisted, turned and kicked away from Ryan's jaws
Then the wolf's fangs snapped and slashed, and scar
let spurted from Ryan's chest. The beast squirmed
backward out between Ryan's locked legs and in
flicted a bite on his right calf.

The wolf bounded out of reach and watched as the
maddened man-beast got to all fours and sprang
again. The animal moved like a great gray wraith, and
Ryan fell facefirst to the ground. Before he recovered
his balance, the wolf smashed him to one side with
its heavy weight, and claws raked Ryan's rib cage.

Ryan didn't cry out or even pause. He leaped again
managing to close his hand around Blood-sniffer'
leg. The wolf snarled in pain and anger and its fang
ripped bleeding furrows in the back of Ryan's hand
forcing him to let go.

Rolling, Ryan came back up to his knees as Blood
sniffer bounded forward. He fell over on his back
beneath the wolf, coming up with one foot into the
belly and kicking. The beast's hindquarters flew up
with the impact of the kick, and it tumbled snout over
rump to land gracelessly on its back.

Before Blood-sniffer could rise, Ryan was up and
over and on top of the wolf. He secured a headlock
one arm around the furry throat, the other pressing
forward from behind.

The wolf struggled, muscles like steel cables covered with fur, hind legs kicking and flailing. Ryan heaved the animal's body up, then smashed it against the ground. The wolf grunted noisily as air was driven violently from its lungs.

With a convulsive effort, Blood-sniffer twisted inside Ryan's crushing grip. Fangs fastened around his forearm, and he was forced to release his hold or have his arteries ripped open.

Back-somersaulting away, Ryan kicked the wolf so hard in the rear that its hindquarters rose off the ground and it rolled in a tangle to the edge of the arena. He thought he heard Sisoka cry out.

The pair of combatants paused, glaring at each other. The hot, sweet taint of fresh blood tinged the air, and the spectator wolves sniffed and wrinkled their snouts in snarling grins.

Blood-sniffer stood on wide-braced legs, flanks heaving, head hanging low, ears laid flat. Blood and sweat wetted the gray fur.

Ryan trembled with fatigue. As the first rush of adrenaline faded, he began to feel the pain of his wounds, feel weakness as his blood streamed from them. Perspiration formed beneath the heavy wolf skin, trickling down his body and into the raw lacerations on his chest and ribs. Though they stung fiercely, surrender wasn't an option.

Slowly he scanned the spectators. Pizi and his human warriors were as blank-faced as before. Only Sisoka showed any emotion. An expression of pity, of sorrow, was in her somber eyes, but Ryan had no idea if it was for him or Blood-sniffer.

Though the dulled fire of beast-rage still burned within him, Ryan's reason told him that he couldn't hope to chill his opponent. It was doubtful if Blood-sniffer could chill him, either. They were too evenly matched. The best that could be hoped for, after a protracted and bloody battle, was a stalemate. Even if that was the outcome, he would be so chewed and clawed he would have to spend days, maybe weeks convalescing.

Taking and holding a deep breath, his face set in a grim mask, Ryan slowly climbed to his feet, noting distantly that standing erect felt a little strange. He tugged the wolf cowl back from his head.

From his position on the slope, Pizi barked, "On all fours, outlander!"

"Fuck you," Ryan snapped. "I won't perform for you any longer. Neither of us will. Come and chill me yourself—if you have the guts."

At Ryan's words, expression and emotion formed on Pizi's face. His brows lowered, and a monstrous wrath flared in his eyes. His lips writhed, and hefting his lance, he made a motion to jump down into the arena.

Blood-sniffer suddenly bounded forward, taking a position between the two men. The wolf took three soft padding steps toward Pizi, and sunlight gleamed on bared fangs. The meaning of the low, menacing growl was unmistakable.

As though that was a signal, a burst of sound broke from the assembled spectators—the shouting of humans and the long, undulating howls of wolves.

Looking smugly at Pizi, Sisoka said in a loud, ringing voice, "It is over. Blood-sniffer has accepted Ryan Cawdor into the pack. He is now a Wolf Soldier."

Since she made the announcement in English, Ryan knew it was for his understanding alone. He stood in the center of the arena. Breathing was an agony

Blood oozed and took his strength with it, and every muscle, ligament and joint was a separate ache and pain.

He wasn't sure what to do next, so he did the first thing that occurred to him. He lifted his head and joined in the chorus of howls.

Chapter Twenty-Six

Joe's finger tightened on the trigger of the Uzi, his knuckle turning white. "If any of you have the least bit of influence over your young friend, now is the time to exert it."

Jak's crimson eyes were locked in a sardonic challenge with Joe's black, unblinking gaze. The blade in his hand was rock steady.

Silence fell on the room. A child's laughter from outside sounded huge and hollow. Joe's dark eyes shadowed with menace.

"One knife against two blasters," he said. "Don't be stupe."

"For smart man, you stupe," Jak replied. "Chill me, sure. You die, too."

Krysty edged forward, hands up, palms open, fingers spread. "Enough, Jak. Put away the blade. You can only chill Joe."

"What I want."

"What about you?"

"Don't care."

"I care," she said in a tone deceptively casual. "We all care. And you've got to care, too. When you drop Joe, Little Mountain will open up with the scattergun. All of us will die."

The teenager's gaze wavered slightly.

"It's not necessary," Krysty whispered. "Joe said

we're in a fix, and he's right. But we've gotten out of plenty of fixes and fixed the fixers. Remember?''

The knife didn't so much as tremble in the white fingers.

Krysty kept talking, kept moving slowly forward. "You fixed the General, remember? Took you a while, but you fixed him.''

At the mention of the man who was responsible for the murders of his wife and child, Jak blinked, his gaze wavering even more.

"Give yourself, give all of us, that same while to fix Joe.''

Jak lowered his arm and dropped the knife, and it sank point first into the wooden floor. His white face was grave, his eyes angry and bitter with memories and frustration.

Doc made a muffled exclamation, and Mildred sat on a bunk, running a hand over her face. The moment of relief quickly came to an end when several warriors swarmed into the room and bound their wrists with strips of rawhide.

Joe dabbed at the fine dew of perspiration on his upper lip. "Young Lauren is in your debt.''

"So are you,'' Krysty said coldly as a man tightened the knots binding her wrists together. They were held out before her.

Two warriors collected the blasters from the table. J.B. winced at the clatter and the rough handling.

"Now what?'' he demanded. "You going to chill us before you ride down on the Wolf Soldier encampment?''

"No,'' Joe answered. "You will ride with us. Your presence is required to spur on my more superstitious warriors. Their vanity will not allow them to stay behind while *wasicun kagas* fight in their stead.''

"*Wasicun* whats?" J.B. asked.

"White demons," Joe explained.

"If you inspire so little confidence among your troops," Doc ventured, "then how can you hope to succeed in your military endeavor?"

Joe shrugged. "Do you think me naive, Dr. Tanner? I have traveled far, farther than any man in this valley, and seen many lands, many people. I have lived among the whites and read many books. I know the fears of my warriors are smoke. With your weapons in their hands, they will know it, too."

He spoke sharply to Little Mountain, who gestured toward the door with the barrel of the scattergun.

"I'll fetch you when I need you," Joe said as they walked past him.

"That," Mildred muttered, "is what we're afraid of."

ONE OF THE FOUR HUMAN Wolf Soldiers acting as an honor guard pulled aside the flap, allowing Ryan, Sisoka, Blood-sniffer and Pizi to enter the tepee.

Ryan began to strip off the wolf skin, then demanded, "Where are my clothes and weapons?"

Pizi picked up a tied deer-hide bundle from the floor and tossed it to him. Opening it, Ryan saw all his possessions, including his gun belt, SIG-Sauer, a spare ammo clip and his panga. Only the golden wafer was missing. He quickly started to take off the skin of Deathmaul.

Sisoka helped him to unlace the harness, saying, "I will treat your wounds. You need a bandage on that arm."

Ryan pulled on his pants and buckled his gun belt around his waist before allowing Sisoka to minister to him. He sat on a buffalo robe, and with a bowl of warm water, a cloth and some sort of stinging, stinking ointment, she cleaned his scratches and lacerations. The bite on his forearm burned like a hot coal, but he knew it wasn't as severe as it could have been.

Blood-sniffer sat on his haunches, licking the bite Ryan had inflicted. The wolf had fought with a restrained savagery, obviously not wanting to kill him unless there was no other choice.

As she bathed and bandaged his injuries, Sisoka murmured, "Tell us about yourself, Ryan Cawdor. You are now a Wolf Soldier, and we need to know of your history, of your place in the world."

Ryan shifted uncomfortably, feeling the pressure of Pizi's stare against his back. He rarely spoke of his past, but slowly, reluctantly, drawn out by Sisoka's gentle encouragement and questions, he began to talk. He told her of his privileged youth as the third and youngest son of Baron Titus Cawdor in Front Royal, the largest ville in Virginia. He spoke of losing his mother, his oldest brother, his father and his left eye to his middle brother, Harvey, during an assassination attempt. He told of how he was wounded, not only in body, but in spirit, and how he fled his past and his birthright to ride with Trader on his war wags, fighting what seemed an endless battle with the human and inhuman spawn of the Deathlands.

When he spoke of Krysty and Dean, Sisoka's lips pursed momentarily in what he interpreted as disappointment.

"I've seen the ruins of all the great cities, the centers of predark civilization," he said in a monotone. "I've roamed in the unknown regions south, east and west and even across the sea. I've been a gunner, an explorer, a father—I've been everything except content, and I hope to be that before I die."

He shrugged his shoulders. "This is as good a life as any and better than most."

Sisoka shook her head and leaned forward to help him on with his shirt. Her breasts pressed briefly into his upper arm. "A sad tale."

"Compared to your lives here, mebbe. But to the rest of Deathlands, compared to some of the suffering I've seen that passes for life, not sad at all."

"In bygone days," Pizi said, "you would have died long before you even saw the pass to the valley. You found your way here through a traitor's cunning, a traitor's treachery."

Turning to face him, Ryan said, "According to Touch-the-Sky, you're the traitors. You refuse to use the powers at your command to heal the earth."

Pizi shook his head vigorously, not in disagreement, but in disbelief. "Touch-the-Sky is a vain fool. He found us, several seasons ago, and immediately devoted himself to protecting this valley. He felt he was more worthy of the guardianship of the Cavern Keepers society than Sisoka and so attached himself to Towasi, my brother. When Towasi died, the hereditary title of Guardian automatically passed on to Sisoka, a tradition that has been observed for generations."

"He told me Towasi intended for him to assume the title, because he had no sons. He said that neither he nor Sisoka had been initiated into the secret knowledge of how to call upon the cavern's powers. He feels you practice low laws, not the high laws."

Sisoka snorted. "First of all, Ti-Ra'-Wa is not a patriarchy. The Guardianship mantle is inherited by the first-born child of the Guardian, regardless of the sex."

"Were you initiated into the secrets?" Ryan asked.

"There are no secrets," Sisoka declared. "Therefore, no initiation rites."

"Touch-the-Sky believes there are initiation rites, and secrets to learn."

"We know what he believes," Pizi growled. "The vainglorious fantasy he built up around the valley and the cavern wouldn't allow him to believe anything else. Nor does he understand that Ti-Ra'-Wa acts as a balance between the high and low laws, achieving a balance between the heavens and the earth. He doesn't know enough about us to even begin to realize he doesn't know enough."

"Didn't his ancestors live here?"

"According to some," Sisoka said, a note of amusement in her voice, "everybody's ancestors lived here, tens of thousands of years ago."

"So he has no real tie to Ti-Ra'-Wa, no valid claim to the guardianship title?"

"He has nothing but a rabble-rouser's abilities," Pizi replied. "He convinced some of our people— young ones, mostly—that a wonderful magical gift lay buried in the cavern and Sisoka wanted it all to herself. He persuaded a few warriors, a few dreamers, that with the gift, he could transform the entire world into a mirror image of Ti-Ra'-Wa, and the planet would be restored to its state before the whites ruined it. As chief of the Wolf Soldiers, and uncle to Sisoka, I supported her against his accusations. We didn't expect him to mount an attack against us and drive us from our own city."

"When he left here," Sisoka said, "Blood-sniffer and I shadowed Touch-the-Sky on the plain. He then went to Amicus and we followed him there, where Blood-sniffer saw you and your friends. He had an instinct about you."

Ryan glanced at the wolf. The animal was stretched on its side, evidently asleep. "An instinct?"

"That you and his kind were kindred. He tested that instinct when you dreamed."

Ryan exhaled a deep breath. "He was my animal spirit guide. My totem. That's why he didn't kill me, even when you ordered him to."

"And that's why you didn't kill him, even when you were ordered to."

He looked again at Pizi. "I know what Touch-the-Sky believes about this place. What do you believe?"

A flame ignited in Pizi's dark eyes. "Our forefathers cultivated Ti-Ra'-Wa, but the forest city was ancient even in our oldest histories. Yes, much of the old knowledge has been lost, but we do not mourn it. Nor has this valley always been a land of peace and plenty. Anger, greed and jealousy made Ti-Ra'-Wa run red with blood more than once. For many years human and animal sacrifices were made to the Grandmother, but she was offended by the taking of lives and it ended.

"For centuries we have dwelt in peace. Tribes fleeing the white government found refuge here, and never spoke its location, even when they were tortured by the whites, the Spanish, the French. Ti-Ra'-Wa endured the purification and it will endure until the Grandmother Herself perishes."

"And the intelligent wolves? How do you explain them?"

Pizi shrugged, as if the matter were of no consequence. "Our brothers were always here."

"And the senders? Where did they come from?"

"Again they were always here," Sisoka answered. "The technique of their use was taught by the first Guardian, Nanabozho."

"Who made the senders?"

"The First People," Sisoka replied. "They vanished many, many centuries ago."

"Where did they come from? Where did they go?"

Pizi answered Ryan's question with a long, convoluted story of dark and mysterious matters, of Nanabozho conjuring magic from the catacombs of the cavern. Ryan wasn't interested in old legends, but he listened anyway, realizing the cavern still exerted a terrible elemental power over the people of the valley. It filled their whole lives, a strange obsession that had shut them off from the rest of the world.

When Pizi paused for breath, Ryan asked quickly, "What I wanted to know is what *you* believe is the cavern's secret."

"There is no secret, like I said," Sisoka answered. "The heart of the Grandmother beats there, the life force of the world."

"What does it look like?"

"I have never seen it. I know it is there. That is enough."

Ryan resisted the impulse to shake his head in exasperation. He remembered the Trader telling him that out of mules, women and spoiled children, Indians would win the award for obduracy any day of the week.

Forcing a patience into his voice that he didn't feel, he said, "Touch-the-Sky thinks it's a core of energy, trapped in the cave since the very beginnings of the universe."

"Yes," Pizi grunted.

"He thinks your ancestors once had the knowledge to use that energy to manipulate the planet."

"True," Sisoka agreed.

"All right, then," Ryan said, "why do you think

he's a traitor for wanting to use the energy in the same way your ancestors did?''

Pizi's hands clenched tight, and he pounded them on his knees. "He thinks our ancestors used the power as a woman uses a needle and thread. Our ancestors were but vessels for the power. They obeyed its bidding.''

Ryan leaned back, staring at the man incredulously. He glanced at Sisoka. "I don't get it.''

Sisoka sighed wearily. "It's not complicated, Ryan Cawdor. We cannot use the power in the cavern to heal Grandmother Earth. The power *is* Grandmother Earth.''

Ryan was struck speechless for a long tick of time. He opened his mouth to voice a question, then shut it again. He hunched his shoulders and looked around the tepee, as if expecting to see someone.

"What is it?'' Sisoka asked.

Eye narrowed, he half whispered, "Krysty?''

Chapter Twenty-Seven

The little bark lodge faced west, and since it was still morning, the sun shone against the far wall. The light peeping in around the edges of the animal pelt hanging in front of the low entrance was dim. They sat on the ground, leaning against the wooden walls, their bound wrists resting on their knees.

No one had spoken for what seemed like a very long time. Finally Jak said softly, "Waiting room in Hell."

"I've got to get out of here," Krysty stated.

"All of us have to get out of here," J.B. replied sourly.

"No," Krysty said impatiently. "I need to reach the crystal chamber. Mebbe I can contact Ryan—if he's still alive."

"If he is, and he doesn't have the sender," Mildred contended, "you won't be able to communicate with him."

"I didn't say communicate, I said contact. With the crystals enhancing my own natural psionic abilities, I might at least be able to sense his mind."

"And if you do, then what?" Doc inquired. "And more importantly, if you do not, then what?"

Krysty didn't answer for a long moment. Finally, in a hushed voice, she said, "I don't know."

All of them jumped at the sharp collection of sounds driving into the low-ceilinged lodge from outside. They recognized the sounds—the dry-twig snapping of the Smith & Wesson 640, the deeper boom of the Colt Python, the slamming bang of the ZKR, the heavy thump of the Le Mat and the whip-crack of the Steyr.

After the fusillade of noise ceased, they heard Joe's voice, shouting impatient orders and instructions in Lakota.

"They're practicing with our blasters," J.B. said. "Didn't hear the Uzi or the scattergun, so I guess Joe and Little Mountain are keeping hold of them."

He sighed and added bitterly, "We've got to get out of here."

Raising her bound wrists to her mouth, Krysty sank her teeth into the thongs. Everyone saw what she was doing and followed suit, though Doc gave up after a few experimental bites. The leather strips were tough, but they were sure they could chew through them given enough time, provided they had much of that commodity.

The thongs tasted awful, but their flavor reminded Krysty that they hadn't eaten in nearly sixteen hours. She kept gnawing until her jaws ached and the rawhide was slippery with saliva. She took a break.

Suddenly the pelt hanging in front of the door was pushed aside, and Sunlata entered. She was holding an earthenware bowl full of water in one hand and another bowl containing some sort of steaming stew.

Jak and Krysty exchanged quick glances. As Sunlata stooped over to place the bowls in the center of the lodge, Jak's wire-taut muscles gave a heave and the thongs parted.

Sunlata's head whipped toward him at the sound, and she began a backward step, but she backed right into Krysty's out-thrust leg. As she began to fall, Jak threw himself across the young woman's body, locking his hands around her slim throat to prevent any cries of alarm. He started to squeeze with all his strength when he realized Sunlata wasn't struggling or even trying to pry his fingers away.

Jak stopped trying to choke her into senselessness. She was staring up at him with a strained smile on her face.

"Stupe," he said, astonished. "Triple stupe."

Mildred laughed softly. "No, I think she's in love with you. Though that might make her more than a triple stupe."

"Let her up," Krysty said.

Jak complied and Sunlata pushed herself to a sitting position.

Doc chuckled. "We're of such a novelty value, especially you, Jak, that whatever loyalty she may have to Joe's cause is vitiated."

"I'm betting she doesn't have much loyalty at all," Krysty said. "He's fairly new here and has caused a split in the society. Mebbe she'll help us."

Using sign language and the few words of Lakota that J.B. could speak, they were able to get Sunlata to understand that Krysty wanted to visit the crystal chamber.

Sunlata frowned for a moment, tapping her full underlip, then her dark eyes brightened with the enthusiasm of an idea. Pointing to Krysty with one hand, she tugged at her doeskin smock and mantle with the other.

"She's suggesting I wear her clothes," Krysty said. She pointed to Sunlata's black tresses, then her own fiery mane, and shrugged questioningly.

Sunlata pulled up her fringed mantle over her head like a hood and nodded.

Krysty smiled. "I suppose it's worth a chance."

She nodded at Sunlata, and the young woman stripped out of her clothes so quickly not even Doc had the time to avert his eyes.

"Uninhibited little minx, isn't she?" he mumbled.

As Sunlata sat naked and beaming at her from a corner, Krysty put on her clothes. She didn't take any of her own off except for her boots so she could pull on the high moccasins. With Mildred's help, she pulled the mantle over her head and tucked all of her red hair beneath it. J.B. emptied the bowls and kicked dirt over their contents.

"I'll be back as soon as I can," she said, picking up the bowls. Sunlata sat very close to Jak, smiling gayly as though she were part of a vastly amusing game.

Pushing through the pelt covering, Krysty quickly scanned the area for a sentry and she saw one. He was a young man, a teenager, standing about two hundred feet away. He leaned on a lance, his shoulders slouched. He was humming to himself, obviously extremely bored with the duty. He glanced up at Krysty, then glanced away disinterestedly.

As she walked unhurriedly through the forested avenues, she realized that Joe had set a hard task for himself, to turn a basically trusting, unwarlike people into soldiers. The young guard was probably the best choice out of an undisciplined lot.

She heard more shots, and more angry shouts from Joe somewhere to her left, and she turned in the opposite direction. She might have been able to fool a boy with her haphazard disguise, but she knew she would give herself away to Joe if he caught the briefest of glimpse of her.

She followed a circuitous route between the gargantuan tree trunks and finally reached the one that had served as their quarters. She entered carefully, eyes down, but she encountered no one. She assumed almost everyone was either taking part in the blaster lessons or observing.

Krysty stepped into the crystal chamber and put down the bowls, moving to one of the translucent mineral points. She put both hands around it and pressed her forehead against it, then closed her eyes to begin her preparations.

A rich warmth blanketed her as she followed the route of blood through her circulatory system, tracing the autonomic functions back to the controlling portion of her brain.

She slowed her respiration rate and concentrated on the mantra to Gaia her mother had taught her.

Her heartbeat speeded up, then slowed, and at the same time she increased the amount of adrenaline into her bloodstream.

Krysty's mind went here and there through her body, adjusting it, manipulating it, honing and revitalizing her reflexes and responses. The warmth spread from the center of her belly, flowed through her arms and legs. Her fingertips and toes tingled with energy.

She repeated the invocation, and in her mind's eye she saw a white blossom opening, the petals reaching out to engulf her. She felt as if she were floating, hovering between the solid material world and one made of warm, insubstantial light.

Then, within the white blossom, she saw Ryan's face and she called out to him.

"THE SENDER I HAD on me," Ryan demanded, "where is it?"

Pizi scowled. "Only a Guardian may touch the Mazaska Wakan and the Inyan Wakan."

Ryan snarled wordlessly. Blood-sniffer raised his head from the floor and blinked at him curiously. Forcing himself to keep calm, Ryan rose to his feet. Bravado, threats and reaching for his blaster would only shatter the tenuous bridge of trust he had built between Sisoka, Pizi and the wolf.

The sudden, insistent pressure in his mind was a new experience, yet the faint, almost intangible touch was familiar. He pulled Sisoka to her feet. She stared up at him in wonder.

"I need the sender," he said in a measured, deliberate tone.

"How do we know you won't contact Touch-the-Sky?" Pizi growled.

"You'll have to trust me. I wouldn't ask you for it if it wasn't important."

Sisoka gave him a searching stare, then knelt and felt around beneath the robe upon which they had been sitting. She brought out the golden wafer and handed it to him.

"Thank you." Gingerly Ryan pressed the crystal disk to his forehead, trying to form thought-words.

The force of the mental energy flooding into his mind nearly bowled him over.

Ryan! Lover! Oh, Gaia, where are you?

I'm here, Krysty.

Her emotions crashed into his consciousness like a sunburst, all golden and glorious. Ryan tried to orient himself. Krysty's riot of emotions became coherent thought-patterns. She told him of Joe's betrayal, their imprisonment, how Sunlata had helped her reach the crystal chamber. Then she told him of Joe's plan.

Fire?

Ryan was surprised by the depth of horror he experienced. His warrior's mind appreciated the beautifully simple plan, but he recoiled at its unutterable cruelty. A fire in the valley was far worse than their blasters in the hands of Joe's warriors.

What do you want us to do? Krysty asked.

Stay there. Don't start trouble unless you have to. Go back to your cell and send the girl away. I'll come for you.

Where will we go?

Here, the encampment of the Wolf Soldiers.

He felt her wordless reaction of surprise, but he didn't waste time explaining or repeating everything Sisoka and Pizi had told him.

Wait for me, lover, he said. *Stay alive.*

You, too, lover.

Ryan lowered the wafer and wiped at the sweat on his brow. He swept a fierce blue gaze over Sisoka, Pizi and Blood-sniffer.

"Touch-the-Sky has made prisoners of my friends," he said grimly. "He has armed his warriors with our weapons to use against the Wolf Soldiers."

Sisoka and Pizi said nothing, but they stood quite still and fixed, waiting.

"They'll be coming with fire for the forest," he continued roughly.

"Fire?" Sisoka's voice was strained, trembly with shock.

"That is death for the valley!" Pizi bellowed, outraged.

"Unless we stop them," Ryan replied. "I must free my friends and recover our weapons from your—our—enemies."

"I will alert the soldiers and the packs," Pizi said. "We will attack the city."

"No," Ryan said. "A frontal assault pitting bows and arrows against automatic blasters will only get yourselves chilled. Your ancestors learned that lesson the hard way."

Pizi flung his arms wide. "The blade has been drawn!" he shouted. "There is no turning back. Blood calls for blood, and vengeance should fall swiftly on this coward!"

Ryan made a spitting sound of derision. "You sent assassins to kill Touch-the-Sky along the trail. That may be expedient, but it means you got no place to brand him a coward. That's the one thing he ain't."

As Pizi sputtered in baffled anger, Ryan turned to Sisoka. "I'm going to the city. Who'll go with me?"

Blood-sniffer rose and pressed his shoulder against Ryan's leg. He reached down and stroked the wolf's broad head.

"While we're gone, get your soldiers ready. No matter what else happens, Hell is on its way."

THE WEAPONS DRILL wasn't going well. In fact it was proceeding badly. Touch-the-Sky had chosen the best bowmen in the city to wield the blasters. Either their marksmanship could only be applied to arrows or they were too disconcerted by the flame and noise that accompanied each squeeze of the trigger.

Only a few of the man-size targets that had been erected in a clearing showed lethal hits. Many of the targets showed no hits at all.

Touch-the-Sky had railed at the men, demonstrated the proper way to fix target acquisition and over and over he had shouted at them to squeeze the triggers, not to pull them.

By midafternoon, the warriors had fired a lot of the outlanders' ammunition and were milling about in a disheartened circle, muttering to one another, complaining and criticizing.

Touch-the-Sky spoke bitterly to Little Mountain about the lack of aptitude and enthusiasm displayed by the warriors. "Are they fighting men or children?"

Little Mountain shook his head mournfully. "You came here from outside and you do not yet fully understand our people. We have followed you against our traditions because you have proved yourself a strong warrior and have said you hold a power to make the world whole again."

The men with the blasters overheard Little Mountain's words and stepped closer.

"My words are true," Touch-the-Sky said. "The power within the cavern is the legacy of our forefathers. It is kept from us."

A warrior holding the Colt Python shook his head. "The First People reared our city in the dawn of the beginnings of day. We have lived according to their ancient ways, and Ti-Ra'-Wa was spared the purification. Even if what you say is true, our actions violate those traditions. You brought outlanders here, and you want us to fight in the outland way against our own people. The valley is no longer the Ti-Ra'-Wa we knew."

"We may bring forth the anger of the Grandmother from the cavern," another man said. "She may purify Ti-Ra'-Wa so it will be as it once was."

The warriors shuddered involuntarily.

"Why did the Grandmother not come forth when the outlanders first entered the valley?" Touch-the-Sky asked. "If I have broken her laws, why has she not expressed her anger?"

"We have not entered the Cavern of Creation," Little Mountain answered. "Yet."

Touch-the-Sky started to speak, gazed at the stubborn, uneasy faces and realized the futility of further argument. He raised his rifle to waist level, but he didn't point it at anyone.

"I am war chief here," he snapped. "You all agreed to it. I have not suffered and bled for all of you to be balked at last by groundless fears!"

He faced them, his eyes bright, and the warriors shuffled away, cowed by the force of his fanaticism. "We have gone too far to turn back," he said tightly. "We will follow through on our path. Even if it leads to the Grandmother Herself."

Chapter Twenty-Eight

The pony galloped across the grasslands toward the forest city. Ryan kept a close watch for Blood-sniffer, who had slipped on ahead, scouting for guard outposts or patrols. So far the wolf had brought them safely to within a mile of the city.

Blood-sniffer appeared a hundred yards ahead, like a wisp of gray smoke blown on the wind. The wolf tilted its snout skyward and snapped at the air, signaling the way was clear.

The sun had sunk behind the highest peaks by the time Ryan reached the outer perimeter of the city. He dismounted, leaving the pony to graze in a stand of cottonwood trees. He wasn't concerned about the animal wandering away, since if he couldn't steal mounts for his friends, one horse wouldn't do him much good, anyway.

Blood-sniffer joined him and they crept forward, threading their way through the high grass, taking advantage of every fold, rise and depression of the ground. Even so, they were almost discovered by a warrior on horseback, trotting less than an arm's length away.

As man and wolf slipped into the shelter of the first line of massive tree trunks, the sun disappeared completely. As silent as shadows, they followed the winding forest ways.

The long avenues were deserted and silent. Only

dust and dry leaves blew lonely on the wind. Ryan detected the acrid odor of cordite, as did Blood-sniffer, his muzzle wrinkling.

The crystal disks glistened as cold as ice sculptures under the spreading boughs, and where the open doorways fronted the footpaths, they gaped empty and lightless. Lamplight flared in only a few of the trees, but there was no sound of talking or laughter. Ryan had been in such an atmosphere before; the city was preparing for war.

Ryan and Blood-sniffer made their way to a small bark lodge, which was identical to the image Krysty had transmitted to him. Also, as she had mentally communicated, there was only one sentry, a young man some distance away. He leaned on his lance, head bowed, either half-asleep, bored or depressed.

Blood-sniffer dropped into a crouch, belly almost on the ground, but Ryan touched him and shook his head. He had no doubt the wolf could take down the man, but he doubted Blood-sniffer could take him before he raised an outcry.

Ryan drew his panga and stepped out of the shadow of an overhanging branch, walking quietly, heel to toe. He intended to clamp a hand over the sentry's mouth and slide the eighteen-inch blade of tooled steel between his third and fourth ribs. It was an act he had performed many times in the past, and he could have done it with patches over both eyes.

When he was within six feet of the man, he realized the sentry wasn't a man at all, but a boy, a stripling maybe fourteen years old, only a few years older than Dean.

The boy shifted, uttering a sigh of ennui. Ryan swiftly reversed his grip on the knife and snapped the heavy pommel across the base of the boy's skull, where it joined with the neck. The thud of impact was muffled, and consciousness fled his dark eyes with the suddenness of a candle being extinguished.

Ryan caught the body and lance before they hit the ground. Blood-sniffer padded up, sniffed briefly at the boy and yawned.

Gathering a fistful of deerskin tunic in one hand and holding the lance in the other, Ryan dragged both toward the lodge.

The blow to the nerve center at the base of his skull was probably good for ten minutes of uninterrupted unconsciousness. By the time the boy revived, he would be trussed up and gagged.

Pushing aside the pelt hanging over the doorway with the lance, Ryan hissed, "It's me," before entering. He didn't want to be clubbed senseless by his friends.

Though everyone was happy to see him alive and apparently whole, there was no time for a reunion. J.B. bit back a startled curse when Blood-sniffer entered.

"It's that double-crossing wolf!" he said in an angry whisper. "What's it doing here?"

"Helping us," Ryan answered, laying the sentry out on the ground.

Krysty knelt over the boy. "He's alive," she said in a mildly surprised tone.

Ryan grunted. "Tie him up and gag him."

Krysty and Mildred attended to that, tearing strips from the boy's breechclout to fashion a gag. Mildred quickly knotted the thongs that had previously bound the friends and hog-tied the young man, ankles to wrists.

J.B. and Doc eyed Blood-sniffer distrustfully and not a little fearfully.

"Joe's got our blasters," the Armorer said, not removing his gaze from the wolf. "He's been trying to train his warriors how to use them."

"I know," Ryan replied.

After the sentry was tightly bound and gagged, the six people slipped from the lodge. Blood-sniffer followed the odor of gun oil and cordite through the dark avenues, and they followed at his heels.

The wolf went to the monstrous tree that had served as their guest quarters. While the humans waited in the underbrush, the animal circled the great trunk, casting for a scent of guards. After one circuit Blood-sniffer paused before the archway, looking toward them.

They joined the beast there and crept inside, the wolf pausing every few feet to sniff the air. The corridor was empty.

They came to a small room and found Joe and Little Mountain. They had a jug of liquid before them, and their faces in the flaring lamplight weren't the faces of happy men. Laid neatly on a low table against the far wall were all of their weapons, including Jak's knives, Doc's swordstick, and the rucksack containing ammunition. Joe's rifle rested at the edge of the table, within easy reach.

Blood-sniffer entered first, and when they saw him, they sprang up, grabbing for blasters. Ryan stepped in quickly, the SIG-Sauer leveled. Both men stopped, frozen in midmotion.

Joe let out a long, harsh breath. "Ochinee. I'm gratified you still live, but not gratified you sold us out to the Wolf Soldiers."

Little Mountain looked from Ryan to the wolf with fear-widened eyes.

As his friends pushed around him into the room to

recover their weapons, Ryan said coldly, "'It's no sin to betray a betrayer,' as Sisoka said."

Joe shrugged, his hard, ruddy face tight. "I didn't betray you."

"You kept us in the dark about what this conflict is really about," Ryan said. "You'll bring death to this valley because of some dream, some theory you cooked up, based on nothing but bitterness and ego."

"You've been seduced by Sisoka."

Ryan caught Krysty's swift sideways glance toward him. "Joe, you're going with us to Sisoka."

His obsidian eyes narrowed. "Pizi will kill me."

"Probably." Ryan showed his teeth in a humorless, smile. "I don't know if you deserve it or not. But I do know you're the man who brought war to this valley, and you brought us here to help you wage it."

"You came here for gold," Joe replied. "If you turn on me now, you'll lose it all."

"Don't be so sure all white men are as greedy as history makes us out to be. Now, both of you, let's go."

Joe didn't move. "Go where?"

"To get horses. When we go out, keep it looking natural and friendly, just a friendly stroll with the *wasicun kagas*. No talking unless I ask you a question. You fuck with me, I'll chill both of you where you stand."

Joe exchanged a quick look with Little Mountain, nodded brusquely, then moved toward the door. All of them filed out into the corridor and then into the brooding, quiet night.

"Who seduced you?" Krysty asked as they walked around the tree.

Ryan sighed. "Later."

They reached the compound, which was unguarded, though Blood-sniffer's ears were pricked up and he stared around as if sensing something that couldn't be seen. The horses snorted and shifted when the wolf scent reached their nostrils.

While Joe and Little Mountain were held at blasterpoint, Krysty, J.B., Doc and Mildred selected the mounts from the others and put pad saddles on their backs. Krysty picked out a sturdy pony for Ryan.

Mildred handed Joe the lead rope of his pinto. As he checked out the braided bridle on the horse, he said, "You're making a mistake, Ochinee."

"Mebbe," Ryan replied. "Mebbe I'm trying to correct one."

Sighing, Joe reached out to pat his pony's velvety muzzle. Abruptly Blood-sniffer stiffened, hackles rising, a growl rumbling from his throat. Ryan made a move toward Joe, raising the SIG-Sauer to club the man down.

Stridently Joe yelled, *"Kicizapi!"*

The pony instantly screamed, rearing on his hind legs, hooves and forelegs lashing out. Ryan avoided a fractured skull by the thickness of a fingernail. As it was, a hoof dealt him a glancing blow on the side of the head, staggering him. Joe and Little Mountain moved so fast that individual motions couldn't be distinguished. They dived toward the horses, shouting shrilly, and the animals neighed and milled in a panic, jostling J.B. and Doc off their feet. Voices yelled from the darkness beyond the compound, and Joe and Little Mountain shouted back.

"Fireblast!" Ryan snarled, grabbing the bridle of the pony Krysty had chosen for him. He vaulted onto its back, squeezing off three shots into the night. The reports sounded obscenely loud, but he wasn't aiming at anything. He hoped the blasterfire would keep the warriors at bay long enough for his friends to get mounted.

With Jak's help, Doc managed to get astride Judas Redux, and when everyone was more or less mounted up, Ryan kicked his horse into a gallop. Blood-sniffer raced beside him.

They drummed up the avenue and veered toward the open plains. Glancing back once, Ryan saw warriors darting for ponies, trying to calm them enough so they could be saddled and ridden.

All six people let their horses run flat out across the grassland for five miles. Only when the black woods rose before them did they slow the horses to a canter.

Blood-sniffer had dropped back due to his injured leg, and Ryan waited until the wolf had trotted up, sides heaving, tongue hanging out with exertion.

Mildred twisted in her saddle. "I don't think they chased us."

"There must be a reason," J.B. said grimly.

Blood-sniffer uttered a low bark. He was sniffing the wind, then he whined, lifted his head and voiced a loud howl. A few moments later the howl was answered from deep in the woods.

"He's warning his pack of something," Ryan muttered. He glanced behind him but saw nothing but the nighted plains. The wolf trotted toward the forest. They followed him, the wolf loping ahead. All through the dark forest they heard howls, an alarm spreading up the ridge, across the river and to the encampment. Krysty's hair was coiled. She felt the fear rising on the wind. Ryan told his friends what transpired at the encampment, and of Pizi's and Sisoka's beliefs regarding the Cavern of Creation.

"So your vision of the wolf as your animal totem came true," Doc commented.

"Especially," Krysty said, "if what Joe said about a seduction has any foundation."

"It doesn't," Ryan muttered.

When they struggled up the hill to the crest, they found Pizi and Sisoka waiting for them. Before Ryan could make introductions, Sisoka said, "It has begun."

The wind brought the first, faint taint of smoke. Looking back in the direction they had come, they saw pinpoints of flame dancing at the far edge of the dark forest.

"The doom you helped bring here is sweeping toward us, outlander," Pizi said somberly.

Ryan didn't know what to say. He simply stared at Pizi and Sisoka. She waved a hand toward the distant crags and peaks.

"You are free to leave Ti-Ra'-Wa," she said. "All of you. The packs guarding the pass are being recalled, so none will molest you."

J.B. gave his pony's reins a jerk. "Let's get moving before that crazy Joe sets the whole valley on fire."

"I'm staying," Ryan said. "I'll try to undo what we helped do here."

He gazed at his friends. "This is my decision alone. The rest of you can get to the pass, and I'll join you when I can."

"You can't make that decision only for yourself, Ryan!" Krysty said angrily. "Anything and everything that any one of us chooses to do affects the others. You know that. We came here together and we'll leave together or not at all."

Everyone murmured in agreement, though J.B. and Doc sounded a little unsure and uneasy.

"Long as we don't have to fight wolves," J.B. said softly.

"They'll fight with us," Ryan told him.

He looked toward Sisoka. "Won't they?"

Her eyes searched his face, seeming to search his soul. "Yes, Ryan Cawdor. They will be your allies. Your help can be valuable in this hour."

Blood-sniffer voiced a staccato series of yelping barks and then a few howls, almost like a vocal Morse code.

"He tells the pack leaders that the outlanders fight with the Wolf Soldiers," Pizi said. "They will pass it along to those beyond hearing range."

Ryan looked again at the forest. He could see tendrils of smoke curling into the sky and dancing orange flames. "That fire will be here in a few hours, and Touch-the-Sky and his warriors will come after it."

Sisoka nodded. "We hope to stop it. While you were gone, our people have labored to cut a firebreak on this side of the river."

"If those dry woods get going," J.B. said, "no firebreak will stop it. It'll jump it, mebbe even jump the river. You've got to start a backfire."

"Use fire as a defense against fire?" Pizi looked worried and surprised. "Our people will not like it."

"Either that or the blaze will burn your encampment to the ground by midnight," Ryan warned.

Sisoka nodded and said, "I will give the order."

They started down the ridge toward the river, leading their horses. Sisoka and Pizi walked ahead of them.

"Joe said he could put only about three hundred warriors into the field," Ryan said to J.B. "What's our ammo situation?"

"I checked on the way through the woods," J.B. replied. "All of us, except your pistol and my Uzi, average about twenty shots per blaster. Joe and his idiots burned up a lot of rounds today."

"Doesn't sound like we can afford to fire warning shots," Mildred put in.

Pizi overheard the exchange and glanced at them anxiously. "But your experience of war will be invaluable to us. We know little of war in Ti-Ra'-Wa. We Wolf Soldiers have not had to fight in over a century, mebbe longer."

"I think—I fear—you may make up for a hundred years of lost bloodshed before this night is over," Doc said bleakly.

Chapter Twenty-Nine

The whole sky over the ridge was a wall of black smoke laced with livid, bloodred flame. The flames were eating through the forest and scorching their way up the hill. Smoke rolled densely, blotting out the stars. The air was thick with it. Panicked animals, like running shadows, streamed over the ridge.

Pizi, Ryan, J.B. and Krysty stood at the firebreak the people of the encampment had been digging for hours. It was a ragged, hundred-foot lane, cut only a few yards from the riverbank.

Krysty groaned. "That'll never stop a forest fire."

"We've got to get a backfire going," J.B. said. "Stop it before it jumps the river."

Pizi reluctantly gave the order. The Wolf Soldiers and the people of the encampment didn't like it. A few of them argued, and Pizi shouted at them in furious Lakota.

With Pizi translating, Ryan and J.B. supervised the task of starting the backfire. Their torches kindled the dry brush all along the ridge facing the fire lane. Undergrowth, cedar and fir blazed up, and the edge of the lane became a new wall of flame moving up the hill toward the oncoming wall of fire.

The wind was against them. Burning twigs and leaves whirled across the lane to land and ignite new fires at the edge of the riverbank. Half-stifled by smoke, sweating and coughing, Ryan, Krysty and J.B.

stamped and beat out each new spark. The wind was like a living, malignant demon, taking delight in hurling fresh fire across the gap.

Yet through smoke-stung, watering eyes, they saw that the backfire was steadily if slowly creeping up the ridge to scorch a belt across which the giant firestorm couldn't leap.

Coughing, sounding half-strangled, Krysty said, "Let's get across the river, see how Mildred and the others are doing."

They made their way through the smoky haze toward the massive log bridge. As they were crossing, Pizi in the lead, they heard a distant crackle. At first they all assumed it was from the flames. But Pizi grunted, caught at his midsection and stumbled and slid toward the edge. Krysty managed to grab his arm and prevent him from pitching into the river. Then she saw the streaks of crimson on his rib cage.

She wrestled the man down to the smooth surface of the log, shouting, "Pizi's been shot! Somebody's shooting at us!"

Ryan and J.B. fell facedown, and they felt the wood beneath their bodies shudder beneath multiple impacts. Looking upriver, Ryan saw the first of a score of bark-and-hide canoes, loaded with warriors, emerging from the pall of smoke. In the prow of one of the lead canoes was Joe, his automatic rifle at his shoulder.

Ryan clenched his teeth so hard they squeaked and grated. He should have realized that Joe's only possible strategy was to use the river as a safe highway behind and past the conflagration he had set. He had probably seen them setting the backfire and swung through the screen of smoke while they were occupied.

Ryan unholstered his blaster and began to squeeze off shot after shot, all the while yelling at Krysty to get herself and Pizi to safety. J.B.'s Uzi stuttered, but the range was too long for handblasters to be very accurate.

Still, miniature waterspouts spumed in front of the canoes, and the flotilla was rowed toward the bank.

Krysty had managed to edge the wounded Pizi off the bridge and onto solid ground. She tried to support him as they ran toward the encampment.

"Get the Wolf Soldiers!" Ryan shouted at her back.

J.B. and Ryan kept up a sporadic fire, hoping to keep Joe and his warriors from leaving the sheltering foliage at the edge of the river. From the direction of the Wolf Soldier village came a multitude of howls, roars and screeches.

Beasts and men clad in beast skins ran across the open ground, screaming war cries, swinging knives, tomahawks and holding crossbows. Ryan and J.B. were forced to stop shooting as the Wolf Soldiers and the packs crashed through the brush and trees at the edge of the red-lit river. They swept into battle, and not even the rapid-fire barking of Joe's automatic rifle stopped them.

The Wolf Soldiers ran up and down the riverbank, their lances stabbing, their arrows flying, fangs tearing, claws flaying. They fought breast to breast with their brothers from the forest city. Great, shaggy bodies leaped and rolled, and slashed and clawed. Bodies fell on the banks or splashed into the shallows. The warriors fought over them, treading faces with their feet, slipping on blood and viscera.

Ryan and J.B., watching from the bridge, were held in a horrid fascination. Lit by the leaping, gouting flames from the forest and the backfire, the scene took on an unreal, deranged, almost hallucinatory quality, like something out of jolt-inspired dementia.

A crackle of autofire broke the stunned spell, and they left the bridge, running toward the encampment. Halfway there they met Jak, Doc and Mildred. Krysty and Sisoka were kneeling beside the fallen Pizi. His breathing was labored, rattling, and a crimson froth spilled out of his mouth.

"Got him through the lungs," Mildred said grimly.

"Get me up," Pizi husked.

Sisoka patted the man's cheek. "No, Uncle. We'll take you to your tepee."

"No," he rasped. "Let me make one last appeal to our people, to stop this war before all of Ti-Ra'-Wa is destroyed, before it succumbs completely to the curse of the outer world."

Summoning all the strength he had left in his bullet-shattered body, Pizi, with Mildred's help, stumbled and staggered to his feet. He began a shambling walk toward the screaming chaos at the riverbank. Sisoka made a motion to go with him, but Ryan restrained her.

"It won't do any good," he said, holding her tightly by the upper arm. "It's gone too far for a peace-making speech to make a difference."

"Guess he has to try," Jak said.

Pizi managed to shuffle to within a few hundred feet of the boiling mass of men and animals. He stood outlined in the glow of the firelight on the opposite bank, his arms raised as his voice rolled out onto the river. He spoke in Lakota, so Sisoka had to translate for them.

"Men of Ti-Ra'-Wa!" he bellowed. "Will you destroy our ancient land in blood and fire? Wrath of the

First People, wrath of Ah-badt-dadt-deah, will fall upon you if you follow this road farther.''

An instant of comparative quiet followed this pronouncement. The combatants didn't fall completely silent, but some of the blood-mad screams decreased in intensity.

The burst of autofire that came from the brush on the river's edge was short and contemptuous. Pizi folded in the middle, clutching at his belly. He sat down, then slowly stretched out on the ground, trying to arrange his feet and hands in positions of grave dignity before he died.

A mad cry, a cry of fury that exploded from human and animal throats, rose into the smoke-choked air.

Sisoka buried her face in her hands and turned, pressing against Ryan. Krysty caught his eye, raised an eyebrow, but said nothing.

A sudden, bright flare caught his eye and he turned toward the river. The land between the bank and the encampment was ablaze. The backfire had jumped both the firebreak and the river. Ryan realized that Joe had mounted his attack in order to draw the Wolf Soldiers away from their fight against the firestorm, and the strategy had worked. The flames had overrun their line of defense and were now moving on the wings of the wind toward the encampment.

"Shit," J.B. groaned. "The fire will be into the camp in an hour. We've got to retreat."

Retreat was a lesson the Wolf Soldiers had never learned or never knew was an option. Though they had recovered from the stunning shock of their chieftain's murder, they were slowly being pushed back.

It was the death fight of warriors who courted death in order to deal death, blind, panting and merciless. Back and forth the battle rolled, blades sinking into chests, blood spurting, feet churning the ground into crimson sludge. The Gewehr started hammering from the press of bodies, and more Wolf Soldiers crashed to the ground.

Joe's warriors were outnumbered, but the effect of his automatic rifle was devastating. Ryan saw him moving through the whirling, eddying mass of men and animals, shooting and clubbing. Again and again a Wolf Soldier who heaved a tomahawk or lance at him found a bullet in his head or chest before he could strike. Arrows missed Joe as he moved like a lithe, phantom panther.

Then the screaming wave of combat surged and spilled away from the riverbank and spread out across the smoky, flaming ground.

Ryan, Sisoka, Krysty, J.B., Mildred, Doc and Jak ran toward the nearest ring of tepees. Great scorching winds whipped and hissed behind them, flinging blinding smoke into their path. The steady crackling of the sky-high towers of flame atop the hill had grown to a steady roar. Sparks and embers whirled in corkscrew patterns through the air.

The warriors left to guard the encampment shouted excited questions at Sisoka when they caught sight of her. She answered them in Lakota, and they gave a great cry of woe.

"You must get everyone out of the camp," Ryan said to her. "The fire will be here in an hour, Touch-the-Sky in half that."

She repeated what Ryan had said, and the response was angry mutterings and shouts. She responded firmly and pointed to the sky over the ridge. Already the flickering, crimson glare was casting red highlights on the tepees.

"Tell them they can fight Touch-the-Sky later,"

Ryan instructed. "When the ashes cool, they and the
acks can come down from the hills and attack
gain."

Sisoka spoke briefly but determinedly for less than
minute. Then the Wolf Soldiers turned and went
hrough the camp, rousing human and animal alike.
Mothers with their children—human and wolf—
moved out of the encampment in an organized exo-
dus. Watching them, Ryan felt their fear, anger and
confusion.

"Joe won't wait for the fire to burn down the en-
ampment before he makes his move for the cavern,"
e said to his friends. "That's where we'll stop him."

Sisoka looked at him with wide, shocked eyes.
"You cannot enter the cavern!"

"Mebbe not. But Touch-the-Sky thinks he can.
We'll lay in wait for him outside of it."

Sisoka nodded in resignation. "Come."

The encampment was almost deserted now. The
ast stragglers were disappearing northward across the
grasslands. Ash fell like a dingy snow, and the wind
vas so hot they felt its breath burning their skin. Be-
ind them the flames leaped triumphant, flaring in
great, twisting tongues from the treetops, roaring and
dancing.

They reached the crude fence where they had cor-
aled their horses and sprang onto their backs, Sisoka
iding double with Ryan. The horses coughed and
norted from the drifting smoke and whinnied when-
ver a flying spark alighted on them.

Pushing their horses into a gallop, they raced up
he slope toward the tumble of huge boulders at the
barren base of the mountain ramparts. Between the
ock tumble they saw the throbbing, pulsing light.

After they reined in their horses at the foot of a

house-sized boulder, Ryan helped Sisoka down. He remained astride the pony while the others dismounted.

"Everybody find some cover," he said.

"What's your plan?" Krysty demanded.

"I'll stay on the hoof," he replied. "Fight a harassing action. That's something he might not expect."

"I expect Joe is expecting everything," Doc retorted.

Ryan handed the Steyr to Mildred. "I doubt he's expecting to be picked off by sniper fire."

The woman's face was an expressionless mask, smeared by gray ash. "I don't feel good about doing that, Ryan."

"Think I do? Give me an alternative." He spoke more harshly than he intended.

When there was no answer, Ryan turned his mount and rode among the immense pillars of stone. He was too tense to feel awed by the cyclopean rock formations. The gray- and dun-colored columns and outcroppings were deeply scored and eroded by aeons of exposure to the elements. They loomed bleakly above him like cold, uncaring colossi, too far gone in old age to pay the tiny humans scrambling at their feet any heed.

He picked a smear of shadow cast by an upthrusting finger of granite to lie in wait for whoever came up the slope. He didn't have to wait long.

Seeming to materialize out of the pall of smoke came several bloodstained men. They were heavily armed with lances and crossbows. There were only five of them and they scanned the foot of the slope before moving forward, in close single file, treading as lightly as panthers. One bent down to stare at the ground. They saw the trail of the horses and they halted instantly, their black eyes questing the shadow-spotted outcroppings.

They saw nothing and moved again, more rapidly now. Ryan kept a tight rein on his pony, waiting for Joe to appear. He doubted the man had been chilled or wounded too severely to walk. If either had happened, his warriors would have lost heart and retreated. More than likely, Joe had sent this small scouting party ahead as a feint, to draw a reaction.

Ryan couldn't allow the warriors to reach the rock formation. Knowing he was showing his hand, allowing Joe to see his ace, he heeled his pony from the shadows and rode for the line of warriors.

He leaned over the animal's neck, the SIG-Sauer spitting bullets. As one, the men wheeled toward him. A warrior catapulted backward, trailing a streamer of blood from high in his chest. Another clapped a hand to his leg and fell twisting to the shale-covered ground.

A third warrior held his position and launched his lance in a smooth, beautiful arc. Ryan pulled on the reins, turning the pony aside. The lance point missed his mount's right flank by a fraction of an inch, but the animal's hooves struck loose rock, which turned beneath them.

The pony stumbled and slid out from under Ryan, slamming into and crushing the warrior who had thrown the lance. The one-eyed man hit the ground rolling, keeping his body turning over and over to minimize injury. He stopped, slamming heavily into a boulder the size of a wagon wheel, and his blaster was jarred from his fingers.

Groggily Ryan flung himself onto his side to see a warrior racing toward him, his painted face a ferocious grimace. He raised a long-handled ax, then his head burst apart in three pieces.

Carried by his momentum, he continued to run for several paces before his bullet-blasted brain stopped working and he fell, draping himself over the boulder. Only then did Ryan hear the faint echo of the Steyr's cracking report.

Though he had no idea where she was, Ryan got to his feet and waved toward the massive rock formations as a thanks and a signal he was all right. He reached for his SIG-Sauer, but the remaining warrior came savagely in to the attack. He swung a tomahawk at Ryan's chest even as the larger man swiftly backpedaled, whipping the panga from its sheath.

The warrior swung again with the ax, an overhead blow meant to split his enemy's skull. The long knife checked the downward sweep and struck the weapon aside. Ryan ripped upward with the blade into the man's belly.

An awful howl burst from the warrior's lips as he crumpled, thrashing, disemboweled. The cry of baffled agony was answered by a wild chorus of yells from the smoke. Some twenty warriors burst through the gray fog, shrieking like the demons they feared.

As they saw Ryan, their screams rose to a bloodfreezing crescendo and they increased their speed, loosing arrows as they came. Ryan snatched up his blaster and started to run, shafts showering and breaking on the rock around him.

Over the warbling war cries, he heard the crack of the Gewehr, and dirt exploded in a foot-high fountain near his right leg. Rock fragments stung him, but he continued to race toward the towering rocks and crags.

Chapter Thirty

By the time Krysty had moved to a vantage point atop a flat, house-sized boulder, she had a clear view of Ryan being pursued up the slope. Steadying the Smith & Wesson with both hands, she chose the closest warriors and fired a full cylinder into the horde massed behind him.

Several bodies convulsed, then fell. The warriors hesitated, slowing, and Ryan sprinted between a pair of outcroppings and out of her range of vision. Within a moment she was under attack herself by a dozen warriors who had fixed her position by her blaster's muzzle-flash.

Arrows rained around her, clattering and rattling against rock. She leaped desperately to a crag ten feet below.

Hitting the stone, rolling, jumping up and running, she saw Mildred and J.B. on a ledge above her. They gestured frantically for her to climb and join them. She began to climb, tearing the skin from her fingers as she forced them into rough-edged handholds.

She hadn't quite reached the ledge when some of the painted warriors raced around the base of the boulder she had leaped from. Arrows whistled up at her, the steel points cracking against rock, and one bounced off the metal band encircling the heel of her right boot.

The stuttering hammer of the Uzi sounded from

above, and from below she heard the whines of ricochets and the screams of wounded or dying men.

Mildred reached down her arms and hauled her over the rim of the ledge. She lay glaring down at the warriors, her breasts heaving as she drank in the air in great, shuddering gasps.

Only a few more arrows whipped up toward the ledge; the warriors knew their enemies could kill them from above if they exposed themselves. They turned and ran back through the labyrinth of stone.

After regaining her wind, Krysty pushed herself to a sitting position, opened her blaster's cylinder and emptied the spent cartridge casings. She put them in a pouch on her belt, then thumbed in fresh rounds.

"Ryan?" she asked.

J.B., on his belly, scanned the stony maze below. "Haven't seen him since he was chased back up here."

"Jak and Doc? The girl?"

"Sisoka's with them. Don't know where they are. Haven't heard their blasters so far."

Krysty glanced at Mildred. "And Joe?"

The woman cradled the Steyr in her arms and shook her head. "Haven't been able to get a clear shot at him. If it's not the smoke ruining my shot, he has his men around him. He must suspect we'd try to take him out from a distance."

They heard the distant boom of Doc's Le Mat, then the deep cracking of Jak's Colt Python.

"We've got to hook back up," J.B. said grimly. "Joe knows this layout, even if his warriors don't. We got them outgunned, but they got the advantage of familiar turf."

Below, the outer ring of the hide-and-wood structures erupted into flame, blazing like huge torches.

'urning slightly, Krysty tried to focus on the waver-
ng luminescence from the mouth of the cavern.

"Only place we can go is the cave," she stated.
'If we can get inside there before Joe does, we'll be
•n more or less even terms. He's never been there,
•ither."

J.B. and Mildred considered Krysty's words for a
noment. A war whoop echoed, then came the familiar
•lapping sound made by Ryan's SIG-Sauer.

"Let's do it," J.B. said, moving away from the lip
•f the ledge.

Krysty descended first, hand over hand, while J.B.
ind Mildred covered her from above. Mildred
dropped the Steyr into her waiting arms, then climbed
down, followed by J.B., who tossed her the M-4000
•cattergun before clambering from the ledge.

The three friends wended their way through the
•hadows, creeping among the looming masses of
•tone, keeping their eyes on the glow from the cave
•pening. They moved into a fissure splitting a mon-
•trous rock, so narrow they walked in single file. Pon-
derous chunks of half-dislodged granite hung over
•hem. They made their way with extreme care, knowing how easy it was to start a slide by accidently
kicking a keystone.

A ghostly silence settled over the tumbles, crevices
and boulders, the only sounds the clinks of stone beneath their feet and the ever-present, rising and falling
roar of the firestorm consuming the Wolf Soldier encampment.

They reached the end of the fissure but had walked
only a few feet when the scuff and scutter of stealthy
footfalls caught Krysty's ears. She raised her handblaster, sinking to one knee in a wedge of shadow.
Behind her, J.B. and Mildred melted into the dark-

ness. By the dim light provided by the distant flames and the shimmering glow from the cave mouth, they saw four figures shuffle out of the darkness.

The figures halted, as if sensing their presence. For a long beat of time, nothing happened, no movement, no sound. Then Ryan's low voice said, "The silver toes of your boots are a giveaway, lover."

The surge of relief washing through Krysty left her momentarily weak. She rose to her feet and ran joyfully into his arms.

Doc, Jak and Sisoka were with him. Ryan quickly explained how he had been drawn to them by the sound of his friends' blasterfire.

"Joe and warriors crawl all over place," Jak said. "Looking for us. Trapped."

"It's me he really wants," Sisoka said softly. "Perhaps I can convince him to let all of you go."

"And take the location of this magic valley back to the world?" Doc asked. "Not very likely, child."

"Our only escape route is the cave," Ryan said.

"My strategy exactly," Krysty agreed.

Sisoka heaved a deep, forlorn sigh. "I have no choice. Even if I surrendered to Touch-the-Sky, he would still defile the sacred place."

"Then let's move on it," J.B. said impatiently. "Not stand around talking about it."

They moved deeper into the twisting labyrinth, squeezing through narrow places and clambering over heaps of shale, scrambling for footholds on chunks of granite and sandstone.

Sidling around the bulging base of a boulder, they faced the cavern entrance. It was smaller than Ryan had estimated, a cleft wider at the bottom that the top, seemingly punched into the mountain wall. A narrow stair of handholds had been niched into the rock, extending upward to a shelflike threshold ten feet above their heads.

The wavery glow from inside the cleft was a bluish fog, more like a phosphorescent mist than an actual light.

Everyone stopped to stare for a long moment, then Sisoka moved forward. The others followed, scalps tingling at the prospect of entering the cave.

A dark shape bounded from a patch of gloom between the rock, and as one, blaster barrels snapped up and fingers crooked tight around triggers.

Blood-sniffer nosed Sisoka's hand, then glanced at Ryan and showed his fangs and red tongue in a grin. They all released their suddenly pent-up breaths in gusty sighs.

"Damn wolf again," J.B. growled. "Hoped it'd been chilled."

Ryan eyed Blood-sniffer and saw the beast had only narrowly avoided that fate. A bleeding gash stretched along its right side, and a red-rimmed notch had been chopped into the base of its tail, probably with an ax. Still, the wolf's condition and spirit seemed sound.

A thunderclap came from the rocky maze on the far side of the entrance, and a bullet splashed cold air on Ryan's right cheek. As his blaster came up, he heard the rattle of stones, a breathless exchange of Lakota and running footfalls from the murk.

Ryan and Jak opened up with their blasters, providing covering fire for the others as they scrambled up the stairs chiseled into the rock. Surprisingly J.B. helped Blood-sniffer climb the niches by pushing him upward with a shoulder against his rump.

Rock chips scattered under the impact of the Gewehr's subsonic rounds. Ryan scaled the steps as quickly as he could. He heard a *whup* of displaced air over his head, followed by the whine of a ricochet. Pulverized stone sprinkled him.

When he reached the shelf, he lay flat and fired the SIG-Sauer in the direction of the autofire. Jak bounded up the niches, not using his hands, his finger working the trigger of his Colt Python.

He stumbled slightly at the top, put a hand over his right hip, brought it away and stared with rueful eyes at the blood glistening on his white palm.

"Shit," he muttered, and staggered, putting out a hand to catch himself.

Ryan slid an arm under his shoulders and half carried, half dragged Jak past the threshold of the cleft. The thundering hammer of the automatic rifle ceased.

Everyone was waiting for them around a bend in a narrow of the corridor of stone. While Ryan reloaded, Krysty and Doc watched the cave entrance. Mildred gave Jak a quick examination, forcing him to drop his pants. Sisoka was listening to the words from outside that floated in.

"Touch-the-Sky is having difficulty convincing his warriors to follow him into the cave," she said. "They're arguing."

Krysty looked tense and impatiently shook her head. "We need to get on the move before the argument is resolved."

Mildred told Jak he could pull up his pants and she said, "Not too bad. The bullet exited his hip above his right buttock. It's deep, sheared through some muscle and might have cracked the bone."

Ryan looked at him. "Can you walk?"

Eyes a bit glazed from trying to control the pain, Jak only nodded, as he shoved fresh rounds into the Colt Python's cylinder.

They moved out, Sisoka in the lead, striding quickly along the stone passageway, peering through the dim, misty blue light. The corridor widened and the ceiling grew in height. Irregular stalactites stretched from above, and they wended their way around stalagmites thrusting up from the floor. Ryan kept listening for the approach of Joe and his warriors.

The light was confusing; it was just bright enough for them to see a few feet in front of them, but too dim to make out shapes clearly. Suddenly Sisoka halted, lifting a hand. They stopped so quickly that they trod on one another's heels.

Dropping to all fours, Sisoka crept forward, her hand groping through the bluish mist. Ryan and Doc stepped forward and knelt beside her. Ryan experienced a shuddery sensation of imminent peril. He stretched out his left hand and found that the tunnel floor dropped straight down into the misty light. Doc picked up a pebble and flipped it over the edge. He counted aloud. When he reached "six," they heard it strike, far below. He backed away, murmuring, "No, thank you, sir, indeed."

"A dead end," Ryan said grimly. "We'll have to make our stand here."

As Doc backed away, something brushed the top of his head, hanging from above. "Look at this."

It was a length of frayed rope, and they craned their necks to look up to see what it was anchored to. The end of the rope was lost in shadows.

Ryan reached up and tugged gingerly on the length of hemp. Nothing happened, so he pulled harder. His effort was rewarded by a loud creaking sound. He pulled hand over hand, and a long, flat slab descended from the rocky ceiling.

The slab was made of rough-hewn, splintering timber and lashed together with rope. It was a bridge, affixed to the tunnel roof by a pulley system of some kind. Creaking, the bridge lowered until its outermost edge rested on the tunnel's lip, spanning the chasm.

"Who wants to take the first step?" Ryan asked.

Before anyone could reply, Sisoka stepped cautiously on the bridge. Though the timbers squeaked, it appeared secure and solid enough. She walked quickly across and was swallowed up by the mist. She called to them that everything was fine. Unhesitatingly, Blood-sniffer trotted across.

One at a time, as if they were walking on eggshells, everyone softfooted across the bridge. Ryan went last, guarding their rear. When the others had safely crossed, he followed. He was the heaviest of his companions, and the timbers didn't simply squeak beneath his weight; they groaned and a couple of them trembled. He tiptoed the remaining yards to the far side of the chasm.

When he joined his friends, J.B. said, "No rope on this side. We can't raise the bridge to keep Joe from crossing."

"He has no choice if he wants us," Ryan replied. "We can just stay here and pick him and his warriors off as they come across."

"No!" Sisoka blurted. "You cannot kill in the heart of the Grandmother, not in the Cavern of Creation."

"If we don't," Ryan said, "we'll all die."

"No," she repeated stubbornly. "Find another way."

"There's another way," Mildred said. "Jak, since you're the lightweight among us, you can ease out on the bridge and cut the ropes supporting the timbers. It won't be able to support another crossing."

"That tactic will leave us stranded here," Doc objected, "perhaps to wander the subterranean rings of Hades for all eternity, like Virgil."

Ryan turned to Jak. "Do it."

Jak nodded and crept back out across the bridge. His motions were a little stiff due to his wound, but they heard the faint snicking of razor steel cutting into hemp and the squeak of timbers. After a moment he returned, backing up on hands and knees.

"Done," he whispered. "Heard voices from entrance."

The seven people and the wolf walked quietly away from the chasm. After a few minutes they heard a far-off noise, a distant rumble as if a great-wheeled machine were approaching. Then there was a crash and splintering of wood, a noise that swiftly faded except for a brief echo. A faint scream trailed behind the splitting roar.

Chapter Thirty-One

Their path took them along the edge of a jagged rock wall on their right, but on their left was an unplumbed darkness dropping to inconceivable depths.

J.B. peered into the abyss, muttering, "Kind of makes you want to spit, doesn't it?" Then he stiffened. "I can see some kind of light down there."

Ryan and others moved cautiously to the edge and gazed into the dark void. A faint greenish glow filtered from far beneath, flickering in a rapid, almost hypnotic rhythm.

"That must be the source of the light," Mildred said.

"Light in here is blue," Jak argued. "That green."

She shrugged. "See that strobing pattern? Any light source pulsing at a high speed is red-shifted on the electromagnetic spectrum. Blue becomes green, yellow becomes orange, green becomes yellow."

J.B. looked at her blankly. "So?"

"So nothing," she said impatiently. "Let's go."

The path wound downward, slanting steeply. The throbbing green glow shone far in the distance. The tunnel debouched to the right, shrinking to only a dozen feet wide. Almost immediately it opened up again into a hollow chamber. Sisoka, still in the lead, came to a jarring halt and cried out something in her language.

The chamber was a catacomb, or a vast crypt.

Around them were hundreds, maybe even thousands, of animal and human remains. Most were skeletons; others appeared to be completely fossilized.

Other skeletons appeared more recent, scattered close to the entranceway. Dozens of skulls bore back-sloping foreheads with barred ridges jutting out over empty eye sockets. All of the skeletons were bare, the flesh that once covered them long ago disintegrated.

"Fireblast," Ryan breathed.

"Gaia," Krysty muttered. "This is a cemetery."

"Or a charnel house," Mildred whispered.

Ryan turned to Sisoka. "What is this place?"

"Where the First People worshiped the Grandmother and made their sacrifices to Her. Where they came to die."

J.B. stepped forward, and his foot struck something that rolled noisily. He gazed down at the yellowed human skull that had fallen to pieces at his feet. The teeth grated under his boot.

"We cannot go back," Doc said. "As disrespectful as it sounds, we must pass across the remains of the departed."

"Not bother me," Jak said.

The party moved through the catacomb, trying not to step on bones but finding it almost impossible. The crunch and clatter beneath their feet sounded unnaturally loud.

The farther they walked, the fewer skeletal remains they encountered. The chamber opened up into a vast cavern, a city of stalagmites and stalactites. Towers of multicolored stone disappeared into the darkness above, where flying buttresses and graceful arches of rock stretched overhead.

There were the marks of pick work in the walls, and the light reflected dull yellow gleams. With every step, the floor became more level, as though by design. The green light grew brighter, until it was at the level of twilight on an overcast day. They could see easily now, their vision no longer obscured by the phosphorescent mist. Here and there they saw cavities gaping in the wall and floor and a scattering of crystal shards. They saw petroglyphs painted on the walls, ancient word-pictures in the form of incomprehensible murals.

The sound of their footfalls rebounded and reechoed like the irregular beating of a gargantuan heart. The level floor ended abruptly in a series of stairlike steps, chiseled out of the rock, leading downward through a round orifice. The green glow pulsed from its other side, like brilliant, cool moonlight. Sisoka hesitated, exchanging a quick look with Ryan, then she carefully walked down the steps. Blood-sniffer whined and followed at her heels.

The stairs ended in an enormous chamber, so vast they could only see part of it at one time. It was shaped like an upside-down bowl, with smooth, curving walls. The party stood on a narrow stone walkway encircling the entire circumference of the cavern. They jolted to an unsteady stop, blinking and shaking their heads, trying to absorb the unreality of what they were seeing.

The walls were patterned with thick, sinuous veins of gold and silver. The floor was scattered with heaps of rough nuggets, smoothly finished ingots, as well as bracelets and artfully fashioned figurines. There was a quartz-crystal cluster the size of a child's head sitting atop a pile of golden pebbles.

The floor inclined in a gentle curve and at the center, surrounded by a collar of interlocking silver and gold slabs, was a perfectly round hole. Ryan guessed

t to be fifty feet in diameter. A terrific blaze of green
ight shimmered from below the collar of metals, almost painful in its intensity. The light was a shifting,
dancing column that appeared to swirl, to twirl, to
shrink, then grow.

In the steady, unearthly blaze, all of them saw
things that astounded and bewildered them. On the
floor, arrayed around the well of light in a circular
pattern, were wafers of gold, some studded with single crystals, others with three or four. Several of the
rectangles were missing, showing the rock beneath.
Either the weight of ages had pushed them out, or
greedy human fingers had pried them loose.

Ryan tore his eye away from the glittering splendor
of the dancing light and looked up, catching his breath
in awed wonder. On the far side of the well, in a place
that the shimmering radiance had first hidden from
him, reared a five-tiered ziggurat of silver-encrusted
stone. Atop the ziggurat sat an effigy gazing down at
him, causing his flesh to crawl and his mind to reel
with impossible possibilities. Ryan, Krysty, Doc, Jak,
Mildred, J.B. and Sisoka stared, stunned, shocked,
awed.

And terrified.

Enthroned in a massive chair that looked to be
fashioned from gold was the huge, skeletal figure of
a man. On closer inspection they saw that the figure
wasn't quite a skeleton, nor quite a man. No man, at
least none that they had ever seen, even in the most
rad-blasted hellpits of Deathlands, had ever attained
such a height or stature.

Though it was hard to tell in the wavering emerald-
hued light, the figure appeared to be at least seven
feet tall—sitting down. The figure was outfitted with
a weird array of trappings: a threadbare buffalo-hide

cloak, a beaded belt and rotting boot moccasins. On its head, canted at a jaunty angle, dented and dull with age, was a casque from the days of Coronado and his conquistadores. A dented breastplate from the same era encased the torso.

Lances decorated with feathers and beads leaned against the side of the throne, and at its feet were shattered, rust-eaten matchlocks. The skin of the figure was brown and stretched drum-tight over the bones. The shadows the shimmering light cast across the mummified face lent it an expression of indescribable, inhuman ferocity.

Ryan finally got his lungs and voice working again. He dragged in a great breath and asked, "Nanabozho?"

Sisoka only nodded, too numb to speak. Then she lifted her eyes, her arms and cried, "Nanabozho! *Unci!*"

J.B. and Ryan recognized the word for "grandmother." The cavern walls threw her voice back.

Ryan continued to stare at the figure atop the hand-hewn altar. He was sweating, and his heart threatened to glide up his throat. He remembered what Joe and Sisoka had told him of the cavern's history, and though he hadn't flatly disbelieved it, he hadn't truly accepted it, either. If the history was true, then what Mildred had theorized about the nature of the energy trapped within the cavern might also have truth to it.

He stepped over to her. She was gazing in stupefied wonder at the light, and he had to call her name twice before she managed to tear her eyes away from the shimmer.

"Is this like the quantum-stream stuff you were talking about?" he demanded.

She blinked her eyes, shook her head and let out a

dry, humorless laugh. "God, Ryan, I don't know. Physics isn't really my field. But now, to see this—I don't know what the hell it is and I'm afraid to find out."

Ryan pointed to the giant cadaver on the throne. "And him?"

"Maybe the First People were the sources of legends about giants in the earth, the Grigori mentioned in the Bible."

Krysty suddenly moved forward, walking around the edge of the floor that overlooked the lip of the well. She stepped down and walked toward the rim.

"What are you doing?" Ryan shouted, starting after her.

"I want to know what the hell it is, and I'm not afraid to find out."

"Krysty, that light wavelength could be radioactive for all we know!" Mildred shouted.

J.B. checked the rad counter attached to the inner lapel of his coat. "Nope," he said with satisfaction. "The needle hasn't moved."

Krysty reached the outer edge of the crystal-studded, golden wafers arranged on the floor. As Ryan rushed toward her, she knelt and pressed her forehead against a crystal. She seemed to freeze, paralyzed by some cold, hidden power.

"Krysty!" he called.

She didn't respond, didn't seem to hear.

At the same time the dancing pattern of the light changed. It leaped, then sank, and the strobing effect slowed. The green color deepened.

Ryan reached Krysty, his fingers biting her arms as he pulled her back and up. Her eyes were slightly glazed. Everyone crowded around them.

"Are you all right?" he demanded angrily.

She ran a hand over her face and murmured, "What I saw—"

"Saw what? You touched the crystal for a second. You didn't answer when I called you." He was angry and a little frightened.

"The ancestors of all the tribes, leaving this valley and spreading out over Earth..." Her whispering voice faltered and broke.

She shuddered, hugging herself. Ryan tried to put an arm around her shoulders, but she pushed it away impatiently. She spoke quickly, tersely, as though she were trying to keep her excitement bottled.

"An entire culture based on science of the mind, of wholeness with nature and the planet itself."

"That's what you saw?"

She gestured to crystal disks inset on the gold slices. "Those are sculpted memory crystals, like the ones used in the computer databases in the redoubts. I accessed the entire history of this place, and even what I can't explain, I understand deep down."

Doc, Mildred, Sisoka and Blood-sniffer made their way down and joined them. Krysty repeated to them what she had told Ryan.

"Does this energy source bear any resemblance to Dr. Wyeth's hypothesis?" Doc asked. "Is it a manifestation of the quantum stream?"

"It is the heart of the Grandmother," Sisoka stated stolidly.

"Yes and no," she answered. "It's both and neither. The information I accessed is chaotic, but at least I can make a pretty good guess to its true nature. It is a focal point of earth energy, what Sisoka calls the Grandmother and I call Gaia."

"Are you saying this *light* is sentient, self-aware?" Mildred demanded.

"It's more than light," Krysty replied firmly. "My mother taught me that a harmony, a balance, exists between energy forces we can't see, but can still affect us. Ancient peoples constructed megalith structures to serve as conductors of the earth energy."

"Lea lines," Mildred said, understanding dawning in her eyes.

"Exactly. This power was utilized to aid the propagation of crops, fertility and good fortune. I saw that what's in this cave is a natural phenomenon, a convergence of lea lines, a hub of geomagnetic energy. It's the external manifestation of what used to be called 'geofire.'"

"That does not answer my question," Doc declared stiffly.

Mildred laughed. "Doc, your question can't be answered." She waved toward the glowing waves of light. "That's the only answer you're likely to get."

"Why did Sisoka's people worship this place, if it's not supernatural?" Ryan asked.

"It is, in a way." Krysty smiled wanly, glancing toward a puzzled Sisoka. "I saw that her ancestors knew how to interact with the energy. They existed in a cause-and-effect relationship with it, like dropping a stone into a still pond, which causes ripples of water to spread out in circles. The First People figured out how to work with the naturally occurring crystals, and through the enhanced electromagnetic energy of their brains, they manipulated the geofire on a nonphysical level in such a way as to affect the physical level."

"I get it!" exclaimed Mildred. "Quantum theory states that all physical forms are of energy, but vibrating at different rates. Nothing exists in a vacuum, so when the First People and their direct descendants focused their thoughts, accidently at first, I'll bet, they interacted with the vibrational field of the geoenergy. The field absorbed, then carried the intentions of their thoughts. The more focused the intention, the more empowered was the vibrational wave of the geoforce to effect changes in their physical environment.''

She gazed at the shimmering green radiance. "That doesn't explain everything, but it explains most of the mysteries of Ti-Ra'-Wa, including the intelligent wolves. Over the centuries belief in the kinship with the animals manifested itself in a human-level intelligence in them.''

Ryan was more than a little at sea, but he understood enough to be a little disappointed. "So Joe was right. It's a power that he can manipulate.''

"No, he was wrong.'' Krysty's voice was flat. "What he wanted was to make an overnight change, all over the planet. That can't be done. The energy is focused in this valley, and one man, no matter how willful, can't bend the earth powers to do his bidding. Ti-Ra'-Wa evolved over centuries, and it became what it was due to concerted, generational effort.''

Ryan gazed at the glow and tried to absorb all that he had heard. It still sounded fantastic, but no more than many other things he'd heard and seen in his life. Pizi had said that much ancient knowledge from the First People had been lost, and Ryan realized with a sense of sadness the Ti-Ra'-Wa that had so entranced him was but a mere shadow of its former glory.

Suddenly Blood-sniffer whirled and snarled, lips curling back from his fangs.

"Touch-the-Sky comes now,'' Sisoka said calmly.

Chapter Thirty-Two

Ryan pivoted on his heel and looked toward the steps leading up through the stone opening. He couldn't see anything, yet he trusted the wolf's instincts. "How many?"

Blood-sniffer voiced seven grunting growls.

"Seven of them made it over the bridge, or they found another way. I'll try to get them as they come through the passage. Triple red, everybody."

Ryan gave no one the opportunity to object, but as he ran toward the stone stairs, Blood-sniffer bounded at his side. Man and wolf exchanged one glance, then they crept into the shadowy mouth of the opening.

At the top of the steps, Ryan crouched, blaster in one hand, the other restraining Blood-sniffer's taut, shaggy body. The SIG-Sauer had a full clip, but only three rounds remained in his gun belt. He couldn't afford to fire bullets indiscriminately. Every shot had to find a target.

He heard the slipping, scratching sounds of moccasined feet, and the wolf tensed beside him. "Not yet," he breathed. "Not yet."

The scuffing of feet grew louder. Ryan waiting, counting seconds silently. He couldn't lift his head above the round entrance without giving away his position, so he waited until he felt sure they were only yards away.

He raised himself and squeezed off three rounds.

Thunderous echoes rolled and died, then there was utter silence in the cave. When he heard a mechanical clicking, Ryan grabbed the wolf by the scruff of the neck and dragged him down the steps.

The rapid-fire cracking of the Gewehr rang out, murderous wads of lead ricocheting off the rim of the opening and whizzing down the stairs. They burst into the cavern, Ryan cursing himself for failing to realize that the amplification of sound in the hollow chamber had tricked his ears.

Blood-sniffer's hair bristled, and his fangs gleamed in a snarl. He was angry, and Ryan wouldn't have blamed him for sinking his teeth into his ass.

He and the wolf ran along the walkway bordering the well and reached the others on the far side, near the base of the ziggurat.

"They're still coming," he said grimly.

Sisoka nodded. "I think Ti-Ra'-Wa dies tonight. If it does, I have no wish to live in a world without it."

Joe's calm voice came to them, floating from the area of the stone stairs. He and his companions hadn't come out into the Cavern of Creation. Ryan knew why—they were afraid of being outgunned.

"Ochinee!" he called. "Are you ready to stop behaving like a fool?"

"How'd you get here, Joe?" Ryan shouted back.

"I lost two men on that booby-trapped bridge." The Lakota's voice was flat, toneless. "But farther down we found a ledge that almost spans the chasm. I knew that from my research into the legends. Something Sisoka evidently forgot or never knew."

Joe paused, then declared, "Ochinee, you joined the losing side. You and your friends are trapped, but I see no reason to kill you. Give yourselves up, and you and your people are free to leave Ti-Ra'-Wa."

"You'd let Sisoka go with us?"

"No!" Joe's voice was tight with anger. "She stays here, where she belongs."

"Why? Aren't you the Guardian? What do you need her for?"

"My affair."

Ryan forced a mocking laugh. "I think you're afraid, Joe, to mess with this place without having the hereditary Guardian on a string. You know your claim is bogus, and you want to cover all your bets."

"Your answer," came Joe's stern voice.

"There's nothing in the cavern that will do you any good," Ryan shouted. "A light show, an old mummy. Lots of crystal, gold and silver, but you're not interested in that, anyhow. The power you crave isn't here."

When Joe's response came, it was infuriated, full of flaming fury and frustration. "Decide, you one-eyed bastard! Don't waste any more of my time! Decide to die in there or not! I'm sick of talking to you!"

Ryan thought swiftly. This situation wasn't much different from the one in which Hatchet Jack roared a similar ultimatum. And like then, he still had one ace on the line. It wasn't a particularly good one, but it was worth playing.

"I don't trust your pals, Joe," he called out. "We'll give our blasters to you if you come to us. Only you. Alone."

There was a long silence, so long that Ryan was on the verge of repeating his words.

"All right, I'll come to you. Remember, if you kill me, all of you will die. My warriors will bottle you up in there until you perish of starvation or thirst."

Ryan patted Blood-sniffer's head. The wolf looked

up at him, its eyes showing comprehension, then slunk around to the left, past the ziggurat. It took up a position on the far side of the well, where its lean, shaggy form was hidden by the green radiance pouring upward.

Joe stepped out onto the walkway. He had his automatic rifle in hand and he froze, gaping at the well, at the ziggurat. His head was tilted back, and his mouth slowly fell open in awe and astonishment. That was the instant Blood-sniffer charged him.

Joe managed to catch the streaking movement and bring his blaster up. The weapon blasted over the wolf's head with a fiery breath and voice of thunder as the animal hit him low and brought him down, its snout buried in the man's breechclout. Joe screamed.

As the echoes of the scream still bounced from the walls and ceiling, three of the warriors who were supposed to have stayed topside charged out onto the walkway. One of the warriors was Little Mountain. They didn't know whether to look at Joe and the wolf or the heart of Grandmother Earth. They opted to stare with fear-widened eyes at the green blaze.

Ryan squeezed the SIG-Sauer's trigger three times, and three men were hit. One of the 9 mm rounds tore through a warrior's forehead, blowing the back of his skull all over the stairs behind him. His companion turned and gaped as the warrior spun and fell, and the second bullet drove through the right side of his head, taking out both of his eyes and most of his left cheek as it exited.

Part of Little Mountain's upper left shoulder dissolved in a gout of blood and sheared tissue. He dropped his lance and tried to clap a hand over the wound as he kicked himself backward toward the stairwell.

Ryan was already running before Little Mountain reached the first step. He was trying to draw a bead on Joe, but he was in a clinch with Blood-sniffer and they were rolling together over the walkway. Behind him Ryan heard Krysty's boot heels beating a rapid tattoo on the stone as she raced after him.

He got to within five feet of Joe just as the lithe, muscular man managed to swing the barrel of the rifle up and around. He squeezed the trigger and flame and lead tore along the right side of the great wolf.

Blood-sniffer yelped in pain, body spasming, crimson strings spilling from his fur. Ryan roared in anger and jumped in front of it, sweeping the wolf aside with one arm, aiming his blaster at Joe.

The rifle spit a narrow tongue of fire, and the bullet chunked into Ryan's right wrist, just below the swelling muscles of his forearm. Blood sprayed, slicking the butt of the SIG-Sauer, and he felt the shock in the soles of his feet. His fingers immediately lost all sensation and strength, and the blaster clattered to the stone walkway.

With his left hand Ryan backfisted the barrel of the Gewehr aside and dived on Joe. Peripherally he glimpsed more warriors running down the steps, and he heard Krysty and Jak shout his name.

Arrows sailed through the air, and J.B., Krysty, Mildred, Jak and Doc plunged from behind the ziggurat, running along opposite sides of the walkway. They opened fire, short sprays of flame erupting from the barrels of their blasters.

Ryan pummeled Joe's face with his left fist and pressed on the rifle with his knees, trapping it lengthwise between Joe's hands and his chest.

They were locked too closely for the warriors to

risk loosing a flight of arrows, but the Lakota raced forward with knives and short stabbing spears.

The steady blasterfire from Ryan's friends converged on the warriors, and he glimpsed a bare-chested man jerk and stagger backward, a crimson spray jetting from a bullet-severed carotid.

Behind him, over the thunder of blasterfire, he heard Krysty cry out in pain and surprise. Instinctively his head turned in that direction.

He saw Krysty, her back against the curving cavern wall, slowly sliding toward the floor of the walkway. Her left hand was pressed against her chest, just below her left breast. A feathered shaft jutted between splayed fingers. She kept her hand there as she eased into a sitting position, as though she were trying to catch the blood. The barrel of her Smith & Wesson clunked against the stone.

For an instant their eyes met. Krysty's showed a dull green in the bright green glow. Ryan saw death in them.

Then Doc was at her side, and before Ryan could make another move, a heavy, deerskin-shod foot slammed the side of his head, twisting him backward. He flailed at the air, landed heavily on his back. He blinked back the cloud of gray the kick had brought to his vision.

Little Mountain loomed directly over him, his muscular torso streaked with a sliding stream of scarlet. He held a tomahawk back over his head, and he let out a scream of anger as he brought the blade flashing down.

J.B.'s Uzi let loose with a long burst. Twisting, literally jumping from the impact of the bullets, Little Mountain crashed back inside the stairwell. Bullet holes sewed dark little periods across his pectorals.

The bore of the Gewehr inscribed a short half arc and centered on Ryan's face, staring at him with a hollow cyclopean eye. Joe squeezed the trigger.

No jet of flame spit from the muzzle, and even over the sound of blasterfire, Ryan distinctly heard the click of the firing pin striking an empty chamber.

Ryan catapulted forward wolfishly, his left hand striking like a great snake, closing tightly around Joe's throat. The Lakota snarled, and his own hands darted to Ryan's neck.

They struggled, rolled and fell over the edge of the walkway and dropped onto the floor. They half slid, half rolled toward the lip of the well and the curtain of green radiance.

Fighting to their knees, they locked together like statues. Ryan exerted all of his strength in his arm, his fingers tight around the slim column of Joe's neck. A choking gasp burst from the Lakota's bloody lips as he sought to tighten his double-handed grip on Ryan's throat.

Their faces were grinning snarls, veins standing out on their temples, hair damp, sweat pouring down their faces.

Fear suddenly flooded Joe's eyes, and the wind whistled from between his parted teeth, blowing droplets of blood. His face darkened, taking on a purplish tint. Ryan's fingers ground deeper into the man's throat tendons, crushing them in upon jugular and windpipe.

Removing his hands from Ryan's throat, Joe began a frenzied wrench and heave, trying to throw himself backward or to one side. He grasped his adversary's wrist, trying to tear away the steely, strangling fingers.

Ryan maintained the grip, but his arm was shaking with the strain. Joe stopped trying to pull away, and his left hand swatted down for Ryan's right, lying bent and numb at his waist.

Joe's fingers closed over the ripped, bloody flesh of his wrist, over the shattered bone. He squeezed, twisted and yanked.

It wasn't pain that flooded up Ryan's arm to take possession of his body and mind. It was a hellish wave of indescribable agony, crashing over him, blotting out everything, even the blazing green glow.

Dimly he heard an animal howl of pain and he realized it had burst from his own lips. He wasn't even aware of his fingers slackening, of his body sagging to the floor. His entire body seemed to literally fly apart.

The pressure on his wrist eased, the wave of agony drew back and his senses returned in a piecemeal fashion. His arms and legs were back where they belonged, and so was his eye, and there was Joe, leaning over him, face a blood-smeared mask of savage satisfaction.

"Huen, iciante mawaste," he crooned through mashed lips.

He was fumbling at Ryan's hip, and distantly, as though he were watching a not very interesting play, it occurred to him Joe was seeking to draw his panga, the better to cut his throat.

Then Joe's body lurched, his eyes flying wide, flicking down to stare in horrified incredulity at the spear haft that projected from his upper right chest, the slim column of wood standing up at a forty-five-degree angle from just below his collarbone. His hands came up and wonderingly traced the pattern of rawhide thongs wrapped around it.

Sisoka's strong, clear voice carried through the cavern. *"Taku ehe kin ekta' Unci!"*

Swiveling his head slightly, looking up, Ryan saw her standing atop the ziggurat, in front of the enthroned cadaver. She had hurled one of the old decorative lances through the veil of shimmering light. Her face was tearstained, enraged, grief stricken all at the same time. She was shrieking something about breaking vows to the Grandmother.

Joe made a convulsive effort to stand. The thick pain-fog in Ryan's mind was scattered by an eruption of fury, the old homicidal rage that always waited in a corner of his subconscious to jump in and take over.

His left hand shot up, closed around the spear haft, heaved up on it. Joe screamed, and Ryan got his legs under him and rose to a crouch. Holding the spear as if it were a fulcrum, Ryan pushed up on it, forcing himself to stand, struggling to attain his full height. He heard flesh and muscle tear, wood grating against bone, even over Joe's shrieks.

The Lakota's moccasined feet scrabbled on the slick lip of the well, failing to gain a purchase on the polished gold and silver. Ryan hooked the wooden shaft above his left elbow and lifted, raising Joe completely clear of the rim, like a buffalo-hump steak impaled on a skewer. His legs kicked at empty air, as if he were running in place.

Ryan took one lunging step forward and, overbalanced, fell. He dropped the spear haft, and Joe vanished into the fountain of light.

No scream, no sound of impact came up out of that dancing pillar of cold fire. The light shifted, shimmering, the colors sliding from yellow to orange, then to a deep, deep red.

Ryan lifted his face from the gold-and-silver plates and snarled, "Give my regards to Grandma, you triple-stupe bastard."

Chapter Thirty-Three

The arrow was planted deep in Krysty's chest, right below her heart. Her breathing was harsh and shallow, and her eyes didn't open.

"Will she live?" Ryan asked, oblivious to the blood dropping from the nerveless fingers of his right hand.

Mildred didn't answer. She was grimly probing the flesh around the sprouting shaft.

"Will she live?" he demanded, louder.

Krysty's eyes flicked open. "Yes," she said, and closed them.

Only Ryan and Krysty had suffered wounds in the fight. Blood-sniffer was dead, and Ryan found himself mourning the great gray wolf as he would a human friend. He didn't allow himself to dwell on the loss. Though racked with pain, he kept his mind focused on Krysty's condition.

In the aftermath of the battle, J.B., Doc and Jak dragged the bodies of Joe's warriors up the steps and into the sacrificial cave. They placed Blood-sniffer's corpse there, as well, after wrapping it in a robe taken from the cadaver on the ziggurat.

The three of them had gone to backtrack Joe, searching for the method he used to jump the chasm. Ryan knew they couldn't bear to see Krysty in pain, and they welcomed the opportunity to perform a task, any task, so they wouldn't have to consider the likelihood of her death.

With Sisoka's help, Mildred carried Krysty over to the base of the ziggurat, laying her on a pallet made of pelts taken from the throne. Ryan was too numb to thank Sisoka for throwing the ancient spear and saving his life. He knew that if Krysty died, Sisoka's effort wouldn't make much difference to him.

One part of Ryan's mind accepted the inevitability of death. He had become accustomed to inevitables over the course of his life in Deathlands, but one inevitable he could never accept was Krysty being taken from him. It was impossible to imagine his life without sharing it with hers.

Ryan took a deep breath and shook his head angrily. Pain jumped around the walls of his skull. He recognized the symptoms of shock, and he wasn't surprised by them. The ulna and radial bones of his wrist were shattered, and his arm was dead up to the elbow. The bullet had missed major veins and arteries, but the delicate network of nerves was damaged. Neither he nor Mildred had any idea if the damage was permanent. She hadn't had the time to give his wound more than a cursory examination.

Standing up, moving away from Krysty, Mildred led Ryan aside. Her dark eyes misted. "The arrow is too deep, too close to her heart. It can't be withdrawn without major blood loss and organ damage. If she's moved, the arrowhead will open up arteries, and she'll bleed to death internally."

"Something can be done," he said.

"In an operating room, with decent equipment and a staff of specialists and heart surgeons standing by, yes. But not here."

"Yes," Sisoka said quietly. "Here."

She had drifted close to them, voice and eyes soft. "The heart of the Grandmother will heal her heart."

Mildred scowled at the young woman. "No more mystical rants, please. This is a surgical matter, not a ceremony for the corn to grow straight and juicy."

Ryan managed to push away a little of the pain and lethargy. "Wait, Mildred. Krysty said Sisoka's ancestors exerted their force of will on the geofire to change their physical surroundings."

"So?"

"Mebbe we can exert our own force of will on it to keep Krysty alive, to heal her."

Mildred's brows knitted skeptically. "We'd be laying her life on the line."

"It already is," Ryan replied darkly.

He looked at Sisoka. "You know how to do this?"

"The technique has been known and practiced by my people for ages. But all of us must take part. There must be no resistance to the chosen intent."

"There won't be," Ryan promised.

J.B., Doc and Jak returned within the hour. They had followed an out-thrusting finger of rock that crossed the chasm and gone on through the tunnels for a recce.

"Joe's warriors are gone, chilled or run back to the forest city," J.B. reported. "The Wolf Soldiers are coming back, even though their camp is burned out. I managed to get one of them to understand Joe was dead, and they're marching on the city to retake it."

Doc and Jak were carrying water-skins and food wrapped in cloth, which they had managed to salvage from the remains of the camp.

"Good thinking," Ryan commented.

"I assumed we would be unable to leave for a time," Doc replied.

"How Krysty now?" Jak asked.

"She'll live," Ryan answered. "But all of us will have to work at it. I'll let Sisoka explain."

The woman assembled everyone around the well and told them what to do. Kneeling on the golden wafers, they stooped over and pressed their foreheads against the crystal disks. Though there were a few complaints, primarily from Doc regarding his back, everyone complied. J.B. was the most skeptical, but he restricted his disbelief to a raising or lowering of eyebrows.

The process began that very hour, everyone focusing his or her thoughts on healing Krysty's wound, envisioning her whole, alive and vibrant. It wasn't easy for such tough, pragmatic minds accustomed to dealing with a harsh, uncompromising reality, to invoke their imaginations. But all of them did their best.

THE PROCESS TOOK a week, and the passage of days and nights ceased to have any meaning to the people within the Cavern of Creation. To Ryan the hours blurred into an endless montage of kneeling, concentrating, envisioning, hoping, dreaming. He barely ate or drank or shaved or bathed. It wasn't important.

Sometimes, when he was kneeling and focusing, there seemed to be too much light above him. It would move and pulse and swim to the movement of his blood, match the rhythm of his heartbeat.

Other times the light seemed too dim, and he was angrily aware that his mind was drifting down other paths, floating into unwanted channels. The pain of his wrist impaired his concentration.

One day he was sure he heard a million little bells, chiming softly, the cheerful sound speaking of love and kindness.

On another occasion he saw Joe and John Hatcher striding out of the green light, entering his mind, moving side by side like a pair of lions. Ryan thought hard and swatted them away.

Once, he was sure he saw Dean, sitting at a desk, reading a book, moving his lips, forming the words. Dean glanced up, puzzled, and his lips shaped the question, "Dad?"

Then, on another day, Ryan realized his fingers were hurting, and he was able to flex them. It occurred to him that perhaps an overspill of the green energy, of the geofire, was healing his wound, but he didn't want to remove the splint made of wood and rawhide to check on it. He didn't need any more distractions.

Krysty stayed calm, quiet and dignified during the entire process. She drank and ate whenever she was offered food and water, and she didn't touch the arrow in her chest.

When he wasn't kneeling and concentrating, Ryan stayed by her side. She rarely spoke, though she wrinkled her nose at his odor. Once, with great effort, she whispered, "A long life. None of it wasted, lover."

Ryan didn't reply. He didn't have one. He thought of all the wandering, all the chilling, all the traveling, and it all seemed like a waste.

She managed to smile. "Not the chilling, not the bloodletting. You and me, together. A long life. Not wasted."

"Yes," he forced himself to say. "Shining times."

Then, one day—and he had no idea if it was day or night, morning or afternoon—Sisoka pulled him away from the well rim and led him over to where Mildred knelt beside Krysty. Her face was startlingly pale, surrounded by her thick cloud of red hair, but her eyes were bright, more brilliant than the green geofire.

"Now," Sisoka said quietly. "Now we will learn if our intentions were pure."

Swiftly, unhesitatingly, ignoring Mildred's word of warning, Sisoka seized the feathered shaft and yanked it from beneath Krysty's breast. It came free as easily and as smoothly as if it had been lodged in cotton wadding.

Black fluid bubbled from the puncture wound, then came a flow of bright red blood. Mildred, her eyes dull with fatigue but registering astonishment, plugged the puncture with a mixture of buffalo tallow and yarrow. No blood seeped around the edges of the wound.

Sisoka touched Krysty's face three times in a ritualistic fashion. "You are well now."

And she was.

Chapter Thirty-Four

It was the third morning after they had left the cavern, and they were guests in the forest city. All of them had been given separate rooms. Ryan in particular was far too grateful for a place to bathe and rest to think about their next course of action.

He rose from the bunk he shared with Krysty and stretched. Pain flared along his right forearm, and he groaned. He parted the bandages and touched the discolored, scabbed-over flesh, wondering again how he had regained the use of the hand so quickly. The image of the green glow flitted through his mind and answered his question. Even Jak's wound was almost completely healed.

Krysty touched his back. "Are you all right?"

"Fine," he replied. "What about you?"

She sat up in bed, her hair tumbling about her bare shoulders and breasts. Only a faint, puckered scar showed where the arrow had pierced her, and according to Sisoka, with applications of aloe juice, that soon would fade.

He and Krysty dressed. "How long are we going to stay here?" she asked.

"That depends on how long you want to stay."

She put on her boots. "If it was up to me, I'd say for the rest of our lives."

He paused in buckling on his gun belt. "Why isn't it up to you?"

Krysty shrugged. "The others may not see it that way. May not feel we should stay in this place. And besides, there may be other factors involved."

"Like what?"

"I don't know," she responded, running her fingers through her hair. The locks stirred. "I sense something."

They stepped from their quarters into the cool air. J.B., Mildred, Doc and Jak were already outside, their faces downcast. Sisoka was with them. Ryan immediately felt a change in the city's attitude. The past two days and nights had carried with them a snap of good spirits, almost a buoyancy.

The Wolf Soldiers had retaken the city two weeks before without meeting any resistance. With Touch-the-Sky dead, the whole basis of his campaign had been swept away. The Cavern Keeper society was sick with guilt. They vowed to redress their grave wrong and to make Ti-Ra'-Wa the valley of peace again.

Much of the valley was blackened and blasted by fire, though the land near the forest city was untouched. Sisoka had said fatalistically, "It is enough. It will grow again."

They had missed the ritual period of mourning the dead while in the cavern, and when they arrived back in the city, they were greeted pleasantly enough.

Now, this day, the air of mourning seemed to have returned. Ryan and Krysty approached Sisoka, and they saw she was dressed in her costume of office: a long buckskin dress, leggings adorned with tufts of fox fur and a necklace made from alternating disks of gold and silver hung from her throat. A buffalo robe was draped about her shoulders. Her dark eyes were inscrutable.

"You can go now," she said. "You can go from Ti-Ra'-Wa with clear consciences. You redeemed any guilt that was yours in bringing death to the valley."

Ryan wasn't so quick to have their responsibility discharged, or the debt he owed Sisoka. "We could stay, to help keep Ti-Ra'-Wa as it is."

Her eyes searched his face, then all of their faces.

"No," she said stiffly. "The stain, the taint, is upon you. The valley cannot fully recover, not heal in your presence."

"Girl, we *bled* for Ti-Ra'-Wa," Mildred said angrily.

"And you spilled far more blood than you shed," Sisoka replied softly. "It will take a long time for that blood to be absorbed back into the heart of the Grandmother. Until that time, all of you will be a reminder to my people of how close we came to turning her land of happiness into a land of horror."

Her eyes softened, and she laid a hand on Krysty's arm and on Ryan's wrist. "I regret this, I truly do. But it is my duty as Guardian to protect the valley. Besides, it won't be forever. Grandmother Earth will heal, as she always has, and banish the demons of hatred and greed and ambition."

Under the watchful eye of several Wolf Soldiers, the six companions collected their mounts from the compound and prepared to leave. Sisoka stepped in front of Ryan's horse.

"*Pilanaya,* Ryan Cawdor," she said in a voice barely above a whisper, her eyes wet. "*Wakan Tanka nici un.*"

They rode out of the forest city, passing silent men and women and children. At the grasslands they turned toward the mountain pass.

"What did she say to you?" Doc asked.

"'Goodbye and may the Great Spirit go with you and guide you,'" Ryan replied.

Their horses carried them across the plain at a walk. The colors of the sun danced across the snow-capped mountain peaks. A breeze, bearing a refreshing hint of autumn, ruffled their hair and the manes of their horses.

As they rode, they listened to the chirp of the birds, the drone of insects. The soft blue mountain ranges rose beyond the grasslands. A hawk glided lazily across the face of the sun. All of them were content to simply ride quietly and observe and listen to the life-rich valley.

Doc finally broke the silence. "The gates of Eden have swung shut again, and the demons have been given the boot."

"Not funny, Doc," J.B. said.

"It wasn't meant to be, John Barrymore," he replied.

They reached the slope that crept up to the pass, and they urged their ponies forward, reining them to stop on the shelf of rock overlooking the valley. Ryan gazed at the great piles of white clouds, the wind-ruffled grasses, then to the charred, fire-blackened tract.

Krysty touched his arm. Though she was still a little pale, she was strong, alive and healed. "Are you okay, lover?"

"It was peaceful here," he answered. "Might have been good to stay a while longer."

"We can come back," Mildred said. "The promise of returning to Ti-Ra'-Wa is a very strong inducement to staying alive."

"What'll we do until then?" J.B. asked.

"What we always do, what we've always done, what we do best," Krysty stated. "Survive."

J.B. tugged at the brim of his fedora. "In Deathlands I reckon that's the best we can hope for."

"'It is the Devil, and the uncharitable votes of Hell, that desire our misery in the world to come,'" Doc quoted quietly.

"I liked your 'ride, boldly ride' stuff better," Krysty told him, a strained smile crossing her face.

"Me, too," Mildred added.

Turning his pony's head toward the crack that separated Ti-Ra'-Wa from Deathlands, Ryan said, "Let's do that very thing."

He kept his back turned toward the valley as he led his friends through the pass.

Watch for the new **James Axler** series in June 1997. EXILE TO HELL launches the Outlanders saga into a bleak and dangerous future, where Kane maneuvers a small rebel group between clashing forces to fight an enigmatic and sinister enemy.

Kane and Salvo returned to C Level. By the time the lift car deposited them on the division floor, Brigid Baptiste had already been escorted to detention, at the far end of the operations suites.

Kane followed Salvo into his office. "Why are we here?"

Salvo sat down behind his desk. "Where else should we be?"

"Down in Tartarus, putting the arm on Guana Teague. He was behind the ambush, used a little albino tramp with a bogus chip as a lure—"

"Drop it, Kane," Salvo demanded. "Forget Guana."

"He chilled a magistrate," replied Kane hotly. "And tried to chill another. Once word spreads, not a single mag will be safe in the Pits."

"I said drop it!" Salvo's angry bark brooked no debate. "The matter will be dealt with on my terms. You've got a very full evening ahead of you."

"I don't get you."

Salvo gestured sharply. "Take off your coat. Remove your sidearm."

Kane didn't move. "Are you suspending me?"

Spots of red appeared on Salvo's cheeks. "Do as I say, or you'll be hoping for something as soft as a suspension."

Kane hesitated, then with deliberate slowness

shrugged out of his coat, draping it over the back of the chair. He unstrapped the Sin Eater from his fore-arm and dropped it with a provocative clunk on the center of the desk. Salvo made no move to touch it. Inclining his head toward the chair, he said, "Sit."

Spinning the chair around, Kane thrust it between his legs and sat ass-backward, in a position where he could see the door and Salvo at the same time. "Now what?"

"Now we wait."

"For what—a disciplinary tribunal to convene?"

"Keep your mouth shut and your ears open and you'll find out."

They waited. The minutes dragged by like broken-legged turtles. Salvo said nothing. Kane said nothing. His mind was focused on Baptiste, on whether she had really used him. Or had he used her? He desperately wanted to talk to her or Grant. Or anybody else but Salvo.

Silence enfolded the office, and not even the fa-miliar sounds of normal division activity seemed to filter in. When the transcom unit on Salvo's desk war-bled, the sound was so unexpected and startling that Kane nearly jumped out of the chair.

Salvo didn't open the circuit. The unit warbled once more, then fell silent. From a desk drawer he produced a set of goggles. The plastic lenses were thick and a deep black in color. He stood up. "Let's go."

"Go where?"

"Where I tell you."

Kane rose, reaching for his Sin Eater. Salvo snapped, "Leave it." When he started to pick up his coat, Salvo repeated, "Leave it."

Kane refused to dog Salvo's heels, so he fell into

step beside him as they strode down the corridor, past
the evidence room and the recessed sec door of the
armory. When they passed it, Kane almost slowed his
pace. All that lay beyond the armory was the detention area. His lips moved in a thin half smile. If Salvo
intended to lead him there and expected him to
meekly enter a cell, he would receive one of the most
painful surprises of his life.

Instead, they turned right down a narrow passage.
It dead-ended at a locked service accessway door.
Salvo handed him the goggles. "Put these on."

"Why?"

"Consider it an order."

Slipping them over his head and eyes, Kane was
rendered almost completely blind. A thread of blurry
light peeped through a seal at his cheek. He heard a
rustle of cloth and Salvo adjusted the elastic strap,
securing it tightly around his head. The darkness was
total and impenetrable.

"Can you see?"

Kane chuckled dryly. "Think I'd tell you?"

"You'd better." Steel slipped into Salvo's voice.

"No," replied Kane. "I can't see a thing. Satisfied?"

Salvo grunted and Kane heard a metal-on-metal
clicking and clacking, then a faint squeal of hinges.
He felt Salvo's hand on his elbow, tugging him forward. Kane resisted.

"Relax." Salvo's voice purred with amusement.
"If I wanted to chill you, I wouldn't go to all this
trouble."

Kane thought the statement over for a moment and
agreed with it. He allowed Salvo to guide him a few
steps, then position him against a wall.

"Don't move until I tell you."

He heard the squeak of hinges again, the snap of a locking mechanism and then a faint electric hum. He felt a sudden rising sensation in the pit of his stomach.

"We're in an elevator."

"Astute."

"And we're going up?"

"Yes."

"To where?"

"To where we get off."

The lift car rose, ascending far above the B Level and even A Level. It hissed to a pneumatic stop and Salvo urged him away from the wall. The floor was slick and smooth beneath his boots, their footsteps echoed hollowly, and Kane guessed they were walking across a big, high-ceilinged room.

"From this point on," Salvo whispered to him, "No talking."

Kane only nodded, feeling tension climb up the buttons of his spine. With a hand on his elbow, Salvo guided him forward. The echoes of footfalls suddenly became muffled, muted. They were now on a thickly carpeted floor. At the same time he detected the acrid odor of spicy incense, of unfamiliar resins.

Salvo gently tugged him to a stop. The scent of incense was stronger, almost overpowering. Kane reached for the goggles, but Salvo hissed, "Not yet."

The aromatic air shivered with the steady beat of a gong. Kane felt the vibrations against his face. The gong sounded thirteen times. After the final heavy chime, Salvo whispered, "Take them off now."

Carefully, Kane lifted the goggles away and off his head. His eyes were narrowed, prepared to be blinded by light. Instead he saw only a gray gloom, and his eyes quickly adjusted. He stood upon a thick Persian carpet. Figures shifted around him, and although he could see only shadows, he knew they were men.

Then a blade of white light speared down from somewhere above and impaled him. The suddenness of its unmerciful brightness seared his optic nerves and he blurted out a startled, pained curse. His hands came up to protect his eyes.

The whirling spectrum of light dimmed, diffused like pale sunlight barely penetrating a great underwater depth. As he stood there, blinking, a voice spoke to him. The voice was silvery, musical, its pitch exactly the same as that of the gong, which still echoed from the far corners of the room.

"You are Kane, a servant of order, a soldier of the Ville, a warrior of the Baron."

Kane's vision slowly cleared, and he saw a dim shape standing before him. It looked strange, hazy, and he realized the figure stood behind a semitranslucent curtain, like a veil of gauze dusted with iridescent gold particles.

"Answer me," the figure said. "Are you Kane?"

"I am."

"Do you know who I am?"

Heart hammering, throat thick, Kane replied, "You are the Baron."

"Do you know why I have had you brought here?"

Kane breathed unsteadily. He wondered insanely if Baron Cobalt was speaking or if he had merely imagined it. He couldn't seem to focus on his figure—he moved, swaying gracefully, almost as though he were performing some bizarrely beautiful ritual. There was only a fragment of an overall impression, of pale golden skin, long arms, lean cheeks. Although he couldn't see the eyes, he knew the Baron was looking at him, waiting for an answer. He bowed his head and whispered, "No."

"Because you belong to me. From the day of your birth, you have belonged to me, as did your father and grandfather."

Kane didn't dare look around, but now that he remembered that other people were present, a bit of his fear ebbed. "Who am I to Baron Cobalt?"

"I offer you the chance to be one of my chosen ones."

"Why?" he asked quietly. "Chosen for what?"

"To hear the truth, to serve the truth, to protect the truth. And in doing so, protect all of humanity and what we have managed to build here from the ravaged ruins of the Deathlands."

Kane didn't understand. He just stood there, cringing inwardly, knowing he was the focal point of critical stares from the shadows behind him. He could scarcely believe what he was seeing, and he was afraid to speak. He waited for the Baron to explain.

"Do you wish to hear the truth?"

He hesitated only half a heartbeat. "Yes."

"Be warned, then, Kane. Once you hear it, you must swear to serve it and protect it with your life. If you do not, then you die. Do you still wish to hear the truth?"

Even with his reason clouded by fear, Kane knew that he was in too deep to back out. An audience with Baron Cobalt was an event that had swift repercussions—it meant either a swift reward or a swift demise.

Kane lifted his head, cleared his throat and announced, "Yes, Lord Baron. I wish to hear the truth."

And the Baron spoke.

"They are here among us...."

From the creator of Deathlands comes...

An all-new series by James Axler!

Enter the future—a postholocaust world where the struggle between the classes takes on a whole new reality...where the misery of the final conflagration gives way to a promise of a new beginning...and where the inhabitants of the entire planet find themselves facing a new, all-powerful and alien enemy....

Available this June
wherever Gold Eagle books are sold.

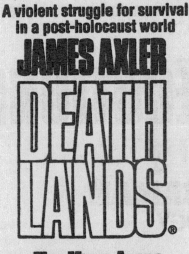

When terrorism strikes too close to home...

Don Pendleton's
THE EXECUTIONER®

THE ★ AMERICAN TRILOGY

An ultraright-wing militia force is using acts of terrorism to splinter American society. But a greater conspiracy is at the heart of the violence on U.S. soil as a foreign enemy seizes the chance for revenge against a nation in turmoil. It's up to Mack Bolan to infiltrate the group and bring it to its knees—before it's too late.

Available this June, July and August wherever Gold Eagle books are sold.

AT-G

It's a jungle out there—and the Destroyer may become the next endangered species

THE Destroyer

#108 Bamboo Dragon

Created by
WARREN MURPHY
and RICHARD SAPIR

Deep in the Malaysian jungle a group of scientists gets a lethal surprise, and a lone survivor rants about a prehistoric monster who eats men alive. The survivor dies with bizarre symptoms—and CURE's Dr. Harold Smith wants answers.

Look for it in July wherever Gold Eagle books are sold.

**America faces a double threat
from the Russian mob**

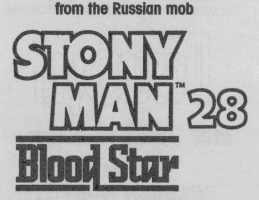

STONY MAN™ 28

Blood Star

The ops center of a covert defence force, Stony Man is
mandated to safeguard American interests and to deploy
worldwide against overt aggression. Now the Russian mob
poses a double-edged threat, joining a turf war in America
and in mother Russia as suppliers of materiel to terrorists.

Available in May at your favorite retail outlet.

D0102690

THE HITE REPORT

3,000 women between the ages of 14 and 78 describe in their own words their most intimate feelings and answer such questions as:

* How does orgasm feel—with and without intercourse? Is it important to you?

* Do you enjoy masturbation? How do you masturbate?

* Do you have orgasms more easily by clitoral stimulation than by intercourse? Are the orgasms different? How?

* Is (are) your partner(s) well-informed about your sexual desires and your body?

* How does it feel *not* to have orgasm during sex? Do you ever fake orgasm? How do you feel about it?

An open look at how women feel about sex and a startling new cultural interpretation of female sexuality.

"REAL, SIGNIFICANT AND POIGNANT . . . THE WHOLE RICH VARIETY OF FEMALE SEXUALITY IS SPREAD OUT IN PANORAMA."

—Mary S. Calderone, M.D., President, American Sex Information and Education Council of the United States

Other Books by Shere Hite

SEXUAL HONESTY, BY WOMEN, FOR WOMEN

THE HITE REPORT ON MALE SEXUALITY

THE HITE REPORT ON WOMEN AND LOVE

THE HITE REPORT

A NATIONWIDE STUDY OF FEMALE SEXUALITY

Shere Hite

A DELL BOOK

Published by
Dell Publishing
a division of
Bantam Doubleday Dell Publishing Group, Inc.
666 Fifth Avenue
New York, New York 10103

ISBN: 0-440-13690-3

Reprinted by arrangement with Macmillan Publishing Co., Inc.

Printed in the United States of America

Two Previous Editions

September 1987

10 9 8 7 6 5 4 3 2

KRI

The author gratefully acknowledges permission to reprint material from the following sources:

Basic Books, Inc. for material from *Understanding the Female Orgasm* by Seymour Fisher. Copyright © 1973 by Basic Books, Inc., Publishers, New York. Brunner/Mazel, Inc., New York, for material from *The New Sex Therapy*. Copyright © 1974 by Helen Singer Kaplan, M.D., Ph.D. Ernest Benn Ltd., London, for material from *The Sex Factor in Marriage*. Copyright © 1947 by Helena Wright. Andre Deutsch Ltd., London, for material from *The Sex Researchers*. Copyright © 1970 by Edward M. Brecher. The Institute for Sex Research and W.B. Saunders for material from *Sexual Behavior in the Human Female* by Alfred Kinsey, et al. Copyright © 1953 by W.B. Saunders Co. Little, Brown and Co. for material from *The Sex Researchers*. Copyright © 1969 by Edward B. Brecher, by permission of Little, Brown and Co. The National Council on Family Relations for material from "Sister Love: An Exploration of the Need for Homosexual Experience" by Janis Kelly from *The Family Coordinator*, October 1972. Copyright © 1972 by the National Council on Family Relations. Reprinted by permission. Penguin Books, Ltd., England, for material from *The Female Orgasm: Psychology Physiology Fantasy* by Seymour Fisher. Copyright © 1973 by Basic Books, Inc. First published in Great Britain by Allen Lane, a division of Penguin Books, Ltd. Random House, Inc. for material from *The Nature and Evolution of Female Sexuality*. Copyright © 1966, 1972 by Mary Jane Sherfey. Dr. Pepper Schwartz for material from her paper "Female Sexuality and Monogamy." Available from the Department of Sociology, University of Washington, Seattle, Washington. Drs. Pepper Schwartz and Philip Blumstein for material from their paper "Bisexuality: Some Sociological Observations." Available from the Department of Sociology, University of Washington, Seattle, Washington.

A minute portion of this book originally appeared in slightly different form in *Sexual Honesty By Women For Women*. Copyright © 1974 by Shere Hite. Published by Warner Paperback Library. All Rights Reserved.

CONTENTS

ORGASM

INTERCOURSE

PREFACE

Women have never been asked how they felt about sex. Researchers, looking for statistical "norms," have asked all the wrong questions for all the wrong reasons—and all too often wound up *telling* women how they should feel rather than *asking* them how they do feel. Female sexuality has been seen essentially as a response to male sexuality and intercourse. There has rarely been any acknowledgment that female sexuality might have a complex nature of its own which would be more than just the logical counterpart of (what we think of as) male sexuality.

What these questionnaires have attempted to do is to ask *women* themselves how they feel, what they like, and what they think of sex. This is not to imply that the only thing that stands between a woman and "satisfactory" sex is her realization of her own physical needs. "Sex" as we define it is part of the whole cultural picture; a woman's place in sex mirrors her place in the rest of society.

This book presents what the women who answered said—in their own words and in their own way. The intention is to get acquainted, to share how we have experienced our sexuality, how we feel about it—and to see our personal lives more clearly, thus redefining our sexuality and strengthening our identities as women. This book is also meant to stimulate a public discussion and reevaluation of sexuality. We must begin to devise more kind, generous, and personal ways of relating which will be positive and constructive for the future.

In addition, this book presents a new theory of female sexuality, which unfolds gradually, chapter by chapter, and can best be understood by reading the book in chapter order. The first half of the book is devoted basically to a discussion of orgasm, and the second half to a critique of our culture's definition of sex.

The experience of receiving these replies has been enriching, warming, and enlightening—for me, and, I hope, for all who read them. What these women have shared (anonymously), with so much love and honesty, comes from the wealth of female experience that is usually hidden, but which foreshadows women's great courage and potential for the future.

It has been my privilege to conduct this project for the last four years, and it is with great joy that I present the results.

Shere Hite
February 1976

It would be preferred if women readers of this book would answer the questionnaire on page 635.

Thank you.

NATIONAL ORGANIZATION FOR WOMEN,[†]
N. Y. C. CHAPTER
47 EAST 19 ST., N. Y. C. 10003

1. ORGASM

1. Do you have orgasms? If not, what do you think would contribute to your having them?
2. Is having orgasms important to you? Would you enjoy sex just as much without having them? Does having good sex have anything to do with having orgasms?
3. Do you have orgasms during the following (please indicate whether always, usually, sometimes, rarely, or never):

    masturbation:————————

    intercourse (vaginal penetration):————————

    manual clitoral stimulation by a partner:

    ————————

    oral stimulation by a partner:————————

    intercourse plus manual clitoral stimulation:

    ————————

    never have orgasms:————————

    Also indicate above how many orgasms you usually have during each activity, and how long you usually take. Space for comments, if desired:

* Questionnaires I, II, and III can be found in the Appendices.

† This project is connected with the National Organization for Women's New York chapter only in that, as a member, I was granted permission to use the name and address as a heading for the questions, to give the reader some idea of their orientation. There was no funding involved, although part of any profit which this project may make will be donated to the chapter.

4. Please describe what an orgasm feels like to you. How does your body feel?

5. Is there more than one kind of orgasm? If you orgasm during vaginal penetration/intercourse, does the orgasm feel different than orgasm without penetration? How?

6. Are you more aroused before or after orgasms? Would you use the word "satisfied" to describe your feeling after orgasm? "Loving"? "Elated"? A "feeling of well-being"? What word would you use?

7. Is one orgasm physically satisfying to you? Do successive orgasms become stronger or weaker? Does the place to be stimulated change or "move around" slightly, from one orgasm to the next?

8. Please give a graphic description of how your body could best be stimulated to orgasm.

9. If you are just about to have an orgasm and then don't because of withdrawal of stimulation or some similar reason, do you feel frustrated? When does this tend to happen?

10. What bodily "symptoms" do you show at the moment of orgasm? For example, does your body become tense and rigid, or are you moving? What position are your legs in? What is your facial expression?

11. Is an orgasm something that "happens to" your body, or is it something you create yourself in your own body?

II. SEXUAL ACTIVITIES

12. What do you think is the importance of masturbation? Did you ever see anyone else masturbating? How did they look? Can you imagine women you admire masturbating?

13. Do you enjoy masturbating? Physically? Psychologically? How often? —————. Does it lead to orgasm always, usually, sometimes, rarely, or never? —————. How long does it/do you usually take? —————. How many orgasms do you usually have? —————.

14. How do you masturbate? Please give a detailed description. For example, what do you use for stimulation—your fingers or hand or the bed, etc.? *Exactly* where do you touch yourself? Are your legs together or apart? What sequence of events do you do?

15. Do(es) your partner(s) stimulate your clitoral area manually? How? Is it usually for purposes of orgasm or arousal? If for orgasm, does it lead to orgasm always, usually, sometimes, rarely, or never? Is this form of sex important to you?

16. Do(es) your partner(s) stimulate you orally (cunnilingus)? Is this stimulation oral/clitoral or oral/vaginal, or both? Is it for orgasm or arousal? If for orgasm, does it lead to orgasm always, usually, sometimes, rarely or never? —————. Do you like it?

17. Is breast stimulation important to you? What kind?

18. Do you like vaginal penetration/intercourse? Physically? Psychologically? Does it lead to orgasm always, usually, sometimes, rarely, or never?

19. If you orgasm during vaginal penetration/intercourse, are other accompanying stimuli usually present? What would you say is your method of obtaining clitoral stimulation during intercourse: a) long foreplay, b) simultaneous manual stimulation of the clitoris, c) indirect stimulation from thrusting, d) "grinding" or pressing together during penetration, or e) some other method?

20. If you orgasm during intercourse, which kinds of movements do you like to make during penetration

to increase your stimulation—soft or hard, slow or fast, complete or partial penetration, thrusting in and out or holding still, etc. Which positions do you prefer for orgasm? Are your legs together or apart at orgasm? Do you use vaginal or other muscles to help you orgasm?

21. Do you ever have physical discomfort during intercourse? Do you usually have "adequate" lubrication? Do you sometimes feel less excited the longer intercourse continues?

22. Is the emotional or psychological relationship more important during penetration than during other forms of sex? What is your emotional reaction to penetration?

23. Is it easier for you to have an orgasm by clitoral stimulation when intercourse is not in progress? If you had to choose between intercourse and clitoral stimulation by your partner, which would you pick? Why?

24. Do you like rectal penetration? What kind?

25. What forms of non-genital sex are important to you (for example, hugging and kissing? talking intimately? looking at each other? smelling?) Do you enjoy these activities as much as regular genital sex? Is the best sex genital?

III. RELATIONSHIPS

26. Answer whichever are or were relevant to you: (Answer in space at bottom of page.)

If you are *married,* how many years have you been married? Do you like being married? What is the effect on sex? Have you had "extra-marital" experiences (how many and how long)? If so, what was the effect on you as an individual, and on your marriage? Were they of the "open marriage" type, or unknown to your partner? What is your opinion of the "open marriage" concept?

If you are *single*, do you enjoy being "single"? Or is it difficult? Do you think of "single" as a temporary way of life or a basic one? Do you have sexual activities very often? What kind?

If you have a *regular sex partner* (not married), how does this compare with other life styles you have tried? Would you rather be married? Do you consider this temporary or permanent? Are you comfortable?

If you are a *lesbian* (relate sexually to women), please answer any of the preceding questions which may have applied to you, and also: How many years have you been relating physically to women? How do you feel sexual relationships with other women "compare" with relationships with men (or would compare, if you have never had heterosexual sex)? Physically? Psychologically? Please also explain how to relate to another woman physically, as this information is not always widely available.

If you are still *living at home* with parents or family, how do rules against sex for younger women affect you? Do they protect you or hurt you or what? Would you like less or more restrictions on sex? Are parents or relatives willing to discuss sex realistically with you? Friends? Teachers? Is getting information a problem? And finally, if you have had sex with a partner, do your parents know? How did they react?

If you have *not yet had sex with a partner*, what do you think sex will be like? What physical sensations have you enjoyed most so far?

If you are currently *asexual or celibate* (that is, you have no sexual relations except perhaps masturbation), how do you like this way of life? Would you recommend it to other women? How long do you plan to remain asexual?

27. Which "life style" do you feel *would* be best for you? Extended periods of monogamy? Two or

three or four regular lovers? Casual sexual relationships? Relatively long periods of no sex at all?
"Swinging"? Or some other style which has not yet
been invented?

28. Rate the following in order of their numerical importance to sex (1, 2, 3, etc.), adding comments, if
desired:

passion
romance
friendship
non-romantic love (deep caring)
long-term commitment, marriage
being "in love"
economics
hostility and feelings of violence

29. Describe the first time you fell in love. How did
you feel? How did the relationship develop and
grow, or die? If you have fallen in love more than
once, do you think there is a pattern of emotional
developments which takes place in romantic sexual
relationships?

30. What have your deepest relationships been like,
with both men and women? How were they satisfying or unsatisfying? Emotionally? Physically?

31. What are your deepest longings for a relationship
with another person(s)?

IV. LIFE STAGES

32. How old were you when you first masturbated?
————. To orgasm? ————. Did you discover
it on your own, or did you learn how from someone,
or somewhere, else?

33. How old were you when you had your first orgasm
with another person? ————. During what activity? ————.

34. What were your feelings about "losing your virginity"? Was there any pain or bleeding involved? How old were you?

35. Can you remember your sexual feelings during childhood? Grade school? High school? What were they?

36. Do you think that child and/or teenage sexuality should be repressed? Why or why not? Why is it presently repressed?

37. Have you had sexual feelings for members of your family? Brothers or sisters? Parents? Have your children (if applicable) ever shown sexual responses to your touch, or have you ever had sexual feelings for them? How did you react?

38. Did pregnancy and childbearing/birth have sexual aspects for you?

39. Have you had sexual contact with people who were quite a bit younger or older than you? Was it different in any way, either physically or psychologically, from other sex you have had?

40. How does age affect sex? Does desire for sex increase or decrease, or neither, with age? Enjoyment of sex? Does this have anything to do with age of your partners?

41. Does menopause ("change of life") affect sexuality, either physically or psychologically? How? Did it affect your partner(s)'s reactions to you?

42. If you have had a hysterectomy, did this affect your sexual activities or feelings? Physically? Psychologically? How?

43. What is your age and background—occupation, education, upbringing, race, or anything you may consider important?

V. THE ENDING

44. Have physical sexual relations with men followed any particular patterns? What were they? (How have most men had sex with you?)

45. Is (are) your partner(s) sensitive to the stimulation you want? If not, do you ask for it, or stimulate yourself? Is this embarrassing?

46. Do you ever find it necessary to masturbate to achieve orgasm after "making love"?

47. Do you often feel your partner(s) is (are) not emotionally involved during sex? Or, what emotional responses do you most often feel from your partner(s)?

48. Do you ever fake orgasms? During which sexual activities? Under which conditions? How often?

49. Have you ever been afraid to say "no" to someone for fear of "making a scene" or "turning them off"? If so, how did you feel during sex? Would you define this as rape?

50. How do you feel about fellatio (mouth stimulation of the penis)? To orgasm? How do you feel about "performing" cunnilingus (oral sex) on another woman?

51. Do you think your vagina and genital area are ugly or beautiful? Smell good or bad? What other parts of your body do you like or dislike? Are you comfortable naked with another person?

52. Do you fantasize? (During masturbation, or during sex with a partner?) Is it to help bring on an orgasm, or just for general pleasure? Do you think of stories with plots, or just visualize specific images? What are they?

53. What do you think of sado-masochism (domination-submission)? Have you ever experienced them?

54. What books on sex have you read? What did you think of them?

55. What do you think of the "sexual revolution"?

56. Do you think that sex is in any way political?

57. Is there anything on your mind you would like to speak about which was left untouched by this questionnaire? If so, please add it here.

58. Why did you answer this questionnaire (*thank you!*), where did you get it, and how did you like it?

WHO ANSWERED

QUESTIONNAIRE DISTRIBUTION

This questionnaire and the three different versions printed on pages 573–590 have been distributed to women all over the country since 1972. Their purpose was to discover how women view their own sexuality. Great effort was put into mailing and distribution of the questionnaires in an attempt to reach as many different kinds of women, with as many different points of view, as possible. Early distribution was done through national mailings to women's groups, including chapters of the National Organization for Women, abortion rights groups, university women's centers, and women's newsletters. Soon after, notices in *The Village Voice, Mademoiselle, Brides*, and *Ms.* magazines informed readers that they could write in for the questionnaires, and later there were also notices placed in dozens of church newsletters. In addition, *Oui* magazine ran the questionnaire in its entirety, and 253 replies were received from its women readers. Finally, the paperback *Sexual Honesty By Women For Women*,* which contains forty-five complete early replies, has asked readers to send in their own replies since its publication in 1974. All in all, one hundred thousand questionnaires were distributed, and slightly over three thousand returned (more or less the standard rate of return for this kind of questionnaire distribution).

Replies to Questionnaire II include, besides answers from the women's movement distribution, answers from readers of *Mademoiselle, Brides*, and *Ms.* magazines. Questionnaires III and IV represent a mixture of wom-

---

* Published by Warner Paperback Library.

en's movement distribution and church newsletter distribution.

Replies to Questionnaire I include those received from readers of the *Village Voice, Oui* magazine, and again from general distribution through the women's movement and various church and religious groups. Although these groups tended to be quite different in manner of expression, and in perspective on their situation (as will be readily apparent in the quotes), their answers did not differ in basic content—i.e., type of masturbation, stimulation necessary for orgasm, etc.

Statistics given in the book are generally broken down into the three populations—Questionnaires I, II, and III as a way of demonstrating how closely results from all of the groups resemble each other. Since Questionnaire IV was distributed while tabulation of the results was already in progress, only replies to Questionnaires I, II, and III are presented statistically (1844 women total); however, quotes from replies to Questionnaire IV are included in the text. Also, replies from women who had read *Sexual Honesty* were not included in the statistics, since they might have been influenced by what the other women had said, but quotes from these replies are occasionally included in the text. The total number of women's answers received from all the sources is 3,019.

GEOGRAPHIC DISTRIBUTION OF REPLIES

Answers, according to postmarks, were received from the following states:

TOTAL FROM STATE:		TOTAL FROM STATE:	
3	Alabama: 3 (city unknown)		Anchorage—3
6	Alaska: 1 (city unknown)		Fairbanks—2

TOTAL FROM STATE:		TOTAL FROM STATE:	
15	Arizona: 5 (city unknown)		Burbank—1
	Flagstaff—1		Canoga Park—2
	Litchfield Park—1		Carson—1
	Mesa—1		Chula Vista—1
	Temple—1		Clovis—1
	Tucson—6		Cypress—1
5	Arkansas:		Danville—2
	Bentonville—1		El Cajan—1
	Camden—1		Escondido—1
	Little Rock—2		Freemont—2
			Fresno—1
	West Helena—1		Goleta—1
248	California: 74 (city unknown)		Hayward—4
			Hemet—1
			Independence—1
	Alameda—2		Inglewood—1
	Albion—1		La Jolla—3
	Alhambra—1		Lakewood—1
	Altadena—1		La Mirada—1
	Anaheim—2		Loma Linda—1
	Arleta—2		
	Atascadero—1		Long Beach—3
	Belef—1		Los Angeles—17
	Bellflower—1		Marina—1
	Berkeley—17		Mendocino—2
	Beverly Hills—2		
	Blythe—1		Menlo Park—1
	Boulder Creek—1		North Hollywood—2
	Boulevard—1		
	Buena Park—1		Oakland—3

TOTAL FROM STATE:

TOTAL FROM STATE:

New Haven—1
Norwalk—2
Southington—1
Stamford—1
West Hartford—1
West Redding—3
Willimantic—1

13   Delaware: 7 (city unknown)
Dover—1
Ellendale—1
Newark—1
Wilmington—3

49   Florida: 27 (city unknown)
Clearwater—1
Coral Gables—1
Coral Springs—1
Delray Beach—1
Fort Lauderdale—1
Gainesville—4
Hollywood—1
Indian Harbor Beach—1

Lake Placid—1
Miami—4
Ocean Shore—1
St. Augustine—2
South Daytona—1
Tampa—2

18   Georgia: 7 (city unknown)
Atlanta—3
Augusta—2
Brunswick—1
Carrollton—1
Jonesboro—1
Marietta—1
Rome—1
Warner Robins—1

1   Hawaii: Honolulu—1

1   Idaho: St. Maries—1

64   Illinois: 9 (city unknown)
Bloomington—1
Carbondale—1
Chicago—30
Dundee—1
Elgin—1
Evanston—1
Granite City—1

TOTAL FROM STATE:

TOTAL FROM STATE:

La Grange—1
Lakeview—1
Lawrenceville—1
Lisle—1
Mt. Sterling—1
North Aurora—1
Northlake—1
Oak Forest—1
Oak Lawn—1
Oak Park—2
Palatine—1
Park Forest—1
Peoria—2
Rock Island—1
Roselle—1
Springfield—1
Waukegan—1

20 Indiana: 2 (city unknown)
Bloomfield—1
Evansville—2
Fort Wayne—1
Frankfort—1
Gary—1
Hammond—1
Hanover—1
Indianapolis—5

Lafayette—2
Monticello—1
Princeton—1
Terre Haute—1

7 Iowa: 2 (city unknown)
Cedar Rapids—2
Grinnell College—1
Klemme—1
Mt. Pleasant—1

10 Kansas: 3 (city unknown)
Dodge City—1
Edwardsville—1
Kansas City—2
Lawrence—1
Merriam—1
Mound City—1

7 Kentucky: 3 (city unknown)
Berea—1
Lexington—1
Richmond—1
Russell Springs—1

15 Louisiana: 5 (city unknown)
Arcadia—1
Baldwin—1

TOTAL FROM STATE:

TOTAL FROM STATE:

La. State U.—1
Metairie—2
Monroe—1
New Orleans—4

12 Maine: 6 (city unknown)
Booth Bay Harbor—1
New Bedford—1
N. Bellerea—1
Orland—1
Waterford—1
Winter Harbor—1

30 Maryland: 9 (city unknown)
Aberdeen—1
Annapolis—1
Baltimore—8
Chaptico—1
Chevy Chase—1
College Park—1
Gaithersburg—1
Mt. Rainier—1
Pikesville—1
Rockville—1
Sherwood For.—1
Sparks—1

Takoma Park—1
Wheaton—1

66 Massachusetts: 33 (city unknown)
Allston—1
Amherst—1
Boston—14
Cambridge—2
Chester—1
Dartmouth—1
Great Barrington—2
Holyoke—1
Lynn—1
Newton Highland—1
Orange—1
Plymouth—1
Provincetown—2
Springfield—2
Worcester—1
Worthington—1

38 Michigan: 12 (city unknown)
Ann Arbor—4
Brighton—1
Clarkston—1
Detroit—2
Flint—2

TOTAL
FROM
STATE:

TOTAL
FROM
STATE:

Grand
   Rapids—5
Kalama-
   zoo—7
Muskegon—1
Pontiac—1
Southfield—1
Westland—1

27   Minnesota: 14
(city unknown)
Cologne—1
International
   Falls—1
Minneapo-
   lis—1
Mora—1
Osseo—1
Richfield—1
St. Cloud—1
St. Paul—4
Virginia—1
Zim—1

1   Mississippi:
Tupelo—1

13   Missouri: 3 (city
unknown)
Bridgeton—1
Kansas
   City—2
Lemay—1
St. Louis—6

3   Montana:
Browning—1
Clute—1
Helena—1

14   Nebraska: 2
(city unknown)

Ainsworth—1
Alda—1
Lincoln—4
North
   Platte—1
Omaha—5

1   Nevada:
Reno—1

13   New Hampshire:
3 (city unknown)
Claremont—1
Durham—1
Franconia—1
Hanover—1
Keene—1
Lebanon—2
Manchest-
   er—1
Nashua—1
White River
   Jct.—1

88   New Jersey: 21
(city unknown)
Atlantic
   City—1
Billing-
   boro—1
Bloom-
   field—1
Bridgeton—1
Camden—2
Cranford—1
East Bruns-
   wick—1
Elizabeth—2
Fanwood—1
Fort Dix—1

TOTAL
FROM
STATE:

TOTAL
FROM
STATE:

Glassboro—1
Hacken-
    sack—1
Hights-
    town—1
Jersey
    City—1
Kearny—2
Lakewood—1
Long
    Branch—2
Madison—1
Maple-
    wood—1
Mendham—1
Midland
    Park—1
Montvale—1
Moores-
    town—1
Newark—2
New Bruns-
    wick—11
New Provi-
    dence—1
Old
    Bridge—2
Paterson—2
Parsip-
    pany—2
Perth Am-
    boy—2
Plainfield—2
Princeton—1
Rahway—1
Raritan—2

Ridge-
    wood—1
Stockholm—1
Teaneck—3
Trenton—1
Ventnor
    City—1
Vineland—2
Washing-
    ton—1
Wayne—1
West
    Orange—1

12   New Mexico: 7
(city unknown)
    Albuquer-
        que—2
    Jemez
        Springs—1
    Los Ala-
        mos—1
    Socorro—1

485   New York: 106
(city unknown)
    Albany—1
    Andover—1
    Athol—2
    Baldwin—2
    Bingham-
        ton—1
    Branting-
        ham—1
    Brent-
        wood—1
    Bronx—7
    Brooklyn—34
    Buffalo—2

TOTAL FROM STATE:		TOTAL FROM STATE:	
	Greensboro—1		John Day—1
	Greensburg—1		Portland—16
3	North Dakota: 1 (city unknown)		Shedd—1
	Bismarck—1		Springfield—1
	Vermillion—1		Sutherlin—1
59	Ohio: 16 (city unknown)		Wolf Creek—1
	Akron—2	107	Pennsylvania: 33 (city unknown)
	Athena—2		Bloomsburg—3
	Bowling Green—2		Boyestown—1
	Cincinnati—1		Clifton Heights—1
	Cleveland—7		Downingtown—1
	Columbus—5		Glenside—1
	Dayton—1		Greensboro—1
	Eastlake—1		Greenville—1
	Kent—11		Hatboro—1
	Marietta—1		Haverford—1
	N. Canton—1		Huntingdon—1
	Oberlin—2		Johnstown—2
	Springfield—1		Lancaster—3
	Steubenville—1		Malvern—1
	Toledo—1		Media—1
	Youngstown—3		Mehoopany—1
	Zanesville—1		Morrisville—2
3	Oklahoma: 2 (city unknown)		Neffs—1
	Tulsa—1		
25	Oregon: 2 (city unknown)		
	Ashland—1		
	Beaverton—1		

TOTAL
FROM
STATE:

TOTAL
FROM
STATE:

New
   Castle—1
North-
   brook—1
N. Brad-
   dock—1
N. Ver-
   sailles—1
Philadel-
   phia—34
Pittsburgh—2
Port Ma-
   tilda—1
Pottstown—1
Radnor—1
Spring-
   field—1
State Col-
   lege—1
Sumney-
   town—1
Temple—1
Wayne—2
Wilmer-
   ding—1
Windber—1

11 Rhode Island:
11 (city un-
known)

9 South Carolina:
8 (city unknown)
Columbia—1

3 South Dakota: 1
(city unknown)
Sioux
   Falls—2

9 Tennessee:
Knoxville—2
Nashville—4
Sewanee—2
Tulla-
   homa—1

32 Texas: 13 (city
unknown)
Austin—3
Cleveland—1
College Sta-
   tion—2
Dallas—2
Denton—4
El Paso—2
Fort
   Worth—1
Galveston—1
Houston—2
San An-
   tonio—1

3 Utah:
Layton—1
Logan—2

13 Vermont: 1 (city
unknown)
Burlington—3
Middle-
   bury—1
Mont-
   pelier—3
Plainfield—4
Putney—1

21 Virginia: 12
(city unknown)
Alexan-
   dria—1

Charlottes-
ville—4
Halifax—1
Lynch-
burg—1
Springfield—1
Virginia
Beach—1

48 Washington: 12
(city unknown)
Bellevue—1
Belling-
ham—4
Centralia—2
Chehalis—1
Cheney—1
Edmonds—1
Ellensburg—1
Everett—1
Moses
Lake—1
Olympia—2
Quilcene—1
Seattle—8
Spokane—2
Sunnyside—1
Tacoma—5
Tri-Cities—1
Trout
Lake—1
Yakima—2

35 Wisconsin: 19
(city unknown)
Augusta—1
Elcho—1
Eleva—1

Ft. Atkin-
son—1
Green Bay—2
Kansas-
ville—1
Kenosha—1
Madison—2
Milwau-
kee—2
Racine—1
Ripon—2
Waukesha—1

3 Wyoming: 1
(city unknown)
Cheyenne—2

36 Canada: 9 (city
unknown)
Calgary, Al-
ta.—1
Courtenany,
B.C.—1
Grand Forks,
B.C.—1
Lethbridge,
Alta.—1
London,
Ont.—1
Montreal,
Queb.—4
Newfound-
land—1
Newmarket,
Ont.—1
Ottawa,
Ont.—1
Sask.
Regina—1

TOTAL FROM STATE:		TOTAL FROM STATE:	
Scarborough,	5	APO: 5	
Ont.—1	28	Washington,	
Toronto,		D.C.: 28	
Ont.—5	13	Foreign:	
Vancouver,		Australia—1	
B.C.—2		France—2	
Wembley—1		Germany—3	
Willowdale,		Mexico—2	
Ont.—2		Puerto	
Windsor,		Rico—3	
Ont.—2		Singapore—1	
Winnipeg,		Sweden—1	
Mani-			
toba—1		TOTAL:	1817
	27	unknown	

"MARITAL STATUS"

The following categories refer to the ways in which women described their own lives. The division married/single is no longer sufficient for the classification of sexual relationships. This question was not asked on any of the questionnaires.

	Q.I	Q.II	Q.III
Married (number of years not given)	182	250	46
Married 1–5 years	19	28	4
6–10 years	6	15	5
11–15 years	4	12	4
16–20 years	5	3	4
21–25 years	3	12	5
over 25 years	2	8	3
Divorced, now single	52	74	30
Widowed, now single	12	15	3
Single	186	246	55

	Q.I	Q.II	Q.III
Boyfriend	70	81	19
Living with lover*	75	104	43
Celibate	3	7	1
Total	619	855	222
Did not answer	71	64	13

*Includes lesbian relationships.

Breakdown by Percentages
(percentages of those who answered the question)

	Q.I	Q.II	Q.III
Married	36.0	38.0	32.0
Divorced and widowed, now single	10.0	10.0	15.0
Single	30.0	29.0	25.0
Boyfriend	11.0	9.5	8.5
Living with lover	12.0	12.0	19.0
Celibate	0.5	1.0	0.5
Total	99.5	99.5	100.0

AGE, RELIGION, EDUCATION, AND OCCUPATION

Statistics on age, religious background, education, and occupation are not available for Questionnaire I, since this information was not requested in that version of the questionnaire. Since so many survey results have given the impression of categorizing and labeling people on a superficial basis, it was hoped that by not asking these types of questions, the questionnaires could break through to a deeper level of communication with the person answering. Quite a few women did appreciate this approach:

"I almost don't know how to handle not being required to put down age, sexual experience, marital status, occupation, etc. It was very objective and remarkably impartial. Great!"

"The questionnaire was good in that it completely avoided questions about age, how long you've been having intercourse, and whether it's with one partner or many. Statistics are easy to answer and to add up, but they encourage you to stereotype yourself on the other questions as well."

"You never asked if I ever had children or was married! Hooray for you!"

"I answered this questionnaire because it was the only one I've ever seen that didn't make assumptions or seem to be overconcerned with placing me in a sociological pigeonhole—like how many men I've slept with, how much experience I've had, that kind of thing."

However, information about age, religious background, education, and occupation was requested in Questionnaires II and III, and these results follow:

Ages of Respondents

AGE	Q.II	Q.III		AGE	Q.II	Q.III
14	3			31	28	8
15	2			32	26	12
16	6	3		33	22	5
17	10	5		34	14	5
18	22	3		35	14	6
19	28	6		36	21	7
20	38	6		37	13	4
21	33	10		38	15	4
22	44	6		39	18	7
23	47	7		40	13	4
24	41	4		41	10	4
25	63	7		42	16	4
26	57	11		43	14	2
27	31	12		44	10	4
28	39	10		45	9	1
29	28	7		46	7	3
30	38	5		47	7	1

AGE	Q.II	Q.III	AGE	Q.II	Q.III
48	4	1	66	1	
49	5	1	67		
50	8	6	68		
51	8	3	69		
52	5	2	70		
53	6	4	71	1	
54	2	1	72		1
55	9		73		
56	2	1	74	1	
57	2		75	1	
58	4	2	76		
59		1	77		1
60	4	3	78		1
61	1				
62	1	1		853	213
63				66 ages	22 ages
64	1			unknown	unknown
65		1			

Religious Background

	Q.II	Q.III
Catholic	252	41
Jewish	198	40
Protestant	309	73
did not answer	160	81
total	919	235

In addition, over 95 percent of all the women who answered indicated that they had been brought up with the idea that sex was "bad," or at the very least a subject that was never mentioned—implying that it was bad.

Race was not specifically asked, and since only a small number of women identified themselves by race, these figures are not included here.

Education

	Q.II	Q.III
less than high school	12	4
high school	145	24
some college	264	60
currently in college	139	31
nursing degree	12	1
B.A./B.S.	179	35
graduate school/ law school	39	8
M.A./M.S.W./ M.B.A.	82	33
Ph.D.	23	12
travel	11	—
"well educated"	14	3
total	741	211
	(178 did not answer)	(24 did not answer)

Occupation

(The following terms are those used by the respondents.)

	Q.II	Q.III
Accountant	4	1
Actress	4	2
Administrative assistant	11	4
Advertising executive	2	—
Air Force	2	—
Artisan	1	—
Artist	17	10
Auditor and tax consultant	1	1
Barmaid	1	—
Bookkeeper	—	2
Broker	—	1
Cab driver	—	1
Call girl	1	1

	Q.II	Q.III
Cashier	4	—
Chemist	1	—
Child care	—	1
Clerical	13	—
College administrator	1	—
Computer coder	1	1
Computer service	1	—
Conservation service	1	—
Costume design	1	—
Consultant	1	—
Counselors		
abortion	2	—
disability determination	1	—
drug	—	1
guidance	1	2
problem pregnancy	—	1
sex therapy and counseling	1	2
vocational	7	1
Cryptanalyst	1	—
Dancer	3	—
Day care	1	—
Dental hygiene	1	2
Department manager	4	1
Diamond cutter	—	1
Dog trainer	1	—
Drug dealer	1	—
Editor	5	2
Factory work	1	—
Food economist	—	1
Greenhouse worker	—	1
Government job	1	1
Health food store stocker	1	—
Hospital worker	14	—
"Housewife"	262	34
Insurance	1	—
Interior designer	1	—
Key-punch operator	—	1
Librarian	3	4
Masseuse	1	—

	Q.II	Q.III
Medical field	11	
Medical technician	2	2
Microbiologist	—	1
Minister	1	—
Model	2	—
Music business	1	—
Nun (ex)	3	—
Odd jobs	6	1
Own a business	1	—
Own a secretary service	—	1
Personnel	1	—
Physical therapist	2	—
Physicist	1	—
Probation officer	1	2
Professional woman	15	5
Program dircetor	3	—
Proofreader	2	2
Psychiatrist	1	—
Psychologist	2	3
Psychometrist	1	1
Public relations	1	—
Radical collective	—	1
R.N.	17	4
Reporter	5	—
Research	6	3
Sales clerk	2	—
Sales representative	1	—
Scientist	1	—
Secretary	89	24
Slave	2	1
Social worker	9	6
Sociologist	2	—
Songwriter	—	1
Speech pathology	1	—
Stewardess	11	—
"Street rat"	1	—
Student total:	139	31
College breakdown:	(95)	
Graduate school	(11)	

	Q.II	Q.III
High school	(10)	
Law	(2)	
Nursing	(6)	
Ph.D.	(4)	
Pre-medical	(1)	
Unclear	(10)	
Switchboard operator	8	1
Teacher		
College	3	7
H.S.	75	11
Testing electronics systems	—	1
Unemployed	23	5
Waitress	5	—
Work for senator	1	—
Writer	25	12
X-Ray technician	1	1
	867	207

"Why did you answer this questionnaire? How did you like it?"

"I answered this questionnaire because I think the time is long overdue for women to speak out about their own feelings about sex. As for whether I liked it, I can only say it was a great relief to say these things out loud at last. I for one am heartily sick of reading what men have to say about my sexuality."

"This was a great questionnaire. I really enjoyed thinking about how I felt about things. Women need to communicate with each other so much more, because we can really give so much to each other. I've learned a lot about my sexuality the hard way—but it doesn't have to be so hard. Sharing is easier."

"I am grateful because finally I got to tell how I *really* feel about sex and my sex life. There's no one I can talk to that would understand, and now I really feel good, like a burden's been lifted. I'd felt like this for so long I was ready to burst."

"I answered because I like the whole idea of it—that

for once a group of women are going to be able to say what we like and don't like and what we want and don't want. I am tired of having some man tell me what I should want and feel and what my sexuality is or should be. I would never try to tell a man what his should be because I have no way of knowing."

"Because I believe the findings will be significant. Since this is anonymous and written, instead of verbal, one can be completely honest without any discomfort. I would find it very hard to have to *say* all these things to another person, and I'm sure many women would feel the same as I. I believe it's terribly important for all women to know what most other women experience— not just what the more sexually free women experience, like those who don't mind relating publicly their experiences, or who could manage to perform in a laboratory situation. I don't believe those more uninhibited women represent the general female population. And if we are to help the rest of us, we have to know what the *average* woman experiences, women we can all identify with."

"I answered this questionnaire because I hoped that in some way it would shed some light for other women, so that they might not go through what I went through to realize they are not 'frigid,' 'inadequate,' or 'have something wrong with them.' Even though more is being written about sex, many psychiatrists, psychologists, M.D.s, etc., are still too uptight and unknowledgeable to be of any service at all. Even in some large metropolitan areas, the heads of psychology departments at universities, for example, don't yet feel that it is important or necessary for women to orgasm! My own O.B. in a large metropolitan area six years ago told me orgasms 'would come' one day when I was 'least looking for them.' I'm glad I didn't just sit back and wait!"

"I really enjoyed this questionnaire. I found out a lot about myself and quite a few things are really clearer to me after writing them down. I sure didn't think it would take so much time but it was worth it. I wish I could keep a copy for myself but if my husband found it, it would hurt him too much and I can't do that to him, because he has been good to me. I do wish he were more of a feminist, but that's the way it goes. I hope my answers have helped."

"I answered it because I'd like to help add to our collective knowledge of ourselves, and it seems a good approach to begin to define female sexuality without theorizing. I trust the answers you might get more than the answers male gynecologists and male analysts have gotten on women's sexuality. We need to know, but we don't get to know with all the studies being done by men. I liked the questions—they made me feel very deeply about things."

"I suppose I just wanted to tell someone how I really feel and get it out in the open. My partner knows most of my feelings but not all of them. I would like to know more about sex, but most of the books I have read are not very revealing. They don't answer the important questions. I really hope that when this book is published it will answer these type of questions. I have found no such book or information yet. All my friends don't know the answers either. At our age (I am eighteen years old—almost nineteen) we really are in the dark about sex."

"It was *great*! Had to do with *my* sex life, not how to please a man!"

"Before this questionnaire, I was content to end the sex act with my husband's ejaculation, sometimes feeling unfulfilled. I now demand more attention, and my husband is very happy to oblige."

"My husband has read through the questionnaire—but not through my answers—and I am going to try to discuss the questions with him, though some of them may be painful. I wanted to answer them all first, however, without getting any comment from him. Perhaps we can find out more about what each of us wants and needs, though that wasn't what the questionnaire was set up for."

"It helped me to be clear about my sexual needs. I am happy that it demanded my being explicit. It also succeeded in putting me in touch with areas of my sexuality that I need to work on in order to get more gratification out of sex. I'm thinking in particular about my inhibition in asking for what gives me pleasure."

"Glad to be able to say what I feel for once. Relieved. Cried some. P.S. I hope the good doctors learn something (smile)."

"I have a great deal of anger about my sexual hang-ups and a great deal of confusion. I am at a point of seeing how much of what I have learned of sexuality has really been slanted and sexist. I am trying to dump that garbage, and trying very hard to *listen* to what is in me. I think it is high time we let those mucho macho jobs know they're doing a lousy job of making women happy. And if they want it for themselves, they'd damned well better make it better for us."

"I answered it for cheap therapy, and introspection. I'm glad I did it—I was able to tie together patterns that I hadn't thought about before, despite the fact that I do think about these things and introspect a lot. Looking over it, I want to go back and rewrite and explain and qualify it all—but probably I wouldn't do a better job than this on a second time around, only a different one—there are lots of contradictions and inconsistencies and complexities in my thinking. I do think the questionnaire is aimed toward women who have done a lot of sex with a lot of different people; I feel defensive about having been with one man so long. But on the whole, thank you greatly—I don't spend my average day writing ten pages on my sexuality and it's been a good thing to do."

"The questions sure got me thinking about myself! I was slightly embarrassed writing out the answers, thinking at certain points the questions were too personal—if it hadn't been anonymous I never could have answered. I learned more than you have about myself."

"I answered because it seemed like a good way of having a dialogue with myself—only incidental to sharing me with you. Now I'm glad I did it. I've kept a journal for fourteen years without ever being able to write this candidly about my sex life. I was able to let out hidden things I'd otherwise never tell a soul!"

"What I like best about it is the thought that I'm talking to other women."

"I am only grateful I don't have to sign this, as all hell would break loose if this ever got into the wrong hands. I can't say I liked answering these questions, I would die of embarrassment to do so in person. This way I don't mind. My only reason for doing so is to be of some help and that is all."

"I cried when I first read through this. There is so much I've lied about for so long; I'd already come to understand that, but wanted to fill out the questionnaire to make myself write it all down. Undoubtedly, you will have helped many women in just this way, and publication of the results will reach many more who as I did, will read the truth they couldn't tell themselves."

"I had an experience into myself, my past and my sexuality in answering. I can only say it brings to mind the lack of areas for 'aging' sexually active women to find satisfaction whether in or out of love relationships."

"I wanted to make sure you had at least one questionnaire with my viewpoint. It was difficult for me to answer this, but I did so in the hope that I could reach someone out there."

"I answered because I think your results are going to be based on a 'skewed distribution' of super-liberal and radical reformer types—and for balance you need some 'straight' *happily* married folks!!"

"I thought that some input from a person who was extremely slow and conventional in sexual development might be helpful to you. Not being a swinger—I had to force myself to be frank in my answers. It was worth it."

"Anything that helps women define their own sexuality on their own terms, and thus have more control over their own lives, is something I want to be part of."

"After I wrote reams, you ask me why I answered this—hah! I feel that all people regardless of age and experience have to be more open and honest and learn from each other. *Some* young people feel they have the market on sexual experience. They have a lot to learn!"

"Because I felt there were not enough statistics about women septuagenarians nor enough understanding of the widows' situation. At my age and without responsibilities I do not want matrimony, but I have a continuing sex drive. Also I had heart surgery two years ago, which has completely rejuvenated me. I want to live to the fullest extent of my capabilities."

"I have a twenty-three-year-old daughter, to whom I still owe much in the way of truth-telling. So, what I have to say here is for her as well as for all young women."

"Saw an ad in the paper, thought you should have the opinion of a middle-aged woman concerning her sexual attitudes. Interesting questions, thought-provoking; some were hard for me to answer because I had never thought about them. I would not have answered honestly without anonymity, and I would not have answered as carefully had it been a multiple-choice questionnaire. For the most part I enjoyed seeing my reactions to many of the questions; but I found most of the questions dealing with masturbation disturbing . . . and I guess that only shows I have not dealt with my feelings regarding it. And if I haven't dealt with my 'hangups,' will I pass them on to my children?"

"I've read the results of a few sex questionnaires before, and all the women seemed happy, well-adjusted, and in control—that is, they all had orgasms. I felt lonely, left out, and odd. I answered this because I wanted you to hear from someone like me who is still struggling with it—but putting up a good fight, too!"

"This questionnaire was hard to answer. I felt blanked out, confused. I didn't want to face what's hard to look at for me. I didn't feel as lucid or as happy with my answers as I usually do when I write. I usually feel clear when I write. I can express myself well, get more in touch with myself, through writing usually—not here; this was hard. But I wanted to hear about/from women who were where I'm at or who had hassled through the same shit and this seemed like the only way to do it."

"Being non-orgasmic, sex is often on my mind and

takes a lot of my energy. So it helped me feel a little better to have a chance to voice my frustrations."

"I answered because I feel the women's point of view should be publicized. I have read many of the sex books available, and they are all written of the male, for the male, and by the male. I would like to ask Dr. Freud how many orgasms Mrs. Freud had?! And Dr. Reuben is another one."

"I think real information on women's sexuality should be made available to other women. It's time we began understanding each other instead of only trying to understand men."

"Actually writing out the answers to it was a chore for me; I did it doggedly to help other women."

"I feel that I owe the women's movement a lot for my own personal sexual satisfaction, which I might never have discovered otherwise. That's why I filled out this questionnaire. I hope it shakes male assumptions to the roots."

"It made me uncomfortable and especially the questions I don't have answers to. But I think it's an important body of knowledge—so I forced myself to be honest. I feel very strongly that sexual education for women will be one of the greatest single factors in our liberation. That's why I answered."

"I answered because I'm sick of all the lies that are printed about women's sexuality—especially that of lesbians."

"I answered it because I am hoping it will be compiled to give a true, realistic picture of female sexuality. I get annoyed at all these men who write about women and how we should or shouldn't feel. They can't possibly know how we feel."

"Wow—let's let women tell it like it *is*, instead of all these men telling us like it '*should*' be!"

"I answered this questionnaire because I was intrigued by the idea of sex information collected by women from women. This project seems to me to have real constructive possibilities and I hope there will be more of the same in the future, and that women will just throw out old assumptions about their sexuality and try to find out what's really happening. And what could happen. I hope no new set of assumptions ever assumes the coercive, limited character of the old Judaeo-Christian and Freudian assumptions. I also hoped, through answering questions, to help jog myself out of old ruts and to get more of an idea of what sort of woman *I* am, sexually. Good luck to you!"

"I liked the questionnaire. I've been doing it at work for the past week and have hurried home at five o'clock sharp every day horny horny horny. As I've said, I've started becoming more creative sexually thanks to these questions. Also, I've become more insistent on climaxing, which is great."

"I got the questionnaire from my mother-in-law's copy of *Sexual Honesty*, and I was moved and fascinated by the diversity of replies. Women telling it like it is! I'd never really thought before about how arrogant men are telling us what we feel or should feel. I felt for those women who wonder if there is something wrong because they don't have orgasms, as I had this problem for many years. I'm sure many women read the book and realized that they were not abnormal after all!"

"I thought this was a very good questionnaire. The different questions seem to give an opportunity to think about various aspects of sex from more than one angle. This type of study is much needed. The book was very supportive, especially in clearing up my own feelings of uncertainty about how long it takes me to have orgasms and that I didn't have orgasms during intercourse. It was helpful to see that there do seem to be wide differences in the amounts of stimulation and time women take to have orgasms and that many women don't have orgasms during intercourse at all, or only very rarely. The most immediate results of this for me was that I decided to ask my husband to help me have an orgasm when I wanted one during intercourse instead of not asking because I had felt maybe I was somehow asking for too much."

"I answered because I went through such hell figur-ing out what was 'wrong' with me, and only after reading the results of the women in *Sexual Honesty* did I start realizing that maybe there wasn't anything 'wrong' with me but that there was, in actuality, something 'wrong' with the information I had been reading or hearing, mostly from male psychiatrists and doctors."

"It was most fascinating, but not surprising, to read in *Sexual Honesty* how many women got off on cunnilingus rather than penetration. It was a surprise to me to learn of the many women who masturbate and the many ways they do it, and of course that was very helpful to me. This book is totally unique, and I recommend it to all women, and men. It's really going to explode the door on a lot of myths. It must be a very interesting task to read all these confessions; I think it is the first and only time most women can really tell it like it is, because with women friends there is usually a block against telling all (she has orgasms and I don't) and men, no matter how genuinely interested some of them appear to be in female anatomy, you can't tell them how it feels since, well, since they have a prick and you have a should-I-say-it cunt. Many thanks."

ANALYSIS OF REPLIES

One woman who answered wrote, "This is the most fascinating sex survey I ever participated in, but I am baffled how you could compile an essay type of study in an accurate form." Had I not written my Master's thesis on the methodology of the social sciences, undoubtedly it would have been more difficult than it was. Actually, it was difficult and time-consuming, but the results made it more than worth it. There were probably over thirteen thousand woman hours involved in analyzing the answers, plus at least another ten thousand put in by the women who answered the questionnaires.

Specifically, the information was analyzed in this way: first, a large chart was made for each question asked. Each person's answer to the question being analyzed was then copied onto that chart (which was usually many pages long), next to its individual identification number. The many days required to copy the 1844 answers to each question were actually very valuable in that they provided extensive time for reflecting on the answers. Once the charts had been prepared, it was a relatively simple, though again time-consuming, process to categorize the answers. Usually patterns had begun to stand out during the copying process, so that the categories more or less formed themselves. Then figures were prepared by totaling the number of women in each category, following which representative quotes were selected. This procedure was followed for each of the 50-odd questions.

In addition, one main chart was kept onto which much of the information from other charts was coded for each individual woman, including preferred type of stimulation, type of masturbation, number of orgasms desired, age, and many other facts. This chart, which acted as a kind of handmade computer, was the basis for the majority of statements in the orgasm, intercourse, and clitoral stimulation chapters.

PROJECT FINANCING

There was no foundation grant or other funding involved in this project. Originally, extensive funds were not needed, as printing was inexpensive. Luckily, there is a free press (Come! Unity Press) in New York that makes space available for non-commercial printing—for whatever donation you can afford, as long as the material printed is free to everyone.* Eventually I printed all the hundred thousand questionnaires at this press, with the help of other women—in many different colors, and on many different kinds of paper, including scrap from old bingo score cards. Thus, until the analy-

* Of course the questionnaires were always free, and *Sexual Honesty* was available free to anyone who wrote me for it. Unfortunately, the present book could not be offered free but many N.O.W. chapters are receiving free copies so that anyone who is interested, member or not, can have access to the book.

sis of the information was begun, the main expense of the project, besides paper and moderate contributions to the press, was postage, since over 75,000 questionnaires were mailed.

The larger the project became, the more apparent it became that the results could best be made available in book form. *Sexual Honesty by Women for Women* was an early attempt to share these replies in the form of an inexpensive paperback. However, since paperbacks do not generally receive as much attention as hardcovers (in terms of publicity or book reviews), it seems that in the long run, the information in hardcover books reaches more people. As for contributing to the financing of the project, the book advance for *Sexual Honesty* was of course small and only contributed to the continuing printing and mailing of the questionnaires. It was really the generous advance, through the sponsorship of Regina Ryan, which made possible the time necessary for the analysis of the answers. The debt I owe to Regina Ryan is enormous. Without her perceptive understanding of the project and belief in its importance from the very beginning, and her unerring good judgment at so many points in the work, the wheels of progress would undoubtedly have ground to a halt many times.

Eventually, it also became necessary to borrow money from friends, some of whom went into debt themselves to loan me money. For this very important support for the project I am especially grateful to Cecile Rice, Michael Wilson, and Virginio Del Toro. However, since loans must eventually be repaid, and since book advances are in themselves a sort of loan, in a very real sense it will be the people who buy this book who will, in the long run, have financed this project.

WOMEN WHO CONTRIBUTED

There were many people who contributed to this project, to whom I am deeply grateful. I am indebted to Veronica di Napoli for so freely and ably giving of her intelligence, time, and resources for two years, not only preparing and analyzing the charts, but also in many other critical aspects of the project. She also made some funds available to the project at a time when they were greatly needed, for which I send her my warmest personal regards. Dylan Landis also gave enormous amounts of time and energy to the project, and waited for over a year to be paid. Without the help of these two women, this book would undoubtedly have taken another two years to complete. Other women who worked painstakingly and with great dedication for hours and weeks on end, for very low pay, were Claire Cowdery, Helen Ferraioli, Maria Finchenko, Diane Maller, Ruth Matthews, Susan Olup, Andrea Selkirk, Julia Spears, and Carol Timko. To all of them I send my thanks and personal greetings.

Many other people helped in other ways, including Sydelle Beiner, Jan Crawford, Stefanie Erickson, Heather Florence, Polly Kellog, Helen Kirschner, Barbara Love, Carol Lowenberg, Naomi Mankes, Mercure, Frances Moulder, Trudy Rosen, Joyce Snyder, Laura Spadicini, Lee Walker, Vicki Wilson, C.K. Yearley, and Sara Zarem. I would also like to thank Dorothy Crouch for her great support for the project from the very beginning. In addition, I am deeply grateful to Barbara Seaman for her own book, *Free and Female*, and for her enthusiastic support and encouragement throughout the entire period of this project, which was a source of great help to me, and a real example of sisterhood.

I would also like to thank the women who produced this book. Not only were the questionnaires printed by women, and the replies analyzed by women, but some very talented women were responsible for the production of the book. Again, without Regina Ryan one wonders what the fate of this book might have been. I cannot thank her enough. At every step of the way, her criticism was invaluable, and her long-term vision and enthusiasm regarding the project provided me with an infinite source on energy and encouragement. Lindy Hess was also extremely important in producing this book, and deserves a large amount of credit and praise for her skillful work in many areas and her intelligent and carefully considered criticisms of the book's content, which influenced the shape of the book. She was enormously helpful, and enormously kind, and I am very grateful to her. Suzi Arensberg took on the gigantic job of copyediting the manuscript, and did so in a remarkably sensitive, skillful, and thoughtful manner. Christine Aulicino is responsible for the book's beautiful design. Finally, had it not been for the women who answered the questionnaires, there would have been no book, and to them I send my warmest greetings and my deepest personal appreciation—and congratulations.

MASTURBATION

INTRODUCTION

Masturbation is, in a very real sense, one of the most important subjects discussed in this book and a cause for celebration, because it is such an easy source of orgasms for most women. Women in this study said they could masturbate and orgasm with ease in just a few minutes. Of the 82 percent of women who said they masturbated, 95 percent could orgasm easily and regularly, whenever they wanted. Many women used the term "masturbation" synonymously with orgasm: women assumed masturbation included orgasm.

The ease with which women orgasm during masturbation certainly contradicts the general stereotypes about female sexuality—that women are slow to become aroused, and are able to orgasm only irregularly. The truth seems to be that female sexuality is thriving—but unfortunately underground.

How women masturbate is one of the most important keys to understanding female sexuality (from the point of view of orgasm): since it is almost always done alone and since in most cases no one is taught how to do it, masturbation provides a source of almost pure biological feedback—it is one of the few forms of instinctive behavior to which we have access. Although some women did not masturbate until after they had had sex with another person, most women discovered it on their own, very early: "I've never needed anyone to tell me where I have to be touched to have an orgasm; I've just been masturbating ever since I can remember."*

* As Betty Dodson has written in "Liberating Masturbation," "Masturbation is our primary sex life. It is *the sexual*

Surprisingly, most researchers have not shown much interest in masturbation. Generally, they approach the study of sexuality through intercourse, with masturbation as a sidelight—since, it is argued, the "sex drive" is fundamentally for purposes of reproduction. However, to take intercourse as the starting point is an assumption†—one that has led to widespread misunderstanding of female sexuality. To assume that intercourse is the basic expression of female sexuality, during which women should orgasm, and then to analyze women's "responses" to intercourse—is to look at the issue backwards. What should be done is to look at what women are actually experiencing, what they enjoy, and when they orgasm—and then draw conclusions. In other words, researchers must stop telling women what they *should* feel sexually, and start asking them what they *do* feel sexually. This is what these questionnaires have attempted to do.

The fact that women can orgasm easily and pleasurably whenever they want (many women several times in a row) shows beyond a doubt that women *know* how to enjoy their bodies; no one needs to tell them how. It is not female sexuality that has a problem ("dysfunction") but society that has a problem in its definition of sex and the subordinate role that definition gives women. Sharing our hidden sexuality by telling how we masturbate is a first step toward bringing our sexuality out into the world and toward redefining sex and physical relations as we know them.

---

base. Everything we do beyond that is simply how we choose to socialize our sex life."[1] In addition, primates also masturbate more or less instinctively from childhood on.

† The basis for this assumption is analyzed in the chapter on intercourse.

FEELINGS
ABOUT MASTURBATION

Masturbation seems to have so much to recommend it—easy and intense orgasms, an unending source of pleasure—but, unfortunately, we are all suffering in some degree from a culture that says people should not masturbate. This deeply ingrained prejudice is reflected in a quote from a woman who was in other ways very aware of the culture's influences on her: "A problem is definitions and usage of words. Probably one of the most offensive statements I've seen in this regard in a long, long time is your question, 'Do most men masturbate you?' To some extent, my difficulty with that is that I give a negative connotation to masturbation when compared with intercourse; that is, I would rather have intercourse than masturbation. I take masturbation to mean what I do to myself, alone. Intercourse is what I do with another person, regardless of what takes place. To call vaginal stimulation of the penis intercourse, and to call manual stimulation of the clitoris masturbation, insults me and makes me angry."

Actually the term "masturbate" had been used (really, misused) as a euphemism for someone giving someone else manual clitoral stimulation with the express purpose of gauging the reaction to this usage. The meaning was perfectly understood by the overwhelming majority of women, but the implication was *hated*: sex with a partner legitimizes the activity, whatever it is, and to call it masturbation demeans it.

We have arrived at a point in our thinking as a society where it has become acceptable for women to enjoy sex, as long as we are fulfilling our roles as women—that is, giving pleasure to men, participating in mutual activities. Perhaps in the future we will be able to feel we have the right to enjoy masturbation too—to touch, explore, and enjoy our own bodies in any way we desire, not only when we are alone but also when we are with another person. "The importance of masturbation," as one woman put it, "is really to love and care for yourself totally, as a natural way of relating to your own body. It is a normal activity that would logically be a part of any woman's life."

"Do you enjoy masturbating?"

Most women said they enjoyed masturbation physically (after all, it did lead to orgasm), but usually not psychologically.

Psychologically, they felt lonely, guilty, unwanted, selfish, silly, and generally bad. Other words that were frequently used included "uncomfortable, adrift, uneasy, pathetic, ashamed, empty, cheap, dirty, self-centered, silly, disgusted," and "self-conscious." As one woman said, "To me, masturbation seems lonely, childish, self-absorbed; everything I'd rather *not* have as part of my sex experience. I do it sometimes, but I wouldn't brag about it in public." Other women gave similar opinions:

"Physically, I enjoy it, especially if I'm not in a hurry. Psychologically, I sometimes enjoy it, but often I feel too self-conscious or embarrassed or even guilty, to really get into it. I don't masturbate too often, because I'm sort of prejudiced in favor of sex with a partner, and I'm living with a man (my husband) from whom I'm almost never separated and who usually wants to have sex with me as often as I want to with him. But sometimes I just feel like masturbating and sometimes if we fuck and I don't come, I masturbate afterwards, and sometimes we like for him to hold me while I masturbate, but not really all that often. I probably only masturbate about once a month at most."

"Yes, I enjoy masturbating. Psychologically, I'm not sure. It's not so much that I feel I am doing something 'dirty,' but it does tend to reinforce my fears of being 'frigid' or just fucked up (I'm afraid I've been terribly influenced by all that 'literature' that says if you masturbate but can't orgasm during intercourse, you are very screwed up). I always orgasm when I masturbate. It's more intense alone. I usually orgasm once or twice."

"I enjoy masturbation physically, but psychologically, as much as I 'know' that it is good and there is 'nothing wrong with it,' I also know that it is not socially acceptable by the majority, and I suffer a guilty fear of being 'discovered' and rejected for it."

"I only started to masturbate recently, after a long abstinence since childhood. It was hard to begin—I felt self-conscious and a little silly. Physically I enjoy it, but psychologically I still have difficulties—a fantasy is necessary. I masturbate about once a week under the bathtub faucet. I do it only for the orgasm—it takes about half an hour to orgasm, but I try to prolong it."

"I very often feel that sex is not quite proper behavior. I always enjoy it very much, but I feel an indefinable uneasiness afterward (even after masturbating). This is only the second time in my life that I have admitted to masturbating. The first time was when my sexual partner asked me."

"I'm rather bored with masturbation, truthfully. If anything I enjoy it more physically than psychologically. If I am dependent upon it, I sometimes masturbate twice a day and it usually leads to orgasm. I think it would be more intense with someone although most men consider 'playing with yourself' something not quite to be shared—unless they are at the same time playing with themselves—I have found men's hands often go toward their genitals when they relax, yet I have been criticized for touching myself by my partner who could not accept the idea that after *he* had come, I was still unsatisfied and he was already on his way to the bathroom."

"Physically yes, psychologically no—there is a feeling of foolishness attached to the act—I prefer mostly waiting for the 'real thing.' I know my associations of loneliness, rejection, childhood punishment, and social ridicule are non-rational. But physical sensation is also non-rational, and it doesn't help to lecture myself."

"I enjoy masturbating. The physical stimulation and the orgasm is nice, but I often feel ashamed afterwards like there is something wrong with me because I should have a man to do this any time I want, and I don't."

"No, physically it's okay but it's the mind thing that throws me. I always feel cheap and dirty. So I don't do it much and when I do, I have orgasm. Really, I just like to block out the entire thing."

"Yes, I like masturbation. Physically, the only times it is uncomfortable is when my bladder is too full; sometimes then there are sharp pains in my urethra. Psychologically, it has definite ups and downs. Some of my sexual fantasies wouldn't even make grade C movies. And god, the number of reruns in a season. Couldn't really say how often I masturbate. At a guess, somewhere between every seven to fourteen days. It used to always lead to orgasm, but sometimes now my heart just ain't in it (I have been known to fall asleep halfway through). Oh, about the ups psychologically with masturbating. I started masturbating around age twelve, but it wasn't until age twenty-two that I actually made love to myself, if that makes any sense. Up to then there had been more dislike and disgust than tenderness. It has only happened half a dozen times or so since (I'm twenty-five now), but I'm sure it is significant. I have never masturbated in anyone's presence."

"I enjoy masturbation physically, but *not* psychologically. I masturbate maybe three times a month. It always leads to orgasm and is equally intense by myself or with someone, but I feel more at ease by myself. A partner's ego is hurt because you can achieve so many orgasms to his one climax! I usually have only one orgasm with a partner, but several if I'm alone."

"First of all I don't know if we both have the same definition. To me it means to have sex with yourself and I think of that in terms of also being by yourself and not with someone else present. Physically I enjoy masturbation; psychologically, I have a lot of guilt and 'dirty' feelings although in my head I recognized fully that

I shouldn't feel bad about it. I think it's as valid as any other sex, and to be alienated from your own body would not be good. I look forward to an orgasm when I masturbate and that's probably because it's an active experience for me since it's hard to have passive moments when you're alone."

"Physically, yes. Psychologically, no. Actually I haven't lived long enough with the fact that, yes Virginia, girls do masturbate. I did it often when I was young (eleven to fourteen years old) and then I 'prayed' for the strength to give it up. My sinful ways! But all too often 'strength' would fail me and I'd be back praying to god that lightning wouldn't strike me. I knew I was a Sinner."

"Physically, yes. Psychologically, I'm just beginning to appreciate the sexuality of it. I've learned about feelings and sex from it, although not too long ago, I experienced much guilt. I always have an orgasm, sometimes up to three at one time. If I wait after each one, I can have nine or ten, but that's rare. It's usually exhausting after three. It's more intense alone since I find I hold myself back when with someone."

"I'm liking masturbation more and more, both physically and psychologically. Physically, it's quick and easy and satisfying. Psychologically, it's a little lonely, sometimes, but then, so is making love with a person who doesn't love you. I masturbate most evenings before I fall asleep. I always have at least one orgasm and usually am satisfied with half a dozen. It is the same intensity, whether alone or with a partner."

"Yes, I enjoy it a lot, but I feel that if I masturbate too often, it will be harder to reach my goal to give freely with a man. I masturbate almost daily, with a vibrator. I almost always orgasm, but manually I have just recently learned how, so I only orgasm sometimes. A vibrator takes five to twenty minutes; with my hand, thirty minutes or longer. I'm too inhibited to masturbate with a partner yet."

Some women used to feel guilty about masturbating, but had gotten over it.

"Yes I enjoy masturbation physically, but only recently psychologically. Before other women began to talk about it I was sure there was something wrong with me for needing it. (I usually masturbate two times a week, and have three or so orgasms each time, in about one hour's time.) I resent not learning how to masturbate until I was an adult. I was too much of a prude to experiment and invent it until I had already been married for several years. I could have had a lot better time in adolescence if I had."

"I like to masturbate physically. I used to feel a little guilty (or frigid) psychologically but not any more. It always leads to orgasm. It's more intense alone but it lasts longer with someone. I usually have about eight when masturbating. There was much guilt involved with my early masturbation as mother always sneaked around on tiptoe trying to catch me at it."

"Yes, in all ways. For a long time I had a psychological hangup, because I felt it was wrong, but it felt so good I didn't want to quit it. But when I started reading that it was natural, I began to feel more relaxed and realized I wasn't weird or perverted."

"At first I thought it was wrong to masturbate, because that's the way I was brought up and because nobody talks about it now, either, so I assume they all think it's bad. But I personally enjoy it and think it's a healthy part of my life."

"From about eleven on I started to feel guilty about masturbating. I was always afraid of being caught. At nineteen, after I finished once, I thought: this cannot be a sin. It always makes me feel better afterwards and I'm not harming myself or anyone else. So God cannot think it wrong. So I went to an old and very strict priest for confession and asked him about it. To my surprise and relief he said it was not a sin. That *every* woman and man did it. There had been new research in psychology and it was found to fulfill a psychological and physical need and therefore it was normal and natural.

This was from a priest who was not liberal or new church. He was so compassionate. After that it didn't bother me any more."

Other women could not let themselves enjoy masturbating, even physically.

"I enjoy masturbation in all ways, but I still have trouble overcoming my upbringing on this one. Masturbation is not as satisfying. I reach orgasm, but don't really enjoy it terrifically. I only have one orgasm because I feel ashamed to have more, although I easily could."

"I seem to prefer suffering with my own horniness to masturbating. I guess I don't blame others for doing it, but I was taught that it was indecent and to hold myself 'above' such behavior. So I developed a tolerance for others' masturbation, but not mine. It's a matter of pride and inhibitions. Basically, I'm a snob."

"I only masturbated once—to find my clitoris so I could show my husband. I became very aroused but stopped because it scared me—I felt I was doing something wrong and might get caught—maybe my husband would come home and find me 'wet' and suspect—although intellectually I know it is not wrong and he does not think it is wrong. I suppose this must go back to some early experience with my parents, although I can't remember any. I can't even remember being that interested in my body. Then I began to develop breasts. I was surprised and only then began to notice them on other women."

"I have too many mental blocks about masturbation. Physically I would like to. Kids in elementary school had the attitude that people who 'played with themselves' were somehow emotionally incomplete. At this time I masturbated but quit because of what they were saying."

"I don't enjoy masturbation at all. It's my only sexual release right now but I dislike it intensely, not because of any moral objection but because it's not what I want; it's lonely, cold, and not satisfactory at all. I have one orgasm, alone, and try to forget it."

"When I masturbate I psychologically feel guilty or disgusted with myself. I did it once and that's all for me."

"I have very strong inhibitions about masturbating myself, and do not, and cannot bring myself to discuss it."

"I've only tried it once and I actually broke down in tears because I felt so guilty. It felt good, but I missed having another body to grab and being fondled myself."

"Masturbation could be very damaging to me, so I try to avoid it unless it's absolutely necessary."

But some women completely enjoyed it.

"I never masturbated when I was young, and when I found out about it, I was filled with a sense of power and liberation. Masturbating helped me learn a great deal about the changes my body goes through in achieving orgasm."

"I enjoy physical masturbation at least five days a week. Ninety-nine percent of the time I do it alone simply because most males think it is 'dirty' to see a female masturbate. If the prejudice weren't there I would do it in front of them."

"I love it. However it would embarrass me to admit it to most (not all) of my friends, mainly because I have the feeling that they would disapprove—they would tell me to find a man. But my faucet never disappoints me— and men usually do."

"Yes, I enjoy masturbating, physically mainly. How often—I don't know—usually when I have no one to fuck with, like when I am temporarily separated from my partner—although masturbation is not *only* a substitute for fucking because I enjoy it immensely as something *different*. I always have orgasms, at least three or four. It's more intense when I'm alone, as I'm more relaxed and less inhibited."

"Masturbation is my only sexual activity at the moment, as I have been a widow for the last two years and haven't yet felt like making new friends. It really isn't bad. I did masturbate all my life, off and on, whenever the need arose, but now it has become a more regular daily part of life. Actually, I rather like it."

"At this point I must make my masturbation confession. Masturbation has not been important to me until last night when I masturbated for the first time, after reading several confessions in *Sexual Honesty*. This is not shit, masturbation was always a sort of vague abstract concept to me because I never knew how nor felt the need to. Of course I had read a lot about it in high school and even made a few attempts to try it, but I didn't know my body and sensations then so I lost interest. After last night I will venture to say that it will definitely become a regular part of my sex life. It was great!"

"Masturbation is one of the sacred rituals that women can enjoy amongst themselves. I say it is 'sacred' because it is *self*-initiated, *self*-controlled, and *self*-gratifying—coming from a position of strength. It is not only about a physical or emotional (they are inseparable) closeness to one's own body, but a conquest of all the fears that families and men have instilled in women about their bodies and sexual dependencies. Try it—you'll like it."

Almost all women had been brought up not to masturbate.

"The earliest I remember masturbating was at age seven, although I didn't know what 'it' was until I was fifteen. Up until then, it was just something that felt good—but that I was feeling very guilty about, because it was in a 'naughty' part of my body."

"I don't think my mother ever taught me anything about masturbation that I can remember. When I was a teenager, and started to masturbate, I had read in a book that it was normal and not wrong, and my mother had not said anything to me, nor had anyone else that I can recall, yet I felt, if not guilty, then at least that I had to hide about it. I still can't talk about it as comfortably as I can everything else about sex."

"When I was almost fifteen, I had my first experience of kissing and light necking with a boy. These times left me sexually excited (though I didn't realize that's what it was at the time). After coming home and going to bed I touched myself and had almost immediate orgasm. So I began my secret, guilt-ridden life of masturbation. I tried not to do it, but couldn't keep from it, it felt so good!"

"When I discovered my clitoris at age eighteen, I thought I was queer and I alone had one. I left home and masturbated a lot and thought I was the only woman in the world who did it. Now I know that is ridiculous, but my first lover (for four years) didn't know either."

"The first time I made myself come I was nineteen. I was sitting on the toilet in the college library. I felt totally guilty about it. I was living with a guy at the time. When I went home I was scared to look him in the face."

"My first experience with myself was in the preschool age. I would masturbate (I didn't know that was what it was) by clutching stuffed toys between my legs and sort of wiggling up and down. I remember it very clearly for two reasons: it felt so good, and my mother was so completely horrified when she noticed me doing it. She got very angry, and threatened to take my toys away."

"At about eight I made a very feeble attempt at masturbation, at which I was caught by my mother, who gave me a very long lecture on how this would cause me to become insane. This was my last attempt at masturbation until seven years ago, when I had my first orgasm. I am now fifty-one."

"Once my mother caught me masturbating (just last year) and she was shocked, although she pretends to be enlightened and liberal about sex. She also told me about every part of my body except my clitoris."

"I used to feel terribly guilty about masturbating, and up to the age of fifteen or so, I periodically confessed to my parents that I had been doing it, and promised never to do it again, but always found myself unable to keep that promise. I knew that the modern point of view is that the guilt and fear I suffered was unnecessary, deplorable, and unhealthy. But I place great value on the whole experience, guilt and all: I view the fact that I did continually masturbate, in spite of my guilt and my fears, as a very positive act of courage and self-assertion, as a dawning recognition of, and respect for, a power that I did not understand, a power greater than my parents and other authority figures, a power greater than reason."

"I have been masturbating since age five, at least. I can remember, at that age, my parents' gentle but nervous attempts to prevent me from touching my genitals. I also remember, at that age, being sick (some infection, I suppose) and having to take medicine that looked like water but tasted truly horrible, and believing vaguely that there was some connection between my innocent (as I saw it then) activity and my illness."

"I definitely 'discovered' masturbation by myself, although I believe that my parents' selectively negative reactions helped me to focus my interest on this forbidden part of my body. At first, I just enjoyed exploring. Gradually, as I became older, the feeling that I was doing something shameful and bizarre became part of the pleasure. I began to have masochistic fantasies about being alternately encouraged (by dirty-minded, leering men) to be 'naughty,' and then being punished for it (by the same men or by other adults—not my parents though). These fantasies, of which I felt terribly ashamed, became an essential part of masturbating. When I was about ten, a girl my age had a bout of serious illness. My father told me that her illness, of which she had almost died according to him, had been caused by her doing 'that.' So I began to realize that perhaps other children masturbated too, but still couldn't quite believe it—it was such a crazy thing to do. The first time I came I was about twelve, I think. I was frightened—I thought I had really screwed up my body, and this strange spasm was the onset of some kind of fit. I sort of held my breath and waited to see what would happen next. Nothing further happened and I seemed to be all right. Still, I decided I better cool it. But after a few days I had calmed down, and cautiously tried again, and came again, and this time I was less frightened. Soon I accepted the orgasm as a natural event, and began to enjoy it."

"What is the importance of masturbation?"*

Most women felt that the main importance of masturbation was to substitute for sex (or orgasm) with a partner.

If some of these answers sound a little cold or stiff, it is merely a reflection of the deep embarrassment the question aroused in women:

"I suppose it's important to relieve some of the frustration of not being able to get a good lay."

"Masturbation is satisfying, but not a substitute for male attention and affection."

"It keeps you from going nuts when you need sex."

"It is relatively important when *real* sex is not available."

"It is my only present form of sexual activity, and it serves the purpose of giving relief from sexual tensions."

"It enables you to be less demanding of your partner when he is not able."

"Masturbation is okay when you have no partner. But I have a full-time man."

"It's only a substitute for successful coitus."

"It's important to women without men who can gain relief that way."

"I think masturbation is essential to one's health. One cannot always have a partner, and—as I learned in my marriage—a partner is not always good sexually, though he may be wonderful in other ways—so I think everyone should know how to masturbate, know her own body."

"The difference between this and sex with a partner

---

* See page 591 for a statistical breakdown of the answers. Generally, statistical breakdowns of all the main topics in this book will be found in the appendices at the back of the book.

is that the intense heat of another body is missing, plus the stimulation of other parts of the body. But you can do it alone, quickly, and you're always sure of an orgasm."

"If your partner rolls over and goes to sleep, you can do it yourself."

"If I can come to an orgasm by myself, I don't feel I have to have sex for that reason alone and can really dig knowing a guy without sexual tension there and really dig just touching and enjoying both his body and mine. Since I usually don't have orgasm with my partner, this is very important for me."

"It's important for survival: my husband can't spend as much time as I'd like in bed."

"They used to say it made you crazy—but I'd *go crazy* without it."

"It's a safe, readily available means of sexual gratification. Better than bad sex with an incompatible partner."

"The importance of masturbation for me is that it's my only source of orgasm. But basically I feel that the exclusiveness and compulsiveness of masturbation is probably unhealthy. I think it's very sad that the only way I can have an orgasm is by masturbating. It makes me feel diminished in my soul."

"Second class fun."

Others saw it as a learning experience.

Many women mentioned that masturbation was also important as a way of learning about sex:

"Masturbation has helped me know how to have an orgasm, and to recognize the stages of arousal I go through."

"It teaches you to have orgasms and how to accept them; what they feel like, how you react and feel after, what you feel like after you climax."

"Masturbation was a release valve when intercourse did not lead to orgasm for long periods of time. It allowed me to examine and learn about my own sexuality: what actually happens to me during arousal, orgasm, what I find pleasurable. It has made it easier for me to tell what feels good, has made me like myself more, and given me insights into the depths of me."

"Masturbation gave me the knowledge I *could* achieve orgasm. Now I know what it feels like and know I'm *normal.*"

"It's a way to explore and learn about your body without depending on a man to show you. The first man I slept with assumed I'd never had an orgasm before— that I needed him to show me how. Of course I wasn't supposed to assume such things about him."

"It taught me a lot, mainly how to reach orgasm. Up until January 1973 I thought it was dirty. Now I know how wrong that idea is. I've learned to enjoy many aspects of sex since then and I feel masturbation helped a great deal."

"I'm convinced auto-erotic stimulation is essential to most women—it may be the only adequate introduction to their bodies they receive."

"Through masturbation I can learn how my body can feel and how it wants and likes to feel."

"It's important in finding the stimulation points of your body, discovering your own body."

"It's a way to explore one's sexuality without the self-consciousness of having anyone there."

Some women also felt masturbation helped them to have better sex with another person.

"Masturbation teaches you to know your own body, and to gratify it, which leads to increasing your sense of independence and may also increase your ability to relate to someone else; being able to tell someone else what gives one pleasure can do a lot for a relationship."

"If you feel guilty about touching yourself, you can't be very free in giving yourself to another, or touching someone else."

"How can you love or satisfy someone else if you can't satisfy your own self?"

"Masturbation develops one's sexuality, because you learn how to touch yourself and therefore others. Perhaps the danger is that you can make it *too* good, because you can make it as you like it, which lovers may not be able to do as well."

But some women saw it as a means of independence and self-reliance.

"Masturbation is the only way I can come without embarrassment and self-consciousness and 'trying to succeed' for my partner's sake."

"It gives me control over my own body because I don't have to be dependent on another person for sexual fulfillment. Because this is possible, I have control over my relationships."

"Masturbation gives you the ability to relieve your own tensions at will, without having to run out and find a sex partner that might not be able to satisfy you anyway. And there is no emotional entanglement."

"It's important because it is always there as an alternative. It has given me a sense of dignity since I realized that I could have sexual pleasure without a man."

"It feels good without feeling guilty about having sex with just anyone, or feeling like he has just used you, and also you don't have to worry about getting pregnant or V.D."

"It relieves tension and preserves human dignity vis à vis other people."

"Masturbation enables you to have self-determination on when and how much sex to have."

"Masturbation is sex on a solo level—that's like saying I can take care of myself. Get in touch with my body and self. I am *here*. I am sexy. I am okay. I *like* myself."

"Masturbation is important for women who are taught to rely on men for sexual satisfaction and who are taught our bodies are ugly and mysterious. And that's just about *all* of *us*!!"

"Maybe if more women were able to find sexual release through masturbation, they wouldn't be forced into relationships they did not want. Many women just don't know how, I hear, which is amazing to me."

"Masturbation relieves frustration and releases energy. It's a way of having sex in which one completely controls the situation."

"It was originally very important to me in giving me a way of finding out about my own sexual nature, and now it is nice because I don't feel so dependent on men and can make up for their sexual mistakes."

"A way of taking responsibility for my own body. I should be able to make myself as happy as others make me."

"Given the historic horror of our culture for masturbation, I suppose being able to masturbate and not be upset by it in others is some small degree of freedom."

"It gave me a feeling of power and liberation when I found out about masturbation and that I could orgasm that way—which was only last year."

"To me its importance is in being able to have an orgasm all by myself, which means: I'm proud of myself. Right after orgasm I usually feel overwhelmingly proud of myself and fond of myself for having given me such a wonderful thing!"

And some women described it as pure pleasure, important in its own right.

"Masturbation is important for pleasure, as a different aspect of any person's sexuality, just like heterosexuality and homosexuality. I don't think enough people have thought it all through. I also strongly feel that my church is wrong in saying that masturbation detracts from sex with other persons. It doesn't; it's just different."

"The attitude that masturbation is just for when you can't relate to someone else sexually for whatever reason is nonsense. Masturbation is another form of sex and should be seen as such."

"I thought of masturbation as a last resort before, but now—it's just another alternative. I used to feel guilty if I masturbated while I was living with someone, but now I think that's ridiculous."

"Masturbation is self-love, giving yourself pleasure, a natural part of regular, everyday life."

"Masturbation is important to relieve tension, to indulge in fantasies, plus, I feel I owe it to myself, as a belated form of self-love. Until I was twenty-nine I never masturbated despite the fact that I was tempted to. As an adolescent, masturbation meant 'self-abuse.' After shyly joining the women's movement, however, feelings of worth and self-respect grew and I gradually dropped the mantle of 'professional Martyr' which my husband, Church, and mother were only too willing to help me possess. A door mat feels she doesn't deserve the pleasure of masturbating. So masturbation had a symbolic meaning for me. It was one of my first overt expressions of self-love, of the dissolution of guilt and the beginning of self-confidence."

"The importance of masturbation is for you to be able to love and care for yourself totally, an expression of self-sufficiency and completeness."

"I think the importance is for pleasure. I used to masturbate in the bathtub with my girlfriend, under the faucet, taking turns. It makes me feel good seeing someone I care for having pleasure that intense."

"For me, masturbation was symbolic of getting rid of attitudes about sex being bad. Being Catholic, I was brought up to think that I should not obtain power or pleasure from my body, nor should anyone else. Furthermore, I felt that my body was dirty and I equated sex with being dirty. I had intercourse before I learned to masturbate. So for me the act of masturbating showed me that I had learned to accept my own body as a means of deriving pleasure."

"I think masturbation is an important exploration and enjoyment of one's own body, and a release of tension at one's own control. I think it can be very beautiful, like a dance with oneself. T. and I are just now learning to watch each other masturbate, but I find it embarrassing. I guess I have some inset rules about 'sex is supposed to come from the other person.' "

"It helps me calm down, feel warm (I get very cold at night), go to sleep, work out my fantasies, and meet the sexual needs of the day."

"It is important to relate to one's own body in a total

way. Loving and respecting oneself should include physical love."

"Masturbation helps you feel good about your body, and liking to touch it, and also it's a good release for those who like orgasms (including me)."

"The importance of masturbation is to come to an orgasm."

"Masturbation wakes me up in the morning. An energy-starter."

"I think it is important that women be freed from the myth that the only road to pleasure is the penis in the vagina."

"Masturbation is important because sometimes I don't feel like sharing my body. It's just for me and I enjoy it."

"Masturbation is important to feel you can give yourself pleasure, can take as long as you want, do what you want, fantasize, etc. Also it gives you a sense of incredible sensuality."

"Masturbation is a beautiful fulfilling gratification of the needs and pleasure of your body—almost a revitalizing force."

"It lets you satisfy yourself best, when you really, really want to get into having an *intense*, very heavy, strong orgasm."

"Often when I've had sex with a man and no orgasm, masturbation has been frustrating and bad, and I can't come. But other times, it's been self-love, beautiful and clear and kind. Then I can rarely stop and get up even after three or four climaxes."

"It has taken me a long time to realize my sexuality is *mine* to *enjoy*, not something I owe my husband or anyone else. It's nice to have fun all by yourself!"

TYPES OF MASTURBATION

Six basic types of masturbation were found.

%	TYPE	DESCRIPTION
73.0%	I	Stimulating your clitoral/vulval area with your hand while lying on your back.
		IA. (47%) Clitoral area stimulation.
		(17%) Clitoral area stimulation with variations:
		IA, direct: direct stimulation of the clitoris itself
		IA_1–IA_5: clitoral stimulation sometimes accompanied by vaginal entry
		IB. (8.8%) Clitoral/vulval area stimulation.
5.5%	II	Stimulating your clitoral/vulval area with your hand while lying on your stomach.
		Same subheadings as I
4.0%	III	Pressing and thrusting your clitoral/vulval area against a soft object.
		Sometimes also includes vaginal entry: III_1–III_5
3.0%	IV	Pressing your thighs together rhythmically.
		Sometimes also includes vaginal entry: IV_1–IV_5

%	TYPE	DESCRIPTION
2.0%	V	Water massage of your clitoral/vulval area. Sometimes also includes vaginal entry: V_1–V_5
1.5%	VI	Vaginal entry.
11.0%		Women who masturbate in more than one of the above ways:

4.4%	IA	1.2%	III
.3%	IB	.9%	IV
1.5%	II	2.1%	V
		.4%	VI

In view of the difficulties women sometimes have in explaining to another person the stimulation necessary for them to have an orgasm—especially in view of the general misunderstanding of female sexuality—these classifications may be useful as "labels" of basic body types. They can be used to provide a convenient means of discussing things that heretofore required lengthy and sometimes awkward explanations.

TYPE IA

Type IA (manual/clitoral)* was used by the overwhelming majority of women who answered. Fortyseven percent of the women who described how they masturbate (plus 2 percent who could also masturbate in other ways) used this type of masturbation, and another 17 percent used it with variations. Basically, it means lying on your back and stimulating your clitoral

---

* It is important to clarify the usage of the word "clitoris" in the following quotes. "Clitoris" is a term that came into popular usage only recently, thanks particularly to Masters and Johnson and feminist writers; a drawing of it can be seen on page 180. In most of these quotes "clitoris" seems clearly to be used to refer to the general clitoral area, and not the clitoris itself, which is only approximately one fourth of an inch in diameter.

area with your hand (or a vibrator). This type of masturbation is so classic that popular usage of the term "masturbation" seems to be synonymous with it.

"To masturbate, fantasizing, or getting into an aroused state mentally is important. Also, for me, being alone is important. I use the tips of my fingers for actual stimulation, but it's better to start with patting motions or light rubbing motions over the general area. As excitement increases I began stroking above the clitoris and finally reach a climax with a rapid, jerky circular motion over the clitoral hood. Usually my legs are apart, and occasionally I also stimulate my nipples with the other hand."

"If I'm in a hurry (pressed for time), I use the vibrator on the base of the clitoris, with my legs open. But usually I use my fingers rubbing around the base of my clitoris, and when I'm near orgasm, I move my fingers to a circular motion on top of my clitoris. My legs are always apart, and I alternate hands because one gets tired. My other hand will caress my breasts or just rest. And I move my body a lot when I have the orgasm."

"Wow! What a question! Usually I lie on my back, my legs apart. I almost always have my panties on, as rubbing the clitoris itself directly is just annoying. I use one hand, two fingers together, rubbing up and down in short, quick strokes right over my clitoris. As I get closer to climax, my legs tend to spread apart and my pelvis tilts up more. I don't move around too much, but sometimes during climax I roll from side to side."

"I use my hands and my imagination, and have probably tried every imaginable position and motion—the basic stimulation remains the same. I use my finger to stimulate the clitoris, sometimes inserting another finger into my vagina at the same time. I touch only my genital area when I masturbate, because I am not stimulated by touching my body in general, as I am if my partner touches me all over."

"I stimulate the clitoris on either side with my legs apart, and do not move any other part of my body. It is as though I allow myself very efficient masturbation without guilt because anything else (touching myself all over, etc.) would be sick."

"When I masturbate I simply think locally stimulating thoughts, then a brief touch of fingers and it's over. Ha! Sneaky, isn't it!"

"I masturbate with my fingers on my clitoris, and other fingers gently pinching, pulling, scratching, across the surface of my nipples. It is necessary to maintain moisture on the clitoris. Sometimes I rub up and down, sometimes in circles. And my legs are sometimes together, and sometimes apart. It is especially exciting to hold my hand still and get the friction by movement of the body against the stationary finger. I also like to see and feel my breasts in motion. Usually I stand in front of a full-length mirror."

"I masturbate with my middle finger rubbing around my clitoris very fast until I come again and again and again. I rarely fantasize during masturbation, I simply want the sensation."

"First there is an up and down rubbing of the clitoris, then a slight pressure, then faster rubbing with pressure all over my mons area. I use my fingers first then my entire hand (palm for clitoral pressure). My legs are flapping or crossed, and high muscle tension is a must."

"I use my middle finger in up and down or circular motions on the clitoris and the area around it. I get stimulated better with my legs apart. I use the other hand on one of my breasts: I rub the nipple and pinch it, pull on it, etc. Sometimes I move a lot, sometimes I don't. I like to feel the erection of my clitoris with my finger."

"I masturbate in bed with my hand. I lie down, pet my skin all over then go straight for the clitoris and move in very rapid motions—sometimes touching the clitoris directly, sometimes just near it."

"I must still have hangups because it sort of embarrassed me to answer this. I rub the thumb of my left hand (I am right-handed) with a circular and up and down motion on my clitoris, legs together, starting out slowly and then more forcefully, sometimes massaging my breast with the other hand. I almost always fantasize and use 'dirty words.' And by the way, I have just turned myself on by writing this."

"Oddly enough, although I'm right-handed in most things, I always masturbate with my left hand. I lie on my right side and use my left hand from underneath me, the second and third fingers stroking my clitoris up and down the shaft. Usually I use a little vaseline to lubricate it. With my right hand, I gently press down on my lower abdomen. Sometimes I cross my left leg over my right leg and press down as I feel the orgasm coming. I move about a bit—sort of wriggling. I would like to try a vibrator, but I haven't had the opportunity yet."

"Sometimes I dress in erotic costumes and view myself in the mirror. Usually I smoke a cigarette, and sometimes put on makeup. If there is time, I lubricate my breasts and genitals with oil or cream. I prefer looking in the mirror rather than directly at myself. Usually I begin playing with my breasts, rubbing my thighs together, then concentrating on orgasm, using the fingers on my right hand in a circular motion on my clitoris. I start with my legs apart, but enjoy having them tight together at orgasm, squeezing the muscles. At that point, I can't move very much."

"I use only one hand and mainly rub up and down. Does everyone answer these questions so frankly? I feel a little wanton, but I feel you must be true or else why try to understand yourself? My legs are apart and I touch only my clitoris."

"I just start right in rubbing my clitoris. I used to touch my breasts and stomach, but it seemed redundant. Now I just rub my clitoris, and generally admire the qualities of me!"

"I masturbate by manipulating my clitoris in a side to side massaging manner, starting gently and increasing in intensity of pressure. I use my finger (one hand). The motion is slightly circular combined with side to side, mainly. The other hand is manipulating the nipple of the left breast (the larger and more sensitive one). Legs are apart. I don't move much, in terms of body movements, until orgasm, when there is a raising of the buttocks (whole pelvic area) and a total kind of stiffening of the body, but especially the legs and feet."

"I make circles with my hand until I almost climax, then fierce, hard, up and down motions around my clitoris. My legs are apart and straight and I don't move much."

"I use my right index finger and press around in clockwise circles, near my clitoris. I only start moving when I am about to come. It's inadvertent, my body just gets excited sort of like it likes what's going to happen and wants to help it along."

"I masturbate lying in bed at night. First I take my nightclothes off and just relax. I like to touch my breasts softly and stimulate them, then use my finger to stimulate my clitoris in circular and slow motions and then faster. I like to touch myself very lightly. As my body tenses, my legs close and I don't move much. I just concentrate on my feelings in the area that I'm masturbating."

"I just apply steady, fast, side-to-side motion to the clitoral area while I fantasize, and eventually I come. It helps if my legs are apart, but it's not absolutely necessary. I don't move much at all."

"I masturbate in bed with the door shut (four roommates!). First, I lean a pillow against my bed and sit in a reading position. I put a dab of vaseline on my clitoris, and get some pornographic literature (maybe a questionnaire!), and then I spread my legs a little and begin to gently rub back and forth on my clitoris with my index finger. I become excited, stop reading and turn out the light, take off my glasses. Then I return to more rapid back and forth rubbing on my clitoris and fantasize, then I orgasm. I continue to rub my clitoris until it is over. Usually my knees are bent up with my left hand gripping the edge of the mattress as pelvic thrusts increase in intensity, sometimes closing my legs on my hand and rolling onto my side and rubbing my clitoris."

"Yes I enjoy masturbation, and occasionally plan it and look forward to it. But it is for physical reasons, these days, and also during periods when my lover would be away. At present, I am getting old (age sixty), and I masturbate as a matter of course when I feel the need of it. I have tried many ways of masturbation, especially in these latter years, but I have sort of settled down to the vibrator-on-the-clitoris technique, turning it off just as I reach climax. With the finger, I use my middle finger. Also, pencil erasers when I was very young were nice, since they kind of fit into the clitoris. I can remember when I used a picking-up motion of the clitoris."

"My best 'quickie, one-minute special' is standing up with my vibrator, on my toes, totally tensed, dropping my pants to mid-thigh, and pulling up my top to uncover my breasts, with the vibrator tip against the clitoris and holding the body of the vibrator out, so it looks like a penis—in front of the mirror. I get turned on by my image doing this and come in a minute!"

"I am very faithful to one way: on my back usually lying down (in taxis or public places I can be seated or standing up), I touch my clitoral area with my right hand's knuckles (hand in a fist), actually, vibrating my hand over my clitoral area or the mound just above it, meanwhile pressing my legs together rhythmically, sort of pumping up to orgasm. Thinking sexy thoughts!"

"I usually lie down, with my legs apart, maybe my knees up. I touch myself very gently, especially the inside of my thighs, then proceed to manipulate my clitoris directly with the middle finger of my right hand. I start slowly around my clitoris, and lubricate it with saliva or soap if necessary (soap if in a tub). I make my whole body 'vibrate' by tensing my arm and moving it back and forth as fast as possible. I stop every so often, especially if I'm near climax, so I can enjoy the period of arousal. My whole body moves rapidly upon reaching orgasm, and my pelvic area moves spasmodically up and down. Otherwise I lie quite still except for my hand moving."

"I used to use my electric shaver—i.e., I held the side of it to the side of my clitoris. Since I've stopped shaving, I don't use it any more. (I'm not liberated enough to have the world, at least my roommates, know when I'm masturbating!) Generally, I begin with clitoral stimulation, usually with my right third finger. My left hand stimulates my breasts sometimes, but usually just massages my body. I think about someone I would like to be with sexually and generally just continue this until I reach orgasm. I don't move or utter very much sound. Legs are far apart, except at orgasm, then they are clamped together. I generally use a circular motion, but as excitement builds, up and down movements stimulates me better."

"I spread my legs, knees bent up (or else I do it standing up in the shower). I rub my clitoris with the middle finger of my right hand, pressing down, moving it in a circular motion. Sometimes, I squeeze my right nipple with my left hand. It feels strange to write this! I seem to get more and more tense all over, with both voluntary and involuntary squeezing together of vaginal muscles, until the tension in the vagina breaks into spasms and relaxation, and contractions of my whole body."

"I just rub with my fingers, up and down, usually using my left hand (I'm left-handed). I go for my clitoris and don't worry about my legs. I move some—but not enough to disturb my husband in bed beside me. He complains if I do."

"I masturbate usually after seeing an X-rated movie or reading erotic material. I can mentally recall the act and proceed to massage my body with a fur thing or sometimes just my hands. Then I moisten my fingertips with my tongue and lightly touch my breasts as if a tongue were licking them. The same with the clitoris. I hold my legs together and crossed at the ankles."

"I usually start out patting my clitoris, then after it starts to throb a little, I start an up and down type of motion, then finally a circular type motion where at times I press the labia against it (my clitoris) to make a sort of covering. Usually my legs are apart. My movements vary from being very still to jerk-type movements."

"I caress my breasts and stomach lightly. I spread my legs (very important) and rub my clitoris in circular motions with my hand or first two fingers. As I get aroused my body trembles and my hips jerk forward. It takes me maybe fifteen to twenty minutes to get to orgasm."

"Masturbation tends to be very functional; clitoral stimulation (squeezing and rubbing) by hand only. The use of jelly avoids irritation. My legs are wide apart. I touch my clitoris and squeeze it between the labia, continually rubbing the area."

"I have masturbated using my hand in circular motions, with my legs held tightly together. I have also used a vibrator, during which it is not necessary to have my legs crossed but I do find it necessary to keep them together."

"It depends. If I want it to be very pleasurable, I usually begin with *some* clothes on. Touching of the breasts and genitals through clothing is very exciting to me. As my body begins to respond, I go inside the clothing and touch my breasts gently, then move to a gentle caressing of the pubic area, moving slowly to the clitoris. I stroke it in a circular fashion, usually, and as the excitement increases, so does the tempo, so that as I approach climax, the stroking is almost a vibration, very rapid agitation until, like a starburst, I orgasm and all too quickly the climax recedes."

"I begin by stimulating my nipples with my fingers or sometimes with an object, anything that provides stimulation. An ash tray, pencil, book of matches, comb, whatever is handy. I used to have a feather which I used for this purpose, but got rid of it because of guilty feelings. Then I start to fantasize and do just this, no bodily stimulation at all. When I am ready to have an orgasm, I touch my clitoris usually applying firm pressure with my finger (or object) and moving it slightly up and down, while still touching it. I climax almost immediately. My legs have to be together tightly. I cannot reach orgasm if they are not, either with myself or partner. No, I do not move very much. I feel that it is possible for me to have an orgasm just through fantasy, without even touching my clitoris. This has happened once or twice, I believe, but it is more pleasurable to touch. I could reach orgasms very quickly if I touched my clitoris sooner, but I like to prolong it as long as possible."

"I use a simple battery-operated vibrator. I usually apply it to the right side of my clitoris, using a slight circular motion. I start with my legs apart, but they usually come together involuntarily and a thrusting motion takes over—quite involuntary. I really think what goes on in my mind (just who I am fantasizing I am with) is more important than the mechanical aspects."

"I have more intense orgasms with a hand-mounted vibrator, but more fulfilling orgasms with my fingers. I prefer a circular motion. The base of my clitoris is better to touch than the tip, which is too sensitive. I prefer my legs together. I usually squirm rather than move violently."

"I masturbate with my two hands, rather, my fingers, on or around my clitoris, up and down. Sometimes I use a wet warm towel. Psychologically, it's better if my legs are apart. I move but not frantically. The best times are long and quiet."

"I lie flat on my back, with the finger next to my thumb (always my right hand) rubbing up and down around my clitoris, thinking or reading happy thoughts and bang. If being helped, I prefer to work the bottom and them the top."

"With my forefinger, I rubbed the clitoris up and down. I use the past tense because I haven't had occasion to masturbate in thirty-three years."

"I use my second and mostly third finger in circular motions, or side to side, up and down. I do this mostly on the top (opposite from where the hole is), the very top. I start off with the legs in the middle between being together and apart, and then gradually I spread them."

"I use my middle finger and usually use a circular motion, but once in a while I'll use an up and down or side to side. Sometimes, I use a very fast motion (side to side) almost like a vibrator effect and I start up where my labia begins (right below where the pubic hair ends) and slowly masturbate around that area to build up subtle excitement, and eventually move closer and closer toward my clitoris, building more intense excitement the closer I get. I try to make this procedure last long, but sometimes it's hard to not get carried away real fast. Finally, I usually climax during direct contact around the clitoral area. I suppose it would work with my legs together, but it's easier for me with my legs apart. I don't move very much (sometimes I move my pelvis up and down); but usually my abdominal area jerks up and down once or a few times while I am climaxing."

"I lie down and begin to fantasize in my mind my favorite fantasy, which is a party where everyone is nude and engaging in group sex, lovely, lovely sex, all positions, kissing, caressing, cunnilingus, and intercourse. After about five minutes of this I am ready, very lubricated. I lift one knee slightly and move my leg to one side, put my middle finger on or around the clitoris and gently massage in a circular motion. Then I dream of being invited to this party and all those delicious things are happening to me. I try to hold out as long as possible, but in just a minute or two I have an orgasm. It is very simple, all in the mind. After the first orgasm I do not fantasize any longer, but concentrate entirely on the delicious feeling in my vagina and surrounding areas, continuing the same movement of my finger, but slightly faster and in about one minute I have another orgasm. I am very quiet, but do moan some during each orgasm. After several orgasms in this manner I start thinking of what's for dinner and the party is over."

"I masturbate with my hand. I usually lie on my back but sometimes on my stomach. I borrowed a friend's vibrator once but I don't think it can come up to the sensitivity of the hands. I have many different movements. Flat of hand sideways across the entire mons area, fingers alongside of the clitoris and then up and down or sideways, circular movement with hand or fingers. The movement is not so important as that a rhythm be maintained and that the pressure be firm and increasing in firmness until orgasm. I usually leave my legs closed. I do not move very much, perhaps only to raise my hips. I'm not really conscious of what the other hand is doing. Probably holding on tight. I concentrate on the clitoris and do not stroke or pet myself except sometimes the vaginal area. I guess I really want to get down to business."

"Usually, when I have a period of time alone, I love to masturbate. I usually use my fingers and rub in a circular motion. Sometimes for variety I use objects to rub my clitoris, such as the rounded handle of my hairbrush, any object I have on hand at the moment, but I don't usually do that. I like my legs to be very apart. And I've never used a vibrator, although I'd love to."

"I press my thighs together, and press my fingers downward from the top of the genital hair into the outer lips."

"I use my index finger and the middle finger of my right hand, gently rubbing the hair above the lips, then the lips, then my clitoris. The motion is circular, with a kneading motion. My left hand rests on the pubic area. My legs are together, my buttocks tense. I move very little. I learned to do it this way when I was in college, so my roommate wouldn't know what I was doing."

"I use my right hand, the second finger on my clitoris moving in a circular pattern. My left arm is stiff, legs are slightly apart. I don't move, scarcely breathing, staring blankly."

"I usually do it when I'm reclining or lying down. I like to be reading (or talking on the telephone with my lover). I use my right hand and rub my clitoris along the shaft or round and round the tip of it. I also like to fondle my breasts and pull my legs up and in. Sometimes I scratch the folds of flesh (labia minora) and smell and lick the wetness on my fingers. When the pleasure becomes very intense my hips move back and forth and then to orgasm. I like to masturbate best when I'm wearing close fitting pants. Sometimes I want to lick myself and I do lick my own breasts."

"I prefer masturbation to ninety percent of my sexual experiences. I use both hands, usually in the tub or in bed. I kiss my own shoulders and caress my own breasts and watch the nipples erect, which increases vaginal lubrication. Then I use a circular motion on my clitoris."

"I usually use the middle finger of the right hand on my clitoris, with a circular, up and down, firm, vibrating motion that gets faster. I usually have to stiffen my body and hold my breath. Usually I keep the other hand at my side, but sometimes when I'm coming I place it under my ass."

"I prefer to be wearing tight blue jeans and pulling so that the seam presses against the tip of the clitoris. Otherwise I use my fingers to provide gentle press-release pressure to the top of the clitoris. My legs are usually together, and I move very little. I can even do it in public without being observed, I think, with the tight blue jeans method."

"I masturbate with one finger in a circular motion, usually with my legs together. I don't move much. Touching myself through my pants is usually better because the material spreads the vibrations over a greater area. Stopping a few seconds just before orgasm and then rubbing again intensifies the climax."

"My right hand pulls my pubic hair above the clitoris toward my navel, and my left places the vibrator on top of my clitoral shaft. There is a drawing in of the muscles of the pelvic and rectal areas. I raise my hips, place my left hand (when not using the vibrator), second and middle fingers between the clitoris and outer vaginal lips, and rub from left to right in about one-inch sweeps with a very fast rhythm (like six strokes per second), push out on vaginal muscles then pull in, say something sexy to myself vigorously indicating I want orgasm, and hold onto the orgasm, pulling the orgasm in."

"I like to scratch my hair to get the kinks out, then proceed with my forefinger making back and forth movements on my clitoris. When that hand gets tired, I switch to the other."

"I begin by stroking the clitoral area, then stiffen my legs and vibrate the skin around my clitoris rapidly with my fingers."

"Masturbation never worked until I got a vibrator—a large one with several attachments and heat. With two hands, I hold it steady or use a slight circular motion. My legs are apart, and I hold it on my clitoris. Involuntary jerking or spasmodic movements indicate I will orgasm."

"I masturbate with a vibrator, my legs together, the sheets clutched in my left hand. Then I hunt for where it feels the best around my clitoris, moving either the vibrator or my hips back and forth gently. At orgasm I hold it quite still."

"Would you believe I'm not really sure how I do it?! That is, I had to do it while thinking about it to be able to write this. I place three or four fingers in between my large lips, the tips on the area above my clitoris, and start rubbing slowly in a circular motion, while fantasizing. I rub faster and faster until I then explode into orgasm. Sometimes I try to stave off orgasm for as long as possible, but this can be a mistake because sometimes I lose it or it's not as intense."

"I masturbate on my back, with my legs spread apart, knees bent, the index finger of my right hand stroking my clitoris and sometimes my lips. My left hand strokes my anus, not penetrating, just feeling around the opening, slightly lifting my left hip. Lately I've been turning over on my stomach, massaging my clitoris with my right hand, my knees pulled up."

"I fully enjoy masturbation—both with a partner and without. The intensity varies, but it is different without a partner than with one. I am able to reach orgasm much more quickly by myself and usually have three or four orgasms within five to ten minutes. I start by lying on my left side with my legs crossed, and slowly rhythmically massaging my clitoris with the index finger of my right hand. I move my legs, bending them at the knee, and increasing pressure on the clitoris until orgasm."

"I lie in bed on my back or side, with my legs apart, and apply the vibrator to the top and then to the left side of my clitoris. When I feel myself start to 'rise,' I slack off and then build up again. Sometimes I put the vibrator on the bed and spread my legs and then, well, 'sit' on it sort of!"

"When I masturbate, I begin by massaging the area

of my clitoris with my whole hand. The massaging is usually soft to begin with, and it gets harder as I get more and more excited. I usually rub my fingertips back and forth over the sides of my clitoris because when I rub the tip of my clitoris the sensations are so strong that they are almost painful. I prefer that the rhythm of these movements be fairly constant, but I like to speed them up or slow them down as I desire. When I am having sex with a partner, I try to get him to duplicate these methods that I use when I masturbate."

"I masturbate in a sitting position as much as I do lying down. I prefer circular or up and down movements with my whole hand and fingertips. I usually use my other hand to stimulate my breasts and nipples. As I said above, my legs are only slightly spread when I begin, but I spread them more and more as I go along. I also wiggle them back and forth. While I am stimulating my clitoral area with one hand, I like to stimulate my breasts with my other hand. Thus, I am usually gently bouncing and massaging my breast with my fingertips while I rub my thumb back and forth over my nipple."

"If I am dressed I usually take off all of my clothes, or I open and undo my clothes enough to have access to the areas of my body that I want to touch. Sometimes I begin to massage my clitoral area with my panties and/or pantyhose still in place and then, when I am ready, I will remove them, pull them down, or reach inside them. While I am starting to massage my clitoral area, I will also begin to caress my breasts."

"I enjoy masturbation immensely, but only in private. I usually pick out a fantasy, get into the role emotionally, then start by exciting the nipples, then working down to my clitoris. I like a fast tickling motion of the same speed on nipples and clitoris. I usually have a dildo at hand, but come before using it—just the fact that it's *there* turns me on!"

"I masturbate in many ways. I can lie flat on the bed, couch, floor, or in the tub and explore my whole body—breasts, belly, legs, ass, vagina, and clitoris. I love to rub my clitoris between my fingers, to grasp my whole vagina in one or two hands, to insert my finger in my vagina, to play with my huge breasts and beautiful nipples. I like to fantasize while doing this. I also like to do the same while using a vibrator."

"I have had an orgasm while playing with my breasts on several occasions. Then I rub my clitoris up and down and around until I find the right spot to have an orgasm. Then I continue it there, usually with my legs together, by then moving my hips up and down on it (my fingers or a vibrator). Sometimes, I hold the vibrator with one hand and play with my breast with the other."

"How I do it: if I'm bored, it's easiest to describe. I stimulate my clitoris with the third finger of my right hand (I find it very difficult to do it with any other finger) until I begin to feel excited. Then I use my left hand to stimulate my nipples at the same time. I hardly ever come without simultaneous nipple stimulation. I guess that's the way I do it when I'm not bored, also, except that I begin breast stimulation immediately— sometimes even just playing with my breasts alone in the beginning to titillate myself. Once I used a long ruler to be able to stimulate both nipples at once (with one hand), passing the ruler back and forth over my erect nipples. I find that if I am not in the mood for sex, my nipples and clitoris are relatively insensitive, whereas if I am excited, they are very sensitive. For my clitoris, I usually use circular or back and forth motions—very rarely patting motions for a short while. I often find that I have to stop at intervals—as though the clitoris had become desensitized by the friction, and I have to let it build up sensitivity for a few seconds. Also, I alternate with my nipples for the same reason. It seems that I must have my legs wide apart (usually knees bent out) and I have found that if I can arch my back (including having my head flat on the bed rather than bent forward on a pillow) I am much more sensitive. I don't move when I do it, except when I'm coming, at which time my hips raise and my back makes the reverse of an arching motion, sort of bending inwards. I think moving would simply be distracting."

IA direct

A small number of women (4 percent) stimulate the clitoris more directly. They generally hold the skin or lips stretched tight around the clitoral area, then stimulate the clitoris *itself* directly with the other hand. Many of these women mentioned that lubrication of some sort is necessary and that after one orgasm the clitoris was too sensitive to touch for a while.

"I use my third finger, moistened, to stroke and rub on and around my clitoris. My other hand pulls back the lips, keeping a gentle tension on the clitoral area. I alternate the rapid clitoral rubbing with a slower rub of the vaginal entrance. (Actually, 'rub' is hardly the right word, since it is a very light touch until just before orgasm, by which time I am very wet.) My legs are wide apart, my knees up—not much torso motion until orgasm, when there are strong muscle spasms in my torso and pelvis."

"I masturbate with one hand only—mostly around the head of my clitoris, then gradually switching onto the head—always with a rubbing, back and forth motion. My other hand helps to hold the skin so firm contact can be gained. I alternately have my legs together and apart."

"I lie on my back with my legs together tightly. I use my left hand to pull the top of my genitals tight and apart so I can use my right hand to stroke my clitoris. I use a circular motion starting slow with a light pressure, and then increase the pressure until I start to come. Then I slow down according to the sensation I wish until the orgasm is completed. If I want to come again I start over."

"I masturbate with an electric toothbrush. I put a dampened washcloth over the toothbrush and lubricate my clitoris with lotion. I lie on my back with my legs spread. With my left hand, I spread the labia to expose the clitoris, and I hold the vibrator with my right hand and gently press it on my clitoris. Sometimes I move it up and down, sometimes I leave it in one spot, depending on what feels good. But I never really get excited until I start fantasizing. I do not move my hips. The action is all with the hand/vibrator and my clitoris."

"I use my fingers only. My left hand holds the outer lips of my vagina open, and my right forefinger and second finger rubs the right side of my clitoris. Sometimes I rub up and down, but usually I rub in slow circular motions. My legs are closed, strained and straight out. Sometimes I will do this lying on my stomach, but not usually. It's a lot harder—I usually do that after I've masturbated a few times and I'm still frustrated. I don't move very much, in contrast with having orgasm with a partner, and I also make much less noise."

"I use my fingers, usually holding the labia apart from the clitoris with one hand, while with the other hand I flick my clitoris with one finger, and/or rub lightly, pinch and pull it between my thumb and index finger. Sometimes I fondle my nipples, and also like to feel my pubic hair. Legs are sometimes closed, and sometimes comfortably apart. I don't move much, just lie back and enjoy."

"Mostly I masturbate when feeling very good about myself, or mildly aroused. I use one hand in a light, circular back and forth stroking motion, while separating the labia with the other hand—usually sitting or reclining. Mostly the stroking is on the clitoris, but also near the vagina with an occasional thrust into the vaginal opening. Tightening the crotch muscle hastens orgasm. Also, occasionally I use mirrors to heighten the pleasure. My legs are apart until orgasm, then crossed firmly at the thighs."

VARIATIONS ON TYPE A: IA_1–IA_5

There are many variations of the basic IA type (stimulation by hand of the clitoral area) all of which involve varying amounts of vaginal entry while clitoral stimulation continues:

5% IA_1 Women who, during *some* of the times they masturbate, enter their vaginas.

5%   IA₂   Women who *always* enter their vaginas during masturbation.

1%   IA₃   Women who enter their vaginas at the moment of orgasm.

1%   IA₄   Women who use one hand for simultaneous clitoral/vulval stimulation and vaginal penetration: keeping the palm on the clitoral area, while a finger or fingers are inside the vagina.

1%   IA₅   Women who occasionally enter their vaginas to obtain lubrication.*

IA₁

Type IA₁ is the basic type, IA, with the occasional addition of a finger or something else in the vagina. Five percent of women who masturbated indicated they sometimes entered their vaginas, but not always.

"I usually masturbate by gentle stroking of the clitoral region, not the clitoris directly, but on the skin above and around it; then I place the fingers around the clitoris and move them back and forth rhythmically and with a bit of pressure. Thus, to achieve orgasm, pressure is one factor, rhythmic movement is another, and protection of the clitoris from direct stimulation is another. This last one is achieved by using the surrounding skin to stimulate the clitoris. Finally, tightening my asshole and concentrating on having an orgasm helps bring it on. Sometimes I stick my finger in my vagina as this seems to stabilize the clitoris and is a bit exciting. My legs are apart. I don't move very much."

"I usually start out rubbing my clitoris on the side of it, with my finger. Sometimes I use a mirror and watch—I used to stand up in front of a large mirror. Then, usually because my finger doesn't really turn me on much, I get out the vibrator. Sometimes I read por-

* The reason for the separation of all these varieties of vaginal entry or penetration will become apparent in the orgasm chapter, when the sensation of orgasm with or without vaginal penetration is discussed. The separation was important for statistical purposes.

nography, sometimes I fantasize. Sometimes I get out the baby oil and rub my breasts and stomach. I move the vibrator up and down along the slit between my legs. One leg is usually with the knee in the air, the other, opened, on the bed. I move my lower body up to meet the downward motion of the vibrator. Sometimes I lick my fingers and wet my tit, and just manipulate it, shake it around, etc. Sometimes I stick the vibrator in and out of my vagina, like screwing."

"I use my fingers rubbing back and forth on my clitoris, with the other hand massaging my nipples and/or sometimes inserting several fingers in my vagina. My legs are together (it's better that way because everything is tighter). Usually I move up and down, whether lying down or standing up. Now this always leads to orgasm, but it took me quite a while to learn what stimulated me quickly or slowly to an orgasm."

"One of my hands plays with the clitoral area, the other is in my vagina or playing with my anus. I touch all over first, then my more sensuous zones. I play in every way and position until I reach orgasm. Dancing nude and sexy is a good way of exciting yourself, and legs spread gives more room to move."

"I masturbate different ways at different times, sometimes beginning in the clitoral area, sometimes on my breasts. I use circular motions in both cases, often using two hands, one on my breast, one on my clitoris; or one on clitoris, one in vagina, or at its entrance. I achieve very large orgasms by running my finger between clitoris and vagina (in that channel) to stop orgasm before reaching it and then begin again until I cannot stop it any longer, all the while spreading my legs further and further apart. Except for raising my lower body up, up, up, my body per se does not move very much."

"To masturbate, I almost always need to be turned on by something like pornographic literature (and believe me it's hard to find anything even halfway decent). I lie in bed, on my back, slide out of my panties or pajama bottoms because I like to be free to move. I rub my two middle fingers up and down and around the clitoral area. Sometimes I put two fingers of my other hand into my vagina. I rub for a few seconds and tense up my body. I can usually feel a definite fuzzy feeling when I know the orgasm is coming on and then I rub harder, mostly up and down. My legs are apart. The vaginal area is usually moistened as a result of my pornographic reading, otherwise I use spit or, very rarely, cold cream. I usually arch my back slightly when I am really turned on, at which point I take the fingers of my other hand out of my vagina and I push down on the uterine area just above the pubis."

"My earliest masturbation was with tub water, and later with my hand, which is what I still do. I use the middle finger of my right hand in vigorous up and down motions which speed me up even more toward climax. Sometimes I put a finger deep inside my vagina with my thumb maintaining clitoral contact. Recently, since reading the literature, I have tried contracting my vaginal muscles, which does seem to enhance the act. Sometimes I thrust my whole body up, moving with my feet under my behind, ending up with my chest and torso and sexual area pushing up and facing the sky. My greatest release is with my legs pushed way apart to give the sensation of the greatest opening. I once tried a cucumber, and also a vibrator, but that gave me the feeling I was out of myself a little—not just me, that is."

"There are a variety of ways, but usually I put my fingers together and rub them back and forth fast over my clitoris. That much friction of the tender skin is uncomfortable, so I usually do it over my underpants. Sometimes I don't have on pants and I put a finger in my vagina, thumb remaining on my clitoris, and squeeze them (the two fingers) toward each other. This way I fantasize and sometimes get vaginal spasms, but it's milder than the first (just fingers on my clitoris). But sexier. In childhood through my twenties, I used to put things in my vagina, from ice cubes to lipsticks—whatever—and once my mother found me asleep with the flashlight on between my legs. The warmth was nice."

"I have several moods and modes of masturbation. First is the quickest, when I have clitoral discomfort from lack of sexual satisfaction. A few seconds with the electric toothbrush, my water pic, or vibrator and I am up and away. But when I want to give myself more full-bodied sexual satisfaction, I make more of a time sensual body thing out of it. I get out my dildo and sometimes my pot pipe and really let myself go on memories and fantasies of beautiful sex and people experienced thus. I can give myself an hour or two free-flow body sensuality this way."

IA₂

Type IA$_2$ is the basic method of manual/clitoral stimulation, but *always* with some form of vaginal penetration. Five percent of the women who said how they masturbated did it in this way.

"I put one finger on my clitoris and with the other hand I move a bottle in and out of my vagina (a plastic bottle). I have my legs apart at first until I orgasm, and then I put them together. First I rub my clitoris and then insert the bottle. When I come I close my legs with the bottle in me as far as it will go."

"I use my fingers first to penetrate my vagina, for purposes of enlarging the sensation in the general area, but then for orgasm I lightly and then more firmly rub my clitoris in circular or up and down motions. With my other hand (left hand), I'm generally turning the pages of the pornography book I'm reading. Yes, it's awkward. Legs apart."

"I fantasize first until I am lubricated. Often I tease myself and hold off touching until I am quite aroused. Sometimes I rub my whole body on the bed, lying on my stomach, and occasionally come that way, but usually I am on my back. First I caress the outer labia, then around the clitoris, using a circular motion, then I insert a finger in my vagina, while lying on my back or side, and move with it. I can come very quickly if my legs are together, but there is a better orgasm when my legs are apart and I work harder for it."

"My husband works a dildo in and out of my vagina while I press a vibrator to my clitoris. I do not touch myself because I am holding the vibrator. My legs are usually slightly apart, but sometimes together."

"I hold a vibrating dildo on my clitoris, with the nozzle of a douche bulb deeply in my vagina. This brings me intense pleasure and orgasm in thirty seconds. I just rotate my hips and move the vibrator, with my legs alternately apart and together."

"I begin with manual stimulation of my clitoris. Then simultaneous stimulation of both clitoris and vagina. Sometimes I use the finger/fingers (first and second or just second) of the other hand for vaginal stimulation. Sometimes I use an object—usually the nicely rounded, smooth handle of my hair brush (no spiked dildoes for me, thank you) for vaginal stimulation. I am defensive about mentioning that I use something other than my hand. Among all my associates there seems to be an unspoken taboo against all such 'unnatural' things. I have no object fetishes. I am not into hurting myself. It's just easier—it's hard to reach inside one's own vagina. My wrist gets tired, especially if I'm slow in coming. Also I guess I find needing vaginal stimulation is also unfashionable and I'm somewhat sensitive about that too."

"I wet my clitoral area (saliva or vaseline) and use an electric vibrator, the kind with attachments. I like to use my other hand with the fingers against the vibrator, so I get the sensation from both the vibrator and my hand. I like to have something (smooth bottom end of a candle, or a bottle) moved in and out of my vagina at the same time the vibrator is rubbing the clitoral area. I keep my legs apart. Sometimes I hold the vibrator still and move against it, sometimes I move very little and let the vibrator move. Lately I've pulled the skin under my pubic hair up toward my stomach so I can see my clitoris as I'm masturbating. Super exciting! Occasionally I use a mirror so I can see myself."

IA₃

A few women (1 percent) inserted a finger or fingers at the moment of orgasm.

"When I was a child, I would masturbate by holding

both hands between my legs very tightly and gently bouncing my whole body. Now I usually use my fingers to rub the whole genital area in a circular movement. Then I usually put one or two fingers inside my vagina before orgasm to feel the contractions."

"Just after I climax I often put a few fingers just inside the mouth of my vagina to feel the contractions—not just to see if they happen; it is very satisfying sexually."

IA₄

Type IA₄ (1 percent) is basically just a certain hand position: the palm is on the pubic area (clitoral area), and the fingers reach around into the vaginal entrance, making a kind of semi-circular shape of the hand. The motion most women mentioned here seemed to describe a very rapid movement of the entire, rigid hand— "a rapid slapping in and out, also circular," "very rapid patting." Generally, the inserted finger(s) was kept near the vaginal mouth to increase the sensation caused by pulling around the opening. This method seemed to provide good generalized sensation.

"I hold my hand palm flat on the clitoral area, and fingers inserted in my vagina about one inch or so, and just massage gently."

"I begin stroking the vaginal opening, then insert two fingers in my vagina and stimulate my clitoris with the palm of my hand with very rapid patting motions. My legs are together."

"I use one hand and clutch the mons, vibrate my hand over it until I get a warm feeling, then open my labia with a finger, and make it wet up and down, then insert a finger into my vagina and move it up and down very fast while the palm vibrates the mons. My legs are wide apart."

"I caress my nipples to get started, and look at pornography. Then I gently massage my mound until I am generally aroused, then insert my fingers into the vagina and at the same time rub my clitoris with my palm. Sometimes I suck on a rubber penis."

"My legs are apart, my middle finger is inserted deep into the vagina, with the palm of my hand making a circular motion over my clitoris."

"I use the heel of my hand and arm against the clitoris, and three fingers inside against the preliminary ridges of the vaginal wall—*not deep*. Legs apart always. I massage the external area and clitoris. I once used a carrot internally."

"My palm is against the fleshy mound toward the top front of my genital area, and one or two fingers are inserted in my vagina. I make very rapid slapping in and out and circular motions. Sometimes I rub the exterior of my anus simultaneously with the other hand."

IA₅

The final variation is the basic IA accompanied by a momentary entry into the vagina (1 percent) for the purpose of increasing lubrication.

"I start out squeezing my outer vaginal lips together and sort of rubbing my clitoris in a circular way through them. After a while I stick my forefinger into my vagina to get it wet and then rub the hood around my clitoris lightly in a forward and backward motion, which gradually gets a little more circular. I like to feel all around my whole vulva, but concentrate on the clitoral area. I always try to prolong the arousal state by moving very slowly, but I never can resist speeding up. I vary the pressure a great deal, but gradually rubbing harder as I get more turned on. Sometimes I feel my breasts with my other hand. I play with my hair. Sometimes I put my other hand in an 'innocent' position that doesn't appear to be involved in any way, because one of my favorite masturbation fantasies is that I have to appear as if nothing were happening at all, whereas secretly . . . sometimes my finger gets tired and I switch hands, but my left hand is always so much more awkward that I always switch back. When I'm just on the brink of coming I stop for a few seconds, if I have any self-control at that point, and wait till I calm down a little before starting again. I do this as many times as I can stand it (three or four) because I like to be so hot that my heart is pounding and shaking my whole body by the time I come. When I come, I thrash all over the mattress and gasp a lot; but if my partner's asleep I try to control it and not make too much noise. If he's awake, he usually gets into watching me, but for some reason the idea of waking him up by coming is too embarrassing for me to handle, unless I told him before he went to sleep that I was going to masturbate. I retain more guilt about masturbation than I do about any other sexual practice I engage in, and I don't know why that is, unless it's a fear of being self-sufficient. I seem to be feeling less guilty about it as I become more independent and self-assertive in other areas of my life, so maybe that's a good sign."

"I lie on the bed with my legs open, and run my hands over my body, massaging my breasts and feeling the sensations inside and outside my skin. My right hand rubs over my genital areas and my left presses my inner thigh and rubs my outer labia. I use my index finger to rub the labia, while my middle fingers rub the clitoris in circles. One finger moves down to my vagina and stirs around the inner folds, feeling the satin-like skin and bringing moisture back up to my clitoris, which I gently rub up and around and down. Meanwhile my left hand drifts around massaging my breasts and thighs."

IA with anal penetration

A few women in all these types also occasionally penetrated themselves anally:

"Upon thinking certain sexy thoughts my blood pressure feels like it's increasing, my heartbeat instantly becomes quick and hard. My clitoris tickles and within a few seconds my vagina gets slippery. I rub my clitoris with my left index finger. I penetrate my vagina and/or rectum with the index and/or middle finger of my right hand and move them in and out at whatever speed I wish. My genitals reach two or three stages of tickling intensity—each tickling more than the one before. I rub my clitoris in a back and forth motion. Sometimes I use household items which have the shape of a penis, for penetration."

"I masturbate in a darkened room. I sometimes read erotic literature, especially anal-oriented. I stimulate myself with lubricated fingers or a vaginal foam applicator or douche or enema tip. I usually make circular motions on my pubic area with one hand and touch my anus with the other hand, sometimes inserting my finger or an object in my rectum. It does not matter if my legs are together or apart. I move very little."

"Sometimes I use my fingers on my clitoris with one inside the vagina, one on the anal area, or just on the clitoris. Usually I use one of two sizes of vibrators—a small one for my anus and a large one for my vagina. One hand is used for the clitoris, the other holds the two vibrators in place. Legs are usually apart. Circular motions."

TYPE IB

Type IB involves a kind of masturbation in which it is important to stimulate not only the clitoris but also the other parts of the vulva (external genitals). The stimulation in this type seems to be a more generalized rubbing and massaging of the whole vulval area. Almost 9 percent of the women answering masturbate in this way, with approximately a sixth of them occasionally also inserting something into their vaginas.

"Dig this. I use the side of my electric women's razor to masturbate. I rub up and down and sideways and usually use the other hand to stimulate the rim of my vagina meanwhile."

"I use my fingers primarily. I begin by softly caressing my body and breasts, and genital organs. Sometimes I use two hands on my genitals, but not always. I try to wait until I feel moist before touching myself, because if I am not moist I usually have difficulty in achieving orgasm. So I rub and stroke my external organs, gently, and then I raise my legs into the air (wide apart) and then rub a little more vigorously—which leads to orgasm or orgasms. It seems necessary to raise my legs or I don't come. I often wonder if other women are the same."

"Slow light finger pressure below the clitoris and back and forth, sliding to below the vaginal opening. A slight pause, then up, then down, etc., pressing in just a little at the lowest point, while my mind's eye sees and feels all that is happening. I use one hand (the middle and two adjoining fingers for the lips), with the other hand propping up one leg as I lie on one side. There are definite rhythmic motions of the pelvis. After a while in this position, I turn over to my back and raise my legs enough to achieve tension, still pressing my entire vulval area up and down, sometimes with my middle finger in my vagina. Intensity varies with my degree of physical well-being, but this orgasm is long, sweet, and intense."

"I use my fingers and hands, circularly on my abdomen, and up and down on my vulva. My legs are stretched out and apart, with the knees bent. I touch my abdomen, mound, hair especially, thighs, clitoral area, and around my vagina. I start by lying down and playing with my nipples. Just for the record, I've found that a circular massage of the lower abdominal muscles, pushing toward the hand, then starting from the mound, up and out to the abdomen, helps alleviate menstrual cramps, plus is generally comforting and relaxing. Anyway, I cover and stroke my vulva and mound with the palm of my hand or with two hands until I am warm. Then, keeping one hand on the mound for continued calmness, I stroke the whole vulval area with my fingers (other hand), gradually narrowing down to the clitoral area only, increasing the speed and hardness of friction. I use two or three fingers (index and the one or two next to it) on my clitoral area, with other fingers spread around my vulva. As I near orgasm, I stretch my legs up and out and raise my torso, at the same time removing my hand from my mound."

Masturbating in Type I means lying on your back, and using your hands, fingers, or vibrator; Type II is very similar, except it means lying on your stomach instead of your back. Five point five percent (plus an additional 1.5 percent who could also masturbate in other ways) of the women who answered masturbated on their stomachs, using a hand or a vibrator, and of course Type II also contains all the variations discussed in conjunction with Type I. However, the pressure of the body seems to make an important difference; some women felt this increased their stimulation, while other women said they could not orgasm at all on their stomachs, or only with difficulty.

Some women of Type II move their bodies against their hands, while others move only their hands and not their bodies; generally, however, they move both.

An interesting sidelight of Type II is that a much higher percentage of women hold their legs together than in Type I. This will be discussed in detail later in the chapter. Only one fourth of the women who described the position of their legs held them apart—an unusually low percentage.

IIA

"I use my forefinger. I lie on my stomach and hug a pillow with my other hand. I use a circular and up-and-down motion on my clitoris and usually keep my legs a little apart, but as I get closer to orgasm, I bring them tight together. Sometimes I move a lot and other times just a little."

"I masturbate mainly on my stomach and use my right hand to stimulate my clitoris in a hard up-and-down movement, using my middle finger, index, and ring fingers. My left hand fondles my breasts. I move a lot in a rotating motion and up and down. I mmmmm a lot and say 'fuck.' I keep my legs open in the beginning and as I feel myself coming to an orgasm I close my

legs and pull my body up off the floor, bed, whatever.
Sometimes I masturbate standing up and use the same
motion and move quite a bit. Occasionally I masturbate
on my back and I find it hard to reach orgasm that
way."

"When masturbating, I lie on my stomach with my
legs slightly apart, using both hands, the knuckles of the
right hand providing the direct pressure to the mons,
with the left hand adding more pressure to the right
hand. The motion of a moderately rapid front-to-back
movement provides the clitoral friction I need."

"Sequence: I put a towel on the bed, put the vibrator
on the towel with the pulsator pointed up (the pulsator
has a rubber cup of about 1 inch in diameter). I usually
wet the pulsator before starting. Then I lie completely
quiet on my stomach with my arms and legs making a
wide V, with the pulsator working the mons area. I
don't use any hands until orgasm approaches, when I
move the vibrator slightly with the left hand so that it is
at exactly the right place. Just before orgasm, my hands
and neck become rigid and my hands rise into the air a
bit just before I move my left one to manipulate the
vibrator at the critical time."

"I masturbate on my stomach with my right hand between my legs and gently and circularly massage my clitoris. I rarely touch my breasts or the rest of my body
because I've found that physically that does little for
me."

"I can only achieve orgasm through masturbation
myself. I *must* lie on my stomach—legs together. I hold
a small towel over my hand. The edge of my right hand
below the thumb toward the wrist manipulates the clitoris, while my left hand in a fist forces my right hand
against the pubic area. I accompany a rhythmic movement of the right hand with pelvic movements. I've
done this in exactly the same way since fourth grade
(I'm twenty-five now), and nothing else will do it.
Sometimes when masturbating I must take all my
clothes off and perhaps rub my breasts on some rough
material. Sometimes I jam something up the vagina and
accompany this by a masochistic fantasy involvement.

Sometimes I arouse myself by laying a hot water bottle over my genitals. I must repeat that with me orgasm is *impossible* without an appropriate fantasy. Sometimes I cannot reach orgasm, and must cast around in my mind for the right one."

"It is fastest lying on my stomach with both hands under me, thumbs inside, next to one another, rubbing myself in a circular motion or up and down. It is also fastest with my legs together because then I constrict the muscles at the same time, which applies pressure."

"I lie on my stomach, elevating my ass, using one finger of my right hand rotating it on my clitoris directly. I move a lot."

"Usually I'm on my stomach gently touching my entire genital area with my left hand. My right hand is stimulating my right nipple. When I'm particularly horny, I manage to put my nipple in my own mouth. Sometimes I use a circular motion around my clitoris. My legs are usually together. I do not move very much."

"The middle finger of my right hand is my strongest and most important stimulator. First I stimulate my clitoris by patting, and tickling, and then I move my whole hand in a circular motion, then I tease my vagina with my middle finger by patting or an up-and-down motion across the outer opening. (I never put anything inside because of infection.) I always lie face down on the bed, to get maximum pressure on the clitoris. Usually I move my hips around and up and down. I become greatly stimulated with my legs apart but have to have them together in order to orgasm. When I am ready to come, I increase hand stimulation till I am on the brink, then press down hard and enjoy. After, I quickly remove my hand and lie there relaxing."

"I masturbate by lying face down, putting both hands over my pubic area, with my legs together. While rotating my hips, I put pressure in an upward direction (sort of pulling the skin toward the heels of my hands) rhythmically—mostly with the index finger of my right hand and the second and third fingers of my left hand. My leg muscles are all tensed up. In short, I put my legs together, get a good clutching grip on my pubic area through whatever clothes I have on, start a sort of thrusting motion with my pelvis while applying rhythmic pressure with my hands, and orgasm."

"I lie on my stomach, my arm around the pillow, my other hand between my legs touching my clitoris with my forefinger. After five minutes, my body starts to move so that I'm all in motion. As I come closer to orgasm, my legs come closer together. The massaging of my finger on my clitoris must be constant and monotonous so that I can come."

Some Type IIs depend mostly on body movements, rather than hand movements:

"I lie face down on the bed with my arms underneath me, both hands over my genital area. Sometimes I need a soft substance between my hands and my genitals, as I move my body, not my hands. I have my legs together, with my ankles crossed. Oftentimes I cannot come when someone else is stimulating me clitorally because they don't know I need something soft there."

And Type IIs have all the variations of Type Is:

IIA₁—Clitoral stimulation, sometimes with vaginal entry.

"I masturbate on my stomach with my legs together, pressing on my clitoris with the fingers of both hands (index and middle fingers), one on top of the other. Sometimes I fondle my breasts or buttocks with one hand, or insert my fingers into my vagina, but not usually. I move much less than in intercourse."

"I am on my stomach lying with a pillow between my legs, either rubbing against the pillow or also using my fingers. My body is rigid and stiff as I rub my clitoris in a circular motion. My other hand is on my nipple, squeezing it, and sometimes I have a vibrator in either my vagina or ass. Legs vary."

IIA₂—Clitoral stimulation, always including vaginal entry.

"I lie on my stomach with my legs as far apart as possible and put about three pillows under me to further arch my back. I massage my body at the genital region and insert the middle finger of one hand up my vagina and press my other hand hard against it, at the region of my clitoris. This way I can strongly stimulate both my clitoris and my cervix (which is often sensitive, but not as much as the clitoris). My breath becomes short and gasping and my body starts pulsating and contracting violently, as my body comes down on the finger and the hand behind it. I have tried using two or three fingers, but this had the disadvantages that then it doesn't extend up as far as one finger."

"I use my hands beginning with a general overall rubbing of myself to warm my hands and my body. Then I move to my crotch and slowly apply pressure with the tips of all four fingers. Then I turn onto my stomach. I begin to use a circular motion with two fingers on my clitoris and occasionally an up and down motion with my clitoris between my fingers. With my right hand I check to see if my vagina is wet, and fantasize. I continue to stimulate my clitoris with my left hand and then insert two fingers into my vagina. I love the folds and crevasses. It is amazing to feel the inside of oneself. I also sometimes stimulate the opening of the urethra, but that can be painful. My legs are usually closed, but sometimes open. If I haven't orgasmed by then, then I flex all my muscles in my legs and ass, and sometimes begin to move my whole body up and down, or maybe just move my hands. I often enjoy having my ass out from under the covers—cool air stimulates it or perhaps it's a desire to be exposed, I really can't say. Anyhow, turning on my stomach really improves my ability to reach my fingers deep into my vagina."

IIB—Clitoral/vulval stimulation.

"On my stomach with both hands (one over the other) cupping my outer genital area, lips remaining closed. I gently squeeze the area with a finger pushing up against the back curve of the lips and the palm of my hand pushing pressure on the front and the pubic bone. Legs together. I have been doing this every day since I was four or five. When my partner joins me he simply lies on my back and helps me squeeze."

"I use the curved plastic back, not the pad, of a small vibrator. I prefer this because I very seldom have long enough periods of time alone to use the manual methods, which I find too slow and not as interesting and more fatiguing. I kind of hold the vibrator more or less steady under me as I lie face down, and move my body on and around it. I use it pretty exclusively against my clitoris and vaginal lips. I like my legs together. That way, with my ankles crossed, I can use my legs to control the amount of contact with the vibrator. Sometimes I move a great deal, sometimes very little. The more aroused, the more movement."

"I lie on my stomach with a pillow between my legs starting at my waist and kinda bunched up in the middle. My hands are under the pillow just under the clitoral region, and I hump the pillow rhythmically. Then I put my vibrator just above my clitoris, and while it remains stationary, I rub against it for a few moments, until I am so gluttonous I have to turn it on, at which time my left hand steadies it or plays with my clitoris or my vaginal area. Anyway its mere presence is erotic. It is important that my right hand keep it from vibrating too much (the reason for the pillow). Sometimes the vibrator points toward the left, sometimes toward the anus. My legs are tight together, and I fantasize. Sometimes I tap the muffled vibrator in a special way."

IIB₁—Clitoral/vulval stimulation, sometimes with vaginal entry.

"I place my vibrator on my clitoris and labia minora and vaginal entrance, plus sometimes a candle in my vagina. Legs together is easier, especially with ankles crossed (it makes muscular tension greater and satisfies a reflex desire to press my knees together). I used to touch my breasts and stomach, but it seemed redundant. And I used to move my hands more than me, now I move me more."

TYPE III

Type III means masturbating by thrusting into a pillow or other soft object. Four percent of the women masturbated in this way, plus an additional 1.2 percent who could also masturbate in other ways. Type III is similar to Type II because it is done on the stomach, in the face down position, but different because no hands are used. It involves thrusting or grinding the pelvis, especially the pubic area, against the bed, some pillows, or a clump of clothing, or perhaps moving one's body in pressing movements against the bed. Legs are usually together, and often there are some sheets of fabric wadded up and held between the legs. Thus stimulation is spread over a rather wide area in an indirect way. Six of the Type IIIs are unusual, and four of these quotes will be found at the end of this section.

"When I masturbate, I usually lie face down on the bed with some cloth, like a blanket or spread, pulled together so there is a mound I rub back and forth on."

"I lie on my stomach with some material pulled firmly between my thighs and pressing against my entire mons area, then bounce gently until orgasm."

"Yes I enjoy masturbation. I have masturbated since babyhood and I don't see any reason to stop ever. However, I prefer sex with a partner because I like company. I always have an orgasm and usually several of them, depending on the mood I'm in. I don't masturbate like anybody else I ever heard of. I make a clump in the bedding about the size of a fist (I used to use the head of my poor teddy bear, but since I became too old to sleep with a teddy bear, a wad of the sheets has to suffice) and then lie on my stomach on top of it so that it exerts pressure on my clitoris. I then move my hips in a circular motion until I climax—very simple. It works with legs apart or together—either one, although when I am in a particularly frenzied state, together sometimes feels better. I usually end up sort of with my weight on my knees and elbows, so I can't do too much else with my hands."

"I cross my legs, thrust my pelvis against a soft object (a pillow is best) and fantasize. This is the tried and true way. I do enjoy touching myself, but it's just not as good as this. I really move very little; only when ready for orgasm do I get into any real action."

"Masturbation: I usually 'hump' a pillow or a rolled-up robe or even a laundry bag—I ride it like a horse, pressing down and easing up repeatedly—pressing harder and harder. With or without clothes on."

"I lie on top of a firm pillow and push a lump in it, then move up and down against it, my weight being on my elbows and groin. At orgasm, I embrace the pillow, close my eyes, faint and moan with delight."

"I move up and down along someone's leg to stimulate my clitoris. I move slowly and then more rapidly, but still with long, exaggerated movements."

"First I use my hands to excite my clitoris and genitals, then I use the pressure of several large pillows against my chest, abdomen, pelvis, and clitoris to increase arousal. Underpants keep the pressure generalized and allow a slippery sensation so it doesn't become painful. I move my body, especially my pelvis, against the pillows. The movement takes the form of several extended pelvic thrusts with all my weight on the pillow."

"For me, masturbation is an active process. I lie on my stomach, place a pillow between my legs, with my legs slightly spread, and rock back and forth."

"I have experienced masturbatory activities through several methods, but the way in which I achieve the deepest, most intense series of orgasms, although it is physically exhausting, is lying on a bed face down, stimulating my clitoris by pressing against the bed in a thrusting action."

"I use a towel rolled up and rub myself against it in an up and down motion. I never use my hands. This method seems to arouse some sensations that the hand cannot reach."

"I don't masturbate. Well, a little rubbing against the sheets maybe."

"Generally, I straddle a pillow (lie over a pillow between my legs), and rotate my hips with the pressure of the pillow against my clitoris."

"Usually I masturbate on the corner of a chair or something similar with a pillow between my legs. I hump up and down with my legs together. I discovered this method by accident as a child of four, having no idea what I was doing; it just felt good and I've been doing it ever since—up until about a year ago, when I had very strong guilt feelings about it, but now I don't anymore—but I still don't think I'd tell anyone about it."

III—with vaginal entry

"Lying on my stomach with something small (like a Tampax) in my vagina and a pillow clamped between my legs, I move up and down slowly, then faster and harder. The sequence is like this—I insert the object, roll over on the pillow, then move rhythmically to orgasm."

Another Variation

The final version of Type III, referred to earlier in this section as unusual, involves holding yourself off the ground with your arms, and rubbing the pubic area against something while suspended:

"I stand on a chair with a protruding but low wing back and rub first against it, then raise myself so I am above it, and stroking downward. This method allows much freedom of movement for my body, which I like. I first learned it as a child while playing on a chair my mother had."

"I draw myself up slowly against a bathroom sink, and press my mons against it very hard. The sink is stimulating because it is cold. Sometimes I revolve my legs to press harder, and sometimes 'flap' them to vibrate the vulva."

"I usually suspend myself against a piece of furniture and rub myself against it in an up and down, slow, circular motion. I never heard of it being done like this before, and I don't know where I picked it up, but at an early age it gave me a quick orgasm, or several. It's a good way, only it gives you calluses on the palms of your hands."

"When I was eleven years old I was playing around our swimming pool near the ladder. I leaned across the top of the ladder and felt a wonderful sensation in my genitals. I had no idea what it was, but I learned I could reproduce the same feeling if I leaned on the back of a chair. I continued this for years. I didn't know I was having orgasms until I was fifteen, but I knew that it was something special to me and that it wasn't something to advertise around the neighborhood, because this was something happening near or in my vagina, and that was a no-no to talk about. Anyway, I still masturbate this way, only now I've advanced to sinks! If I go into the bathroom and straddle the corner of the sink, and rock back and forth I can have wonderful orgasms! I have tried to stimulate myself while I'm in bed, but it's futile. This upsets me, because my lover (he doesn't know about my masturbating—yet!) can't make me come either. I can be stimulated, but not to orgasm. An interesting note to add—throughout my teenage years (I am now twenty) I used to hop on the back of my desk chair and put a book in front of me on the desk and read and have orgasms for as long as I wanted! I went through *In Cold Blood* in total bliss!"

TYPE IV

Type IV is a way of masturbating in which you cross your legs very tightly and squeeze rhythmically. You can be sitting, or lying down, or on your side, just strongly tensing and untensing your legs, especially the upper thigh muscles. Sometimes there is a pillow between the legs, which can help to center *and* generalize the stimulation.

Most of the 3 percent of women who masturbated this way (plus the additional 9 percent who could also masturbate in other ways) simply squeezed their thighs together or contracted their muscles:

"I lie on my back, with my legs together, and move quite a bit until right before I come; then I am pretty rigid, squeezing my vagina on the inside, moving slowly. But it's the clitoral stimulation and squeezing inside that make me come. I squeeze the whole pelvic area that way and the cheeks of my ass are very tight."

"I masturbate by rubbing my thighs together, usually lying down, but it can be done sitting up (in an office, on a bus, etc.). I rub them rhythmically, putting subtle pressure on the clitoris. The tension gradually builds to an orgasm."

"I lie flat on the bed, lock my ankles together, rhythmically squeezing my thighs together, fantasize and occasionally touch my nipples if I have difficulty reaching orgasm by thigh-squeezing alone."

"I cross my legs twice—that is, cross them and tuck an ankle around the other leg, which creates a pressure on the clitoral area. I never use hands or touch myself—don't have to. I squeeze my legs until I achieve orgasm, moving only slightly. I have very easy orgasms."

"I lie down (mostly when I bathe) and cross my legs; I caress my breasts and lightly bounce up and down as the stimulation builds. I keep squeezing my breasts and then I have an orgasm."

"I can rarely take much direct clitoral stimulation. Therefore I am more inclined to tense and release vaginal muscles in my upper thigh area. Crossing legs helps. Occasionally tapping the clitoris helps, but I do this very rarely."

"When I'm sitting (like in school), I cross my legs and contract my leg muscles together—a technique my lover (a woman) showed me."

"When I masturbate, I sit up in a chair or on the bed, cross my legs right over left at the knees and use the pressure of my inner thighs, exerting all the energy in my body and centering it in my genitals."

"I either read a sexually explicit passage in a book (keep several on my night table) or run through a sexual encounter mentally, and with ankles crossed press my thighs together—no manual contact. Have tried vibrator or manual stimulation, but usually don't bother. I first masturbated to orgasm accidentally by this method and have so continued. I saw no reason to change ever."

Some women who masturbated this way also held something—usually a pillow or towel—between their legs.

"Initially, I get stimulated either from the outside, or I tell myself stories or I fantasize, then I lie down and put my right arm through my crotch with my wrist or lower arm on my labia and clitoris (I can be either clothed or naked) and my hand or my ankle or calf, and close my thighs on my arm. My left hand may support me (if I lie on my side), or else play with my nipples. I rock my hips or pelvis for friction. Occasionally I use my fingers or hand for my labia, on my clitoris, or up my vagina."

"I bunch up a blanket or sheet, place part of it between my legs, which are tightly pressed together, and then I rub the sheet into and on my cunt, especially my clitoris, using no hands, just hip and leg movements. I begin to fantasize a situation and come in minutes."

"My legs are crossed as I tightly squeeze some object which touches my clitoris and the entrance to my vagina—like any slightly elongated object. Usually I keep it on the outside of my underwear. I rarely use my hands, I just press my uppermost thighs together against the labia. My masturbation is just basically the placing of objects and rocking of my pelvic region, with pressure on my uppermost thighs against the labia."

"When I masturbate, I usually press my legs hard together (or wind them around each other) and use a towel, pulling it against my clitoris rhythmically until I come."

"I use a pillow or some other object that is firm but soft. I hold it between my legs and rub it up and down or squeeze it with my thighs. I can get stimulated somewhat by rubbing my fingers directly on my genitals, but can't touch my clitoris, as it is too sensitive. In fact, I'm better off wearing pants so I don't become too directly stimulated. My legs have to be clasped on the pillow, they can't be apart. I move quite a lot but don't need to if my fantasy is strong enough. I need lots of air, so therefore I prefer it out of the covers, with my ass and feet, especially, exposed."

"I masturbate on my side, squeezing a quilt between my thighs, moving up and down. This is the way I did it the first time orgasm happened to me, and I've had no reason to change, although at times I've thought I should practice lying on my back to learn to please men."

"I lie in bed on my stomach, my arms around my pillow, fantasizing. Then I put a soft pillow between my legs, and push it against myself with my legs together tightly around it. By moving up and down, I orgasm within five minutes in a really beautiful way."

"I put a blanket between my legs, stuffing as much as I can of it between them, and then close them together tightly. I push the blanket especially against my clitoris and move up and down rhythmically, tightening and releasing my thighs at the same time. And sometimes I put one finger of the other hand inside my vagina or anus, from behind."

"I lie on my stomach and pull one or two pillows between my legs. I press against them with my pubic area, while pushing with my hands in the front of the pillow (both hands). My legs are apart and moving as in a butterfly stroke in swimming—like a butterfly! A few times I have used the hose of a hair dryer to blow warm air on my vagina for initial stimulation, as a kind of 'foreplay.' I also push pillows against my breasts."

"I use a small pillow between my legs and use both hands on it to apply pressure to my clitoris. I move up and down until orgasm, which takes half a minute."

"I am sixteen and have no boyfriend. I have hardly ever 'fooled around,' so all of my orgasms have resulted from masturbation. I have at least one orgasm every time I masturbate. I enjoy masturbation physically. I masturbate very often, from once to six times daily.

Usually in school or in public I just cross my legs and press my thighs together, then relax, then press. By myself I do one of three things: 1) lying down on my back or side, I cross my legs and press my thighs, then uncross my legs when at the height of tension and raise hips off the bed; 2) lie on my stomach with some material (or a nightgown or something) pulled firmly between my thighs and pressing against the entire mons area, then bounce gently until orgasm; 3) or rub my clitoris with my finger, legs apart."

"In my teens I branched out into public masturbation in boring classes and during the sermon when I was a member of the choir. All I did was cross my legs and squeeze the thigh muscles together repeatedly for two or three minutes. But even with the utmost control it was impossible to avoid a slight convulsion at the moment of orgasm, which I would disguise by a coughing fit or having to lean over and scratch my leg. Must have been pretty horny."

"I get completely naked and lie on the floor. I place a towel between my legs so it's in contact with my clitoris. Inside my vagina is some object like a penis, and the towel is also in contact with the tip of this. I put my legs together tightly and rotate my hips. Sometimes I read pornography first."

A few women also described another highly unusual variation similar to one mentioned at the end of Type III. Here again the whole body is off the ground, although there is no outside pressure on the pubic area as in Type III.

"I masturbate by tightening (clenching) my vaginal muscles. I don't usually touch my clitoris at all, but can do it just with my muscles. I can do it sitting up and pressing myself up with my hands or arms, i.e., sitting at a desk I can lean on my arms, raise my pelvis and tense my muscles and have a great orgasm."

TYPE V

Type V (water massage) is masturbating by running water (usually warm) over the genitals to orgasm. Two percent of the women who masturbated (plus another 2 percent who also masturbated in other ways) used this method. The most common way of doing it is to turn on the faucet with a strong, hard flow, lie on your back with your legs up on the wall and your clitoris positioned under the rushing water. Legs are usually apart.

"I masturbate with shower water only. I aim it at my clitoris, legs spread apart. Sometimes I hook up a hose and sit on the side of the tub, and use a nice steady stream of water. Or I lie down in the tub, and let the shower water strike my clitoris if it is hard enough."

"I lie in the tub on my back with a stream of very warm water on my vagina, mons, and clitoris. The harder the pressure and hotter the water, the quicker the orgasm."

"I remove the head from my shower to allow a steady stream of water to come out. I open the vaginal lips, exposing my clitoris. The water can be slightly hot for more stimulation, and hips can be moved slightly to tantalize and prolong the enjoyment. I usually do it standing up. Lying down is more beautiful, but you get your hair and face wet. This orgasm tops them all for me, and can be multiple."

"I masturbate with water, preferably a half-inch stream that is arched so my butt does not stop the drain. My feet are braced on the wall about two feet apart, and I am lying on my back."

"Occasionally I bring myself to orgasm in the bathtub. First I excite myself with fingers, then I let the water on and get into an acrobatic position so my vagina is directly under the faucet. I start with the water warm or cool and at a low pressure on my clitoris. When I have gotten excited I run the water harder and I lift myself closer to the water and let it pound into my vagina and then I come and it's the most fantastic feeling."

"For masturbation, I have used a vibrator, but I usually masturbate when I take my bath by letting the gush of warm water run over my genitals. My legs are apart and the water usually hits right on my clitoris, until I go into orgasm."

"I use the hand shower (very efficient). I regulate the flow and the heat and pat my clitoris up and down with water. My legs are almost closed, otherwise it hurts. I do not move my body. I almost always come this way. When no hand shower is available I use an object, but then it takes a very long time for an orgasm to come, if any."

"I get in the tub without water (usually this occurs immediately following a shower) and turn on the faucet only part way, adjusting the water to warm. Then I maneuver my buttocks as close to the running water as possible, arranging my body so the water strikes directly on the clitoris. Sometimes I 'rock' to and fro just slightly. I always come in a few minutes."

"I regularly have orgasm in the bathtub by allowing the water from the tap to flow over my clitoris and labia, and moving my body so that the flow 'strokes' the area. In this way I can achieve orgasm rapidly and fully, and feel quite satisfied after. I turn the water on, lie under it, adjust it for the right pressure and temperature (I like it slightly hotter than body temperature). Then I lie on my back, directly stimulating my clitoris and labial area with the water flow from the tap, and moving my body—sometimes a little, sometimes a lot. I like to spread my legs apart when I do it, and to cry out or moan with pleasure when I have the impulse to. As the sensation becomes stronger I move faster and faster until orgasm occurs. I lie there a few moments after, then sit up and wash myself."

"With the hose in the shower was how I masturbated for eight years at home and then when I moved to the place I have now, my dear old landlord (eighty-nine years old), gave me a hose you hook onto the shower (I have no bath). If he only knew. I first put the nozzle of an intense spray right against my clitoris, spreading the vulva area apart with my fingers of the other hand a little. At the same time I would stand, sometimes inserting the two tubes from my vaginal foam in my rectum and vagina. This was a little difficult because it's hard to relax while standing up and holding the tubes in me at the same time. It also gave me helpless feelings of great pleasure, standing there and reaching an orgasm. Finally I tried sitting down on the cold floor with my legs out in front of me. This is much better because I can brace my feet against the wall and relax better. It doesn't take very much pressure before I get the aching feeling and then I come. It's pretty hard to get up and take a shower after that."

TYPE VI

Of all the women who described how they masturbated, only 1.5 percent masturbated only by vaginal insertion, plus another .4 percent who used this method sometimes. Over half of these women stimulated their clitoral areas first manually.

What was inserted?

candle	5	women
fingers	13	women
one finger	4	women
vibrator	6	women
dildo	3	women

"I usually masturbate with my finger and touch my breasts with my other hand, but not always. Sometimes when I'm lying in the sun in my bathing suit and I'll start to feel sexy, I end up going inside to masturbate (when I'm alone in the house). I usually use a back and forth movement in my vagina, or just hold my fingers there for a while. My legs are quite wide apart with my knees up near me. Sometimes I move a lot, depending on the intensity of my feeling at the time."

LEG POSITION

An interesting and important, but as yet unanswered puzzle about female orgasm is why some women need to have their legs apart for orgasm while others must have them together; still others prefer to have them bent at the knees or up in the air. Just as different women need different kinds of stimulation for orgasm (the masturbation types we have just seen) they also *need* different leg positions to orgasm.

Unfortunately, many women did not answer this final part of the masturbation question, probably due to the length of the question, and because they assumed their leg position was the same as everyone else's. However, most of the women who did answer usually had their legs apart. Still, a significant number of women in all the masturbation types did hold their legs together.

Reasons women gave for keeping their legs together included the following.

"I like my legs together because then everything (the whole genital area) is tighter and the vibrations travel better."

"If I have my legs *apart,* I feel almost nothing, no matter what I do!"

"Legs *together* intensifies orgasm—to have everything as tight and tense as possible is best, like a drum."

"When I masturbate I tense my legs up real tight and squeeze them together in order to come. It is almost impossible unless I do this 'tense and squeeze.' Then for the few seconds I am releasing I feel out of this world."

"It is much stronger if my legs are together and I contract my pelvic area and hold my whole body tight."

"Legs together is better, easier, quicker."

On the other hand, some women could feel nothing with their legs *together.*

"I prefer to be on my back with my legs raised and open wide. There is such a strong feeling in my legs accompanying orgasm that if my weight is resting on my legs the orgasm is different."

"My body is still, I think—my face is 'distorted' (as though in ecstasy). And my legs must be apart and straight up in the air."

Some women who liked their legs apart also liked their knees bent.

"My legs are apart, either with my knees bent while my feet are flat on the bed, or with my knees at right angles and my feet together. I can masturbate sitting also, and standing, but I prefer lying down in this position."

"I prefer to be on my back with my legs somewhat apart and bent and holding quite stiff. My movement is like a gradual increased vibration."

"Legs apart, knees bent, sometimes touching my chest. I move very little, as this stillness seems to heighten my pleasure."

"Legs bent up and somewhat apart. It helps to have the pubic area pulled up taut."

"I lie on my back, knees bent, legs up and apart. Then I move the bottom half of my body a lot in a sort of pumping motion."

Some women moved their legs together for orgasm, as the feeling intensified, after having them apart during stimulation (and a very small number did the opposite).

"As my body begins to tense, I put my legs tightly together."

"I like my legs far apart when direct stimulation begins, but it is torture for me to try to keep them this way as the 'good vibes' heighten."

"I have my legs apart first then grip them together later on."

"I lie on my back, legs apart at first, then put them tightly together near orgasm. I move very little except to tense and relax my body."

"Sometimes I squeeze my legs together a bit after sex just to make the last bit of orgasm."

Some women also moved their legs alternately together and apart, perhaps increasing the stimulation by "pumping" the genital lips and interior bulbs.

"I prefer to lie quite still; then, when the orgasm starts to happen, I get into this rhythm thing, usually lifting one leg, then the other."

"As I'm building up to orgasm, I sort of pump my legs back and forth slightly, especially my upper legs. Each time they come together I feel a spark of the orgasm feeling, then I go apart (a few inches) to build it up more (!) and after about ten times, wow! It's beautiful!"

Most women had only one basic leg position that worked best for them, but a few women found leg position interchangeable.

"I hold my legs together or apart depending on the type of fantasy I am using."

"My muscles usually tense up, and then right before orgasm my hips start moving back and forth. My legs are the tensest of all, usually bent at the knees, one up and one sideways when I'm by myself. With a partner, there are other considerations that determine what I do with my legs—sometimes they stiffen out straight."

The reason for the importance of different leg positions to different women is still a mystery. Does it depend on how the woman first learned how to orgasm? Or does the anatomy of our genitals (both interior and exterior) vary just enough from woman to woman to make different positions necessary for different individuals? Answers to these questions are simply not known.

ORGASM

IS ORGASM
IMPORTANT?

"Orgasm feels great! Like a combination of intense pleasurable sensations plus an ecstatic frenzy of love, energy, and emotion, all mixed together."

"Orgasms are a renewal of all my senses, an awakening of life, spring, refreshing, sparkling, exciting, and complete relief of everyday boredom."

"They make me incredibly happy, everything on the way to orgasm is heavenly. An orgasm cancels out all rage and longing for at least forty-eight hours, and the day an orgasm bores me, I think I'll commit suicide."

"A marvelous happiness, comparable to no other."

"Orgasm is the *ultimate* pleasure—which women often deny themselves, but men never do."

"Orgasm. The most fantastic sensation I've ever experienced."

"At best, an organ-moving cataclysm: my ovaries, uterus, breasts, and brain become one singing dark pulsating sea of the most exquisite feeling."

"Whoever said orgasm wasn't important for a woman was undoubtedly a man."

Are orgasms important to women? Although the answer would seem clearly to be yes, it has often been said, and written, that women do not *need* orgasms, at least in the same way men do. It is said that ours aren't as strong, and don't feel as good as theirs. One woman answered these claims perfectly when she said, "Whoever said orgasm wasn't important for a woman was undoubtedly a man. Good sex expresses love, relaxation, and letting go, plus pure body pleasure."

Most women agreed:

"Only physicians and clergymen tell women we should comfort and pleasure our husbands, and to 'stop chasing rainbows' when our turn comes around."

"The idea that it doesn't matter if women have orgasms or not is an absurd lie women tell themselves."

"I am entitled to orgasms. If I have to masturbate to get them, then my man should also have to masturbate for his and that does not mean masturbating in my vagina—i.e., intercourse when he's the only one who has orgasm."

Women are now under great pressure to perform by having orgasms, especially during intercourse.

It does seem clear that women should have a right to orgasms during sex as part of the natural course of things. However, now that the idea has become popular that women should enjoy sex "too," this new "right" has sometimes turned into an oppression. Women are made to feel that they must have orgasms more to please the man than to please themselves.

"It is only fair to him, and makes him feel 'as a man' and successful."

"I 'perform' and boost his ego and confidence and love for me with an orgasm. I do not *like* to think of myself as a performer, but I feel judged, and also judge myself, when I don't have an orgasm."

"There's this pressure there is something psychologically wrong with you if you don't have an orgasm."

"Yes, alas, I still feel I must have an orgasm to make him feel, er, macho."

"An orgasm is not necessary to make you 'normal,' but men do expect it, so I often force myself, especially because he enjoys watching. Besides, it's better for him to feel a contracting vagina, but you can also do that at will if you practice."

"Yes, I feel the need to perform orgasmically, competitively with other women at large in the community. I wish I didn't. It really got started when I used to feel pressure from my former partner, because if I didn't come, it proved he wasn't a 'real man.' But I'm not a star or a two-ring circus."

"I'm very wary about telling new partners I don't have orgasms because then they make it a contest to see if *they* can be the one to make me come. I really resent being expected to come, and almost *forced* if I don't."

"Sometimes I have felt that reaching orgasm was more a matter of satisfying my partner's desire to satisfy me than my own need for orgasm."

"You're supposed to be uninhibited and have orgasms, and when I do it makes him feel confident and secure. Orgasm is important, but not as important as *he* thinks: my orgasm is actually more important to my husband than to me!"

"Yes, I must have an orgasm. Otherwise, I'm not a real person and making him feel bad and maybe he'll abandon me. Men enjoy making love more to women who have orgasms."

"I would enjoy sex with no orgasm at times, if I felt other people weren't uptight about it, and if the reasons were my own. Maybe sex would be better if we'd never heard of orgasm."

"I'm afraid that new partners will think I'm weird and not as sexy as other women if I don't have orgasms—or that I'm selfish and aggressive if I do!"

"I wish orgasms didn't exist. Then maybe sex would be fun."

There is also a social pressure that says a woman who has an orgasm is more of a woman, a "real" woman.

"I don't think orgasms are that important; the literature has given women another burden. But I'm ashamed to admit, because of the myth, I feel 'good' having an orgasm—like I'm a *real woman*! Arrgh. . . ."

"I can enjoy sex without orgasm, but psychologically I feel like I'm a failure, like a not totally functioning woman."

"Orgasms are continually talked about. Therefore if I don't have one, I feel inadequate."

"The idea of having orgasms is important to me, but I can certainly enjoy sex without having them. Worse than not having the orgasm is the feeling that I've failed or that I'm frigid or unsexy. I feel a lot of pressure, both from men and from women's liberation, to have orgasms or insist on having an orgasm. I don't have sex in order to have an orgasm—I suppose part of me wonders whether I will 'this time'—but generally I have sex because I want to have a loving fucking tenderness with that person. Or because it seems like a good idea at the time. Or because I want to possess them in some way for a while."

"Yes orgasms are important, but the symbol of 'Orgasm' has probably been exaggerated as a symbol of being 'sexy,' 'fiery,' 'passionate,' 'alive,' etc."

"All the publicity about orgasm is making me nervous."

"It's a big credential to have orgasms—I feel sort of commended when I do."

"Having an orgasm unlocks the door to my being a full woman."

"When I have an orgasm, I show open, clear womanness."

"My mate says I look and 'perform' like a woman, so I'm not bothered about whether or not I have an orgasm. However, I must admit the old myth of being 'less of a woman' lingers in the back of my mind."

"Orgasms are important, but I don't know if it's because of their own sake or because I think I ought to have them. I rarely feel I *need* one."

"Now there is so much emphasis on orgasm, a person would feel abnormal not having one."

A few women reacted strongly against this pressure to perform.

"Once in a while a desire to impress someone with my 'tremendous sexuality' appeals to me, but usually I am just very happy to have lots of orgasms. Basically I'm too selfish to bother to prove anything to my partners—and especially, too intelligent to want to do *anything* to prove I'm a real woman! Bullshit on that!"

"I only want to have orgasms for my own pleasure, not for his appraisal of my womanliness!"

On the other hand, not having an orgasm with a man could be frustrating too, because you could wind up feeling left out and cheated watching him have his.

"I want to have orgasm, not so much for the feeling of the orgasm itself as for the frustration and anger I feel when I don't."

"When I see my partner having one, I feel I should enjoy one too."

"It's rarely that I have an altruistic, non-orgasmic intercourse. Without orgasm I feel robbed."

"I always felt cheated when he had orgasm and I didn't."

"Having sex without an orgasm makes me feel like I was along for the ride, but why? (except when I'm really emotionally involved)."

"Consciously, I don't care, but perhaps I resent the absence of orgasms on a more unconscious level."

"Yes, when having sex with someone I become furious if I don't have at least one orgasm. I don't enjoy sex without them because I get terribly built up. I wouldn't even bother with sex without orgasm."

"Orgasm is important to me for two reasons: 1) physically and 2) I feel cheated when I do not experience one. I feel many times my sexuality is not important to certain men."

"*Never* having orgasms would be indicative of something being wrong with 'our' sex life. He always has one, so why shouldn't I?"

"If I am engaging in sexual activity with the same partner repeatedly, never achieving an orgasm, I become very angry and frustrated and increasingly frigid—really turning off on things that would normally turn me on."

"I *deserve* a climax after working him up to one. He has one so why shouldn't I? No matter how long it takes I make him rub my clitoris until I orgasm."

"I regard orgasm as a natural end to sexual experiences—when I kiss passionately I want and expect to go on to intercourse and orgasm. When the man doesn't seem to notice or care or try to help me to have one, I become *infuriated*."

"Intercourse is okay sometimes for the emotional and physical warmth of the sharing, but it's better with orgasm and I interpret a man's understanding of my desire for orgasm both as an indication of his sincerity and of his caring."

"Because I never orgasm during intercourse, I still enjoy intercourse but sometimes I do feel cheated and angry when he has his orgasm because I can't orgasm."

"Orgasm is important—especially if my partner has one."

"If I don't orgasm, when intercourse is over I am left frustrated and unfulfilled and bitter/guilty. The more orgasms the better."

"Always watching the joy of my partner would be intolerable."

"I prefer no sex to bad sex, which to me means sex with a fumbler or a male chauvinist pig, who doesn't let me have an orgasm."

"Before we settled into a pattern of clitoral stimulation to orgasm and then intercourse, I sometimes enjoyed sex a lot without orgasm. But usually I felt very frustrated and pissed off, especially if I almost had orgasm but then didn't. Unfortunately, I was and still am too inhibited to masturbate in a situation like that."

"There is no reason for sex unless I orgasm too, otherwise I get mean."

"Sometimes I feel slighted if my partner doesn't bother to give me one, and just goes on and enjoys his own and then falls asleep."

"Why would a woman want sex without them? Sick!"

"Sex play with no orgasm is lovely sometimes, but not intercourse where he does orgasm—it makes me feel short-changed and inadequate."

"Sometimes I get hung up on the thought that I *could* have had an orgasm when *he* did."

"We have had lots of sex without *me* orgasming—sometimes it's very frustrating and I'm upset but I love him and I keep trying."

"I feel cheated and in pain and angry—so frustrated that I am seriously considering getting a divorce."

"I must have an orgasm, or I climb a wall. I have to go somewhere private and masturbate. Before I knew about orgasms, I loved to be aroused, and just come down naturally after the man had his. I would go to sleep just pleasantly horny but not disturbed. Now I can't and I won't."

"The rare times when sex was a tool for healing, or emotional relating when extra warmth and intimacy were needed, orgasm was unnecessary. Also, before I learned how to have an orgasm, sex was a service of intimacy to my partner. Still I always enjoy it more with one, and usually it's not fair if he does and I don't, do you think?"

"If he comes and I don't, I feel short-changed and like crying and like I don't want to have sex ever. But once in a while I feel satisfied and warm and cuddly."

"It is okay without orgasms if my partner isn't being selfish, or taking advantage, and if he is tender and considerate—but inside I still feel kind of pissed off."

"I feel confused and cheated when I don't have an orgasm and I lie there watching him have his."

"Sometimes I tell my husband I don't *need* to come to enjoy sex, but I think that's *bullshit* on my part."

"How would a man feel if he made love and never achieved orgasm?"

"I must orgasm because sex is supposed to be an exchange. If I'm going to serve his physical needs, he has to serve mine. Also, orgasm is such a great experience, I like to let a man share it with me. I think men should get used to giving this pleasure to women. I don't like just getting fucked."

Sometimes women focused on the man's orgasm as a surrogate for their own.

"I guess I get very tied up in how he is feeling also, and so when I can make him climax, I feel as though I have also, so that I don't need to any more."

"Sometimes I can have mental orgasms helping my

partner reach an orgasm—and find it just as stimulating."

"Sometimes it's more fulfilling without orgasm because it's possible to experience my partner's orgasm more completely."

"I think sometimes it's okay not having orgasm during intercourse, but perhaps I am too concerned with making the sexual experience whatever he wants."

"Giving is more important than taking, therefore if there is a choice between my partner's and my orgasm, I take theirs."

Some women came to the conclusion that orgasm during sex was not important.

"Orgasms are exceedingly pleasurable and as I haven't given up masturbation, I guess you could say they're 'important' to me. But that's exactly the point of something else—I totally associate orgasm with masturbation. *I don't have to come,* and often when he comes, it's the peak of sex for me."

"To me orgasms have nothing to do with regular male/female sex. Orgasm is not necessary because I can give them to myself in masturbation."

"Since I don't have orgasm during intercourse, therefore I enjoy it without."

"Personally, I don't mind very much if I don't have one with a man. I don't expect to."

"Orgasm is something I am able to give myself any time—so it's no big deal to not have one. Cuddling and touching is more important to get from my partner."

"I think orgasms are overrated. When I masturbate, it is to achieve orgasm, but with my lover I really don't care if I do or not. I just want to feel warm and close."

"Orgasm is not always necessary during intercourse. It's still okay because of the warmth and comfort and just to let someone know you accept their physicality."

"Orgasms are only important in context. If all I wanted was orgasm, I'd masturbate. If someone wants to give me an orgasm, and it is an act of love and affection and consideration, then that is important."

"It's okay not having an orgasm if you love your partner and there is lots of affection and caring. If I love my partner, I get emotional satisfaction even without orgasm."

In a sense these women were *right*: to experience sex as a race for orgasm is a narrow and unimaginative view. However, most women are not speaking from a position of strength in this regard. We are not always *having* orgasms (or able to orgasm) during sex, and *then* saying they are not important. To bring our sexuality up from underground, we must bring our own orgasms (and the stimulation and body positions necessary to have those orgasms) out of hiding, and feel free to make them a natural, comfortable part of sexual relations.

The right to orgasm has become a political question for women. Although there is nothing wrong with not having orgasms, and nothing wrong with empathizing with and sharing another person's pleasure, there *is* something wrong when this becomes a pattern where the man is *always* having an orgasm and the woman isn't. If we make it easy and pleasurable for men to have an orgasm, and don't have one ourselves, aren't we just "servicing" men? If we *know* how to have orgasms, but are unable to make this a part of a sexual relationship with another person, then we are not in control of *choosing* whether or not we have an orgasm. We are powerless.

Isn't this just like the traditional female role—watching and nurturing, always acting as helpmates to the lives of others? Isn't it the same sense of martyrdom and self-sacrifice that women have always shown in other aspects of personal and family relations? We are the sensitive and understanding ones, while men are the physical and mechanical experts who "get things done." In sex, supposedly, men know what to do: they initiate and carry out the main activities. We "respond" to them. But what men have generally initiated has had little to do with our needs for orgasm. And even worse, being necessarily passive gives us no sense of our strength and autonomy. It is time we reclaimed our own bodies, and started to use them *ourselves* for our own pleasure.

WHAT DO THE STAGES OF ORGASM FEEL LIKE?

AROUSAL

What does arousal feel like?

Judging from the rapturous descriptions of feelings during arousal, its pleasures would seem definitely to rival those of orgasm itself. *No one* disliked arousal; there wasn't a single negative description of how it felt. Words used to describe it often included "tingly," "alive," "warm," "happy," feelings of wanting to touch and be touched. Most women felt the sensations all over the body; few mentioned genitals. And in these descriptions most seemed to be describing their experiences during sex with another person—emotional terms were abundantly used.

"I feel (without touching them) my skin, breasts and legs and hands and neck. It's like my body has expanded and wants frictional warm type contact."

"There is an exquisite tension, an ache, a hunger—and my breasts get tight and feel as if they must be touched."

"I have a sort of fainting type feeling—tingling warmth, fullness, dampness, energy."

"Blood pressure rising . . . every part of my body feels each and every touch made on it—I am hypersensitive, in heaven."

"A sense of well-being, I am radiant, like a gradual awakening."

"A feeling of being loved and wanted. Exhilarating."

"A crawly feeling all over; I want to get closer and closer."

"My body feels poised, alive, pulsing—glowing, 'high.'"

"A quickening of all my senses."

"Urgency, an irresistible pull."

"Moderate arousal is lovely and is intoxicating in many ways; severe arousal is practically painful but *wonderful* with the final orgasm."

"I'm high—I breathe fast—also lightheaded, in a dream world, sounds are distant, time suspended."

"At my best with the person, happy, and, in general, warm."

"It feels like tenderness and caring."

"Happy and joyous, tingling."

"Could go on forever—will go insane."

"Warm and good, secure, caring."

"It is a pleasure to be aroused. I become more sensitive and alive to everything."

"Great, like in good health."

"A total focus of attention, while time stands still, body alert, waiting."

"Heightened sensitivity all over; I become aware of part of me I am not usually aware of."

"Floating."

"Supreme sensitivity to touch—waves of butterflies in my stomach."

"I love it when it turns into a fiery, driving force. I become conscious of my vagina and it seems to beckon through a longing feeling."

"I am aroused by some people just by closeness and tenderness. I feel like I want to touch all my skin to all of their skin."

"Like an awakening and the beginning of life."

"Fantastic, almost unbearably ecstatic."

"Like wanting someone so close you just can't touch enough."

"The physical state of wanting—a feeling in the back of my throat, deep emotion and desire."

"Emotional well-being, affection, intimacy."

"Very free and uninhibited about my body, and very close to my partner. I want to rub my body all over his and get as physically close as possible."

"Attractive and wanted."

"Blood throbbing."

"Reckless!"

"Being aware of all parts of my body, wanting to give caring touches—in touch with my own cosmic energy, and my partner's—there is no past and no future."

"My whole body feels wide awake, *super*-stimulated."

"Wow! My whole body is alive, sensitive, fantastic, tingling, positive!"

"My body becomes soft and fluid, and completely in harmony with the universe."

"Happiness, energy, thrills, ecstasy, lying in whipped cream."

"On the edge of an earthquake."

"Warm, tingly, heady. Specific parts of the body come into focus as they are touched, and I feel loved, wanted and worthwhile."

"I feel sensual, excited—and a trifle wicked."

"I am completely sensitized."

"Hot, want to be close and touch her."

"Beautiful and *alive*."

"A rush—hot—yearning in my breasts to be touched —a desire to kiss."

"Warm and wet inside and out, electric—open and languorous."

"Electric currents blowing through my body to my clitoris and vagina—I want to touch and hold him and want my body up against his."

"Heightened alertness, mental health, euphoria."

"I would describe arousal as an increasingly powerful beautiful tingling I always felt was the step past the shivers we gave each other in the sixth grade."

"Electricity with outward streaks, like drawn outward from stars."

"Buzzy, like being mildly aware of every bit of my body, especially my genitals, breasts and neck, stomach, mouth and ears. Also, pretty, desirable and *good*!"

"Very emotional, completely alive, with my entire body urging toward my partner. I just can't get enough of being felt all over and would like to merge with the other person and their body."

"My whole body reacts with a feeling of aching and releases great feelings of love within me."

"A heightened sensitivity all over, a vaguely burning sensation in the clitoral area, and a sort of yearning to be touched on my breasts, stomach, ass, and vagina—great!"

"Tremendous excitement, losing control of my body, I feel desires and needs which I can't deny, and might do things which I would never do in an unexcited state. My body becomes acutely sensitized and simple touches or caresses in various places give me excruciating pleasure."

"My vulva feels still and hot and sexy—my skin feels funny."

"*Joy* is the only word I can use to describe the feeling with someone I love."

"Warm and loved and content and not lonely and 'together' with the other person."

"I lose control, do things impulsively—feel shaky and weak and at the same time tense and supersensitive all over—I have a good feeling that I can't describe because it's better than any other feeling I've ever had."

"*A feeling of power, strength.*"

"A racing of my heart, an intense feeling of closeness, wanting to touch bodies."

"Somehow it gives me the chance to climb above myself—to wake up from the fogginess of daily existence."

"Like being outside of my body, outside of my mind, not really caring what is important to my usual self."

"Sometimes I feel aroused generally, without having been touched—it feels like a kind of tension, a sweet tension, and there is a dreaminess in the desire to touch and be touched. Then again, arousal from touching and being touched can be more acute, a kind of pang in my vagina; nerves stand up under my skin. Being *too* aroused is painful."

"All touch feels exquisite and I want it to go on forever."

"It feels like freedom or power, in the cunt and gut. My body feels uninhibited and *strong*."

"Gorgeous pleasure like baths and sun."

"Senses alert and energizing."

"Sweaty hotness all over my body."

"Like a strong emotion."

"Physical *yearning*."

"Suffusion of delicious feelings."

"Alive everywhere."

"I am alone in the world with my partner."

"Suspended animation, like an eternity in one second. Intense communication through drinking and tasting of their body."

"Voluptuous, elegant, and sensuous."

"Eager for more!"

"A strange feeling, another dimension of myself, melting away from my anchors."

"A feeling of swelling heat, dense, engulfing, sweet."

"Warm, pulsating, dark. All over my body, an intensity of feeling."

"My whole body burns."

"Do you enjoy extended periods of arousal? Arousal for its own sake?"

Arousal is highly enjoyable. But is it pleasurable for its own sake, without an orgasm following?

Many women said that long arousal does feel good.

"No sexual experience has probably ever quite equalled those old high school days in the back seat of a parked car when arousal was an end in itself."

"I wish making love were more sensuous touchings and less direct genital activity. My most exciting times were the hours I used to spend just touching my best friend, and she me."

"Arousal is the ultimate part of sex. During a stage of heightened arousal, I prefer *not* to have orgasm. (It brings me down off it.)"

"I don't remember, as my sexual experiences in the last eight years always led to bed. But as a teenager, getting hot was always neat."

"I often find I like the period of lengthy arousal better than the relatively brief orgasm. After two or three hours of it, I'm as exhausted as if I had had an orgasm."

"When I am with someone I love, sometimes being close and not going for an orgasm can be beautiful."

"I have often enjoyed just passionate kissing and then lost interest when more involved sex followed."

"I like the 'befores' better than intercourse."

"Yes, I like arousal, but I've been conditioned *not* to, so when I get really aroused, I cop out and turn it into intercourse."

"A very intense state can be achieved and maintained—I call it skimming."

"Yes, arousal is more important than orgasm. It was this that sustained me through all the sexual encounters I had that didn't end in orgasm."

"Yes, I am so ungenitally oriented that I find it difficult to make it with my lover. I just tend to caress and be loving rather than get directly involved genitally. Sex is the only legitimate way to get enough skin contact."

"Plain old-fashioned necking and petting can go on for hours, as far as I'm concerned, including touching, kissing, nuzzling and rubbing."

"If I had to choose, I would give up orgasms rather than this feeling."

"I like to keep this state for as long as possible. It just feels very alive and responsive. And it removes the loneliness and isolation more than anything else."

In other words, women really loved the feelings of arousal and being together physically with someone. Many of them would like to see the imaginative mix of activities expanded and revalued—not always necessarily aimed so mechanically at orgasm.

But some women complained that men wouldn't wait for long periods of arousal.

"I like to prolong my states of arousal until the desire for orgasm is irresistible. Unfortunately, many men are too impatient to allow this."

"I never reach this state with a man. They are much too uptight."

"Yes, I love long arousal, especially if it is clear we

are not going to have intercourse. I had one of the best times ever last summer necking with a man for several hours. But I haven't found anyone to do this kind of thing within a situation of possible intercourse. It's always cut short and I guess I haven't yet been able to say, 'I want to do this and I don't intend to do anything else.' "

"I like long arousals but it usually doesn't last as long as I need because he is rushing me to move along toward orgasm."

"It makes me sad I have to control my actions and miss so much of this because my partner is still conditioned to want intercourse whenever we touch practically."

"A long period of arousal is very important to me, and sometimes I'm disappointed if my partner becomes too excited to continue."

"Sometimes when I'm having sex, the guy comes just as I'm beginning to be turned on. I don't like it. It's disappointing."

"I like long periods of arousal. That's why my husband I are not too compatible—I talk to him and he's sensitive for five minutes, then it's 'business as usual.' "

"Who has such choices?? Not me!"

"I like it prolonged, but I know very few males who can or are interested in doing so."

And arousal is not so much fun when the man goes on to orgasm, leaving the woman aroused with no orgasm.

Many women have often had sex without orgasm, and feel resentful that men almost always do orgasm. Thus they made it clear that although arousal is enjoyable, they expect to have an orgasm too.

"I enjoy simple touching just for its own sake without overtones of 'this has to conclude in intercourse.' But getting me aroused so that the man can be satisfied—that is a sexual ripoff as far as I am concerned."

"It's pleasurable to be caressed extensively, but I don't want any man getting off on me if he isn't willing to work to get me off too."

"I generally find men unable to accept arousal alone.

They demand fulfillment, their *own,* of course—but rarely mine!"

"It's like a big letdown and makes me very quiet and sad when I don't orgasm, and he is already lying there quiet and happy and not interested any more."

"If I see I'm not going to have an orgasm, I feel resentful, bored and frustrated."

"If it doesn't lead to orgasm, I have a feeling of being cheated and a lot of anger."

"Sex for me until recently was a long series of one-nighters, and I never felt that I had plenty of time to be physically satisfied. Usually the man would just hop on and pump away and suddenly it was all over. I resented it more and more each time it happened, and now I never *let* it happen."

"If I'm with a man I'm sure will satisfy me eventually, I enjoy prolonging it. But if I'm doubtful, I have to try to 'get mine' before I lose the chance."

Other women pointed out that long arousal without orgasm at some point is extremely frustrating—especially when it becomes a pattern.

"It is very frustrating to *repeatedly* become aroused and not orgasm. Now I refuse to let myself become aroused in this situation."

"It can become painful both physically and psychologically. I guess I resent non-orgasmic stimulation because I associate it with the years I couldn't come, and would hate myself and the men I was with."

"After a certain point, non-orgasmic sex, even just non-genital sex, dragged out over a period of months, makes me lose interest."

"Yes, but if it happens continually without a release it soon makes me ill. I'm on edge all the time and feel sluggish and congested. Teasing is fun—for a while."

"Heightened sensitivity and sensual experiences are great especially when shared. But genital arousal without orgasm is frustrating."

"The longer the better, up to a point. I feel like I plateau at several levels, but then must finish."

"When orgasm is in doubt, I have conflicting feelings

about arousal. It is pleasurable for itself, but after a certain point I am left tense and angry and disappointed, and . . . depressed. Ultimately I have to come and know I will enjoy it."

There were no mixed feelings about how it felt to be on the edge of orgasm, and then have the stimulation that brought you there changed or withdrawn: it felt terrible.

Questionnaire III asked, "If you are just about to have an orgasm and then don't because of withdrawal of stimulation or some similar reason, do you feel frustrated?":

"If my husband comes before I have a chance, I am left shaken and sick to my stomach and resentful and angry."

"Men often have orgasm and roll over and go to sleep, leaving me in a state of high excitement but no orgasm. This is mentally infuriating and has a terrible psychological effect on me. They can be trained to satisfy me but most men seem to assume that women don't need orgasm like men."

"At first I think, oh, it doesn't matter, it was pretty good while it lasted, and then I think, *no!* why should I settle for that?"

"Frustrated and angry, and potentially violent. It usually happens when my husband decides that his method of stimulating me is not working fast enough and so changes it—without asking first."

"I feel extremely frustrated. I'm almost doubled over in pain and I'm furious, and would like to kill my partner."

"I feel frustrated and disappointed and a little hurt and resentful that his work (the next day) should take precedence over me."

"Frustrated, cheated, angry. Usually he comes too quickly. I sometimes think my husband only cares about his release, like he doesn't think I need one."

"Yes, very frustrated and sad, and sometimes I cry."

"Damn yes. I feel sad, let down, that something is wrong with me."

"Yes, I feel furious and insist my partner continue. It is the ultimate in frustration. It makes me feel like I could commit murder."

"I feel frustrated and disappointed and sometimes physically ill, and hurt and rejected emotionally. However, I usually hold my emotions together by trying to reason with myself."

"If the stimulation has been sufficiently long and strong, I feel a discomfort in my genitals and down the back of my legs. Then I'm uncomfortable for hours."

"This happened repeatedly during the early part of my marriage before I turned myself completely off as a means of survival. Now I'm somewhat resigned that this is what happens with men, and don't expect to climax. So it's not too bad. I haven't gotten to that 'just about to' point for a long time."

"No orgasm is frustrating and worse than no sex at all. It makes me feel depressed and discouraged. I would give up a partner I didn't orgasm with."

"If I am really aroused, and don't have an orgasm, I am frustrated to tears."

"It's okay without sometimes when I am mentally into it. Otherwise, not having an orgasm is disastrous, disgusting, and depressing."

"I feel a great frustration when I don't have an orgasm, which destroys all other pleasure for me. Especially if I am very aroused, and still don't have an orgasm, I often cry as an alternate form of release."

"Not having orgasm *hurts*."

"In the beginning of my sexual experiences I didn't mind, but after a while, after a few experiences with guys who just cared about their orgasms, or were ignorant enough to believe all women would just come at the sight of their penis, I got disgusted, and now it makes me feel extremely frustrated. I hate the man and will never see him again."

"Yes, frustrated, angry, frightened, insecure, and humiliated."

"Frustration comes in the form of abdominal cramps, I don't know whether in the uterus, ovaries or where, but around there, and also involves bitchiness, irritability, nervousness, depression, pessimism, self-doubt, and lack of energy to accomplish anything."

"I feel slightly frustrated, mostly inadequate and greatly disappointed at *myself* for being too slow or perhaps incompetent."

"I feel frustrated, tense, bitter, scrappy, resentful, and guilty for feeling bitter and resentful."

"It feels like someone is trying to kill me, like God hates me by not letting me be gratified."

ORGASM

Suddenly, after the period of arousal, which can vary greatly in time from a minute or so to hours, with appropriate stimulation there is a sudden, intense sensation known as orgasm, climax, "coming." What does this, the moment just *before* the contractions, feel like?

"There are a few faint sparks, coming up to orgasm, and then I suddenly realize that it is going to catch fire, and then I concentrate all my energies, both physical and mental, to quickly bring on the climax—which turns out to be a moment suspended in time, a hot rush—a sudden breath-taking dousing of all the nerves of my body in Pleasure—I try to make the moment last—disappointment when it doesn't."

"Before, I feel a tremendous surge of tension and a kind of delicious feeling I can't describe. Then orgasm is like the excitement and stimulation I have been feeling, increased, for an *instant,* a hundred-fold."

"It starts down deep, somewhere in the 'core,' gets bigger, stronger, better, and more beautiful, until I'm just four square inches of ecstatic crotch area!!"

"The physical sensation is beautifully excruciating. It begins in the clitoris, and also surges into my whole vaginal area."

"It's a peak of almost, almost, ALMOST, ALMOSTTTT. The only way I can describe it is to say it is like riding the 'Tilt-a-Whirl.'"

"Just before orgasm, the area around my clitoris suddenly comes alive and, I can't think of any better description, seems to sparkle and send bright dancing sensations all around. Then it becomes focused like a point of intense light. Like a bright blip on a radar screen, and that's the orgasm."

"There is an almost frantic itch-pain-pleasure in my vagina and clitoral area that seems almost insatiable, it is also extremely hot and I lose control of everything, then there is an explosion of unbelievable warmth and relief to the itch-pain-pleasure! It is really indescribable and what I've just written doesn't explain it at all!!! WORDS!"

"I can't answer this question. The charm of an orgasm is that, when it's there, all your concentration is on it, until a feeling of intense relief encompasses your whole body and mind—then when it's over, it's impossible to describe it accurately or catch any remnant of the feeling. So you go at it again and it seems all fresh and new again, but then the moment it's over it's as elusive as ever: pure *amnesia* seems to set in the minute you try to explain it."

Perhaps slightly easier to verbalize is exactly where this orgasmic sensation, this rush, is felt—although subjective perceptions such as these are notoriously tricky.

"Just before orgasm, my clitoris is burning and tingling and vibrating until there is a sudden orgasmic gush of heat and burning into the vagina also, that followed all too suddenly by my contractions, the clapping of the walls together."

"It begins with great pressure and tightness in the clitoris, like the organ itself will explode. Then it grabs my pelvis and vagina."

"The clitoral area builds up the tension, with the release being in the vagina. Arguments over vaginal versus clitoral are irrelevant. They work together."

"It starts at the clitoris and surrounds the vagina like a hoop."

"It goes spreading from the clitoral region descending to deep in the vagina and makes me want penetration."

"It begins with an incredible throbbing in my clitoris

and then progresses upward including my vagina and belly and finally my head."

"During masturbation or cunnilingus, there is a strong feeling of the clitoris expanding and filling and becoming unbearably pleasurable, after which at about the moment of orgasm there is some shift to the vaginal area and then strong contractions of the vagina, with me, trembling and swooning."

"Orgasm starts as a pressure from within and a tingling tension near the clitoris, which spreads to the vagina inside my abdomen. There is a general stretching tension throughout until orgasm breaks."

In other words, clitoral area stimulation (direct or indirect) is necessary to have an orgasm, but the orgasm itself is felt in an undifferentiable area around the clitoris and vagina, often including the upper part of the vagina. Similarly, men need stimulation on the tip of the penis to orgasm, but feel the orgasm itself inside their bodies.

Some women described the feeling in the vagina at this time.

"I feel it in the depths of the vagina. I have a strong urge to be penetrated, which, if I allow before I've begun coming, makes orgasm virtually impossible." (See page 190.)

"It feels like a balloon in the abdomen filling up and then exploding rapidly through my body."

"I feel a tense tightness for several seconds midway in my vagina."

"I feel it at the base of the vagina—a burning, tingling feeling, then I feel like jumping and screaming."

"There is a burning, aching feeling in my vagina, and the feeling that the rest of my body will follow."

"I have burning warm feelings in the upper opening of the vagina."

"I am unaware of my body except for a center core deep inside my vagina."

"It comes as a sort of bearing down/opening feeling in the mouth of the womb."

"It is a hard pulling throbbing sensation. The harder

the orgasm, the further 'up' or 'back' it feels—that is, from the clitoris on back or up toward the uterus."

What does your body look like during orgasm?

Picture book and pornography examples of female orgasmic passion often show women writhing and arching like wild horses during orgasm. This is more accurate as a depiction of passionate arousal than as a picture of a woman during orgasm. During orgasm, women (and men) become rigid and tense—and for most women this means lying stiff and still. (If movement continues, it tends to have a spastic quality.*) Women who continue moving are often the same women who masturbate by moving their entire bodies and not just their hands.

"I stiffen into a long hard teeth-gritting stretch that seems to bear down on my orgasm and squeeze every marvelous feeling out of it."

"During the orgasm, every muscle (that I'm aware of) tenses completely. Sometimes my stomach buckles up and afterwards I convulse with what may look like the 'dry heaves.' I kind of shudder and shake spasmodically as the muscles in my vagina contract."

"Just before orgasm my whole body clenches and becomes completely rigid, with a kind of intense trembling. It is completed when I feel a rush of heat up my body."

"My legs stiffen and point out. My eyes automatically shut, and my lower body becomes sort of spastic."

"I feel sort of epileptic—veins in my neck stand out, my face is red, I am rigid and mostly motionless, but the motion that does take place is spastic. It sounds awful, but it feels great!"

"I always feel a hot flash just before orgasm. My body is tense and fairly rigid. My legs are usually spread apart but not always. I don't know my facial expression."

"My actions get very spasmodic. My body becomes

---

* Kinsey has pointed out the similarity between epileptic movements and the movements both during and after orgasm.

rigid and often shakes and vibrates with the tension."

"I gasp, breathe heavily, grip him tightly, then dissolve, during which there is a regular rhythmic pulsating of my vagina."

"I breathe heavier and heavier, gasp, have rigid and frenzied pelvic movements, my face contorts, I go rigid, and then I relax dramatically."

"I flush, my vaginal muscles tighten and loosen repeatedly, I moan, and at the peak, my body tightens to the point where I'm paralyzed and I usually say something like, 'Don't stop!' "

"Tense, legs straight out, back arched and body in convulsions. I imagine my face looks like it is in pain."

"My body is usually tense, with legs straight out, my pelvis thrusting erratically. I think my facial expression is a bit pained—brows knit, eyes closed, mouth open."

"I get a sex rash, usually have my legs extremely wide, around the man, and my pelvis is very tilted; I move uncontrollably up and down across the man's pubis."

"I move some, especially my hips, but I do not writhe or twist. I think my face must remain fairly expressionless. What's happening goes on primarily inside. I'm told that I give few indications of what's happening."

For women who don't move their whole bodies against the point of stimulation, this stillness at orgasm can be misinterpreted by a partner to mean lack of interest!*

"Does your partner realize you are having an orgasm when you do?"

45	usually
226	my regular partner, yes; others, almost never
51	yes, because I tell them

* Many primate researchers seem to have been confused by the very same stillness, as they are frequently unclear as to whether the female primates they observed had orgasmed or not.

50	yes, if the partner is experienced
40	no
9	"I think so"
13	"I don't know"
42	yes, because I cry out, and utter moans and sighs
3	"I hope so"
——	
479	

Some women did show physical signs.

"Yes. I'm vibrating and spastic and probably moaning. I *hope* he notices!"

"Yes, probably. Other than vocal heights, I get a rocking motion in the pelvic area and my thighs begin to really squeeze together. Since he's between my legs, he soon knows I'm coming. I also sometimes experience shudders for up to five minutes after orgasm."

"Usually he knows unless he's in the middle of orgasm himself. I moan and groan and lose control of my pelvis. With my hands I grab my partner's buttocks and guide him in his movements if he isn't already doing what I want."

"Yes, I show the same signs as for faking: rapid breathing and interior contractions, willful or not."

"With intercourse, he can feel the contractions, but clitorally, I have to tell him just before."

But most women did not show signs—or, that is, not the mythical signs of writhing and arching, etc.

"This is one of my hangups. I have a tendency to grow suddenly passive just before orgasm, and it bothers me. I wish I knew if other women have felt this. I feel like I am waiting for something. The stillness of it bothers me. Why can't I accept it?"

"Up until my early thirties, I didn't know if I was, or wasn't, having an orgasm, since the type of orgasm I *thought* I was supposed to have was not what my *partners thought* I should have. And to this day I haven't come across one man who knows *when* or *how* a woman has an orgasm. They all think it is the same as theirs with thrusting, ejaculation, etc. And, of course, only one orgasm."

"Before orgasm, I am absolutely motionless myself, almost not breathing, for a while, while he's stimulating me. They get turned off by this lack of motion and response."

"A lot of my partners think I'm strange because I'm very quiet and I get very much into my head when I have an orgasm. They think because I don't pant, scream, and claw I haven't had one."

"I used to go out of my way to offer all the mythical Hollywood signs of female orgasms, but now I offer only some subdued signs or sounds."

"No, he doesn't. I hold on tighter, but I don't show the signs you're supposed to."

"I wish I could show him more, but I get so high during orgasm I don't speak or even hardly move."

"Women always can; men never could. They don't know what a real flesh-and-blood woman is like—all they know is *their* own image of us."

"Nope. Sometimes when I'm groaning and shaking they think I'm coming but I'm not. When I really come, I'm stiff and rigid and epileptic."

"I am surprised when they are not aware. Sometimes they mistake when I am just getting very aroused or excited, and think *that's* it."

"They only think I orgasm when I fake it."

"They keep telling me that I don't come, because I don't thrust and writhe and scream."

"I don't move convulsively the way women in books do. I don't know if anyone does. I guess I just hold on tight. Sometimes it bothers me when a man hasn't been able to tell that I climaxed."

"Sometimes—but I don't think I show much different responses when I'm really excited from when I come; only after several orgasms do I relax my whole body."

"I guess not, since he usually asks. But it is hardly mistakable—I go into simulated rigor mortis."

"It is not always obvious when a woman has an orgasm. I suppose the main indicator would be my body stops moving."

"My partner thinks I do when I show signs, like special hard breathing and body movements. But I never have orgasms—*never*."

"My body lies very quietly while it happens. I don't seem to show any vivid signs. But the different type of movement and feeling of the body should be evident to any sensitive partner."

"Usually not. Sometimes they ask, and sometimes they assume I do, or else couldn't care less."

"When I masturbate, I'm constantly amazed at how I managed to fool so many men in the past about whether or not I had an orgasm. After all, I have intense vaginal spasms and involuntary pelvic convulsions."

"Are you shy about having orgasms with a partner? Only with new partners, or always?"

Some women move a lot at orgasm, while others don't move at all; it all depends on how you're getting the stimulation. But even women who move usually move in a spastic, rigid way at orgasm, with the whole body tense and stiff. Women, aware of this, are sometimes concerned that they might look strange and unattractive to their partners, and this fear has inhibited some women from having orgasm.

Although the majority were not shy with their regular partners, quite a few women did express these feelings.

"Yes, so I am very noncommunicative about letting it be known when I have orgasm."

"Well yes, sometimes all that feeling seems out of place, overwhelming."

"Yes, but it helps me to remember that he will enjoy any contractions my vagina might make. But I still fear I will become only an animal and he will get all messed up."

"Yes, his watching me while I'm out of control seems undignified, embarrassing. I'm also embarrassed when he does."

"Yes, with all my partners. I'm afraid they'll think I'm doing something weird."

"I haven't orgasmed with a partner yet because I'm

afraid they will find it offensive. I feel another person would be turned off to see me like that."

"Yes, I am, because I need to hold him, open to him, cry out for more, and make noises that sound almost desperate. I feel it's too heavy and I'm afraid of sounding animal."

"I just don't like my face hanging out when I'm experiencing orgasm. I notice the same is true with my husband."

"Yes, I'm shy because I don't like the way my face and body *look* when I'm feeling that way."

"Yes, but maybe it's because we're taught that convulsive movements and loss of control are unattractive. Whereas maybe, theoretically, they *are* attractive."

"Yes, I'm even shy about expressing appreciation for anything my partner might do for me. And I'm especially shy about asking for the *amount* of stimulation I need to have an orgasm."

"With new partners it's a problem all right—letting them know what they have to do and taking the time to do it."

"Yes, with a new partner. I worry because I don't feel they really want to satisfy me—and perhaps it takes me longer than other women?"

"I'm afraid that new partners will think I'm weird and not as sexy as other women if I don't have an orgasm or that I'm selfish, or aggressive, if I do!"

"Yes, I'm especially shy with new partners because I'm ashamed I don't have orgasms during intercourse."

"Yes, I am with new partners because maybe he will think of me as oversexed if I achieve a strong orgasm."

"With a new partner I'm shy because I have to explain the masturbation business (clitoral stimulation). About the orgasm itself I have no fears. The thing is so damned powerful, it can't fail to boost his ego about four miles."

"With new partners, especially. I turn off all the lights, but it still isn't dark enough."

"Well, with new partners I tend to be quieter. But also, I feel proud to have come with a partner—'There,

I did it, it's my accomplishment, I got what I wanted out of this.' "

"No, I used to be, then I said fuck it! I'm not going to be such a product of society that I can't even enjoy my own body!"

CONTRACTIONS

The intense feeling of orgasm lasts for only a second, and is followed by contractions. The peak itself is so brief that many women didn't separate the two concepts.

What do the contractions feel like?*

"I feel a spasm starting inside my cunt (a regular pulse beat) but also extending down my legs and through my body."

"There is an intense sensation in my vagina and clitoris (orgasm), and then intense pulsations close to pain."

"My clitoris vibrates at some unbelievable speed, and the muscles in my vagina and further back contract intensely, my head seems de-burdened, my toes curl, my abdomen feels strong—and my whole body pulsates along with my clitoris and vagina."

"I feel pulsating white lines of intense pleasure with a lovely throbbing in my vaginal area."

"My body runs itself, with no thinking on my part. I feel a rhythm in my vaginal canal, a throbbing or muscle contraction, and my upper legs are very tense."

"Waves of muscles in my vagina are pulsating, tingling, alive."

"Vaginal contractions radiate out over my body in waves."

---

* It is interesting to find that *"no part of the vagina itself produces the orgasmic contractions.* The muscular contractions engendering the actual sensation of orgasm are produced by the extravaginal muscles contracting, not against the vaginal wall directly but against the circumvaginal venous chambers. The lower vaginal wall is passively pushed in and out by these contractions."[1]

"Orgasm occurs to me like an intense tickling in the front of my vagina, with a sudden release through rolling pulses inside my vagina."

"I feel involuntary highly pleasant spasms in my clitoris, vagina, and anal areas. Sometimes my whole body seems to be in spasm. The pleasure is basically in my genital area, but my whole body does react."

"I experience a series of profound contractions in my vagina with immediate reactions of sweating, hyperventilation and *release*."

"I feel vaginal contractions at the moment of release, and in a strong orgasm, uterine contractions also. (Sometimes my whole body jerks, but I'm not sure how involuntary that is.)"

"The sensation of orgasm feels to me like fantastic excitation of my clitoris and a general explosion through my entire body. There are definite contractions of the uterus and vagina, which were most apparent to me when I was a good deal pregnant."

"I feel the muscles in my vagina rippling open and shut, sometimes powerfully, sometimes lightly. A few times it has been so intense that I felt brief cramps in my uterus."

Although a *slightly* arched position may be natural during arousal, and the moments up to and just including orgasm, during the contractions the hips tend to move forward somewhat, as does the head, in a kind of bending inward.

"I arch back before orgasm, then during the contractions my hips raise and my back makes the reverse of an arch, sort of bending inwards—almost a fetal position."

"During the orgasmic contractions, I convulse toward the direction of my stomach, like doubling over."

This bending inward sometimes takes the form of whole body spasms, reflecting the uterine spasms that often accompany orgasm. "During the arousal period (buildup), my whole body's muscles tense, and my limbs may jerk. Then the release is accomplished in about four vaginal spasms, during which my upper body sort of lurches forward slightly, either simultaneously or sometimes after."

How did women describe the whole orgasm, from arousal to contractions?

Finally, to sum up and get the complete picture of how orgasm feels to women, following are some complete descriptions of orgasm from some very articulate women.

"At a certain point, I know I'm on my way, but it's hard to put into words. Physically my breathing is faster, my body tenses and strains to make my clitoris as open and vulnerable as possible. My vaginal and clitoral area gets absolutely hot and I seem to switch into a pelvic rhythm over which I have no conscious control; every contact with my clitoris at this point is a miniature orgasm which becomes more frequent until it is one huge muscle spasm!"

"To begin with there is increasing heat and pleasure focused in my clitoris and genitals. Then a piercing localized pleasure, a feeling of inevitability which grows until there is a rapid, skyrocket-like burst of piercing pleasure, beginning clitorally then radiating to my whole groin. It only lasts a minute, then there is some trembling, diminishing shudders, some residual heat, breathlessness and some residual piercing-like pleasure. Then I rest."

"First, various parts of my body tingle and feel strange, then at different times there is the feeling of an orgasm but only for a split second, then all of this becomes more and more frequent until orgasm comes like waves. At that time all else is non-existent. Orgasm is centered in my clitoris releasing waves to my vagina, and ends after an intense but brief amount of time, very slowly again emitting the split-second sensations for a few minutes getting more and more infrequent and less intense."

"Orgasm is a feeling of warmth, first, all over me. In fact, my general mood and the atmosphere around me before sexual activity begins is a great part of the buildup of this warm or excited feeling. After the general warmth comes tension in my legs (particularly thighs), my abdomen, and, of course, my breasts and genitals. My clitoris feels very 'tingly.' I feel very strong just before the orgasm and my 'insides' seem to be alive and powerful. The moistness, heat, and strength are all very satisfying. Sometimes my buttocks and pelvis feel the need to be very frenzied and move a lot, and sometimes I feel more like pushing strongly against something with my pelvis and legs. The orgasm itself reminds me of a dam breaking. I can feel contractions inside me and a very liquid sensation. The best part is the continuing waves of build-up and release during multiple orgasms."

"It starts out feeling like a sweet, good, slightly intense feeling. This feeling occurs every now and then, then it increases in intensity and more often; the time lapse between each feeling gets shorter. Just before orgasm the feeling is very intense and almost all the time, with glowing good feelings radiating on the inside of my thighs. During the climax, it feels like everything around me stops existing and I am fully concentrated on this good feeling which seems to intensely buzz for a while. Sometimes I am aware of twitching or contractions in my vagina especially around the opening. Afterwards, my genitals are very touchy and just seem to glow with the same slightly intense 'sweet' feeling that I started with. This feeling I have been describing is also an aching feeling that is centered at the top of my vagina. When my clitoris is being stimulated, I am also aware of that feeling in my clitoris, but when orgasm occurs, somehow the two feelings (vaginal and clitoral) get together and become one."

"Orgasm is the greatest physical pleasure, by far, of any in life. The greatest pleasure is just *before* the first contraction. At first, sexual tension is localized in the genitals but as the orgasm starts, pleasure spreads through the entire middle part of my body and down into the legs. Then when the contractions start, they feel like what they are—contractions of the uterus and cervix and perhaps the circular muscles around the cervix end of the vagina."

"Orgasm feels like an intense drawing together sensation, located in my genital area (I can't differentiate in feeling between my clitoris and vagina at that point), then my whole body tenses and the sensation is one of total involvement without any 'will' or thought involved. 'It' takes over completely. The physiological sensation is best described by the word 'outrageous' in terms of its devastating total effect. It's over within seconds, but fantastic when it occurs. The only awareness I can state is a certain stiffening all over, in addition to the intense 'implosion' in the undifferentiable genital area."

"I don't have orgasms like they describe in books. (Not skyrockets or total relaxation, etc.) What I have starts as a diffuse 'good feeling,' most strongly genital, but all over my body. This feeling gets more and more genitally focused, and I can predict the quality of the climax—if it is *too* focused, it's not as good an orgasm: the best climaxes seem to involve more of my body. The quality of the orgasm can vary from almost a frustration (the climax coming somehow before the buildup is completed) to a total release—waves of relief involving my whole body."

"My thoughts tend to focus on myself—moving and positioning, so that I can feel the greatest stimulation. I become aware of pulsating sensitivity in the area of my vagina. I have some anxiety about whether I can climax or not, and so attention is focused on completing the sexual act and not being 'left hanging.' Then there is a convulsive muscle activity, occurring in a wave-like rhythmic cadence, which lasts about four to five seconds. Then, generally, a lot of muscle relaxation and frequently I feel very tender toward my partner."

"First, tension builds in my body and head, my heart beats, then I strain against my lover, and then there is a second or two of absolute stillness, non-breathing, during which I know orgasm will come in the next second or two. Then waves, and I rock against my partner and cannot hold him tight enough. It's all over my body, but especially in my abdomen and gut. Afterwards, I feel suffused with warmth and love and absolute happiness."

"There is a gradual tensing of my body which reaches a sharp peak then hits a thrilling plateau, a kind of screeching, sliding across a plane, then lets go in five to six fluttering convulsions, at first sharp and quick, then duller, slower and smoother."

"I feel it beginning with intense pressure and tightness in the clitoris, like the organ itself will explode. Then it grabs my vagina and pelvis. I feel hot, usually sweaty, my head buzzes, everything blocks out but the excitement—it's like being one big, hard clitoris."

"Before it begins, I feel a vibrant pulsing in my clitoris and pent-up tension in my vagina, then the tension explodes and I feel my vagina contracting, my heart pounding, my body moaning, and my voice going 'oh, oh ohohoh.' There is a feeling of intense pleasure when it starts, then disappointment that it cannot be sustained. Then my husband becomes a person again, and I am very aware of him and the feeling of closeness."

"An orgasm feels like a powerful force somewhere in the middle or deep in my vagina that is a release of the tension. A sensation of waves or contractions in my groin, and I curl up my body, usually moving in different directions with the feeling, almost pushing with the contractual sensations. Toward the end it turns blissful and relaxed and instead of squeezing my lover's arm or the sheet, I just lie there. Toward the end or afterwards my vagina usually actually contracts in pleasant squeezes from one to six times. I feel usually very conscious and aware during my orgasms, and if I were interrupted it would probably ruin one in progress."

AFTER ORGASM

How did women feel after orgasm? Did they feel "satisfied" and "fulfilled"? Ready for sleep? Relaxed?

It is now widely accepted in sex research that women can have many orgasms in a brief period of time, and that orgasm does not return women physiologically to an unaroused state but rather to pre-orgasmic levels of arousal, which recede only slowly. Mary Jane Sherfey has made an important contribution to our understanding of this capacity. As her point of departure, Dr. Sherfey quotes Masters and Johnson:

> If a female who is capable of having regular orgasms is properly stimulated within a short period after her first climax, she will in most instances be capable of having a second, third, fourth, and even a fifth and sixth orgasm before she is fully satiated. As contrasted with the male's usual inability to have more than one orgasm in a short period, many females, especially when clitorally stimulated, can regularly have five or six full orgasms within a matter of minutes.[2]

Sherfey goes on to explain, in more detail than anyone else has ever done, the physiology behind this capacity:

> . . . the popular idea that a woman should have one intense orgasm which should bring "full satisfaction," act as a strong sedative, and alleviate sexual tension for several days to come is simply fallacious . . . Each orgasm is followed promptly by refilling of the venous erectile chambers, distension creates engorgement and edema, which create more tissue tension, etc. The supply of blood and edema fluid to the pelvis is inexhaustible.
>
> Consequently, the more orgasms a woman has, the stronger they become; the more orgasms she has, the more she *can* have. To all intents and purposes, *the human female is sexually insatiable in the presence of the highest degrees of sexual satiation.*[3]

Sherfey adds:

> I must stress that this condition does not mean a woman is always consciously unsatisfied. There is a great difference between satisfaction and satiation. A woman may be emotionally satisfied to the full in the absence of *any* orgasmic expression (although such a

state would rarely persist through years of frequent arousal and coitus without some kind of physical or emotional reaction formation). Satiation-in-insatiation is well illustrated by Masters' statement, "A woman *will usually* be satisfied with 3-5 orgasms . . ." I believe it would rarely be said, "A man will usually be satisfied with three to five ejaculations." The man *is* satisfied. The woman usually wills herself to be satisfied because she is simply unaware of the extent of her orgasmic capacity. However, I predict that this hypothesis will come as no great shock to many women who consciously realize, or intuitively sense, their lack of satiation.[4]

Helen Kaplan, in her book *The New Sex Therapy*, puts it this way:

> . . . apart from the fact that he often feels placid and sleepy after intercourse, the male returns to his pre-aroused resting state, both psychically and physically, rather rapidly. In contrast, the woman returns to the non-sexual state much more slowly. If she has achieved orgasm the woman can experience profound and prolonged sensuous pleasure during the resolution stage and, as mentioned above, can be brought to orgasm again at any point during this period, if she is open to this.[5]

Most women in this study did not seem acquainted with these facts, the great majority reporting a desire for only one orgasm,* and being unaware of how many they might be capable of.† It is possible that the phrasing of the question—"Is one orgasm sexually satisfying to you?"—may have been somewhat responsible for eliciting "yes" answers, plus the cultural pressure to see "one" as the norm. Or perhaps, as Dr. Sherfey suggests,

---

* There was no correlation found between women's desire for more orgasms, and their age, amount of experience, or number of children.

† In response to: "How many orgasms are you capable of?" many women replied that they did not know. Figures can be found on page 602.

one may be satisfying, although not satiating. A larger number of women did indicate that they were less inclined to be satisfied with only one orgasm during masturbation than during sex with a partner.

How do you feel after orgasm?

Although women in general indicated satisfaction with one orgasm, when asked how they felt after orgasm, they did *not* indicate a return to a state of a relative lack of sensitivity. There were two basic kinds of feelings described:

Feeling tender and loving, wanting to be close.

"It varies, but the instant my consciousness returns to my head (after the contractions) I feel this overwhelming passionate love for my lover, sometimes to the point of crying."

"A feeling of closeness and relief, and *intense* affection for my sex partner."

"A feeling of crazy friendliness, sometimes unfounded."

"My orgasm subsides into a warm glow of well-being. This afterglow is short if I am not emotionally close to my partner, otherwise, it is long and rich and almost the best part."

"I want to 'hold' my partner, a sort of tightening time that is my arm and vaginal muscles and emotions wanting to hold my partner tight, and then there is a gradual loosening and lessening of this 'holding action.' "

"I feel deep spasms, several in a row. Then I always cry and feel a fierce tenderness."

"I am more aroused after an orgasm, more loving, needing."

Feeling strong and wide awake, energetic and alive.

"I feel the most alive of any time except after vigorous exercise. A feeling of well being, feeling beautiful."

"There is a prolonged energy release during the following hours—in other words, a desire to do and be physically active."

"After, I feel exhausted and totally relaxed, with a

feeling of well-being, then either sleepy or recharged with energy."

"Fulfilled. I could conquer anything."

"I feel exhaustion, for a few minutes, lying around sleepy, and then a lot of energy, more aware than to begin with and usually in a more positive state of mind."

"I experience a warm burning tingling—a supreme sense of health, vitality and even power immediately after."

"It varies. Some leave me exhausted, some light and bouncy and I *receive* energy."

"I like best this feeling of my own muscular *strength* at orgasm."

"I used to masturbate before I got up in the morning, and I felt like singing, optimistic, friendly, generous. I always marveled how nice people seemed to me at those times."

"Orgasm is *magnificent*—it is the absence of all thought or thinking for me, sheer body sensations—tingling, tension, tremendous heat and strength—my body feels *alive* and *powerful!*"

Both of these reactions represent continued arousal. *The descriptions of arousal earlier in this chapter are very similar to these descriptions of feelings after orgasm.* It seems to be only a matter of perception as to whether we interpret what we are feeling as driving us on toward orgasm or as just general good body feelings. Of course there are many degrees of arousal, and some do point more strongly toward orgasm than others. To repeat Dr. Kaplan, "If she has achieved orgasm the woman can experience profound and prolonged sensuous pleasure during the resolution stage [or] . . . can be brought to orgasm again at any point during this period, if she is open to this." Of course there is no need to interpret arousal as a need for orgasm, whether it occurs before or after an orgasm.

Women who are very physically active in obtaining orgasm may also feel more satisfied physically after orgasm; according to one woman: "There is a sense of physical relief after orgasm, but the degree of satisfaction depends on how strenuous the sex has been, and how long." Orgasm and physical exercise have much in common in terms of release of tension. Vigorous sex may be the most strenuous exercise many women get, and this may also account for some women's emphasis on the pleasurable feelings of body strength and well-being during and after orgasm.

The truth is that all women *are* capable of many orgasms *if* they want them. However, this does not mean that more are necessarily better, or that women who don't have or want more are not "performing" correctly. The point is that women seem unaware of their capacity, and in that way limit themselves. The decision to have more than one orgasm must be based on the knowledge that there is a choice, and on the freedom to act on that knowledge.

MULTIPLE ORGASMS

Why don't women realize their capacity for orgasms?
Why don't women realize their capacity for orgasms? Why don't they perceive their arousal as continuing?

There often seemed to be an unconscious rejection of the possibility of having more than one orgasm.
If men can only have one, perhaps it seems greedy or aggressive, challenging, to want more when with a man; perhaps a woman who does is "unnatural" or a "nymphomaniac." We are told, by inference, that one *should* satisfy us. Even during masturbation, some women (although less than during sex with a partner) felt guilty or self-conscious about wanting more than one.

"It's hard for me to indicate I want more than a single orgasm in lovemaking, and I almost always leave it to my lover to take the initiative. Continued caressing now satisfies me as much as another orgasm."

"I've never felt that I couldn't come again with pleasure, but am hesitant to pursue it."

"Although I've often felt vaguely unsatisfied with one orgasm, I've never attempted to have more."

"One, so far, is just great, and then I concentrate on *his*."

"I think I could have several if he used his tongue, but I don't like to make him stay down there that long."

"One never is enough, two sometimes (rarely) is, but I usually 'need' about five once I have the first one. (The five is for masturbation. On the rare occasions in the past when I came during sex with my partner, two or three was 'enough'—i.e., I couldn't admit to the man I wanted more. . . .)"

"I have at least three during masturbation. But my male partners usually stop after I have come once."

"I get worried about his exhaustion, and that inhibits me during clitoral stimulation."

"I feel like I want twenty. However, because my husband seems to want only one I have had to adjust to his pattern."

"With a partner, I feel lucky if I even get one, and usually, I wouldn't attempt even *wanting* more. Usually I get 'none' and feel starved!"

"One orgasm is usual for me, via clitoral manipulation (cunnilingus or manual stimulation). I *have* had five or six orgasms due to self-manipulation and fantasy. With men, I have never had more than one. I have had the uniform feeling that men, no matter how much they talk about 'taking you higher and higher,' aren't really interested in your capacity for many orgasms."

"One orgasm is usually satisfying to me because I'm so damned lazy. I usually wait until I'm stoned or so tired that one orgasm leaves me without any energy and I fall asleep. As far as I know, however, I'm capable of going on indefinitely when I'm wide awake. In the past, my partner has generally gotten worn out before I'm ready to quit. During masturbation, I usually come two or three times, depending on how worked up I was before I started. When I was little, and before I started having sex with men, I used to spend half the night masturbating over and over and over again."

"I found with women—after having sex with men for years—that I wanted and could enjoy many orgasms, and continue lovemaking for a much longer time. Men, because they only had one and then collapsed, assumed that I was satisfied and I told them I was. The truth is, I was still aroused after orgasm—even more than before."

Some women didn't even know it was possible to have more than one, and confused the idea with multiple orgasm.

This made answers to the question "How many orgasms do you want?" even more confusing to interpret. Few women really seemed to know what multiple orgasm is; and several wondered if each contraction was one orgasm, and four to five contractions "multiple orgasms":

"I am not sure whether I have one long orgasm or several shorter ones."

"I have a lot of contractions grouped together. Is that one orgasm?"

"I wish I could have a continuous orgasm for a long time—say one half hour. Is that possible?"

"Last night I masturbated. I've always never been quite sure if I have 'multiple orgasms' or not. But last night I felt I did. Or was it just multiple 'contractions' or 'convulsions,' or is that the same thing? This was in the space of less than a minute, and whatever it was happened maybe four to five times, the first one being the strongest."

"Yes, one is fine. I usually feel so content, and exhausted, actually, that I don't have any desire for another. However, having heard about 'multiple orgasms,' I wanted to know what it was like, but actually find it uncomfortable to continue clitoral stimulation immediately following an orgasm. My orgasms are usually so prolonged that I wonder if they may represent 'multiple orgasm.' I don't know how many I'm capable of."

What is multiple orgasm? Sequential orgasm?

Multiple orgasm is *not* the same thing as restimulating yourself every few minutes to have another orgasm—which we will call *sequential orgasms*. Multiple orgasms, which are much rarer, are several orgasms with no break in between (with the stimulation continuing, of course). Sequential orgasms can be continued indefinitely by many women. To have a sequence of orgasms, *you must wait for a few minutes after each orgasm, until you feel the return of the focus of sensation, and desire for another orgasm.* Then, when the feeling is centered again, stimulation of that spot should bring the second orgasm very quickly. Restimulating yourself too quickly, before sensation refocuses, could diffuse and dull the feeling and make another orgasm impossible. Sometimes subsequent orgasms increase arousal, and so you may feel the spot that is sensitive moving lower, deeper into your genitals.

Unfortunately, the whole concept of being able to have more than one orgasm, and multiple orgasm, has taken on a competitive ring, as in "Am I a 'complete' woman? If other women are having multiple orgasms, why can't I?" and so on. The Orgasm Olympics, as one woman called it.

"I have read that one woman had fifty orgasms within an hour—I struggle to have one mini one a week. How jealous I am!"

"I can't believe this multi-orgasm business. I once had two about five minutes apart. It was a pretty grubby affair, and the second one was weak. By grubby I mean I had to work awfully hard, and had a desperate feeling. Afterwards I felt totally wasted. I only want one. Like the average man, I could get it up again, but why?"

Once again, merely discussing women's capacity for orgasms does not imply that we would necessarily always want many orgasms. The point is that we must become aware of and acquainted with our bodies' potential, so that *we* are in control of defining ourselves and making our own choices—not the people around us, or our lack of information. And, after all, many orgasms can feel very good.

Many women mentioned that one orgasm (or none) could be emotionally satisfying.

"Yes, one—but as I've described it, with its aftershocks. I don't know how many I'm capable of. I haven't experimented. It seems to me, though I may be wrong, that there is an emotional quality to the experience and that immediate repetitions of that aspect of it probably aren't possible. At least not for me."

"Depends on what has gone before, whether or not he is having his. Generally, I am satisfied by his orgasm, regardless of how many I have had or not had. My body is capable of an indefinite number, really limited only by how energetic I am at the time. I couldn't answer 'How many do you usually want?' It seems somehow inapplicable."

"One orgasm is always sexually satisfying for me. I don't know how many I'm capable of because I never want to go beyond just one. I think I reach such a high, such a state of ecstasy that to go beyond it would take away from that peak. It takes a while for my body to feel normal afterwards anyway."

Also many women felt that their arousal was physically diffused and "satisfied" by intercourse. This will be discussed later in the chapter.

Some women stated that they could not have more than one orgasm because their clitoris became too sensitive to touch after orgasm.

"I'm incredibly aroused before orgasm. After I come I feel like I can't move, very very satisfied, but also as if I could do it ten times over. I can't though—when I am touched again it feels irritating. I like to lie there and flex my vaginal muscles because it gives me a curious electric tingling sensation on the soles of my feet, believe it or not. I feel content and full of love for my lover. We usually talk about how our orgasms felt and laugh a lot."

"I've often wondered about 'multiple orgasms,' but I

never go on, for being so sensitive—sensitive is a better word than hurt."

"Afterwards I can't bear to be touched directly. Usually I feel a return to gentle lapping accompanied by the pleasurable sensations that precede orgasm, but I just can't do anything about it."

"After orgasm I am relaxed, drowsy and contented, and my clitoris is hypersensitive and touch is irritating—I only want to cuddle."

"One is satisfactory—after which I'm extremely sensitive and ticklish for at least twenty minutes. I could go on all day with pauses after each orgasm, but seldom have the opportunity."

"One is fine. I had three once, but never more. I had two with masturbation, but had to wait fifteen minutes between them. My clitoris was so sensitive I couldn't touch it for a while."

It is possible that in many cases this problem is caused by "too direct" stimulation of the clitoris (for example, masturbation type IA direct), perhaps in combination with a buildup of something appealingly called "smegma," under the clitoral hood. It is important every so often to pull back the foreskin or hood of the clitoris, and using your fingertip or fingernail, remove the partially hardened (harmless) whitish deposits that tend to collect there. This can be slightly painful to do, but these deposits can lessen the flexibility of your clitoris. In any case, these deposits would probably not interfere with your capacity to enjoy renewed stimulation unless you stimulate your clitoris very directly, more directly than most women do.

Other women did prefer more than one orgasm.

"The first orgasm is just the beginning. I find that I become more aroused generally (not just in the genital area) after the first couple of orgasms. I arouse slowly, but once aroused, the feeling grows larger and more intense and sweet, engulfing me."

"One is okay, but many are nice too. I have had as many as six within a half hour; I prefer one at a time, with time in between to relax and enjoy it, and then being restimulated."

"I prefer half a dozen smaller ones, building into a crescendo."

"One orgasm is enough, but I can usually have several after the first one, and very quickly—everything builds!"

"During cunnilingus I can achieve up to five orgasms if vaginal and clitoral stimulation are alternated."

"I find I am still aroused after one orgasm and am able to have several. Then I am still not satisfied. I still feel localized arousal in the clitoral area, but I am tired and I stop and wait for the feeling to subside."

"During my period I am very excitable and the more I masturbate and have orgasms the more my clitoris tickles and after ten orgasms my clitoris sort of itches and can be insatiable—it'll tickle more and more and instead of relieving the tickling the orgasm makes it tickle more."

"The first orgasm is hard, but after that it's easy. Once I'm really going, I can enjoy six or seven."

"One good one. It's nice to orgasm from clitoral stimulation first, then intercourse. When I have all day, several times is great. I always want to come a million more times."

"After the first orgasm I want to be aroused and have another almost right away. I am capable of several in one session but how many depends on the partner, my mood, how we make love, etc. and I think it would be silly to set any definite figure."

"One is intense, but I usually want more, usually two. If manual stimulation is going on, I can have five or six, but sometimes this is even more frustrating, because then I have a hard time coming down—which is not true with just one orgasm, because I haven't really gotten going yet."

"The more the better. Each one is deeper and more stimulating and I get less inhibited with each one."

"I like a few in a row after one gets going. It's nice to orgasm from clitoral stimulation first, then again from intercourse."

"One is just a warm-up and the best is to go on until I drop from exhaustion. They just keep getting better and better."

"The more the better—but also, to be satisfied, I have to feel that communication has occurred."

"Sometimes one's okay, but other times I could go on until I can't move."

"The more the better. Once I start having orgasms, it is one long series of orgasms."

"In masturbation, two to three, sometimes five to six; with a partner, it's too much work and I just make it once."

"Yes and no—an orgasm from intercourse is tiring, and feels as though my pubic bone is getting pulverized—so one is okay that way. But I want more if I am masturbating or am being masturbated. Usually two but I also like three to five."

"Males I have been with tell me my sex drive is unusually strong and sometimes make me feel like a freak. I'm very interested to hear if other women have had similar experiences. According to Masters and Johnson, women are capable of having sex the entire night, while men are not. Although many men I've known think they're liberated, they're not. They don't grasp the significance of this idea about women's sex drives."

Do subsequent orgasms feel different?

"Each subsequent orgasm is stronger than the preceding."

"Orgasm is a sharp explosive feeling followed by a series of contractions. After several consecutive orgasms, the feeling becomes more like a 'melting sensation.' "

"When highly aroused for a long period of time, my feet tingle, and my clitoris responds readily. After several orgasms, it is very sweet to be still and allow the sensation of heightened sexuality to suffuse the body, vagina, lips, etc."

"In a good situation, orgasms keep going and going and getting stronger (as long as restimulation is continued) until when I am finally finished, I cry to release the tension or whatever it is—leave my body and fly!"

"My orgasms get more intense the longer I stimulate myself."

"My first orgasm seems to involve a definite generalized excitement—i.e., a metallic taste in my throat or my clitoris expands, etc., then a feeling wanting to have a penis inserted, then a rapid rise to intense bodily shaking with my legs thrown up, then rapid vaginal contractions, then a lessening of tension but not a complete release—for which I need three or four orgasms. The first orgasm does not involve a great deal of vaginal sensitivity, which generally develops with continued intercourse or a return to sex play or whatever. Second, third, or fourth orgasms are more likely to involve changes of consciousness where I do not seem to hear or be aware of what is going on around me but feel inside a vast inner space."

"Each orgasm brings its own exquisite sensations, each different and sweeter than the last. . . ."

"At the best times, I reach frenetic peaks over and over in rapid succession."

"One orgasm is almost never enough. Successive orgasms become stronger and usually deeper, more satisfying. I don't know how many I might be capable of. In fact, I often feel frustrated and a bit scared by this multi-orgasmic capacity. I've rarely had 'sessions' where I've felt like I really had enough. I get tired by myself and I haven't been with many men who can sustain a long enough period of arousal in themselves. So, too often, my reaction when I feel horny is 'oh, no.' "

"Each level of orgasmic satisfaction only seems to open a new level of frustration. So, most often, I avoid getting aroused—not always successfully. I find myself wishing something would zap away the frustration, but not the desire or pleasure. I would love advice on this."

"I am sixteen, living at home and a lesbian. For me, sex is a beautiful experience and important in showing my love to my lady and feeling my *sexual* love I have to hide so often. Orgasms are a part of my sexual life and important to it. My lover satisfies me because both of us can continue in bed having orgasms over and over again and never really coming down off them."

"Years ago I tried a couple of times to see how many orgasms I could have and reached about fifteen. Up to about eight they were very strong and then they started to weaken. I have slept with other women a few times and they all had a similar pattern of enjoying loving and caressing by the hour, but after one orgasm they did not want to continue. I always felt they were ashamed to try for more. The most thrilling thing for me was a woman in my arms during her orgasm, hearing her moaning."

"Each orgasm is deeper and more stimulating and I get less inhibited with each one."

DOES ORGASM FEEL DIFFERENT WITH OR WITHOUT INTERCOURSE?

Even after the well-known work of Masters and Johnson has conclusively proved that all orgasms in women are caused by clitoral stimulation (whether direct or indirect), there is still enormous confusion over the terms "clitoral orgasm" and "vaginal orgasm." Why does this confusion continue? There are several reasons: the first is that we lack complete understanding of our anatomy, mainly because most of our sexual organs, unlike those of men, are located inside our bodies. The following description of our sexual anatomy will try to give a fundamental picture of the basic underlying structures.

ANATOMY

Sherfey's book *The Nature and Evolution of Female Sexuality* is, although technical, definitely the best and most complete explanation available of our anatomy, and worth the time a thorough reading requires. Here we will quote from Edward Brecher's analysis of her main points, in *The Sex Researchers:*

> The truth is . . . that the glans and shaft of the human clitoris are merely the superficially visible or palpable manifestations of an underlying *clitoral system* which is at least as large, as impressive, and as functionally responsive as the penis—and which re-

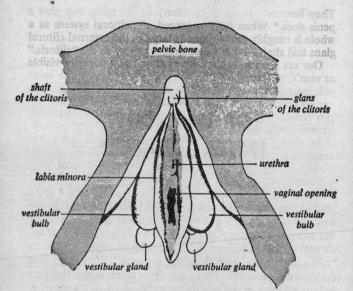

The vestibular bulbs and the circumvaginal plexus (a network of nerves, veins, and arteries) constitute the major erectile bodies in women. These underlying structures are homologous to, and about the same size as, the penis of a man.

Redrawn by Charlotte Staub from Atlas der deskriptiven Anatomie des Menschen *by J. Sobotta, Berlin: Urban and Schwarzenberg, 1948.*

sponds as a unit to sexual stimulation in much the same way that the penis does.

The penis, for example, has two roots known as *crura* which play an essential role in its functioning. During sexual excitation these crura become engorged with blood and contribute to erection of the penis. The clitoris, too, has two broad roots, of approximately the same size as in the male. The clitoral crura, too, become engorged with blood early in the woman's sexual excitation.

Again, the penis contains within its shaft two caverns or spaces known as *corpora cavernosa*, which fill

They become engorged (swollen) in the same way that a penis does.* When fully engorged, the clitoral system as a whole is roughly thirty times as large as the external clitoral glans and shaft—what we commonly know as the "clitoris."

Our sex organs, though internal and not as easily visible as men's, expand during arousal to approximately the same volume as an erect penis. The next time you are aroused, notice how swollen your vulva and labia majora become; this reflects the swelling of the vestibular bulbs and other tissues, which lie just below this area.

In short, the only real difference between men's and women's erections is that men's are on the outside of their bodies, while women's are on the inside. Think of your clitoris as just the *tip* of your "penis," the rest of which lies underneath the surface of your vulva—or think of a penis as just the externalization of a woman's interior bulbs and clitoral network.

---

* Masters and Johnson refer to this as the "orgasmic platform." Helen Kaplan explains that "local vasocongestion forms the basis of the responses of both genders. However, in contrast to the male, where the local genital vasocongestion is limited and shaped by the penile sheath, the female congestive response is more diffuse. . . . The thickening of the orgasmic platform results from this general distention of the blood vessels surrounding the vaginal barrel and the 'bulbs of the vestibule.' These structures, which are located deep within the labia and surrounding the vagina, are analogous to the cavernous bodies of the penis."

---

with blood during sexual excitation, and contribute to the expanded size of the erect penis. The female clitoral system has a precisely analogous pair of bulbous *corpora cavernosa*, which similarly fill with blood during sexual excitation. They are not inside the shaft of the clitoris, however. Rather, they are located surrounding the vestibule and outer third of the vagina.†

† Sherfey has provided an imaginative way of helping us visualize this: "We may say that the external genitalia of the female are homologous to the entire penis split open along its undersurface and the split-open scrotal sac."⁶

(They are therefore known as the vestibular bulbs.) The spongelike body (*corpus spongiosum*) inside the penis is paralleled by a similar spongelike structure in the clitoral system which functions in the same way.

The penis, Dr. Sherfey continues, is associated with sets of muscles which help to erect it during sexual excitation. The clitoris is associated with precisely homologous sets of muscles which serve to retract it, too—though, as Masters and Johnson have shown, at a somewhat later stage in the sex act. Other male muscles contract during orgasm, forcing the ejaculation of semen. Precisely homologous muscles function during the female orgasm, causing a rhythmic contraction of the outer third of the vagina. Indeed, as Masters and Johnson have also shown, the male and female sets of muscles respond in the *same* rhythm—one contraction every four-fifths of a second.

There are also differences, Dr. Sherfey concedes, between the penis and the clitoral system—but the differences, astonishing as it may seem to readers brought up in a male-dominated society, are in favor of the clitoral system. That system, for example, includes at least three (and possibly four or five) networks of veins called *venous plexi*, which extend diffusely throughout the female pelvic area—but especially through the regions immediately to the left and right of the vagina. These networks are also, Dr. Sherfey reports, a part of the clitoral system; and in addition they merge with the venous networks of the vaginal system. Together the clitoral and vaginal networks become engorged with blood during female sexual excitation.† Thus the clitoris itself, far from being

---

† Ruth Herschberger has made some pointed comments about terminology in her chapter of *Adam's Rib*, "Society Writes Biology": "The patriarchal biologist employs *erection* in regard to male organs and *congestion* for female. Erection of tissue is equivalent to the filling of the local blood vessels, or congestion; but erection is too aggressive-sounding for women. Congestion, being associated with the rushing of blood to areas that have been infected or injured, appears to scientists to be a more adequate characterization of female response.'"

a vestigial or rudimentary organ, is merely the visible tip and harbinger of a vast anatomical array of sexually responsive female tissue. When fully engaged, the clitoral system as a whole overshadows the clitoral glans and shaft *in the ratio of almost thirty to one.* The total blood-vessel engorgement of the clitoral system during sexual excitation may actually exceed the more obvious engorgement of the male.[8]

As Barbara Seaman has explained in *Free and Female,* our sexual structures expand as much or more during arousal as men's; the only difference is that male erection (engorgement) takes place outside the body, and is therefore more visible, while ours takes place underneath the surface—under the vaginal lips. The total size of our engorgement is no smaller than the size of an erect penis.

Helen Kaplan, in *The New Sex Therapy,* explains a further anatomical cause of the continuing confusion between "clitoral" and "vaginal" orgasm:

. . . it is now believed by many authorities that all female orgasms are physiologically identical. They are triggered by stimulation of the clitoris and expressed by vaginal contractions. Accordingly, regardless of how friction is applied to the clitoris, i.e., by the tongue, by the woman's finger or her partner's, by a vibrator, or by coitus, female orgasm is probably almost always evoked by *clitoral* stimulation. However, it is always expressed by *circumvaginal* muscle discharge.

Apparently, it is this dichotomy—on the one hand, the location of orgasmic spasms in and around the *vagina* and concomitant perception of orgasmic sensation in the general vaginal and deep pelvic region; on the other hand, the location of the primary area of stimulation in the *clitoris*—which has served to perpetuate the myth that the female is capable of two distinct types of orgasms, and has also given rise to the incredibly stupid controversy surrounding female orgasm. The orgasm is, after all, a reflex and as such has a sensory and a motor component. There is little argument over the fact that the motor expression of this reflex is "vaginal". . . ..

The entire argument really only revolves around the location of the sensory arm of the reflex. Is orgasm normally triggered by stimulating the vagina with the penis? Or is it produced by tactile friction applied to the clitoris? The clinical evidence reviewed above clearly points to the clitoris.[9]

In other words, clitoral stimulation evokes female orgasm, which takes place deeper in the body, around the vagina and other structures, just as stimulation of the tip of the male penis evokes male orgasm, which takes place inside the lower body of the male.

THE CLITORAL-VAGINAL CONTROVERSY

"Do orgasms with the presence of a penis (intercourse) feel different from those without? In what way?"

Another reason the clitoral–vaginal controversy remains with us is that the mystique of orgasm during intercourse is still very strong. The idea is that orgasm during intercourse ("vaginal orgasm") feels much better than orgasm without intercourse ("clitoral orgasm"). It is this idea which will be examined here. The fundamental question is: Does orgasm with a penis inside feel different from orgasm without a penis inside? Have women who orgasm during intercourse, by whatever means, defined their orgasms in any way that is different from the general definition of orgasm? And what comparisons have they made when asked if orgasm felt different with or without the presence of a penis during intercourse?

Most women felt that orgasms during intercourse were more diffuse, while orgasms without intercourse were more intense.

"I feel they are different, but it's difficult to say how. With a clitoral orgasm* the feelings seem centered, right there, while an orgasm with penetration seems more to pervade the body."

"Yes, they are different, but I'm not sure how. Non-penetration orgasms are more intense, almost disturbing in intensity. Penetration ones are usually lighter, almost fleeting."

"With penetration they are less sharp."

"Penetration orgasm is softer, more diffuse."

"Yes, with vaginal penetration, there is a lesser sense of your own orgasm."

"Intercourse involves the whole body, not just the genitals."

"Intercourse orgasm involves the musculature of the abdomen more, gives more of a feeling of being shaken (like an earthquake) than being electrified, as clitoral does."

"Clitoral are sharper but lonelier."

"Clitoral orgasms are more intense, longer; intercourse orgasms are dull, no edge, very short."

"Clitoral orgasms are stronger, more definite."

"Clitoral orgasm is higher, more exciting, the peak of sensitivity."

"Masturbatory orgasms are stronger, but I prefer the diffusion and variety of intercourse and the warmth and pressure of a man's body and the sounds and smells of two people."

"Clitoral is stronger and more localized. Intercourse is more total body."

"Clitoral are specifically located and very intense. Intercourse are more whole body, stronger, longer lasting, and more satisfying."

---

* "Clitoral orgasm" in these replies refers to orgasm without a penis inside, while "vaginal orgasm" refers to orgasm with a penis. This is true for all the quotes in this chapter.

"Clitoral are stronger; intercourse is weak and unsatisfying and extremely frustrating!"

"Masturbation orgasm is stronger, more erotic."

"Clitoral is stronger and more physically satisfying. However, during intercourse, the emotional closeness of being together is also extremely satisfying."

"My most satisfying ones, both physically and psychologically, are those during intercourse. My most *intense* ones are those from masturbation."

"During intercourse, the sensation of orgasm is more diffuse because of the presence of the penis inside me."

"Clitoral orgasm is more piercing, intercourse orgasm more deep, widening, pulsating—the difference between sharp and dull pain."

"I can tell when I have a clitoral orgasm when I masturbate, because it's such a distinct climax, but sometimes when I'm with a man, I can't always tell if I've had an orgasm—I just sort of heat up and die away."

"Orgasm can't be felt with penetration and seems more like a state of mind. I *wish* I could have the same kind of orgasm as I have during masturbation then."

"Orgasm without penetration is sharp, well-defined, spasmodic—goes on almost unbearably—orgasm after orgasm until I could scream—and do—vaginal penetration is softer, longer, and less well-defined—different, more tender, less scary."

"I have orgasms during masturbation, by clitoral stimulation. During intercourse I sometimes have a type of "release" which may be another type of orgasm (??). It's not as intense as with the masturbation orgasm. The way I know something happens during intercourse is that sometimes I feel satisfied after intercourse and other times I feel hornier than when we started."

"I never have the same sort of violently physical orgasm with vaginal penetration with the penis as I do with direct clitoral stimulation. I'm not even sure if I come. I get a great sensation of pleasure, but it never peaks like it does the other way. I wish it did. I'd love to come right when he does without any extra attention."

"I do also have orgasms in coitus, but they are less

specific as they happen. More or less just a release that makes it unnecessary to fuck any more."

"Most people (and I previously) think of orgasms as only that muscle spasm that is obvious, but I found out I have orgasms very quietly and many times I only realize afterwards that I'm relaxed and don't feel like moving for a couple of minutes."

"I have recently had my first intercourse. It was strange—I was used to the sensation of vaginal contractions, but when his penis was in me, it seemed to prevent the contractions. I still had them, but it was hard to feel them, and if he had been moving during the orgasm, I might not even have known that I had one."

"Orgasm during intercourse is more of a diffused total mental and physical trip, whereas a clitoral orgasm involves a tremendous sense of physical pleasure and tingling in the whole lower pelvic area and vaginal contractions."

"Intercourse orgasm has a deep tingly effect over my whole body; orgasm during masturbation is a concentrated extreme tingly effect in basically my pelvic area."

"Orgasm is more diffuse when I am emotionally aroused with my partner, but more specifically genital during masturbation."

"During clitoral stimulation, the unbearable pressure is suddenly dissipated, my raw nerves stripped. During intercourse, my whole body is involved and feels tingly, especially my hands and feet, and my husband says the vaginal walls quiver."

"Masturbation is the most intense type of orgasm I have. It is centered in my genital area and upper legs. During intercourse when I am on top, there's no center of feeling, but my whole body, especially my arms, hands and face, feel a very intense tingling."

"I have two types of orgasm: clitoral (during masturbation or oral sex) in which I feel warmth and pressure in the genitals, my muscles become tense, and then there is a fantastic rush from my toes to my head, then an explosion in my clitoris. Afterwards I feel high for a half hour or more. It is very intense. During intercourse, it is not as intense. I feel the deep thrusts, then a general rush from toes to head, and after, I'm numb in my arms and legs."

"During masturbation, I experience a clitoral orgasm that approximates my idea of male orgasm—a buildup of over-all sensation in the general area of my clitoris, and a 'muscle spasm' feeling. A vaginal orgasm is a more pervasive sensation through the whole body, less concrete to describe—wider waves of feeling."

"A masturbation orgasm is physical and somewhat localized. It involves a building of tension in my legs and buttocks and probably my whole body. When released, there is a throbbing contraction of muscles in my anus, vagina and if I am really with it, my whole body jerks with the contractions. Non-masturbatory orgasm is very subtle. I can build up to it like in masturbation, and then there is some sign of orgasm, or it can come upon me and even I don't know it's there until I become aware of the post-orgasm symptoms."

"Orgasms not during intercourse are usually more 'defined' due, I think, to the concentration of attention. However, I find intercourse more erotic and hence more satisfying."

"Clitoral orgasm is more explosive and intense; vaginal is a slower rise and slower decline in feeling."

"Clitoral is more intense, intercourse orgasm vague."

"During clitoral stimulation, the orgasm is so intense I can't believe it; during intercourse, it comes on by surprise, just flowing smooth and deep."

"Clitoral orgasms are more tense, but not as good an all-over feeling."

"With direct stimulation, the orgasms are stronger; without, they are often weak and unsatisfying and extremely frustrating! My orgasms when I masturbate are fantastic and make orgasm during intercourse (usually) seem awful."

"Clitoral orgasms are stronger and sharper. Sometimes during intercourse I have almost a 'missed' feeling."

"Orgasm is more locally intense by clitoral stimulation, but more diffusely satisfying through intercourse."

"I have clitoral orgasms when I masturbate and occa-

sionally vaginal orgasms during husband-wife intercourse. I wish I could have the same type of orgasm I
have during masturbation when I have intercourse with
my husband."

**However, some women emphasized the over-all body
pleasures of orgasm during intercourse and thereby
saw orgasm during intercourse as "stronger."**

"Intercourse orgasms are stronger and better and satisfy my whole body rather than just the genital area, the
way direct stimulation does."

"Masturbation is the fastest and most technically pro-
ficient, but the over-all and entire body effect of intercourse is the richest and longest lasting."

"Intercourse is better, because the pressure of the
penis adds to the pleasure, also the weight of the body,
the caresses, etc."

"Intercourse is more intense because it has more
emotional impact."

"Intercourse is more emotional, abandoned, high,
joyous."

"Orgasm during intercourse is more violent, muscular, rather than just that warm good feeling."

"With no penetration, orgasms seem lighter and
freer."

"Clitoral orgasms involve less of the body and seem
rather shallow and empty, less satisfying."

"Clitoral stimulation orgasm is more intense and
wracking, but less pleasurable, slow and sexy."

"Orgasms with my vibrator are stronger and more
prolonged, and not distracted by all the other stimulation. However, the pleasure and other sensuous reinforcement during intercourse make up the difference."

"Intercourse is stronger emotionally and is a better,
more whole feeling. But for outright getting it done, me
wanting five or more orgasms, masturbation is better."

"Clitoral contractions feel more intense and it is easier to differentiate one from the other; during intercourse, the sensation is more diffuse, and it is hard to
count the contractions. The feeling is felt all over. Both
types are groovy, but intercourse is better usually be-

cause I like the sensation of closeness and the pressure of my whole body and especially my breasts against the man's. But clitoral orgasm is more intense and sometimes gives more complete relief. Often, I have both types of climaxes in one evening."

"Masturbation orgasm is quicker and more intense physically, but there is an emptiness or isolation following."

"Clitoral orgasms are more intense and make me feel tingly all over. On the other hand, intercourse orgasm is a deeper, and more overwhelming, feeling."

"Clitoral is very intense but less deep and full; there is no qualitative difference, only a difference in richness, fullness and emotional satisfaction."

"Orgasms with penetration seem to involve my whole body and mind more. They sort of flow, whereas orgasms I have while masturbating just seem to involve satisfying my horniness."

"There is more total physical and psychological involvement during intercourse orgasm, which is less focused on my genitals."

"Vaginal orgasms are deeper, more releasing, more satisfying, better both psychologically and physically. They are like an underground volcano. A manual orgasm is sharper and more piercing, more superficial."

"Clitoral orgasms are more violent but less satisfying."

"During intercourse, it goes through my entire body; during clitoral orgasm, it is an outer body sensation."

"The direct stimulation of the clitoral area leads to a different kind of orgasm, which is less satisfying. It is stronger because it is more concentrated in one physical area, but it doesn't envelop me. There's an intense pulsating and then it's over."

"I prefer orgasms with penetration, and it is easier for me to have them that way, catalyzed by clitoral stimulation of course. This is because the closeness to my partner resulting from the penetration turns me on more. I also feel like I'm doing more for him during penetration. Orgasms during penetration are more satisfying psychologically."

Despite their seeming surface contradictions it seems clear that both of these groups of women are saying the same thing. While one group terms clitoral orgasm "more intense and focused," the other group calls it more "localized" and therefore more "limited"—in much the same way as one person will see a glass as being half full of water, while another sees it as half empty. While some women found orgasm during intercourse "more diffused" and more "whole body," and therefore not as exciting as the locally intense clitoral orgasm, other women found the "whole body" feeling during intercourse more fulfilling than the "locally intense" and "limited" clitoral orgasm.

Which way you interpret these feelings is a question of your own individual feelings, what is going on in your life regarding feelings for another person (that is, especially in this case, for a man), and of course the cultural pressures to find intercourse more fulfilling. Whichever way you interpret the physical feelings, however, there is no argument that the sensations differ: a clitorally stimulated orgasm without intercourse feels more locally intense, while an orgasm with intercourse feels more diffused throughout the area and/or body.*

Thus, it can be concluded that the presence of a penis seems to diffuse and generalize the sensation of orgasm. This is not to say that orgasm without intercourse is "better" or to make any other value judgment, since only individuals can make those. The sole purpose here is to define the actual physical feelings as most women experience them.

The fact is that clitorally stimulated, nonintercourse orgasms—especially in masturbation—are physically stronger than orgasms during intercourse. Masters and

---

* These findings are quite similar to those of Seymour Fisher's study of three hundred women. Fisher wrote: "Scanning the comments the women offered, I was struck by how often clitoral stimulation is described with words like 'warm,' 'ticklish,' 'electrical,' and 'sharp,' whereas vaginal stimulation is more often referred to as 'throbbing,' 'deep,' 'soothing,' and 'comfortable.'"

Johnson have also reported that not only were contraction patterns stronger in masturbation orgasms than in intercourse orgasms, but also that their study subjects gave the same subjective opinions. As a matter of fact, the highest cardiac rates of all the orgasms they studied occurred during female masturbation.

Is the feeling of orgasm weaker during intercourse because of the presence of the penis, or because of other factors?

There may, for some women, be an increased intensity in orgasm during masturbation because of being totally unself-conscious when alone.

"My orgasm is more powerful when I am alone than when I am with a partner. As I am coming, when I am alone, I usually wish someone were with me to hold me and be in me, but when someone is there, the orgasm isn't as powerful, because I'm holding back and thinking about what they are thinking of me."

"Masturbation orgasm is better, probably because of psychological factors like not having to concern myself with someone else's pleasure, or with my own feelings of fear and insecurity about their feelings about me."

But other women felt just the opposite; intercourse is more acceptable than masturbation, and therefore one can "let go" more then.

"Physically, I feel much more excited with penetration, and this affects the depth and intensity and loss of self-consciousness of my orgasms."

Also, the women in the Masters and Johnson experiments were not alone when they masturbated, and Masters and Johnson found their orgasms to be stronger during masturbation than during intercourse.

Perhaps orgasm during masturbation is stronger because you can get the stimulation more perfectly centered and coordinated, including your leg position.

"For me, the intensity seems to depend on 1) not rushing the orgasm but trying to hold on as long as pos-

sible, when the peak excited stage has been reached.
The longer I hold on (I can't wait longer than about 1
minute at that stage) the more intense the orgasm. The
second factor is 2) letting go at just the right moment.
This leads to very intense orgasms. If I let go too soon,
or a little too late, I have a less intense orgasm."

"What I mean is, have you ever had that feeling that
it was almost getting it, but not quite, and you wanted
to say, 'Move over just a little bit'—but you didn't and
you came but it wasn't just really making it?"

**Another reason why orgasm without intercourse could
feel stronger is the absence of body movement of the
other person that is going on during intercourse.**

"I am more aware of every nuance when I'm not at
the same time engaged in vigorous intercourse. My
body seems more wholly responsive and involved and I
can feel shock waves traveling to every extremity."

"Clitoral stimulation-orgasm is better because I am
not distracted. I cannot concentrate on my orgasm when
somebody is pushing themselves in and out of my vagina."

"Penetration with clitoral stimulation feels good, if
the penetrating 'object' is not moving."

"If my partner is moving too fast, I don't feel the
orgasm as effectively as I would otherwise."

"Clitorally stimulated orgasm is more erotic and sensitizing, whereas, with intercourse orgasm—maybe the
discomfort of the partner thumping on my body dis-
tracts me."

**On the other hand, orgasms during intercourse may feel
stronger psychologically because of very real feelings
for the man, or because we are culturally conditioned to
feel intercourse is the highest expression of our sexuality.**

"I can't answer which feels best, because conditioning has been too important a factor for me to be definite about it. Because I have striven for a vaginal orgasm, I probably attributed undue intensity to it in

relation to clitoral orgasms, which I considered almost illegal."

"I feel that it is more acceptable to orgasm during intercourse, that it shows my womanness more, and so I guess I let myself revel in the sensations more."

"I guess the mystique of joining affects me. I attach a quality of transcendence to orgasm with penetration that orgasms without don't have."

Orgasms during intercourse may feel more "whole body" partially because there is usually a longer build-up period than during masturbation.

"Sometimes, if it's an orgasm that occurs early in the lovemaking then it's more limited to excitement and tension and a sort of explosion/relief in the clitoral area; but when the lovemaking is more lengthy it affects my whole body—really from head to toe."

"My second husband used to make love with a sort of massaging motion of my entire body, and this may have made me enjoy vaginal orgasms more. Orgasms were more localized in fast fucks, and more diffused in longer lovemaking."

However, none of the factors just mentioned changes the basic conclusion that the physical intensity of orgasm per se is greater for most women when intercourse is not in progress, and especially during self-stimulation.

Despite this, a majority of women stated flatly that, no matter what the difference in feeling might be, they would always prefer orgasm during intercourse because of the psychological factors of sharing with and being loved by another person, the warmth of touching all over, body to body.

"Love of another is what makes intercourse orgasm better, in its way, and self-manipulation is more intense in its way."

"Orgasm during intercourse is less intense, but more emotionally satisfying."

"With penetration I feel more whole and loved."

"I feel the contractions less during intercourse, but I

enjoy the feeling of fullness, and psychologically, being seen as complete."

"Clitoral orgasms are more intense, but intercourse with love is more fulfilling."

"Clitoral orgasms are stronger, sharper, but intercourse orgasms are better, probably because I like to hold onto him. Masturbation is lonely."

"Intercourse orgasms are better. They involve my soul, while masturbation simply staves off insanity."

"During masturbation I may achieve orgasm five times and really enjoy it—but not be fulfilled; the orgasms are not as satisfying as through intercourse—they are less emotional, less deep, less meaningful."

"VAGINAL ACHE"

There is a very specific but important question that has been saved until last, something that will be referred to throughout this book as the phenomenon of "vaginal ache," that is often perceived as the desire for vaginal penetration. It is part of the same question just discussed, i.e., the difference in feeling between orgasm with intercourse or without. This feeling of intense desire, or "ache" (desire to be filled), comes during the buildup to orgasm, very near the moment of orgasm itself, and then spills over into the orgasmic contractions.

What happens is this: sometimes building up to and just at the moment of orgasm there is an intense pleasure/pain feeling deep inside the vagina, something like a desire to be entered or touched inside, or just an exquisite sensation of pleasure, which we call "vaginal ache." It is an almost hollow feeling, and is caused because the upper end, the deeper portion, of the vagina is ballooning out, expanding into what has theoretically been pictured as a little lake for the collection and holding of semen.

Some women perceive this feeling as hollow, empty, and unpleasant, while others find it intensely pleasurable. Whether you prefer to have a penis there or not at that moment depends on your own personal preference, of course. For most women, "vaginal ache" is not felt so intensely with a penis present; the penis seems to "soothe" and diffuse the feeling, so it depends on whether you prefer to feel the sensation or not.

Without intercourse the sensation of "vaginal ache" was described like this.

"I feel an urgent yearning way deep inside to envelop and take him inside me."

"During arousal, there is a craving in my vagina—which is, by the way, disappointed if satisfied."

"I feel empty without intercourse after clitoral stimulation. My vagina throbs and is screaming to be filled."

"First I stimulate my clitoral area, pulling the skin up toward me. My vagina begins to feel open, wanting to be filled, or penetrated—but it ruins the whole thing if it occurs, maybe because it is too generalized. Maybe if the particular spot could be touched—wow! At the moment of orgasm the feeling is the most intense. But if there is penetration at that moment, I lose the whole thing."

"My vagina becomes very aroused during clitoral stimulation and I start to crave contact there (either penetration of the penis or just reaching in and touching with a finger)."

"Sometimes while masturbating, I'll feel the urge to push something up me—usually always I am disappointed with the result."

"After cunnilingus, just at the moment she reaches orgasm, she likes me to place my tongue in her vagina, as it seems to soothe the ache."

"Just at the moment when I orgasm, there is a beautiful, painful feeling in the vagina."

"Clitoral orgasm makes me want penetration. It feels like the top of the vagina is screaming for pressure."

"Vaginal orgasms are more releasing; clitoral orgasms leave you wanting the other kind."

"Clitoral orgasms make me desire intercourse."

"I can get high on clitoral stimulation, but I like intercourse after."

"Clitoral orgasm is exciting and a great prelude to penetration, while vaginal orgasm is a feeling of completeness."

"Yes, the two orgasms are different but hard to explain. Vaginal penetration is more like the storm followed by calm, whereas orgasm without penetration is still one of desire."

"My vagina feels like a 'desiring hole' just before orgasm. But then orgasm causes me intense pleasure as long as I *don't* put anything there (at least, sharper pleasure). My feelings get diffused with something there—I feel less desire for another orgasm but also less satisfaction."

"This itchy feeling can continue after a clitorally stimulated orgasm (no penis pressure) because clitoral orgasms (with no penetration) only leads to more arousal."

"I feel as if I can have orgasm after orgasm clitorally, but I am completely satiated with one or two orgasms by intercourse."

"During intercourse, there seems to be more finality and less desire to continue having more orgasms, whereas clitoral are more easily repeated."

"Orgasm during penetration gives me a deeper satisfaction, ordinarily. I think it's the hitting of his whole body against my lower legs and bottom that triggers this relaxation, in addition to the penetration. Clitoral orgasm is great as far as it goes, but I still feel quite tense, by comparison, when it's over."

CONCLUSION

We have seen in this section that, with the presence of a penis, the orgasm and contractions are felt less concretely, and that the "vaginal ache" as well is either soothed or not felt during intercourse. In general, then, vaginal penetration or the presence of a penis seems to have a soothing, diffusing, or blanketing effect.

There are two ways of interpreting this phenomenon. You could say either:

1. During intercourse the penis works as a pacifier—the touching and rubbing kills feeling, allows less intense contractions and sensations, and disperses and diffuses the focus of orgasm—making it less intense and less pleasurable.

2. During intercourse the penis, by soothing or quieting arousal, gives more of a feeling of peace and completeness, relaxation and satisfaction, than non-intercourse orgasm, which in many cases only leaves you a second later with continued arousal. Thus, intercourse (actually, with or without orgasm) is more "fulfilling" than orgasm without intercourse.

Whichever you prefer is a personal decision and a matter of temperament—whether you define pleasure as desire or its satisfaction. Is the greater pleasure desire (arousal), or its fulfillment?

Finally, you could prefer either sensation at different times:

"I cannot describe the difference, it is neither better nor worse, just different. Sometimes I want penetration, and other times I am happier engaging in other activities. It depends on my mood."

"Just a general thought about the relationship between the type of orgasm I have and the frequency I desire. I find that if I don't have intense orgasms due to clitoral (direct) stimulation often enough, I go through sex always thinking about that, and wanting it and focusing fantasies on it. I'm never as completely satisfied. If a week goes by without that type of orgasm, my desire and need for it builds up. When I finally do have one, it's fantastic. But if I never have penetrations, I also get hungry for that. It's important to strike a balance."

If orgasm during intercourse is vague, "more or less just a release that makes it unnecessary to fuck any more," how can you be sure you have orgasmed at all? In some cases, it was not even clear to the woman herself whether there had been an orgasm or merely high levels of arousal:

"When I'm on top, my mouth is near his right ear and I whisper what's happening in a variety of explicit ways. When I actually come, my body stops moving and I moan and sigh. Afterwards, I kiss his face all over. This whole thing varies, of course. Sometimes I think I'm coming, and then don't; sometimes it feels almost as good as if I had come. We often ask each other afterwards if there was any doubt, and describe how this time felt different from some other time."

"Now, with some experience, I can distinguish between an orgasm and it just feeling good . . . but there have been many times during intercourse when it was a draw. I guess what I'm saying is that a good fuck without an orgasm is as pleasurable as most orgasms during intercourse."

"There is a deep throbbing inside my vagina when I orgasm—but I have not always been sure whether it was my orgasm or my lover's throbbing."

"My masturbation orgasm is very intense. My stages of excitement are *very* distinct and I usually don't spend much time to do it. But there have been many times in sex with a man when I have been very excited and I have felt a rise and somewhat of a plateau, and satisfied after. Then I wonder 'did I come or didn't I?' and I honestly don't know, because I didn't feel the explosive charge and super-release. I think orgasms vary in intensity, so I sometimes think maybe I had a little one. But it frustrates me when I don't know for sure."

Probably, in many cases, no regular orgasm has occurred; perhaps at other times there was an orgasm but the sensations were dulled or diffused by the presence of the penis. Some women who think they are having orgasms during intercourse probably are not. In any case, an orgasm, with or without intercourse, although it may be perceived differently, is the same basic orgasm: orgasm is always due to clitoral stimulation in some form, and always follows the same physiological pattern. Therefore, from now on in this book the terms "clitoral orgasm" and "vaginal orgasm" will not be used, since they carry so many confused and outdated meanings. Instead, we will refer to orgasm simply as "orgasm"—adding any other descriptive phrases that may be necessary.

EMOTIONAL ORGASM

Some women who mentioned that they have a different type of orgasm during clitoral stimulation or masturbation than during intercourse meant that they have "real" orgasm during clitoral stimulation and something else during intercourse—what has often been called "vaginal orgasm." By this they did not mean they felt vaginal contractions, or intense clitoral or vaginal sensations, but that they felt an intense emotional peak (sometimes felt as an extreme opening sensation both in the vagina and the throat)—accompanied by strong feelings of closeness, yearning, or exaltation. We will call this "emotional orgasm":

"Clitoral orgasm gives me a full-blown climax. During intercourse, none of the flash sensations occur, but there is a tremendous calm and loving feeling that makes me cry—kind of like having an emotional (rather than physical) orgasm."

"With a man I care about, penetration leads to an emotional climax that has physical aspects, but not to orgasm. I tremble, sometimes overtly, sometimes psychologically. There is a feeling of direct 'communication' with another person, without defenses, and expressed through the touching and vibrations of our being together, as we two become one. If it's really good, I feel an intense wanting to suck his penis into me, inside my vagina deeper and deeper."

"It's difficult not to use clichés I've heard or read, but some of them are so accurate. It is a full, warm sensation in the vagina, lips, and surrounding pubic area, that spreads out, plus a feeling of tremendous exhilaration in my chest. If the man is an important part of my life, I find myself wishing his penis could reach clear up to my neck, that he would just crawl inside of me. He can't seem to get deep enough or close enough."

"It's silly to explain what an orgasm feels like to me because it sounds so sentimental. I love my fiancé very much, to where my heart feels like it will burst. Sometimes it does and I get a feeling of great contentment. Well, when I have an orgasm it's like my whole body is consumed by this bursting forth of love that it can't contain, and I get a feeling of great inner peace. I'm usually laughing with happiness for myself and my man."

"First all feeling seems centered in the genital area and it spreads through my entire body in great waves of sensation and sensitivity. Sometimes I feel as though I want to sing, as though the sensation has traveled to my vocal cords and has set them vibrating in a key yet to be discovered."

"Penetration leads to a great and large feeling. It is difficult to describe—my body is electric all over, and I desire physical and spiritual union with the other. Sometimes I am praying to God, being one with Him, and it is ecstatic joy."

"This kind of orgasm for me is metaphysical immersion in another world, religious, ascending a mountain. It happens mostly in my mind, which is flushed with sensation, and sends me very close emotionally to the person I am with."

"Orgasm: a compelling sensation of light pouring from his head and into mine. I start pouring out light to match. My vision dissolves into brilliance behind my eyes, blinding me; my body dissolves into pure light. I see nothing but light, hear nothing at all, feel nothing that can be named—but every blood cell is dancing and every pore outpouring radiance—and the spiders in the closets and the ants on the floor must be full of joy at receiving the overflow of love."

Emotional orgasm is a feeling of love and communion with another human being that reaches a peak, a great welling up of intensity of feeling, which may be felt physically in the chest, or as a lump in the throat, or as a general opening-up sensation, a feeling of wanting deeper and deeper penetration, wanting to merge and become one person. It could be described as a complete release of emotions, what one woman called "a piercing feeling of love," or an orgasm of the heart.

Sometimes emotional orgasm was felt as the desire to conceive, to be impregnated, to keep the person there, inside you, mix the two as one in real flesh and blood: "When I was married for sixteen years I had an all-pervading thinking that was not really fantasy about having the baby implanted in me. Especially if I really am involved with my partner, at the moment of orgasm I want his baby so much I can only think of that." Physiologically, there are some rather remarkable parallels between child birth and regular sexual orgasm, as pointed out by Dr. Niles Newton in an article in *Psychology Today*. A few women mentioned childbearing as another kind of orgasm: "What I consider was the biggest orgasm of my life was the birth of my first daughter—I saw her coming out of me in a mirror above me. Never, never, before or since was there anything like that."

Drs. J. and I. Singer of M.I.T. have emphasized in a paper on orgasm the physical components of the emotions felt during the emotional orgasm, especially in the throat. They quote from Doris Lessing's *Golden Notebooks* to illustrate their point:

> . . . the response is a kind of laryngeal spasm in the throat, accompanied by tension of the diaphragm. The breath is inhaled cumulatively, each gasp adding to the amount of breath contained previously in the lungs. When the diaphragm is sufficiently tense, the breath is involuntarily held in the lungs, and the cricopharyngeus muscle tenses, drawing the larynx down and back. The feeling is one of "strangling in ecstasy." Finally the cricopharyngeus snaps back to a resting position, and the breath, simultaneously, is exhaled. The suddenness with which this occurs produces the explosiveness without which the term "orgasm" would hardly apply. . . . For me, the relief from sexual tension which this cricopharyngeal orgasm brings is analogous to the relief from pent-up nervous tension which

an acute sobbing spell may bring. Both involve crico-
pharyngeal action.[10]

The Singers also mention that this physical reaction
in the throat and the tension in the diaphragm are characteristic of a variety of emotions, including grief, surprise, fear, and joy. For example, crying can be considered another kind of orgasmic release. In fact, many
women mentioned crying after sex with no orgasm, to
let out the feeling of frustration: "There were times
when I used to feel tremendously unsatisfied following
sex without orgasm and if I were near enough, I'd begin
to cry following my partner's climax as an alternate
form of release."

As long as women are not pressured into using emotional orgasm as a substitute for *real* orgasms (as they
have been and still are now), there is no reason why
many types of releases should not be enjoyed. However,
their existence should never be used to discredit the fact
that women have, enjoy, and need regular physical "clitoral" orgasms:

"Without bona-fide, clitoral orgasm, sex would have
no greatness about it. When I orgasm, all the tensions,
emotions, and feelings that go into sex come out in the
orgasm. I feel flooded with relief and also with remorse.
Everything seems to come out in a strange mixture that
leaves me refreshed and renewed, and happy with the
world."

"Orgasm is an explosion which clears my mind, a
force collected from my entire body, revitalizing and in-
spiring—like waves of fire, like becoming one with the
rhythms that run the universe, like receiving a personal
message that life is good and beautiful. . . . "

WOMEN
WHO NEVER ORGASM

Women who have never had orgasms often felt extremely depressed, or cheated, since society glorifies orgasm so much, and, indeed, it is a great pleasure that is being missed. The purpose of this section will be to look at what these women say and to try to suggest what they might try.

Almost every woman who didn't orgasm would like to.

"I feel I'm less desirable since I don't or seldom have orgasms. I often wonder if having orgasms is partly an individual physiological response. I don't really believe that differences in this area are all psychological. I wish our culture put less emphasis on orgasm and 'tiger' lovers. It would be easier for people like me to accept ourselves."

"Half of my sex life seems to be in search of having an orgasm. It took seven years before I experienced my first orgasm and I feel like I keep falling into a negative failure pattern about it; I almost *never* have them."

"Never have and never will. I am frigid."

"It would make my lover happy. I don't really want one until he gives up. Orgasms are a big myth to me. What is an orgasm?"

"I read about orgasm and hear about it constantly. How would you like to be colorblind and keep reading about rainbows and butterflies?"

"The questionnaire is okay except it is oriented to the orgasmic woman and I have become very depressed since beginning it. I feel cheated and envious of women to whom all questions apply!"

"I need to talk with other women about sex but it is

so impossible. I am embarrassed about my not having orgasms and wonder whether my friends share this problem. My best friend is highly orgasmic and I could cry when she says something because I can't share my problem with her. I felt comfortable with my male shrink and gynecologist but feel inadequate around women— probably because I know that many women have orgasmic problems and experienced men are aware of this and of the fact that a woman can be a good sex partner and enjoy it without orgasm, but a woman, such as my best friend, thinks it must be torture not to come—that a woman must be very unhappy, tense, and screwed up and that it would destroy a marriage or relationship. I can't expose that much of myself in the face of such judgments and can't stand the pity."

"God, I feel like a whole part of me is just *shut off*. I think there are a couple of things blocking them, both concerning my head. One is some bad personal history (rapist stepfather) and the other is such a strong need to maintain control over my head that I cannot surrender it even in sex."

"Having orgasms is an unreached, seemingly far-fetched goal for me. I think orgasm would relax my tensions—especially sexual ones. I feel that orgasm is a fulfillment. I feel it is necessary for me to have them. At times, I would fake them and get so involved I could almost believe it was really happening."

"I would like to have them. I do enjoy sex and feel satisfied, but maybe I'd answer differently if I knew what I was missing."

"I've tried everything, but I've never had one. I feel that having an orgasm would leave me more satisfied and satiated. Now I never feel contented when we are finished. I feel very frustrated and insecure without them. It causes me more unhappiness than anything else in my life. I'm not sure that I want to stay married to my husband because of such an unfulfilled sex life."

"Orgasms escape me no matter how hard I try and God knows I've tried. I dig getting there but swear to God before I die, I'm going to orgasm at least once even if I'm eighty-five at the time!"

"If others enjoy them, I want them too. And also, my husband has trouble getting an erection, and so I usually don't have much hopes of its being completed with my having an orgasm, and so I don't get as turned on as I used to."

"It's like being the only person with cake with no frosting—you feel you're missing something but you're not sure what."

"Not having orgasm used to matter to me. I felt a lack, an incompleteness, a yearning. I felt I was a disappointment to my husband, and also felt a deep self-hatred."

"I never really enjoy sex anymore because I'm obsessed with the possibility of having an orgasm, and disappointed for the millionth time when I don't."

"Since I'm not sure if I have orgasms, they have assumed importance to me. I am ashamed of the fact that I don't seem to have any. I still enjoy sex with my husband, but I wish I had them."

"I haven't had an orgasm during my marriage (twenty-seven years) or with the two other men with whom I had sex besides my husband. I remember an experience when I was fourteen or fifteen and at the movies and from descriptions I have read, I believe I had a mild orgasm. I was very warm, my legs felt weak, and there was a most pleasurable, tingling sensation in my pubic area. That's the closest I've ever come to it. I have masturbated occasionally, but nothing happens. I have no idea *what* would cause me to respond. God knows I've tried everything except anal sex. I still believe it's possible for me but I'll be damned if I can locate what's wrong and I don't have the money to go to a sex clinic."

"I have never yet come, so having sex usually ends up a little sour. I have been very excited and feeling very good when the man I'm with comes—which is the end of really active exciting lovemaking—but still I feel very depressed, unloved, and I feel like crying—sometimes I have cried (though I usually tried not to, so I wouldn't upset my lover). It's hard to describe how bad and totally alone and ignored this makes me feel."

"I am very uptight about not having orgasm, generally unhappy about relationships with men. Am I alone? I want to know where I stand, I want to be heard, because I am certainly not ashamed about any aspect of myself and my feelings."

"My female lover also received the questionnaire to answer, and when I asked her if she was going to complete it, she said she'd gotten through Part I and gave up—felt funny because it seemed to center on orgasm and she had never been sure if she actually *has orgasms*. (I think she does have them, certainly reaches a peak and relief; without convulsive movements, however.) Anyway, she said she wasn't going to send in what she had, and I could not convince her to, though I suggested other women may also be confused about orgasm. She said she was defensive about it, from the questionnaire."

"I am living in friendship with my sixty-year-old husband. I *am* and always have been sexually anesthetized and believe I always will be. I enjoy sex psychologically (closeness, intimacy, feeling feminine, meeting a man's needs, etc.) but I have no way of knowing what sex *with* orgasms would be like, to compare it to. I feel extremely unique, sexually isolated, and disgusted."

"Sometimes I feel psychologically inadequate because the feeling in the air is that modern liberated women have orgasms most or all of the time, whereas I do not seem to have the need to have orgasms. Probably I have a low sex drive. Nevertheless I resent the pressure placed on me and other women to have orgasms. Every time I read a survey that says Masters and Johnson or other researchers have found that x percent of women almost always have orgasms, I feel psychologically inadequate. But except when I read about the expectations for women's sexual performances, I feel quite satisfied regarding my sex life."

Only two women didn't *seem* to mind not having orgasm:

"I am not interested to the point of pursuing the matter, it's not too important anyway."

"I have to consider (at this point, it seems to me) that maybe I'm just not very orgasmic, and that it's nobody's fault, including my husband's."

One woman who never orgasmed gave a description of her feelings during sex with her husband:

"At first during foreplay it is pleasurable, usually—but sometimes there is no sensation—except like rubbing—I hate that. I feel so defeated. A couple of times as I got more excited I felt as if I might urinate. It was like a welling over. Then later it feels like something is happening to my body, but I'm not always in it, sometimes it feels a little like pain. I used to never have anything or else have pain which was quite severe. It is a lovely feeling to be held and to hold my husband."

Some other women weren't sure if they were having an orgasm or not.

"For a long time I didn't know if I was having them because of verbal myths surrounding them and no means of comparison with other women."

"To tell you the truth, I'm really not sure. I have read so many descriptions and heard so many concepts of what an orgasm is and should feel like. I used to be terribly worried because I didn't think I could have one. I was expecting something really exciting and dynamic to happen—you know, bright lights, psychedelic flashes—but they never did. Also I read, I think in Dr. Reuben's book, that your back will arch and you'll have uncontrollable vibrations in the vaginal area. I never had this happen either so sometimes I would fake it and almost believe it was really happening. Now I say—whatever happens, happens. It's usually quite nice but I don't know if it's an orgasm. I always know what I'm doing and I'm always in control of my faculties."

"I get very wet, then start getting dry. I don't know what an orgasm is, and occasionally I feel slightly unhappy or cheated after sex, but if the wet/dry happens, I always feel tired, relaxed and content. Is this an orgasm?"

"Throughout this questionnaire, every question relating to orgasm finds me in somewhat of a puzzle. I'm not all that sure what it is, but if it means a very pleasant feeling of being loved (even if your mind tells you it's a one-night stand), then I guess I know what it is. But I never noticed if I have any tingling sensations or vibrations, etc. I always secrete a lot . . . even if I'm just talking to a sensual guy. So does this mean I have orgasm with my clothes on and no body contact? Oh well. It is pleasurable."

"I have had a lot of sexual experiences and still can only say that I am not sure if I have orgasms or not. If I have had, they must not have been so outstanding because I do not hold in my memory any memory of them in particular."

"I don't know, but I've heard that if you're not sure then you aren't having any."

The best way to learn to orgasm is to masturbate.

One method for helping women to learn how to orgasm is masturbation. The percentage of women in this study who never had orgasms was five times higher among women who never masturbated than among the rest of the women. Eleven point six percent of the women in this study never orgasmed,* and most of them also never masturbated.

Of course this may only mean that if they felt free enough to touch themselves they would feel free enough to masturbate, and so learn to orgasm. If a woman has never masturbated because she is disgusted with the whole idea, and still refuses to try on the same grounds, "treatment" would then involve getting her to overcome these feelings.

---

* It has been estimated that approximately 10 percent of the women in the U.S. population do not orgasm. According to Masters and Johnson, 94.5 percent of the women in their study who never masturbated also never orgasmed in any other way.

There were some women who never orgasmed but *did* masturbate, though not to orgasm.

"I enjoy masturbation while I'm doing it, but afterward I feel bad about it. I can't get over the things my parents taught me about masturbation being bad. I used to do it once or twice a month, but I've only done it once since I got married. I've come closest to having an orgasm when I was masturbating, but I've never had one. It's more intense alone because I'd be too embarrassed to do it with anyone else around, including my husband. I've seen my husband masturbating, but he doesn't know it."

"I get started by playing with my breasts. When I've gotten myself started, I begin playing with my clitoris, but I keep playing with my breasts too. I stick my finger into my vagina and move it back and forth like a penis would go. At the same time I use my thumb to press and rub around my clitoris. I have to press or rub real hard to get much of a feeling in my clitoris. My legs are apart, and I don't move much. I lie there quietly and enjoy it, even though I never have orgasmed yet."

"I have rubbed my clitoral area with my forefinger, starting slow then faster. I usually quit before orgasm from loneliness, some slight discomfort, some fatigue and some boredom. My legs apart and sitting."

"When I am undressed, I enjoy just feeling my body. On rare occasions I become aroused enough by feeling my body that I masturbate. When I masturbate, I continue to feel my body in general, but I concentrate on my breasts. I feel them, stroke them, massage them, etc. When I get more aroused, I concentrate on my nipples, and I tickle them with the tips of my fingers. I continue to feel my body in general too, but I do not concentrate on doing that the way I concentrate on the things I do to my breasts. It never leads to orgasm, of course, since I never have, nor ever expect to have, orgasms."

"I don't enjoy masturbating, and have never reached orgasm when doing it. Every six months to a year or so, I will rather idly try it, but usually abandon the effort after a few minutes."

"On the rare occasions when I masturbate, I use one hand to gently stimulate my clitoris by stroking it. It is more intense if my legs are apart, but it would be stretching the point to call it exciting. When I was six, I masturbated by straddling a little padded armchair in my mother's bedroom and rubbed vigorously up and down. I sometimes bounced a little. I didn't bother to close the door—it never even occurred to me. When my mother discovered me doing it she very simply told me not to—climbing on the furniture was forbidden. After that I did close the door, and tried to remember to listen for her. She never caught me again, but she eventually got rid of the chair (to my sorrow) and the rocker that replaced it was in no way suitable! There was a good chair in the living room, but it was a little too tall and tipped over with me several times."

"I masturbate frequently (every other night or more) but only enjoy it on a limited basis since I rarely come this way (am working on it though). I find it too lonely and even with a fantasy I miss a lover's touch."

"I've been experimenting but usually I start with a fantasy of the best lover I ever had and imagine that my hands are his and caress my body the way he would, rolling over and caressing everywhere, lightly fondling my breasts. I use all different motions on my vagina—patting, circular, pressing and releasing, and up and down, while I keep one hand free to stroke my breasts. I find the insides of thighs very sensitive. Usually my legs are apart and my hips move rhythmically. I have been thinking of trying a vibrator for an aid toward more consistent orgasms."

"I've had no good feeling from hand manipulation of my vaginal area. As I said, I haven't found my clitoris yet, nor has my partner. I enjoy warm water from the shower on my pubic and rectal areas."

"I have considered this more lately than ever before in my life. I think I have a hangup about it because when I begin to feel great doing it and become aware of impending orgasm, I always stop. I have thought about getting a vibrator to see if I could succeed with that method."

"I have never masturbated for sexual pleasure. I have at times fondled my breasts, wondering what men thought of them, but that is the extent to which I have masturbated."

"I stimulate my own breasts, sometimes my thighs, but I never put my own fingers or objects in my vagina. When I touch my breasts I feel warm and I feel psychologically okay about it. But, it's usually not for orgasm. In fact I've never done that. I do 'squeeze' my thighs and that feels good, but I've never brought it to an orgasm. I think I could if I wanted to."

"I rarely do it and only to see if my parts are still working—they don't. Nothing ever happens—I could go on for hours and only get tired. I don't discuss the subject—when my husband asks if I masturbate, I never give him a straight answer."

"I know I must have masturbated, but I don't know what it really entails. What gives me a lot of pleasure when alone is to dress myself up by draping scarves over my breasts and other places on my body and taking nude pictures of myself. Also stimulating my breasts in front of the mirror, standing up."

"I raise my legs and spread them apart and rub my clitoris with a finger or other object. Sometimes I thrust my fingers into my vagina rather forcefully like a male thrusting his penis, but I never get an orgasm."

"Usually after intercourse, I rub from my clitoris to my rectum in a circular pattern with my legs apart. Often I can get into a frenzy but cannot get an orgasm no matter what."

"I masturbate two or three times a day. I use my fingers; usually I press my middle finger against my clitoral shaft and exert and release pressure very quickly. The effect is much like a vibrator. I keep my legs pressed tightly together. Sometimes, the other hand fondles the small lips or inserts a finger into the anus, sometimes violently—but my hangups take over before I reach that point usually and so I never orgasm."

"I masturbate with my fingers or my husband's genitals. First I get warm feelings, then breathe faster, and feel an increasing physical response in my genital area, then it just drops off to lack of feeling. I use circular and up and down motions, move very little, and it's better with my legs slightly apart."

"I enjoy masturbation, but I feel ridiculous! Which is why I hardly ever do it. Also it never leads to orgasm, another reason I gave it up, although sometimes I get horny when alone and do it anyway. I never tried a vibrator on myself. I probably would if I had any time to myself. When I was younger I just used to rub my whole hand over my genital area and keep my legs more or less together and I didn't move much and I felt really dumb. Now I use two fingers and rub them up and down on either side of my clitoris and down the insides of the labia. My legs are always wide apart—just spreading my legs makes me feel sexy! I move a great deal—thrash around—and make weird noises. And I feel *ridiculous!*"

"I've never had an orgasm but I'd like to. Having sex is important because it's a very nice thing, a nice way of being close to someone. I've never worried *too* much about not having an orgasm, but mainly because I don't know any ways of working toward it so I just accept it."

"I like masturbation best with a vibrator. I use it in a circular motion—soft—all around the whole vestibule. I like to go straight up and down the sides slowly. I like to press it kind of hard on the pubic bone and sometimes directly on the clitoris—it drives me so wild that I can't hold the vibrator to my skin but I still don't come—I usually end up kind of squirming and jerking so bad that I can't keep the vibrator on but I don't come—and this is from very soft stimulation. The same thing happens when I masturbate. Sometimes I use the whole palm in a circular motion, kind of pulling all the skin around—and it gets so intense I can't do it any more but I still don't come! I haven't done enough masturbation with other people to know if they could make me come. I keep my legs apart and usually kind of lie down and leave my other hand just lying down."

Where should you stimulate yourself?

A book written in 1947 by Dr. Helena Wright still has good advice to offer on getting acquainted with your anatomy:

> Arrange a good light and take a mirror and identify all the parts described. To find the clitoris, the thighs must be separated widely enough for comfortable vision, then if two fingers hold apart the larger lips, the mucous membrane-covered hood will be seen immediately inside the front end of the space between the larger lips. The hood can be gently drawn backward by the finger tips and inside will be seen a small, smooth, rounded body (sometimes it is very small and only just visible), which glistens in a good light. This is the clitoris. Its root runs upward under the hood and the junction of the outer lips and extends for about an inch. The two inner lips begin in the mid line close together just under the clitoris, and extend downward and backward on each side of the smooth space in the middle, and come to an end by fading away at about the middle of the ring-shaped opening which is the entrance to the vagina.
>
> When all external parts of the sexual equipment have been carefully and thoroughly identified, it is next necessary to prove at first hand the truth of the statement that the clitoris does possess a unique kind of sensitiveness. It is best to do this with something other than the owner's finger, because the fingertip is, naturally, itself sensitive to touch, and if it is used, there may be confusion of effect between the feeling finger and the part felt. Any small, smooth object will do, such as an uncut pencil, or a toothbrush handle. The procedure is one of comparison of response by a very light touch. One hand separates the outer labia without touching the inner ones, and the other hand, holding the chosen object, touches first one inner lip and then the other, and then the clitoris, through or under its hood. If the hand movements are watched in the mirror, it is easy to get the touches accurately in the right places, but without a mirror and a good light, it is not easy, because an inexperienced woman

has practically no sense of accurate position if she tries to use a finger unguided by her eyes. The effect observed is that the instant the clitoris is touched, a peculiar and characteristic sensation is experienced which is different in essence from touches on the labia or anywhere else.

This difference has to be experienced; it cannot be described in words.[11]

Perhaps it is important here to say something about what most women mean when they say they stimulate their clitoris. In most cases they do not mean they stimulate it directly. The preceding quotation was intended basically for purposes of getting acquainted with your own anatomy. What happens for most women is that they feel around the general clitoral area until they find a spot that feels good—and actually, the "good feeling" is really stimulated by the movement of the hand, fingers, or whatever, and lies *beneath* the surface skin. Some women described it like this:

"It's a matter of exploration of your body; you hit upon a spot that tingles and you just exploit it."

"At first, I just piddle around the entire clitoral area, looking for a good spot—then I stimulate it directly."

"I don't feel the excitement exactly at the spot I am touching, but more buried, more underneath somewhere."

"It seems to 'catch fire' about one inch inside or behind the mons area. One inch inside the clitoris."

"It comes from directly *beneath* my clitoris."

"When the rhythm and pressure is right, the sensitive spot will reach out."

"It's like when someone rubs your back, you know the spot you want them to do next, and you move your muscles around, put your back in the position where you can feel the rubbing the best, and you tense your body to feel it better—to focus the feeling. That's what I do with my legs."

To put it another way, as general stimulation continues, usually one spot begins to stand out as the focus of feeling, an almost burning sensation, which flares up on and off, as you make contact, and then you strive to make total *longer* contact with that spot. You adjust your movements to cause that feeling to continue and increase to orgasm.

Some women had learned how to have orgasms, sometimes after years of not being able to.*

"I rarely had an orgasm during the first three years after I started having sex on a regular basis. I have gradually learned how to enjoy sexual relationships and I really always do have an orgasm now. My last sentence implies that I once didn't enjoy sex, which is not true. I have always enjoyed sex. I have always become very aroused. I just didn't know enough about sex or myself to know how to climax. Having an orgasm is important to me, but I don't think that it is necessary to orgasm *every* time to have good sex, but if I didn't climax most of the time, I think it would be very frustrating. I do have orgasms by many different means. I have not yet experienced an orgasm in intercourse with a man, but I think the situation is probably due to the fact that I don't slow down and initiate the type of things needed to bring me to orgasm. I have always been too concerned with making the sexual experience whatever he wanted and was too self-conscious to let myself go enough to be able to climax. I experience orgasm generally during masturbation, oral sex, and manual sex."

"I am thirty-five years old and never experienced an orgasm until I masturbated and made myself have them!"

"I did not have an orgasm until I was twenty-one, through masturbation. I did not have one with another person until I was thirty-three, despite the fact that I was married at eighteen."

"I didn't orgasm until a year ago. Masturbation showed me the way. I discovered what stimulated me

---

* The age range of women who never orgasmed was from eighteen to seventy-seven.

and then encouraged my lover so that he would bring me to orgasm."

"I do now. I didn't for a long time. I had to get better acquainted with me and my body—practice has made perfect."

"I didn't for years—six years of marriage and two before. Mostly it was inexperienced partners and at the very first it was guilt; I thought sex was 'wrong.' Later it was a reluctance to masturbate—which I later overcame."

"Unfortunately, I didn't know how to masturbate until I had been married about five years; I enjoyed sex, but I kept waiting for an orgasm I didn't know how to achieve."

"First, I read a lot about women and sexuality, sex manuals. I began to accept and appreciate myself. Then I ventured beyond my old limits, in all directions, and learned to orgasm too."

"I just started having them about one year ago. Before that, I was very interested, perhaps obsessed, about it. I came to the realization that I should learn to masturbate to orgasm, which I'd never done. I bought a vibrator, and had one the first time I touched myself with it!"

"I thought I had had orgasms but I didn't know until my partner spent a lot of time stimulating my clitoris in different ways and then all of a sudden, whammo! Orgasm! And a whole new world for me."

"I have had orgasms ever since I discovered my clitoris—which unfortunately happened after *seven* years of vaginal sex."

"For four years I was frigid—this was because of my partner's selfishness and indifference and my guilt over sex."

"I never had orgasms during my entire marriage and its aftermath. I think what cured my frigidity was becoming my own person in other ways as well: which I did through psychotherapy and a love relationship. Orgasm, for me anyway, is part of selfhood."

"I couldn't orgasm, I think, because of overcontrol and my inability to relax. Once I convinced myself that having orgasms was possible and beneficial to me and my husband and that I was *entitled* and deserving of them, I started having them."

"During seventeen years of marriage, I didn't have orgasms. Since then I have had them sometimes. And with the lover I have *now,* every time we are in bed together, I have *multiple* orgasms! It is a surprise to me to know that I have this capacity (other than theoretically). I really thought that it was some other kind of woman who had that much response. I have tried to figure out what makes the difference. His incredible concentration on me is part of it. He totally enjoys me."

"I used to not have orgasms. What started me off into having them was a great deal more confidence in myself which has been a steadily growing feature of the last several years, talking plainly about sex and the sex that we were having with my husband and experimenting with different things to do in bed."

"I went several years without orgasms. Sometimes I wanted them but I wasn't quite sure how it would be different from the sex I was having. My husband's help and patience and me knowing and accepting myself better helped free my mind. Now, as I get older, they have become easier to achieve, longer and more intense."

"I was thirty-five years old and faking orgasms with my husband since I was eighteen, when I 'fell in love' with a man who was married also. I faked with him too but he saw through it and told me that he was very unhappy that he could not make me happy physically and give me an orgasm and that it bothered him so much he feared it would destroy our relationship. I decided to level with him and tell him what really turned me on . . . spankings were what my fantasies were about and I thought I would enjoy his acting it out. It turned him on too, although he had never thought of it before. We tried it (he spanked me) and later I was able to have an orgasm with him through manual clitoral stimulation. I can't describe the full meaning this had for me—that I could have orgasm with another person! I have not since found another partner who digs this kind of thing but it lost its importance and I have always been able to climax since."

"I enjoy having orgasms a great deal. I didn't have them until about two years after we were married, and went through a period of becoming aware that such an experience existed and feeling very frustrated that I didn't have orgasms. Especially as I knew that when I was younger I had had something that I figured was an orgasm (it turns out that it was really more just a feeling of being very turned on). As a teenager I used to put the covers between my legs in bed at night and would get sensations of mild arousal from that that I liked, but I never knew that had anything to do with orgasm. As I recall my mother explained orgasm to me as something you had when you were married and had sex with a man, so I assumed that was the only time you ever had one, and of course had a very foggy idea of what it was. I learned to have orgasms by experimenting, and got a vibrator which I used to help learn how to have them. I am not ever bored by them. I don't believe I would enjoy sex as much without having them, as otherwise I would probably rather just cuddle than have intercourse. I have just lately, since reading your book, *Sexual Honesty,* decided that I have a right to have an orgasm during lovemaking when I want one; previously I often didn't do anything about asking my husband to help me have one because I felt guilty about how long it takes me unless we use a vibrator, and uncertain about using that and possibly making him feel unneeded. However, he doesn't mind that at all; those are really my feelings of uncertainty and guilt about asking for something just for myself, and I am finally getting over that. It has improved our sex life already."

"I faked orgasms continuously throughout my marriage, but I didn't do that as a conscious malicious deception. I simply didn't know what an orgasm was—I thought it was when you felt really terrific and in love and surrendering and what not—like a 'climax' of feeling. Also, I was totally into the business of not being a frigid woman. I didn't have an orgasm until six months after we separated. It was then I realized I had never even been fully aroused. And even now I'll fake an orgasm just to get the whole thing over with, but I'm trying not to do that at all any more."

"I am thirty-eight, married and have two children. I had intercourse for the first time with my husband when I was twenty-seven years old, three years before we were married. He was and is the only person I've slept with. About three months ago I had my first orgasm, except for a few in the past two years during my sexy dreams. I really wanted that first orgasm, worked at it, and rejoiced when it happened—during masturbation. Now I have orgasms all the time and I love it; they get better and better. I masturbate at least two times a day, usually more, and always have orgasms. It took longer to learn to have them during intercourse, which happens with us every two or three days, but now I always do. When I was an adolescent and young woman I had very intense feelings about other women only, and my sexual experience was nil. My sexual fantasies didn't get beyond tender caressing and I didn't even imagine myself having an orgasm. I didn't even masturbate. Only about two or three years ago, after years of psychoanalysis and the sexual revolution and the women's movement gradually changed my image of myself, could I begin to open up. Now I can't imagine sex happening without orgasm."

Some women were able to orgasm only with a vibrator.

"I have tried dozens of times, maybe hundreds of times, to stimulate myself to orgasm by clitoral stimulation and have found it impossible except with a vibrator."

"The vibrator is a tremendous aid, especially if you've never had an orgasm. You must develop a technique which is just right for you, and this may take some time. I've found the direct contact of the vibrator is too much, causing pain/pleasure. By turning over and muffling the vibrator with a pillow, or using the vibrations in your fingers caused by holding the vibrator, you can muffle the intensity of the vibrations. Some people say women get addicted to a vibrator, but if it gives you pleasure when you thought your genital area was deadened to pleasure, why not use it?!"

"I get the most feeling so far with a vibrator and believe I've come close to orgasm. I like to touch it to the side (usually right side) or top of the clitoris—the top feels 'sweeter' when stimulated with a vibrator—that is, the 'pangs' of pleasure shooting through the whole area (vulva) are sharper, rather than deeper, and earthier, which I feel when I move the vibrator from beneath the clitoris slowly upwards, which I also like to do. I have to put a towel or hanky between me and the vibrator and so far have felt the vibrations to be too intense as my muscle contractions cause my body to jerk forward and I lose my place."

One woman suggested sex workshops for women: "A sex workshop would probably help, with an atmosphere of openness and understanding, erotic films and literature, *no pressure,* a workshop just for women."* Another felt that she would be able to learn from intimacy with another woman: "I would like to make love with a woman I felt really close to. I think another woman would want to teach me about my own sexuality—be both sympathetic and empathetic and truly tender and a turn on for me—I wouldn't feel the need to put on an act with a woman and I would want to be honest."

If you can't orgasm, you could also read books on sex therapy, feminist literature, and try to talk to friends about how they have orgasms.† You could also try a local women's self-help group, perhaps a sex therapist, or a lover who was sensitive enough to help. *Don't give up.* Many women *have* learned to orgasm after years of not knowing how, and it is never too late to discover what works for *you.* I hope that reading many of the things other women have said in this book will help.

---

* Such workshops are listed in *The Catalogue of Sexual Consciousness,* published by Grove Press, and *The New Woman's Survival Sourcebook,* published by Alfred Knopf.

† Good books in this area are *Liberating Masturbation* by Betty Dodson, and *For Yourself* by Lonnie Garfield Barbach.

INTERCOURSE

DO MOST WOMEN ORGASM FROM INTERCOURSE?

"This is one of the last questions I've answered—I'm afraid to admit it—but I'm not really sure yes or no—although I've had many orgasms through masturbation, I'm not sure what orgasm from vaginal intercourse is like—I've had very high feelings, but I guess since it wasn't like a masturbatory orgasm I didn't think it was an orgasm. At first, this questionnaire made me feel totally inexperienced—but it's just that I guess I don't always *think* about these things during sex. Like I remember when I had my first coitus I just kept thinking, 'My god, I've got to remember all the details about this—the big important time of my life, when I chose to give up my virginity' and you know something—I don't really remember that much about that specific time."

"I really don't know if I've had an orgasm with a man, unless it's just that I don't really know what to be aware of because if it's supposed to be like when I'm masturbating then I think not. I would like to know if that makes me abnormal."

"I don't think I've ever really experienced an orgasm. In any event, not the way I've read about them. My husband's clitoral stimulation usually leads to a climax for me but never during vaginal stimulation. I keep hoping and working at it. Sometimes I tend to think maybe I'm not supposed to experience a vaginal climax. Sometimes it bothers my husband more than it does me. He really feels badly that I don't experience the same type of pleasure he does. Sometimes I think we work at it too hard and sometimes we think we're getting closer to it, but I never experience anything physically ecstatic."

"I am rather hung up when it comes to orgasms. Because I never have them during intercourse, I feel deeply ashamed and inferior. I grew up with that wretched word 'frigid'—and I think that a lot of my desire to have orgasms during intercourse comes from this shame and feeling of inadequacy. I think the only thing that will contribute to my having them is when I change the feelings I have mentioned before—when I stop pressuring myself and hating myself because I don't have orgasm—hell, I don't know—I've been in therapy for two years and it has helped me personally a lot, but I'm still no closer to having them during intercourse. I think it will take some radical change in my perception and attitude toward myself."

"I went along for thirty-four years carrying the burden of not having vaginal orgasms, never telling anyone because I felt something was wrong with me—I thought I was frigid."

"Is it uncommon to not have orgasm while you are having sexual intercourse? Could you give any suggestions on how to have one?"

"I want to find out where we can go to cure my own impotence in intercourse. I haven't got the money to go to Masters and Johnson's clinic. Will your book mention this?"

"I read *Sex Without Fear* some years ago and was diminished when I read that clitoral orgasms are the sole property of immature sexuality and only vaginal orgasms represent a mature woman. I bought that for a few years but after a time I said, 'So what, I'm immature but enjoying myself just the same!' "

"I would like to have orgasms during intercourse *without* having to play with my clitoris at the same time! If I didn't do that I would almost never come."

"I don't feel that I'm in any way abnormal because I don't have orgasms during intercourse, but I do feel much emotional frustration. It's going to take some time, and I believe eventually a woman will have to tell me how to have an orgasm during sex. Right now I don't know who to ask plus I will have to be quite careful in discussing this—because I wouldn't want someone to think I was abnormal."

"I like intercourse in every way and that's why I feel like a sickie! At thirty, and having screwed for over fifteen years, and still not able to come! I'm fed up."

"I have been married to one partner for over twenty-six years, and it's been very satisfying. I have only one wish: for vaginal orgasm during intercourse—I would like to experience this."

"Sex in the best of all possible worlds? My clitoris would be in my vagina, for Christ's sake, so I could come when I fuck!"

"I feel that some men's egos are wounded when I don't come with them during intercourse, but I don't feel that I'm abnormal. Mostly, the fact that it's difficult for me irritates me. I'd love to be one of those females who can come at the drop of a hat, but since I'm not I'll just keep trying to relax more and experiment with new ways. At times I've considered the theory that the position of my clitoris is responsible, as it just doesn't seem to be stimulated by anything in my vagina. Perhaps I should try masturbating by penetration, but when I'm actually feeling horny I want to come as quickly and easily as possible."

"I've never had an orgasm during intercourse. Till I was around twelve I felt guilty about masturbation, then when the guilt about stopped, I read all these things saying, 'You *must* have an orgasm, and you have to have it *this* way.' That gave me a new worry and blocked my really letting go when I later began having sex. I have orgasms clitorally when I masturbate, but it takes a while, and still not during intercourse."

"I still feel a constant need to know I'm 'normal' sexually. All the new information and discussion of sex has made me too conscious of performance. And I still feel inadequate or immature that I require manual stimulation to reach orgasm. I think there are lots of women like this, but no one is admitting it and saying it's okay."

"Yes, I'm especially shy when I have sex with new partners, because I'm ashamed I don't have orgasms during intercourse."

"After three years of trying, I'm beginning to wonder what's wrong with me. From other women's descriptions I wonder if I could have better ones and I wonder if vaginal orgasms are different and if they exist and how to have one."

"My husband is the best lover I ever had, and I hope we have sex till we're a hundred and ten years old! I have orgasms from masturbation and clitoral stimulation *only*. I feel very little, and rarely, from penis penetration, and I've *never* had an orgasm from penis stimulation. We've worked that out, so that he knows what I need, provides it, and I almost invariably (ninety-nine percent or more) have an orgasm when we have sex."

"I would like to have orgasms during intercourse *without* having to play with my clitoris at the same time. If I didn't do that I would almost never have orgasms. I would like to be able to have them with just intercourse. Maybe when I develop a long-standing trust with someone, and more confidence in myself, this kind of orgasm will come to me. They say it is a question of letting go, and of trusting enough to let go."

"When friends and I began discussing our sexuality a few years ago at 'consciousness raising' sessions, we found very few of us had orgasms during intercourse, although we had always expected to and been expected to—almost automatically. Being able to admit to each other that we didn't gave us a sense of relief and elation about feelings about ourselves—that we weren't abnormal, weird, or 'different,' and we began to feel really good about our sexuality for the first time."

"I expected to have vaginal orgasm as soon as we began fucking after marriage. I took the pill at marriage though I never relaxed about getting pregnant (Catholic) the first year. Both of us were disappointed because of no vaginal orgasm and he considered cunnilingus orgasm second best. I used to pout and beg him to finish me after intercourse and he was reluctant, thinking we could achieve vaginal orgasm if I just got horny enough. In those days I had a lot of congestion after arousal. I suppose I had learned to have clitorally stimulated orgasms and couldn't vaginally. It took about five years for us to be convinced cunnilingus orgasms were just fine and he decided he really liked cunnilingus."

"I love my boyfriend and had sex with him when I was twelve. I got pregnant when I was thirteen, my parents flipped and tried to break us up, but our love grew. My parents and seven sisters tried to push me to give up my baby. But I had a baby boy and I kept him. My boyfriend has supported me since my parents first discovered I was pregnant. He lives with me now without my parents knowing. We love each other very much. I'm on the pill now and we have sex often. But when we have intercourse I can never feel anything. He feels bad because he can't make me happy and because of that he doesn't want to fill his needs. He kisses me and talks to me but no matter what he won't let his self enjoy me, because of my disadvantage. What could I do about this? Please write me back."

FINDINGS OF THIS STUDY

Did most of the women in this study orgasm regularly during intercourse (the penis thrusting in the vagina), without additional clitoral stimulation? No. *It was found that only approximately 30 percent of the women in this study could orgasm regularly from intercourse*—that is, could have an orgasm during intercourse without more direct manual clitoral stimulation being provided at the time of orgasm.

In other words, the majority of women do not experience orgasm regularly as a result of intercourse.

For most women, orgasming during intercourse as a result of intercourse alone is the exceptional experience, not the usual one. Although a small minority of women *could* orgasm more or less regularly from intercourse itself, since almost *all* women orgasm from clitoral stim-

Do Most Women Orgasm from Intercourse?

TOTAL POPULATION	NEVER HAS ORGASM	NEVER HAD INTER- COURSE	HAS ORGASM REGULARLY FROM INTER- COURSE
Q. I : 100% =	12%	2.6%	29%
Q. II : 100% =	11%	3 %	25%
Q. III : 100% =	13%	3 %	23%
	12%	3 %	26%

TOTAL POPULATION WHO DOES ORGASM AND HAS HAD INTERCOURSE	HAS ORGASM REGULARLY FROM INTERCOURSE*
Q. I : 100% =	34%
Q. II : 100% =	29%
Q. III : 100% =	28%
	30%

* How many women orgasmed regularly from intercourse? These figures are based only on women who have had inter- course and who do have orgasms at any time, and who an- swered "yes," "usually," or "always" to the question: How of-

HAS ORGASM RARELY FROM INTERCOURSE	HAS ORGASM DURING INTERCOURSE WITH THE ADDITION OF SIMULTANEOUS CLITORAL STIMU- LATION BY HAND	DOES NOT ORGASM FROM INTERCOURSE
16%	15%	25.4%
19%	15%	27 %
22%	18%	21 %
19%	16%	24 %

HAS ORGASM RARELY FROM INTERCOURSE	HAS ORGASM DURING INTERCOURSE WITH THE ADDITION OF SIMULTANEOUS CLITORAL STIMULATION BY HAND	DOES NOT ORGASM DURING INTERCOURSE
17%	17%	32%
22%	17%	32%
26%	22%	24%
22%	19%	29%

ten do you orgasm during intercourse? Figures do not include those who used simultaneous clitoral stimulation by hand, or defined a different type of orgasm during intercourse. See appendix for complete breakdown of findings.

ulation (during manual stimulation with a partner or masturbation), henceforth we will refer to the stimulation necessary for female orgasm as *clitoral*.

As the figures in the chart on page 230–231 show, it is clear that intercourse by itself did not regularly lead to orgasm for most women. In fact, for over 70 percent of the women, intercourse—the penis thrusting in the vagina—did not regularly lead to orgasm. What we thought was an individual problem is neither unusual nor a problem. In other words, *not* to have orgasm from intercourse is the experience of the majority of women.

We shall see later on in this chapter that, often, the ways in which women do orgasm during intercourse have nothing much to do with intercourse itself. In fact, these methods could probably be adopted by other women who wished to orgasm during intercourse—if this was felt to be a desirable goal.

But do these findings reflect women in general? Or do they only reflect the women in this particular study? Let's compare these findings with those of other researchers.

Seymour Fisher, The Female Orgasm (Basic Books, 1972); Understanding the Female Orgasm (Bantam Books, 1973).

Dr. Fisher conducted a five-year study of some three hundred women, all relatively young, married, and of middle economic standing. Of these women, about 39 percent reported to him that they orgasmed always or nearly always during intercourse. However, "during intercourse," in Fisher's study, could include clitoral stimulation by hand. *Only 20 percent of these women said they never required a final push to orgasm from manual stimulation.*

In addition, Fisher says that when the women in one of his samples were asked to answer the question: "If you had the choice of receiving only clitoral or only vaginal stimulation, which would you select?" 64 percent stated they would choose clitoral stimulation, while 36 percent chose vaginal.

These results are well within the ranges of the figures

obtained in this study. That is, only 30 percent could orgasm regularly from the stimulation of intercourse itself.

Alfred Kinsey et al., Sexual Behavior in the Human Female (W. B. Saunders, 1953) (Pocket Book edition, 1965).

Kinsey and his associates conducted the famous and precedent-setting research that led to the "Kinsey report" so talked about in the 1950s. In many ways, this is still the standard that sex researchers refer to when trying to establish the validity of their findings for the U.S. population as a whole, since Kinsey made every effort to insure that his research did include women representative of all parts of the population. A large-scale random sample has never been done to this day in sex research, since so many of the people who might be chosen at random would refuse to answer. Kinsey, now dead, went to enormous trouble to give us this measuring stick, and the institute is still carrying on this work.

Kinsey and his associates affirmed from the beginning the importance of the clitoris in female sexuality, although here (as in Fisher's work) there is a blurring of meaning of "orgasm during intercourse" that makes it difficult for us to discern useful figures from their findings. The Kinsey report refers to orgasm during intercourse, orgasm during petting, and orgasm during masturbation. But what does orgasm during intercourse include? Wardell Pomeroy, one of Kinsey's associates, has stated that Kinsey did mean an orgasm attained by *any* means during intercourse. With this criterion, Kinsey found that most women, especially after they had been married a while, did have orgasm during intercourse. But the fact that Kinsey brought up over and over again the problem of inadequate stimulation for women during intercourse, and the ease with which women could orgasm during masturbation, tells us that clitoral stimulation by hand must have played a large part in how these women orgasmed during intercourse. As Kinsey put it, "The techniques of masturbation and of petting are more specifically calculated to effect orgasm than the techniques of coitus itself."

Kinsey went on to explain several times that the basic problem for women was *not* an inability to orgasm, but only that "a substantial minority" did not orgasm during "coitus." Furthermore, most of the women he studied who achieved orgasm only sometimes during "coitus" orgasmed promptly and regularly during masturbation. As Edward Brecher summarizes it, "Note that Kinsey did *not* say that masturbation is more enjoyable than coitus, or that it is preferable in any other way. What Kinsey did report was a very simple fact that tens of millions of women know from their own experience: regardless of the joys of coitus, and regardless of its emotional rewards, it is less likely than masturbation to terminate in orgasm—and for some women it always or almost always terminates without orgasm."[1]

Helen Kaplan, The New Sex Therapy (Brunner/Mazel —Quadrangle, 1974).

Dr. Kaplan is a sex therapist and psychoanalyst of high repute. She has not done specific research, but her clinical experience is extensive, and it is this experience on which her statements are based. Her position can be summed up by her statement, "It is difficult to believe that the millions of otherwise responsive women who do not have coital orgasms are all 'sick.'"

As she says:

> Our own impression, which is based solely on our clinical experience, is that in our society 8 to 10 percent of the female population has never experienced an orgasm, while approximately 90 percent of all women seem to be able to achieve orgasm by some means. However, it is also our impression that only about one-half or even fewer of these orgastic women regularly reach a climax during coitus without additional clitoral stimulation. These impressions are in sharp contrast to the view held by many experts, and shared by the general public, that coital orgasm is the only normal form of female sexual expression and

that orgasm attained primarily by direct clitoral stimulation is somehow pathological.[2]

In other words, Kaplan estimates that perhaps one half or fewer of those 90 percent who can orgasm do so during intercourse without additional clitoral stimulation. "Half or fewer" of 90 percent remains within the general area of this book's findings, although the figure, which is an estimate, is slightly higher.

William Masters and Virginia Johnson, Human Sexual Response (Little, Brown and Company, 1966); Human Sexual Inadequacy (Little, Brown and Company, 1970).

Masters and Johnson have given no specific figures with regard to the prevalence of orgasm from intercourse; indeed, their research was not undertaken with this question in mind. Their aim was to study and understand orgasm itself. The crucial finding of their work, with regard to female sexuality, is that there is only one kind of orgasm, not two; that orgasms during intercourse are caused by indirect clitoral stimulation, not vaginal stimulation.

With regard to the question being asked in this chapter, what does their work have to tell us? First of all, Masters and Johnson chose their basic study population only from women who did have orgasm from intercourse; all others were eliminated. Then in their findings, they labeled not having orgasm from intercourse "coital orgasmic inadequacy." However, Masters and Johnson obviously recognize that women orgasm more easily from masturbation and clitoral stimulation and they report the strongest and most frequent orgasms occurring in women at this time, even going so far as to say with regard to intercourse/coitus:

> Sociocultural influence more often than not places woman in a position in which she must adapt, sublimate, inhibit, or even distort her natural capacity to function sexually in order to fulfill her genetically assigned role (i.e., breeding). *Herein lies a major source of woman's sexual dysfunction.*[3]

Still, one of their major goals seems to be to "treat" women so that they will be able to orgasm during intercourse. There is nothing wrong with this, except that it still leaves women with the impression that not having an orgasm during intercourse is "sick" and "abnormal"—a dysfunction. This is especially true since Masters and Johnson's statement that the clitoris is indirectly stimulated during thrusting has received so much publicity. We will have more to say about their theories in the section of this chapter dealing with the ways in which women orgasm during intercourse.

In summary, the over-all consensus of these studies is that most women do not automatically have orgasms from intercourse—in the sense of simple thrusting without additional stimulation. Not only is "failure" to orgasm during coitus (intercourse) the most common female sexual complaint found in sex therapy clinics, but the fact that women very frequently do not orgasm during intercourse has been general popular knowledge for a very long time. For a woman to have orgasm during intercourse, from intercourse, is simply not the majority experience.

Why is this? Even the question being asked is wrong. The question should not be: Why aren't women having orgasms from intercourse? but, rather: *Why have we insisted women* should *orgasm from intercourse?* And why have women found it necessary to try everything in the book, from exercises to extensive analysis to sex therapy, to *make* it happen?

THE GLORIFICATION OF INTERCOURSE

Why have we thought women should orgasm from intercourse?

There are three basic reasons for this insistence, which will be developed in the following pages:

A. The explanation of sexual pleasure as the means of insuring reproduction.

B. The crucial role of monogamous intercourse in patrilineal inheritance.

C. The widespread influence of the Freudian model of female psychology.

A. Sexual pleasure and the reproductive model

First the idea that since nature gave us a "sex drive" and the capacity for sexual pleasure in order to insure reproduction, therefore coitus is "the real thing," and all other forms of sexual gratification are substitutions for, or perversions of, this "natural" activity.

It is important to scrutinize this assumption. Intercourse *is* necessary for reproduction, and sexual pleasure and orgasm *are* involved with reproduction. But exactly how? Looking closer, one sees that only *male* orgasm during intercourse is necessary for reproduction. It would make sense, from the point of view of the necessity to deposit semen inside the vagina, that intercourse provide almost automatic, perfect stimulation for male orgasm, and, of course, it does: men orgasm as regularly during intercourse as women (and men) do during masturbation.

However, since female orgasm is not necessary during intercourse for reproduction to occur, why should nature provide stimulation for female orgasm during intercourse? (As a matter of fact, what is the reason for the existence of female orgasm at all?) There are several possibilities:

1. Some researchers claim that female orgasm helps "suck" the sperm up into the uterus. However, Masters and Johnson believe that this is doubtful, since the contractions of the uterus progress downward, and so are "more likely to have an expulsive action than a sucking action." To check this, they placed a fluid resembling semen but opaque to X rays in a cap covering the cervix, so that if there were any sucking, the fluid would be taken into the cervix. However, X ray films showed no significant gaping of the cervical opening at all. Several respondents in this study mentioned that their contractions move downward, or outward. One woman described her orgasm this way: "A clitoral orgasm is a

sharp, shuddering, breath-taking pleasure/pain gripping of the muscles in my rectum and vagina. Whatever is in me—a finger, or penis, or dildo—is gripped and pushed outward."

2. Dr. Mary Jane Sherfey says: "In general, the orgasm in the male is admirably designed to deposit semen where it will do the most good, and in the female, to remove the largest amount of venous congestion in the most effective manner."[4] But orgasm does this for men too, and Sherfey herself has made a point of emphasizing that after one orgasm, women do not completely decongest but remain in a state of partial arousal, and sometimes after one orgasm arousal can become *stronger*. Can this be, then, the only function of female orgasm?

Dr. Sherfey has also given a reason why, from the point of view of reproduction, women should *not* have orgasms during intercourse: "In a woman with a lax perineal body who has borne children, semen easily escapes with premature withdrawal, whereas if the woman does *not* have an orgasm, the still-swollen lower third acts as a stopper to semen outflow. . . ."[5] Masters and Johnson have also mentioned that there is a greater chance for impregnation for some women if they do not orgasm, for the same reason.

3. Another possibility is that perhaps our orgasmic contractions are for the purpose of further insuring male orgasm, gripping the penis and pulling slightly downward rhythmically. In this model of intercourse, thrusting would not be considered as necessary as it now is, and perhaps intercourse in another culture would be less gymnastic and male-dominated—more a mutual lying together in pleasure, penis-in-vagina, or vagina-covering-penis, with female orgasm providing much of the stimulation necessary for male orgasm.

4. On the other hand, perhaps the function of female orgasm is to provide arousal and "receptivity," or interest in the woman in initiating intercourse. Most female primates have a period of estrus, a specific period of time during which arousal is more or less constant, which guarantees that fertility and intercourse will coin-

cide. Women do not have estrus; they are theoretically capable of becoming aroused at any time. We become aroused in many ways—by kissing, hugging, and even talking. During all these activities, if we find them arousing, a warm, tickling sensation—the desire for clitoral stimulation, perhaps—becomes stronger and stronger. If clitoral stimulation follows, it often leads to a kind of vaginal tickle ("vaginal ache") that feels to many women like a desire to "be penetrated." While continued stimulation brings orgasm, and, for many women, a return to arousal, intercourse seems to quiet this feeling. Perhaps one of the functions of our orgasm is continuing arousal—and "receptivity."

It is unclear whether the "vaginal ache" part of the outline just presented holds true for most women, or even for very many women, since most women generally don't use any kind of vaginal entry during masturbation. However, the general idea of our orgasms perhaps serving the function of continuing our arousal and keeping it at just manageable levels for the body is an interesting possibility.

In the same way, it could be argued that since women do not have estrus, it is necessary for our clitoris to be located on the outside of our bodies rather than closer to the vagina, so that stimulation might happen in the normal course of things. In other words, since we are not periodically receptive like other mammals, there must be some mechanism provided for arousal that can be activated at will and that will not leave us constantly in a state of arousal.

However, none of these theories may be right. For example, if the purpose of arousal and sexuality in general is really connected only with reproduction, why can we have just as much if not stronger arousal and orgasm(s) at times when we are not capable of conception—i.e., during pregnancy, after menopause, during menstruation, and at other times of the month when conception is not possible, and during childhood?

Perhaps orgasm is basically a release mechanism for the body, as are other spastic body reactions, such as laughing, crying, or bodily convulsions. Maybe one function of orgasm is the discharge of *all* kinds of tensions through this release. Or could it be possible that there is no "reason" for the existence of female orgasm other than pleasure? In any case, whether or not continuing arousal is the function of female orgasm, or the release of all kinds of bodily tensions, it is definitely clear that there is no logical reason for insisting that we have our orgasms during intercourse.

B. Patriarchy and monogamous intercourse

A second reason for insisting women (and men) should find their greatest sexual pleasure in intercourse, and for seeing intercourse as *the* basic sexual act, *the* basic form of sex—is that our form of society demands it. With a very few isolated exceptions, for the last three or four thousand years all societies have been patrilineal or patriarchal. Family name and inheritance have passed through men, and religious and civil laws have given men authority to determine the course of society. In a non-patriarchal society, where there is either no question of property right or where lineage goes through the mother, there is no need for institutionalizing intercourse as the basic form of sexual pleasure. In the earliest societies we know about, families were mostly extended groups of clans, with aunts and brothers sharing equally in the upbringing of the child; the mother did not particularly "own" the child, and there was no concept of "father" at all. In fact, the male role in reproduction was not understood for quite a long time, and intercourse and male orgasm were not connected with pregnancy which of course only became apparent many months later.

But with changeover to a patrilineal or patriarchal society,* it becomes necessary for the man to control

---

* Books related to this subject include *The First Sex*, by Elizabeth Gould Davis; *The Mothers*, by Robert Briffault; *The White Goddess*, by Robert Graves; *The Cult of the Mother Goddess*, by E. O. James; *Woman's Evolution*, by Evelyn Reed; and *Prehistory and the Beginning of Civilization*, by Jacquetta Hawkes and Sir Leonard Woolley.

the sexuality of the woman. Nancy Marval, in a paper
printed by The Feminists, explains this further:

> In a patriarchal culture like the one we were all
> brought up in, sexuality is a crucial issue. Beyond all
> the symbolic aspects of the sexual act (symbolizing
> the male's dominance, manipulation, and control over
> the female), it assumes an overwhelming practical im-
> portance. This is that men have no direct access to
> reproduction and the survival of the species. As indi-
> viduals, their claim to any particular child can never
> be as clear as that of the mother who demonstrably
> gave birth to that child. Under normal circumstances
> it is agreed that a man is needed to provide sperm to
> the conception of the baby, but it is practically impos-
> sible to determine *which* man. The only way a man
> can be absolutely sure that he is the one to have con-
> tributed that sperm is to control the sexuality of the
> woman.[6]

To do this, he had to insist she be a virgin at marriage, and monogamous thereafter. As Kinsey put it:

> Sexual activities for the female before marriage
> were proscribed in ancient codes primarily because
> they threatened the male's property rights in the fe-
> male whom he was taking as a wife. The demand that
> the female be virgin at the time of her marriage was
> comparable to the demand that cattle or other goods
> that he bought should be perfect, according to the
> standards of the culture in which he lived.[7]

With regard to keeping her monogamous, Marval
comments that a man could do this in several ways:

> He may keep her separate from any other man as in
> a harem, he may threaten her with violence if she
> strays, he may devise a mechanical method of prevent-
> ing intercourse like a chastity belt, he may remove her
> clitoris to decrease her erotic impulses, *or* he may con-
> vince her that sex is the same thing as love and if she
> has sexual relations with anyone else, she is violating

the sacred ethics of love. This last method is the one
used most commonly in the United States today.[8]

In addition to these practical reasons for controlling
sexuality (to maintain the form of social organization
we know), in the early period of the changeover to patriarchy there were political reasons as well, in that
other forms of sexuality represented rival forms of social organization. For example, it is generally accepted
by Bible scholars that the earliest Jewish tribes mentioned in the Old Testament accepted cunnilingus and
homosexuality as a valid part of life and physical relations, as did the societies around them—which were
not, for the most part, totally patriarchal. In fact, prior
to the seventh century B.C.,* homosexual and other sexual activities were associated with Jewish religious rites,
just as in the surrounding cultures. But as the small and
struggling Jewish tribes sought to build and consolidate
their strength, and their patriarchal social order, and to
bind all loyalty to the one male god, Yahweh, all forms
of sexuality except the one necessary for reproduction
were banned by religious code. The Holiness Code, es-
tablished at the time of their return from the Baby-
lonian exile, sought to fence out the surrounding cultures and set up rules for separating off the Chosen
People of God. It was then that non-heterosexual, non-
reproductive sexual acts were condemned as the way of
the Canaanite, the way of the pagan. But these activities
were proscribed as an indication of allegiance to another culture, an adjunct to idolatry—and *not* as "immoral" or as sexual crimes, as we consider them. They
were political crimes.

These codes have continued in our religious and civil
law up to this day. Judeo-Christian codes still specifically condemn all sexual activity that does not have reproduction as its ultimate aim. Our civil law is largely
derived from these codes, and the laws of most states
condemn non-coital forms of sexuality (in and out of

---

* Although according to the *Jews: Biography of a People*,
by Judd Teller, it was the sixth century B.C.

marriage) as punishable misdemeanors or crimes. Thus, intercourse has been *institutionalized* in our culture as the only permissible form of sexual activity.

Forms of sexuality other than intercourse are now also considered *psychologically* abnormal and unhealthy, as we shall see in a few pages. However, the full spectrum of physical contact is enjoyed by the other mammals, and their mental health has not been questioned. Furthermore, intercourse is not the main focus of their sexual relations either, but only one activity out of many. They spend more time on mutual grooming than they do on specifically sexual contact, as Jane Goodall and many other primate researchers have described in great detail. They also masturbate and have homosexual relations quite commonly. Among the animals for whom these activities have been recorded are the rat, chinchilla, rabbit, porcupine, squirrel, ferret, horse, cow, elephant, dog, baboon, monkey, chimpanzee, and many others. Although our culture seems to assume that since sexual feelings are provided by nature to insure reproduction, and therefore intercourse is or should be the basic form of our sexuality—even though women's sexual feelings are often strongest when women are *not* fertile—it is patently obvious that other forms of sexuality are just as natural and basic as intercourse, and perhaps masturbation is more basic, since chimpanzees brought up in isolation have no idea of how to have intercourse, but do masturbate almost from birth.

To try to limit physical relations between humans to intercourse is artificial. But perhaps it was also necessary to channel all forms of physical contact into heterosexual intercourse to increase the rate of population growth. A high rate of reproduction is the key to power and wealth for a small group, and in the early Jewish tribes, barrenness was a curse. In fact, children have been the basic form of wealth in almost every society up to the present. From the point of view of the larger society, increase in numbers provides the ability to consolidate more territory and to defeat other tribes. On a personal level, children could inherit one's property and also consolidate the family's holdings, and they could till the fields, hunt, gather food, or tend flocks (and later, work in factories) for their parents.

The desire for maximum population growth was institutionalized in our culture, and out of this grew the definition of women as basically serving this ideal. The glorification of marriage, motherhood, and intercourse is part of a very strong pro-natalist bias in our culture, which is discussed in detail in the book *Pronatalism: The Myth of Mom and Apple Pie*, edited by Ellen Peck and Judy Senderowitz.

In summary, since intercourse has been defined as the basic form of sexuality, and the only natural, healthy, and moral form of physical contact, it has automatically been assumed that this is when women should orgasm. Heterosexual intercourse has been *the* definition of sexual expression ever since the beginning of patriarchy, and is the only form of sexual pleasure really condoned in our society. The corollary of this institutionalization of heterosexual intercourse is the villainization and suppression of all other forms of sexuality and pleasurable intimate contact—which explains the historic horror of our culture for masturbation and lesbianism/homosexuality, or even kissing and intimate physical contact or caressing between friends.

C. The Freudian model of female sexuality

The third and final basic reason why women have been expected to orgasm during intercourse is the general acceptance of the Freudian model of female sexuality, the model of female psychology based on it, and in general the acceptance of the concept of "mental health."

Freud was the founding father of vaginal orgasm. He theorized that the clitoral orgasm (orgasm caused by clitoral stimulation) was adolescent and that, upon puberty, when women began having intercourse with men, women should transfer the center of orgasm to the vagina. The vagina, it was assumed, was able to produce a parallel, but more mature, orgasm than the clitoris. Presumably this vaginally produced orgasm would occur, however, only when the woman had mastered important major conflicts and achieved a "well-integrated," "feminine" identity. The woman who could reach orgasm only through clitoral stimulation was said to be "immature" and not to have resolved fundamental "conflicts" about sexual impulses. Of course once he had laid down this definition of our sexuality, Freud not so strangely discovered a tremendous "problem" of "frigidity" in women.

These theories of Freud's were based on faulty biology. Freud himself did mention that perhaps his biological knowledge was faulty and would turn out, on further study, to be incorrect—and indeed it has been demolished, for some thirty years now. Undoubtedly, Freud would have accepted this research by now, but the profession he originated has been unwilling or slow to do so. All too many psychoanalysts and various "authorities" writing in popular women's magazines continue to insist that we should orgasm through intercourse, via thrusting, with no hands, and still see "vaginal primacy" as a crucial criterion of "normal" functioning in women. They continue to regard orgasm produced by intercourse as the only "authentic" female sexual response, and climax caused by any other form of stimulation (like "clitorism," as they call it) as a symptom of neurotic conflict.

Freud's theory of female sexuality has also been refuted on psychological grounds. Not only, in Freudian psychology, must a woman orgasm by the movement of the penis in the vagina, but if she doesn't, she is "immature" and psychologically flawed. Her difficulty is supposedly a reflection of her over-all maladaptive character structure. She is seen as being significantly disturbed and lacking in "ego integration." It is said that she is struggling with unconscious conflicts that make her anxious and unstable; and her lack of orgasm is only one facet of this general unhappiness.

No major studies in the field of psychology have detected these correlations between personality structure and ability to orgasm during intercourse. If anything, as the most recent large-scale study has shown (Seymour

Fisher, *The Female Orgasm*), there is almost an opposite correlation:

> There seems to be good reason for concluding that the more a woman prefers vaginal stimulation, the greater is her level of anxiety. The strongly vaginally oriented woman is tense and has a low threshold for feeling disturbed. This was demonstrated not only in her overt behavior but also her fantasies. As reported, the relatively high anxiety of the vaginally oriented woman was detected by multiple observers who got to know her while she was in the psychology laboratory. It was also revealed in her self-ratings of how disturbing it was to experience the stress of being delivered of a child in the hospital. Variously, too, it was revealed in her difficulty in dealing with learning tasks; in her ink-blot responses suggestive of discomfort and dysphoria; and in her autobiographical accounts of past emotional turbulence. These findings, as already mentioned, represent a reversal of what might have been expected within the framework of most current theories of female sexuality. It has been fashionable to regard a vaginal orientation as indicative of maturity and good adjustment, while assuming that a clitoral preference denotes inadequacy in personality development. Obviously, the facts, as they have emerged in the present studies, blatantly contradict existing theories. If these facts receive support from other investigators, a gross revision of such theories will be required. If anxiety is greater in those who are more vaginally oriented, the question arises as to its origin. Unfortunately, there is no solid information available to answer this question. . . . [9]

However, Fisher cautions:

> . . . although the vaginally oriented have been described as more anxious than the clitorally oriented, this in no way implies that they are less "healthy" or that they are seriously maladjusted. There is no intent to replace the equation between vaginal response and maturity which has so long been common in the psychoanalytic literature with a reverse equation. The

women who where studied were without major psychiatric symptoms and generally functioned at what would be considered a "normal" level. The fact that the vaginally oriented woman is more anxious or has experienced more psychological distress than the clitoral oriented does not mean that she is less mature or that she is somehow psychologically inferior. . . .[10]

In addition, Fisher reported that,

Numerous dimensions of the woman's body images were evaluated. One, called Depersonalization, turned out to be of special importance with respect to vaginal–clitoral preference. It concerns the extent to which an individual perceives her body as alien or foreign, lacking sensory vividness. . . . It was found that the more a woman describes her body as "depersonalized," the more she prefers vaginal rather than clitoral stimulation. This finding impressed me as having an intriguing congruence with the fact that the woman with high-vaginal preference was inclined to describe her orgasm as lacking "ecstatic" quality. Just as the high-vaginal woman apparently experiences the body state called orgasm in a nonecstatic fashion, she also refers to her body as lacking experiential intensity in a more general characteristic fashion. . . .[11]

Fisher goes on to speculate that the vaginally oriented woman might

believe that an intense body experience like sexual arousal should occur only when someone else, a male partner, becomes so closely involved with her body that he is sharing in the responsibility for it. When her body is fused sexually with his, she can think of her sexual arousal as a joint event. She can perceive the experience as not primarily for her own satisfaction but also for another. At the other extreme, the clitorally oriented woman would, from this viewpoint, have the opposing need to experience her body autonomously and to be reassured that an event like intense sexual excitement belongs clearly and personally to her. She would respond negatively to conditions which seriously challenged her sense of body autonomy."

Despite all these demonstrations of the fallacies of Freudian theory about women, "treatment" of women along Freudian lines is still being widely performed, with the large majority of psychiatrists having complete faith in this version of female sexuality and female psychology! Even with all the advances in biological knowledge that make Freud's biology obsolete, and even with the findings of Masters and Johnson, and Fisher, and many others, psychoanalytic theory has not changed! As Sherfey, herself a psychiatrist, asks, "The question must be put and answered within the profession . . . Could many of the sexual neuroses which seem to be almost endemic to women today be, in part, induced by doctors attempting to treat them?"[13]

Probably millions of women could agree with one woman who wrote, "It would give me a great deal of personal pleasure to give Freud a black eye."

"If you don't have orgasms during intercourse, you're hung up."

The influence of these psychiatric theories on women has been strong and pervasive. Whether or not a woman has been in analysis, she has heard these unfounded and anti-woman theories endlessly repeated—from women's magazines, popular psychologists, and men during sex. *Everyone*—of all classes, backgrounds, and ages— *knows* a woman should orgasm during intercourse. If she doesn't, she knows she has only herself and her own hangups to blame.

"I see my failure to have orgasms during intercourse as *my* failure largely, i.e., I've had plenty of men who were 1) adept, 2) lasted a long time, 3) were eager for my orgasm to occur, and 4) etc. but none of them were successful. I guess I have a fear of childbearing, a fear of responsibility—I don't know."

"I am interested in having orgasms during intercourse because I see it as a normal natural release which I cannot achieve. My obvious underlying mistrust of men and disgust for their sexuality which keeps me from totally letting go disallows my sexual freedom."

"I could have them if I freed myself of anxiety and felt totally vulnerable."

"I'm interested in having orgasms during intercourse because I want to have that experience when I'm so close to Mike. I just don't know what would contribute to my having them. I believe in my head I can't fully let myself go during intercourse, though I don't think I'm 'trying' to have them. I just feel it must be some sort of hangup—Mike is really a fine 'lover'—though we're both rather lazy and don't do more out of the ordinary things during sex, for instance. We don't try hard at all to do anything about me having orgasms."

"The fact that I cannot come during intercourse must mean that I do not like it, or have a shame or fear of it, even though I think I like it. I realize this, but since I don't know *why* I am this way, I do not know how to go about overcoming it."

"I think my mental attitude is wrong, that I have a mental block. But with a mutual atmosphere of trust and faith and love, I am sure I could let go of control and have orgasms."

"I can have an orgasm with clitoral stimulation but I have never had one with intercourse. This is purely a fear thing, as before I thought something was wrong with me, but a while ago I realized I didn't want to come with a man inside me, because basically I never respected any of the men I went to bed with—although I was not conscious at the time of this. My therapist helped me see it."

"I've never come with a man inside me, only by hand or mouth. Personally I think it's because I don't want to. I have very mixed feelings about men—anger vs. love, and I've never been with a man who I totally accept and respect as an equal to me."

"Orgasms probably multiple will come with penetration when I relax my vagina and give up the rigid control over what's happening to me, i.e., to not be afraid, to let myself be as vulnerable as I really am."

"I think I don't have them because I don't want to

truly 'open up,' to me it's a submission, and the final conquering of me as a woman and person."

"To have orgasms during intercourse I need to culti- vate a more sincere loving of self—my whole self, body and soul and mind; and a continuance of a relationship in order to get into and share many experiences harmo- niously with each other."

"I wish I knew the answer. I take my lack of orgasms during intercourse very personally and very hard. Trying so hard as I do doesn't seem to be the answer. I seem to need the situation in which the sex act takes place to be perfect emotionally and physically."

"I can never forget that I want to come. Men have said that if I'd just forget about it and relax, I probably would come. I try very hard to come and to forget it too."

"I must let go, relax and trust, unlearn my taboos and defenses against violation, resistance to my feel- ings. . . ."

"Yes I have orgasms but I'm not satisfied with them entirely because it took me twenty-eight years to get there with masturbation and I still can't give myself completely to a man yet."

"I am one of the few females I know that really doesn't have some sort of psychological hangup about screwing. No matter how slight, they all do."

"During eighteen years of marriage, we did every- thing but stand on our heads, but there were few or- gasms for me—due to the deeper mental attitudes, probably. Masturbation has always worked."

"Orgasms are very important, and since I don't have them during intercourse, I have wondered if I am nor- mal, what's wrong with me since I cannot have them, is it my fault or my husband's?"

"I will learn by vacuuming the fear out of my mind and learning to relax."

"Unless you work out your rage and fear about pene- tration, some energy will be taken by these emotions rather than letting yourself be completely taken over by the emotions and orgasm."

Fisher has something to say about this idea in particular:

Another factor often mentioned in the psychoanalytic literature as inhibiting a woman's orgasm potential is fear of being penetrated. It is said that anxiety about the consequences of the penis entering her body not infrequently prevents a woman from becoming sexually aroused during intercourse. Presumably the penetrating penis stirs up fantasies about internal injury, potential body damage consequent to becoming pregnant, and so forth. Relatedly, it has often been said in the analytic literature that most women envy the penis; and this envy may evoke competitive fantasies which, when intensified by sexual interactions, interfere with loving and being loved, and thus prevent orgasmic levels of excitement. No support has been found in the empirical data for either of these two formulations.[14]

"It's very difficult for me. I can't forget past hurts. I know I must hold back as a punishment. In therapy I hope to learn to forget, and to relax and not be uptight, to be open and free with someone else."

"My problem is refusal to lose control with someone else, to let my feelings, physical responses take over for a few seconds of vulnerability. I need to truly love and trust the one I am with."

"With my husband, I don't trust him with my innermost being. He would probably consider my having orgasms *his* accomplishment anyway."

"There is some mental block I don't know about."

"In order to have orgasms, I have to deal with my own hangups. I don't think it has to do with any failure on my lover's part."

"I do feel I'm not sexually normal because I've never had an orgasm during intercourse, and I've lived with this guy for *years*. I know it's because of my guilt feelings toward sex and it's not him because he's a good lover. It's my own inhibitions."

"Although I do have clitoral orgasms, I do not have spontaneous vaginal orgasms. I have been in several relationships where there was warmth and tenderness but not the kind of love, I guess (or trust, or commitment, etc.), necessary to get me over the hump. I hover so close to vaginally coming but panic at the last minute—block out my intense feelings. I guess I have a fear of being overwhelmed. Of letting a man have complete control over me. If I only come clitorally, if the relationship ends, no great loss."

There was a lot of psychiatric jargon in those answers. The women may have been in therapy, but it's just as easy to pick up these terms from numerous articles by therapists and others in the women's magazines, and also from male "experts" with whom you may have "sex."

The idea that if we would "just relax and let go" during intercourse we would automatically have an orgasm is, of course, based on the fallacious idea that orgasm comes to us automatically by the thrusting penis, and all we have to do is to give ourselves over to what our bodies will naturally and automatically do—that is, orgasm. As one woman put it, "It's our fault that we can't be as natural as they are."

I wish we could have back all the time and energy we have spent blaming ourselves and searching our souls about why we didn't have orgasms during intercourse. And all the money we spent "flocking to the psychiatrists" looking for the hidden and terrible repression that kept us from our "vaginal destiny." I would like to have what we would have built with that energy.

Another reason frequently given for not having orgasms during intercourse was that the "Right Man" (Mr. Right) was lacking.

"In order to have orgasms with a man, I would have to have a deep trust in him. He should be a really sensuous and intensely sexual man with a lot of patience and very perceptive, but easygoing. I think once I *knew* someone could satisfy me, I'd be able to come."

"If I could find a sex partner with whom I felt *completely* at ease sexually, I would probably have an orgasm during intercourse or at least other than during masturbation."

"I would very much enjoy having more orgasms with a partner. I guess I'm a bit of a perfectionist now in my expectations regarding sex, and becoming more realistic would contribute to my having more orgasms with a partner. I demand a fairly total understanding of myself by a partner, and expect the same of myself toward him—and this is rarely possible. I've had a few orgasms—(um) I can count only one or two *total* in all my life with approximately fifteen lovers to date. Good grief. That's no average—that's a total! Two orgasms with a partner in my whole life!!!"

"I must seem to have a low threshold of sexual need, to anyone reading this. You see, I've never known what sex is like with a dear, dear *friend* (in my experience marriage and friendship are *not* synonymous). I'm sure an orgasm during intercourse would be possible in a real *friendship*, a *companion* relationship."

"Maybe having sex with someone I knew well and deeply cared about would help."

"I don't know what would help but I think I have to know beyond a doubt that I'm the only piece of pussy he's interested in at the moment, the past ones were substandard, and that he'll be damned lucky to find another like me if he lives to be a hundred. I am in counseling now and hope this helps. Doctors have said I'm built alright and shouldn't have any problems."

"I must relax and feel secure and happy with a man I know loves me completely."

"If I could find the right man—one who cares deeply for me and I care deeply for. A man who feels I am beautiful and I feel he is beautiful."

"I don't know what would give me orgasms during intercourse. I suppose thinking it was worth doing. If you have to work so hard for it, if it doesn't come naturally or easily, then it seems pretty artificial, or wrong to force it. If my body wanted me to have orgasms, I'm sure it would see I did. I'm healthy, normal, well-balanced, and all that, so if I don't have orgasms, there must be something wrong with the act—or the man.

I've tried lots and lots of them, from one-nighters to long, long affairs, almost always with men who must meet a very high standard, but none of them made me have an orgasm from intercourse, so I guess they just weren't good enough (meaning I guess I just didn't like them well enough) or else the whole act of intercourse is a concoction of the imagination. You can think yourself into almost any kind of fantasy, especially with a little psychology to help it along: like you aren't fulfilled unless you have orgasm. I think most of those men I was with were jerks (though I tried to pretend at the time they were giants of some kind) and that's why I couldn't get excited enough to have an orgasm. A stream of water is a lot more accommodating, it doesn't try to dominate you, insult you, use you, etc., etc."

"If I could feel my lover was more involved emotionally, if he made me feel secure, then I could come."

"I need to feel absolutely sure of my partner in every way to enable me to feel absolutely free to let go."

"I am only interested in trying with someone I care for and who cares for me, someone I really trust and believe in, and who feels the same about me."

Waiting for the Right Man to make us orgasm is like waiting for the prince to come. However, a partner who is more sensitive and understanding of the realities of female sexuality *can* make a difference in what the experience involves, and so there is some truth to the idea, at least on this level:

"I would like to come more consistently and more frequently. I know what would contribute to this and have already discussed it with my boyfriend, and that is his inability to give of himself more on *all* levels. In sex, for example, he's just too quick—not enough foreplay on my clitoris."

"In a very equal relationship (current) orgasm is the primary if not the only area where we aren't at the same level with each other in our relationship. I guess I need to abandon myself to my own sensations a little more, and not worry so much about responding and making *him* feel good."

"Sex is a failure without orgasm, as far as I'm concerned. I think I could be able to have them with a partner if I could feel an equal with the man, if I could feel he really enjoyed doing good things to me—not just preparing me for *his* orgasm—if I could get rid of the feeling that I am solely responsible for his success and pleasure, for instance, like if I don't do everything right he won't get much out of it and I will have failed."

"The vast majority of men I have had sex with had little understanding of female orgasm and, worse, some of them think a woman who does not have orgasm through intercourse needs a psychiatrist."

But the point still must be: don't wait for the Right Man to be dependent on, but create your own good situation—which can include yourself as being the Princess Charming, who knows pleasurable things to do and who finds another person to do them with.

Of course, the thirty percent of women who said they *could* orgasm regularly during intercourse often bragged about it:

"Yes, I always orgasm during intercourse. I do not require a lot of play."

"I have a natural desire for sex, I do not need to be clitorally stimulated."

"Most men don't know the difference until they meet a *woman* who can show them what they have missed with the passive pussycats who hop into bed and fake it."

Like the competition among women fifty years ago as to who made the best pies, we're still competing for male approval and haven't yet come into our own.

We are quite frankly desperate, all too often, to have orgasms during intercourse, no matter what:

"When a woman says, 'I have clitoral orgasms from manual manipulation or cunnilingus, but I never have orgasms from stimulation by my husband's penis, and we're unhappy about it,' and she is told, 'There is only one kind of orgasm, the vaginal orgasm is a myth, so since you're having orgasms, you don't really have a problem, *you only think you do*,' I don't see how the woman's problem has been solved."

"I would like to experience a vaginal orgasm to know what it's like, it must be great! But I don't know why I don't. Neither does my gynecologist."

"I would like manual clitoral stimulation during intercourse, but feel shy about asking for it since I have a fear of making the man feel shut down about the effectiveness of his penis. Equally or more important, I have felt I ought to be able to do without it."

"I would love to hear from someone who is able to have a super orgasm during intercourse without any direct clitoral manipulation. I suppose it's possible. I wonder if I could 'learn how' the way I've 'learned how' the other way."

"There is an area on the roof of my vagina that actually provides a greater amount/level of arousal and stimulation than does my clitoris. This area can be stimulated by a finger but is best stimulated when I am on my stomach with my ass slightly raised and my male partner is lying on top of me, thrusting in and out in long hard strokes with his penis. This brings me right to the peak of orgasm in a much more intense way than clitoral stimulation *ever* can, but will not actually cause the orgasm. For me to orgasm, either I or my partner reaches underneath my belly and stimulates my clitoris, and I'll come almost immediately. This stimulation is definitely preferable to clitoral stimulation by either one of us, but I do need the clitoral stimulation to have an orgasm. If I had to choose, though, at this point I'd choose clitoral stimulation because I don't want my sex to be purely orgasmless arousal. But I think since I took two years just to have an orgasm when a guy stimulated my clitoris, I could definitely reach a point where this intense vaginal stimulation could bring me to an intense orgasm."

"I would like to have orgasm during intercourse *without* clitoral stimulation. The only way I can get orgasm during penile introduction is by pushing my clitoris to the penis with my fingers—which is very painful."

"Do you ever fake orgasms?"

The pressure on women to orgasm during intercourse is so great that an enormous number of women fake orgasms—some infrequently, most "sometimes," but some women said they do it every single time.

DO YOU FAKE ORGASMS?

Yes	567
No	775
Used to	318
"It's no use, it's not convincing"	4
	1664 total

"I used to fake orgasms all the time, and always with vaginal penetration. I came from the school of it's not right—you'll emasculate the man—if you don't let him think he's satisfied you. With the onset of the women's movement, and its personal effect on me, I've stopped faking them. My husband used to ask, 'Did you come?'—and when the answer was 'yes'—even if I was faking it—that was cool for him. Then when I started saying 'no' a couple of times, he quit asking. Now, if I complain I didn't come, he's either asleep, or says he's sorry and turns over and goes to sleep."

"I never fake orgasm. I am angry with other women who do, because then men can tell me that I am incapable sexually, because I do not have vaginal climaxes, and other women they have slept with do. Since I have never had a vaginal climax, I question their existence, or at least their general prevalence, and wonder if another woman's faking an orgasm has made it harder for me when I am honest."

"I fake it during clitoral stimulation and during intercourse when I'm not in the mood. It's easier and faster than saying 'no' and then worrying about my husband's ego and feelings for me, etc. He, like most other men, gets really frightened and hurt when I say no and I hear about it in passing a week later."

"I have, and occasionally still do fake orgasms during intercourse, but not often. When I do it now it's because I know I'm not going to have an orgasm but my man is really working hard for me and really wants to give me one and would be very disappointed to know it's no use. As we live together longer it becomes less necessary because our sex is better and we know each other better. In the past I would do it to protect the man's ego and occasionally (with one man) because he would be mad if I didn't have one. I hate faking it, though, and I really hated it with that one man, but he was a typical dominant egocentric chauvinistic horse's ass."

"During my marriage I was excellent at faking orgasms and so for maybe four years I never really had any satisfying sexual experiences. Unfortunately, I was totally faithful to my husband so I was pretty miserable physically. I masturbated a whole lot! After my separation I explored sex with a variety of partners and had a sexual awakening, so to speak."

"Yes, I used to, more to give a positive reinforcement for something I liked even though I didn't orgasm."

"I used to, when my husband had a complex about sex and a marriage counselor told me I should build up his ego."

"No, but I may act more excited than I really am."

"I used to, because my partner was comparing me to another woman he was sleeping with. He made me feel terrible with descriptions of how she went into a screaming orgasm before he even entered her."

"Yes, when I haven't had one for quite a while, I do it so my partner won't think he isn't pleasing me. I don't feel orgasms are all that important (he seems to) and I don't feel it's his fault if I don't come but . . . sometimes it is his fault, though, I guess."

"I was afraid to appear 'less of a woman' and emasculate my partner. So I did it, but he found me out."

"Sometimes it builds a man's ego to let him think he's successful. Therefore if I really like a man and want him to think I enjoyed sex more than I did, I do it."

"Only to get me or him 'off the hook.' "

"He thinks if I don't have an orgasm, he has failed me, even though I've explained that it isn't that way at all. Anyway, sometimes it just seems easier to do it. I used to sometimes when I thought he was anxious to have an orgasm, or getting bored, or impatient, or disappointed."

"I fake orgasms to save his pride and prevent arguments."

"Never. I consider it a denial of all that shared experience means."

"Sometimes I fake them, if he keeps pestering me with 'did you come yet?' "

"I used to, because men would enjoy watching me pant."

"Yes, a couple of times with a partner who thought he was fantastic in bed. He would have to penetrate me almost immediately to prove his prowess, and there was no way he would get off again unless he thought I'd had an orgasm."

"I used to, to avoid having men make a big fuss or act critical or pitying."

"I used to fake them in order not to leave the other person out on a lonely psychological limb."

"Yes, I always fake orgasms. It just seems polite. Why be rude?"

"I have promised myself—no more. I used to because my man expected me to have an orgasm; I thought I was unable to, and I thought faking it was the only way he would continue to want me."

"I used to, to please men and get their approval, and make them believe I was a sexy chick, etc., etc. I remember faking them on acid trips and even on my wedding night, etc. It was grizzly and at the time I was sure I was the *only* woman who did this."

"I used to fake orgasms until I started having them at age thirty. I faked them to avoid confrontation with a man, to avoid explaining why I was like I was, to avoid their trite responses of lesbianism, frigidity, etc."

"I did until we were married, because I thought getting married would do the trick. Ha!"

"I used to, but not since I learned the submissive implications of it and the fact that I had a real right to genuine pleasure."

"I fake them often. He and I have had such an abysmal sex relationship that I don't want to burden him with the knowledge that I don't come during intercourse."

"I *always* did. (I'm sixty-two now.) I was told to do it by male doctors to keep my husband happy (bless me). I was thinking there was something missing in my makeup for about thirty-five years—and that's a long time to imagine you had to fake it!"

"Yes, and especially I fake passion—sometimes to excite myself and sometimes to get the guy off my back and save myself."

"Yes, I used to think the male ego was more important than me."

"I have been faking orgasms for thirty years, because I need approval—I lack self-esteem—I'm ashamed as though I had a club foot or one eye—and because I don't want to hurt my husband, who is also insecure."

"I used to fake them to keep my husband from straying."

"Yes, to please men. It makes me feel a bit empty to do so."

"I used to fake orgasms because I felt it was my duty, and my own inability to orgasm during intercourse."

"Only with my first lover for the first few months—I knew how to pretend great passion and he thought he trained me. I just conformed to his male demands to gain other non-sex privileges of dates to good places. I was a free whore."

"I used to fake them all the time until we discovered my clitoris. I had always thought intercourse was the only right way and that it was my inadequacy—but once I found masturbation I was all set."

"No, I told him that I don't orgasm during intercourse."

"When I've felt insecure and negative about myself: Goddamn, any *normal* woman would have had an orgasm ten minutes ago. He must think I'm weird. This kind of feeling comes from the miserable social pressure for women to be what they're not—if you have brown hair, you *ought* to be blonde. If you have small breasts . . ."

"By omission. I don't say I didn't, and they assume I did."

"I used to, sometimes. When he wouldn't stop until I came, but I wanted him out—or I felt sorry for him—shit!"

"I used to fake orgasms on a regular basis because I was too shy and ashamed to tell the man what I wanted him to do and that it didn't turn me on just to be screwed."

"Fifty percent of the time—when you just aren't getting there, you know it, and you just want that blood ritual over."

"Several times I faked orgasms when I couldn't stand a heavy, hairy, rough body crushing me. Men outweigh women. Men are stronger. Men use penises as guns and straddle you as they please."

"I always fake them during intercourse. I know it would hurt the guy I live with if he knew otherwise, so I always tell him that it was great."

"Yes, usually I orgasm during foreplay and then fake it during intercourse. He would be concerned if he felt I wasn't orgasming during intercourse."

"I wouldn't know how."

"Rarely—only with an inexperienced guy who's going to lose a lot of self-esteem and is too mortified to talk about what's happening."

"Yes, it's easier and faster than struggling."

"For many years, I thought faking was a part of the game! Then I discovered how much healthier we both were with no fakery, much conversation, description, and exploration together."

"No, I don't owe anyone an orgasm but myself!"

"I used to when my husband's patience was running out."

"Four or five times a month—if we have built up to a certain point. I feel there's something wrong with me, so I fake it out of pride. It does make me feel strange, that after all the stimulation I still can't reach an orgasm. I have often thought that I'm trying too hard. I don't feel like less of a woman, but I do feel embarrassed that I have some kind of a mental block. I fake because I can't make him feel inadequate when it's *me* who's having a psychological problem."

"I don't know if my partner always knows when I have an orgasm. I always enjoy sex so it may be difficult for him to tell."

"I used to but I got tired of it and quit. I felt I had to do what he expected of me."

"I faked them when I was first married and wasn't really sure what I was supposed to feel. I thought for a long time that I was actually achieving it and that it was somewhat overrated."

"No. It's degrading. The most insulting thing that ever happened to me in bed was being accused of faking an orgasm. If a man can't give me pleasure, let *him* stew about it."

"When he asked if I came, I said yes. Sometimes he would even tell me how many times I came, and I didn't have the heart to tell him that I hadn't come at all."

"No, he doesn't care if I have one or not anyway."

"I always fake them—because I never have them."

"I have never consciously faked an orgasm. Sometimes, though, I start the moaning and other signals that indicate the onset of orgasm, and then my partner finishes too quickly for me to come, only he doesn't realize this—in this situtation I will allow my partner to keep his assumption that I've come because it makes him feel better and wouldn't do me any good to straighten him out. If he comes right out and says, 'Did you come?' then I refuse to lie; I'll say something like 'almost.' "

"A few times, to keep a man. Never again."

"I used to, when I wanted an orgasm so badly I'd even try to fool myself."

"Yes, during intercourse. If asked, I will tell the truth, but I have often tried to show more enthusiasm than I feel. I do it under pressure from my partner's disappointment because he couldn't stimulate me adequately."

"Yes. With women, rarely. If I'm too tired or she's getting tired and I don't want to make her feel inadequate. Sometimes no matter how skillful or thoughtful one's partner is, it's more trouble than it's worth to really have an orgasm, if one is tired or upset or distracted for some reason."

"I never have. I'm a very honest person. If my partner mistakenly thinks I did, I may not correct him, though."

"Frequently, yes. To get the social obligation over with for the night."

"Rarely. Only when I come close, then he orgasms and 'freezes up' right when I needed just a bit more."

"No, but I fake pleasure."

"Constantly, during intercourse, I faked them to please my husband. However, this week I had my limit and told him the truth, as gently as possible, and promised never to fake again."

"I always used to. I thought I should so he'd feel successful. Men never believed I could enjoy sex without an orgasm."

"Most men either take it for granted that you had one, or they don't care. So sometimes I do it to get it over with."

"Sometimes when I hate the partner and feel the state of my mind might lead him to violence."

"I never needed to fake—no man ever noticed I didn't come."

"Yes, during intercourse. I can fake vaginal contractions that feel like orgasms to my partner. I do it because not having an orgasm makes me a 'challenge' to him."

"No more! I think it's a testimony to male insensitivity that faking an orgasm fools them."

"With my last husband, I used to fake orgasms. I also faked love and other things for financial security."

"I used to. I just wanted to love; I wanted to please and I was desperate for affection."

"I used to and often cried after intercourse."

"No. But I never insisted on stopping in the middle when I wanted to, which was often."

"How do you do it? I would like to."

"Like asking if the sky is blue. Yes, during intercourse; I usually don't want men to know I *never* have them."

"Yes, often, during intercourse, when I felt my partner would be crushed otherwise. I also used to have the idea that I should be a hot tamale and always come."

"Not usually. Sometimes I kind of 'share his orgasm' even though I'm not having one myself and kind of grunt and groan along with him while he is having his."

"No, I'm afraid of being caught."

"I used to, through two marriages and two years of being 'kept.' The men who demand you do it, and the abundance of ignorance that accompanies this scene is ludicrous! No more."

"Yes, during intercourse I fake a number of times. I want him to have his orgasm so I can go to sleep. Often I have tried to communicate during intercourse what would excite me, but he is unresponsive and I just give up."

"Yes, if I like him, I don't want to put him down."

"Yes, for ten and a half years! I didn't want anyone to think I was frigid."

"No. But my husband is convinced that his other sex partners always reach orgasm. Are they faking? I feel inferior."

"I faked orgasms during intercourse with one man. And when I finally told him, he absolutely blocked any kind of sharing communication and mutual learning so that I might enjoy it also."

"Yes, I just go along with his orgasm and try for some vicarious emotional climax."

"If suddenly, in the middle of everything I realize I've made a mistake and I didn't even like him, I'll just squeeze hard around four or five times and moan like I'm coming, and that makes him come, and then it's over."

"Definitely—some men want to fuck me till I come or drop dead."

"Before I had orgasms I used to fake it to get the man to stop and let me sleep. With my first husband I didn't even know what I was faking. I thought maybe orgasms were just high levels of erotic feeling that gently subsided after reaching a nice sturdy peak of enjoyment. So I faked that. Now, no. Women still faking orgasms are holding all of us back, and betraying their men as well."

"I used to, the whole B movie scene, with groans and everything. However, now my groans distract me from what I feel."

"I used to in intercourse until I learned to say 'go slower' or 'my turn now.' "

"Yes, during intercourse, when a man is anxious to get it over with because he's satisfied."

"I used to, and then stopped, and found that men didn't seem to care!"

"Yes, if I particularly like a person but I feel they are vulnerable and will blame themselves if I don't come. After that I don't sleep with them again."

"Yes, with one man whom I loved, but who was a lousy lover in bed, I had to do it every time we made love! Can you believe that?"

"Always, unless I'm angry with my partner."

"Yes, when I cannot come and the poor fellow is exhausted and doing his best."

"Rarely. If the person would be made to feel very inadequate and hurt, I will fake an orgasm."

"I fake orgasms when I'm scared of disapproval."

"I faked them to hide my hurt because the other person had an orgasm."

"I felt I couldn't have my partner believe he was inadequate as he had suffered from impotence early in our relationship."

"Yes; as I said, I don't need sex as often as my husband but he gets upset if I don't have an orgasm, so to keep him happy I fake one. I tried playing it straight with him, once, but he got into a terrible thing trying to have it only when I wanted an orgasm, so I fake it. It's really the most satisfactory way. I do not feel put upon or abused—it's part of the TLC."

"I also realize now that many males who seem so concerned with whether you were satisfied or not are only interested in inflating their egos by hearing a 'yes' reply. I'm sure if I said 'no' they'd just be angry and wouldn't think of trying to do something about it."

"I should think it would be lousy to have a wife that came with a touch but never by your penis. I feel badly about this."

"I have faked orgasms until recently, even though I feel it is wrong to do so. I have faked orgasms many, many times. They just didn't have any idea of what to do with the clitoris and I hate to give an anatomy lecture in the middle of lovemaking."

"No, this is a big mistake, as the man will never learn."

"I have faked it without exception, because I felt men, without exception, need to feel that they are good in bed, usually to feel that *they* are the best in bed."

"I said 'no' to my husband for some time after my second pregnancy, but after a while I began to feel quite guilty about that and so I compromised and faked a response that I did not feel. The trouble with that was that having faked once, I was committed to faking again and again. The end result of such sexual dishonesty was that eventually I was really quite unable to feel any sexual arousal and I became frigid. Sometimes after sex with my husband I found I was so in pain that I had to go into the bathroom and satisfy myself. The interesting thing about this period is that I had never insisted on or even cared about fidelity from my husband and I thought then, and do now, that satisfying himself with someone else, someone more eager than I, would have been much better than turning this very real problem into a contest of who loves who how much. But, being presented with the problem in those terms, I had no choice but to fake what I did not feel. Well, orgasm is all too easy to fake and I doubt that any man can tell the difference between real and simulated orgasm."

"For fifteen years I was the world's best faker. Honestly—they should have a phallic trophy—mounted on a pedestal (like in the art history books) for *all women*—I think they all fake it with men."

CONCLUSION

Insisting that women should have orgasms during intercourse, from intercourse, is to force women to adapt their bodies to inadequate stimulation, and the difficulty of doing this and the frequent failure that is built into the attempt breeds recurring feelings of insecurity and anger. As Ann Koedt* put it, in *The Myth of the Vaginal Orgasm*:

> Perhaps one of the most infuriating and damaging results of this whole charade has been that women who were perfectly healthy sexually were taught that they were not. So in addition to being sexually deprived, these women were told to blame themselves when they deserved no blame. Looking for a cure to a problem that has none can lead a woman on an endless path of self-hatred and insecurity. For she is told by her analyst that not even in her one role allowed in a male society—the role of a woman—is she successful. She is put on the defensive, with phony data as evidence that she better try to be even more feminine, think more feminine, and reject her envy of men. That is: Shuffle even harder, baby.[15]

Finally, there are two myths about female sexuality that should be specifically cleared up here.

First, supposedly women are less interested in sex and orgasms than men, and more interested in "feelings," less apt to initiate sex, and generally have to be "talked into it." But the reason for this, when it is true, is obvious: women often don't expect to, can't be sure to, have orgasms:

"I suspect that my tendency to lose interest in sex is related to my having suppressed the desire for orgasms, when it became clear it wasn't that easy and would 'ruin' the whole thing for him."

"I want orgasm to make myself feel content and fulfilled—but also it's very important to have them with

---

* Ti-Grace Atkinson has also written about this in *Amazon Odyssey* (Links Books), 1974.

my boyfriend—because the more I have, the better he feels and if I don't have any—then it's my fault, and my boyfriend doesn't want to have intercourse very much if I am frigid. He figures I'm uptight about something and ignores me. I went through one period of being frigid— it was after I moved in with my boyfriend—and he suddenly got 'too tired' most nights, and sex went down to twice a week. I developed a guilt complex that I was oversexed and asking too much from him, especially when I held back and never came. I felt horrible and selfish. But I was still horny and very frustrated every night. To avoid frustration I would think myself into a state of frigidity. This curbed the 'hornies,' but then, when my boyfriend *wanted* to have sex, I found it harder and harder to defrost myself in time. He would work hard to get me aroused, and often spend a lot of time before I would begin to thaw out and start allowing the feeling. By then, he wouldn't be able to hold out any longer and he'd come. Then, I'd be *left* 'warmed up,' horny and frustrated. He'd go to sleep, I'd feel bitterness and hatred and guilt, and finally I would put myself back into the deep freeze. I would never try to communicate my problem to my boyfriend because I felt it was my fault and that it would be selfish and unfair for me to 'force' him to have more intercourse unless *he* felt like it. I was pissed off."

"I am fifty-six years old, a housewife, morally straight Presbyterian, Mother proper and believed in duty first, fun second. Fit myself into the role of 'Good Christian Woman' and I *am*! I have sexual activity about twice a month with my husband, who usually initiates it. I think about it more often than I act on it. I need to find some method to turn me on more often—I guess laziness keeps me from pursuing it—it's easier to just go to sleep or read a good book. Our biggest problem is timing—he's ready for early morning sex and I like it in the evening or is this a cop out??? He adores it when I do initiate it—I wonder why I don't do it more often? I wonder what it feels like to ejaculate? Guess I'll never know. I like to think I please him even though I don't have an orgasm during intercourse. It's pleasing to receive that certain look—wow!"

"This is my first sexual relationship. I am eighteen—almost nineteen. I must say that I had expected much more. (Probably my conditioning.) Maybe I am too young to feel anything, really (as a doctor told me) but I really do wish I would. I get very frustrated when I don't have an orgasm or feel satisfied. In fact, at one point in this relationship I was so frustrated that I lost interest. Right now I still don't feel any great need for it usually, and I wish I knew some way of getting satisfied and really liking sex. I'm really not quite sure what an orgasm is or what it is really supposed to feel like. When masturbating, I get a satisfied feeling, so I assume that is it. When I am having sex, I don't really feel anything. Sometimes I feel him in me but not usually. This I don't understand. I really thought that I would be able to feel his penis in me but I usually don't. Yes I have felt very frustrated."

The other myth involves the mystique of female orgasm, and specifically the idea that women take longer to orgasm than men, mainly because we are more "psychologically delicate" than men, and our orgasm is more dependent on feelings. In fact, *women do not take longer to orgasm than men*. The majority of the women in Kinsey's study masturbated to orgasm within four minutes, similar to the women in this study. It is, obviously, only during inadequate or secondary, insufficient stimulation like intercourse that we take "longer" and need prolonged "foreplay." But this misconception has led to a kind of mystique about female orgasm:

"I believe that a woman needs much more than a man—it's a more complex totality of physical and emotional stimulation for her to have an orgasm."

"Women have orgasm when the spirit moves them. They don't just have or seek functional orgasms that you can always predict."

"All most men need is the up and down friction on the penis. I believe that a woman needs much more. It is a much more subtle combination of physical and emotional feelings."

But female orgasm is *not* particularly mysterious. There is no great mystery about why a woman has an orgasm. It happens with the right stimulation, quickly, pleasurably, and reliably. As we saw in the first chapter, women don't need "foreplay" in masturbation to orgasm. The whole key is adequate stimulation. In the next section, we shall see how some women get this in intercourse.

HOW DO WOMEN ORGASM DURING INTERCOURSE?

"Penetration is one of the nicest feelings I know, mentally and physically. It practically always leads to an orgasm and takes from twenty to forty minutes. My lover is capable of two and sometimes three orgasms so we are not really slow but we do luxuriate in our lovemaking. I like to feel him inside of me and to hear him moan and sigh and feel him pulsating. Mentally I enjoy the secure feeling I have when he is in me and I like for him to stay inside as long as possible. Sometimes we go to sleep this way."

Another woman wrote after reading *Sexual Honesty* to ask if she was "weird" because she *did* have orgasms rather easily during intercourse. There is certainly no reason for this reverse stereotyping. Some women *do* orgasm during intercourse, but the causes aren't mysterious; it results from very concrete kind of physical stimulation, which we shall try to describe here.

MASTERS AND JOHNSON: A RUBE GOLDBERG MODEL?

Before we describe the methods women in this study used to orgasm during intercourse, it remains to mention how Masters and Johnson have explained the way in which orgasm during intercourse occurs.

Stressing that all women's orgasms are caused by stimulation of the clitoris, whether direct or indirect, they have explained that orgasm during intercourse comes from the indirect clitoral stimulation caused by thrusting: as the penis moves back and forth, it pulls the labia minora, which are attached to the skin covering the clitoris (the hood), back and forth with it, so indirectly moving the skin around over the clitoral glands. In Masters and Johnson's own words:

> A mechanical traction develops on both sides of the clitoral hood of the minor labia subsequent to penile distension of the vaginal outlet. With active penile thrusting, the clitoral body is pulled downward toward the pudendum by traction exerted on the wings of the clitoral hood. . . .
> When the penile shaft is in the withdrawal phase of active coital stroking, traction on the clitoral hood is somewhat relieved and the body and glans return to the normal pudendal-overhang positioning. . . the rhythmic movement of the clitoral body in conjunction with active penile stroking produces significant indirect or secondary clitoral stimulation.
> It should be emphasized that this same type of secondary clitoral stimulation occurs in every coital position when there is a full penetration of the vaginal barrel by the erect penis.[16]

In other words, the clitoris is surrounded by skin known as the "clitoral hood" that is connected, in turn, to the labia minora. Supposedly, during intercourse the thrusting penis (notice the assumption of female passivity) exerts rhythmic mechanical traction on the swollen labia minora, and so provides stimulation for the clitoris via movements of the clitoral hood. Sherfey has termed this the "preputial-glandar mechanism" wherein "the thrusting movement of the penis in the vagina pulls on the labia minora which, via their extension around the clitoris (the clitoral hood or prepuce) is then pulled back and forth over the erect clitoris."[17] That is, the final stimulation is provided to the clitoris by friction against its own hood.

The development of this theory was a great advance in that it no longer said friction against the walls of the vagina had anything to do with stimulating female orgasm. However, the existence of this model, and its publicity, has left women with the impression that orgasm during intercourse is still to be expected as part of the automatic "normal" course of things.

Masters and Johnson developed this model of how women's sexuality works by observing the women they had selected for study, all of whom were chosen only if they were able to have orgasms during intercourse. It would seem that to analyze what is probably an unusual group of women, and then to generalize from these women, is a mistake. Indeed, it is only possible if you assume that to orgasm during intercourse is somehow "normal," and not "dysfunctional." (Masters and Johnson have labeled the "inability" to orgasm during intercourse "coital orgasmic inadequacy"; "primary sexual dysfunction" is never having an orgasm in any way.)

Besides the fallacy of generalizing from a special population about just that very thing which makes them special, there is a second problem with this model. That is, there can only be traction between the penis and vagina when the woman is already at a certain stage of arousal, because only then do the labia swell up enough to cause traction (the stage Masters and Johnson call late plateau arousal). In other words, the penis can only pull the labia back and forth with it if the woman is at the last stage of arousal before orgasm so that there is sufficient engorgement of the area to cause a tight fit between penis and vaginal opening. (You can check how well this mechanism works for you, by the way, by placing a dildo or similarly sized inanimate object in your vagina when you reach this state of arousal, and then moving it in and out and seeing what you feel.)

Masters and Johnson have not explained how they arrived at the conclusion that this mechanism is the means of orgasm during intercourse of the women they studied. It does seem clear that this mechanism is indeed the means by which most women orgasm during clitoral stimulation or masturbation, in that during masturbation the skin of the clitoral area, or the upper lips, are pulled around or moved around slightly, thus causing the skin to move back and forth over the clitoral glans. As Sherfey puts it, "Mons area friction will have exactly the same effect on the prepuce-glans action as the penile thrusting motion: *the prepuce is rhythmically pulled back and forth over the glans.*"[18]

It seems that the thrusting activates this mechanism for very few women, however. Most researchers and sex therapists agree that thrusting is less efficient in causing female orgasm than clitoral area stimulation. Pulling your ear slightly back and forth can also pull the skin on your cheek. Just so, it is possible for thrusting to pull the skin near your clitoris in just the right way to stimulate you to orgasm, and it may happen regularly for a small percentage of women—but not for most women most of the time.

This brings to mind the fact that Masters and Johnson have insisted on treating women, but not men, with their *usual* sexual partners, whom they must bring with them. (Men were allowed surrogates.) This is usually understood to imply adherence to a moral double standard, but the reason for this rule may in fact have been that, for a woman to orgasm during intercourse, she must adapt her body to inadequate stimulation, and so it is essential that she work out this procedure with a regular partner.

More recently, in lectures and private therapy, Masters and Johnson have emphasized the specific techniques women can use to orgasm during intercourse, such as being on top of the man, doing most of the moving, and etc. Perhaps they have too found that the "preputial-glandar mechanism" does not work for most women. However, if this is indeed the case, the message has not reached the general public. The woman-in-the-street (most of us) still has the impression that it is "normal" to orgasm from male thrusting.

There is nothing wrong with saying that the movement of the clitoral hood over the clitoris is what is responsible for orgasm; this is true. What *is* wrong is to say that thrusting in itself will activate this mechanism in most women. As Alex Shulman has pointedly remarked:

Masters and Johnson observe that the clitoris is automatically "stimulated" in intercourse since the hood covering the clitoris is pulled over the clitoris with each thrust of the penis in the vagina—much, I suppose, as a penis is automatically "stimulated" by a man's underwear whenever he takes a step.[19]

But let's apply this same logic to men with more scientific precision: As Dr. Sanford Copley put it, when interviewed on the television show "Woman," this indirect stimulation of women could be compared to the stimulation that would be produced in a man by the rubbing of the scrotal skin (balls), perhaps pulling it back and forth, and so causing the skin of the upper tip of the penis to move, or quiver, and in this way achieving "stimulation." Would it work? Admittedly, this form of stimulation would probably require a good deal more foreplay for the man to have an orgasm! You would have to be patient and "understand" if it did not lead to orgasm "every time."

Masters and Johnson's theory that the thrusting penis pulls the woman's labia, which in turn pull the clitoral hood, which thereby causes friction of the clitoral glans and thereby causes orgasm sounds more like a Rube Goldberg scheme than a reliable way to orgasm.*

It is not that the mechanism doesn't work. It does: if you pull any skin around the area it can stimulate the clitoris. But the question is, does thrusting do this effectively? The answer would seem to be that, for most women, without some special effort or some special set of circumstances, it does not.

Perhaps, finally, it is important to point out that, if this mechanism works so well, why hasn't it been working all along, for centuries? Why is "coital frigidity" the well-known "problem" that it is? And why don't women masturbate this way sometimes? No, having an orgasm during intercourse is an adaptation of our bodies. Intercourse was never meant to stimulate women to orgasm.

* This analogy may have first been made by Dr. Pauline Bart.

WOMEN WHO ORGASM DURING INTERCOURSE: HOW THEY DO IT

Orgasms during intercourse in this study usually seemed to result from a conscious attempt by the woman to center some kind of clitoral area contact for herself during intercourse, usually involving contact with the man's pubic area. This clitoral stimulation during intercourse could be thought of, then, as basically stimulating yourself while intercourse is in progress. Of course the other person must cooperate. This is essentially the way men get stimulation during intercourse: they rub their penises against our vaginal walls so that the same area they stimulate during masturbation is being stimulated during intercourse. In other words, *you* have to get the stimulation centered where it feels good.

Answers seemed to define about six basic ways of having orgasm during intercourse, descriptions of which follow.

1. The position of woman on top.

There isn't anything that *automatically* makes this position work—it is the freedom of movement it gives the woman to seek her own satisfaction, which in large part explains why it is so effective for so many women, and especially women of masturbation type III (thrusting into a pillow). Also it can allow you to have your legs together, or to adjust the amount of penetration to hit your pubic area against his pubic bone in a good way for you. And this position is the one seen in the earliest Stone Age drawings, as well as on the wall murals at Pompeii.

"A very exciting feeling is for me to rub myself up and down while sitting on the man's pelvis, with his penis inside. Then I have the right stimulation for me physically, plus the psychological stimulation of his excitement."

"How I orgasm involves being on top and moving

back and forth so my clitoris rubs against the base of the penis without the penis moving in and out of the vagina."

"I have an orgasm during intercourse when I assume the 'dominant' position, and rub my clitoris against his belly and pubic area."

"He sits or half reclines, I above him, with his penis in my vagina at just the right angle and to get pressure on my clitoris from his pubic bone. At the same time he plays with my nipples while I move my pelvis whatever way feels good."

"My ideal position would be in the female above position with a slow but complete penetration in a rather rhythmic rocking motion, with my legs together, and breasts being fondled. But with prolonged 'straight' (missionary position) intercourse, my interest lags."

"I like to be on top, because I can better control the amount of friction in the right places. My legs are usually apart and there has to be a lot of the 'right kind' of movement."

"I prefer lying down, stomach to stomach, with me on top. This gives me more freedom in setting the pace, and much more clitoral stimulation from our intercourse."

"When I am 'on top' my chances of orgasm are improved because I can look for my orgasm and my partner waits till I make mine before he makes his."

"On top I prefer the man not to move at all but they simply don't pay attention and move anyhow."

"I do it by sitting on top of him after he comes and rubbing up and down. Sometimes he comes again when I do this."

"I had my most satisfying orgasm on top of a man who was lying exhausted and still, after *his* orgasm. I rubbed myself (my clitoris) against him and had a very easy total orgasm."

"On top, I could have orgasms during intercourse, but I've always felt that essentially I'd be masturbating—i.e., being on top, rubbing my clitoris against the man's pubic hair or something. This prevents penis–vaginal movement (thrusting in and out) and thus has always hung me up—made me feel selfish or infantile (thanks to Freud, I guess) or something. So I don't *seek* orgasms during intercourse. The vaginal trip feels good in itself."

"We have intercourse with me on top. I create my own rhythm through up and down back and forth movements until I achieve orgasm or until I know the capacity has passed."

"In heterosexual intercourse, after being generally aroused, I reach a climax by getting on top, in the female superior position, and moving my pelvic area around in a sometimes up and down, sometimes circular, motion. It usually takes less than a minute if I'm really turned on."

The woman on her stomach.

A position that can work for many women, especially those who masturbate by type III, is lying face down on the bed, with the man entering from the rear, since this enables the woman to rub against the bed or sheets in her accustomed manner, with the added pleasure, perhaps, of the other person's body on top of her.

2. Grinding pubic/mons areas together.

Very similar to the position of woman on top is the grinding friction method, although it can be done in any position. Grinding involves complete penetration, with little or no thrusting, one person moving around and around so that the two genital areas are rubbing together and massaging each other, especially the female lips and vulva, or the mons area.

"My orgasms during intercourse are usually triggered by a thick penis buried deep for me to grind slowly on."

"We lie side by side with legs entwined, so that one of his legs is between my two legs, which makes one of my legs between his legs, with the penis inserted, which causes my clitoris to be riding on his front muscle or pubic bone. Then wriggling around."

"Very close body contact. I enjoy it when the penis is completely inserted and when we sort of rub together more than making bouncing motions."

"I prefer the top position and/or grinding together, face to face. The problem here is that both positions he finds uncomfortable and appears to accommodate me resentfully and passively. Naturally this affects my state of mind negatively so I rarely insist upon these two positions."

"I lie on the bottom with my legs around him, then grind my pelvis and pubic area against his."

"I can orgasm by pressing and rubbing my pubic area, which is spongy and very sensitive, against him, with the penis inside but not going in and out."

"I press my clitoris rather hard against my man and move my pelvis back and forth or in circles. Sometimes he keeps moving when I do this, and sometimes he stops. I can either lie on my back with my legs up on his shoulders, or with them around his hips. Sometimes I sit on top and he lies underneath, or sometimes we both sit up and face each other. Sometimes I tighten my vaginal muscles and hip muscles to speed up the orgasm."

"We use the missionary position with the man's body (the part directly above his genital area) pressed against my clitoral area. Until the orgasm is reached, it is necessary for him to remain in contact with my clitoral area, rubbing and pressing, and he should not prop himself up on his elbows until after I come."

"Most men move too much for me. I like him to penetrate deeply, press to the front and then remain still for a while but few men seem able or willing to do this. At orgasm, I want the man to be very hard, in very deep and remaining still. It always diminishes the intensity of my orgasm if the man is moving fast as I orgasm. And most men, sensing I am coming, immediately rush their own orgasm and this often spoils mine."

"There is a particular rhythm I find most helpful. It is that when the man pushes in, he stays pressed against me for a few seconds, instead of backing up right away. Also that he does not back away as soon as I press against him, which some men have a tendency to do."

3. Touching of pubic bones together during intercourse.

Getting clitoral stimulation by the man's pubic bone hitting against the woman's with each thrust was another method used by some women. In most of the examples, the man was doing the moving. Positions included the man on top, or one or both sitting up; the women's leg positions included everything from together to apart to up or bent up and back. The thrusting makes it hard to keep the stimulation on just the right spot, so it is important to have freedom of movement for yourself.

"I prefer having the man on top, but I move a lot because I am finicky about the timing and thrusting that's going on. It requires a lot of squirming around to get certain places that are pleasurable. Also, if I keep my legs together, my grasp regulates the pressure as I like it."

"Usually I receive clitoral stimulation by pressing my mons area against the pubic area of my partner in a rhythmic fashion. It is difficult for me to come in a standing or rear entry position, because the vital pubic bone to pubic bone pressure is missing. When he is on the top, I usually grab my partner's buttocks with my hands and guide him in his movements, if he isn't already doing what I want."

"We have intercourse with him on top, bodies arched slightly so that my clitoral area is exposed and receiving stimulation by the natural thrusts of our bodies together."

"During intercourse, I am on the bottom. I am scooted down so that the penis is more at a right angle to his body. The energy required to resist his weight, and to move my hips seems to concentrate in the clitoral area of my pelvis. At this point, I lift my feet to concentrate the energy even more."

"There is one position with me underneath with my legs up over my partner's shoulders that I can come in with no arousal. It blows my mind."

"I like not too deep penetration, long and smooth

strokes, my legs straight out or close together, and pubic areas rubbing together."

"I use slow and gentle movements trying to touch my clitoral area to his pubic area, then faster."

"To have orgasms during intercourse, I had to learn to make use of my vaginal–perineal muscles, and I had to learn to position myself and move my body in such a way as to maximize the pressure I received on the mons area. I also learned to give my partners the feedback they needed to know what I needed; usually this communication is nonverbal but occasionally verbal when I have difficulty getting the point across. I had to adjust to a lesser intensity of stimulation to obtain orgasm during intercourse. I had masturbated for several years before I fucked, and was used to intense, direct stimulation right on and around the clitoris. Of course, the movements of the penis in the vagina do not provide this intensity. I had to learn how to focus on the vaginal sensations, the more subtle 'pressure' sensations on the clitoris, and the deeper sensations."

"We have intercourse with me on the bottom. My husband inserts his penis and moves his pelvis, and I move my pelvis so my clitoris moves against his pelvic bone."

"During intercourse, if he is very active and regular, not altering the rhythm or pressure, and if I actively pursue the feeling, sometimes I have orgasms. It also depends on the partner and his particular body aligning with my particular body."

"I think that this is a matter of anatomy as well as psychology—i.e., with one man in particular our bodies fit together in such a way that the in and out motions of his penis did stimulate my clitoris to orgasm. But usually this doesn't happen."

"I think the positioning of a couple's genitals (due to their respective sizes) has a lot to do with stimulation. One of my partners fit me perfectly."

"I need the rhythmic movements of two bodies together, which doesn't have to be interrupted due to the man's 'almost' ejaculating every minute or so. If I can feel the penis at a steady timing going in and out of the vagina, I can get the feeling centered for myself, and begin my own steady climb to orgasm."

"My most recent steady boyfriend is the best lover I've ever had (i.e., I respond best), and I think it is because he fucks me rhythmically and continuously for long periods (e.g., half an hour to an hour). This steady rhythmical uninterrupted thrusting by him is over-all very soothing, and enables that degree of relaxation necessary for the delicate quivering response of the vaginal walls to begin."

"His penetrations/thrusts are very smooth and continuous and unhurried for a long time, *then* whenever I begin to react a little, he quickens his thrusts, penetrates more strongly and excitingly and thereby heightens the response from what it started as. The excitement builds like this, then he returns to steady quiet soothing movements, then again I begin to respond delicately, etc., etc., etc. It is the first time I really enjoyed sex *enormously* and it's all vaginal."

However, not everyone can orgasm in these ways, so don't expect too much of yourself: position, whether you are on top, or grinding your pubic bones together, or whatever, does not work for many, many (most?) women. It is always an individual adaptation for each woman. If it doesn't work for you, don't be surprised; as one woman commented, "I haven't found a position yet that works. And I've tried everything."

Position is a very tricky way of having orgasm, as are the other indirect ways yet to be discussed. They require your partner's full cooperation or, at least, some cooperation. And even then you may find that the same way doesn't always work regularly, or with a new partner—because his body is shaped differently, or his sense of rhythm may be different,* and this type of

---

* "For the past twenty years or so, I have not had orgasms during intercourse, although I once did, over a period of nearly five years, with my first husband. I have literally racked my brain for the intervening twenty years to try to figure out *why* with that one man, during intercourse, and never since (and never before), I was able to have orgasms."

touch-and-go indirect stimulation requires that everything be perfectly meshed. That is why many women said that the best sex came after practice with one individual. As one woman put it, "With each new partner, I have to relearn to have orgasms with them."

Perhaps it is important to mention here that the emphasis on the mechanical and technical aspects of intercourse in this section is not meant to minimize the importance of the individual feelings and emotions experienced during intercourse. Actually, as will become apparent in other chapters, the emotional context is the primary value of intercourse for most women. However, the point here is to dissect and analyze the various parts of our *physical* sexual experience, disassembled from the whole, so that we can become not only "emotional experts" but also knowledgeable "physical experts."

Preferred type of movement during "pubic bones together" stimulation, when the man is doing most of the moving.

"Slow, tender, sensitive, firm."

"Not a battering ram, not rammed to the floor."

"Soft then harder. (Most men do 'harder' too hard. If a man could use his penis like his hand, it might be more fun.)"

"A definite rhythm I can count on for some time."

"Hard, slow shoves, with a grind when penetration is complete."

"Gentle entry, then slow, full-length strokes of the penis in and out, getting faster. I've found that when the movement is generally rhythmical, I can relax and have an orgasm easier because I don't have to concentrate on what is coming next."

"I dislike being roughly ridden and prefer a more slithery approach."

"Slow, prolonged gentle lovemaking and not a demonstration of semen-power and muscle thrusts."

"Tender and passionate."

"Gentle. I do not like being raped, if you know what I mean."

The only persons who liked rough treatment were generally those who didn't have orgasms during intercourse. One woman wrote, "I like rough treatment. Why? I often think of it as massive frustration—like, I don't care what you do to me, just do it and do it soon, because I want to come in the most desperate way, and what you're doing now just isn't going to get me there."

Preferred type of movement during "grinding" stimulation.

"Soft but deep—almost no thrusting, sort of just lying together in a *deep* penetration."
"Deep 'hugging positions.' "

It should also be kept in mind that women require continuous stimulation to orgasm, as opposed to the discontinuous stimulation adequate for men. This is one of the few *basic* differences in female and male sexual physiology. As Sherfey explains it:

> A universal feature of the response cycle in women is the necessity for continuous stimulation. If stimulation is stopped even in the middle of the orgasm, the orgasm stops. This is true with clitoral area and vaginally induced orgasms.[20]

To depend on thrusting to bring your pubic bones together is risky since a *very* steady, dependable rhythm must be maintained, at the very least. Since this rhythm is more important to the woman than the man, because she needs continuous stimulation, perhaps she should be the one in control of the thrusting.

Leg position/body position.

Remember too that the kind of intercourse that may work for you may very well depend on the leg position you require and the general orgasm type (masturbation type) you are. If you have to have your legs together, or knees bent, or if you have to be on your stomach, this will influence the positions you find most appealing during intercourse. In general it is important to have enough freedom of movement so that whatever body movement and especially leg movement you may need to orgasm is not blocked.

4. Partial holding of the penis in the vagina, without moving in and out.

This is a kind of positioning wherein the head of the penis is just inside the vaginal lips, with the base of the penis pulled up toward the clitoris, sort of draped around the vulva, as it were. This can be a hard position to maintain.

"The only partner with whom I had orgasm during intercourse was Mickey and it was because his pubic bone was constructed so it pressed down on me during intercourse. I felt exactly like I was masturbating. Also, with Mickey, my legs were together. This way, his penis couldn't enter me very deeply and so it was sort of draped up over/bent around from my vagina to my clitoris—i.e., the base of his penis wound up being against my upper vulva. It was great. I was younger then, and I got off on the idea that I was finally coming through intercourse! (like a grown-up). It kept us together for the longest time, even after we really had nothing much more in common."

"During intercourse, I actually position the male so his penis touches my clitoris. This is probably the reason I prefer the missionary position and avoid overweight males. Slender males are best for this. Besides, you can really move under them if you need to."

"I like to have my clitoris against the base of his penis, then I want my partner to move in concert with me, gently, slightly, but in the same rhythm. When the partner breaks through my rhythm, it disrupts my progress toward orgasm. The only exception is when we have not been together for a period of time. The first intercourse following separation for a long time is a joyous spontaneous explosive experience."

"Best is him going in and out, slowly rubbing the base of his penis over my clitoris. I know it sounds like it's impossible, but the penis ends up hitting the opposite wall of the vagina toward the back."

However, the irony is that what feels good for the woman often doesn't for the man:

"No man I've met will agree to partial penetration."

"Unfortunately sex for me is like a fight. I put the penis where I want it; I say 'it feels good there.' He shoves it deep inside and says, 'No, *that's* where it feels good.' This may sound far-fetched, but it's true; God, I wish it weren't. I usually lose the fight."

5. Frequent re-entry of the penis into the vagina.

There is also a type of intercourse with even *less* penetration than partial. It involves just basically moving the penis around the outer lips, or coming completely out with every stroke, so that the entranceway or lips are constantly being pulled and stimulated.

"I appreciate fairly slow, deep rhythmic thrusts, nearly leaving the vagina as he prepares for the next thrust. Too many men give short thrusts mostly inside their own skins, which result in too little friction on the vaginal opening. I also like the poking of the vaginal entry with the penis head for a bit before intercourse starts."

"What feels good is any pulling or stretching at the vaginal opening. Coming all the way in, then out again, etc."

"With one lover, an older experienced man who was not able to get an erection, I found the soft penis at the mouth of my vagina very exciting. I was able to have 'vaginal' orgasm with him. My only one."

"I need a rotating, building process around the lips with some clitoral stimulation and a final, deep penetration."

"I like my hips elevated, with considerable withdrawal and re-entry of the penis—actually requiring more time that most men can allow for."

"I orgasm when I feel the head of his penis enter and move slowly in and out, but not entering more than just the head itself, moving around the vaginal lips."

"Well, it takes a lot of kissing and hugging, possibly some oral stimulation, then me on top with only very limited penetration, and much withdrawing, bumping, and nuzzling, then when I'm coming, deeper penetration but still not too far in—until I'm coming. Also sometimes he puts his hands around my buttocks and his fingers between my labia minora and majora, which is nice."

Orgasm on entry of the penis.

In this way of having orgasm during intercourse, the orgasm is actually in progress as entry occurs, and therefore it is not listed in the statistical tables. Since it depends on the woman being already in the throes of orgasm when entry takes place, usually the woman must tell the man when the time is right. Once again, as in many of these methods, orgasm during intercourse is more of a victory by virtue of a "technicality" than by anything having purely to do with the presence of the penis in the vagina. However, if this provides a feeling of satisfaction, there is no reason not to do it.

"I usually have an orgasm when I have been stimulated prior to penetration . . . and then the nature of the penetration is the critical finishing touch."

"I have orgasms by kissing, sucking on my breasts, then his fingers stimulating my clitoris, the penetration of fingers into my vagina, the penis touching my clitoris, and then one hard thrust and the penis kept there."

"Sometimes, if my clitoris is stimulated enough, and his penis is inserted very fast and hard at the right time, and kept still, it is easy for me to have an orgasm."

"I like vaginal penetration only when I'm ready for it but I usually get it when I'm not ready so it usually doesn't lead to orgasm. A really important thing is letting him know I'm definitely *not* ready for intercourse, even if he is."

Trying to penetrate just at the moment of orgasm can actually ruin or make orgasm impossible for many other women. In the first place, if the focus of sensation is suddenly drastically changed, just at the most critical moment, it can stop the orgasm. And second, as we have seen in the chapter on orgasm, many women do not feel the pleasure of orgasm as well during penetration:

"Last night, for example, he was giving me manual clitoral stimulation, and then just before I orgasmed, he penetrated and it just ruined the whole thing. All of a sudden, he took his hand away—I mean, you should have seen the look on my face, I was shocked! and then he dived in. I was to the point where I was rigid and shaking a little with the orgasm but when he put it in, it just stopped it and the more he just kept on going in and out, in and out, the more it just started fading away."

"I mean, I can have orgasm on penetration after a lot of clitoral stimulation, but I have to really press against the guy and even then it is really hard and usually one of those orgasms that never really makes it and just kind of fades away."

6. Extended "be-fore play": Clitoral stimulation or other stimulation to pre-orgasm, then followed by entry or joining.

Another method, very similar to the preceding one, is extended "foreplay," which is recommended by many sex therapists, and seems to be very traditional if one remembers all the clichés about women needing longer "foreplay" than men.

The difference between #5 as a type and this one is that here orgasm does not occur at the moment of joining, but rather, usually shortly thereafter, and orgasm is considered to continue to be "worked up to" during actual intercourse via one of the means mentioned earlier.

The term "foreplay" is a very strange one. *What is "foreplay"*? "For me to have an orgasm, intercourse must be preceded by foreplay. But I don't like that word because it makes it sound more subordinate than it is." Well, it is common knowledge that "foreplay" is all of the body stimulation prior to, "before," intercourse. There is no "before-play" to speak of in masturbation for most women. Why is "foreplay" necessary before intercourse*? Obviously because there is so little real stimulation for women involved in intercourse. The term "be-fore" has been retained here because its meaning is so clear, but in general it is important to emphasize that there is no reason why "be-foreplay" must come "be-fore" anything.

The question of what else these activities could be called is interesting. The lack of an appropriate word for them in our language reflects the way our culture has rigidly defined the ways in which we touch each other: only activities surrounding intercourse have been considered legitimate. Thus "clitoral stimulation" and general touching is referred to only as "foreplay," which everyone "knows" precedes intercourse, and which everyone also "knows" will end in male ejaculation. In short, all our terms are geared to a linear progression: "foreplay" is to be followed by "penetration" of the penis into the vagina, and then intercourse (thrusting in and out), followed by male orgasm, and then "rest." If one does not accept this pattern as being what "sex" is, one is left with almost no vocabulary to describe what *could* be alternatives. Of course the *possibility* does exist for many different patterns of sexuality, and many different kinds of physical contact between people that are sensual/sexual, and that do not necessarily have orgasm (or anything else) as their goal, as we will discuss in the chapter on older women.

In any case some women did have orgasm during intercourse through the use of extensive "be-fore play":

"My best sex has always been when foreplay and sexual stimulation (without actual penis insertion) was carried out and engaged in for long periods of time before actual intercourse. Having my partner tease me and cause me to have orgasms time and time again during the afternoon and evening and finally leading up to intercourse late in the evening. Excitement runs so high that when you finally do have intercourse it is a terrific

---

* Of course this is not to imply that people would not enjoy caressing each other simply for its own sake.

experience. This is so much better than getting all prepared for it and then it is over so quickly with little
anticipation."

"I like: a romantic mood, being undressed, stroking
my entire body, putting pressure to my pelvic area with
hands and fingers, his nude body held tightly to mine,
talking to me about our bodies and feelings while I
watch in the mirror, then oral stimulation, soft, wet
kisses, rectal stimulation while having my vagina stimulated with fingers, biting all over, blowing in my ear,
then finally penis penetration and intercourse with close
contact of our pelvic areas."

"I think the feeling that allows me the most pleasure
is of unhurried, unpressured, undisturbed time for lovemaking. I like my whole body to be stimulated with another's whole body—our bodies touching at as many
points as possible. I like to be caressed with hands and
arms and fingers and held tight. Then I like to have my
vulva stimulated, first with fingers, then with a tongue
lapping my clitoris and labia. If I'm having intercourse
with a man (I've never made love with a woman), I
like him to insert his penis in my vagina. I need a lot of
freedom to rock and sway and move my pelvis for pressure stimulation, and eventually without rushing, go on
to orgasm."

**Orgasm during intercourse after having the first orgasm,
or several orgasms, by more direct stimulation.**

Actually, the longer one is aroused (whether by extended be-foreplay or successive orgasms), the deeper
into the outer vulva and lips the arousal may reach.
Therefore some women found they could have orgasms
during intercourse after their second or third orgasm.
As one woman described it:

"First I can have a clitoral touch orgasm, then lower
for the next orgasm, then lower again, then finally my
outer vaginal area can be stimulated to orgasm. But
when not at the height of intensity, intercourse can turn
off my responses altogether and even stop me from
coming."

CLITORAL STIMULATION BY HAND
DURING INTERCOURSE

Of course, the women in this group were not counted as part of the thirty percent of women who did orgasm from intercourse. However, it is perhaps the best way for most women to orgasm during intercourse, and therefore there are many quotes offered here of women telling how they adapted this stimulation to their needs during intercourse.

This way is very popular because you can be sure the stimulation is right "on target." Although stimulation by hand during intercourse has been recommended by marriage manuals for a long time, it is unfortunate that now it is often considered to be "second best" or "cheating." All too many women explaining their use of this method had some special rationale concerning why they did so, or worried about why they needed to.

"I was not *ever* having any orgasms all through four years of college and I was *mortified* and thought something was terribly wrong with me. I could masturbate to orgasm *very* easily but couldn't feel a damned thing during intercourse. Well, I was with my long-standing boyfriend one day and we were making love and I got really pissed at my not having orgasms so, with him in me and moving, I just reached down, rubbed around my clitoris and decided that, by God, I was going to get off, and 1 to 2 minutes later, I sure did—I had a fantastic orgasm, and have been successful ever since, *every* time, by using this method!"

"I believe that the current emphasis on pleasure coming from the clitoris has given me the courage to go after that—which has improved my sex life enormously. I always found it very frustrating to get my clitoris stimulated just enough by trying to rub it against my partner—who was moving around in ways that were intended to achieve his orgasm and didn't necessarily correspond to what I needed. That is really catch as catch can, and my clitoris never seemed to be fitting right anyway so that it could really be rubbed. I have decided that it's much better to do it with a hand."

"During intercourse, sideways, I place my hand around that part of the penis not in the vagina, massage it, and at the same time create clitoral stimulation and orgasms occur!"

"My partner is lying on his back, I am on top of him with his penis inside my vagina. I am kneeling with my upper body raised up away from his chest so that my breasts are hanging down in such a way that he is able to lift his head and suck on my nipples. One of his hands is down between us, and his fingers are directly stimulating my clitoris and the area around it. With his other hand he is feeling other areas of my body, especially my bottom. Meanwhile, I am free to move in whatever way gives me the most pleasure."

"I can't squeeze my legs together during regular intercourse. That is still necessary for me to make myself come. And I never have the same sort of violently physical orgasm with vaginal penetration with the penis that I do with direct clitoral stimulation. I'm not even sure if I come. I get a great sensation of pleasure, but it never peaks like it does the other way. I wish it did. I'd love to come right when he does without any extra attention. The only way we've been able to achieve this is if he lies on his back, and I on mine, with my rear on his pelvis. In this manner, his penis can be inside me, but my clitoris is free to be stroked by him and my stomach and leg muscles are unrestricted so they can react freely in the often violent spasmodic way they do when I'm coming. I would love to hear from someone who is able to have a super orgasm during intercourse without any direct clitoral manipulation. I suppose it's possible. I wonder if I could 'learn how' the way I've 'learned' how the other way."

"I have orgasms during intercourse only by masturbating simultaneously. While I'm doing this I don't like my partner to move around too much because it's distracting."

"I have often had the desire to have an orgasm with penetration and have tried to have my partner penetrate me, lying on my side across him, and stimulate my clitoris at the same time, but this doesn't work too well, because sometimes he can't hold his erection and also I have the problem of having to keep my legs tightly together in order to climax."

"Positions and movements are better or worse for all sorts of things, both physical and psychological, but they have never yet led to direct enough clitoral stimulation to lead to orgasm for me without a helping hand."

"Intercourse is okay providing some form of clitoral stimulation is continued during intercourse. If we are in such a position that makes penis/clitoris contact impossible or at least impractical, then my mate would need only to use a free hand to manipulate my clitoris."

"My most beautiful sexual experience ever was one afternoon I spent with my lover. He sat with his penis in my vagina while I was lying down, and he vibrated me from one orgasm to another while pushing himself in and out. There was so much love coming out of him, I'll never forget it."

"I am on top, sitting up, during intercourse. He touches my clitoris lightly with his finger, hand, or both hands, in a way that I can move against it as I want to."

"I have not found a lasting position that will give me maximum clitoral stimulation during intercourse. Direct stimulation with a hand is necessary to orgasm."

"I enjoy entry from behind, so I can stimulate my own clitoris at the same time."

"We have intercourse with slow, writhing movements on both of our parts, pressing my labia around his penis while my hands caress his stroking penis, or while I masturbate and/or close my legs tightly together."

"If I am feeling especially 'horny' and feel the need to be penetrated, then intercourse itself is good. But physically, it is satisfying only if accompanied by clitoral stimulation. I don't feel overly excited by vaginal penetration. Psychologically, it can be exciting by just the thought of what the man is doing to you and at times I'll experience a physical excitement which is a feeling that is not as intense or high-pitched as clitoral stimulation, but definitely a sexual feeling in the vagina during penetration. Intercourse *without* clitoral stimulation has *never* led to orgasm (so far for me, anyway)."

"So far, I have only had one partner who *really knows* what I like, and provides it without my actually directing him. Usually, I try to let it be known what kind of stimulation I want, but if my partner does not catch on, I think nothing of stimulating myself in front of him. It doesn't embarrass me to do this. I have no qualms about manually stimulating myself during intercourse. To hell with what the guy thinks of me; I deserve satisfaction as much as he does!"

"None of the positions of intercourse bring the penis into a position where it offers direct or frictional contact to my clitoris. I have been embarrassed to touch myself during partner sex. I'd like to do it but it would feel inappropriate."

"It is hard to get a hand at the clitoris during intercourse, but it can be done in almost any position with a little effort."

"He is on top. I reach down—pretending to just rest my hand on my stomach—and touch my clitoris. I've only done this a few times. Those times I came very close to orgasm, but I think my inhibitions kept me from coming."

"We do male on side, woman on back with one leg over both of his, penis inserted, I or he masturbates me. And the woman controls the body movements."

"I like to lie on my belly, over a pillow, so I can be clitorally stimulated by my partner's hand at the same time as he penetrates me."

"I sit on him with his penis inside my vagina. Then I lean back until I am on my back and he stimulates my clitoris with his fingers."

"Best for me is doggie position (on my stomach with penetration from behind) plus manual stimulation with his hand on top of mine."

"If I like him, and am not angry with him at the time, and he is not clumsy, he can make slow movements in my vagina, holding me with one arm, and stroking my clitoris with the other, saying sweet things. We can lie on our sides with his stomach to my back, and he is a tender and loving partner—he starts with kissing and fondling of my breasts, ears, arms and legs, almost all over until he begins to concentrate in the genital areas—then he touches the clitoris, then orally, until I want to feel his penis inside me. He lies on his back, and I kneel over him with my knees around his chest and I sit on his penis. His left hand is free to stimulate my clitoris. And we very gradually and very gently begin the long climb to orgasm until I want more and faster and harder pressure, and I come."

"Some men say they ought to be able to make me come by themselves, without my helping. But it just won't work that way. And I *do* try. If a man understands this, and we can talk about it, then the sex works out. For the few minutes that I play, there are many compensations for him in the over-all scene, and usually, his stimulation is combined with mine. However, if he can't work this out after we've talked, then I won't let him make me feel guilty again. I'll change partners."

"The way we work it is, my man keeps his dick inside me sort of poised for action while I manually stimulate myself just to the point of orgasm then actually come by pushing against him. The clitoris hits the root of his dick or his pubic bone or something—anyway, it works. I used to be concerned because it still isn't the famous 'no-hands' orgasm till I realized how stupid it is to take such a competitive or comparative point of view. Maybe eventually I will be able to come from intercourse alone but it doesn't hang me up. He's happy and I'm happy, so what the fuck?"

"You know it's weird that in porno films people who are fucking always seem to go faster toward the end—we do the opposite. When it starts to get into the 'build-up' stage we slow down to almost no movement at all. My man has incredible control of his responses, he can stay right on the edge of orgasm for a long time (and keep me there too) with tiny, subtle, intricate little riffs. If sex is an art form, he is the Picasso of it. The only thing is I just can't come unless I can get a finger in there—this has to be purely a mental problem. After a long period of 'build-up' I feel a slackening off in my response, and that's when I bring myself to the verge and push against him."

"All different kinds of movements are nice at different times. In one session of lovemaking my present lover uses the whole spectrum of choices as far as soft, hard, back, front, partial, complete, etc. If a particular way of doing it is good for him, I usually 'catch' his excitement and he keeps it up until he starts to lose the maximum effect, then tries something else. If the method is good for me, he catches my excitement and keeps it up until I lose it, then goes on to something else. When a particular method doesn't do it for either of us, it's abandoned and another one is used. If I am being the active one and moving either underneath while he holds still or sitting on him, I do the same thing, experimenting with this way and that till somebody strikes pay dirt."

"We use three different positions. If I'm going to come first, he lies sort of on his back but kind of on his side, I lie on my back at a ninety-degree angle with his dick inside me from the rear. He can reach my tits and I can reach my clitoris. If we are aiming for more or less simultaneous orgasm, we go in the missionary position. He fucks me for a while, getting aroused to a certain point, then sort of leans sideways so I can play with my clitoris while he's still inside. When I get to a certain point, he takes over the action again. We take turns till somebody gets tired or can't take it any more. If I come first, intercourse is not painful as I have read in some alleged sex manuals, but is extremely pleasant. I am super-sensitive inside and can feel the surges or waves of his orgasm. If he comes first, he stays on me and in me till the last sensations have subsided, then lies beside me lending encouragement while I bring myself off. I'm glad we discovered that idea of taking turns to gradually build, each using our own peculiar rhythms. I get off on being both active and passive in this; each feels wonderful in its own way. He may give me clitoral stimulation in any one of these positions, and sometimes he does it better than I do!"

Length of Intercourse.

Many people believe *long* intercourse is the key to having orgasm during intercourse; that is, "premature ejaculation" in men is what prevents orgasm during intercourse in women. But it seems that unless there is some specific form of good contact, of one of the kinds referred to in the preceding section, long intercourse is not helpful to most women. In fact, there were several complaints about intercourse going on too long:

"If intercourse lasts more than ten–fifteen minutes, it begins to irritate me and then the next time I urinate I get a burning feeling."

"If the man is grinding away in a boring fashion, then I get bored. If he'll let me be active (get on top, for example), I can keep interested for any length of time."

"After too long my lubrication decreases."

"The moment of penetration is usually the most exciting and then it's usually downhill."

"Sometimes I get 'numb' if the activity is too heavy, and I feel unhappy. Sometimes I am too lubricated to feel anything. Then I feel too much like a receptacle instead of a participant."

"I usually find intercourse with men a struggle; it doesn't usually flow, so usually the longer it goes, the less interested I become. I get too physically tired."

"After thirty minutes, I ask to stop."

"It becomes no more stimulating than someone shoving a hand on my arm."

"I have a terrific emotional reaction to penetration right at the beginning. After that it fades."

"I love the first few penetrations, then I just go downhill after that."

"Yes, I like intercourse, if I am aroused. Excitement leads to a desire for deep vaginal penetration. I don't like too much of it though (pumping). It just makes me sore or I get a urinary infection."

"Although the initial penetration is exciting and satisfying, penetration in general (intercourse) is disappointing and without any specific attempt to get simultaneous clitoral stimulation by position or manually—just jiggling."

Variations in Anatomy.

Some researchers feel that a possible cause of "coital frigidity" may be variations in the sexual anatomies of individual women. This idea seems to have caught the fancy of many women who—for good reason—would like to find a non-psychological reason for the fact that they don't have orgasms during intercourse:

"My clitoris is hooded, therefore I do not come during intercourse."

"I think my clitoris is placed too high to have an orgasm during intercourse—or maybe it's psychological; I don't trust me."

"I guess I could have an orgasm during intercourse if my clitoris could be in the right place, getting the right kind of pressure—which never ever happens when I'm with a dude."

"I went to a doctor and he said my clitoris is hooded and is very small so therefore it would take more to get me to come. He did not want to operate because he said it is a dangerous operation. I felt he would not have said that if it were a man who was having that problem. Anyway I have orgasms through masturbation with a vibrator and if I am sitting on top of the man and moving forward and backward so my clitoris is rubbing on his bone."

"I have a very small clitoris so maybe that is why it is hard to stimulate it through 'normal' intercourse. I do not feel my clitoris being stimulated at all when his penis is inside me."

"Although I have not read Masters and Johnson, so maybe it is covered there, it seems to me my clitoris is *too far away* from my vagina to be stimulated by normal intercourse, unless it is already stimulated. Is it possible that breaking a hymen early tends to allow the clitoris and vagina to grow apart?"

"I wonder if I'm like other people. I don't feel abnormal, but perhaps the position of my clitoris is responsible. It just doesn't seem to be stimulated by anything in my vagina."

"I really believe my clitoris may not be physically positioned quite right because I almost never can find a position for stimulating it while his penis is in my vagina."

The truth is that clitoral and labial anatomy are highly variable, in size, shape, placement, texture, and other factors. However, that does not mean that our anatomy is *wrong*, deformed. It is the cultural pressure on women to orgasm during intercourse that is wrong, and the stereotyped way in which we define sex.

It is doubtful whether anatomy is an important factor in whether or not we orgasm during intercourse. Masters and Johnson found no evidence to support the belief that differences in clitoral anatomy can influence sexual response. However, Barbara Seaman, who wrote *Free and Female*, cautions that "this must be viewed as a highly tentative finding since they were unable to observe any clitorises during orgasm." Sherfey also feels that more research should be done in this area. Masters and Johnson have said that they think certain *vaginal* conditions can operate to prevent the thrusting penis from exercising traction on the labia and clitoral hood. But it's all animal crackers in the end. The real thing to keep in mind is that it is more unusual than not to orgasm from intercourse, especially without making some kind of special effort to do so by getting additional clitoral stimulation at the same time.

It is possible to learn to orgasm during intercourse.

"I didn't orgasm for the first seven years of sexual intercourse with my husband; I thought pleasing him was enough, and also I took pleasure in the act itself. But eventually I became frustrated and went to a lot of trouble to learn how to please myself too."

"I almost never had orgasms with my husband during the ten years I was married. I thought I was frigid, but when I was taught by a man who seduced me two years after my divorce, I was shocked to learn how unfrigid I am. In a sense I had to learn—that is, what positions, etc.—were best and most likely to produce my orgasm. I wish I had learned earlier."

"Orgasm during intercourse is definitely a learned response; if I were illiterate and had never heard anybody talk about how to do it, I'd probably still be lying on my back, looking at the ceiling and wondering if that's all there is to love. But thanks to the Little Yellow Book by Berg and Street, I learned how to have orgasm pretty regularly during intercourse, me on top so I can control the pressure. Although the regular male thrust is stimulating and fun, what brings me to climax is my own lateral or circular writhing on the pole. Rarely do I have a non-orgasmic encounter."

Finally, in this study there was no apparent correlation between ability to orgasm during intercourse and age, number of children, or amount of experience.

Other women felt that, although they could orgasm during intercourse, they would rather just enjoy it for its own sake than concentrate on working toward their own orgasm.

"Orgasm requires almost no effort at all, as long as there is direct stimulation of my clitoris. However, the effort required to orgasm during intercourse is prodigious. So I usually don't bother. Now I just relax and enjoy the closeness and his orgasm."

"Thrusting in and out and moving while the penis is in me, so that I can control the amount of clitoral stimulation, are the most exciting. I guess I have given up, though, on trying for an orgasm during penetration. In the traditional way, I focus more on my partner's satisfaction. I find it's more enjoyable in the long run, and then I can relax and enjoy mine after, with manual stimulation, with all the attention on myself."

CONCLUSION

To have an orgasm during intercourse, there are two ways a woman can increase her chances, always remembering that she is adapting her body to less than adequate stimulation. First and most important, she must consciously try to apply her masturbation techniques to intercourse, or experiment to find out what else may work for her to get clitoral stimulation; or, she can work out a sexual relationship with a particular man who can meet her individual needs.

Do it yourself

The women who had orgasm during intercourse were usually those who, in a sense, did it themselves. They did not expect to "receive" orgasm automatically from the thrusting of the partner:

"The main thing I suppose is that a woman is more involved in the intercourse and lovemaking bit than I had thought originally."

"It's important for women to be able to stimulate themselves. If they just accept what a man does, it's no wonder they don't experience orgasm."

"For a long time I didn't have orgasms because I was so concerned about responding correctly to my partner and breathing hard when he came—to fake it. I think it's all part of the Catch That Man game. I didn't have them until I really started looking for them."

"In sex, the more I involved myself in going after my own pleasure, in following my own genital feelings (by thrusting and placing my body) the closer I get to orgasm. I used to worry that such seriousness, working for your pleasure, was unfeminine."

"I once experienced definite clitoral sensation while balling. I was on my back, but we were turned slightly to one side. Perhaps I should be more aggressive but men I've known seem to lose momentum while I try pressing against them, or make verbal suggestions."

The cardinal rule is you must make it happen yourself, not just wait for it to "happen," or for him to happen to hit the right spot out of luck:

"When I can freely rotate my pelvis, I can determine where I want the pressure, and in what pattern."

"During intercourse I am quite active and talk to him, saying what I like better than other things, etc."

"I have orgasms during intercourse by very subtle fucking—attention to nuances of feeling and sensation—great slowness and also I am very careful to stay 'on' where it feels good."

The most successful women have adapted their masturbatory techniques unabashedly and unashamedly to relations with others—or else have just been unusually lucky in having a very sensitive and knowledgeable partner.

You have to care about yourself and *want* to please yourself, and you have to feel it is your *right*. You have to do it, whatever it is—or ask for it, very clearly and very specifically.

THE CONNECTION BETWEEN ORGASM DURING INTERCOURSE AND MASTURBATION

There is an old myth that masturbation causes "clitoral fixation" and "frigidity":

"Perhaps if you masturbate, you can get a fixation on your clitoris and are thus unable to come during intercourse."

"The fact that I've been masturbating since I was ten has made it more difficult for me to orgasm vaginally."

"Having been used to masturbating for years as a teenager and repressing my desire for actual intercourse with boys, I feel I developed a conditioned reflex that did not allow me to have a vaginal orgasm with my husband even though I enjoyed the act itself."

"I don't penetrate myself in masturbation because for

some reason, when I insert something into my vagina, when I'm about to climax, the orgasm isn't as intense. I'm afraid I'm getting hooked on masturbation and should stop."

The truth, however, is just the opposite: masturbation increases your ability to orgasm in general, and also your ability to orgasm during intercourse. Why not? It's the same stimulation. Only 19 percent of the women in this study who did not masturbate orgasmed regularly from intercourse—quite a drop from the 30 percent in the over-all population. Of course, masturbating to orgasm does not automatically enable you to orgasm during intercourse. There is no mystical connection between the two—just the practical experience with orgasm—how it feels and how to get it.

"Are your techniques in masturbation similar to your techniques for orgasming during intercourse?"

Was there any correlation between type of masturbation and method used for having orgasm during intercourse? Are some types of masturbation easier to adapt to intercourse than others?

Some women felt their methods were similar during masturbation and intercourse.

"Masturbation for me involves the circular rubbing of my clitoris and the edge of my vagina, and intercourse is basically the same."

"They are the same when his penis is rubbing directly against my clitoris, or his body is pressing against the area of my clitoris. Otherwise, when I masturbate, my stimulation of the areas that are most sensitive for me is much more direct and intense."

"Yes, it's the same during intercourse as during masturbation. It's the difference between rubbing my clitoris around on the base of a penis as opposed to rubbing my clitoris around on a clump of bedsheets."

However, most women who answered this question (and especially, almost all the women who did not orgasm during intercourse) felt that stimulation during masturbation and intercourse were not the same at all.

"I attempt to use the same technique, but intercourse often makes this difficult, as my clitoris becomes less sensitive, and sometimes seems to be sort of submerged."

"No, for one thing, I can't squeeze my legs together. That is still necessary for *me*, to make myself come. I never have the same sort of violently physical orgasm with vaginal penetration with the penis as I do with direct clitoral stimulation. I'm not even sure if I come."

"I don't think I will ever have many orgasms during intercourse because masturbation has accustomed me to close my legs hard and this doesn't work too well with a man."

"No. During intercourse there is more pushing pressure; in masturbation it's more back and forth with one finger against my clitoris."

"No. In masturbation, I mainly play with the clitoris—just inserting my finger in my vagina to satisfy the need that was created by my orgasm causing my vagina to throb for something in it."

"In masturbation it is important that the muscles are massaged so as to provide a kind of stretching and release of the clitoral area. The same stretching and release has not been accomplished by any up and down or in and out movement on my partner's part."

"No, the different position and the closeness of the partner prevent a successful masturbating technique."

"Supposedly you should be able to have a climax with a man if you masturbate by rubbing the outside of your vagina, sometimes penetrating the inside. I have a climax fairly easily by myself. I have since I was a little child. It seems like it shouldn't be too hard to have one with a man but so far I have been unsuccessful. Is there a way to have a climax with a man's penis in your vagina if one masturbates in the way I described?"

Actually, most of the answers to this question were

unintelligible or very confused; most women did not seem sure what the question even meant, so compartmentalized has our thinking been. In this sense, perhaps the preceding quotes are not representative. What really emerged from the answers was the fact that most women had never even thought about a possible connection.

Finally, was there a correlation between type of masturbation and "ability" to orgasm during intercourse? Were some orgasm types more likely to orgasm during intercourse than others? My impression was that these figures are imprecise because too many women were disqualified from being counted; they included those who did not specify how they had orgasmed during intercourse, those who masturbated in more than one way, and the "questionable-orgasm-definition" group. This left a very small number from which to make correlations.

However, despite all these problems, two definable trends did appear. Most likely to orgasm during intercourse were those who masturbated on their stomachs, especially those who did not use their hands (type III). Least likely were those who held their legs together or crossed.

Other than this there were no really clear-cut correlations, and many women whose type suggested they might be able to were still not able to orgasm during intercourse. A lot seemed to depend on how interested the individual was in applying her own knowledge of her body to intercourse and actively directing the stimulation unabashedly to herself.

Of course it remains an unanswered question whether these body types are made or born. That is, once you learn to orgasm a certain way, does that become a basically fixed pattern for you? For example, if you learned with your legs together, could you later learn with them apart? Or, are some types of bodies only able to orgasm in certain positions?

This question is, however, important only academically. Women who masturbate with their legs together, for example, can just as well adapt this position to intercourse as other masturbation types. No one body type is "better" than another. While a woman who needs to have her legs together to orgasm may have slightly more trouble teaching new lovers ways to have intercourse in which she can orgasm, it is also true that women who hold their legs together are more likely to be able to have many sequential orgasms than other women, since they do not stimulate their clitorises so directly (the bunched-up skin forms a protective cushion). Whatever body type a woman has, she can have fully as much pleasure as every other woman. All she has to do is be active and explore.

What is the difference between "to orgasm" and "to have an orgasm"?

This idea that we really make our own orgasms, even during intercourse, is in direct contradiction to what we have been taught. Most of us were taught that "you should relax and enjoy it"—or at most help him out with the thrusting—because *he* would "give" you the orgasm:

"If you try too hard, you will never have an orgasm; it should come naturally as a result of the loving."

"You don't have to make it happen, it's a response. You should just naturally be grasped in the flow."

"Orgasms are as natural to women as ejaculations are to men. If a woman is in touch with herself physically and emotionally, I think orgasms will be very natural for her."

"In a normal woman orgasm is a natural part of sex."

"No effort should be necessary . . . it just happens when the time is right, two people caring for each other. Learn to accept and love your body and yourself, and you will have orgasm."

"I feel you shouldn't have to concentrate so much on having an orgasm, but on the glory of what's happening at that moment when your two bodies are one. The beauty of that time will make you come."

It should be mentioned that many of the women who answered in this way were also not having orgasms regularly in sex. As we saw in the preceding section, orgasm is most likely to come when the woman takes over responsibility for and control of her own stimulation. You always, in essence, create your own orgasm.

"I create my own orgasm. Sometimes no amount of stimulation will turn me on, because I don't want it. I really resent men who boast of 'giving' a woman a good come. I always feel I have created it myself, even if he was doing the stimulating."

"My orgasm is my own. I control it, produce it, and dig it."

"Although I think mutual pleasure is wonderful, the orgasm is in the end one's own. You have to put in the concentration and physical effort yourself."

We do give ourselves orgasm, even, in a sense, when someone else is providing us with stimulation, since we must make sure it is on target, by moving or offering suggestions, and by tensing our bodies and getting into whatever position(s) we need—and then there is a final step necessary in most cases: we need to focus on the sensation and concentrate, actively desire and work toward the orgasm.

"Is having an orgasm a concentrated effort?"

"Yes, you can't just lie there and wait for an orgasm. You sense that one is approaching, and so of course you concentrate on helping it."

"Yes, I willfully strain the muscles of my upper thighs, rectum, and vagina. It has taken a long time to learn to concentrate on my body and what's happening during sex rather than only on what he's thinking or is he ready."

"Yes, each person probably has to learn her own body's way to reach it, how to tense it, maybe even what thoughts or words help it happen. For many years I was unable to have orgasms with another person; then finally I taught myself to tense my body so much that I'd push myself over the brink."

"I forcibly contract my vaginal muscles during cli-

toral stimulation, and it helps a lot to cause my orgasms."

"Sometimes I really have to make an effort—tense
my muscles, tremble, sort of force myself. A man I
dated suggested I force myself to as he did from time to
time, and it worked."

"Yes, I concentrate all of my energies. Every muscle
and every nerve."

"When I feel an orgasm approaching, I often make a
concentrated effort to make sure that I reach it. That
means moving on my own and/or telling my partner
what to do."

"They *can* happen, and do, without great effort, but
unless you take control and make them happen the way
you want them and when you want them, they are probably going to be inadequate and infrequent."

"Just before orgasm, my mind and senses focus down
to controlling one area rather than the coordinated system."

"I try to position my pelvis to my best satisfaction by
rhythmic movements and then concentrate my body energies to this great explosion."

It would almost seem as if there is a definite break
between sensuality (diffuse, non-focused physical feeling, and sexuality (drive toward orgasm), and that in
order to have an orgasm, at least most of the time, it is
necessary to think and work and concentrate toward
one.

"At a certain point you have to stop relaxing and
having fun and build yourself up to this earth-moving
experience, orgasm, and sometimes it seems like too
much trouble."

"Occasionally when I am feeling passive and very attuned to being touched all over my body, I will sort of
'forget' to get super genitally stimulated and not come
unless I roll over and work at it."

"I could not have an orgasm if in the last few moments before the orgasm I didn't give it complete concentration. If this isn't the case with other women, I
envy them."

"The more involved I am with active interaction with my partner, the more aroused I am. But if I become too involved with someone else's stimulation, I don't stay in touch with my own."

"During orgasm, I concentrate on my body, not on him."

"It is a totally personal experience and during orgasm especially there is *no* way to share that with your partner. But I like that he is there."

"I have always wanted to keep my eyes open during an orgasm but I have never succeeded. I thought it would make me feel closer to my partner, but during an orgasm the only thing I am conscious of is my own pleasure—and in the back of my mind, how my partner is moving so I can coordinate my movements."

This process of concentrating or focusing on physical sensations as you make the effort to have an orgasm is probably the same thing Masters and Johnson have called "sensate focus."

"Full concentration like hypnosis is needed to attain orgasm—your whole mind and body is focusing on it."

"Yes, I definitely have to concentrate to orgasm. If I think about anything other than the sensation, or any unsexual thoughts, I immediately lose the excitement."

"You have to form your attention in your genitals."

You can bring on an orgasm, not exactly by fantasizing (that is, thinking of a story or situation, which is often used more for arousal), but by a kind of self-hypnotism, sort of "picturing" the feeling and the "organs" involved:

"The specific act sort of fantasies are almost always used to bring on an orgasm faster while masturbating, and never have a story. Sometimes, in fact, they don't even have a real character, simply a fantasy that 'someone' is sucking my clitoris, or that a cock is in my cunt. These fantasy people are sometimes identified at least as far as being 'a man' but are other times so vague as to be only 'a long tongue' with no person attached."

"I do not fantasize during sex with someone. I only

have a mental picture of the penis moving and penetrating in my vagina."

"I am *thinking* of the friction of the man's penis."

"The concentration of your mind must be focused with all your might between your legs—*on the vagina*."

"I have to concentrate really hard on my clitoris or my thoughts wander and I don't feel sexual at all. It took me a while to learn to concentrate like this and that's how I learned to come."

"Yes, I have to *want* to come and think about only that. Forget everything except what I am doing and what is being done to me. I close my eyes and picture it in my mind."

"At the beginning, I just think of what I'm doing, and then I feel like waves on a beach are coming in and out, and I think, 'do it—do it—do it—.' "

"I concentrate very hard on the inward, outward movement of the penis. And what it looks like as it's going in and out."

"I concentrate on body 'wanting' sensations."

"I like pornography which leads to anticipation—for example, I think of someone bent over and waiting to be entered."

"I concentrate on mentally thinking of what he is doing to me."

"I have fantasies of Swiss or U.S. woodlands, generally with a directional left or right pathway, very pictorial and recallable visually. They serve to keep me closed up in myself and free from distraction in the last five minutes leading to orgasm and they are wholly mental. They are my 'movies' and I invariably have them."

"To have an orgasm for sure if I'm nervous or in a hurry, I say to myself: he cannot get up, he must keep doing what he is doing, I cannot make him stop, I have no choice but to be here, and to have an orgasm. Then I concentrate real hard on my vagina. It always works."

Finally, did most women have to learn to have orgasms during intercourse?

"I had to learn to make an effort, not lie back and wait for Jove's thunderbolt."

"One has to develop freedom and skill in mutual interaction."

"You have to learn to not be afraid of your partner's response."

"Not learn, but perhaps on a larger level learn how to handle the whole thing."

"It's quite a struggle sometimes! I don't think orgasms come naturally during intercourse. They do come easier, however, once you learn from trial and error experimentation."

"Maybe in the beginning it's accidental, but then you learn what stimulates you the most, or not to stop something when it's working or encourage something that started to work."

"You have to learn to move your body to get maximum stimulation for an orgasm. The thrust of the penis or finger or tongue or whatever may not be in the right spot or be firm enough or last long enough, so that I have to thrust my vagina or clitoris against the penis, etc., in a way that feels most intense at the time that I feel ready to explode."

"In my experience I never had to learn anything but to be forward enough to demand clitoral stimulation."

"Yes, a woman often has to learn how to achieve orgasms in *spite of* her partner, not *because* of him."

"Yes, and the devil of it is that each woman will probably have to learn how for herself."

In conclusion, it could perhaps be said that the two reasons women don't orgasm during intercourse are: they are given false information, specifically they are told that the penis thrusting in the vagina will cause orgasm; and they are intimidated from exploring and touching their bodies—they are told that masturbation is bad and that they should not behave "aggressively" during sex with men. They do not control their own stimulation.

This emphasis on getting your own stimulation does not in any way imply a lack of feeling for the man you are with during intercourse. However, orgasm has been very importantly the focus of this discussion, because it is symbolic for women: the ability to orgasm when we want, to be in charge of our stimulation, represents owning our own bodies, being strong, free, and autonomous beings.

CLITORAL STIMULATION

HOW HAVE MOST MEN HAD SEX WITH YOU?

The following answers represent the overwhelming majority of answers received to this question: that sex—whether enjoyable or exploitative—generally follows the reproductive pattern described in the chapter on intercourse: "foreplay" followed by "penetration" and "intercourse" (thrusting) followed by orgasm (especially male orgasm), which is then defined as the "end" of sex. Answers not falling into this category, not including the lesbian replies, composed less than 5 percent of those in the study.

"In bed with the man above me, in the dark."

"I've only had sex with my husband. (We were just married for a few months.) He always initiates it. We kiss and he plays with my breasts. He puts one hand down and sticks his finger into my vagina and moves it back and forth like a penis would go. When he's doing this, I lie on my back, and he lies on his side so his body is pressed against my side. He moves his hips back and forth so that his penis rubs against the side of my leg. When he's ready, he has me get on my hands and knees, and he gets in back of me. He sticks his penis into me and moves it back and forth until he finishes."

"Most of the men I've slept with have had absolutely no idea of what I want or need and no interest in finding out. There have been several men who seemed to care whether I was happy, but they wanted to make me happy according to *their* conception of what ought to do it (fucking harder or longer or whatever) and acted as if it was damned impertinent of me to suggest that my responses weren't programmed exactly like those of mythical women in the classics of porn. All I can say is, after years of sexual experience that ranged from brutal to trivial to misguided, etc., it's a wonder I didn't just blow off the whole thing a long time ago. I'm glad I stuck with it until I found a partner whose eroticism complements mine so beautifully."

"I find that a lot of men care nothing about sex foreplay and are only interested in 'getting it off.' These are the kind that really burn me up. Usually, they are the type that have never had or never wanted to really love someone for the sake of love and the pleasure it brings; they are only interested in themselves. I find that most men like for you to perform orally on them."

"There has always been some kind of preliminaries, only the length has differed. The preliminaries consisted mostly of vaginal stimulation and necking. Not as much breast fondling and sucking as I would have liked."

"It's usually a short period of foreplay then male on top, female on back, with legs drawn apart, standard slam-bam-thank you ma'am."

"Most men do it on top of the girl and would probably continue to do so if I didn't suggest different positions."

"We undress separately, start making out, he does foreplay not very long then he goes in and we're rhythmic. Generally I get to the verge but he comes first. It's very tense for me and that's the usual."

"Very perfunctory. A little kiss, a little feel, a finger for arousal, a touch of breast and he's on top, wham it's over."

"A lot of it used to be get it up, get it in, and get it out."

"There was from a minimum to a maximum of kissing and touching. Usually once our clothes were altogether off, the screwing began. All the sex I have had with men, they were on top, bouncing up and down. I always wished a little bit of kissing or even tight holding would go on during it, but the men seemed to be off in their own world."

"Most men, if left to their own devices, will engage in a little (ten to fifteen minutes) foreplay of a not very imaginative kind, paying little attention to my clitoris. They then go immediately to penetration in the 'missionary position,' have a whale of a good time, and go to sleep immediately afterward. This is an extreme picture, but is too well defined to ignore."

"They undress me and try to penetrate at once. It's horrible."

"Whenever I have had sex with a man they always are trying to get there, of course. That seems standard."

"A little foreplay, to one end."

"Unfortunately most men just get into you."

"In general, they tended to minimize foreplay and to concentrate just on intercourse. I can't generalize about technique other than usually foreplay and just good old hugging and kissing. Gets less and less once we get to know each other."

"Foreplay with constant pressure to have intercourse."

"They try to arouse me, then as soon as possible, start intercourse. Some *few* do not hurry and wait for *me* to advance to the next step."

"Nothing really standard except the bed, the penetration, the ejaculation, and orgasms (real or faked)."

"In and out."

"Caressing my body, breasts, vagina . . . asking me to caress their penis . . . then bang bang. . . ."

"Kiss, pet, go down on me, then lay me on the bottom and unless I've really wanted this person for a long time this isn't satisfactory."

"Men are very uninformed about women's sexual desires. Most men will engage in a little manual stimulation but expect a woman to reach orgasm during intercourse. They cannot understand that some women prefer clitoral stimulation."

"They jumped on and rode."

"It used to be pretty standard until we saw that fucking mechanically was damaging to us. Now usually we are tender, sometimes intense and passionate, sometimes just affectionate and close without 'real sex.' Our sexual times are very varied."

"With some recent and beautiful exceptions, the encounters have been too short, not affectionate enough and too impersonal."

"Small amount of foreplay, then intercourse till he comes, The End."

"Preliminaries—kissing, foreplay, clitoral massaging—then he jumps on top and all of a sudden I don't matter any more. Sometimes, I'm not even there to him."

"Most didn't seem to be aware that what brought them to climax was not what brought me to climax. That about sums it up."

"They climbed on top, after what they thought was enough foreplay, and pumped away. A few knew about the clitoris but generally they overlooked it completely."

"Most often: one or two kisses, if any, maybe some (very little) breast stimulation or vaginal stimulation, then jump right in till he's finished."

"Some men just kiss, feel, finger, and fuck. Then come and light a cigarette."

"Most men have fucked me with a minimum of foreplay, have been reluctant to touch me (not from repulsion just lack of interest), and have shown more interest in demonstrating their longevity and great prowess in various gymnastics, etc., than in real mutual pleasure."

"First comes kissing, then the taking off clothes ritual, then breast and body kissing, sucking, nuzzling, then cunnilingus, cocksucking, direct clitoral stimulation (order of last three items can change), and intercourse."

"Foreplay, *always* too short, then penetration."

"Begins with kissing, which gets deeper and more passionate, proceeds to body caresses, undressing, usually he leads me to the couch or bed, we lie down, kiss and pet some more, then he gets on top of me, inserts his penis and comes. If I know him well enough, he knows that I need to have my clitoris stimulated and places his hand between my thighs for me to rub myself on."

"Men can be put into two groups: straight intercourse men and foreplay men. Straight intercourse men I have had are usually less experienced, they just screw.

Others indulge in a great deal of foreplay including oral-genital contact, which they often want to bring me to climax in."

"Most men just kiss and stick it in. These are the creeps. The few good men who I've had and stuck with, ask my desires and then proceed very slowly and tantalizingly."

"Most were speed demons."

"They move too quickly to enter and move to their climax too fast for me to keep up. I often do, but at the expense of my feelings. It becomes a 'job' to come."

"Most of them start kissing, petting, really get off on the breasts—then the fingers in the vagina bit, some love talk, when we're ready, cunnilingus and fellatio simultaneously, then I get on top, then he does. This is fairly standard with a lot of guys."

"Most of them the same way—take what you can get and don't give any. Before my husband, that is, who is the most erotic, imaginative man I ever met."

"The usual pattern is lovemaking, then oral sex upon each other, and then whatever position he wants."

"American men come within ten minutes; Europeans take time and give *beautiful* head!"

"Most climb on top of me. We don't even have a chance to get acquainted and love and kiss first. They are too anxious."

"I find *most* men are willing to experiment with several positions of intercourse, and a significant number do not like oral sex and all but two or three wouldn't even have sex if I was having my period."

"A little foreplay by them and wanting a lot of foreplay by me, then they just sort of start getting on and getting it over with as soon as possible. Sometimes one of them will really take their time and give me a real good time."

"Before my present lover, they would *expect* me to jump into the hay whenever they got horny, go through a perfunctory foreplay, enter me, thrust rapidly for fifteen to thirty seconds, shoot their wad, graciously condescend to 'finish me' with their finger, roll away and let me sleep on the wet spot. It was monotonous, drill-like, and boring."

"When you think about it like *that,* it's a wonder it isn't boring: Most men seem to go in for minimal fore-play, and prefer the man on top, woman on bottom, face to face position."

"Lately, I've detected a very specific pattern. He comes over, we sit around on the living room floor, drinking wine and listening to music, move on to kiss-ing, stroking, and at this point, he whispers, 'Let's go into the bedroom,' whereupon we disrobe, get in bed, embrace, indulge in further foreplay, and then inter-course. I'm beginning to think there must be something like a sexual 'Robert's Rules of Order' which every guy follows."

"My sexual encounters have followed very traditional (or so they seem to me) patterns. Kisses and general caresses moved to caressing of my clitoris and vagina, then usually to oral stimulation of my clitoris. Often then either oral or manual stimulation of my partner's penis and then fucking. Written here, this sounds rather cold and 1, 2, 3 but embroidered with all the details that really *are* sexual contact, it takes on a warmth that isn't part of these words."

"All the men I have had sex with have been alike, except for *one* who took time to sufficiently arouse me before intercourse."

"There is a pattern but it's too boring to tell about."

"Men differ, but most do not seem to understand a woman's body. They seem to think that vaginal penetra-tion is the only important thing and that all else should be done only to 'get you ready.' They think that once you are lubricated you are immediately ready and want to be penetrated then."

"With the first man I slept with, sex was tender, in-nocent and beautiful—it was basically kissing and light petting as foreplay to coitus. But then my appetite be-gan to decline and I was afraid to say so. So it became very forced. I was submissive and resentful. It became more of a chore than anything else. With the second, sex was tender, exciting and fulfilling in a way it had never been with the first man. Foreplay included kissing and heavy petting. Coitus takes place in the male dominant and female dominant position. I feel he makes love more emotionally than the other did and shows more genuine concern for me."

"I feel guilty when the man appears disinterested. A sensuous man (one in a million) enjoys a woman's body—touching it and giving her pleasure seem to turn him on. Most men, though, seem to consider it a waste of energy and just want to get on with the intercourse part."

"The only pattern I can discern is one of brevity. Men arrive and depart as if they had a round-trip ticket. It has reached the point that I almost know it is no use starting any more."

"Usually the man has been on top and had the most pleasure—I like sex, but I know it hasn't been as good as it should be and could be for me. The men have assumed that they should make the first move, and all that bull. They've been pretty sensitive, gentle, they've tried, but obviously not enough."

"I hate the usual pattern—kiss—feel—eat—fuck, simply because it's usual. I like when people talk to me and moan a lot. I like when people are expressive and creative with me."

"I find that many men expect fellatio but don't want to perform cunnilingus, after I've washed and they haven't."

"Many men are far more hung up about sex than I am. They are not as curious, as explorative, as into just touching. They are squeamish about my vagina. They aren't as talkative or as open nor do they feel as much of a desire to rid themselves of all inhibitions as I do."

"I have very limited experience so I'm not sure—but there may be one: they ask what you like, find out it's hard for you to have orgasms, try very hard to make you orgasm *one* night, then thereafter, pretty much please themselves thinking you won't orgasm anyway or just being caught up with their own sensations."

"Most men I have been with have been conventional

lovers—missionary position and came too soon. Men don't seem to have much imagination about sex. They don't readily accept new ideas or suggestions."

"Most men—brief foreplay (which gets briefer every time) then missionary position, unless I climb on top first. Most men don't continue kissing during climax. It's a breath problem, I guess, but I would like it."

"I have found most men to be very unimaginative and prosaic in their approach to sex. Most go about it in the so-called 'missionary' manner."

"Slam-bam-thank you ma'am. No, that's a simplification. He tries to make it last long, so I'll come, but he just isn't able or willing to indulge in the foreplay I want and need."

"It's hard to remember any patterns since I've been happily married for thirty-five years—but I do remember that most of the men seemed totally unaware of what I was really feeling; they thought their penises were fantastic instruments that drove a woman insane with desire and satisfaction just by being in the room with her! Only two of the many I slept with made a real effort to stimulate and satisfy me. And I was too young, embarrassed, and unaware myself to do much but keep quiet and/ or pretend orgasm or excitement."

"With the exception of my husband, most of the men I have had sex with have just satisfied themselves and that's all. They seemed concerned that I reach climax but did nothing to make it happen. And most men seemed more sexually hung up than I was. For the most part, the encounters were more of an ego booster for me than physically satisfying."

"There is no particular pattern except that I have always done as was expected, put on whatever sexual performance, or done whatever act was demanded of me. The majority of men I have had sex with wanted the ordinary man-on-top position, or fellatio. Most have believed the rough, tough approach was best."

"Most of them have been basically dominant— though consistently 'gentle.' Some have had a partial aversion to female genitalia (oral stimulation or actually looking at what it looks like, etc.) None have ever seemed concerned enough about my satisfaction to continue manual stimulation after they have 'come.' "

"Mostly with an excess of activity. It's too much too fast and I don't even have a chance to begin to feel involved before he is all finished. Perhaps that is why I have been monogamous for the last few years. I feel something *deeper* should develop each time."

"When I'm first going out with a man, there is usually much kissing on the mouth, ears, and neck, then graduated play to fondling of breasts, on to my genitals, touching, hopefully oral stimulation, then intercourse, usually in the old Missionaire. Then, after having sex once or twice, most men like to get a little experimental with positions; me on my back, me on top. Then, unfortunately, sex begins to deteriorate for me. First, it's the kissing of my mouth that goes. Sex is just preceded by a few short kisses, and then on to the rest with increasing brevity. Stimulation of my breasts is sometimes cut out entirely, or else reduced to five seconds of attention to each one. Making love becomes strictly (and restrictingly) genital. Most men get to the point where sixty seconds of head is it, then the old in-out for five minutes and it's over. It seems that they must feel that they have to seduce a woman to get her to 'give in' to their lust at first, and then, once she's fallen, she's only to expect intercourse in the narrowest sense. They don't seem to realize that a woman doesn't necessarily have to be convinced to have sex—and the reason why so-called seduction practices work is that she simply is an erotic being in her own right, and with the proper attention and stimulation she'll be at a point where she'd rather have sex than anything! At least that's the way it is for me and my girlfriends. If the only reason a man spends two hours making love to a woman is that he wants a hole around to fuck regularly, let him carve one out of a meat loaf and keep it in bed with him. I want to be with a man who feels the way I do, that making love to the other person is the most important thing— you both get what you want and need that way. As it stands, few women are making it clear that they expect men to make love to them the way that is best for a

woman—we've been come buckets for them long
enough."

"The first time a man fucks me, he seems to be extremely aroused but wants to put in a good performance. There is usually a long and passionate foreplay,
but once intercourse begins he's been dying to fuck
for so long that he may come pretty fast. If time permits
he may fuck me a second time, and this is longer and
better. Some men with a lot of experience and control
have run a real enduro with me on the first fuck, but
this is the unusual case. The better lays will usually go
down on me the first time, and I am very hot to do the
same for them, particularly to help them gain a strong
second erection. For me, the first fuck with most men
may be the most passionate and spectacular, but is not
the loosest nor the most orgasmic by a long shot. Sex
seems to improve over time, up to the point where boredom, laziness, or apathy sets in. At this point the partner is not so eager to please and the routine is seldom
altered. The routine? Quick (if any) foreplay, quick
fuck in one of two positions (man or woman on top),
an orgasm for each of us, then crash. Unfortunately, if
it's been *too* quick for me to come, it's too bad, because
sex is officially over. On these occasions I listen to my
lover sleep and wish I had the nerve to masturbate.
Masturbation of any kind is seldom a part of sex, particularly with male partners. I've never masturbated in
front of a man. I've never seen a man masturbate. I
have never masturbated a man to orgasm, and a few
times, with one man, I've been masturbated to orgasm.
I wish my partners and I could learn to be more relaxed
and uninhibited in this respect, because I think we
could learn a lot from each other this way. Although
there have been quite a few situations in which I did not
come or I came but still felt unsatisfied, I have *very
rarely* been asked if I would like to be stimulated to
orgasm when intercourse is over. Almost invariably,
when the man has come and intercourse is concluded,
the sexual encounter is over, irregardless of my satisfaction."

"A few other little patterns I can think of: as a sexual relationship continues, a man will either emerge as the type who would rather not eat you out, or the type who would. If he is the former type he will either never give you head, or only occasionally give you head. If he is the latter type, he will usually, but not always eat you, sometimes as foreplay and sometimes more extended, to give you orgasms. Most men are very responsive to fellatio, but a few men are very touchy about it, and it is difficult to give them a full blow job because they seem so uptight and may not be able to come. Men are usually much quicker lovers in the morning than in the evening. Most of my male partners have shown themselves to be distinctly non-adventurous. They have a limited repertoire of lovemaking techniques which they rely on, never seeming to give much thought to trying something new or a bit different. I myself am guilty of staying stuck in the feminine role of never making suggestions, just hoping my lover will make them. I usually keep on hoping . . . I have had a few lovers whom I would call the erotic-adventurers. They will make suggestions that raise my eyebrows and my respiration level. I find myself thinking 'and *what* have you got in mind *now*???' These men seem a lot less inhibited, and exhibit a genuine love for pure eros and sex for sex's sake. Many men dearly love getting their rocks off, but few show this real lust for the erotic."

"How most men have tried to have sex with me can be summed up as Insert A into B. Dulldulldulldull."

"Who decides when it's over?"

"It's over after his orgasm. Isn't that the natural end of sex??"

"Usually it's over when he ejaculates and loses his erection, whether I have had an orgasm or not."

"Ideally it would be both of us who decide but of course it never is. The man decides when it's over for anatomical reasons."

" 'Dick power'—the penis decides when it's over."

"Obviously the man! He goes to sleep at once and snores!"

"The one thing I hate is that no matter how you go

about it, intercourse ends almost always when he comes and becomes limp, which has many political implications."

"It's over when the male ejaculates, unless the woman is lucky enough to have more than one man in bed."

"Nature decides when it's over."

"If the partner is male, the woman is stuck with the limits of his sexuality."

"*He* does, as he ejaculates."

"My partner ends it, but he does make sure I'm completely pleased and satisfied, and then he holds me and touches me until I'm asleep."

"I like getting into the sex experience as much as possible and feel terribly frustrated emotionally if I am not allowed to because he has an orgasm and falls asleep. I would like to have continuing love after and not make an orgasm the end!"

"My partner decides when sex is over because when he comes he usually loses interest in sex. He may be tired if it is in the evening or if during the day he may have other things to do. If he stays in a sexual mood long enough to gain a second erection, then the lovemaking may go on for a long period, but that is the unusual case. I feel it is a great pity that males and females were sexually-biologically built such that males are ready to quit just as females are getting started. I wonder to what extent men realize this? That when he is feeling exhausted and satisfied and sleepy as hell she is feeling hot-wired and dying to come again, and sleep is the last thing from her mind. Of course this is not always the situation, but I know I've played satisfied and exhausted many many times just because I knew my partner was, and I'd damned well better be."

ORGASM FROM CLITORAL STIMULATION BY HAND

Do most women orgasm regularly from clitoral stimulation by hand?

In the reproductive pattern of sex just described, which is far and away the most prevalent in our culture—if not the *only* definition for most people—were women having orgasms during "foreplay" with clitoral stimulation?

FREQUENCY OF ORGASM DURING CLITORAL STIMULATION BY HAND

	Q.I	Q.II	Q.III		TOTAL
"Yes"	279	220	67	=	566
Always	16	36	25	=	77
Usually	9	102	24	=	135
Sometimes	12	40	17	=	69
Rarely	0	14	2	=	16
Total	316	412	135		863
Orgasm Regularly	44%	39%	49%	=	44%

Those who orgasm regularly (those who answered "yes," always or usually) during clitoral stimulation by hand during sex with a partner comprise approximately 44 percent of the total population.

In other words, although nowhere near the over-

whelming majority of women who orgasmed regularly
with masturbation, those who orgasmed with the manual clitoral stimulation of their partners comprised a
much larger number than those who orgasmed during
intercourse (30 percent). But why don't women orgasm
as easily during clitoral stimulation with others as they
do with themselves?

First, a note on the derivation of the preceding figures.

There were here, as there were in the chapter on "intercourse," difficulties with coming to a general, over-
all figure. The main problem here, and with oral sex, is
that clitoral stimulation is often offered mainly for purposes of arousal ("foreplay"); because of this, it was
not always clear whether the woman's answer meant she
had the *ability* to orgasm "usually" or "sometimes,"
etc., through this kind of stimulation or whether she and
her partner "usually," "always," or "sometimes" did engage in this stimulation to orgasm. Women who answered with regard to ability might have caused the figures to be slightly higher than the actual frequency of
the practice of clitoral stimulation to orgasm would warrant. However, as in the intercourse figures, every effort
was made to cross-check answers, and in most cases the
meaning could be surmised.

Further, in Questionnaires I and II, the question was
phrased, "What positions and movements are best for
stimulating yourself clitorally with a partner? Do you
have orgasms this way usually, sometimes, rarely, or
never? Please explain ways you and your partner(s)
practice clitoral stimulation." The active voice was used
as a way of suggesting that the woman herself could be
active about getting clitoral stimulation, but this caused
many women to misunderstand the question:

"I don't understand the question—me stimulating
myself? Is that what is asked? I rarely do this with a
partner."

"I don't stimulate myself clitorally with a partner. He
does."

"What is clitoral stimulation? Is that when the partner masturbates you?"

"I don't know what any of this means."

"This question doesn't make sense. Clitoral stimulation is part of the warm-up exercises."

"I'm not sure what you mean. I've never had a homosexual relationship."

Perhaps to some women even the idea of having an orgasm this way was novel. The ultimate significance of how many women misunderstood or didn't answer this question is that a culture concerning the needs of female sexuality, a way of relating that truly concerns itself with the needs of women's bodies, hardly exists.

When the question was changed to the more usual passive voice in Questionnaire III, it was perfectly understood, which accounts for the higher percentage of positive answers in Questionnaire III.

It would be pointed out that it cannot be assumed that the total percentages of women who orgasm from intercourse (30 percent) and from manual clitoral stimulation (44 percent) can be simply added together to represent the total percent of women having orgasms during sex with their partners. Many of these women are the same women, who can have orgasms in both ways. There were, unfortunately, many women who orgasmed regularly during masturbation but almost never during sex with another person in any way.

The first reason women don't orgasm as frequently from the clitoral stimulation of another person as they do from their own, is that, more often than not, clitoral stimulation is not *intended* to lead to orgasm. The reproductive model of sex has traditionally included just enough clitoral stimulation in "foreplay" for purposes of arousal but not for orgasm—which is perhaps worse than no clitoral stimulation at all, a kind of "cock teasing" in reverse:

"I vividly remember reading in some marriage manual (at an age when I still found the idea of intercourse and genitals disgusting—maybe eight or nine years old) about where the sensitive parts were on a woman, and how the man should stimulate them before attempting intercourse, so the woman would be ready. It sounded so unpleasant and obligatory—and I never wanted a man to do that to *me* in order to get me ready, so that he could get on with what he really wanted to do—fuck. I never got the idea that anyone would want to touch and caress for its own sake. It was always an obligation one did so that he could be proud of his 'technique' as a lover."

"My partners seem to be slow to understand this is what I enjoy most, and therefore I rarely have an orgasm with my partners because they mount me before I've been satisfied."

"When having intercourse, this is used for stimulation only. If I do not attain orgasm during intercourse, then clitoral stimulation *may* be used again, if I'm lucky."

"Men usually do manual stimulation a very short time—they wanna get in there."

"He only does clitoral stimulation before intercourse. If I don't come during intercourse, he figures it's my problem."

"They tell me they want me to come, but they don't do anything about it so I'm suspicious. This 'why don't you come?' talk may be just another way to make me feel badly."

"He doesn't usually give me much foreplay, but I encourage it, sometimes unsuccessfully. If it happens, it's usually before intercourse."

"They have touched me there, but I doubt if they knew what they were doing."

"Most men will finger the genitals, poke a finger inside, etc., without being asked. This is preliminary and doesn't last long. Sometimes some attempt cunnilingus."

"My partners do sometimes stimulate my clitoral area manually. It is usually for purposes of arousal, rather than orgasm. I wish they would *continue* and that I would be able to *let go* enough to *have an orgasm* or to tell them to continue or show them how to do it so that it does lead to orgasm."

And many men did not even stimulate their partners at all:

"We don't practice clitoral stimulation. I could agree with what's in the chapter on the subject in a dozen books, but first hand I have nothing much to say. Basically I dislike the notion of deliberate stimulation—wishing romance would take care of all the lubrication, etc.—just the back and forth of emotional energy. However, it doesn't."

"Sometime in the first year of marriage eight years ago, my husband said he did not particularly enjoy using his hand. I would not consider it after that, and grew to feel disgust when touching him, too. Now I am totally ice cold with him."

"My man is a little hung up about stimulating me so I have to rely on penetration."

"My lovers never have attempted to stimulate my clitoris specifically."

"My partner disapproves of this technique and I can't usually relax and enjoy it for this reason."

"I like it, but I don't think my husband even knows where the clitoris is, and I'm too embarrassed to tell him. He does hit it by accident sometimes."

"I have never been clitorally stimulated to orgasm. Most of my partners have not been really aware of the clitoris's significance."

"My present partner doesn't realize, or doesn't want to realize (he may see it as a threat to his masculinity), that my clitoris is for me what his phallus is for him. He doesn't want to spend the time to stimulate me."

"My partner does not do this too much. He is more interested in penetration."

"Masturbation by men is usually to check if I'm wet."

FEELINGS ABOUT CLITORAL STIMULATION

"Do you feel guilty about taking time for yourself in sexual play which may not be specifically stimulating to your partner? Which activities are you including in your answer?"

Many women interpreted this question to mean, did they feel guilty about needing "foreplay"—rather than interpreting "taking time for yourself" to mean to have an orgasm. This only underscores more strongly the picture already presented—that clitoral stimulation is commonly used for purposes of arousal but not orgasm. And nevertheless, many women felt guilty—even *without* orgasm—for "needing" this kind of "extra" stimulation. As one woman put it, "Women are made to feel *sexy* women don't require it."

"Most men enjoy the girl playing with them usually, more or as much as intercourse, and therefore each partner should have equal rights to this situation, which is not mutually satisfying. But I personally feel ill at ease asking for my share."

"Yes, sometimes I feel guilty, or like I'm intruding, bothering him. I *know* it's ridiculous and masochistic, but I still *do*."

"My boyfriend stimulates my clitoris usually with his tongue and sometimes his finger. This is satisfying but it seems so computerized and mechanical and lustless—he doesn't mind doing it for me but sometimes I experience *enormous* guilt feelings that he has to. I wish I could come during intercourse. If you know how could you please let me know!"

"I feel afraid more than guilty—of how he'll react and how I'll feel if he's angry."

"Yes. I cannot abide the thought that he is working to make me feel something; he works *too* hard and makes a performance of it, so screw it, I won't ask."

"I don't bother with it. It decreases my pleasure if my partner seems the least put out or obliging."

"Long foreplay makes me uncomfortable because I worry that I'm putting my man through too much work, when I know that he could come so much sooner if he let himself."

"I resent men engaging in some activity because they think it will stimulate me. I doubt that clitoral stimulation is even remotely interesting to men except that it makes them feel powerful in getting a reaction from the woman. I do not cooperate with patronizing nonsense."

"Yes. I feel anxiety, distrust, and resentment at being maneuvered, even in disguised forms; I don't like feeling I'm being 'worked on' by someone who feels I should have 'orgasms.' "

"To me, sexual satisfaction is selfish. Each person takes the most she or he can from the stimulation being offered. The trick for women is to unabashedly take and not give a fuck."

"Orgasm by clitoral stimulation occurs seldom with my partner because I feel very self-conscious when being acted upon without doing anything to the other person."

"I asked my lovers to stimulate my clitoris, but my husband always says, 'Only whores enjoy clitoral contact and going down on the man,' so I don't ask him."

"I feel embarrassed because men think it means I masturbate."

"Yes I feel this way about foreplay. I want more of it than my husband does. Sometimes after intercourse (sometimes with orgasm) I want to go on with clitoral stimulation. But I'm slowly getting over this hangup."

"Yes, I definitely feel guilty about taking time for myself in activities such as clitoral stimulation, erotic massage, and cunnilingus simply because these activities are not specifically stimulating to my partner. I feel selfish, I imagine that my partner is either impatient to 'get on with it' or is not enjoying himself very much, or feels uncomfortable because he doesn't quite know what he's doing (which he usually doesn't because he does it so seldom and doesn't ask for any feedback from me, and I'm so reluctant to volunteer it); in other words I can't relax very well when things are being done to me, only, and I don't come very easily as a result."

"Yes, I feel very guilty (or obligated) taking time for myself, because during intercourse my partner is getting at least as much pleasure as I am. This could relate to the fact that I always resented stimulating my partners in the past—especially when I was a teenager—and perhaps I don't want them to resent me the way I resented them. I remember how my hand would get tired, or, with my husband, how my jaw would ache from having him in my mouth too long. I knew I didn't enjoy stimulating them, and I knew it caused me to resent them, and I never want anyone to feel that way about me. Sometimes when my partner plays with my nipples while I masturbate I feel uncomfortable, also because he usually does it after he's come, when he's not excited any more; he's so dispassionate about it."

"I don't feel guilty because I've never taken time for myself or been given the opportunity to do so. I have always rendered a service to the man, even though I didn't realize it when I was very young. It was expected. There has never been a question of *myself* in a sexual relationship. It has never arisen except in my own mind lately."

"Guilty feelings or not, someone who 'doesn't want to play' is a colossal bummer. I just refuse to capitulate to that 'you're making demands on me' garbage. Especially when it's non-verbal. I get out of bed and read a good book."

"I think in terms of debits and credits—I blew him so he should go down on me, etc."

"I don't make much demand for sexual play. It's the mood that sets the situation, not special physical stimulation. Also I kind of hate to ask my man for things, for fear of being a bother."

"Men think they are really being hip and up front in the vanguard if they do it without your asking. Out of all the information popularized about female sexuality since the 'sexual revolution,' the idea of clitoral stimulation has really made the heaviest impact. But still I feel my partner is doing something that for him is a mere technical obstacle to deal with before going on to the 'real thing,' and I resent feeling up tight about having him do that to me."

"When I ask, and receive, I feel inordinately grateful. Yet I just did what *he* needed to come to climax, and I didn't feel he owed *me* anything."

"I have many problems in this area. I need manual stimulation to orgasm, plus gentle fondling of the breasts, and lots of soft kisses. First of all, I have never stimulated myself when I was with a partner, unless one counts rubbing my clitoral area over his thigh or penis as self-stimulation. Yeah, I guess it is; but I could never use my hand then without feeling really weird, exposed. And I hate giving directions to men almost as much as they hate taking them. Even when they say they want to know what I like, and I tell them, they invariably forget the next time—and I hate like hell giving the schtick again. It's embarrassing and humiliating, like I'm the only weirdo who does things this way."

"Both people participate in a clear unity of purpose with penetration, whereas the manual stimulation is one doing it to the other, so I feel funny about it."

"I used to feel guilty and afraid, but it turns out it's fairly easy to ask. It feels like longed-for honesty."

"I ask, but he stimulates me for three seconds and then just goes ahead and penetrates—he thinks women are just like men. Sex is so much easier and automatic for them. I feel cheated to be a woman as far as sex is concerned."

"When I ask a man to stimulate me manually, they become insulting and suggest I've had lesbian experiences."

"It's rather hard to ask. It's nice if they know on their own, because I feel a little embarrassed saying those words."

"Yes, I feel it's an imposition. That's why I like men who dig it anyway; there's never the implicit question 'is that enough?' "

"I don't feel he enjoys my body as he says he does. He does enjoy my breasts, and it shows from the way he does it."

"I feel he must be thinking, 'This is too much like masturbation.'"

"Yes, I would not ask him. In fact, the last time we had sex he told me he was not going to masturbate me. He feels this is a reflection on his sexual abilities, i.e., his penis should do the job. I couldn't tell him that his penis couldn't possibly do the job as well."

"I still have an uneasy feeling that I am inconveniencing him. I really need more foreplay than what my husband gives me and I have told him so frequently, but he usually doesn't bother. He seems very orgasm oriented—that is, *his* orgasm; that's all that's important to him."

"Yes, it's a matter of dependence on a man's willingness to do an aggressive action for me while I am mostly passive—whereas during intercourse a man orgasms through his aggressiveness. Men also are under the illusion that fucking involves two people in physical enjoyment, whereas clitoral stimulation is only for the woman."

"What I believe contributes to my not having an orgasm sometimes with a partner is my unwillingness to risk letting my partner know he/she is stimulating me in the wrong area or not going fast enough or hard enough or not taking long enough. When I realize I'm not going to climax right away and I think my partner is getting bored, I frustrate myself and stop."

"When he comes, I want to too, but then it always seems like him masturbating me, so I get all worried and say let's go eat some berries and yoghurt."

"Do you feel embarrassed asking for clitoral stimulation? Do you feel your partner is sacrificing to give it to you?"

"I've only managed to talk about it a few times. I talked a long time once to one man and told him what I liked and then I did come with him. I think if I had done that with other men, I could have come with them. But it's less exciting that way, at least at first. If men were more honest and sensual it would be easier too."

"I finally managed to communicate the situation to

one man so that he managed to Get It. The others just could never grasp it, evidently, or I was too shy to get the point across clearly."

"He was furious the last time I asked him to stimulate me (as it stopped his readiness to 'dive in'). He's really timid and clumsy and too unsure for me to risk spoiling another evening by coaching. So I accept him this way (it's really okay)."

"I ask for it sometimes even though it's embarrassing—and then it's hard to be very specific on what you like, and you feel like a nut in being so limited in what turns you on."

"I don't think I ever asked for what I wanted. I just thought some guys knew and some didn't, and it was very exciting when they did. I always was intimidated by the concept of a controlling and/or castrating woman—it was holy writ to me not to make a guy feel inadequate (a result of my intellectual male friends and my psychoanalyst), and to suggest that he do something more or different would have been to appear to suggest that he wasn't adequate. Now the women's movement has helped me to be outspoken. I ask for what I want in all sorts of situations—church, work, the supermarket, local government—and in bed."

"It used to be embarrassing, but then my partner and I learned how to touch each other by oral instructions. Dialogue goes like this: me: 'What would you like?' 'Touch my penis.' 'How hard?' 'Harder.' 'Like this or this?' 'The second way.' 'What else?' 'Touch the tip.' 'How?' 'Rub gently.' 'Like this or this?', etc. I really insisted that he be literal and use all the words. Then we reversed it. I had a hard time asking him to touch my breast or clitoris. Now it is easier, but *still* hard to suggest something new."

"No, I don't ask for it usually. That would be embarrassing to me and is something I know I must struggle with. If I can tell them a foot massage feels wonderful, why not feelings related to sex??? I'm trying though, and it's getting better. If my friend ever reads these answers I'm writing to you, it'll be a long night, but it'll be worth it!"

"Yes! He's *always in the wrong place!* and I'm too embarrassed to show him *exactly* how. Funny, I'm not embarrassed to do anything a man likes or that occurs to us, but I am embarrassed to say, 'a little to the right' or 'higher' or 'stroke my back.' "

"My present lover feels even more affectionate when I tell him what I want—but I'm only able to do this because we really love and care about each other and I am very secure with him. With previous lovers I felt uptight and insecure about asking and I rarely did. I don't think I expected very much of them, or, more importantly, of myself. I was too hung up on maintaining *their* approval, which ultimately, however, didn't matter very much."

"It did embarrass me to say 'not there—here.' Then I closed my legs and said, 'Let's make it for real.' "

"I used to resent not coming, but I reasoned it would be better to put resentment aside and ask for what I wanted. This state of mind took a lot of effort to achieve and it involved learning to be willing to ask outright for what I wanted if I wasn't getting it already. I think being open and direct about one's desires is the best way of getting them satisfied. Lying there and hoping he will make the right move at the right time is too maddening."

"Though I have been really shy about saying to a man what I have said here, perhaps the next time I am with one of my men friends, I'll try telling them about all this and see where it gets me."

If women couldn't ask for clitoral stimulation to orgasm, or do it themselves, they were unlikely, in many cases, to get it from the man they were with.

"Are your partners well informed? Are they sensitive to the stimulation you want?"

Answers to this question indicated that in general only regular partners came anywhere near being well informed—and that women often felt that their needs for clitoral stimulation were unusual, evidenced by statements like, "Not all women are the same," or "Some women are different," or "I usually have to explain how stimulation works for me, that I don't come during intercourse."

"Men are uninformed. They must all read the same book. Of course, passivity in women contributes to their miseducation."

"My husband is now well informed because I explained exactly what I like to have done to me."

"Most men are not exactly uninformed; they seem to know about all the right places of a woman's body, but too often most of them seem to be just not tuned into Woman."

"There are many myths about what men and women want and enjoy. Great honesty is necessary."

"My male partners seemed to be well *mis*informed about female sexuality."

"Men feel we're rarely capable of orgasm."

"Nice but dumb men are unaware that orgasm in women is not a chance occurrence beyond their control!"

"The only partner I've ever had who was 'sensitive' is my husband and it's taken years for us to be honest about our sexual desires. I'm still embarrassed if I have to vocally say what I want."

"Men have been brainwashed to think they're the sexual experts, and furthermore, that whatever feels good to them is what feels good and 'fulfills' us also. Most men I have first slept with seemed to have the attitude, 'Here, dear, let me show you how.' Of all the presumption!"

"They are uninformed and they don't seem to *want* the information about the clitoris, as people once refused to believe the earth went around the sun. And women are still being dishonest about telling them, usually as a way of holding the man."

"They are uninformed but I teach them! Sometimes this is thrown up in my face as part of being a 'demanding female.' "

"My husband isn't fully informed, but he's eagerly reading these answers, and I shall try to be more explicit at appropriate times from now on."

"Most of my partners never gave a thought to what pleased me and totally ignored anything I said. They invariably knew what was best for me. I tried a few times to ask for what helped me but was ignored or ridiculed."

"I don't like men who fancy themselves as sex therapists and try to tell you what should feel good. But the male ego is a pretty tricky thing—you have to go to bed with a guy at least three times before you begin to tell *him* how to do it."

"When we first got married, my husband would just stick his penis in and move it in and out—and he had been married before!"

"They are uninformed in any way specific enough to be useful. I feel as though I should have a physiology training course with each new lover. I asked one man if he had ever seen a woman's genitals, and he said, no, it has always been in the dark. . . . "

"They've read those awful manuals, and take a very mechanical approach. They also don't understand their own sexuality very well."

"What should one do? Post a manual over one's bed?"

"It was like they were foreigners. Often they cared but were ignorant."

"I've never met a man who knew how to stimulate me very well until after I told or showed him what to do. Are all men this insensitive to what turns women on? I know what turns men on and have known since I was fifteen."

"My lover, who was an obstetrician, was not well informed."

"Staggeringly uninformed. The more confident they are of their sexual prowess and the effectiveness of their techniques, the more ignorant they seem to be of the facts and realities."

"We are all uninformed. We need to discuss sex openly and freely together, privately and in public, and show each other with our bodies how we do things— just as is done in other fields. I, for one, have told very few people what I am telling you here. Not good!"

"Most of the men I've encountered *lately* seem real concerned about bringing me to orgasm and always try to manually stimulate me after they've come. They seem to feel bad if I don't come. I guess today it worries them."

"He seems fascinated by what I tell him about myself, as if amazed that I have preferences, etc."

"Men are especially uninformed about the clitoris but it's getting slightly better. Now they are aware of its importance, but don't know where to find it!"

"Very few have had any idea of the number of sensitive places and variety of on-turning things to do—most seem to be very limited themselves in what they like and where they're sensitive. It's unaccountably hard for me (impossible in the throes of passion) to tell them about it either verbally or any other way—and even harder to get them to abandon their preconceived and usual methods even if they think they want to please."

"Most partners seemed to think that I would be automatically aroused by two minutes of kissing and touching and then would be just as ready for intercourse as they were. I have had to tell them or show them what I wanted. No one has ever asked me, or known already what would turn me on. It hasn't been embarrassing, exactly, but it's hard to strike the right tone; showing lovingly what pleases without suggesting that the man is an ill-informed, selfish animal (unless, of course, he is!!)."

"Men should ask flat out? *'What do you want?'* "

"Not one man has consistently performed sexually in a way that would be the best possible and most satisfying for me. It isn't that I don't enjoy intercourse or can't have orgasms in intercourse—it's just a simple fact that in order to enjoy it the most I need more direct clitoral stimulation. And it's not so much work—just three minutes done well is enough to help me fly through half a dozen orgasms in intercourse. It doesn't require suffocating, straining, or sacrificing his pleasure. A gentle hand or sensitive tongue can accomplish miracles. And please, no pressure on the clock. Any man that makes it seem like a favor is going to make the woman feel guilty and pressured, two things that aren't conducive to having orgasms."

"It seems like over the past five years I have met a lot of premature ejaculators, and a lot of inconsiderate, selfish men. They either didn't know about a clitoris and foreplay, or they just wanted to get their rocks off and then roll over. Consequently, I built up a lot of fears and expectations and anxiety and learned (I realize now) not to get too turned on. That way I wouldn't get too disappointed. I put blocks up because I figured the man would come right away anyway, so what's the use? Now my current partner is very considerate and very sensitive to my needs, always asking what feels best, etc. But I have been with men who, when I told them what I liked or how to rub my clit, didn't pay attention. I would repeat myself, but only for so long because it began to sound like nagging. The biggest thing I think I've come up against is men don't seem to realize the value of foreplay and that some women take longer to be ready. It was not really embarrassing to ask for a certain stimulation, but I hesitate sometimes, because I don't want to hurt their feelings etc. I have begun to look out for myself more lately, though, and risked."

"No, most of my partners were not well informed about my body and sexual desires—except my husband. It was always difficult for me to ask for something, or correct or instruct. And often, after summoning the courage to instruct, I would notice that my partner would 'forget' the instructions the next time. Few of my partners ever tried to find out what I liked."

"My husband isn't well informed (but right now he's reading *Sexual Honesty!!!*). I am a little embarrassed to tell him what makes me feel good but, strangely enough, I'm not embarrassed with my lover. I suppose that's because my lover and I have a very honest, open relationship which depends a lot on sex. He has only been with four women besides me, but seems surprisingly well informed with what pleases women. He is a very quick learner, and takes criticism very well. My husband, on the other hand, can't handle criticism at all, which is partly why I never tell him.

"I *did* the Masters and Johnson's bit—two weeks in St. Louis. I learned that good sex followed almost effortlessly after good communication. Communication is what they tried to teach my husband and me. I bought it, he didn't. It takes two to talk, tango, or screw."

"The unique men are those who have outgrown the need for techniques, etc., and are comfortable offering themselves. The important thing is just to *listen* to yourself and to the other person."

It is not news that masturbation for women is done clitorally. Why has this—our own silent testimony to what is efficient stimulation for our bodies—been so ignored in favor of the way men think we *should* have orgasms? All too many men still seem to believe, in a rather naive and egocentric way, that what feels good to them is automatically what feels good to women:

"Most men didn't seem to be aware that what brought them to climax wasn't what brought me to climax. That about sums it up."

"Most partners seem to have a minimal knowledge about female desires and anatomy. My women partners have shown an intuitive knowledge of my needs, so I exclude them in this discussion. Most male partners have a general idea about how to please a woman, but each woman is so different that initially a man may not know how to please *me*, as different from any other woman he's fucked. I may have to let him know that the clitoral stimulation he is giving me is *too* direct and too sensitive, or I may have to adjust my body to his so that I get the right stimulation in intercourse that I need. Initially he cannot know how I like to be fucked. If I'm feeling really loose and nervy and horny I may just say, 'heeey, I really love it this way,' and show him what I mean by fucking him in a certain way, maybe really deep or complete thrusts or real grindy and a lot of pelvic and pubic bone pressure. *Most men do not know that a woman may need clitoral stimulation aside from intercourse to get off*. I can't imagine what women who do not come easily from intercourse, as I do, and who can't bring themselves to communicate their needs, do—they must want to climb walls. It is very easy to communicate my desires in intercourse—men seem to have a bit of intuition about this—but very difficult to communicate needs and desires in clitoral stimulation, cunnilingus, etc. Unless a man volunteers to do these things (which most seldom do), I would never even bring it up. I have begun to wonder why this is. It seems that once a man discovers how 'nicely' I come from intercourse, he decides that this is all I want or need. I *do* love intercourse and I usually moan and yell as I come, so the man knows I've come and assumes my satisfaction, I guess. If I was like some other women who don't often come in intercourse then maybe he'd try to please me in other ways, like clitoral stimulation and cunnilingus, which I really miss. There seems to be a tacit assumption on the part of most men I've fucked that fucking is the best way to come, and if you can come that way there's no use bothering with any of that other stuff. It's an odd assumption, though, when you think of it, cause most men I've been with, even though they loved to fuck, still really dug a good blow job or hand job now and then. In short, what is a man thinking when we are both horny, I stimulate him orally to really get him in a mood, he communicates that he'd like to be blown, I lovingly make him come, and then he assumes that sex is over because he has come? What about me? Doesn't he realize that I expect some kind of reciprocation and sexual release? Appareantly not, because this has happened to me so many times. And I'll be damned if I can figure out how to communicate this without making him feel like a real 'dildo' (dumb prick) or making me feel like a demanding bitch."

Often, even when men did clitorally stimulate their partners, they didn't do it well—perhaps because they felt awkward, embarrassed, or resentful.

"Done to suit *me*, clitoral stimulation would be done by somebody who really wanted to do it, instead of just doing it because it was chic this year or because he thought it might finally get me off, and is doing me some big favor, or because if he does it for me I will do it for him. In short, it is the attitude that really counts."

"The men I usually choose I have sensed are not all that into it. I am looking forward someday to somebody being really into stimulating me so I don't have to concentrate on a thing but just that."

"Once I let a man use my vibrator, but he turned it into something of a weapon, jamming it into my vagina, using it roughly, doing what he pleased, playing his own little game, hurting me, and I never tried again."

"Only one partner ever cared about stimulating me clitorally—no that's not right. Some other men did, but I think they were trying to hurt me, they rubbed so hard. The stimulation has to be the same as when I masturbate."

"It seems like he is trying to *erase* my clitoris!"

"They do it sometimes for arousal, and sometimes for orgasm, but it never leads to orgasm for me because they either 'stimulate' too hard, or too directly, or not long enough. I don't explain what I want too well so it's partly my fault, but manual clitoral stimulation is important to me because I do it to them, and I believe turn about is fair play."

"It invariably seems that they're left-handed, and I have a right-handed clitoris."

"Usually we just try to find the damned thing."

"My husband is pretty clumsy in the clitoral stimulation area, and our hangups keep me from telling him how I could enjoy sex more. I've been very disappointed in my ability to deal with this whole area of our relationship."

"I try to communicate with my lover as to what does it for me. Usually they don't like me to rub the clitoris myself and they insist on doing it for me—all wrong, too fast, too hard, just irritating the tissues. When I come to the realization that I'm not going to reach orgasm, I fake one, so he'll stop rubbing the life out of my clitoris and get on to the business of coming and it will be over with. In order to teach him how to do it right would take a major education and psychotherapy job which is only worth going through with someone I really dig."

"My partners usually are very clumsy when it comes to clitoral stimulation—either they press too hard, or right in the center which is agonizing, or they move too jerkily. I use my whole hand and not fingers like they do so that the pressure is evenly distributed and my clitoris doesn't get poked and shocked to death."

"There's just one thing I can't stand—that's when someone rubs my clitoris hard and rough directly on it. It's the most annoying feeling."

"Men always do it too roughly. And they'll change the rhythm at just the wrong time."

"The main problem with having someone else stimulate my clitoris is that he usually doesn't increase the pressure enough or stroke fast enough for me to orgasm."

"I try to show men how I like it, but most of them can't do it right or don't want to, so I seldom have man made orgasms."

"My partner sometimes tries direct stimulation with his hand rubbing my clitoris, but he never gets it on the right spot, or else he doesn't stay on it when he does hit it."

"If he could just stimulate me with his fingers—but he goes around my clitoris and *misses* it."

"My husband does stimulate my clitoris but his touch is much harder than I like and though I tell him this on occasion, he doesn't seem to be able to remember the light touch for long. I do become stimulated from this touch, but it seldom leads to orgasm. It is used mostly as foreplay."

What kind of clitoral stimulation do women like?

Of course, it is impossible to give any kind of quick answer that will be true for every woman every time, because each person is slightly different; the answers contained thousands of subtle but very important nuances. In general it is always necessary to be sensitive, and to feel what the other person's body is saying. Most women like clitoral stimulation to start out softly and slowly, gradually building up to a little more pressure. It is often safer to use the whole hand, or palm of the hand, than one or two fingers.

"Gentle but firm with a rhythm I can count on. But the surprises and unknowns of my partner's fingers make his stimulation of me much more erotic than if I were using my fingers. He strokes gently up and down the groove."

"I like when his fingers are slightly spread and moving the genital area around slowly and softly, then increasing the pressure."

"I like irregular ('clumsy') rhythmic movements—soft—sometimes a little *too* soft (like teasing), so I must press up against his hand."

"Changing the position of the hand or fingers would make me lose whatever height of excitement I had gained. It should stay in one place all the way up to and through my orgasm."

"Four fingers placed slightly above my vagina moving lightly around is just about right."

"Pressure or harsh rubbing irritates my clitoris; there must be an even sort of gentle movement and pressure with much fluid for lubrication. At the same time I move my body in the rhythm to help."

"I usually like a gentle but insistent pressure on my clitoral area (that is, against that upper bone). Direct stimulation of my clitoris is uncomfortable."

"I like direct stimulation of my clitoris with fingers or tongue, round and round, at first not constantly, but at different speeds and tempos, and then finally all the time real fast."

"Firm, quick, constant movements, increasing in strength (firmness) and speed as orgasm comes close."

"Soft first, then the more times I climax, the harder I like it."

"Soft then hard, the position varying for each orgasm, but not varying *within* an orgasm."

"Best for me is sort of shaking my clitoral area with the palm."

"The vibrator *concept* is helpful when showing my lover how to masturbate me. He should vibrate his hand on my pubic area."

"If they do not do it on their own, I place their finger where I want it, then show them the motion I want and the amount of pressure that I desire. It always leads to orgasm, if they are patient and sensitive enough to follow my instructions."

"They should use a light, teasing, tentative touch, not too regular—I like an attitude of playfulness, exploring, sensing."

"I need a certain quality of touch from soft to medium, otherwise my body gets numb and loses the feelings."

"Diddling is what I like—playing around—medium intensity—a rhythm with syncopation—a little jolt, a little surprise—drives me crazy!"

"A break or change in the rhythm can even stop my coming altogether."

"There is nothing worse than a partner who is not knowledgeable in this technique—i.e., fingers planted firmly and directly on the clitoris."

"I like soft and rhythmic rubbing, accompanied by kissing."

"A gentle massage then gradually firmer. Hard massaging causes pain when it is directly on my clitoris—a common mistake men make. The more vigorous massage has to be around the edges—never directly on the clitoris, but softer movements can be direct. I like direct movements around my clitoris, alternating with up and down movements. The rhythm should be maintained—gives me more confidence, I think."

"I find I always have to say, *Don't stop now!* "

"Soft massage, position constant, rhythm constant. Actually stroking is not involved, but pressing and then moving the hand around is."

"I prefer the use of the hand or a larger object because it's softer than fingers."

"I like the very front of me rubbed, higher than my clitoris."

"The fingers should be well-lubricated."

"Direct physical stimulation is physically irritating; I prefer indirect clitoral stimulation where he uses his entire hand, not just fingers."

"Direct clitoral stimulation with a regular rhythm but a variety of methods, sometimes slight interruptions of rhythm plus mouth kissing at the same time; also my partner should appear excited."

"The guy shouldn't act like he's doing seven years of hard labor, he should be creative. It should be gentle, loving, and passionate contact."

"The light touch is better than the gorilla approach."

"Soft and circular movements. I prefer contact over the labia (i.e., fingers push the labia against my clitoris) rather than direct touch on the clitoris."

"Please don't try to push it back into my body, it doesn't do a thing!"

"Stimulate the tips of the labia very close to the front of my body."

"Stimulation of the whole mons area is more important than direct clitoral stimulation for me."

"I like him to draw back the foreskin and rub the clitoris itself."

"Sometimes my husband goes under the hood and touches and lifts, touches and lifts. I once had a lover who seemed to shake it. That was wonderful. As for myself, I just do a simple circular motion."

"Begin slow, and end near a frenzy."

"Soft, rhythmic, clitoral, with 'excursions' to the vagina. Pressure can be increased as I get more aroused, but medium or hard pressure at the beginning will turn me off."

"Toward orgasm he should not slow down—it drives me crazy, I hate it!"

"Mellow and affectionate, yet with spunk."

"The general area but not the clitoris directly. As I become more and more *quiet* this means I am closer and closer to orgasm and until the moment of orgasm when movement begins, it is very important that my partner not interrupt the continuing gentle and rhythmic stroking of the area, by misinterpreting my quietness. The area should be wet and lubricated, not dry, especially when using the hand."

"Rapid side-to-side massaging of the clitoris, by either tongue or finger, starting gently, increasing in pressure as I become more excited. Corollary stimulation of the nipple of one or both breasts helps immeasurably."

"It's best to vary the position at first to find the one which gives the most stimulation, and then keep it consant."

"I like a slow and soft massage that becomes harder and faster, and then goes back to the beginning again (teasing element)."

"It should be a medium massage with rhythm and empathy."

"Soft massage with rhythm and position constant because in that way it builds up; if it is changed, I have to build up again."

"The position should be stable, because the change of position could turn me off at the wrong moment."

"As arousal gets more acute, I need a more firm, rhythmic and quite constant massaging around my clitoris. But too much manipulation of the very sensitive clitoris would end by hurting and immediately closing up and turning off the feeling. A relaxing of the rhythm, or a break or change in it at the final stage—when all the feeling in the entire body, breasts, torso, head, legs and feet, seem to be gushing up and surging toward an overflow point—would be terrible, an awful letdown of the trust put in the lover who got so careless (uncaring)."

"Medium or soft massage, I like to be 'teased' a bit—once the feeling of excitement starts in my clitoris, the movements should be rhythmic and the position constant."

"The most reliable technique is one finger placed along either the length of the clitoral shaft, or just above it, rubbing rhythmically, beginning light and slow, then harder and faster. Doing this for fifteen to thirty seconds, then stopping, then beginning again, repeated five to six times."

"Sometimes, frustratingly, too constant a pressure

numbs me more than anything, and I find it hard to come."

"Barely brushing the skin."

Positions used during manual clitoral stimulation with a partner.

Here again, preferences depend on individual needs, especially with regard to leg position. However, there should always be room for freedom of movement of the legs and lower body.

"I lie on my back or my side, especially with my back arched over my partner's extended leg, while he rubs my clitoris up and down."

"I like him on my left side, me cuddling up with him, while he rubs me with his left hand. (I would like oral, but he refuses to do it or have it done to him.)"

"I stand in the shower with my partner 'sudsing' me clean between the legs."

"She lies beside me, using one hand to stimulate my clitoris—and we're kissing, and I'm holding her."

"I stand in front of my spouse, who is seated. He uses his finger or the vibrator on my clitoris with a slow, moving action, then as I become aroused, he increases the speed of rhythm until orgasm, and then he pushes either his finger or the vibrator up into my vagina."

"My partner rests her hand, palm facing into my pubic area, with one or two fingers on my clitoris with gentle pressure."

"I lie on my back and my partner lies to my right on his side—his left hand under my buttocks with his middle finger inserted in my vagina, stimulating my clitoris with his right hand."

"Usually I'm lying on my back and my husband is on his side kissing me on the lips and neck, while using his middle finger to exert the primary pressure while the other fingers stimulate my vaginal lips."

"I am on my back with my legs apart and his head and hands are between my legs watching what he is doing."

"He lies gently playing with my clitoris, rubbing up and down while teasing and talking dirty."

"I lie on my stomach and he's on my back reaching up under me and makes me come and come and come, and he won't stop and he won't let me up! *Wow!*"

"My thighs are wide apart, but not necessarily my feet. I am on my back. He has a finger on each inner labium, rubbing them against the base of the clitoris."

"I like to be on my side with her beside me on her side, with both of us moving back and forth, with one of her hands on my clitoris, the other on one of my breasts, one of my hands in her hair and the other on her leg or her stomach."

"The man stands behind me with me facing a mirror. He uses his right hand and with the left massages my left breast—or the man lies in front of my open legs, watching closely as the clitoris gets harder and redder."

"I'd rather have a part of the other person's body stimulate me than a hand or finger, so that leaves open a lot of positions."

"We lie facing each other, with our legs entwined and fondle each other's bodies until one of us comes near to orgasm, then I or she concentrates on that person until orgasm. Then it's the other's turn."

"I like to move myself against a man's body, usually his leg or sometimes his penis (though I'm shy about the latter). Also it can be his hand moving but I need to be already aroused, enough to be lubricated, and it seems to be very difficult for men to learn what the right kind of pressure or motion is."

"He rubs around my genital area and then down into the lips—opens the lips and explores until I signify (non verbally) excitement. He continues rubbing through an orgasm or two, then might stimulate my clitoris orally by licking or sucking the area—hard actions are more satisfying and during these actions he is wetting his fingers with vaginal secretion and inserting one or two fingers into my vagina. Sometimes he licks deep into my vagina also."

"I like being backed against a wall, with clothes on, feeling his whole hand pushing up against me—great!"

Stimulation of the clitoral area with the man's penis.*

"Before penetration, I hold his penis and use it to fiddle with my clitoris."

"We lie on our sides, face to face, and I move his penis with my hand so the tip stimulates my clitoris. On top, I can balance the tip of his penis in the strategic area and can stimulate myself with a rocking motion."

"We lie on our sides with my back to him and I take his penis through my legs from behind with both hands and give myself direct stimulation. This can be varied by caressing his testicles and inner thighs but at the same time stimulating the clitoris. Orgasms are great this way."

"I can orgasm by getting on top of him while clothed and moving up and down on his penis, or by moving my hips in a circular motion while straddling him and sitting on the head of his penis."

"I lie on my back, one leg hooked over my partner's shoulder with him brushing his penis and balls across my clitoris."

"We pet heavily and I put my hand down his pants so he gets an erection. Then he moves it up and down on me."

"I hold my partner's penis between my thighs and have him simulate intercourse."

"My husband is on top, not penetrating, moving hard."

"Him on top, with me holding his penis and rubbing it against my clitoris."

"Another way is both lying face down, me on top, while I rub my clitoris on his buttocks. Sometimes my hands play with his testicles and penis too."

"One man had the most stimulating habit of pushing his penis inside my vagina then rubbing it up and down on my clitoral area (holding his penis with his hand) then into my vagina again, then rubbing my clitoris, etc.

---

* This and the following type are not included in the statistics regarding frequency of orgams by manual stimulation, but can be found separately in the appendix.

I don't usually like fingers, because men are too rough and clumsy."

"Lying sideways, he puts his penis between my legs near the clitoral area and then moves back and forth."

"Sitting, facing each other, with the lips of my vulva around his penis and the top part of his penis rubbing my clitoris—marvelously warm."

"Side by side, we place his penis between my lips, and begin stroking."

"After many years of trial and error, my lover and I have finally found a foolproof (almost) way for me to orgasm. His penis is used to stimulate my clitoris after we have had some preliminary intercourse. He pulls out, does not have orgasm and uses his penis to stimulate my clitoris. He or I use a hand to guide his penis to massage my clitoris. I invariably achieve orgasm then, and while I am in the throes of orgasm, he enters, we fuck, then he orgasms."

"Standing (clothed) with his erect penis pressing against my clitoris, breasts against breasts, hands holding bottoms, we press and rub against other."

"For clitoral stimulation, I like to stand between two legs with hands pressing my ass into a stiff cock. In that position, two persons begin to rotate and move and press against each other, and sometimes I have an orgasm this way. It's great on a dance floor."

Tribadism: stimulation by rubbing two clitoral areas together.

"Lying or standing very close to one another, pressing hard with rocking movements against each other's pubic areas."

Tribadism is only mentioned here in passing, as sex between women will be discussed extensively in the following chapter.

Do it yourself.

Is the "answer" to the oppression and neglect of female sexuality and especially orgasm that men should learn to give (better) clitoral stimulation? Yes and no.

Of course men should learn these things but, even more important, we should find the freedom to take control over whether or not we get this stimulation. One way we can do this is to move in ways that increase our pleasure, for example, during clitoral stimulation. Men certainly have control of their own stimulation to orgasm: during intercourse they move and thrust in ways that are best for them to orgasm. Why should this be wrong for women—even if it interferes, at least temporarily, with what the man is enjoying? Here are some answers from the *few* women who did do this:

"I rub against his buttocks. Or I ride him, doing all of the motion—I have to be kinda careful not to press too hard against his pubic area (causes pain for him). My head is always rested on his left side for some reason."

"I prefer to do the moving so I can set my own rhythm or help my partner to understand it."

"Me on top, sometimes sitting with the penis inside. I just move around a lot. Men have tried oral and manual stimulation but it's never worked with me. Maybe I'm too sensitive."

"I lie on my stomach with my legs spread. I need complete freedom of movement, and move my pelvis in a circular thrusting motion. I lift my buttocks up and down rhythmically to vary the pressure. Meanwhile my partner also strokes and rubs my buttocks."

"I used to accept sex without orgasm, faked orgasms, concentrated only on the man's pleasure, tried to convince myself of nonexistent vaginal feelings (like feeling the 'hot' sperm inside me where you can't feel anything), and didn't think I should 'work' or do anything 'unfeminine' in bed. Now I usually do what I want along with what they're doing."

"I rub the top of the fleshy part of my vagina against the man's bone right above his penis."

"I lie on my side facing my lover, with her thigh between mine, and rub my clitoris against her thigh."

"I can sometimes achieve an orgasm by having my partner bring his thigh up between my legs. I then hold it tight by wrapping my legs around it, and by moving my hips I can rub the area of my clitoris against his thigh."

"I hold my legs together tight and even crossed. I squeeze them together hard and relax them over and over again, as I press against him."

And what is wrong with using your own hand, for example, to stimulate yourself—"masturbating" with your partner?

"A partner can't stimulate the clitoris to orgasm. I have to do it myself. He can't feel what the stimulation is doing—I can."

"*I* have to do it. My partners usually can't find it, or are too rough with it. If he is an erotic man, he is fascinated and usually gets turned on."

"I use a vibrator-like motion, moving my clitoris from side to side as rapidly as possible. I do this for myself as no man seems to sustain it for as long as I need."

"If he doesn't exactly know how, I will show him by putting my hand on his hand. The thing is, I don't like being the only one getting turned on. I feel insecure about it—more naked than him."

"He is sensitive but I think it necessary to stimulate myself. I don't like giving orders. It ruins the sensitivity for me. I would rather satisfy myself than give instructions."

"The best thing we've found so far is for me to stimulate myself directly before fucking. This keeps it in the family and lubricates and prepares my vagina for intercourse, which I then enjoy very much. And my husband enjoys watching me do this. So it works."

"I like sucking a man and masturbating at the same time."

"I enjoy mutual face-to-face voyeuristic masturbation!"

"I lie on my back, and he slides my own hand and fingers over my body."

"My body achieves orgasm 'best' by a combined effort of my lover and myself. She uses her mouth and tongue to stimulate my clitoris and then gently blows into my vagina; while she does this I masturbate. This combined effort leads me to a most terrific orgasm."

"I do most of the clitoral massaging while my husband plays with my cunt, runs his hands gently between my legs, plays with and sucks my breasts, and talks to me softly all the time about coming."

These were very unusual answers.

ORGASM FROM CUNNILINGUS

How many women orgasm regularly from cunnilingus?
The other widely practiced form of clitoral stimulation is cunnilingus—oral sex. Do women have orgasms frequently during oral sex? The percentages here are similar to those for clitoral stimulation by hand: whereas 44 percent of the women orgasmed regularly with clitoral stimulation by hand, 42 percent orgasmed regularly during oral stimulation.

Frequency of Orgasm During Cunnilingus

	TOTAL POPULA-TION		NEVER ORGASM IN ANY WAY	DIDN'T AN-SWER	NEVER HAD CUNNI LINGUS	NO ORGASM DURING CUNNI-LINGUS	DO ORGASM DURING CUNNI LINGUS
Q.I	690	=	82	75	15	121	397
Q.II	919	=	102	115	24	131	547
Q.III	235	=	30	39	7	28	131
Total	1844	=	214	229	46	280	1075

Breakdown of Frequency of Orgasm During Cunnilingus

	Q.I	Q.II	Q.III		TOTAL
"Yes"	350*	50	10	=	410
Always	6	95	16	=	117
Usually	3	201	57	=	261
Sometimes	24	122	34	=	180
Rarely	14	79	14	=	107
Total	397	547	131		1075
Percentage of total population who orgasm regularly during cunnilingus	52%*	38%	35%	=	42%

Once again, the problem with counting accurately here was, as with clitoral stimulation by hand, the fact that most oral stimulation was done for arousal and not for orgasm. That is, although most women loved cunnilingus, especially since there was hardly ever any chance for pain as with manual clitoral stimulation, all too often cunnilingus was offered by the partner for very short intervals, and that not continuously on the clitoris, as "foreplay." So here again it was at times unclear whether the woman's answer meant how often she had orgasms during cunnilingus, or how often she *would* be able to orgasm during cunnilingus, if given the chance.

In addition, Questionnaires I and II used only the term "cunnilingus" and did not provide the definition "oral sex," as did Questionaire III. Some women did not know what "cunnilingus" was, and even in Questionnaire III, when it was defined as "oral sex," a few

* The wording of the question in this version of the questionnaire was different, and accounts for the irregular percentage: "Do you usually orgasm during cunnilingus?" Rather than "Do you orgasm during cunnilingus—usually, sometimes, rarely, or never?"

women responded regarding fellatio—perhaps never having experienced oral sex themselves. But the most common reaction was that oral sex was most often a form of "foreplay," not done long enough for orgasm or with the understanding that it would be "acceptable" for the woman to have an orgasm then:

"I've gotten to dislike cunnilingus because I've gotten so aroused without coming. Men seem to think that once they've done that for a while that's all, they can just climb back on and come, having done their best for the good of the cause. I guess it's this feeling I have that they are doing it in a mechanical way because they read that it's a nice thing to do to women and that all women really like it, and that they are good guys to do it."

"I wish I could be told sometimes in the middle of the day or in bed at night, 'Lie down, relax, enjoy; I'm going to give you head for an *hour*.' Ah-h-h-h . . ."

And often, perhaps more often than not, it was done in conjunction with fellatio—"69"—making it a little difficult to really concentrate on having an orgasm oneself.

However, cunnilingus was still described very frequently as one of the most favorite and exciting activities; women mentioned over and over again how much they loved it:

"A tongue offers gentleness and precision and wetness and is the perfect organ for contact. And, besides, it produces sensational orgasms!"

"Cunnilingus is very sweet, tender, and tense."

"It's sexy! What can I say!"

"It's erotic because it's forbidden—another kind of 'soul kissing.' "

"It arouses me *greatly,* but I get tense and don't have orgasms. I have some feeling that neither I nor my husband should be enjoying it!"

"It really puts me in orbit, and I *always* have an orgasm!"

FEELINGS ABOUT CUNNILINGUS

If women find cunnilingus so enjoyable, why doesn't it lead to orgasm more frequently?

Once again, many women were held back by feelings of embarrassment and self-consciousness. The most common worries about cunnilingus were: Is the other person enjoying it? And, especially, Do I smell bad?

"I haven't gotten away from the feeling I'm 'dirty' 'down there.' "

"I never had orgasm during cunnilingus. I hope to soon but I still feel my cunt is dirty and this preoccupies me if anyone attempts it with me."

"I'm afraid I will 'gross him out' if I orgasm then."

"If I were a man I would *never* do it!"

"I am *always* self-conscious that I might smell or look disgusting."

"It's messy. My husband must brush his teeth and wash his face after."

"It feels like I'm being 'serviced' somehow."

"Men seem to be more squeamish about oral sex than I am."

"I am too concerned about my husband's reaction to tastes and smells to fully enjoy it, but I'll *never* use sprays and douches."

"I think it's fine if I feel clean and don't have my period."

"I think perhaps it seems a little gross, or I think it isn't 'ladylike.' I got a big dose of 'ladylike' when I was growing up. Perhaps I think I smell bad."

"I used to always orgasm during it, but now I rarely do because of my current partner's reticence, which sometimes turns into active distaste (pardon the pun) and sometimes he puts on a big martyr act."

"Yes, I like it now, but it took me years to 'allow' it. Why must we feel so unclean??"

"I often wonder if it really does anything for him."

"My man has a mental block here. He thinks the

vulva area smells ghastly and gags when he tries. He's tried, but can't get over it."

"The odor bothers me; but sometimes it really turns me on!"

"I go back to what I now understand is my learned repugnance to my genitals. I find it physically pleasing but can't understand why any man would want to put his mouth there."

"I get uptight if I haven't recently showered, because of my discharge."

"As much as I like cunnilingus, I want it to be over fast. I have a conflict about this because I feel it must be unplesant for him to get his face wet."

"I can't really believe my partner likes it and feel that he is doing it for some other reason he won't admit or tell me."

"I feel that I don't smell or taste right. I feel ashamed."

"I don't like it because I have a feeling he feels obligated to do it, and I don't care for sacrifices."

"I enjoy cunnilingus, although it feels more comfortable for me to eat a man. Men have never made me feel comfortable and beautiful in that position. I hope someday I can enjoy it."

"I enjoy it, but feel a certain amount of distaste about it. I am a little shy about kissing a partner who has just had his mouth on my vagina. Probably a very early hangup, having to do with dislike of the 'lower' parts, etc."

"I kind of enjoy having it done to me, although it makes me feel vulnerable emotionally, slightly like it's something dirty, and the other person doesn't like doing it. I have performed it several times on others, but it seems like they weren't comfortable with it and didn't all that much enjoy it."

"I wonder sometimes if my partner is enjoying it, or if he is only doing it to please me, especially when I like to take a long time. The feeling he is not enjoying it lessens my pleasure and I get self-conscious about coming."

"I am afraid I smell. I also feel that I *must* come when so much attention is paid to my doing just that— and that pressures me, and I don't feel free enough to come."

This concern with cleanliness and odor is part of the more general problem of accepting female genitals:

"I am ashamed of my genitals, and don't want anyone to see them."

"I don't believe our society likes vaginas. I think it finds vaginas dirty, smelly, hairy, wet, etc. They want us to spray them with deodorant."

"They think our vaginas are dirty because we menstruate and eject babies and smell bad from urine, blood, discharges, and sex fluids. Women should stop pretending that they have dry genitals."

Even the word "pudendum," which means "the external genitals of the female," comes from the Latin *pudere*, "to be ashamed." Artist Betty Dodson has done many drawings, personal "portraits" of friends and other women, which can be found in her book *Liberating Masturbation*. They show how varied vulval anatomy can be, and how sensuous and elegant. The fact that there is no "iconography" of women's genitals, while penises are glorified, is a further reflection of the way sex mirrors the general cultural inequality between women and men.

"Do you think your vagina and genital area are ugly or beautiful? Do they smell good or bad?"

"You know what turns me on? The smell of my own human mush!"

"I think my vagina is beautiful, rich, fertile—I especially like my black pubic hair. The smell is at times erotic and this turns me on—but I don't believe in not bathing to keep the smell!"

"I used to dislike touching my cunt to wash it—I used to think it smelled bad and I used deodorant. Now I think it's beautiful, thanks to the women's movement."

"They're ugly, like an unhealed wound. The male genitals are beautiful."

'It's small, cute, and attractive like the rest of me. It smells good if clean.'

"Beauty is in the eye of the beholder. If I'm horny, they're beautiful. Artistically, they're ugly. There's no reason it should smell good."

"It's ugly—lots of extra flabby skin, all wrinkled and flapping. My two-year-old daughter's is beautiful, very firm and smooth."

"Ugly. But then I have a long ways to go in making peace with my body generally, although there's a cyclical nature to it all—sometimes I'm much more comfortable in myself than others. I've tried to see some beauty in my genitals, but without much success. But then I remember that it took me three years of not shaving my legs before I could look at them without getting freaked, so surely it will take a long time to undo the damage of my social conditioning in such a heavily loaded area. . . ."

"I am just beginning to relate to my vagina as something good, personal, and beautiful. Pre-lesbian, I was very unrelated to my cunt, feared it, was ashamed of it, etc."

"The outside is ugly like a plucked chicken."

"I've gone from feeling they were unknown and unmentionable to feeling they're fine and usually nice."

"Logically they're ugly and smell bad, but a man's genitals aren't better. Emotionally, they're beautiful, but I fear he won't think so."

"Ideally, genitals are beautiful and smell sensuous. But really they are bad looking and sometimes stink."

"They're beautiful—the secretions are exciting and smell unusual."

"I put my finger into myself and got so sick to my stomach after a second that I never tried it again, not even to put on a Tampax."

"Funny and crooked."

"I used to be embarrassed by my protruding vaginal lips."

"The vaginal smell is one of the most complex and mysterious."

"It's ugly if viewed from directly below, although the pubic hair is attractive frontally."

"My husband is more beautiful and smells better. I look funny and smell bad during my period."

"Beautiful—and smell womanly."

"Not as pretty as the one woman's I slept with (who I thought was beautiful). Both of ours smelled bad."

"One thing makes me *sick* and that is that a picture of a woman with her legs open is called pornographic and dirty. How dare they call the most beautiful part of me dirty!"

"Very nonsymmetrical with all that loose skin."

"They're interesting, delicate, and fascinating in design."

"Not beautiful, not good. But in good sex, they become supersensitive and beautiful."

"They're ugly, smell warm, moist, and different from anything else—there is a sensuous smell in sex."

"I used to feel bad about the smell and douched and sprayed and washed every minute because one man said it was bad."

"I think it's good, even when it smells bad!"

"It's just 'there'—what's so beautiful about flaps of hair and slimy skin?"

"The vagina's good and natural but not aesthetic. Appealing but not repelling."

"It smells so good, I smell my fingers after masturbation!"

"The genitalia are ugly, but pubic hair is feminine and mysterious and quite beautiful."

"Vaginal and pubic hair look fine and smell good— but the color inside of the lips, no. I would probably have designed them to look different if given the chance."

"Healthy and warm and erotic looking; smell intriguing."

"I used to like them but now after being exposed to men's attitudes, I think they're ugly and bad."

"Beautiful in a strange way."

"Beautiful—fantastic—wonderful."

"I think I smell good and taste all right too. Any

lover that wants me to smell like a lilac or rose is discarded very quickly."

"Lovely, fascinating, curious, mysterious, despite self examination. I like my smell—but will he?"

"The inside of the vagina is gorgeous—outside is weird looking. When young, and when on the Pill, there was only a faint odor, but now I'm on the IUD and it is stronger and not kissable."

"Ugly, but I am trying to accept them. I have never in my life seen another woman's genital area, only my baby daughter's. They are so pink and clean. I'm kind of purple and red and brown. The modesty of my mother's generation dictated that I should ever be humiliated by my private parts. On top of that, the first man I was with spread my legs and told me I looked like a dried prune."

"When I was little I thought 'that' part of me was ugly—the red color reminded me of pictures I had seen of intestines and organs which had grossed me out. Also I remember sitting in the bathroom while my father took a shower talking to him. I thought his penis was ugly because of its shape and color. I was glad to be a girl because I was much prettier and didn't have one of those ugly dark dangling things. (Did you ever notice pornography always shows *erect* penises, not dangling ones?) Now I like to look at my vagina. I don't think of it as beautiful but I like to look at it. To me my vagina is warm, moist and soft, I like to feel it, me."

"I bought a very valid, informative book called *Liberating Masturbation** and I learned a good deal about both myself and other women—especially valuable things such as the fact that my long, uneven labia were not a deformity, but women could look all different ways."

"I think I have a nicely made pretty genital area, but do not belong to the vaginal fascination cult. If not washed, it smells bad but no worse than the penis."

"I don't think it's ugly, but am not sure I'd say it is

---

* By Betty Dodson. Published and distributed by Betty Dodson, Box 1933, New York, N.Y. 10001.

beautiful, more that it seems strange and exotic to me. I love the way I smell. When I was young, and now, I used to masturbate, and then smell my fingers. The odor really turned (and still does) me on, and my mother caught me quite often, and really freaked out. She tried to get me to stop, but I never did. To her it was and is, perverted, and I guess she'll never change."

"Neither. Some faces are so beautiful it takes my breath away. I've never felt anything like that about genitals, male or female."

"They look ugly, but *feel* beautiful!"

"Neither, but I am shy about people seeing them."

"They were nice before I had a baby, but not now. My pubic hair is too long, so I cut it. I wash two times a day and douche every three days."

"Gorgeous. I put my finger in my cunt and rub it behind my ears!"

"Beautiful and soft and warm."

"The smell and the taste excites me. I have begun to taste myself regularly, and wonder why it tastes bland every once in a while? Usually it tastes good."

"Smells bad to others, but I'm used to it."

"When I was in the hospital, some male doctors said I have too much hair there. Now I feel embarrassed when I get undressed."

"I watched another woman become aroused, and it was fascinating to watch the genital/vaginal changes."

"I wish I could truly believe my cunt is beautiful like my husband says, that it smells and tastes good, but deep down, I'm always afraid."

"Ugly, embarrassing. I refer to 'it' in the third person, as not part of my own body. I'm trying to overcome this feeling."

"I don't think of it as *beautiful* just as I don't think of my face as beautiful. But it's part of my body, part of *me,* and that's nice."

"I guess my generation was not taught that the genital area was beautiful, so I have a few hangups."

"Until I met Don, I thought about them as little as possible. After I met him, I felt much better about myself. When we are making love, I see myself and him as *gorgeous!*"

"I worked in a doctor's office once where I saw lots of them and I don't think they are beautiful; I think they are ugly—like a gaping wound with dirty brown edges. On the other hand a female with her legs *together* is beautiful."

"I think they are beautiful. I like the way the pubic hair curls and the smell of the secretions; the colors of the skin, the shape of the lips."

"Women seem to me to be more sexually curious and freer than many men. They like smells and gushiness more."

"Beautiful. I think they smell great. I resent that we've been made to feel dirty and bad-smelling."

"I used to think my genitals were ugly but one day I realized that I only thought they were because I was supposed to feel that way. From then on I admitted that they were quite functional, graceful, and handy. Beautiful like a person you know well becomes beautiful."

"At fourteen I decided to cut off one labia which hung lower but after getting the nail scissors I lost my nerve."

"Basically ugly, but I'm struggling like mad to get rid of that."

"Pleasantly homely, interesting, and complex."

"I like most parts of my body. Those parts I don't think are attractive, I'm fond of."

"Neither. Good if clean. But can I consider any part of me beautiful at fifty?"

"B.C. (before cunnilingus) I thought they were disgusting. But, since I love *hers,* I now love mine too! Smell too."

"At first, when I had not looked at adult vaginas, they looked ugly. Now okay."

"I only looked recently; I like the hair and sometimes brush it after a bath. The lips look funny."

"I used to think I was horribly ugly and deformed until I saw some porno and saw I looked like other women. Now I think all female genitals are ugly."

"Lovely, all the little folds and holes and juices."

"They just 'are.' I wish I were a man."

"I've been told they're pretty, but don't believe it."

"I sense that men think that while they're blessed with a wondrous organ, women are cursed with something downright repulsive."

"Plain, but with charisma."

"Ugly. I pulled one of my labia minora when I was masturbating when I was eleven. It got long and I thought that was the reason. The other got almost as long, later. I always thought I was supposed to look like a nude little girl, except with hair. My mother said my labia majora were separated because I had 'touched' myself. So I had a big guilt about how I deformed myself. I have had to get other ideas piecemeal, for the anatomical drawings of women's genitals look more like little girls' genitals with a scrap of pubic hair than like mine. The S.F. *Chronicle* has or had (I don't see it any more) a Dr. Hip-Pocrates, who gave straight answers. He said something once about a woman who had lips four inches long not being abnormal. Another time he mentioned the fact that the lips of a brunette are brownish. Lolita taught me when I was about thirty that someone else's crotch smelled, for HH smelled the acrid crotch of Lolita's panties. All my life I had tried to get the courage to ask a doctor what genitals should look like, but I never dared, even through two births! Finally at forty-six I asked a doctor if mine were normal, and his answer was, 'I'm not much of a judge.' I did it again at forty-seven but this time I asked a woman doctor at the college and she was magnificent. She said it was an important question and she was glad I had asked, that women don't have the opportunity men have to compare genitals because women's are hidden and they have a tradition of modesty, in contrast to the male tradition of comparison. She said that my genitals were normal, but I was hairier than normal. I was glad to receive a straight answer. I am comfortable naked with another person, if I am intimate with him and we love each other. Then I don't mind my hairy (or prickly) legs and my ugly crotch, because he doesn't. Other than those things I feel proud of my body and take pleasure in its strength and competence and good looks. I have had fantastic breasts—full and high—that I never liked when I was in girls' schools because all the girls made fun of them. When I was young and interested in gymnastics, I wanted to cut them off. When I was older and a good modern dancer, I'd come across the floor and my roommate would say 'jello again.' When I finally got into coed college, I learned they were as beautiful as any breasts in the world. Part of feeling all right about myself, I taught myself by becoming an artists' model— seeing that artists found me beautiful made me feel more assurance (but I tried not to show my crotch and comb my pubic hair over the split in it). I am not comfortable naked with people I am not intimate with. I went with my children and another woman and her children to the wilderness where they all skinny-dipped. I didn't want to. I thought about my dreams of going naked and it was all right; and now I wanted to wear clothes and have it be all right. I don't like encounter groups either—instant intimacy of any sort turns me off. I have no desire to embrace strangers and fondle their faces. It's too good with someone you love. Now I am sorry to see my body age. My breasts are lowering a little, my skin is losing its firm under layer and discoloring, I am out of shape and somewhat overweight. I used to take such pleasure in my body that I am sorry to see it go, and I'm just hoping my mind will hold out, so that I can do for myself in old age what I never did when I was young—learning music, languages, math, chess, writing, writing songs, etc."

One reason women like cunnilingus so much was that they felt that for someone to want to put his or her mouth there was very meaningful. It implied a special kind of acceptance:

"The fact that someone can love 'that' part of me means a lot."

"I enjoy cunnilingus immensely for the obvious physical reason, and for a mental reason as well. The male is exhibiting positive feelings to my femaleness. Its particular odor and architecture is as attractive to him as it is to me. He feeds at the font of my biological femaleness. His penis becomes obsolete inasmuch as it is not needed for cunnilingus. Therefore he is offering me something besides his tool to please. It is infinitely easier for him to offer his penis as it offers him release in using it, but for him to declare by action that the penis isn't necessary for my orgasm is to offer himself as a human being first and a male second. I have thought about my partner's reluctance to practice cunnilingus and maybe this holds true for other like-minded men. If I have an orgasm by cunnilingus it negates the power of his penis. He feels like a pseudo woman, a crippled man perhaps. Nevertheless, the few times I have cajoled him to do this I reached near orgasm in half the time and was going wild with delight. He, sensing the nearness of the orgasm, withdrew, however, and proffered his non-obsolete tool."

"It seems more intimate than the sex act. It's as close as one can get physically to another."

"I like to see his face and mouth down there and know that he's exploring me—with his tongue, his mouth and eyes. And I consider a man to be a *real* lover if he eats me during my period!"

"Men have gotten me very excited that way but I have yet to get over inhibitions making me feel they are doing me a favor, that they don't like doing it, that they will stop soon—now! It is, of course, an act of extraordinary intimacy (to put your head *there!*) and if I don't feel that intimate with the man, it can seem quite embarrassing and inappropriate and fail to get me off. But in most cases it is a real, even a terrible turn on because of the softness of contact, and abovementioned intimacy, and perhaps the verboten thrill."

In the same way that men seemed to resent manual clitoral stimulation, many men also resented or felt awkward during oral sex.

"I enjoy oral sex, but it never leads to orgasm. My partner doesn't like it (or he doesn't seem to). I like it because a tongue/lips are soft and moist and warm and feel good on my soft warm sensitive genitals. I like to just lie back and enjoy—feeling good—not feeling like I have to do anything. But I'm always waiting for my lover to stop too soon."

"Now take cunnilingus. The thing to do is to lie back, stretch out, let fantasies take over or whatever, and don't rush! If I know the man will do it only so long, and will think it's weird and perverted even though it excites him, and will then look up bravely, spitting a pubic hair out of his mouth and run to the bathroom to wash his face . . . yes I felt guilt and who needs this stuff? I've got to feel my partner is psychologically into the activity."

"Sometimes during cunnilingus I notice him watching TV out of the corner of his eye. That a turnoff!"

And as with clitoral stimulation by hand, women often felt they shouldn't need it, they *should* be able to orgasm during intercourse:

"I feel perverted that I can't have orgasms during intercourse and need to have cunnilingus to make me come."

Another objection to cunnilingus was that even though it felt great, many women didn't want to be obligated to perform fellatio in return—or "69"—especially to orgasm/ejaculation.

"I only dislike the slight twinge of guilt I feel about not reciprocating."

"I don't care to do this to my spouse because he usually doesn't smell too great. Also I am afraid of ejaculation in my mouth and I have an excellent gag reflex."

"I like cunnilingus when freshly washed, and when I can succeed in not feeling guilty about not liking fellatio."

"I just don't feel comfortable, especially knowing he expects me to respond likewise."

"I dislike an unskillful partner, and don't like to have him come in my mouth."

"Cunnilingus seems too detached, and one has to reciprocate and that's a bore."

"I guess it's a hangup, but I feel personal distaste for doing it to my partner."

"I like everything about cunnilingus except my having to do fellatio at the same time does cut down on my concentration, but you can't have it all your own way."

"Sometimes I feel that it is selfish on my part because my partner cannot enjoy it *that* much, and I do not like performing fellatio for him. But he says he enjoys it anyway."

"Do you enjoy fellatio? To orgasm?"

"Sometimes I like fellatio although I'm not wild about swallowing semen—it burns my throat. Sometimes, though, it makes me very excited."

"I don't mind doing it, sometimes I really enjoy doing it. I know it makes my partner feel very good, which I like doing."

"I hate to go down on a guy unless I care for him a great deal. Or if I can't have sex (don't want it because I am menstruating or have a vaginal infection or am too pregnant) and he needs relief. The penis is too big for my mouth and I choke. I do it as a present for someone I love. Otherwise I hate it. I don't mind the semen so much, someone compared it to the white of an egg."

"To orgasm is fine as long as the semen does not end up in my mouth."

"I do it to orgasm, but avoid swallowing it."

"With a new partner, I have a problem about what to do with the 'come' in fellatio. I don't like to swallow it but with a new mate I'm embarrassed to spit it out."

"I enjoy it a short time, but don't like him to come in my mouth. I like fellatio mixed in with a lot of body play, not as the main event. My partner really likes it; often I do it mostly to please him. I have never had sexual contact with women, but I think if I did, cunnilingus would be more pleasant than fellatio—I wouldn't feel invaded."

"Fellatio feels like my face is being raped."

"The orgasm feels like big blobs of thick snot being shot down your throat."

"You should perform fellatio and cunnilingus several

times in order to condition oneself before deciding against it."

"Fellatio is okay but my mouth gets tired of being stretched open."

"I'm sure I would choke to death. I cannot stand the idea of sperm in my mouth, and I'm sure he'd urinate."

"My feeling is that I would consider sucking a cock with a loaded gun at my head. No other way."

"He doesn't go down on me during my period like I wish he would. I love his sperm. I love to swallow it and rub it on my face, my breasts. I wish that he found my blood as beautiful and delicious."

"I don't usually mind fellatio. At times it seems a chore, and I have to stop in the middle, but usually when I do it's because I want to. It's often fun. I like it when he comes in my mouth. I like the taste of semen and think the protein does me good. I have never performed cunnilingus, and the idea of it revolts me. And the idea of it revolting me revolts me even more. I hope I'll grow out of this perverse attitude liking it to be done to me but not being able to imagine doing it."

What kind of cunnilingus do women like?

What are the best "techniques" for cunnilingus? Once again, there are individual preferences, and much depends on the situation, mood, and feelings of the person doing it.

"Massages like licking or sucking are great because they involve a constant breaking of contact, which keeps the sensation from being too monotonous. Every time the tongue touches, it is a new and pleasurable sensation, which eventually leads to orgasm. Any great change in position would be distracting, but the slight breaks and expectations are exciting."

"Starting in the lower folds, with your lips and tongue work upward from side to side opening me fully; when the apex of the folds are reached, go all around the clitoris with a simultaneous stomach and buttock massage, then put my clitoris between your lips for my climax."

"Oral stimulation should include the nose, mouth,

and chin. The tongue should *not* be flexed and pointed!"

"I like oral stimulation to be soft and delicate but it must be constant."

"I love being eaten with a very rapid licking tickling tongue on my clitoris, accompanied by slurpy noises and throaty sounds."

"Since she has learned how to exert heavy pressure with her jaw to bring me to orgasm if I have trouble with light pressure, I *always* orgasm. Also, her tongue can touch more area than her finger, which helps."

"I lie on my back with my partner between my legs, flicking his tongue very gently over the same area, over and over. I like not doing anything else except concentrating on the sensation until I orgasm."

"I dislike it when my partner's tongue digs too close to the clitoral nerve inside the hood—it really hurts."

"Orally, he vibrates his tongue very fast (great!) and/or sucks. He also blows air into my vagina, which is strange, yet exciting."

"I like a slow, steady rhythm, very gentle and circular in motion, right at the front part of my private parts, then moving down to my opening, with a deep penetration of his tongue just before I come."

"Nibbling and nuzzling on the clitoris, like simulated chewing is good—but gently and tenderly."

"I like soft gentle kisses above the hair and between my legs. Long laps of the tongue up and down my vagina and anus. Should be moist and with sound."

"If my partner will apply clitoral stimulation with his tongue, and at the same time gently rub my nipples, I can achieve an orgasm within a few seconds. Some men try to stimulate my *vagina,* but that really does very little for me."

Quite a few women mentioned that oral stimulation was better than stimulation by hand:

"A tongue is much gentler than a finger usually and also involves a bigger area."

"The tongue is warmer, wetter, and softer than a penis or finger and makes more delicate motions."

"Oral stimulation is best, mainly because most men do not have a clue what to do manually and are often too rough, whereas the tongue is more gentle."

"The tongue molds to my shape the way fingers can't."

"I prefer the tongue because it's smaller and more versatile than the penis."

"I like it because it is less painful and abrasive than manual stimulation. A tongue feels more alive and direct, not just power and pushing."

"Oral stimulation is better than manual because manual is sometimes too intense, giving more sensation than pleasure feelings."

"I like the tongue's mobility and sensitivity and constant lubrication. I like that it's possible for my clitoris to be directly touched with tongue or lips without causing pain, and because during it I feel completely open and vulnerable to my partner. It symbolizes my being known completely, being accepted and seen openly."

But one drawback was the inability really to caress the other person, because she/he was of necessity too far away.

"I dislike not being able to feel my partner's body next to mine and his lips on mine. I like the fact that he wants to do it to me and the feeling of his mouth and breath there."

"I feel disconnected from him, as though I were alone."

"I like to have my partner's body close and enveloping during orgasm—which is possible in this position."

"It *works* fine, but I feel isolated since she is so far away from my head."

"I miss my lover's head . . . nothing left to kiss."

Did "69" solve this problem? Not very well.

"We tried sixty-nine a few times but each of us felt distracted by too much going on at once."

"I know cunnilingus is not *his* favorite position, but since he likes fellatio, we usually do sixty-nine. But I have trouble concentrating on the feeling this way, because I have to worry about pleasing him. I like to be on top in sixty-nine because I can control how much cock gets into my mouth. On the bottom, I always get choked."

"I really cannot have a good orgasm myself if I am involved in his at the same time."

"On the subject, I don't enjoy sixty-nine at all for many reasons: First, the positions we must assume are unsatisfactory. If he is on top of me, he tends to choke me by thrusting too far into my mouth. I like to have control over my movements when I go down on him. I am not comfortable being on top of him—I can't get used to the idea of shoving my vagina in his face, and I don't like having to have that much control over it. On our sides, my legs are uncomfortable, as well as my head. I also don't like the idea of our noses being in each other's assholes (I realize that's an exaggeration, but that's what I always think of in that position). And I forgot the most important thing—in this position I can't get the kind of clitoral stimulation I need. I like stimulation that concentrates on the 'underside' of my clitoris—and in the position of sixty-nine the stimulation is either too much on my vaginal area, or on the top part of my clitoris."

In cunnilingus a passive activity? Not necessarily. Some women described moving during oral sex:

"I love rubbing my clitoris on his mouth with him sucking it and rubbing his tongue around."

"I sit on his shoulders while he's lying down, with my legs apart. But near orgasm. I begin to close my legs a little. I like to move myself against his tongue, up and down, but I don't move *very* much. *I hate* a man to throw my legs around or move me very much when he's giving me head. I've been with some guys who push my legs up like I was in stirrups ready to give birth, I resent their trying to play a manipulative role like that. They've got to let *me* do it!"

"I would like to try it standing up, with the man on his knees (reverse blow job) but men seem to find this position demeaning."

"I also like cunnilingus because I usually get it sitting up, which lets me be more in control than lying down."

"I like him to grip my ass hard, suck on my clitoris, and just let me *move*!"

Remember how beautiful and enthusiastic the language was that was used to describe intercourse and general arousal? But notice how spare and tight, unenthusiastic and secretive the language has become here. Obviously women do not feel proud about clitoral stimulation in any form. Our culture had discouraged clitoral stimulation, even to the point of not giving it a name. "Cunnilingus" at least is a name, even if its meaning is not clear to everyone, but "manual clitoral stimulation" is just a phrase that is used to describe an activity that has no name. Our language for, as well as our respect for, clitoral stimulation, is almost nonexistent. Our culture is still a long way from understanding, not to mention celebrating, female sexuality.

"Do you ever find it necessary to masturbate to achieve orgasm after 'making love'?"

	Q.I	Q.II	Q.III
Yes	120	170	55
Sometimes	90	117	29
Rarely	35	41	11
No	275	349	73
Used to	19	23	11
Would like to	20	22	19
Yes, *with* partner (or, *he* does it)	12	25	1
Would be embarrassing	6	20	2
I don't bother	2	5	6
It wouldn't be right	1	3	
It doesn't work	6	6	
Do it *during* intercourse!	1	5	
For an *extra* orgasm	5	2	
Total	592	798	207

"I never felt I had to, but maybe it would be a good idea and not so hard on the nervous system!"

"Yes, except when a man has been awfully rough or clumsy or thoughtless, and masturbation wouldn't even help afterwards."

"Sometimes, but I usually masturbate at other times, so that making love with my partner is for me a friendly rather than a sexual act anyway."

"No. If I don't have an orgasm, I generally feel that he's been selfish and using me which makes me feel *shitty and awful* and I'm much more upset about my emotional feelings and his than attaining an orgasm by masturbation."

"Sometimes I do unless I'm afraid I'll be caught doing it."

"No—I just take a cold shower!"

"Yes—sometimes *several* times after intercourse!"

"I never have. I'd feel very self-conscious and insulting if I did."

"Yes, with some regularity. Since I lie fairly still, most of them don't know what I'm doing till I come, and then in wide-eyed surprise they ask me if I just jerked off. After that they sometimes get apologetic like 'Oh, why didn't you *tell* me? I'd have eaten you out for hours,' or some such nonsense."

"I've never tried. I think it's cheating."

"Yes, I did sometimes after my ex-old man had gone off to sleep, slobbering and snoring."

"No, never. With a man like this, I would scream and yell and break things, but not masturbate."

"Sometimes. It's frustrating because he rolls over and goes to sleep, after he's had *his* orgasm."

"Yes. That was how I masturbated for the first time."

"Sometimes. Usually I just forget about it. It seems such a cheap thing at that time."

"Sometimes I would really like to, but it's quite a difficult thing to do if you are still in the man's company. You might feel embarrassed and create strange feelings between both of you."

"Frequently I would like to, but I don't for fear of embarrassing or revolting my partner."

"I feel like it but don't get up the courage."

"No, because it just makes me feel more frustrated."

"Yes, sometimes to re-enact the act after he has left."

"Sometimes I do. My husband seems to understand, but I know it makes him feel he's sort of let me down."

"I've never dared."

"No. It doesn't seem right or fair to the guy (even if he doesn't know). (Brainwashed brainwashed brainwashed.)"

"Yes, but I do it by lying on top of him and rubbing up and down."

"Sometimes, but I feel ashamed."

"Yes, but if I do, I don't think we have 'made love'— I think he has masturbated in my vagina."

"Sometimes it helps to run a spray of warm water on myself when I haven't had an orgasm."

"Sometimes, but then I never sleep with *him* again."

"Not in front of my partner."

"Yes. Most men are lousy lovers."

"I have thought of it at times, when intercourse had ended, when I was just on the verge of an orgasm, but I never did so out of consideration for my partner's feelings!"

"Sometimes when he's not with it I get frustrated so I cut off the session and wait till he's asleep to masturbate and have an orgasm. It makes me either mad or sad."

"Yes, but like a fool I sneak out into the living room so he won't know. Then I hate myself for not telling him he's a lousy lover."

"Sometimes, when I'm alone. I don't know what to do about it. Should I tell him I do it?"

"Yes. Sometimes. I don't want to tell my partner about my need to masturbate during intercourse so I get left out."

"I used to do it secretly in the bathroom. Now my partner does it for me."

"I did it one time then hid in the bathroom crying afterwards. I never thought sex would be so disappointing."

"When I haven't come and I still want to, I have masturbated on occasion. Also I've done deep breathing and relaxation exercises to let go of the sexual tension."

"I've tried (secretly) a few times, but somehow I come down with him *enough* so I can't get up again right then even if I'm disappointed about not having had an orgasm."

"Yes, once in a while. Other times I grin and bear it."

"Yes, sometimes I do. Most of the time though I'm either too exhausted, or so emotionally satisfied that I don't need to masturbate."

"Sometimes I would like to do this, but there is no way to do it without be noticed.

"Sometimes I wish I could but it would be too insulting to the man I'm with. I sleep with him afterwards so there is no chance of being alone."

"I first masturbated when I was extremely frustrated because I'd been aroused by the man I'd just had sex with, but hadn't come. He'd left the room. It suddenly occurred to me that I could do to myself what he'd been doing to me. I had never thought of doing that before. The thought surprised me. So I locked the door. I touched myself with great hesitation at first—feeling distaste. (Now it's hard for me to imagine that because I like to touch myself and the smell from the sexual juices, too.) I remember the thought that passed through my head as I came: 'My God, this is better than with a man.' The thought surprised me as much as the orgasm."

"In fourteen years no partner has ever masturbated me after he had orgasm from intercourse (when I did or didn't) and I have always been too inhibited to ask. I am too inhibited to do it in front of my partner and if I go to the bathroom, I usually feel resentful and thereby tense and just push aside my feeling."

Is it bad for women not to orgasm during sex? It is obvious that it doesn't feel *good*. As shown in the orgasm chapter, most women felt that after a certain degree of stimulation, orgasm became more or less necessary, or else they were left with feelings of discomfort and irritability.

"Orgasm is especially important if I am aroused to the point where my genital area feels bloated."

"Physically, orgasm is not always necessary, but if I am close to orgasm, then I feel a crampy tightness and I don't feel like moving freely if I don't have an orgasm."

"Sometimes it's okay without until I reach a certain level of arousal; then it's either orgasm or a crying spell or a fight."

Are there any physical effects on women who become aroused and don't orgasm? If this is a pattern that occurs on a regular basis over a long period of time, chronic/pelvic congestion can result. Sherfey defines it as "chronic passive congestion":

> An abnormal amount of blood in the vessels of any part of the body due to increased influx and/or inadequate drainage. In women this condition is caused by enlarged varicose veins of the pelvis; it is the usual byproduct of two or more pregnancies and, to a lesser extent, of frequent prolonged sexual stimulation. Vessel relaxation may then render adequate expulsion of blood during orgasms impossible or completely prevent orgasms. This, in turn, increases circulatory stagnation, enhancing the varicosities. If severe, the pelvic congestion contributes to many disorders and may block venous return from the legs. This places increased strain on the heart. In this condition, all the external genitalia become swollen, waterlogged, and purple; this condition is very uncomfortable, and the sensation of unrelieved sexual tension readily passes into cramps and pain.[1]

Of course, congestion is not commonly found in the extreme form described, since most women can and do masturbate to orgasm, even if they are not regularly having orgasms with their partners. However, Masters and Johnson have also described women who are not able to orgasm as irritable, emotionally disturbed, and complaining of pelvic fullness, pressure, cramping, moments of true pain, and a persistent, severe low backache.

However, the worst effect not having orgasms can have on women is psychological. What lesson do women learn as they watch a man enjoying his orgasm, secure in the knowledge that it is his right—every time? This is a perfect object lesson to women that they are inferior, oppressed, and *less*.

Of course this does not mean that the solution is for both men and women to always orgasm every time as the goal of sex. It means that sex and physical relations must be redefined in a way that ceases to reflect these oppressive and outdated cultural stereotypes.

CONCLUSION

The reproductive model of sex exploits women.

It is very clear by now that the pattern of sexual relations predominant in our culture exploits and oppresses women. The sequence of "foreplay," "penetration," and "intercourse" (defined as thrusting), followed by male orgasm as the climax and end of the sequence, gives very little chance for female orgasm, is almost always under the control of the man, frequently teases the woman inhumanely, and in short, has institutionalized out any expression of women's sexual feelings except for those that support male sexual needs.

Many women expressed their frustration about this: "I don't quite understand why for men, orgasm is presumed to occur each time, but for women it must be 'worked at.' Sex as it is defined between men and women is male sex." And, "I think most of the writers I've read don't understand women at all, sexually. They regard sex as an activity engaged in by two for the satisfaction of one. The current writers are worse than the older ones, because they stress the whore-like sexual techniques used by women for men. Women's needs are less and less emphasized, except by female writers."

The reproductive model of sex insures male orgasm by giving it a standardized time and place, during which both people know what to expect and how to make it possible for the man to orgasm. The whole thing is prearranged, preagreed. But there are not really any patterns or prearranged times and places for a woman to orgasm—unless she can manage to do so during intercourse. So women are put in the position of asking for something "special," some "extra" stimulation, or they must somehow try to subliminally send messages to a partner who often is not even aware that he should be listening. If she does get this "extra," "special" stimulation, she feels grateful that he was so unusually "sensitive." So all too often women just do without—or fake it.

Do it yourself

But we can change this pattern, and redefine our sexual relations with others. On one level, we can take control over our own orgasms. We *know* how to have orgasms in masturbation. How strange it is, when you think about it, that we don't use this knowledge during so much of the sex we have with men. Why, in our pattern of sexual relations, does the man have charge of both his stimulation and ours? A man controls his own orgasm in the sense that during intercourse he thrusts his penis against the walls of the vagina in ways that provide the best stimulation for him; this is not considered "selfish" or "infantile" because there is an ideology to back it up.

However, women do not usually, are not supposed to, control their own stimulation:

"I have never tried to stimulate myself clitorally with a partner—I have always been afraid to."

"It seems too aggressive when I act to get the stimulation I want."

"During sex, I must depend on a man's willingness to do an aggressive action for me, while I am passive. (Passive about my *own* stimulation; moving for *his* pleasure doesn't count.) Whereas during intercourse a man climaxes through his own aggressiveness."

"When you're young, you masturbate/touch yourself instinctually, then you stop when you hear it's 'wrong' and 'naughty,' and then you try the rest of your life to get other people to touch you the same way, only they hardly ever do it right!"

"I always dreamed of the ecstasy of physical love. I have never been able to reach this kind of feeling with another person. The sensations, the orgasms I can give myself, are more than just in the sex organs, they are feelings of relaxation and pleasure throughout the body, mind, and soul. A sort of sailing feeling, a flowing, rich in colors, rich in well-being, joy. They are 'multiple orgasms,' each richer than the previous one. A *whole, complete* feeling. I can have orgasms with a partner, but not these complete intense sensations."

But why can't we touch ourselves? Why can't we do whatever we need to make orgasm happen? Although sharing sex with a man can be wonderful, why does "sharing" for a woman mean that the man must "give" her the orgasm? Why can't a woman use her own hand to bring herself to orgasm? In sex as elsewhere, women are still in the position of waiting for men to "mete out the goodies."

We have the power to make our own orgasms, if we want. You can get control of your own stimulation by moving against the other person, or by stimulating yourself directly in the same way as you do during masturbation. Although this suggestion may sound strange at first, it is important to be able to masturbate with another person, because it will give you power over your own orgasms. There is no reason why making your own orgasms should not be as beautiful or as deeply shared as any other form of sex with another person—perhaps even more so. The taboo against touching yourself says essentially that you should not use your own body for your own pleasure, that your body is not your own to enjoy. But we have a right to our own bodies. Controlling your own stimulation symbolizes owning your own body, and is a very important step toward freedom.

LESBIANISM

"Neither male nor female sexuality is limited by 'genital geography,' and it has been one of the greatest public relations victories of all time to convince us it was. The very naturalness of lesbianism (and homosexuality) is exactly the cause of the strong social and legal rules against it. The basing of our social system on gender difference, biological reproductive function, is barbaric and should be replaced by a system based on affirmation of the individual and support for all life on the planet."

"I think we are all born 'sexual'—that is, we are each born with natural desires to relate to all other creatures—animals, plants, ourselves, women, men—when we feel love or communication with them. But society teaches us to inhibit all of these but desires for partners with whom it is possible to procreate, and then works up our enthusiasm for the 'act' by pushing the ideal of romantic love combined with marriage down our throats until we can't think of anything else."

INTRODUCTION

It must be clear by now that female sexuality is physically "pan-sexual," or just "sexual"—certainly not something that is directed at any one type of physical organ to be found in nature. There is no organ especially concocted to fit the clitoral area and the kind of stimulation we generally need for orgasm. From the point of view of physical pleasure, we are free to relate to all the creatures of the planet, according to their individual meaning for us, rather than their specific classification or gender.

Of course it goes without saying that as we move toward a more equitable view of life, the right to love other women will be taken for granted. However, the general villainization of homosexual contacts in our society has a long history. As Kinsey explains:

> The general condemnation of homosexuality in our particular culture apparently traces to a series of historical circumstances which had little to do with the protection of the individual or the preservation of the social organization of the day. In Hittite, Chaldean, and early Jewish codes there were no over-all condemnations of such activity, although there were penalties for homosexual activities between persons of particular social status or blood relationships, or homosexual relationships under other particular circumstances, especially when force was involved. The more general condemnation of all homosexual relationships (especially male) originated in Jewish history in about the seventh century B.C., upon the return from the Babylonian exile. Both mouth-genital contacts and homosexual activities had previously been associated with the Jewish religious service, as they had been with the religious services of most of the other peoples of that part of Asia, and just as they have been in many other cultures elsewhere in the world. In the wave of nationalism which was then developing among the Jewish people, there was an attempt to disidentify themselves with their neighbors* by breaking with many of the customs which they had previously shared with them. Many of the Talmudic condemnations were based on the fact that such activities represented the way of the Canaanite, the way of the Chaldean, the way of the pagan, and they were originally condemned as a form of idolatry rather than a sexual crime. Throughout the middle ages homosexuality was associated with heresy. The reform in the custom (the mores) soon, however,

---

* Especially their non-patriarchal neighbors.

became a matter of morals, and finally a question for action under criminal law.[1]

Kinsey (who was originally a biologist) also tells us that other mammals and other animals routinely have lesbian and homosexual relationships:

The impression that infra-human mammals more or less confine themselves to heterosexual activities is a distortion of the fact which appears to have originated in a man-made philosophy, rather than in specific observations of mammalian behavior. Biologists and psychologists who have accepted the doctrine that the only natural function of sex is reproduction have simply ignored the existence of sexual activity which is not reproductive. They have assumed that heterosexual responses are a part of an animal's innate, "instinctive" equipment, and that all other types of sexual activity represent "perversions" of the "normal instincts." Such interpretations are, however, mystical. They do not originate in our knowledge of the physiology of sexual response, and can be maintained only if one assumes that sexual function is in some fashion divorced from the physiologic processes which control other functions of the animal body. It may be true that heterosexual contacts outnumber homosexual contacts in most species of mammals, but it would be hard to demonstrate that this depends upon the "normality" of heterosexual responses, and the "abnormality" of homosexual responses.[2]

Kinsey mentions that lesbian contacts have been observed in such widely separated species as rats, mice, hamsters, guinea pigs, rabbits, porcupines, marten, cattle, antelope, goats, horses, pigs, lions, sheep, monkeys, and chimpanzees. And, he adds, "Every farmer who has raised cattle knows . . . that cows quite regularly mount cows."[3]

The arguments over whether lesbianism and/or homosexuality are biological or psychological in origin (the origin of the "problem," as it is usually put) are still raging in some quarters,* but the "answer" hardly matters any more. Homosexuality, or the desire to be physically intimate with someone of one's own sex at some time, or always, during one's life, can be considered a natural and "normal" variety of life experience. It is "abnormal" only when you posit as "normal" and "healthy" only an interest in reproductive sex. Discussions of why one becomes *heterosexual* would come to the same nonconclusions. To consider all non-reproductive sexual contact "an error of nature" is a very narrow view.

Not being "allowed" to really touch or be in physical contact with anyone other than a sexual partner—since it might "imply" a sexual connection!—is depressing and alienating. Specifically, vis-à-vis women's connection with one another, this ban on physical contact is oppressive and has the effect of separating women. The dynamic works something like this: you may feel a sudden impulse to kiss or hug a friend—or you may feel subtler desires for greater closeness or contact of which you are unaware—which you must stifle and repress. But when a natural impulse is stopped and is not consciously recognized, it can cause feelings of conflict, guilt, and anxiety. Such repression can then lead to half-conscious feelings of rejection, which engender feelings of distrust and dislike for the same person to whom one was originally attracted. This, of course, is a well-known psychological phenomenon, and commonly happens on a subtle level between friends. The point here is that this prohibition on the exchange of physical contact (*of any kind*) between women is bound to increase the level of hostility and distance between them.

One of the best descriptions of how we more or less "unconsciously" select our sexual partners on the basis of gender (and screen out those of the "wrong" gender) has been given by Pepper Schwartz and Philip Blum-

---

* A good summary of the arguments can be found in Edward Brecher's *The Sex Researchers*.

stein.† To begin with, they explain that given a state of physiological arousal for which an individual has no immediate explanation, "he will 'label' this state and describe his feelings in terms of the cognitions available to him . . ." They continue, "the sources of arousal are likely to be more diverse than the sources to which it is attributed by the most astute laymen," and, "the greater the confidence in, or need for, a heterosexual identity, the more likely that ambiguities will be resolved in a heterosexual direction. When one has strong suspicions about one's homosexuality or has taken on gay identity, then the interpretation is likely to go in the other direction." In other words,

> homosexuality—like heterosexuality—becomes self-fulfilling. This is especially so since the free-floating arousal levels early in one's sexual development tend to be channeled and shaped by sexual experience and strengthening sexual identity. So we believe that untapped or uninterpreted homosexual arousal cues tend not to arouse as one takes on a more firm heterosexual identity and engages in more heterosexual behavior. Likewise, untapped or uninterpreted heterosexual cues tend not to arouse confirmed homosexuals. Our dichotomous views of our own sexual identity thwart any possibility of bisexuality.⁴

With specific reference to women, Schwartz and Blumstein state that:

> Women have a different arousal system from men. Their arousal is a total body response, rather than a genital one. While some women may feel "horny" (i.e., feel sexual tension in the genital area, or lubricate during an exciting encounter), all of these signals are less visible than their counterpart in the male. To put it very simply, a woman can reinterpret her ex-

† "Bisexuality: Some Sociological Observations," a paper presented at the Chicago Conference on Bisexual Behavior, October 6, 1973, Department of Sociology, University of Washington.

citement; a man cannot miss noticing his sexual arousal and labeling it as erotic. . . . If a woman has sexual tension in an inappropriate environment such as during a softball game, a mother-child interaction, etc., she has more freedom than a man in how she can label that excitement.

Likewise, in female/female relationships, the cues that a woman receives from another woman are more subtle than the cues men give each other. Apropos of our discussion of erection, two women do not have to explain away an erection should one of them get excited while they were having a tête à tête and talking about their sex lives. If they are getting excited, and they want to communicate sexual interest in one another, they have to rely on eye contact, intensified attention, and other kinds of interpersonal connections to convey their meaning. The problem, however, is that these kinds of cues are confusing, they are usually associated with heterosexual negotiation and since they seem inappropriate or unreal in a same sex encounter, may be reinterpreted to mean friendship or non-sexual affection. Women may be afraid to believe—even if they want to—that another woman is giving sexual cues to them. If they were coming from another source their intent would probably be unmistakable; but since they come from what has in the past been an asexual source, the receiver may tend to doubt or reinterpret the most direct of signals.

Because of this obfuscation of cues—and because women are not used to being wooed by other women—nor are they trained to do the aggressive part of sexual pursuance—it may be hypothesized that women rarely activate erotic responses to women simply because they do not realize how often the excitement they feel is mutual and has a possibility of being reciprocated. Furthermore, since no sexual negotiation is apparent, women may not realize or admit to themselves that they have been in a sexual encounter, thereby allowing all such attractions to die out. One final hypothesis along these lines follows this same theme of unapparent, passive aspects in the female sexual tradition. That is, that since women have been taught to eroticize people who eroticize them—i.e., interpret their worth and sexuality by the way men "turned on" to them, many women discover their own sexual feelings when they are approached by a man. When they see someone sexually aroused and interested in them, *then* they decide they might be sexually interested in the other person. To some extent, this seems to be true for both sexes—people start to get sexually aroused when someone begins to show sexual interest, begins aggressive moves and makes the other person feel desirable. Sexual tension begins to build and soon the two people must acknowledge its pressence (even if they choose not to act on it). With women, this sexual tension may not get a chance to build because each person is embarrassed, unpracticed and unsure about the validity of the encounter as a sexual experience. Unused to taking the lead (or the responsibility) for such situations, they may back off rather than try to chart something they are unprepared for and unused to. It may be hypothesized that same sex relationships between women will not occur unless at least one person in the dyad is able to take on an aggressive sexual role and dare to make ambiguous cues explicit. If both women are unable to take this role, the relationship may never become articulated.[5]

"Do you prefer sex with men, women, yourself, or not at all?"

A hundred and forty-four women in this study (8 percent) said they preferred sex with women. Another seventy-three identified themselves as "bisexual," and eighty-four women had had experiences with both men and women but did not answer as to preference (another 9 percent).

In addition, fifty-three women in this study said they preferred to have sex with themselves, and seventeen women preferred to have no sex at all. Another fifty women had had no sexual experience with others yet, or had had such extremely limited experience that they felt they could not answer the question. All the remaining women said they preferred men, although many stressed that they did not prefer "men" but rather an *individual* man.

It is impossible to know what relation there may be between statistics and how many lesbian women there may be in the United States population, since, due to the fear of persecution, no one knows how many lesbians, or bisexuals, there are. Kinsey estimated that perhaps 12 to 13 percent of women had "sexual relations to the point of orgasm" with another woman at some time during their adult lives, and that between 11 and 20 percent of single women and 8 to 10 percent of married women in the sample "were making at least incidental homosexual responses, or making more specific homosexual contacts" between the ages of twenty and thirty-five. More recently Dr. Richard Green, formerly of the University of California (Los Angeles) Gender Identity Research Treatment Program, has commented that there may now be an increase in bisexuality and/or lesbianism among women "partly for political reasons"—as one of the ways women can "disassociate themselves from the extraordinary dependency they've had on men all these years."

At the same time, it is important to note that preferences can change during a lifetime, or can change several times; what is called "gender identity" is not so cut and dried as the preceding statistics might seem to imply. As Kinsey explained, there are not two discrete groups, one heterosexual and one homosexual, in other words, the world in not to be divided into sheep and goats. "The living world is a continuum in each and every one of its aspects," and homosexuality and heterosexuality are only the extreme types sitting at the poles of "a rich and varied continuum." In fact, "lesbian," "homosexual," and "heterosexual" should be used as adjectives, not nouns: *people* are not properly described as homosexuals, lesbians, or heterosexuals; rather, *activities* are properly described as homosexual, lesbian, or heterosexual. In other words, it is really only possible to say how many persons have had, at any particular time, a given type of relationship, and that is how the figures in this study should be viewed.

Many other women said they might be interested in having sex with another woman.

One of the most striking points about the answers recieved to the questionnaires was how frequently, *even though it was not specifically asked*, women brought up the fact that they might be interested in having sexual relations with another woman, or at least were curious. This interest was usually mentioned in connection with the question on sexual preference (above), or with the question "What would you like to try that you never have?" Some of these answers follow:

"I have been married for twelve years, but I am not happy with it. I've never had a physical relationship with a woman but I feel it would be more satisfying than with a male. I don't know how to relate to another woman physically, as I've never had the opportunity to do so. There is a woman whom I'm attracted to and feel is the same as me but I am afraid to approach her."

"How I wish I could have a relationship with a man the way I have with my closest woman friend. I want to be honest and giving, caring, loving, supporting, and supportive. I want to be cared about, thought special and worthwhile. That I am a person who has lived through things. I want to be able to say 'I love you' and 'I want you' without the other person feeling threatened."

"I've only had sex with one man—the man I'm with now. He felt like a close friend for a while. I found I wanted to talk to him and be with him in times of happiness and crisis. The relationship has progressed from friendship to 'being in love' back to deep friendly love. Right now my head is in a place where I would like to be in a relationship with a woman as well as keeping my relationship with this man. I am in the process of changing my entire life and feelings about my sexuality."

"I have always admired beautiful women, but have

never had a homosexual experience. So far I've loved fucking. But women excite me more and more."

"There are times when I feel such a warmth from my best friend that I experience it sexually and almost desire her. But I have never let her know I have this feeling, because it might make her afraid of me."

"If my parents had not put so much pressure on me to find a good man and get married, I might have continued the relationships I had with other girls in grade school. My best friend and I, at about eight, used to play doctor and touch and examine each other. Then at twelve she and I would spend the night and take off our clothes under the covers and kiss and mess around, and take turns being on top, trying to figure out how men did it with women. We were horny and curious! And we loved each other too. I still write her (she's married too)."

"I have been brought up to believe women are more attractive and more beautiful and I am beginning to believe it."

"I'd love to massage a woman I liked and was turned on to, and then gradually arouse her sexually through massage and then slowly make love to her and then stop and talk, then love again, then sleep together. I'd like with her to know myself better. But I'd never have the nerve!"

"I would like to have a sexual relationship with a woman. There is one woman I am sexually attracted to but I would never approach her in a sexual way because that would be imposing on her heterosexuality. We are very good friends and her nonsexual friendship is more important than her sexual friendship. It is a new experience for me even to consider lesbianism. Until two years ago, I barely recognized this facet of sexuality, never consciously thought about it, and when I did I thought it was 'disgusting.' I have never met a woman who was a lesbian to my knowledge, although one doesn't broadcast this proclivity yet in this repressive society. Women, even feminists, are sometimes uncomfortable talking about lesbiansim, so I have little idea what their fears and unconscious desires are concerning their sisters vis-à-vis themselves as sexual partners. One must grapple with many possibilities before embarking on a sexual relationship with a woman. 'Am I doing so because men have disappointed me?' 'Am I running from a threatening situation and thus avoiding confronting the problem where it stands?' 'Am I having sex with a woman who cannot handle guilt associated with "deviant" behavior?' 'Am I exploiting her as I was exploited by men?' "

"In school, I had lots of hopeless crushes on boys I wouldn't look at now. I also had lots of crushes on women—friends and teachers which I'm only now acknowledging as sexual. I also really wanted someone to be close to but I thought I wanted a boyfriend, which is not necessarily the same thing."

"I would like to have sex with women. I think I am a lesbian, which is not too helpful since I'm married, and don't feel capable of a divorce at this point, and living on my own, etc. However, someday it'll probably get to be too much, and I'll have to."

"I haven't had sex with another woman, except verbally—I think women often make love by talking a certain way, at least I do."

"I want a woman lover—or more. I generally want *closer* relationships with women; I want to do all the things only *men* are supposed to do! I want to explore!!"

"I never thought of women as such interesting people before this revival of the women's movement. I enjoy their company so much, and we are able to work together with real pleasure. I suppose sex, in another lifetime, would have been a part of this."

"My experience up until now has been with men, but I would welcome a love affair with a woman. I would want to question myself very strongly as to the genuineness of my feeling for a woman, however, because, knowing me as I do, there is a danger that I might enter an affair merely from sexual curiosity. Somehow I wouldn't feel too bad about going with a man out of that motivation, but I would feel rotten if I used a woman that way."

"I've never had sex with a woman but I would like to—although I'm not sure about whether to orgasm or not. I have, after a good deal of thought about things like the fact that I *have* had many deep relationships with women, come to the conclusion that I am, for the time being, at least, straight. The thought of performing cunnilingus doesn't turn me on, and although I have been physically attracted to women friends, it has not been particularly sexual—just wanting to cuddle, hug, etc. Another difference—I can be attracted physically to men I don't know, but I feel physical attraction only to women I love."

"I have never had sex with a woman and can't imagine it, but that is because of my conditioning. I can see why women would want other women, and can accept it. I don't know any lesbians that I know of. I have a close girlfriend who is divorced and we have discussed this a little and it seems we are both 'straight' but I notice we never touch each other. Are we afraid we might be gay and couldn't handle it? Sometimes I think I would like to try but then I realize I'm fairly happy the way things are."

"I guess I still feel strange when I take the initiative, though I don't think it's right that I don't initiate sometimes—I guess I have gotten very used to having things done to me. I think that's the main reason why I haven't had sex with women too—that we are accustomed to not initiating sex and so no one does! That's a hard bit of conditioning to overcome—it's the gap between believing something is right and actually *feeling* good about it, too."

"I have only had sex with men and with myself—more with men than with myself. Sex with women appeals to me, but I think mainly because of curiosity, because in my closest relationships with women I love, sex doesn't seem to come 'naturally.' I still consider myself rather inexperienced in sex."

"I was married for seven and a half years. I didn't like being married, except at first when it was like a new toy, sort of like playing house. Our sex life was disastrous. I had no extramarital experience during marriage. I am now single, and enjoy it, but it is difficult. I do not have sexual experiences as often as I would like. When I was about fifteen, I had what you might call a crush on a woman. She was about twenty-one, I think. We were friends, and I discovered that if we touched (by accident), I liked it. I began to speak of love. We spent a lot of time together, until one day she told me that her father thought she ought to see less of me and concentrate on her studies. Naturally, I didn't believe a word of that, but it was pretty much the end of the relationship. Then, about three years ago, I had a sexual experience with a woman. All we did was lie in bed together naked, and touch and caress each other all over. I liked it very much, though I was a little afraid. Apparently she was even more afraid, for later she sort of pretended that it had not happened."

"I have several friends who are lesbians, and superficially I have no strong feelings about that one way or the other. However, when they talk about their relationships, I find myself becoming rather defensive; it seems I do have very deep and complicated feelings about it, both positive and negative."

How do women relate physically?

"As far as how we relate to each other physically—we hug a lot and kiss and caress each other. As for 'technique,' we masturbate each other with our hands and fingers and orally, as well as combining both. Also, mutually masturbate, with other parts of our bodies. Basically, the same things a man and woman can do without a penis, and *usually don't*!"

"I've made love with a woman only twice, the first time was a year ago—don't think I know enough to tell you exactly how. The basic difference with a woman is that there's no end, where you have orgasms and end—it's like a circle, it goes on and on."

"Some times I think I could go straight from deep mouth kissing to clitoral stimulation to have orgasm. It depends on my state of 'readiness.' I like also to have my lover touch me very lightly, with her tongue and hands, all over my body, especially my buttocks and lower abdomen. There is no one 'best' way of clitoral stimulation—when she uses her mouth it's different than her fingers. Sometimes I like her mouth at first and then her finger, and the other times, just her mouth. Either her tongue gently flicking my clitoris, or her mouth sucking me hard, or her finger moving right above my clitoris in an increasingly rapid up and down movement, usually makes me orgasm. Sometimes she pushes her mouth hard against me and shakes her head rapidly from side to side—I orgasm this way also. No one way works best all the time; different ways at different times work marvelously well. One thing, I guess it's easier for me if we start lovemaking with our clothes *on* and do not have more than a minute's interruption for removal of clothes. Otherwise I get a little self-conscious."

"There is always a great deal of touching and affection, fingers run over each other's bodies, legs entwined, and a great deal of kissing all over our bodies. Then we get into oral sex, mutual or sometimes one person at a time. Sometimes we rest for a while and then start up again."

"Sex is slow with long preliminaries and explorations, conversation, gentle mutual stroking and then clitoral stimulation in unison. Great! It's great to do and feel the *same* done to you."

"She soft and gentle knowing exactly how to rub my clit and what pressure to use—taking as long as we want coming—coming—*coming.*"

"Once, recently, when my lover and I had been making love for hours, I felt that she was beginning to feel frustrated (I had not yet learned her 'style'), so I guided her hand to her clitoris, so I could learn from her what pleased her."

"The women I've been with so far have been more on an affectionate love basis than sexual. I have yet to be more sexual with a woman. The women I've been with have kissed me and I them, we have hugged and gently touched each other; just having our bodies together and being warm sends a fire surging through my body. One woman sat on my pelvic area lightly, with her back to my face, and stimulated me vaginally/clitorally with her fingers, very gently, taking her time and not at all concerned with getting me excited but more exploring—which releases me to take my time and do the same. I enjoy all of them very much and hope to see that I make women a more active part of my life. I am doing this by seeking them out by going to women's and lesbians' activities and putting myself in a position to meet them for the conscious purpose that I want to make love to a certain kind of woman that I love."

"Lovemaking with a woman is always more variable than with a man, and the physical actions are more mutual. While the same places are kissed and touched with a man, the whole feeling is heightened for me when the lover is a woman, and it is so different because of all the psychological and emotional factors involved. The touches become different, the kisses different—the whole aura is different."

"Sex with a woman includes: touching, kissing, smiling, looking serious, embracing, talking, digital intercourse, caressing, looking, cunnilingus, undressing, remembering later, making sounds, sometimes gently biting, sometimes crying, and breathing and sighing together."

"Liz, my roommate, and I have oftentimes made love when one of us has emotional problems—the love of friends. In this case, Liz had a bad experience and I made love to her. I first kissed her forehead, then her lips, and then very gently massaged her breasts. Gently kissing and rubbing them, sucking her nipples. While doing this, she usually either squeezes my breasts or rubs my shoulders. I then caress her vagina and perform cunnilingus on her. I then take the position of the man and let her kiss and hug me. This is when the emotion comes out. If she wants to, she then makes love to me."

"To relate to another woman physically, you just caress her body the way you like to be caressed and/or the way she indicates she likes. You explore lovemaking together and find out what works. I don't know how to answer more specifically. I don't think there are any 'cookbook' approaches that work in all situations—thank goodness. For me it comes more naturally than it ever did with men."

"Technically, women together do what male and female together do—touch and kiss and caress one another, except there's no penis. (And I've yet to meet a lesbian who uses a dildo. I think that is one great big male porno trip.) I earlier mentioned mutal breast playing. Sometimes it feels good to put my nipple into her vagina, or vice versa. Cunnilingus is beautiful too, either as participant or recipient. I don't enjoy sixty-nine, however—it's too distracting, too much happening at once for me to concentrate on either of us. When I perform cunnilingus, I like to not only stroke the inner lips and edges of her vagina with my tongue, but I also like to suck her clitoris. This excites me very much and my partners always seem to enjoy it. I also enjoy tribadism. I enjoy just holding each other very closely, our thighs pressing against one another's genitals; or lying diagonally with each other, our legs in a 'v' sort of scissors around each other's torsos, our vaginas warm, moist, happy, touching, our hands holding."

"Our relationship works on a pretty equal basis, with both of us the initiators at various times, with both of us taking different positions in tribadism, the sixty-nine position, mutual masturbation, rubbing breasts, or breasts against clitoris. There are no particular patterns, except we usually achieve our orgasms during tribadism, which we practice most frequently."

"Sex with a woman for me has involved kissing, feeling one another completely, and *basically* humping—pressing mound of Venus against mound of Venus or each other's leg. Also cunnilingus and manual and even anal lingus! Pressing against her backside, riding her, which feels *good*."

"It's *most* stimulating to be in a sitting position facing my partner. She also sits and presses her hand gently into me. This way I can determine the speed and intensity of the movements. And we can see each other, kiss, talk, and feel each other's breasts."

"Usually with the one woman I've gone to bed with

we would spend *ages* on foreplay and *finally* when we *absolutely* couldn't stand it any longer, we would manually bring each other to orgasm—or else I would perform cunnilingus on her, even though she didn't on me."

"My best sexual experiences were with the first woman I ever loved. I had been married for a thousand years and she was a total virgin. We didn't even practice cunnilingus, yet they were powerful sexual encounters for both of us because they were a dream come true emotionally. We were mad for each other and that's why they were my best sexual experiences."

"I become very aroused by caressing my female lover's breasts and clitoris and vagina and get so hung up on her body that she need not do anything to me, the mere touch and taste of her body is all the stimulus I need. Arousal (and orgasm) is a very emotional experience because somehow it communicates all the love I feel for her."

"Finally, now with my present female lover of two months, I have orgasms. A person's understanding of the clitoris's stimulation, foreplay, cuddling, display of other intimate expressions of caressing and deep kissing are important. She and I spend anywhere from two hours to six hours in caressing, touching, cuddling, hugging, lip kissing, deep kissing and intimate conversation before, in-between, and after sex, lying in bed. This is very important!"

And one woman gave a long answer:

"My lover is very sensitive to what I want. But she asks me, and I tell her, too, because it is better to communicate your desires. Like the other night when she was being gentle and I wasn't responding much and I said, 'I want you to be rough' and so she was and it was strong and wonderful. We like to stimulate ourselves and neither of us minds this or feels embarrassed. Sometimes, usually, if she comes before I do she keeps making love till I come but if she doesn't then I masturbate and she holds me while I do and it's just the same as making love.

"She is always emotionally involved. Sometimes her

mind wanders, like once we were hugging and kissing and starting to make love and all of a sudden she says, 'What part of the world do armadillos live in?' Really, she was serious, and we laughed a long time.

"I must be lying face down to have an orgasm. I must be rubbing my clitoris against a part of my lover's body or a soft object. (Before getting in this position, I like my breasts to be sucked. I like that the best. I also like manual clitoral stimulation and oral.) Then I get in a face down position. Sometimes my lover lies on top of my back and I rub against a pillow or soft blanket and sometimes (usually) I lie on her back and she stimulates herself manually and the feeling of the waves in her hips and legs and my thighs and clitoris moving against her bring me to orgasm.

"I like non-genital sex as well as or better than genital. I like hugging and kissing (we don't usually have big deep penetrating kisses, but when we do it's nice, but mostly little wet ones in nice places). I like talking and laughing and being silly, and just looking at her face and body in the moonlight. I like it when she lies on top of me and looks down into my face. She looks loving and proud. Once my heart had an orgasm when she was hugging me and looking at me and saying how she loved me. Hers did too. It felt like it just jumped up and had a wave like my body does when it comes. I like smelling a lot. The first woman I was in love with (when I was twelve) had a smell like wild woods and autumn leaves, and I loved it. I like to smell my lover's hair and her breast and her melt. I like to suck her breasts and I like her to suck mine. She does all kinds of new and wonderful things to me. I never felt like I do with her. I like the little things she does better than all the orgasms in the world."

Women explained some of the reasons why they preferred to relate sexually to women.

"I have been relating sexually to women for over four years. I have always had strong, warm, loving relationships with women—ever since I can remember. My feelings of sympathy, compassion, and understanding have always been more strongly directed toward women. In other words women have mattered and do matter to me more than men, and even though I've had more sexual relationships with men in the past, they have not compared in depth emotionally to my relationships with women, sexual or nonsexual."

"I am a lesbian. I had my first feelings of sexual desire for another woman eight years ago, when I was fourteen. We both got scared after that (terrified would be much more accurate) and tried to convince ourselves we were heterosexual. In that next three and a half years I slept with seven or eight men but never was very satisfied with the relationships emotionally, sexually, etc. They weren't satisfying because I just don't feel the *complete* relationship—emotional, spiritual, etc. Besides, I like women's bodies much more. When I was nineteen I fell head over heels in love with a woman and realized that I couldn't kid myself any longer. I knew then that I was a lesbian. She was much more afraid than I (this was the first time she had realized that she felt this way about another woman), and our sexuality was not expressed with each other very frequently for that reason. I was in love with her for almost two and a half years. About a year ago I saw my first lover again (from freshman year in high school) and we began to sleep together. In the year since then I slept with two other women before I met my present lover. We've been living together now for three months and we both expect it shall be for a long, long time. We are extremely comfortable with each other in all ways. Neither of us wants to sleep with anyone else (at least right now). I am now twenty-two, she is twenty. She has been out since she was thirteen though she too slept with some eight or nine men in the first few years of her sexual experience. Neither of us would ever get married, even if we weren't lesbians. The political implications are too large and damaging. We live with two other women and really enjoy collective living."

"I believe that this is true for countless millions of wives, in spite of all the claims to orgasm, that they really don't know what orgasm is. Almost no one is willing to admit to not having orgasms—what, me frigid? I used to say, during my marriage of thirty years, and quite sincerely, believe it or not, that yes, I had orgasm almost every time. But then, taken by surprise in a lesbian relationship, I experienced real, buffola total eclipse orgasm for the first time. Wow. I'd never felt anything like *that* before. Suddenly I understood all kinds of strange masculine behavior. The rather pleasant, generalized sensations I was accustomed to feeling with men—vaginal stimulation—were in a class with sensuously warm oatmeal. No wonder women have never made such a big thing out of sex—it's nice, really, but one can do without it. I believe that most women who claim orgasm without having experienced the clitoral detonation are speaking in ignorance."

"I was divorced in September 1974, after being married for thirty-five years, no extramarital experiences, only had intercourse with one man ever—I just didn't like it. After thirty-four years I tried a woman and loved it, so I got divorced. I think I had always been attracted to women but the women's movement and a less inhibited lifestyle, thankfully, caused me to come out. In junior high and high school I had 'crushes' on girls, but I was too young and stupid to know what was going on and what to do about it—information regarding lesbians was practically nonexistent then. I also had scrapbooks of Dorothy Lamour (boy that dates me!) and other women stars—Pat Neal and Lauren Bacall. I am fifty, and I am very enterprising and very resourceful, and run a business of my own."

"I think I've had a lot of experience for being eighteen. A lot of it was bad, but I learned from it anyway. I've slept with about twenty men and one woman. I found the woman much better sex and better love. She was warm and tender. This is because we were friends for five years before sleeping together. Until men understand me as well as she does, I prefer to sleep with her above anyone. I would like to have more experience with women I know. The most important thing involved in good sex is being honest. If you dig another woman, let her know—she may very well feel the same. If it freaks her out, talk to her about it—she needs to loosen up."

"Personally I like girls better, they are more tender and loving."

"I have orgasms—always multiple—in masturbation, but I do not have them too often with my husband. I fake them at times, but at times I don't even bother to do that because it's only for his gratification. I am in my forties—in the past year for the first time I have been involved with a woman. It is entirely different and I always have orgasms."

"My best sex experiences were with my woman friend, not because I was orgasmic, because I generally wasn't, but because (1) she was a woman and it's much easier for me to give myself emotionally to a woman, to surrender my ego; (2) her skin was so soft and smooth, the vulnerability sent me; (3) the opportunity to act the aggressor and the lover was wonderful; (4) lovemaking was so mutual, endless, unhurried, she didn't quickly tighten up into a ball of sweat and demand the old in and out; (5) I didn't worry about coming, there was no program; (6) I didn't worry about my body, whether it was "adequate"; and (7) I didn't worry about her sexual-moral judgment, where I was going to be placed on the spectrum of female frailties (angel or whore?)."

"My best experiences were this past year with my girlfriend. Once we made love in my parents' bed in candlelight and discovered our love for each other as sexual women. Also once we made love all night in great passion and were soft and silly and warm, and great love was built that night. The difference with boys is it is much shorter."

"Sex is not just sex no matter whether hetero or homo. As any lesbian (or bisexual) will tell you, sex is a very different thing with men than with women—a completely different experience which encompasses more than the fact that most women who have sex with other women like women better than men. It has to do more with the way men are brought up to regard their bodies, touching and sensuality, versus the way women learn to do this. All of which is summed up by the phrase 'make love *with*' instead of make love '*to*.' "

"Men were mostly concerned with their own pleasure rather than mine. I found no emotional love, just physical love. I find women better lovers; they know what a woman wants and most of all there is an emotional closeness that can never be matched with a man. More tenderness, more consideration and understanding of feelings, etc."

"With women there is a lot of hugging, kissing, caressing, i.e., a lot more touching and affection. There is not any particular procedure, only there is usually either finger-clitoral stimulation or cunnilingus to produce orgasm at some point. Women are warmer, more mutual, careful to see how I'm reacting, as opposed to most men, and sex is much slower. Women consider the whole body erotic since there is no one concentrated 'tool' for pleasure."

"Women seem to have a more sustained energy level after orgasm, and are more likely to know and do something about it if I'm not satisfied. It isn't all automatically 'over' because somebody orgasms."

"There was clitoral manipulation by hand and mouth, with much more kissing and holding than with men, and much more concern for my pleasure. I felt greater, much more free, than with men."

"I have been a lesbian for two years, and I'm living with the woman I love. Both of us hope this will be a permanent situation and we are happy, comfortable. I don't consider it a marriage, and by my definition of marriage I don't think I'd like to be married. Physically, sexual relationships with women have been *much* more pleasurable than with men. Psychologically too, because the women I've had sex with have been my friends first, which was never the case with men. Being friends sets up a trust that I think is essential for satisfying physical intimacy. Relating to another woman physically seems to me like the most natural thing in the world. You've already got a head start on knowing how to give her pleasure. Gentleness seems to be the key, and is the main difference between relating to men and women. Just follow the golden rule."

"When I first had sex with a woman, I thought, there's something very weird about going to bed with a girlfriend, your best friend and making love to her. 'God am I a *lesbian*? I must be *sick*!' But then, you know you aren't really sick at all. I found out that it's a new experience to make 'love.' It's a different sort of sex when there's emotions behind it. Both are good—yet they are different."

"The first time I made love with a woman, who was my best friend, was a good experience in that I had been waiting to touch her for so long, and finally when I told her how I felt for her she gave me a back rub which led to sex and I was surprised how natural a woman's body felt, and what a rush it was kissing her—it felt prevertedly good—I mean it was supposed to be so perverse but it was great. The sex itself was not too good—we were both freaked out, especially me, and I was afraid to do anything. And we never talked about it."

"I've only been out since early this year. I had chosen a woman to talk my feelings out with and went to her house and realized that considering my emotions, it was ridiculous to talk so I said, 'I want to hold you,' and did. When I kissed her neck I was shocked and delighted to find how easy it was and how good it felt. I am still and probably will always be amazed at how easy it is for me to feel desire or to excite another woman, and how natural it is to act on it."

"Sex is better with women physically and emotionally. Women are much more sensitive to other people's needs probably as a result of our servile programming. However, the benefit is a tuned-in lover! Also, I like the fact that women can't rape each other. I also like the aesthetic symmetry—'twin' aspect—as well as the power symmetry."

"At seven, I used to become highly aroused fantasizing kissing a certain girlfriend. By about twelve, I was fantasizing necking with both sexes. By about fourteen, I wanted to fuck; or, more mysterious and exciting and

forbidden, do whatever it was the lesbians did! Now I
do and it's great."

"My love affair with a woman (a good friend) was
beautiful, even though neither of us came to climax,
she because she couldn't, I because I knew how that felt
for her and said I wouldn't."

"Most of the men in my heterosexual career (when I
was twenty until I was twenty-eight), wanted oral stimulation from me of their penis, after which they would
mount me and reach their climax. After their ejaculation they would ask, 'Didja come?' In general, my female lovers have taken far more creative and varied approaches to lovemaking. All of them, however, began
by being incredibly gentle and aware of my needs, as
well as theirs. The women did not act as though I was a
'masturbation machine' for them, nor did they fall
asleep when it was over. No woman ever asked me,
'Didja come?' They knew. My lovemaking periods with
women have always lasted much longer than they ever
did with men. Twenty minutes for a man, at least an
hour with a woman, usually more. I hope the day will
come when heterosexual couples can universally boast
of having the kind of good sexual encounters I am having now."

"Lesbian sex is very different from sex with men. It
is not an 'exchange' or a 'trade' or services, it is not
physically awkward, it is not something done *to* me (despite the best will in the world men still made me feel I
was being acted *on*), it is not demand (orgasm) oriented. It is wonderful. I can be both passive and active,
relaxed and demanding. There is no anxiety that anything will stop our lovemaking except exhaustion. I enjoy what I do to her almost as much as what she does to
me; we make each other's feeling possible by revealing
our need and pleasure to each other. I have somewhat
forgotten the panic I used to be in about orgasms and I
am angry whenever I feel pressure from that kind of
memory. I'm not even sure if I answered the questions
about orgasm 'right' because I've stopped thinking like
that because now the *act* is not pleasurable, and besides
I don't have to make sure I have an orgasm so I won't

feel left out and cheated when he has his. It is good simply to be with women. I could not have written that five years ago. I hated women, believed affection was male (!) and looked like a fairly successful imitation of a Barbie doll. Except that I kept rejecting Kens."

What is "different" about sexual relations between women is precisely that there is no one institutionalized way of having them, so they can be as inventive and individual as the people involved. Perhaps the two most striking specific differences from most heterosexual relations, as defined in the clitoral stimulation chapter, were that there were generally more feelings and tenderness, affection and sensitivity, and more orgasms. This higher frequency of orgasm in lesbian sexuality has of course been remarked on by other researchers going at least as far back as Kinsey. Also lesbian sexual relations tend to be longer and to involve more over-all body sensuality, since one orgasm does not automatically signal the end of sexual feeling, as in most of the heterosexual relations described earlier.

What types of bisexual answers were received?

"I think my background has a lot to do with the way I feel about sex. I was brought up middle class with parents who taught me that sex was bad unless you were married period. A girl should never go to bed with a man unless he was her husband. So I'm still struggling with some guilt feelings. It hurts me to think how it would hurt my mother if she knew some of the things I've done, but I just couldn't live my life just for what she wants. I had sex with a woman for about two years and it was really a fantastic experience. I have never felt so close to anyone or so loved. I used to think I would always prefer sex with a woman, but now I find I like sex with a man I care for too. Both are really great if the caring is there. I guess I feel more relaxed with a woman because I know about her body and seem to be more in touch with her feelings. At present, I am only having sex with one man but if the opportunity presents itself, I will have sex again with a woman."

"The first time I fell in love was with a woman who had been a close friend for several years. We joined a consciousness-raising group together, which is where we first discussed the possibility of sexual relations with women. We were then apart several months during the summer, and when we got back together she told me she had slept with a woman. Our relationship after that got more and more intense, and several months later we started sleeping together. Falling in love with her was totally unexpected—I had known her for years, but it really changed. We talked all the time, about everything under the sun. We grew to know and understand everything about each other. I am still very much in love with her, and still get chills of anticipation when I'm about to see her. Even though we're apart most of the time, at school, we still share all our thoughts and I've never felt so close to anyone on any level. We understand each other on all levels, and satisfy needs no one else has even realized were there. Since our falling in love, I've also fallen in love with two other people, both male. One was gradual, the other was instantaneous. I feel that somehow, my love for her makes me much more open and able to have intense feelings for others too."

Lesbianism can be political.

Besides the increased affection and sensitivity and the increased frequency of orgasm, some women felt that sex with another woman could be better because of the more equal relationship possible. Sex with women can be a reaction against men and our second class status with them in this society:

"Sex with a man is often the beginning of a political education. Sex with a woman means independence from men."

"Because of my own tremendous conditioning, which I believe is almost universal, it is almost impossible for me to have a truly healthy sexual relationship with a man—probably for any woman."

"Sex with women is more of a communion with self, although society makes it more complicated. But men are usually juvenile in some way and so one gets emotionally wasted with them."

"I am currently thinking of lesbianism as an alternative to abstinence, and to men in general, because they are not very liberated sexually or emotionally or any other way, and I can't stand it any more."

"You can have sex with everybody and say 'up yours' to morality, or, you can have sex with women and say 'up yours' to men and the society that puts you down. Lesbianism in my view is a far-out alternative to always being underneath some man and being a baby machine."

"I see lesbianism as putting *all* my energies (sexual, political social, etc.) into women. Sex is a form of comfort and to have sex indiscriminately with males is to give them comfort. I think it should be seriously considered.'

"Is sex political? Of course. When I quietly parted from my last male lover (for women) I suddenly, for the first time, moved into my own space, my own time zone, and my own life."

Janis Kelly has had some interesting things to say along these lines in *Sister Love: An Exploration of the Need for Homosexual Experience*:

> All heterosexual relationships are corrupted by the imbalance of power between men and women. In order to maintain superiority, males must feed on the emotional care and economic servitude of women. To survive in a male-supremacist social order, women must cripple themselves in order to build the male ego. Due to the stifling effect of this culture and to the damaging roles it enforces, women cannot develop fully in a heterosexual context.
>
> Love relationships between women are more likely to be free of the destructive forces which make [these] defenses necessary. Institutional norms and the restraints of a power-oriented culture have, of course, also influenced women; nevertheless, the domination-subordination patterns women sometimes bring to lesbian relationships cannot overshadow the essential equality of the persons involved. In addition,

many of the responses nurtured in females are extremely conducive to non-exploitative interaction. Sensitivity to the feelings and moods of others, caretaking, and gentleness are among the qualities more encouraged in women than in men. . . .

Because men occupy a superior social position and are schooled to covet power over others in order to maintain that position, they can rarely accept others, especially women, as equals. Human contacts must be arranged hierarchically, and women must be on a lower level. Tension is inevitable when a woman refuses to accept this position and must be "put in her place." In contrast, women are able to start from a foundation of equality and devote their energy to growth and creativity rather than to struggling to maintain identities against the destructiveness of the traditional female role.[8]

It is important for women to recognize their own potential for having sexual feelings for other women. If we want to grow strong, we must learn to love, respect, honor, and be attentive to and interested in other women. This includes seeing each other as physically attractive with the possibility of sexual intimacy. As long as we can relate sexually only to men *because they are "men"* (and as long as men can relate only to women because they are "women"), we are dividing the world into the very two classes we are trying to transcend.

Any woman who feels actual horror or revulsion at the thought of kissing or embracing or having physical relations with another woman should reexamine her feelings and attitudes not only about other women, but also about *herself*. A positive attitude toward our bodies and toward touching ourselves and toward any physical contact that might naturally develop with another woman is essential to self-love and accepting our own bodies as good and beautiful. As Jill Johnston has written: ". . . until women see in each other the possibility of a primal commitment which includes sexual love they will be denying themselves the love and value they readily accord to men, thus affirming their own second class status."

SEXUAL SLAVERY

WHAT IS SEXUAL SLAVERY?

"I have wanted to have orgasms with a man for years—about twelve. Seems like the impossible dream. I can be a loving eunuch with him, but only a full sexual person by myself."

Why does this woman say this? Why, if she can be "a full sexual person" by herself, can she be only "a loving eunuch" with a man? This woman's comment points up a dilemma that has become clearer and clearer throughout this book. We have seen that heterosexual sex usually involves the pattern of foreplay, penetration, and intercourse ending with male ejaculation—and that all too often the woman does not orgasm. But women *know* very well how to orgasm during masturbation, whenever they want. If they know how to have orgasms whenever they want, why don't they feel free to use this knowledge during sex with men? *Why do women so habitually satisfy men's needs during sex and ignore their own?*

The fact is that the role of women in sex, as in every other aspect of life, has been to serve the needs of others—men and children. And just as women did not recognize their oppression in a general sense until recently, just so sexual slavery has been an almost unconscious way of life for most women—based on what was said to be an eternally unchanging biological impulse. We have seen, however (in the intercourse chapter), that our model of sex and physical relations is *culturally* (not biologically) defined, and can be redefined—or undefined. We need not continue to have only one model of physical relations—foreplay, penetration, intercourse, and ejaculation.

Women are sexual slaves insofar as they are (justifiably) afraid to "come out" with their own sexuality, and forced to satisfy others' needs and ignore their own. As one woman put it, "sex can be political in the sense that it can involve a power structure where the woman is unwilling or unable to get what she really needs for her fullest amount of pleasure, but the man is getting what he wants, and the woman, like an unquestioning and unsuspecting lackey, is gratefully supplying it." The truth is that almost everything in our society pushes women toward defining their sexuality only as intercourse with men, and toward not defining themselves as full persons in sex with men. Lack of sexual satisfaction is another sign of the oppression of women.

This, of course, is not to say that women don't like sex, or that they don't enjoy intercourse in many ways. When asked if they enjoyed sex, almost all women said yes, they did. Furthermore, there was no correlation with frequency of orgasm: women who did not orgasm with their partners were just as likely to say they enjoyed sex as women who did. And women who never orgasmed during intercourse were just as likely to say they enjoyed intercourse as women who did. However, the important question is: What is it that women enjoy about sex/intercourse, and what do women mean when they say they like them?

FEELINGS ABOUT SEX AND INTERCOURSE

"Is having sex important to you? Why? What part does it play in your life, and what does it mean to you?"

The overwhelming majority of women answered that sex meant a great deal to them, and the reason almost always given was because it was a wonderful form of intimacy and closeness with another human being.

"Sex is important because during sex you can be as close as possible with another person. During sex I feel so at ease, and the time before, during, and after I can really enjoy how close we are."

"Sex is beautiful because such a complete contact with another person makes me feel my being is not solely confined to my own body. It is one of the most direct ways to get beyond the barriers between 'them' and 'me.' "

"Sex plays a very important part in my life because at this point it is a symbol of the love I am sharing with my man. I know it is his way of showing he loves me. Many times I do not have an orgasm but I still feel a great deal of satisfaction. The closeness and feelings are what is important."

"Sex is primarily important as a vehicle for intimacy, a way of showing my deepest love. It is the very essence of my life with my husband, not in the sense of a transitory emotion resulting from some form of personal satisfaction, but because of its symbolic meaning that we share."

"I become very emotionally involved in my sexual relations. I think I have sex almost always to consummate a bond, to develop and perpetuate closeness. The more sex I have with someone, the closer I feel to them. I love my sex partners more than I would if I wasn't having sex with them. Is this true of other women? of men? Sex is very important to me for this reason."

"Sex is very important because it is the most intense pleasure two people can give each other, and the closest you can be to another person—the one time we express ourselves fully. We drop all barriers and truly communicate as human beings."

"Sex is a form of communication without words based on bodily responses, and is the ultimate in human closeness where a person can express and understand more than the mind can conceive of. It brings me closer in spirit to others in ten minutes than I can get in ten years to people I do not share sex with."

"Sex is important because when there is a feeling of understanding and appreciation between two people— sex can make life together something special. It shows 'you mean more to me than others do.' It recements the relationship between my husband and myself—a reflection of our love."

"Do you like vaginal penetration/intercourse? Physically? Psychologically? Why?"

Since 87 percent of the women in this study answered "yes" to this question,* this includes most of the women who never orgasmed during intercourse. Clearly, there was no automatic connection between not having orgasms during intercourse and not liking it. In fact, even women who did orgasm during intercourse most frequently gave affection and closeness as their basic reason for liking intercourse, rarely mentioning orgasm.

The most frequent reason given for liking intercourse by far was that it is a time of great affection and closeness.

"I love intercourse. Even when I'm not getting off at all or don't really love the man, I still love it (unless

* See appendix for the feelings of women who did not like intercourse.

actual pain is present), because we are so close at that time—closer than at any other time. Even *with* orgasm, I would have to say that this is over half the pleasure of intercourse for me. There's just something about it that brings you closer."

"Yes, I like intercourse, even though I don't have orgasm. It shows affection or the illusion of it—when people are at their most vulnerable moments. Physically I like the total closeness and the sensation of wrapping myself around him."

"Yes, it feels warm, like being hugged more closely than ever. I feel accepted and giving at the same time."

"I love his body and love feeling it. Physically I like having his penis in my vagina, he is in me and we are one. Psychologically it's fantastic because of the love I feel for him and which I show physically and vice versa. It has never led to an orgasm, but I really enjoy it anyway."

"Physically, I love having his penis inside my vagina—which kind of caresses the penis and hugs it. Emotionally, I feel it all through my body and spirit—I feel that we two are merging as one. I feel very alive, very vital. I feel very fulfilled, and I feel as if I hadn't a care in the world, just the supreme ecstasy and happiness of being one with him."

"During intercourse I feel very close and somehow entangled and united with another human being, which I cannot realize in any other way. It is like holding your first new-born baby—someone else is part of you."

"Intercourse is good, warm, close, a reaffirmation of love, an ultimate sharing, and special intimacy—a very private spiritual thing."

"Intercourse is profound—a sense of merging your individual identities and becoming one."

"Yes, the idea of union, both physical and emotional, with another is exciting and satisfying. We are joined in love."

"Psychologically I feel I am truly communicating with my partner—getting as close as one can get, both physically and spiritually."

"Yes, I like intercourse—especially psychologically,

due to the closeness and intimacy, and the sharing, hugging, and togetherness. It is totally satisfying."

"During intercourse I feel secure and wanted—whole, warm, loved, womanly."

"During intercourse I feel secure, assured of his love, and protected. It feels good to my mind, body, and heart."

"I like penetration physically because it feels warm and sweet and mutual. Especially his chest against mine is great! Psychologically I feel more complete, and fulfilled and needed."

"It is an affirmation of love, warmth, and caring, and makes me feel alive and human. My face is near his and I can feel his breath."

"The touching and tenderness then makes me feel warm and secure, safe and close."

"I love it. Feeling your man's penis deep within you, thrusting even deeper, is ecstasy. Psychologically it is warmly intimate—becoming one. It's really tender, acting out our physical love for each other."

"It is a oneness that transcends all else. I feel overwhelmed and in a grand passion, and very close to the person I love."

"Yes, it is the most beautiful thing two people in love can share. Frequently at the moment of penetration there is a tremendous feeling of relief, of becoming one together."

"Yes, I like it, because of what it represents—the ultimate unity of us. It's an inimitable closeness, one is kind of enfolding the other person."

"It is the ultimate of physical and psychological fulfillment. The act is something only God could have imagined that is so beautiful."

"Intercourse is the total integration of two people in love. Didn't you know?"

In addition these answers very frequently included specific references to feeling sure of the man's attention and affection at that time.

"I love intercourse. It feels really close, like he is really mine, and cares for me."

"I love the intimacy of it because for those minutes the man is totally mine and I am loved, happy, fulfilled, high, needed—and sometimes adored."

"The greatest pleasure in sex is simply feeling very special and very close with someone. The greatest displeasure is anxiety about the relationship."

"I like intercourse because it is a time when I get his undivided attention, and feel very loved and secure."

"Intercourse shows my husband loves and wants me."

"The greatest thing is the security I feel when I'm in bed with a man. I feel loved and wanted and powerful."

"Yes, during intercourse I feel a sense of euphoria— I am successful, competent, beautiful!"

"I feel that when he's inside me, I really 'have' him as opposed to always wondering if he cares or what/who he's thinking about."

Similarly, answers to "Is sex important to you? What does it mean to you, and what part does it play in your life?" contained references to the reassurance sex gives about the over-all emotional relationship.

"Our sex life together is important because it makes me feel secure and wanted, and proves he loves me."

"Sex is to please him. What I like is the feeling of security I get when he holds me tight after. It makes me feel accepted and attractive."

"Sex makes me feel I am a woman to my husband instead of just a live-in maid."

"I get self-confidence because my husband desires me."

"Sex is the biggest part in a relationship with a man. If he doesn't want me, I feel something must be wrong with our relationship."

"It reassures me I'm desirable, gives a deeper bond to a relationship."

"My entire marriage revolves around making love to my husband. It makes me feel loved and wanted."

"It keeps me close and affectionate with my husband, and gives me a feeling of security."

"Maybe I like it because when I have sex the other

person is focusing all his attention on me, and I feel important and wanted."

"Sex is important to me as a reaffirmation of my worth that a man would take the time to be gentle with me."

"Sex tells me where I stand with my man. It allows me to ask nitty-gritty questions I wouldn't be able to feel I could without being close. I feel loved."

"Having a man love me and want to have sex with me is necessary to my happiness. It gives me a feeling of being worthwhile if I can turn a man on."

"I've never heard a word of praise from my husband in twenty-one years except while having intercourse. While I resent this, I still love him, and I still enjoy sex with him—but only for this reason."

Another frequently stated reason for liking intercourse involved identification with male pleasure, giving the man pleasure.

"I like the closeness and definitely the pleasure I'm giving the man. I like the feeling the man seems to feel."

"I never had an orgasm this way, but I love to hear him panting, groaning, moving, getting crazy. I like the feeling of closeness it produces, and I am excited by my partner's excitation—the sound of his breathing, the feeling of his excitement through the stiffness of his penis and the way he moves."

"Yes, I like intercourse. I like men, their bodies, and pleasing them."

"Yes, intercourse is a lovely way to share passions, love, devotion. And there's a feeling of power in it—the power to give a man a pleasure that is very important to his feeling of well-being."

"Psychologically I like being in control and having power, feeling close to him during his orgasm—giving the most valuable and personal pleasure possible to my man."

"I like it because I feel very close to my partner. He has an orgasm and I'm very glad to watch him and help him—we do it together and I feel very good. I would

like to have orgasms then too and I'm hoping that
sometime I will."

"Sometimes it is enjoyable in itself, but usually I enjoy it because I am giving pleasure to my partner. I like
the idea of having his penis inside me, although I don't
usually need the accompanying *movement*. However, it
gives him pleasure."

"Intercourse is something I'm finally good for and
the only way he can satisfy his desire."

"No not for its own sake, but during intercourse I get
to have him in the most intimate way, and to be a part
of his body."

"During intercourse I constantly think about if he's
enjoying it, if I'm tight enough, what he's thinking
about, and I try to keep my vaginal muscles contracted.
I guess I like it okay."

"It's only good for me psychologically—I'm too
much involved with making sure the man is having a
really good time. Mainly I worry about whether he will
lose his hard-on if my vagina squeezes his penis too
much."

"Yes, I do like intercourse very much. The only way
I do not like it is politically, because I do not like being
as vulnerable as I am, just physically, not to mention
other ways, which are probably more important. But I
love to feel the man that I love, or even a man that I
just want a lot, come into me. I love to enclose him,
give him pleasure, feel his body all over, wrap my legs
around him, and to feel his strength and show him
mine. Love to feel him come, and hear his heart beat,
and whatever craziness he has to say at that moment.
That, in itself, is a trip."

**Another reason sometimes given for liking intercourse
was habit or "conditioning."**

"It has never lead to a climax for me. I guess I enjoy
it because I have been conditioned to view it as 'normal
sex.' Not enjoying it at all, or not having orgasm during
intercourse, threatens my concept of myself as a 'normal'
woman."

"Yes I like it, especially when I want it. Probably I

like it because I've been conditioned to find it pleasurable."

"Yes I like it in all ways. I feel more at home with this type of stimulation."

"Psychologically intercourse may be more enjoyable because of all my hangups with masturbation."

"Yes, I like it in all ways, but probably more psychologically than any other. I think I like it partly because of fantasies that are a result of reading, seeing films, etc., etc., and all the other attempts of society and the media to make this a 'great' thing."

"Yes. I like to give him pleasure, and also maybe I like it because it's so familiar."

"Yes, especially psychologically because (1) we're sort of brought up to think it fulfilling (I don't know whether it is per se), and (2) because I know I've got a vagina."

"Intercourse is fun—sort of like a carousel ride where you've gone to all the trouble and paid your twenty-five cents and you might as well get a kick out of the prescribed number of ups and downs and the color and glamour and all the pretty lights and people watching you . . . and besides, it's the only game in town."

Intercourse also seemed to make sex "official."

"I feel I'm not really having sex without penetration."

"Yes, I like intercourse in all ways. To go through all the actions without penetration seems like you're leaving something out."

"I love it; to me nothing else is really 'sex.' I love the feeling of our bodies united and confused at their most sensitive points."

"It's okay physically but it's especially valuable psychologically because it makes sex 'official.' No relationship could last for long without it."

Some women said intercourse made them feel "more like a woman."

"During intercourse I feel whole, like a woman."

"I love intercourse because during it I get wild and free. I'm a sexual woman, and I enjoy feeling passionate."

"Yes, I like it, especially the initial penetration. I feel I am fulfilling the reason for my womanly existence."

"Yes I like it in all ways because my cunt is *there* to receive the male organ and naturally it feels good. I feel renewed as a woman."

"Physically it's healthy, psychologically I require it. It's a basic requirement of a healthy physical woman."

"Yes, I like it. What healthy American woman doesn't? It's a normal process."

"Intercourse is beautiful, God-given, necessary to my happiness, and my physical and mental well-being as a woman."

"Yes. I am a woman, he is a man, and it was meant to be this way. It's instinct. Also sometimes I have a tender thought of possible impregnation."

WHY DON'T
WOMEN CREATE
THEIR OWN ORGASMS?

We have seen that the basic value of sex and intercourse for women is closeness and affection. Women
liked sex more for the feelings involved than for the
purely physical sensations of intercourse per se.* As
most women's answers in the preceding section reflected, it is the emotional warmth shared at this time,
and the feeling of being wanted and needed (not the
plain physical act) which are the chief pleasures of sex
and intercourse.

Sex in our society is an extremely important way of
being close—almost the only way we can be really
physically or even spiritually intimate with another human being. And sex is one of the few times we tangibly
feel we are being loved and demonstrate our love for
another person. And yet, in another, as yet unborn (un-
created) society, it would not be necessary to define "sex"
in such a closed and rigid way. It would not be necessary for women to accept an oppressive situation in order to get closeness and affection.

It is not the fact that women don't want or don't like
intercourse that makes them sexual slaves (since they
do like it), but rather the fact that they have few or no
alternative choices for their own satisfaction. Sex is de-

* As far as the physical sensations themselves are concerned,
the moment of penetration was by far the favorite sensation
mentioned by most women. What sex researchers call "proprioceptive feeling"—pleasurable physical sensations having
nothing to do with orgasm—were very rarely mentioned.

fined as a certain pattern—foreplay, penetration, intercourse, and ejaculation—and intercourse is always part
of that pattern, indeed, intercourse *is* the pattern (at
least insofar as it ends with male ejaculation, and this
ends sex). This pattern is what oppresses women, and
in fact it oppresses men too, as we shall see later on.

But the original question of this chapter is still not
answered—If women know how to have orgasms, why
don't they use this knowledge during sex with men?
Why don't they break out of the pattern? There is no
reason why using this knowledge and taking the initiative in new directions would diminish the warmth and
closeness of sex. Or is there?

HABIT

On one level, it could be said that we think of "sex"
as we do—as "foreplay," "penetration," and intercourse
followed by male ejaculation—because we are taught
that this is what sex is, because we are taught that these
are the proper physical relations between people, and
that this is what you are "supposed" to do. Our idea of
sexual relations is structured around reproductive activity, which is defined as "instinctual." Although sexual
feelings of pleasure are instinctual, or at least innate,
intercourse is not, strictly, their instinctive or innate
goal. One of our society's myths is that it is "nature" or
our "instincts" that make us have "sex" as we do. Actually, most of the time we do it the way we do because
we have learned to do it that way. Even chimpanzees
and other animals must learn to have intercourse
(Yerkes; Harlow and Harlow; H.C. Bingham). Sex and
all physical relations are something *we* create; they are
cultural forms, not biological forms. Most often, however, we do not think of ourselves as free to explore and
discover or invent whatever kinds of varied physical relations we might want, or which might seem natural to
us at any given time, corresponding to our own individual feelings and needs. Instead, we tend to act as if
there were one set formula for having intimate physical

contact with other people (who "must" be of the opposite sex), which includes foreplay, intercourse, and male orgasm.

From this point of view, the answers women have given when asked if they like "sex" can be seen as reflecting their feelings about this standard definition: if intercourse is instinctive, and if the way we have sex is nature itself, how can anyone (who is not "neurotic") say they don't like it? Or how can anyone say they would like to change it? Sex is sex, and either you like it or you don't. However, as we have seen, the more specific questions did bring out all kinds of satisfactions and dissatisfactions with sex as we know it.

There is great pressure on women in our society now to say they like "sex." As one woman put it, "With the current spotlight on sex, the knowledge that I have a good sex life protects me from damaging doubts about myself every time I read an article about sex." Women *must* "do it right" and especially they must enjoy it. Any woman who says she does not like sex is labeled "neurotic," "hung up," "weird," or "sick," by the psychiatric profession and others. Women, for all kinds of reasons, *must* like "sex." This means, essentially, that women must like heterosexual intercourse.

In fact, to even hint at questioning the glory and importance of intercourse as a primary value is like questioning the American flag or apple pie. One is not even allowed to *discuss* feelings about intercourse, or whether one likes it, etc., without arousing a strong emotional reaction in many people, who feel you are attacking *"men."* But this is not true. The fact that it is so perceived is merely another indication of how stereotyped our ideas about physical relations are and, further, how emotionally and politically sensitive a topic sex is.

To reinforce us in these ideas of what sex is, and especially that heterosexual intercourse is *the* high point in every case, we have all kinds of people—from physicians to clergymen to self-styled sex experts in books and women's magazines to our own male lovers—instructing us in what sex is, and in the proper ways of having it. But, how can there be a "proper way of touching another human being? Sex manuals tell us with mechanical precision where to touch, how to touch, when to Orgasm, that it is Bad not to Orgasm, and so On. But especially we learn that, no matter what else, intercourse and male orgasm *must* take place. Although this subject will be pursued further in a later chapter, it is important to stress here that, although sex manuals can be helpful, it is *we* who know what we want at any given time, and we who can create sex in whatever image we want. There is no need to follow any one mechanical pattern to be close to another human being.

LOVE

But somehow, the truth is more complicated than the simple idea that women are oppressed in bed as elsewhere out of "habit"—simply because "just as women are used to serving men their coffee, so they are used to serving them their orgasms." It is still remarkable how easily we bring ourselves to orgasm during masturbation, and how totally we can ignore this knowledge during sex with men. It seems clear that we are often afraid to use this knowledge during sex with men because to do so would be to challenge male authority. Somehow it is all right for a woman to demand equal pay, but to demand equality in sex is not considered valid.

Why are women afraid to challenge men in bed? First, they fear losing men's "love." The question of what love is, of course, is very complicated,* but it is clear that as seen throughout this chapter, the importance of sex for women is inextricably bound up with love:

---

* This book has purposely refrained from bringing these feelings into the discussion, since the politics of love still remain to be analyzed. If you would like to contribute, please write me c/o Box 5282, F.D.R. Post Office, NY, NY 10022, for a copy of the questions on love and personal relationships.

"Sex for me is a very private and almost sacred thing. To me sex means the supreme proof of love."

"In my own case, I desire happiness, togetherness, love, etc., and I know that if for no apparent reason I kept refusing sex, I would lose some of the happiness in my life, and I might lose the love my man has for me. He would assume that something was wrong and make changes, perhaps excluding me from his life."

"It's a trade. Like my mother says, men give love for sex, women give sex for love."

It does seem to many sex researchers and therapists that fear of losing a man's love *is* holding many women back from having orgasms with men. According to Helen Kaplan in *The New Sex Therapy:*

> . . . the frank reaching for sexual pleasure may mobilize unconscious fears (in a woman) that she will be abandoned. She may be afraid that her husband will get tired of 'catering' to her. Or, if the patient assumes the superior position in coitus, she may be afraid that her husband will find her unsatisfactory sexually because she is unattractive in that sitting-up position. These fears may have some basis in reality. The husband may, in fact, become impatient or rejecting. Moreover, if he feels that his sexual role has been pre-empted, this experience may give rise to anxiety in the husband as well, and in that event he may defend against this anxiety by behaving in ways that repel or frighten his wife.[1]

Similarly, Fisher found that the *only* difference psychologically between those women who were able to orgasm with their husbands (they were all married) and those who were not involved love. Fisher reported that:

> . . . the prime difference between women who are high and low in orgasmic consistency is their alarm about losing what they love. The low-orgasmic woman feels that persons she values and loves are not dependable, that they may unpredictably leave her. She seems to be chronically preoccupied with the possibil-

ity of being separated from those with whom she has had intimate relationships.[2]

In addition, he remarks:

> It should be pointed out that this fear of loss of love object bears a remarkable resemblance to a type of anxiety that has been found to be particularly characteristic of women . . . women have been observed in several studies . . . to be especially sensitive to potential separation from those with whom they have close relationships.[3]

In his epilogue Fisher says:

> The psychological factors—for example, fear of object loss—which my work suggests may interfere with orgasm attainment in many women may exemplify at another level the general cultural feeling transmitted to woman that *her place is uncertain and that she survives only because the male protects her.* The apparent importance of fear of object loss in inhibiting orgasm can probably be traced to the fact that the little girl gets innumerable messages which tell her that the female cannot survive alone and is likely to get into serious trouble if she is not supported by a strong and capable male. *It does not seem too radical to predict that when women are able to grow up in a culture in which they are less pressured to obedience by threats of potential desertion, the so-called orgasm problem will fade away.*[4] [Italics mine.—Au.]

Although Fisher, as a psychologist, tends to see these fears of loss of love as emanating from childhood experiences, it is obvious that they also can be reactions to very real current, adult conditions, such as fears that as you get older the man you love will stop loving you, that he needs you less than you need him, and so forth.

ECONOMICS

Not only may a woman be afraid of losing a man's love, if she asserts herself, or "challenges" him sexually, but all too often economic intimidation is also involved. This can take many forms, some subtle, some overt. The most obvious form of economic intimidation occurs when a woman is totally dependant on the man with whom she has sex for food and shelter, and has no economic alternatives such as being able to get a job herself if she wants—that is, marriage as it was traditionally defined. We have all seen the connection between affection and economics in a mild form on "I Love Lucy," where affectionate words and embraces were always a standard part of talking Ricky into a new sofa, a new hat, or a vacation. Some of the women in this study also mentioned the connection between sex and economics in their lives, in answer to *Do you feel that having sex is in any way political?*:

"In my circle, generally the man makes twice as much money as the wife. That means if you like your lifestyle—your swimming pool, leisure, shrink, dishwasher, neighborhood—you don't chuck it all to run off with some surfer. I see a lot of marriages held together not with a genuine desire to share a life, but with a need to keep things financially secure. Come The Revolution, when women will really be as prepared to make a living as men are, there will be far fewer of these feudal relationships."

"Yes it is. In my relationship I am forced to give sex because of the marriage vows. My husband has on occasion threatened to withhold money or favors— that is, permission of some sort or another—if I do not have sex with him. So I fake it. What the hell. When the kids are older—I just might lay my cards on the table."

"I'm not sure if it's political, but it's economic. I really felt I was earning my room and board in bed for years, and if I wanted anything, my husband was more likely to give it to me after sex. Now that I am self-supporting, I don't need to play that game any more. What a relief!"

"I think it is used for 'horse trading.' I know I have used it that way, and I think most women have been forced to use it that way (for bargaining purposes and to gain economic support) at one time or another, although this is gradually changing as jobs become open to us."

"It could be, like if you're bartering for a new sofa or a night out."

"I can see no way sex is political, unless you mean the way that women have sex with their husbands if they'll do this or that for them. I don't believe that's right, but I can't say I don't do the same kind of thing with my husband sometimes."

"With my husband, I sometimes feel obligated because I'm his wife and, after all, he does pay for everything. That's why I enjoy extramarital affairs (although I haven't had one in some time)—it makes sex special and exciting."

"I cannot explain my feelings about sex. The celebration of two human beings is very important to me, but happens rarely. I feel that I and other wives pay the price of being available for sex at their husbands' whims by accepting financial security."

"There are times when I feel I'm discharging an obligation, like washing the dishes or doing the ironing. Then I feel like a prostitute."

"For me, I'm glad to have lived long enough to see the light out of the tunnel—the hope that women some day will get an equal shake. Can you imagine what a brainwashed era it was forty years ago? You had to consider yourself lucky you had a husband, and most of the time you were sure something was wrong with you, and you just spent your life catering to men and your children and you touched your forehead to the floor that he didn't beat you—that he provided for you, and all you were was an unpaid domestic. Death freed me, and I discovered a career and life for a woman. Some of

my peers died without ever knowing that there was
hope for the female—died ignorant of the whole thing."

Anyone who is economically and legally dependent
on another person, as women traditionally have been,
and in the majority of cases still are, is put in a very
vulnerable and precarious position when that person expects or demands sex or affection. Although the woman
may genuinely want to please the man, still, the fact
that she does not feel free *not* to please him, and that
she puts his satisfaction before her own and keeps secret
her own knowledge of her body, reveals the presence of
an element of fear and intimidation. Clearly, if a
woman is financially dependent on a man, she is not in
a good position to demand equality in bed. Economic
dependency, even if you love someone, is a very subtle
and corrosive force.

Of course, *legally* in marriage, a woman *must* have
intercourse with her husband. As Kinsey explained it:

> Both Hebrew and Christian codes have emphasized
> the obligation of the wife, and to some lesser degree
> the obligation of the husband, to engage in coitus with
> the lawfully wedded spouse. . . . The position of the
> wife in a marriage is reflected in the traditional atti-
> tude of English and American law which rules that
> she, in consenting to marry, has thereby given her ir-
> revocable consent to accept coitus under any condi-
> tions from her husband, even though he may use ex-
> treme force or violence to achieve his ends. Even
> under present-day American penal codes, a husband's
> coitus with his wife can never be interpreted as rape,
> no matter how much the coitus may be against her
> wishes and no matter how much force he may use.[5]

Even the position most commonly used today—the man
on top of the woman—is a legacy of ecclesiastical law.
Kinsey was writing in the 1950s, but these laws are
still on the books today. Although they are unevenly
enforced in various states, in general, they still are very
much in force. A group known as the Feminists pick-

eted the New York City Marriage License Bureau in 1969 with a pamphlet containing the following question: *"Do you know that rape is legal in marriage? According to law, sex is the purpose of marriage. You have to have sexual intercourse in order to have a valid marriage. Do you know that love and affection are not required in marriage? If you can't have sex with your husband, he can get a divorce or annulment. If he doesn't love you, that's not grounds for divorce."*[6]

Of course, it is not marriage itself that is at fault—that is, the idea of two people wanting to share their lives in common goals. Marriage in the sense of a *real* love contract could be wonderful. However, the reality of marriage now for many women is economic and legal dependency. This dependency can keep women from feeling free to explore and discover their own sexual feelings with their husbands.

Women who are not married can be economically intimidated in other, more subtle ways. As one woman explained her situation: "From early childhood, I felt I was programmed by my family background and society to become a wife and mother with a fallback on a meaningless job. Therefore I graduated with high grades in nothing subjects and went on for one year to a community college to study to be a secretary. For the next five years I worked as a secretary (still am one). During this time I have felt very inferior about my position in life and I am sure this carried over into my sexuality and feelings about myself. I was more vulnerable to abuse from men and my low self-esteem contributed greatly. In the last three weeks I have made the decision to quit my secretarial job and return to school full-time. This decision has worked miracles for me. I have a higher opinion of myself and feel totally unwilling to become involved in any kind of relationship (sexual or other) that is destructive in any way for me. I feel free to enjoy my body on my own terms, and not as some preconceived notion of some sexist man. I do not hate all men at all—I'm sure I'll always have a great love for them, but I can see now how we have been using each other

and how unfair women's roles have been in every aspect
of their lives, and I want to change this. I feel my attitude is very healthy and will not hinder me from developing good relationships with men."

On another level, even a woman who is only on a
"date" with a man can be made to feel that she "owes"
him sex:

"Sex can be political, when the woman is made to
feel obligated, for instance, to pay for a date with sex in
exchange for anything."

"I hate Disneyland dating—the old 'I-took-you-here-
and-spent-$$$-so-now-you-go-to-bed-with-me.'"

"There were times when I was in school I would go
out to dinner with a guy just for the chance to eat some-
thing besides spaghetti—I was very poor. I knew they
usually wanted sex, and the less I was able to afford the
dinner he was paying for, the more I felt I owed it to
him. The more grateful I felt. Isn't that awful? It was
terrible, but I couldn't help it."

As Dr. Pepper Schwartz has pointed out, even when
women are no longer economically dependent, they are
still

> used to modifying (their sexual) desire to fit their
> more important needs: food, shelter, protection, and
> security, and most have ceased to be analytical about
> their sexual situation. Even when the situation arises
> that makes them independent of such considerations
> (personal wealth, a successful career, and a bevy of
> admirers, etc.) they are so used to having other exi-
> gencies define their sexual and marital structure that
> they do not reevaluate their life style. They believe the
> myths they have heard about their emotional and sex-
> ual needs.[7]

There are also economic pressures on single women
to get married—leading to the same financial and legal
dependency discussed earlier; as one women, age
twenty-seven, working in an office, explained her situa-

tion, "Even with the jobs I can get—and I'm a good secretary—I still can't afford to pay my rent. I'm forced to move in with a man, or else have roommates. Roommates do not give you any privacy, and living with some guy—first one guy and then, after a year or two, another guy, and so on—is a horrible way to live. You feel like an itinerant worker, moving all your belongings from place to place. It's humiliating. So you have the pressure to get married and settle down and forget it. And—(!!) if you are just living with a man on a supposedly equal share-the-rent basis, guess who still gets to clean house and cook? And be loving and affectionate and always ready for sex? And if, God forbid, you just don't feel like it for a while—out you go! So—you wind up thinking you'd be better off married."

As the Redstockings put it,

> For many women marriage is one of the few forms of employment that is readily available. Not marrying for them could easily mean becoming a domestic or factory worker or going on welfare. To advocate women "liberate themselves" by giving up marriage reflects a strong class bias in automatically excluding the mass of women who have no other means of support but a husband.[8]*

Of course this is not to say that love (for husband and children) cannot also be involved. Unfortunately, however, economic dependency can eventually corrode and subtly undermine the most beautiful feelings, or even go hand in hand with those feelings, leading to a kind of love-hate situation. But marriage could become a *real* love contract (either heterosexual or homosex-

---

* Dorothy Tennov, in *Prime Time* (a journal "for the liberation of women in the prime of life"), has looked at it another way: Those who recognize that wives who remain in marriage for economic reasons are, in fact, selling sexual services may condemn the practice on the basis of the male-serving edict that there is something wrong with selling sexual services. The thing that is wrong with the wife's situation is not that she gets paid for her services—sexual and others—but that she receives so little for what she provides that she remains dependent.[9]

ual) if the laws that make a woman legally dependent were changed and if women had a real chance for economic autonomy.

The negative effect of economics on women's freedom, both sexual and otherwise, is widespread. According to the U.S. Department of Labor, in 1975 women who worked full time year round (40 percent of American women) still earned only about 60 percent of the wages of similarly employed men, and this figure has not increased in the last five years. Women, despite their education and qualifications, are still largely absent from management and non-traditional professional positions. Federal subsidies of child day care centers have been cut back, and job layoffs have affected women more frequently, as they traditionally have more peripheral jobs. This means that most women—whether single or married—are not financially independent.

In other words, as Ellen DuBois, of the State University of New York at Buffalo, has written me,

> An erroneous and dangerous assumption is that the only thing that stands between a woman and "satisfactory" sex is her realization of her own physical needs. As an oppressed people, what we women lack is not knowledge . . . but *power,* social power, economic power, physical power. To put it another way, it is not our ignorance that has condemned us to sexual exploitation and dissatisfaction, but our powerlessness.

THE SEXUAL REVOLUTION

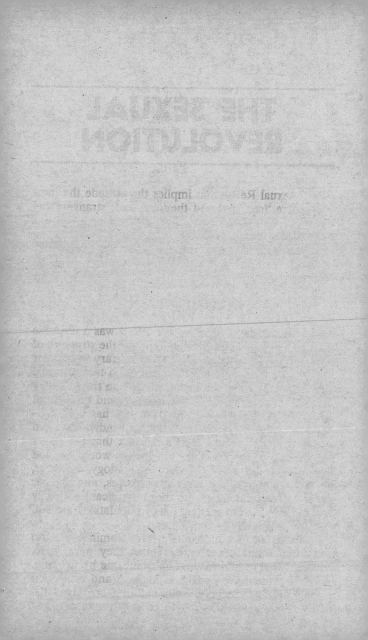

"If the Sexual Revolution implies the attitude that now women are 'free' too, and they can fuck strangers and fuck over the opposite sex, just the way men can, I think it's revolting. Women don't want to be 'free' to adopt the male model of sexuality; they want to be free to find their own."

INTRODUCTION

The "sexual revolution" of the 1960s was a response to long-term social changes that affected the structure of the family and women's role in it. (Contrary to popular opinion, the birth control pill was more a technological response to these same social changes than their cause.) Up until the second half of this century, and throughout most periods of history, a high birth rate has been considered of primary importance by both individuals and society. In social terms, it was thought that the larger the population, the wealthier the society would be, and the stronger the army. Modern technology, however, has ended the need for huge work forces, and nuclear power and technology are far more significant militarily than massive human armies. Large populations are still valuable principally as consumers.

In terms of the individual, large families are no longer the social or economic asset they once were. Children used to add to the family income by working, and they assured the parents of support and protection in their old age. Socially, male children continued the family name, which was felt to be very important, and increased the family's social prestige. Today these assets are considered negligible. Furthermore, children cost a great deal, since their education is prolonged, and after the second or third child, a couple's standing in the community diminishes rather than rises. In addition, most men no longer feel that carrying on the family line is a matter of primary importance—although they may very well enjoy having children and being fathers. But since marriage (in its original form as a property right) had been created so that the father could be sure of his paternity of the child, now that that paternity was no longer so important, marriage (as traditionally defined) was no longer so necessary, and women could be "allowed" sexual "freedom."

This change in women's role was double-edged. In traditional terms, insofar as having many children had become less important, women's status declined. That is, since women had traditionally been seen almost completely in terms of their childbearing role, they themselves as a class became less important and less respected when that role was no longer so important. At the same time, it was said that, now that women were "free" from their old role, they could be "sexually free like men," etc. There was some truth to this idea that new possibilities for female independence *had* opened up. However, as with the slaves, after emancipation, becoming independent was easier said than done. In fact, women did not have equal opportunities for education or employment, and so they were stuck in their traditional role of being dependent on men. In spite of the so-called sexual revolution, women (feeling how peripheral, decorative, and expendable they had become to the over-all scheme of things) became more submissive to men than ever. This was even more true *outside* of marriage than inside, since marriage did offer some forms of protection in traditional terms. This increased submissiveness and insecurity was reflected in the child-like, baby-doll fashions of the 1960s—short little-girl dresses, long straight (blond) hair, big innocent (blue) eyes, and of course always looking as young and pretty as possible. The change in men's attitude toward women (from mother to sex object) is summed up in Molly Haskell's title to her book about women in the movies, *From Reverence to Rape.* This situation eventually led to the women's movement of the late 1960s and 1970s, which was now trying to implement some of the positive potentials of the change in women's role, to make women truly independent and free.

Although anti-feminists advise women to give up pretensions to economic independence and return to their traditional role as wives and mothers, for better or worse, fortunately or unfortunately, there is no real way to retreat en masse to our traditional position. Insofar as the importance of childbearing has diminished, women are, so to speak, out of a job. This change has come about over a long period of time, and is not likely to be reversed. Although women are not yet, as a class, financially or socially independent, we can improve our status (or even keep it at present levels) only by going forward and reintegrating ourselves with the world and perhaps, if we find it necessary, changing that world.

In conclusion, what we think of as "sexual freedom"—giving women the "right" to have sex without marriage, and decreasing the emphasis on monogamy—is a function of the decreased importance of childbearing to society, and of paternity to men. Although this change has been labeled "sexual freedom," in fact it has not so far allowed much real freedom for women (or men) to explore their own sexuality; it has merely put pressure on them to have *more* of the same kind of sex. Finally, it is important to remember that *you cannot decree women to be "sexually free" when they are not economically free*; to do so is to put them into a more vulnerable position than ever, and make them into a form of easily available common property.

THE AMBIGUITY OF THE "SEXUAL REVOLUTION"

"What do you think of the sexual revolution?"

Answers to this question varied, including the following range of opinions:

1. I like it, because it allows more openness. It is basically a good thing, healthy and necessary.

2. It is long overdue, but not over yet and has a long way to go.

3. What revolution? There has been no real revolution. It makes women feel they *have* to have sex and can't say "no."

4. It is a male rip-off and exploits women.

5. It came along too late for me, but is probably fun. I wish I'd been born later.

6. Mixed emotions. I don't understand what it's all about, and sometimes it seems to go too far.

7. I don't believe in it; it is bad and leads to promiscuity, etc.

More women expressed the first opinion—that increased openness is good—than any other.

However, they often shared some of the doubts of other women. Many married women and older women in particular, who had not experienced "sexual freedom" personally, took this long view of the change:

"It's highly important and the only sensible way our society can go. Future young people—my grandchildren—will reap the benefits of it. The sexual revolution is one more step to humanity's adulthood, but it has been exploited and needs refinement."

"I really hope that people are becoming freer and more tolerant of both their own and others' attitudes. I hope we can pass it on to the next generation. Our sexuality is so integral to our everyday lives, that I hope I can see progress in other areas, socially, politically, and intellectually, before I die, as well."

"It's about time we are able to be human and feel normal instead of some quiet closet pervert. Now people can discuss freely many things which years ago were considered vulgar. Women now are beginning to have a say if they want instead of acting like quiet little girls; they can express themselves and their feelings, they can now begin to learn a lot about others and themselves."

"People are finally acknowledging that they have penises and vaginas and that they enjoy using them. I think it's healthy and helps us do away with our cramping inhibitions."

"It's marvelous, because it finally allows those of us who grew up in the fifties to break out of that horrible inhibition, guilt, and unnatural 'respect' for our bodies."

"The sexual revolution (if you could call it that) has brought sex and body communication out into the open a little more than before, along with attempts to make it more natural and better understood. People are just as hung-up as always—but at least they are talking more and realizing they aren't alone with their problems."

"It's good for the most part, especially less guilt about masturbation and more acceptance of sex as a part of life—a healthy reconsideration of our customs and values."

"Generally, I applaud it. For me personally a good marriage is the happiest life style; but any sex that is not harmful or insulting can be good. And a variety of experiences can please, educate, and enrich."

"I think it is great because a lot of people are finally learning to become comfortable with and accept their own sexuality for the first time in their lives. The young ones coming up will not have all our hang-ups to get rid of in the first place."

"It is good that more people are talking about sex and I think that more women are recognizing themselves as sexual beings—not passive objects waiting for a man's arousal. I don't think that my mother ever enjoyed sex though she is beautiful and a strong woman. She doesn't talk about it or read about it, to my knowledge, and I think that she has always depended entirely on my father for sexual feedback. I think that it was always an in the dark, under the covers, ordeal that she tolerated out of a sense of duty. This could have happened to me also if times were not looser now. I am glad for a greater sexual freedom, but see too many women fucking out of a sense of obligation and exploiting themselves, using their sex to manipulate men. It seems to be the only hold we have over them at times."

"No love is 'free'—there are always consequences. But I do approve of alliances outside of marriage so long as children are not involved. I really believe fifty-year marriages are over—especially the gritted teeth till death kind. But still, even now, not many girls get to be 'free.' "

Some of these women, although they thought the sexual revolution was good in general, worried about its effects on their daughters.

"I don't really know—I think that if people feel more, that is great. I have three daughters, twenty-four, twenty-three, and eighteen—and they all have had good sex experiences, which I am quite happy for, although I am concerned a bit about the wisdom of sex so young."

"It's mostly a good thing, though sometimes I think if I see another *Playboy* spread on sex in the movies I'll scream. But I still have an old-fashioned streak. One of my daughters recently had an abortion (at sixteen) and hastened to assure me that the boy who had impregnated her was not her best boyfriend; she didn't want me to be mad at *him!* Well, I wouldn't have been mad at him—to tell the truth, it would have just made the abortion hard to take, because I like him so much I'd have had an awful time signing the papers to condemn the potential baby to oblivion. On the other hand, I found myself feeling regretful that she was having relations with other boys, even though this is acceptable in her crowd. I would have preferred to think the boy I care for is the only one."

"If you mean the free wheeling 'easy' sex present right now, I worry about it because of a sixteen-year old daughter and a ten-year old daughter. I see notes my sixteen-year old writes back and forth with friends and it upsets me very much. She is presently a virgin and I want her to stay that way."

"I think the sexual revolution is basically good. My only hesitations are 1) an almost inevitable development of guilt feelings in those who do not feel 'with it.' Eventually these reactions should subside but I feel sorry for those who will suffer for it. 2) I also am concerned that young people have not been prepared for this. I would categorize this group as those between eight and twenty who have been or will be influenced greatly by traditional attitudes and at the same time by the current new ones. Their traditional upbringing and current level of experience are not sufficient to help in the decision-making process they will inevitably encounter. The traditional viewpoint says 'don't' and the new revolt says 'do.' They are not experienced and frequently cannot accept their personal decision because of the tug of war of the old versus the new viewpoints."

Only a very few women totally accepted it for their daughters.

"I'm all for the sexual revolution. I think a good many of my children's generation are benefitting from the breakdown of many crippling taboos about sex. I like the fact that my children now in their early twenties have good relationships with young people I like; that I was able to speak very candidly and openly with my daughter, answer all her questions about sex long before she had her first experience, and that sex seems to be a healthy part of their lives, not something secretive and apart."

"It is amazing to me that it's this easy to write about these things and yet I never discuss them with women. I recall finding my fourteen-year-old daughter asleep in bed naked with a young man one morning and smiling and tiptoeing out. But I couldn't ask her about her experience, nor could she tell me about it (with a view of comparing notes, giving advice, etc.). However, I told her about this questionnaire and she wants to answer it too. I'm not at all sure she wouldn't think I was pushing for unwanted intimacy if I Xeroxed this and let her read my answers."

"My nineteen-year-old daughter was encouraged by me to have her young man spend the night at our house—rather than 'play games' and pretend it was not happening—and that worked fairly well for us. I never worried about it much with my kids—let them go on camping trips, etc. with their peers and just trusted their judgment, which they seem to have; however, at twenty my daughter did get pregnant and had an abortion (from the same young man) and I supported her through it—feeling proud of her judgment but irritated and concerned that she somehow deliberately (??) let herself get pregnant and now still wonder why—and she hasn't figured that one out either."

Many of the answers reflected very strong reactions against the so-called sexual revolution. Many women felt there was no real revolution.

"I think there is a lot of talk about the 'sexual' revolution but I don't think there has been much change in attitudes. Just having left my husband of eight years, four months ago, I am somewhat shocked by the fact that men still want to play games, that they can't accept me as a person when I am strong, intelligent, and have as much will and strength as they do. It has me quite worried actually because I know in order to relate to me sexually, they also have to accept me as a person—and there aren't many men around who do not feel threatened by strong women."

"It's got a long way to go. If the crap in *Playboy* or *Penthouse* is anybody's idea of a sexual revolution then it's revolting all right. As long as women are exploited sexually, viewed as sex objects and raised from the cradle to accommodate men, the sexual revolution is meaningless. It seems to me that the sexual revolution has just given the con men the chance to sell douches and razors, but that you don't see much in the way of real free expression and happiness, or joy in the body and in sex."

"I think the *idea* of a sexual revolution is very good, but I think that some people are out in left field in their interpetation of what needs to be done. *Playgirl* is no better than *Playboy* and they're both disgusting, and demoralize both men and women."

"Is there one? I hardly noticed. Talking a lot about sex hardly constitutes a revolution. Most 'swingers' are non-swingers. Most men have hardly heard of the clitoris. Boys are constantly looking to get laid, girls are constantly getting hurt—what else is new? Girls are going to bed somewhat more than they used to— nothing revolutionary about that—just a different way of handling a problem one still does not understand."

"What is it? Some journalist's expression? I think that wife-swapping, porno movies, etc. are not necessarily freedom but obsessions."

"It's just words. The 'sexual revolution' has been stimulated by advertising and by the ethics of competition and consumption, etc. It opened up a whole new market. Mini-skirts are not a revolution!"

"I'm not thrilled by it. People have sex more often with more people but the *kind* of sex most people have is still unhealthy."

"Baloney! Men get to look at women half-dressed or undressed more, there are more 'free fucks' around, and there are *more* women faking orgasms."

"What 'sexual revolution'? I am struggling in a feminist revolution! The so-called sexual revolution, from my point of view, did nothing to liberate women or men. Men got a screw for free and it was done out in the open and under the liberal-radical guise of a revolution against antiquated sex attitudes. Women still wanted those men for lifetime companions because they gave away their bodies and minds and found their identity in the man instead of in themselves. Men still maintain the top position on the job market, in women's magazine stories, in bed, and in the mind of the female psyche. So really the sexual revolution advertised something I already knew. Women are treated as objects. Only in this 'revolution' the oppressed didn't gain a thing. The oppressor began the 'sexual revolution' through rock music, the cosmetic market, Hugh Hefner, etc., but we weren't liberated from our roles, only more objectified. It also backfired on the patriarchy, by leading (indirectly) to the women's movement."

"I think it's got a long way to go before it's a real revolution. It's causing harm to women as it is now, especially young women. For older ones, too, I suppose, because the older men are, by and large, not liberated and still operating out of their *pig* assumptions—and we all assume older women aren't very sexy, so they are never asked to sleep with anyone and are considered neuters, expendable."

"The sexual revolution was late sixties bullshit. It was about *male* liberation, women being shared property instead of private property. And we know which kind of property gets better treatment."

"Men have reaped glorious benefits from the sexual revolution, but have acquired no more sense or sense of responsibility. My feeling is, 'Whatever happened to the good night kiss??' "

The crux of the matter—the effect of declaring sex healthy and necessary, and women "free" to do it— was to take away women's right not to have sex. Women lost their right to say "no."

"To me, the sexual revolution is just a simple reversal of the pressure I grew up with to be chaste—now there is another one path for all to follow, and it makes just as little sense. Both enforced sex and enforced abstinence are bad."

"I think the 'sexual revolution' basically pushes many women toward having sex more often and with more men than they want to. Now that women are supposed to enjoy sex as equally as men, they are considered 'square' or 'frigid' if they don't rush into bed, etc. I don't think men's attitudes have changed toward women; they are still threatened by aggressive women and they may dig a sex trip with a sexual woman, but not necessarily want a relationship with her."

"The line I hate the most is, 'You won't ball me because you're hung-up,' which is what the sexual revolution has used to scare women with."

"Now men feel it's *expected,* the cherry on the sundae. When some of those men I've slept with call me they give their first *and* last names, thinking I do it with everybody, I guess—incredible!"

"I think it's destructive and a lot of bullshit. Not that I have anything kind to say about the Victorian idea of marriage either. But a woman retains less independence and integrity when she feels she has to screw every slob she runs into or risk not being a 'hip chick.' The whole freaked-out scene is some dude who's got his dope and his chick, both possessions for his pleasure. You go to a party and you're expected to ball because everyone balls at 'hip' parties. Well, maybe I just don't happen to feel like it. Or maybe I might feel like it after a while but I don't see sex as a prelude to getting to know each other as people, I think the most triumphant moment of my life was finally being able to get up out of bed as we were going through our preliminary rolling around, announcing 'this is a pile of shit,' and walking out of the room, not giving a damn whether I hurt his little ego or not, because suddenly my own ego and integrity were more important. It took me a long time to get to that place, a lot of trying to explain to guys why I don't want to screw them and really wanting them to understand. I now feel that if I go to bed with somebody it's because I want to and because the liking is mutual. It wasn't easy, but it feels good."

"The Sexual Revolution tells me I am abnormal if I don't desire to make it with every Tom, Dick, or Jane that I see. I am only free to say yes."

"I think sex is great but I don't want to sleep with everyone or anyone that comes along. There has to be a special attraction. There shouldn't be insinuations like if you won't sleep with a black guy you're a prude or scared or prejudiced."

"Indiscriminate sex is irresponsible. Loving your

body and your feelings is beautiful. Guys looking for a girl 'who screws' is revolting."

"Some of the sexual revolution is okay. But when we like guys and say no to sex, the guys get all pissed off and will drop the girl. I don't like to be called a whore. If we don't give men the sex they want they call us sluts or bitches or anything else rotten they can think of. There is this girl I know and used to be friends with. She's sixteen. She had sex with one guy. This guy told all the guys at school and now when she doesn't give a guy what he wants, he'll beat her up just to get a good hard fuck."

"When I was a freshman (freshwoman!) at college (1968–69) I thought that a 'liberated woman' was one who could, as freely as men did, pick men up and have sex, with no emotional strings attached. Then I saw how shallow that was, and I got involved in women's liberation. Now I try to live my feminist politics in bed as well as elsewhere. Women sometimes feel they have to submit to sex with men, to keep them around. But I reserve the right to say 'no.' "

"The sexual revolution liberated a vast amount of masculine bestiality and hostility and exploitiveness. Some (few) younger women seem to know how to say no; the others have lost some protection. On the whole, there is a lot of mess revealed as prohibitions disappear; people are then free to be louses in a way they weren't before. It's something one must fight, but expect."

"Most men didn't give a damn about whether I wanted to have sex with them or not; if I didn't want to screw them, they would make a moral thing out of it, and try to lecture me into being 'free.' "

"I've opted out. The only sexual revolution I like is the one that gives equal time and freedom *not* to do what you don't want to do."

"Basically it's progressive but women still get *fucked*—literally, because now you have to prove how liberated you are and men use that."

"I personally have greatly benefitted from the women's movement, which is a sexual revolution for me. I'm not sure whether the 'sexual revolution' is really that at all, and I hope women don't end up in general being even more exploited by it. If a sexual revolution means that either sex has the privilege of initiating and having sex whenever and however they want (between consenting adults) and people are aware of the intricacies of 'choice' and 'consenting' and no one is exploited, then *great*! However, I think we are a long way from that, and I think, as much as I hate to admit it, that among the majority of the population, a lot of guys are getting 'laid' a lot easier, and their responsibility toward the act and the relationship hasn't changed all that much. I think it is the minority of the population that is really involved in a true sexual revolution and I hope it spreads."

Since this issue kept coming up in answers to Questionnaire I, Questionnaire II asked specifically: Are you ever afraid to say "no" to someone for fear of "turning them off"? If so, how did you feel during sex? Afterwards? Many, many women had felt this fear at times.

"I was afraid to say no and hated myself for being weak and submitting. Afterwards I thought, how can anyone like me or me like myself, if I can't say what I feel and not be threatened?"

"Yes. And afterwards I felt like a dead lump. A hole. A cunt."

"When I was younger I did. I felt like hell—angry and unhappy, and just plain powerless. Infuriated."

"Yes, I felt used, and later just disgusted with myself. I hope I have the strength never to let it happen again."

"Yes. I am afraid. I feel lonely afterwards."

"I'm not supposed to say 'no' since I'm legally married. Sex is then all one-sided and I fake orgasms."

"I hate to admit it, but I've said yes when I didn't really want sex. It usually occurred during intercourse and was painful to me. I couldn't wait until intercourse was over and the pain gone, but my feelings toward my partner make me feel that it would be unfair not to satisfy him physically."

"Powerlessness at not being able to say no and experiencing the development of something I don't want. It's harrowing."

"I never believed in the oft-quoted marital advice to a wife that she must always accede to her husband's demands. When I was first married, sixteen years ago, I made the headache excuses, etc., but now I just say 'not interested.' Sometimes I go along with his demands to keep peace in the relationship. On the other hand, if I want sex and he doesn't, that's a bit more difficult; he feels his time is too valuable to interrupt."

"I've never been raped but I've often had a combined feeling of unwillingness and accession."

"Very rarely have I had sex without wanting it. Sometimes I've had my doubts, and in the course of 'fooling around' have gotten turned on, begun intercourse, and then wished I hadn't done it—my emotional reluctance was strong enough to recur fast—then I wish I could just get up and leave the room, sorry, goodbye. But I stay, politely, like a hostess, and wish to hell the guy would disappear afterwards so I could go to sleep alone. But I act like a 'nice person.' "

"My husband has a defensive personality. I have a horror of offending him. I always accommodate him, though it gives me no pleasure. Before, during, and afterwards I think, how can I remedy this situation?"

"Sometimes I hesitate to say 'no' when I would really like to. When I don't, then intercourse is not enjoyable to me. And I want it over with as soon as possible. There is not the feeling of closeness that I value and it leaves me feeling distant afterwards."

"I have never said 'no' to sexual overtures when they occurred during a continuing relationship. I resent my own passivity very much."

"Yes. Stupid. Disgusted, with my lack of spine."

"Sometimes I have been afraid to say 'no' to someone for fear of spoiling what relationship we did have—the trouble is, I often don't know whether I feel good about them sexually till they are worked up, and by then it doesn't seem very fair to say 'no.' But I really hate sex if I don't feel like it, feel a bit revolted physically and very resentful of the person. Afterwards I feel very miserable and usually want to cry."

"Yes, at eighteen a man whose wife had just died used to come over. One day when no one was home he started touching my breast and suggesting more. He may have kissed me. I felt like protecting him from rejection rather than myself and then felt very guilty afterwards, and it caused me to cut off almost all sexual feelings for quite a while after that."

"When I was fifteen, my cousin told me that when a man gets a hard on and doesn't come, it's the most painful thing in the world. I believed that till last year. I believed that if a man got turned on by me, it was unfortunately my responsibility to keep him out of his misery. So I'd be with Professor X or radical student Z who'd suddenly be standing there naked and hard and I'd say to myself, 'Oh shit, oh no, I might as well go through with it and never see *him* again.' "

"We were all taught that he can't control it! *He* is in pain! Shit! It's the same old martyr bit."

Questionnaire IV asked: "Have you ever been afraid to say 'no' to someone for fear of 'making a scene,' or 'turning them off'? If so, how did you feel during sex? Would you define this as rape?"

"I never knew how to say no. I was brought up that nice girls were treated like ladies, and men behaved like gentlemen with them. I never knew girls were supposed to say no, that they were in control of the situation. I define as rape someone you don't know who attacks you. I never defined it as someone you go out with or someone you know. If you define rape that way, every woman has been raped over and over. In that situation feelings vary, from obligation to might-as-well to hatred for that one, or all men, to self-contempt—never any good feelings."

"I have been afraid to say no for fear of incurring a major hassle (if I was just afraid of 'turning them off' I would probably have said no anyway). Sex wasn't much fun on these occasions, as I was plagued with guilt and anger at the partners, and afterwards with shame. I guess these weren't technically rapes except when I feared physical harm, but I think any sex not wholeheartedly engaged in is rape. Even if the wholeheartedness is wholehearted jealousy, or something. The important point is that one makes love because that's what one wants to do, for whatever reasons, without reservations."

"Yes, cold, used, and hateful. I didn't then, but I do now, call it rape."

"Yes, once: I was afraid I was overreacting if I just left, and he kept subtly making further and further advances after persuading me to stay over and promising me my own bed. Eventually I got tired of listlessly fighting him off in bits and pieces and thought okay, let him have his stupid orgasm and leave me alone. I had *no* feeling at all—not even a physical realization of the slight penetration, and did not believe him when he told me he'd been inside. Later, I discovered he had been right; I got pregnant. I used to think it was rape, because he knew my consent was not involved, but no one else seemed to think so."

"I have been afraid to say 'no.' Then if I give in and this person ignores me after sex, I feel angry and sad and humiliated. I don't know if this is rape."

"I was 'ripped off' by my boyfriend when I was a virgin. He really raped me, but not in the legal way. I couldn't prevent him, in other words. As a result I got pregnant and had a child. I gave the child away. This has caused a deep, deep feeling of resentment and bitterness which I can never get rid of. I think this colors my sex life. I have become more enlightened by the new books that I have read—*Free and Female, Sexual Politics, The Female Eunuch,* etc., and now realize how conditioned I am in regards to sex. I am trying very hard to undo all the damage."

"Oh yes. I went to a New Years' party with one guy once and crashed there. I said I didn't want to sleep with him and he said I could have the sofa. I felt I should be more relaxed, and I said no, I'd sleep on the floor too. Then he talked me into a corner: Why was I so afraid of touching? Afraid of sex? We didn't have to ball after all, we could just hug and touch. What, my god, why didn't I have orgasms? What was wrong with me? etc. etc. I felt raped even though we never had intercourse; we had oral sex. He didn't know my cunt from a hole in the wall. If this happened to me now I would have acted totally opposite but this was two years ago and I didn't really know that I could actually say no, and not have to prove that I was a 'woman.' This has been a major change in me—knowing I have the right to say no!"

"Women aren't always free to not have sex. The time I was beaten up by a strange man in a strange city, the police wouldn't do anything—they tried to say that he was my boyfriend, even though I didn't know him and he was trying to rape me. If you don't submit, you can be beaten, killed, and nothing is done. Under less severe circumstances, you don't want to yell and scream, especially if you know the guy, even if you don't want to sleep with him. Some guys understand if you don't want to have sex, or if you don't want to at a certain time, but most think they have a right to have sex with every woman just because she's there."

"Only with my husband. It was a condition of our marriage as it developed, that if I refused him sexually he was insufferable. I think this is a common degradation of women in marriage. But rape is too strong a word, as force was not involved. I felt I was prostituted, being used as a whore, with no regard for my desires. I think it is a barbaric tradition, that men cannot be refused by women in marriage, and this led to my finding my husband sexually repugnant."

How strong is the male "sex drive"?

These quotes graphically illustrate the pressure that is on women now to have intercourse, both inside and outside of marriage. One of the worst forms of this pressure comes from the idea that a man's need for "sex" is a strong and urgent "drive," which, if not satisfied, can lead to terrible consequences. As one woman phrased it, "Men being sexual animals, at least to my way of thinking, their bodies drive them to the culmination of sex, the climax, ejaculation, and depositing of their seed. I feel that most of them could gladly do without foreplay. At times I have felt guilty, especially if waiting for me has robbed my partner of some of the intensity of his climax."

This particular stereotype of male sexuality is extremely commonplace, and reflects the picture most frequently presented by sex manuals, psychologists, psychiatrists, physicians, men's magazines, and many others. Typically, the male "sex drive" is seen as a constantly surfacing and demanding feeling; as Theodore Reik has expressed it in *The Psychology of Sex Relations*:

> . . . the crude sex drive is a biological need which represents the instinct and is conditioned by chemical changes within the organism. The urge is dependent on inner secretions and its aim is the relieving of a physical tension.
> The crude sex-urge . . . is entirely incapable of being sublimated. If it is strongly excited, it needs, in its urgency, an immediate release. It cannot be deflected from its one aim to different aims, or at most can be as little diverted as the need to urinate or as hunger and thirst. It insists on gratification in its original realm.[1]

This glorification of the male "sex drive" and male orgasm "needs" amounts to justifying men in whatever they have to do to get intercourse—even rape—and defines the "normal" male as one who is "hungry" for intercourse. On the other hand, the definition of female sexuality as passive and receptive (but, since the sexual revolution, also necessary for a healthy woman) amounts to telling women to submit to this aggressive male "sex drive." Especially since the 1940s the glorification of male sexuality has often been justified as a kind of natural law of the jungle (the product, we are led to believe, of cave-man hormones), even by some of the most serious social scientists. Actually, the information available does not warrant such conclusions. This idea of male sexual "right" (via biology) is not much more scientifically based than the old idea that kings were monarchs by the grace of god and natural law. Just as kings said that any other political model (like democracy) would be unnatural and would not work, just so men now say that if women are aggressive sexually (i.e., anything but passive), sex will be unnatural, they will become "impotent," and sex will be impossible.

What *is* "sex drive"? Lester A. Kirkendall, in "Towards a Clarification of the Concept of Male Sex Drive," says:

> As the term "sex drive" is now used, it has become a blanket term which obscures the components with which we are actually dealing. We should distinguish between sexual capacity, sexual performance, and sexual drive . . . that is, what you can do, what you do do, and what you *want* to do.[3]

Kirkendall explains that although capacity ("what you can do") has a biological base, sex drive ("what you *want* to do") "seems to be very largely a psychologically conditioned component. . . . Sex drive seems to vary considerably from individual to individual, and from time to time in the same individual, and these variations seem related to psychological factors." In other words, sex *drive* (not capacity) is more a function of desires than "needs."*

A further point along this line is that even if a man has a strong physical desire for orgasm—an erection, for example—there is nothing in nature, nothing physical, that impels him to have that orgasm in a vagina. The stimulation he feels is linked to the desire for *orgasm,* and not to any desire for intercourse per se. The physical "urge" a man feels is a desire for further stimulation of the penis, or for orgasm—*not* a desire to penetrate a woman's vagina. There is no "beeper" or sensory device on his penis that makes him seek a vagina in

---

* For a discussion of possible hormonal influences, see John Money and Anke Ehrhardt's *Man & Woman, Boy & Girl.*

which to put his penis. This pleasurable connection is *learned,* not innate; as mentioned earlier, even chimpanzees must learn to have intercourse, although they masturbate on their own from early childhood. The definition of male sexuality as being "instinctively" drawn to heterosexual intercourse is only another example of the way we define sexuality as reproductive activity.

Finally, there is not even a medical term for the colloquial "blue balls." Contrary to popular opinion, it is no harder on a man not to have an orgasm than on a woman. Men feel no more "pain" then we do. Kinsey gets right to the point:

> There is a popular opinion that the testes are the sources of the semen which the male ejaculates. The testes are supposed to become swollen with accumulated secretions between the times of sexual activity, and periodic ejaculation is supposed to be necessary in order to relieve these pressures. Many males claim that their testes ache if they do not find regular sources of outlet, and throughout the history of erotic literature and in some psychoanalytic literature the satisfactions of orgasm are considered to depend upon the release of pressures in the "glands"—meaning the testes. Most of these opinions are, however, quite unfounded. The prostate, seminal vesicles, and Cowper's are the only glands which contribute any quantity of material to the semen, and they are the only structures which accumulate secretions which could create pressures that would need to be relieved. Although there is some evidence that the testes may secrete a bit of liquid when the male is erotically aroused, the amount of their secretion is too small to create any pressure. The testes may seem to hurt when there is unrelieved erotic arousal (the so-called stoneache* of the vernacular), but the pain probably comes from the muscular tensions in the perineal area, and possibly from the tensions in the sperm ducts, especially at the lower ends (the epididymis) where they are wrapped about the testes. Such aches are usually relieved in orgasm

---

* "Blue-balls."

because the muscular tensions are relieved—but not
because of the release of any pressures which have ac-
cumulated in the testes. Exactly similar pains may develop in the groins of the female when sexual arousal
is prolonged for some time before there is any release
in orgasm.³

In other words, if a man's desire for intercourse is
not shared by a woman, there is no reason why masturbation or other stimulation will not provide him with an
equally strong or stronger orgasm, although the psychological satisfaction may not be the same. Or, there is
no overriding reason why he must have an orgasm at
all. The point is that there is no physically demanding
male sex *drive* that forces men to pressure women into
intercourse. Women need no longer be intimidated by
this argument. As one woman answered, when asked
"Have you ever been afraid to say 'no'?", "*No*. This is
my body, *my* breasts, and *my* cunt, and they are *my*
territory and if *anyone,* even my husband, tries to take
what I do not wish to give, it's WAR, baby."

THE DOUBLE STANDARD

Women who did try to be open and share with men,
having sex in the new, free way, in all too many cases
wound up being disrespected and often hurt—because
the double standard is still operating.

"I think the sexual revolution is very male-oriented
and anti-woman. The idea is that men are telling
women they're free to fuck around with whomever they
want. But the catch is that the double standard is still
employed. A man who has many lovers is 'sowing his
oats'; a woman who has many lovers is a 'prostitute' or
'nymphomaniac.' "

"Usually after they know they 'have' me, I get the
feeling I am a piece of ass. I feel their hostility and their
contempt. The double standard is alive and well."

"I had one experience with a partner—in fact, several partners—who castigated me for indulging in sex

with them at the conclusion of the act. This has left me somewhat fearful of rejection."

"Most males still have the feeling of wanting to conquer and win me. Therefore they try much harder to be nice and to please me before I agree to have intercourse with them. Then afterwards they are never as excited or as anxious to please as that first time (not just in sexual dealings either)."

"I started out when I was very young open, natural, warm, spontaneous, uninhibited and in ten years I've become bitter, cold, cynical, angry, resentful, hateful, frightened, suspicious. I don't like it but that's where I've ended up."

"I suppose I should be totally against sex. I was fucking *many many* guys when I was young because they wanted me to and I couldn't refuse. I've been pregnant twice and have gone through much shit for abortion money, etc. I suppose I hate men except the man who I live with. I think if we ever split I would be alone. I think I am pretty dried up and old for twenty-one but maybe I'll die young. This world's really fucked up."

"I just can't take the attitude that men put into women through the sexual act. When I find *the* rare man whose head is relatively okay I'll really try to hang on to him. Men have been raised in an environment where sex is seen as something *they need*, and that they must trick and seduce women into letting them have, against the woman's better judgment. Thus when a woman really chooses to have sex with a man, he doesn't see it that way. Rather he thinks he has won something, and proceeds to use it. Afterwards he doesn't care what happens to her. This is a terrible down for a woman—although I'm trying to say, 'That's his problem, not mine,' and go my way."

"However casual sex is, it can still be friendly and constructive, which is how I want it to be. Boys have had casual sex with me and have then ignored me or thought less of me. I've been hurt, but in the long run what are they saying about themselves and their own attitudes? If they think sex is wrong and dirty and are disgusted with themselves for having it, all right, but please don't project your disgust onto me. If their semen is 'dirty' and I as the spitoon am therefore dirty, that's their problem. People may try to make me feel guilty, but I don't think I've done anything wrong."

"They generally pretend to care, to be enraptured, and talk bed talk till it is over, and then it's back to reality. The important thing is to not believe these lies, not get involved, just realize it is bed talk and you won't be hurt."

"It's great if you can just take as much of it as you want or need. Men who play off of it to be bigger schmucks than they already are hopefully will suffer appropriately in hell. I mean the type who say, "Sure women are liberated now! Liberated to get laid. . . .' Nobody should put up with that shit. Release your anger and tell that insignificant idiot what you think of him."

"It's definitely healthier but there are too many men who haven't come around and still think 'loose woman, easy lay' and all kinds of other derogatory thoughts. Even if you are aggressive enough to get what you want, the whole double standard is still in effect, hidden under a surface of phoniness and pseudo-hip liberalness, and it always comes out in the end."

"The sexual revolution is the biggest farce of the century for females. Before at least she had the right to say 'no.' Now she is a prude or worse if she doesn't put out whenever asked. And if she does have many short-term sexual encounters, she is considered a whore. The sexual revolution is a male production, its principles still concentrated on male values, e.g., Why get married any more, since we have our pick of slick chicks."

"I think there's still a lot of liberating to do. Women may fuck more, but still have to play old sex roles. And if a woman fucks more than one person, she is still a whore, a call girl."

"In high school, my favorite masturbation fantasy was to imagine that a pornographer was filming my masturbation and directing me. He'd tell me which way to turn, what to masturbate with. While stripping before a mirror, I'd imagine I was stripping for a camera. Later, when I was twenty I started to model. I'd meet men hitchhiking and ask them if they'd be interested in taking pictures of me nude. Soon I was making fifteen dollars a half hour—working at home. Then I got into pornography—fucking for cameras. I made a porno film for some men who own an 'adult bookstore.' We spent six hours making the film. I fucked several men—including the cameraman. I spent about two hours giving blow jobs to the men. By that time, I had not only lived out my every masturbation fantasy, but also overlived every fantasy. The next day my muscles ached, my jaw was sore. My vagina was irritated from so much fucking—with men and wine bottles. Burned out. Satiated. For two weeks, the thought of sex made me tired. By the way, I only got thirty-five dollars for making that film. The men who made it never paid the rest which they previously promised. They knew I had no legal power—for I had signed no contract. I didn't think I needed a contract because they were so friendly, they smoked dope, they had long hair. . . ."

"Incredible as it may seem, there is still a strong double standard. Although people practice sex more, they still have large remnants of their childhood prejudices and sexist ideas of sex. This makes it very hard to freely experience sexuality without fear of censure. Although I live at a college campus which is considered nationwide as a place of avant-garde sexual and intellectual ideas, it is not. Men here still disrespect women who have sex with those they're not 'in love with,' and if a woman cares about her esteem, it is only safe to have sex with either a male who cares about her so he won't make her feel bad and talk about her to other men so they disrespect her—or else with a person no one finds out about (like flings at ski resorts or vacations, etc.). One male, considered a leading radical here, was talking to a supposed female friend of his the day before Halloween. They were invited to a costume party and she, having trouble deciding what to wear, asked him, 'What do you think I should go as?' Very cruelly, he replied, 'Why don't you go as a virgin? I'm sure nobody will recognize you!' "

BE A "GOOD GIRL"!

Almost all the women who answered these questionnaires had been brought up to be "good girls."* And
those still living at home were, for the most part, *still*
being taught to be "good girls." Girls are still being kept
from finding out about, exploring and discovering, their
own sexuality—and called "bad girls" when they try. At
puberty, girls are given information about their reproductive organs and menstruation, but rarely told about
the clitoris! The unspoken message is still that female
sexuality is bad:

"It was drilled into me since early childhood (I'm
twenty-three now) that 'nice' girls don't have sex, they
don't even *want* sex—and if you do, you're a tramp. I
can recall my mother saying to me and my two-year-
younger sister when I was eighteen: 'I certainly hope
you aren't the kind of girls that . . . um . . . *neck* with
boys.' At which point neither of us were virgins! She
also said to my sister after reading some women's lib
book, 'It was very, well, interesting—but what kind of
woman would write that you should try to make love in
different positions?' That about says it for my family
background. All I know is that if and when I have a
young daughter, she's going to know that sex is beautiful. I've tried—when I'm back home, which is rather
rarely—to instill a bit of this consciousness in my
youngest sister, who's now thirteen. I made a point of,
for example, inserting my Tampax in front of her, running around naked, and telling her that soon she'll have
little mounds on her chest, too, and hair on her vagina.
I say to her that even though boys in her grade are repulsive, in five years they'll be much better. I don't
think this can possibly be harmful—I know that the
way my mother raised us was harmful to me."

"When I was eight or nine, our family went on a trip
to the country with neighbors. They had a son about
seven years older than I and during the day he and I
went out around the farm and in exchange for some

* There is an in-depth development of this point in Dr. Leah
Schaefer's work *Women and Sex* (New York: Pantheon Books,
1973).

favor (I think it was shooting his BB gun) I was persuaded to lie down and he laid down on top of me and squirmed around a bit. We were both fully dressed and nothing really happened, except that I felt squashed and extremely uncomfortable, but somehow I sensed the significance of the whole episode, and I felt dirty and degraded. I could never look that boy in the face again and I still can't."

"My father was a career man in the U.S. army. My mother went to work when I was about five. My parents were never home until five P.M. or later at night. They never took interest in anything us kids did except to be home on time and want to know where we were going. Sex was never talked about—what us kids knew about sex was from what we heard or read. My sister got pregnant at sixteen and from that time on my parents were watching me so close, especially my Dad. Every time I would say can I talk to you they'd always reply are you pregnant. When I'd ask if I could go out on a date my Dad always had some nasty remarks about getting laid or knocked up. Believe me I was thankful to get out. I dated a lot and loved it. But I treated the guys terrible because I always felt they wanted me only for a bed partner."

"I was never told that sex was bad or dirty, although my father used to freak out at my sexual activities with boys, and he was constantly warning me that they wouldn't respect me if I let them 'do things' with me. I believed this. When he found out I wasn't a virgin at sixteen, he wouldn't speak to me for months. I'd forgotten this until now because the values they mouthed were contradictory to the way they must have felt. I think of them as liberal because they said they were liberal, you know?"

"My mother is afraid of sex, I always knew that, but I was shocked and saddened to learn finally that my father is also ashamed of his own desire and does not want me to have sex because I am female. In a rare moment of opening up to him once, I asked him if, when a girl refused to kiss him goodnight, he would think that maybe she didn't want to. His answer was,

'No, I would think she was a good girl.' I can't tell you the agony that answer created in me. Probably the only fear I have left about sex now is that men will despise me if I let them make love to me because of their own fear and disgust. I avoided men for years because of this fear, but now I am willing to take the risk, and I feel that any man who loses respect for me because I like sex and give myself to him—that is a man I don't want. Sometimes I even go so far as to think that if men got more satisfaction in bed, more real satisfaction—and that means honest, free giving on both sides and real, openly expressed joy in orgasm—there would cease to be wars. But perhaps that is wishful thinking."

"It's obvious the restrictions placed on women. My parents are both pretty liberal, but somehow it's very difficult for them to get out of that old rut, saying that women should be pure until marriage (my mother was—her daughters aren't) but as long as I am not living home and I don't get pregnant, my mother's adjusting a little. I don't know how my father feels. He doesn't know I have a lover and he's better off not knowing. He would be crushed. When my sister, five years ago, said she was living with her now present husband (they were unmarried then) my father wanted to disown her. He gave me the only advice about life that he's ever given to me—'Watch out for men like that!' Very sad. My daughters will never live through that, not if I can help it."

"One experience which I think affected me deeply was my parents finding out I was sleeping with my lover. I was living at home for the summer. My mother read my diary. I'm sure not three days went by without intense fights, battles, pain, name calling, whore, slut, etc. Five years have gone by; we don't fight any more but we are not close. I've been a lot more frightened and less spontaneous in all my relationships since that time."

"My first experience that I remember was when I was in the third grade. One of my girlfriend's fathers while I was at her house sent everyone else out of the house—or they were in another part of the house—and he took me in the bedroom and pulled my pants down and looked at my vagina and touched it and told me it was pretty. I knew it was wrong so it took me about a week before I told the girl what her father did and she didn't believe me and yelled that I was a liar, so I didn't tell anyone else. A year later a friend of my father did it (at our house). I can remember it really felt nice. My mother found out and he didn't show up any more, but right after that my sister and I started touching each other. That lasted about six months and we stopped that probably because we were afraid of getting caught by our parents."

"I lived at home until the age of twenty-three, and the sexual repression was incredible. My father freaked out every time I as much as mentioned such things as lipstick or dates or dancing. Once, I was about eighteen then, I think, my mother and I went shopping and I bought a beautiful purple velvet cape at a sale. I showed my father the cape, and he called me a prostitute ('street girl' was the expression he used; I think what he had in mind was the Biblical 'harlot'). The next day I gave the cape to the Salvation Army."

"Information was a real problem. When I started asking questions like, 'How come children look like their fathers as well as their mothers?' the answer usually was, 'You'll learn that later when you're older.' Later, when I was older, the answer was, 'We'll get you a book,' but the book never came. When I began to menstruate at the age of twelve, I was terrified; here was the dread disease I had been dreading—I vowed I would never masturbate again. I kept washing myself and changing my underwear, but the bleeding didn't stop. In the evening I told my parents I was bleeding 'down there'; my mother gave me some sanitary napkins, and my father 'explained things' to me. I can't remember what he told me; all I know is that he told me very little, and yet managed to convey the impression that I now 'knew Everything.' That's quite a feat, and I wish I could remember how he did it. When I was about sixteen, I became involved with a boy. All we did was what was called 'heavy petting,' but I was worried about getting pregnant, so I went to the public library and looked at some marriage manuals. I remember I was rather shocked. About three years later (my nineteenth birthday, I think), my mother gave me a big medical book as a present. The book of course had a chapter on male and female genitals, sexual intercourse, childbirth, contraception, V.D., etc., and after several hours of intensive thought, it slowly dawned on me that this was the book I had been promised so long ago."

And one woman gave a long answer:

"My parent's troubles stem from incredibly harsh regimented religious upbringings. They and my sister never swayed. Daddy did briefly, but swung back after dirtying himself with worldly people. . . . I am not given privacy for when I shut my door to write or think my folks get nervous, and after they found some pot my dad wouldn't let me shut my door, not in fear I'd smoke but because I keep to myself. I closed it once to shut out the sound of the TV and when he saw it closed he banged the whole door into the room with his shoulder. He doesn't dig me wearing loose pants—they must fit— and he doesn't dig my clothes even though I dress relatively conservatively. I can't dance in front of them for they'd crucify me if they saw me digging moving with my body. They stress virginity to the extent that they pray that I've never gone beyond kissing, and closemouthed at that. If I am wearing pants and sit with my legs not crossed my father bawls me out. I must always wear a bra, and must always be fully dressed in front of my father—underwear doesn't make it. And my mom won't let me give my dad back massages for she's 'afraid it will put ideas in his head' (that's a quote). I am not allowed over to a guy's house unless his parents are home, and then not allowed to go into his room or to sit on a bed or lean back because it's suggestive. My parents always hassle me for they've told me I'm sensual looking and I move as such and they say I mustn't. My sister and I are not allowed to use the word 'sexy' or swear or anything. This all sounds silly listing this, for I do it anyway. My parents are super against body awareness. I've never seen my father undressed. People used to tell me that I was unique for surviving so well and I said no, but now due to tons of reflection I agree. Man, I never realized how shitty it all was and how strong I am now.

"I was told I had to accept Jesus or go to hell when I was four. I questioned it then and all my life. I wonder why I did and my sister, cousins, parents didn't. The mutant me. I had very strong sexual fantasies and along with them masturbation as a kid and now, and all in secret but they helped me for I accepted them and enjoyed them even though when I was younger I suffered guilt feelings. But I've always been independent minded and when my dad hit me or screamed or my mom did, I kept it in and decided they were wrong. My mom has very warped views of women and they're shared by my dad. As I don't shave my legs or armpits my mom and dad inform me that it's nauseating, etc. My mom's always pleading with me to wear makeup on my eyes and to curl and comb my hair like my sister's. I keep it clean and long and that's me. And I have pride in my body. I don't like girls who dress like dolls and only for guys for I think clothes are for self-expression . . . my mom instilled fears in me by telling me when I was too young about perverts, etc. A release for her but a millstone around the neck for me for I couldn't handle it and I still suffer from them . . . man, the saddest thing is that they don't know and couldn't possibly understand. They don't even realize what they've put me through! I've tried to explain some minor stuff and get met with blank stares and Jesus preaching . . . I remember a time when I was still a virgin and my father didn't take to something, maybe it was my clothes, and he called me a slut and a whore and every name in the book . . . said I opened my legs to every guy who came along. I was very sensitive about my self-respect as far as guys saw it. Everything was imbedded in guilt. . . . Then I was birthed and I've emerged amazon, and he still bellows, but, babes, he knows he's lost me and it's his biggest pain for he loves me and receives none back."

SEX AND EMOTIONS

Some of the sexual revolution ideology stated that it was old-fashioned to want to connect sex with feelings—it meant you weren't "hip." Not only marriage but also monogamy and love or even tender feelings were often considered to be something only "neurotic" women wanted. The idea was that "people should spontaneously have sex and not worry about hurting each other, just behave freely and have sex, no strings, anytime with anybody, just for pure physical pleasure." But almost *no* woman in this study wanted that kind of sexual relationship very often—although a few thought that they *should*: "I saw a TV show the other night and this guy said we need to separate sex and love and I think he is right—that is why women get hurt so much because men for some reason seem to be able to do this while we have a great deal of trouble separating them. At least I don't seem to be able to."

Overwhelmingly, women wanted sex with feeling.

"I think the sexual revolution is fantastic. But I have remained 'faithful' to my husband and will because I know from past experience that sex with me is totally involved with a personal relationship. It's a part of me that I can't separate from the rest of my body and mind. I could not successfully divide my sexual life among two or more."

"I think the sexual revolution has totally distorted the place of sexuality to the point that it has become an end in itself, an escape, or a desperate attempt to achieve love. Writers like Rollo May (*Love and Will*) and the women's movement have helped me to value the integration of love and sex as opposed to casual encounters with partners who do not value me."

"Well, I like being able to have a sexual life even though I am not married. But I do not like the casual and 'cool' sort of relationships as well as what used to be called 'romance.' I like to feel involved with someone."

"I approve of the acceptance of sexual desires and relations. But personally I still believe it is most desirable to have a personally intimate and close relationship, not a casual one."

"Where I see trouble is in people of my generation, many of my friends. In their attempts to be freed by the sexual revolution they have undertaken sexual practices they are not psychologically equipped to handle. In joining group gropes and multiple sexual encounters they seem to mess up their lives . . . leave their partners and families for all the wrong reasons . . . become middle-aged hippies, as though we could ever be twenty again. They seem confused and definitely not content. This older group has simply forgotten that sex should be a thing that fits in nicely with a lot of other things like a good nourishing one-to-one relationship, work, personal growth, strengthening friendships, going fishing and watching sunsets. I get the feeling they've thrown out all commitments, not just the bad ones, and sex has become the mainspring of their every waking moment. The sexual revolution has permitted me to share home and life with a man without marrying, and it gave me the right to choose my way of life without having to be a flag-carrying rebel about it, but if I were not to pick and choose within this revolution to suit myself, to avoid damaging myself . . . then I would not have been freed, and I feel the people I am talking about have not been freed by the so-called revolution either; they've just exchanged one kind of slavery for another. Without doubt though, more good than harm has come of it, and my generation will pass out of it in time anyway."

"I like sex a lot. But it can only supplement a warm, affectionate, mutually respecting, full personhood relationship. *It* can't be a relationship. It can't prove love. It can't prove anything. I have found sex with people I don't really like, or who I'm not certain will really like me, or with people I don't feel I know well, to be very shallow and uncomfortable and physically unsatisfying. I don't believe you have to be 'in love' and married 'till death do us part.' But mind and body are one organism and all tied up together, and it isn't even physically fun unless the people involved really like each other!"

"The sexual revolution is great. But as an individual I feel I could not have sex except with someone I loved. And if I felt such love I'd want it permanently (as permanent as anything can be). I am even at fifty-three a romantic idealist—Damn it!"

"Because I'm very sensitive and afraid of getting hurt (I'm only eighteen), I still imbue intercourse with very strong emotional meaning. It upsets me and leaves me unhappy to be with someone who views intercourse casually and feels no meaningful tenderness afterwards."

"My emotions play an enormous part in sex for me—maybe too much for my liking. I sometimes feel that I'm too 'particular,' or selective or delicate—I have to be feeling very intensely, or in love, or overwhelmed by sexual feelings in order to enter a deep sexual encounter. Sometimes I worry about whether the man will expect too much from me, sometimes whether I will expect too much from him. Sometimes I worry about whether I won't feel enough, or will be disappointed afterwards. At times I have gone out to have a totally casual encounter just to avoid these complications. Most of my relationships—maybe all—begin with a combination of the physical and emotional. I can't get turned on to a partner without an emotional or mental factor being present, even if not primary. And sometimes it is primary, and the physical secondary."

"I think the sexual revolution has caused a lot of suffering. People use it to avoid commitment; they refuse to work at a relationship, preferring to search for the 'perfect' love. They fantasize their way through relationships, always seeking perfection, running scared at the first sign that work is needed to keep two people together. No one knows where the other person is at, and what attracts one may turn off another. Everyone wants to try everything, but not stick to any one thing, so they change from day to day, and are bewildered by the way they and their friends reverse opinions and trade partners. I'm not saying the old way was better, but I'm afraid of what kind of life I can look forward to. I'm not married, but even if I do get married it seems that my marriage has a small chance of surviving. And I don't see the advantages of this style, frankly."

"I'm confused as hell about the 'sexual revolution.' My husband and I lived and slept together for over a year before we were married—and that was fine. We loved each other and there was some kind of commitment between us. The summer before I was married, my (then) fiancé was away and I slept twice with another man because I was curious. Fine. As I mentioned earlier, I lost my virginity to a friend, a bit of a cold way to start out, but I was scared and wanting to get laid, so he helped me out. Fine. But extramarital sex, after a man and woman have made a big commitment to each other—I can't buy. I moved out on my husband when he took on a girl friend because I couldn't stand the pain. A year later, right now, we're negotiating. We seem to be at a stalemate. I hate to think of myself as behind the times, but I just can't hack anything but monogamy."

"I still believe the greatest sexual satisfaction comes from having a partner you care about. I've gone through stages of having several lovers and thinking I was really liberated. But I'm much more fulfilled now with one caring partner."

"I went along with the sexual revolution quite a while until I realized that holding my feelings back was causing me lots of anguish. I was very depressed. I tried opening communication lines up—that was part of the problem, but not all of it. Now, in love with my lover and trusting him, I can see how all that damaged me— made my trust mechanisms inhibited by sex. For a while I stopped having sex with him because I couldn't love and fuck him both. These days things are much better. I think that the loyalty is important."

"It's an overreaction and after years and years of the old double standard, of women expected to be pure and virginal for marriage and to always set the limits, society has overturned itself. Now women are supposed to be willing, ready, and able to have sex with anyone, anytime, no strings attached and so on. Out of the latter swing of the pendulum have come some good opening-ups of certain repressive taboos. But women, and men, remain oppressed by these roles. I have found that I *can't* detach myself from sex and still enjoy it. I can't make love with someone I'm not supposed to trust—and feel good about it. These attitudes don't treat me like a whole person either. Too much mind/body separation results in either compulsive screwers or strained virgins!"

"I have mixed feelings about the sexual revolution. Hedonism seems the opposite side of the coin of puritanism. My daughters tell me that they feel used and abused and refuse promiscuity, although they have had sex with young men they cared about. I personally hate the singles scene. It makes me feel like a walking cunt!"

"I guess I like the idea of intercourse—two people's bodies joined in an act of love or mutual excitement or whatever, but I've become so disillusioned by the whole thing—having met and fucked with a lot of guys who (as I came to realize later) just wanted to get laid and liked the looks of my body but wanted little or nothing to do with me. I have come to regard sex as exploitative—having sex is almost like saying 'here, fuck me, do anything with me that you want, I'm not worth anything anyway.' I guess I'm sort of screwed sexually, my ideas about sex are screwed up, and I hope my therapy will help me there. I've found I have a lot of guilt feelings and a refusal to enjoy sex, or at least that is what my therapist says."

Many women mentioned these same feelings in answer to "What is it about sex that gives you the greatest displeasure?"

"I despise the attitude so many men have that sexual liberation means a woman who will 'put out.' It makes me feel gypped if later I find out I am dirty in his eyes."

"My greatest displeasure is to wake up the next morning with a man who had changed since we'd had sex—he wouldn't talk to me or react to anything the next day."

"I feel very angry that I seem to be more loving toward them than they are to me."

"I need a mutual exchange, knowing he wants to do everything with me. What gives me *least* pleasure is people who are emotionally inadequate, who can give nothing on a wholly human level but rather use the sex act as some kind of device in the pattern of their unhealthy ego needs."

"The absolute worst was all the hassle I used to go through in New York with guys who abused me, who didn't know me and didn't like women, and considered it their prerogative to get laid. I minded the ordinary abuse more than the time I was raped, as the rape I could excuse on the grounds of psychological disturbance."

"One thing that makes sex so pleasurable is being able to share such an intimate part of someone. It is like being in a world with just you and your partner, everything else becomes unimportant at that moment. Then comes the moment when it must stop and after a while, after he goes home, then the total separation things sets in. I don't know, I get kind of depressed after it's over. But it is only slight depression. I suppose I feel that way not knowing if I will see him again."

"My greatest displeasure is feeling myself to be simply a substitute for his hand, a dish of mashed potatoes, or any warm place he can stick it into and come."

BIRTH CONTROL

The pill itself did not bring about "sexual freedom," as mentioned earlier, but merely offered a new kind of protection from pregnancy, which had the effect of pressuring women into having more intercourse.

"The pill doesn't lead to greater freedom but perhaps to greater availability to men: 'Well, baby, as long as you use birth control pills, this ain't going to matter.'"

"I got on the pill, and stayed on that for over five and a half years, which really screwed up my head. It of course allowed me total freedom, that is to screw whenever I wanted to. It of course also allowed men to take advantage of me, knowing that I was on the pill, and therefore not having any excuse not to screw with them. Not loving or liking them was not enough of a reason— you either had to have V.D. or no birth control."

Although there is no space to delve into the subject of birth control here,* it is important to note that many women are dissatisfied with current forms of birth control, for many reasons:

"I feel free to enjoy sex although now I worry about the dangers of the pill instead of worrying about pregnancy. I have tried a few other methods but was terrified of becoming pregnant. I also feel extreme anger that I should be completely responsible for birth control and risk all the dangers."

* For further reading about birth control pills, see *Doctor's Case Against the Pill* by Barbara Seaman (New York: Peter ...den, 1969).

"The pill liberated men from condoms. I demand a return to the old way."

"I think that if there is such a thing as a sexual revolution going on it is, for the most part, to the detriment of women. Men expect that a woman will consent to having sex more often and with less commitment. Men very rarely take responsibility for the birth control and it angers me that women have to be prepared every day for a man's sperm. Women are really wreaking havoc on their bodies and mainly for the explicit pleasure and convenience of men."

"Contraception was a hassle till my hysterectomy. He didn't like his 'sensations' dulled by a rubber. The diaphragm hurt me; the coil caused constant bleeding and pain, and the pill had enough side effects to have probably caused the hysterectomy. I was very bitter that I had to endure all of these gadgets with rarely an orgasm while he could always come even when 'dulled' by the rubber."

"The birth control pill allows a woman to control her fertility but also forces her to take all the responsibility for birth control and to risk her life and health and future fertility."

"Contraception is a pain in the ass to me. I feel very frustrated and oppressed when I think about how relatively unreliable and/or unsafe or what nuisances they all are. I took birth control pills before and after we were married for about a year, then went off them as the doctor I had wouldn't let you use them longer than that if you never had used them before. I never went back on them because I discovered that they seemed to have had a bad effect on my vaginal secretions and made intercourse more painful because I had less lubrication—I still have that problem somewhat, but then it was much worse. They also gave me breast pains that felt like someone was sticking pins in my breasts for about a week before the time you went off them to have a period. Because of that and all the studies that have been done on side effects (my family has a history of heart trouble, and cancer on both sides) I did't used very safe about using them. After that we condoms and I have used foam but don't really trust it and find it always seeps out and is a nuisance therefore. So mostly we use condoms, which I don't like real well either, as I like to feel his penis. I am thinking about asking for a diaphragm the next time I go to the gynecologist."

"The medical establishment, overwhelmingly male, has both not bothered to investigate 'female complaints' and also has withheld information about our bodies and our sexual functioning, plus spreading myths about menopause and vaginal infections (they may be caused by cunnilingus, etc.). *We* must be responsible for birth control, no matter how hard on our bodies, so men can be free to ejaculate into our vaginas; and we have no control over methods of birth, and are usually put to 'sleep' while male doctors do whatever they want with regard to the birth. Having a baby and a D and C and a cervical biopsy made me afraid of my reproductive organs for the first time."

"Contraception or lack of it affected my sexual life as food or lack of it affects a human's chances to survive. I used the rhythm method for five years, complete with temperature taking, chart keeping, and calendar eyeing, turning the bedroom into a laboratory. After my third unplanned baby was born in as many years, I desperately wrote a letter to the good Bishop inquiring if there had been any change in Vatican policy (what a fool I was). He directed me to the local Rhythm Clinic. What a joke that was! After the priest (male) sang the praises of rhythm, a doctor (you guessed it, male again) proceeded to confuse the safe days with the unsafe days. Upon leaving, and this is funniest of all, the priest gave us poor souls a gift—a thermometer wrapped in a baby blue and pink box. I stood on the street corner and laughed hysterically for minutes. The thermometer seemed the final indignity. I never got a chance to use the blessed thermometer as I was already two weeks pregnant with the fourth. My husband was wild with disgust by now and insisted he'd divorce me if I didn't get an abortion. Now, how could I consider abortion at that time if I couldn't even use any birth control!. . ."

"Contraception is a very sore spot with me. For two years I held off with my first lover because I was afraid of birth control and was too chicken to get the pill. I clearly remember the first time I got the pill at age nineteen. I had to go to this dingy-looking doctor in an old health clinic that didn't even examine me and sent me away with three months' supply of pills. At the beginning of every month I was on them I threw up, and since I have a very sensitive stomach, felt sick the first week of every month. Not until a year later did I connect the throwing up with the pill—I always thought I had the twenty-four-hour flu or food poisoning. I also remember crying constantly during that time. I went off them and did not go back on them till six months later. I vomited again, and tried eight different pills altogether. Two more made me vomit, one gave me breakthrough bleeding, one gave me severe periods that lasted two weeks, one gave me tender sore breasts, some made me gain weight, and I cried constantly on most of them. My sex drive also seemed to diminish. I also got raging vaginal infections every time I went back on the pill. That was probably the worst side affect—I have also read and been told by doctors that the pill can contribute to the things needed to get a vaginal infection, by creating a warmer, moister vagina with more discharge. Needless to say, I hate the birth control pill with a passion and think it's one of the most destructive devices ever developed for the female body."

"I think that women ought to withhold sex from any man (husband or lover or acquaintance) who is not willing to do something tangible to fight for their right to free legal abortion on demand. A woman puts herself in great danger by having intercourse, and contraceptives leave a great deal to be desired. I myself would like to feel that anyone who was close enough to me to be my lover would be fond enough of me to go to some trouble to see that I didn't need to worry about unwanted pregnancy. I feel that if I were sexually involved with a man who was threatened with some danger, I would exert some effort to help him. I would like a man to do this for me, too."

HOW IMPORTANT IS SEX?

Is sex necessary for health?

Finally, since the arrival of the sexual revolution and its tenet that sex is no longer "serious" (you don't have to fear pregnancy, and marriage is no longer a requirement), it has become "hip" to have a lot of "sex" (intercourse). In fact, we are often told that the sex "drive" must be regularly expressed to maintain "healthy functioning." Many women resented this commercialization and vulgarization of sex—"beds on the sidewalks and pills in the vending machines":

"We are taught that every little twinge is a big sex urge and we must attend to it or we'll be an old maid. I'm getting sick to death of sexuality—everywhere sex sex sex! So what? Sex is not the end all and be all of life. It's very nice but it's not everything!"

"I filled this questionnaire out because I wanted to think some about my sexuality. I found it helpful and interesting, though I felt uneasy sometimes. I felt divided: it seems progressive for women to affirm sexuality and their control of it but, on the other hand, I have long been oppressed by the overemphasis on sexuality. Also, for both men and women, sex in recent decades has been heavily associated with consumerism and with the ideological separation of public and private life. This overkill is politically bad and creates undue personal anxiety about sex for many people—myself included."

"I wish there wouldn't be as much of a 'hype' about sex as there is now. I hate the media's exploitation of sex and women. I would hope that women wouldn't be looked upon as things to look nice and to have sex with.

For the most part, women are judged by their potential sexual worth. I would like sex to become more matter of fact, and more personal. In a way, I'd almost like to have back the hush-hush good old days when you just didn't talk about sex. It would not be hidden because it was dirty, but because it was a sweet, private thing."

Unfortunately, the idea that sex is necessary for health has become big business. Magazines, books, television ads using sex (or the happy couple) to sell their product, some psychiatrists, counselors, sex clinics, films, and massage parlors—all have a vested interest in the idea. We are constantly being reminded of sex in one way or another, and subtly coerced into doing it: "Why aren't you doing it? Everybody else is. Get on the bandwagon! You're missing all the fun if you don't!" (And you're probably neurotic and mentally unhealthy.) Many women commented on this, or felt defensive that they did not want to have sex more often:

"I think our culture has made sex overimportant. Everyone thinks that everyone else is having a great time fucking all the time and so we all compete against the American myth. Given this, I think that sex in my life has assumed a correct proportion, that is, an expression of love between us; yet, I still feel hung up about the myth sometimes—maybe having sex is less important to me than to others."

"When I'm not seeing anyone in particular, I only feel interested in sex about once every two weeks. This makes me feel somewhat inadequate to say this. I feel it should be more frequent than this."

"If I go for long without sex, my desires drop ridiculously, which worries me. I start to wonder if something is 'wrong' with me, which makes me feel obligated to have sex. I usually think, 'Wow, it's been a long time since I've had it and I guess I ought to!' "

"I feel a heavy social pressure to have lots of sex, but sex is something I do not have time for now, as building my career takes all of my energy. I guess I'm not as interested in sex as I should be."

To be told that we should have a regular "appetite" for intercourse does not coincide with how most women feel: periods of greater interest in sex with a partner, for most women, fluctuate according to attraction to a certain individual, and (to a lesser extent), according to the menstrual cycle.* Most women† emphasized that the appetite for sex with another person became really intense only in relation to desire for a specific person, although of course they could enjoy sex at any time. What causes the awakening of this intense desire or love for another, specific, person is very personal and mysterious.†

"Good sex involves a certain spark between two people. I once had a friend whom I had only to touch and the heat of his skin and his manner of being could arouse me. He had a very sexy way in my eyes, I don't know why. To this day I often think of him."

"Leaving out love and even commitment for the moment, good sex has to be more than anatomy or even 'psyching' yourself into it. It has to involve a certain amount of chemistry between two people. After a singularly disastrous experience trying to make a sexual relationship work when there was no attraction (just affection), I don't want to try to add sex to my friendships (unless I feel attraction too). I don't understand it in any way but 'chemistry,' but there certainly is such a thing as sexual attraction which can't be forced into existence."

"There is an irrational, mysterious element in sexual attraction and experience that I feel is left out here. It is

* See appendix.
† This includes women who do orgasm with their partners as well as women who do not.
† All we really know about our sexuality is that we have a desire for orgasms, and that certain individuals and certain situations stimulate these desires in us more than others. Other primates like chimpanzees become genitally aroused from feelings of frustration or fear, anger, tension, joy, or exuberance, or from playful or affectionate body contact. Arousal, for humans also, is often brought on by tension or frustration, and not only by sexual feelings themselves.

real, but hard to discuss without ending up sounding like the cardboard fantasies of Hollywood movies and romance magazines—but it is real nevertheless."

"I've never been able to figure out what it is that draws me to a certain person; I don't think that it is any one basic trait. But although I can't define what the ingredient of attraction is, I usually know quite quickly after meeting someone when it is present; it is a combination of the physical and emotional makeup of that person. Occasionally, I will discover that I'm attracted to a person whom I've known for a long time—often I am surprised by this late attraction and wonder why I wasn't aware of it sooner."

"The thing I enjoy most is making love with people I have that 'special' feeling for—this is when it's most satisfying totally, even if it never gets down to real sex— it's still beautiful just holding them and feeling warmth and love with them."

"Oy. You know what I think? I think sex is a damned nuisance. For a few weeks of 'rapture' a lot of us suffer and often go weeks of agony with someone we don't get on with, all because of some kind of passion we felt. But I hunger after what ecstasy it can be, even while I distrust it and try to stay away from it!"

Of course, not all sexual activity or physical relations are based on this kind of attraction; some women prefer relationships to be based more on friendship than passion. But they still indicated clearly that their desire for sex with another person is usually based on feelings for another person, and not on a purely mechanical need for "release."*

Do you ever go for long periods without sex? Does it bother you? Do you feel you are missing something when you are not sleeping with a partner?

In fact, there is nothing unusual about spending various periods of one's life entirely without sex (with or

---

* On the other hand, perhaps masturbation and the certainty of orgasm at that time are related more purely to a need for release.

without masturbating). Most of us went without sex until we were fifteen or twenty or twenty-five years old. Also, pregnancy, widowhood, old age, or being "single" are frequently celibate periods.

Many women had spent rather long periods of time in their lives without having sex with a partner—and sometimes without even masturbating—for many reasons.

"My husband and I go through very necessary times of emotional withdrawal from each other and at these times we don't have sex. We have been together for fourteen years and sometimes I am overwhelmed by a feeling of too much togetherness. We once went nearly two years without intercourse (although I did have orgasms by masturbation). It turned out not to be a serious deprivation, and of course, we were still very much in touch physically during this time."

"Having been single all my life, I have had long periods of celibacy in between lovers. I have presently been uninvolved for about six months, and I don't feel I'm missing anything in particular sexually. Once in a while I masturbate. Of course we were all celibate as children; in my case, I went twenty years until I was devirginized. If it didn't kill me then, I guess it won't kill me now."

"I have been divorced one and a half years and in that time I haven't had much sex. At this point in my life, it's just not really important, and I can't find many men that turn me on enough to want to have sexual relations with them anyway. Sex plays a very small part in my life, and I really don't seem to miss it."

"Military wives either endure or masturbate. I do both. I can't say I like a total diet of masturbation, however, because my best orgasms are through intercourse."

"Although reading both the book and the questionnaire make me extraordinarily defensive about this, having sex isn't very important to me for the most part. I lived with one man for most of seven and a half years; our sexual relationship was only active for about the first two and a half of those years. After that it dissolved almost completely—I don't think we fucked more than twice in the last year of it. During all that time I never had or actively desired an affair with another man (or woman), and the relationship with this one man was otherwise sufficiently satisfying and nourishing that I was able to imagine living with him for the rest of my life quite sexlessly. We were not unsensual— we did kiss and hug, and this physical contact was (I now understand) exceedingly important to me. I didn't relish the idea of no sex forever, but it seemed quite livable-with, given the importance of the rest of the relationship to me."

"Since we broke up (eleven months ago), sex has become considerably more important to me, but what I think is operating is that having a relationship with a man is what is really important to me. After my first two sexual encounters after the breakup (both of which were one-nighters), I decided not to do it in the absence of at least the potential for a relationship. There are plenty of days when I feel very horny and very depressed and rather wish that I could take sex casually enough to just go ahead and do it with attractive men, but for the most part I feel okay about it, and would in the end rather spend time with women friends, or nonsexual time with men I like, or sit at home with a good book, or masturbate to relieve sexual tension, than go to bed with any but what someone in *Sexual Honesty* called 'quality men.' "

"I am single now, and my steady sex life is with myself, out of choice. As for sex with others, I seem to get hungry for it every couple of months. Which means I get to want contact with another body sexually enough so that my objections get minimized. Most of the time I feel I don't want to be that close to any man I know, or it's too complicated in terms of his or my feelings and expectations."

"I used to be very straight-laced about sex and did not engage in sexual intercourse until age thirty-four (this is true). I was very religious and thought surely I would marry, so I was waiting for marriage to begin my sex life. But I never found a man I wished to spend my entire life with, so when I reached my thirties and my sexual desires became even stronger, I compromised my religious beliefs. I felt some guilt at first, but quickly got over it because I had never known such lovely closeness and tenderness, or so much pleasure, before. And I realized that anything that made me feel so good could not be wrong. It was wonderful to be so physically and spiritually close to another human being. Now this man has been gone from my life for about three years, but I've been quite happy without sex. I'm good at sublimating, I guess, and sometimes I masturbate. I still can't bring myself to have casual sex partners—I only want to have sex with someone I care about."

"I have had such a poor relationship with my husband for seven years that I no longer have sexual desires. I used to have desires for sex, but never reached the heights of passion I desired. A mental block formed somewhere during the last few years and I just gave up."

Although most women said that they missed the touching and holding of sex, they emphasized that they would not go with "just any man" to get it.

"Going without sex doesn't bother me enough to go out and get laid by someone I don't feel really close and loving with. Meanwhile, I'm happy to sleep with my animals."

"I think I would probably go without sex unless I met a person whom I had deep feelings for. Sex in itself really matters little to me; it only matters what I think is behind it between me and the other person. Besides, it can be refreshing to be alone."

"When I am in love, I cannot tolerate more than two weeks without sex. I feel lonely when I sleep alone, but I can get used to it. I would rather masturbate than just have sex with anyone."

"I can live without it quite a while and did for a year once when I was very religious. If there is a stimulus, someone I love or am attracted to, I may want it a lot— daily for quite a while. But otherwise, I'm only missing a lot of hassle and complications."

"Sex is only important when I think about it. For long periods I can get along quite well, until someone I like touches me. But it is difficult to find someone I can integrate intellectual and emotional love with, and the hassles of splitting up hurt. Sex is a luxury and a comfort, but not an essential."

"I am currently celibate because I haven't met anyone who turns me on. I miss having a regular sex life very much. Masturbation is very nice, but I like to wake up and be held and cuddled, etc. I hope I meet someone I like soon."

"I don't feel I'm missing anything when I'm not sleeping with someone. Like Europe, they're always there, and maybe I'll go someday, but I'm not that interested right now because of other interests here."

Sometimes celibacy could bring an increased sense of freedom and independence.

"Sometimes I get really high on being without any sexual activity. I think it's because I'm not dependent on anyone for anything."

"I haven't had intercourse for six months. At first, I fluctuated between depression and exuberance, but after a while I felt an increased sense of personal freedom and independence, and self-confidence. Now I like it, and I really enjoy having control over my desires."

"Not having any sexual relationships for a while (two years) gave me time to turn my life around—a beautiful and peaceful time."

"I have gone for long periods without sex (up to one and a half years), but not recently. During those periods, I felt a sense of spiritual growth and independence and increased self-confidence."

"I did it for nine months once. It was harder at first, then I got used to it and kind of got high off it, and energetic. I was only horny near my period. To know I can do it if I want is a real feeling of independence."

"I did it once for seven months, and was somehow glad of the time free from lovers to think things over. For a long time sex had been the most important thing in my life and I felt lost if I didn't have a steady lover. I learned to be more interested in me as a person, an individual—my relationships with friends, my career, *my* life. Now I don't feel as frantic about sex and proving my worth through it. It's still wonderful, but not all-consuming."

"About celibacy—I was celibate for about six months, the first six months I was at college. It was a conscious decision on my part not to deal with sex because I was having a lot of difficulty adjusting to being away from friends and lovers; I had had a very sexual year before that, with two lovers, and I didn't have the energy to get involved with anyone and didn't want to have any sex without emotional commitment. Celibacy was a really good thing; I became very content with myself, never thinking about finding someone to sleep with, never having to worry about whether or not I wanted to sleep with someone, being able to take all relationships for what they were on a purely platonic level. I learned a lot about myself, and how I relate to men. It's something I would recommend to anyone who wants time to sort out her feelings about sexuality, as not having sex for a while leaves you remarkably clear about what you really want, and from whom."

"I am currently celibate. I enjoy it but the society makes it hard to be partnerless sometimes. There are activities I avoid because they will be 'couply.' People often think there's something wrong with you if you're not part of a couple, but being independent is worth it."

"I love being single. I would never imagine myself being married. Celibacy is glorious. One reason I am glad I am celibate is that I am not as slavish as some of the women I see around me. 'You said you would call and you didn't.' 'Do you love me?' 'I love you so much.' 'Aren't you going to dance with me?' 'Where were you?' I feel I am in total control of my body and my life."

"Periods of celibacy can be useful for re-evaluating your life and rediscovering your sexuality—the fallow period before new things can grow. I did it for five years on and off once. By not having to please anyone else, I was able to get really deeply in touch with myself, and develop my understanding of the world—

whereas before, always having boyfriends had kept me so narrowly focused on them that I hadn't had time to think about my relationship to the larger scheme of things. I found that giving up physical sex was a small price to pay."

"As for celibacy, I think every woman should see it as an alternative. For years, I was so busy fulfilling male expectations I didn't know *what* I felt. I believe there are a lot of women who are going through what I went through. Now, I just have sex by myself—searching for I don't know what, just discovering myself sexually."

However, other women felt cut off and isolated during periods of celibacy, since sex is almost the only activity in which our society allows us to be close to another human being—since all forms of physical contact are channeled into heterosexual intercourse.

"When I go without sex a while, I begin to crave affection and reaffirmation. I feel closed off from others, and begin to notice an intense need for affection, warmth, and any form of contact with another human being."

"It doesn't seem to bother me physically, but emotionally I tense up. I miss body contact and find it extremely frustrating. There is a special kind of loneliness in being one in a culture that seems to think in terms of pairs."

"Without sex, I start to feel dead, ugly, and alienated—like life is passing me by. I begin to feel that I need to have sex as a psychological release."

"When I go without it, I become preoccupied with it. I especially long for the warmth and comfort it brings. When I was a child I never imagined there could be so little affection in the world."

"After about three weeks I get starved for affection and company, and life feels drastically incomplete. I miss the general physical contact, especially going to sleep and waking up with someone, to be at those moments of partial consciousness and feel that I am not alone."

"I miss feeling wanted and needed, and the body warmth when I wake up. I usually start feeling unattractive and undesirable too—mentally depressed, bored, low-energy. I lose my sense of humor."

"I become withdrawn and feel inhibited and isolated and frightened. I have gone into deep depressions at such times, and had a feeling of disconnection from the human race."

"It really bothers me. I feel lonely and rejected without sex. Sex is great for breaking the shell of aloneness and fear that seems to come down like a curtain between me and the world when I have no one to love. I find sex to be a retreat to comfort, warmth and emotion in a cold world—rejuvenation. A sort of magic area of refuge."

Physical contact, "flesh to flesh, warm and tight," is tremendously important, and sex is almost the only way to get it in our culture—after we are "grown up." As one woman explained, "If I was deeply depressed, cold, lonely, even with a stranger sex could be regeneration to me. The closeness gives me a sense that I am not alone, and that life is not all rough edges after all. It makes me feel loved and special." Another woman said that what she liked best about sex was "the feeling of crazy friendliness it gives, sometimes falsely. And the reassurance, however momentary, of being held. The closeness, intimacy, honesty—and after when you feel alive and happy in a way you never do at any other time."

The idea that we should have a certain regular amount of a kind of genital contact we call "sex" is a very mechanical notion, to say the least. One woman put it very well: "There was a time when all across the country babies were fed at two, at six, and at ten o'clock. Then suddenly there was a revolution: the experts decided that babies must be fed 'on demand'—every ten minutes, if necessary. It took a long time before it became clear that these two methods weren't so different after all: both relied on the authority of ex-

perts. Now they tell us we should have sex 'regularly'—
you should keep up a regular healthy sex life, but before you weren't supposed to do it except once in a
while—shit. I don't need any experts to tell me when to
have sex, how much or what kind. If I feel like it, I
will—otherwise I won't. It's *my* life and *my* body, and
I'll do what *I* want with it."

CONCLUSION

Finally, what was the ultimate significance of the
"sexual revolution" of the 1960s?

Although sexuality is very important, it is questionable whether it is important in and of itself, apart from
its meaning in your life as a whole. The increasing emphasis on sex and personal relations as the basic source
of happiness and fulfillment is a function of the lessening probability of finding even partial fulfillment
through work. In the first place, most people do not
have the luxury of being able to choose work that they
would like to do; for most people it is a question of
finding some way to support themselves as quickly and
as best they can, from the very limited options available
(unless you have some capital to begin with). Now,
added to this, is the fact that since technology and the
growth of large corporate business have taken over almost every aspect of life, most jobs have become very
repetitive, impersonal, and boring. There is almost no
way that most people today can hope to find any real
personal fulfillment through the actual work they do.
As one woman put it, "Sex* is clearly used as a universal panacea, to keep the masses quiet and stop them
from realizing the emptiness, meaninglessness, and alienation of their working lives." It is interesting in this

---

* In the same way that woman's role has shifted from child-
bearer to sex object since the decline in importance of childbearing, just so the emphasis on personal fulfillment has
shifted from family (as a larger group of people) to sexual
and romantic love (whether in marriage or not).

context to note that the sexual revolution came at a time when social and political unrest in the United States was a problem.

Sexuality and sexual relationships can be surrogates for (or obscure our need for) a more satisfying relationship with the larger world—for example, with work. In a way, as long as we accept this schizoid compartmentalization of public and private life, we are abrogating our moral obligation to take an active part in the direction of the larger world, and accepting an ethic of powerlessness. Meanwhile, the commercialization and trivialization of sex advances further and further into our private lives and obscures their deeper personal meaning for us. In fact, we haven't had a sexual revolution yet, but we need one.

OLDER WOMEN

The sexual revolution did not include older women* as among those who could now enjoy sex—although this denial is nothing really new. For centuries it has been a hideous cliché in our culture that older women are not sexual women. I wonder how many younger readers, when reading the descriptions of masturbation or orgasm, for example, were envisioning exclusively twenty- and thirty-year-olds as having written them? In this section we will see how wrong these ideas about older women are, in some very eloquent comments from some very interesting women.

How does age affect female sexuality?

With regard to how menopause (or hysterectomy) affects sexual feeling, Helen Kaplan has explained that:

> While some women report a decrease in sexual desire, many women actually feel an increase in erotic appetite during the menopausal years. Again, the fate of libido seems to depend on a constellation of factors which occur during this period, including physiologic changes, sexual opportunity and diminution of inhibition. From a purely physiologic standpoint, libido should theoretically *increase* at menopause, because the action of the woman's androgens, which is not materially affected by menopause, is now unopposed by estrogen. Indeed, some women do seem to behave in

---

* How old is "older"? Obviously, there is no answer to this question; I can only agree with Ti-Grace Atkinson when she says "the older woman is all of us."

this manner, especially if they are not depressed and can find interested and interesting partners.[1]

Mary Jane Sherfey has also pointed out that female sexual capacity increases as women get older, because they develop a larger and more complex system of veins (varicosities) in the genital area.

Once again, confusion between reproductive activity and sexual pleasure is playing havoc with our lives. It's true that the capacity to reproduce ends at menopause, and that vaginal lubrication *can* decrease, but women's sexual arousal or orgasm capacity actully increases. What happens at menopause is something that happens only to our reproductive organs: sexuality and the capacity to experience sexual pleasure are lifetime attributes. Childhood is another time when, although we are not capable of reproduction, we are certainly capable of sexual pleasure. We should picture our bodies as being sexual all our lives, from birth to death, but with the addition during certain years of the potential for reproduction.

One woman was probably speaking for all "younger" women looking ahead to old age when she said: "I'm only twenty-eight, but I'm already dreading it and thinking of it a lot—I'm angry that society views women's aging as more detrimental than the 'maturity' of men. I see no reason why a woman should feel loss of sexuality or attractiveness at menopause. It's simply another phase in the female cycle, and part of womanhood."

"How does age affect sex? Does desire for sex increase or decrease, or neither, with age? Enjoyment of sex?"

Most women who answered this question felt that their sexual pleasure had increased with age.

"I believe sexual desire increases with age. Enjoyment certainly increases—I can vouch for that."

"I didn't know getting older would make sex better! I'm fifty-one now and just getting started!"

"Sex definitely gets better as you get older. In the

past two years, I have simply done as I damn well pleased when it came to sex. I live every day as if it were my last. It's great."

"I think that men are conned into believing that it decreases in age for them. I don't think it decreases drastically for anyone, *especially* for women. My best sexual experiences are coming out of maturity and self-confidence."

"I am enjoying sex more in my forties than I did in my thirties; I enjoyed it more in my thirties than in my twenties. There's a liberating combination of experience, self-knowledge, and confidence, and an absence of pregnancy fears."

"I am just as horny at fifty-five as I was at fifteen, but my man considers me too old to be sexy!"

"I thought that menopause was the leading factor in my dry and irritable vaginal tract. My doctors thought that it was lack of hormones . . . but with my new lover, I am reborn. Plenty of lubrication, no irritation!"

"Even though I've not been through menopause, I've had a partial hysterectomy. (I'm forty-seven.) For me it's great! Only one partner was adversely affected—he thought he might someday want children and I would not be suitable to his needs, so we parted."

"My roommate (she is in her early fifties) had a hysterectomy five years ago. From what I see of her sex life she changed drastically: more sex partners and sex more often."

"I enjoy sex more since I no longer fear pregnancy. (I'm post-menopausal.) Also it's more enjoyable since my children are no longer home—children *can* inhibit sexual activity. Because I enjoy it more, so does my husband. He finds it a pleasant surprise—in fact, I put the excitement in his life!"

"I am answering your questionnaire because I feel there are not enough statistics about women septuagenarians (I am seventy-eight), not enough understanding of the widow's situation. At my age and without responsibilities I do not want matrimony but I have a continuing sex drive which keeps me looking fifteen to twenty years younger than my chronological age. Also I had heart surgery two years ago, which has completely rejuvenated me. I want to live to the fullest extent of my capabilities."

"I am sixty-seven, and find that age does not change sex much. Circumstances determine it. I have had much more sexual pleasure, both with my husband and other mates in recent years. I love not having menstruation."

"Menopause makes everything better, easier, and less dependent on time. My partners enjoy my physical freedom, as do I. I went through it fairly easily."

"I am sixty-six and sexual desire has not diminished. The enjoyment is as great as ever. I think it might diminish if you couldn't have sex. But enjoying it has nothing to do with age."

"I think that sexual desire, attitudes, pleasure, etc. certainly change with age, but the change is qualitative rather than quantitative. It's a matter of growth and development, from a simplistic yes-or-no view of sex to much greater complexity, variety, subtlety, fluidity. I don't mean this so much in terms of increasing sophistication in 'technique,' though I suppose that's part of it. It's like the difference between a young shoot and a tree with many branches and a unique shape and structure and pattern of growth all its own. This is a natural growth process, but I believe that in our culture this process is often inhibited and retarded; we've all been told that all cats are gray in the dark, and many of us come rather late to the recognition and appreciation of her or his own unique and intricate sexual personality. I find it much easier now to know and accept and act on what I want and feel, instead of worrying about what I should want and feel."

However some women did feel that sex was not that important to them any more.

"I find age (or maybe it is state of mind?? the 'space my head is in') has cut down considerably on my sexual needs—that is, I don't seem to turn new people on *at all*, sexually—nor am I being turned on by them—but also *I* am not 'turned on' by former love relationships. I'm just not interested."

"I am seventy-three—living alone—and I don't miss anything. Male companionship is a bore. I was married fifty years ago. I don't want to concentrate on this questionnaire, but I'd answer it if I were forty or so. Enclosed is two dollars. I wish it were more. Good luck."

Other women were interested in sex, but were having difficulty finding partners they liked.

"I am fifty-four years old, living in a new state and city (I just moved). As yet, I have met *no one* I am interested in sexually—either man or woman. I do not seem to give out sexual 'vibes' at this point. I miss it some, but my sexual appetite also seems very low—I have had an opportunity for sex when I visited some women friends on the way out, but I was not even a *bit* interested. I do masturbate and that seems satisfying enough for now; but recently I purchased a vibrator which does *nothing* for me! I was disappointed."

"I am now forty-four and have had some sensational love trips, but my increased age has made a difference in sex for me, because of the culmination of my choosiness and the world's present insistence on sex as a youth symbol. I had thought that if a person (woman) were terrific in her own right and togetherness, her sexual attractiveness would be maintained self-evident for her lifetime. What a bummer! I think the sexual revolution is great but I just can't wait till they include grandmothers in the race of sexually desirable beings! This is one reason why I've started a concerted project with myself on going into autoeroticism—as far as I can find to take it. With what I know I'm capable of, and with what's available to me on the 'sexual marketplace,' it looks like it's gonna be a long cold winter for us single over-forty ladies. *Damn Damn Damn!!*"

"Menopause does not feel like an 'experience' to me; I am still on birth control pills—for hormones. I am aware that my body is less vigorous, I have less energy—that I look *old*—which I guess I am. It's hard to realize however that I *am* fifty-four years old, but I do not make any effort to conceal my age or years or experience—I just *am*. It doesn't seem to turn men on—

maybe more women (??) but I have some fear of loving a person who might have a long-term illness—senility, etc. I've coped with *that* enough."

"I feel that I could give two sets of answers to these questions—one concerning a perfect marriage and one concerning sex relations in widowhood. I seem to be able to interest only married men and that means clandestine relationships. I have not achieved an orgasm with any of my partners (although I do in masturbation). The more promiscuous I become (I had several short-term relationships since widowhood) the more I believe I want what I had for so many years: the love, attention, and affection of one man. However, life is enjoyable, especially with men, but my ego gets in the way with married men, as I want to be the only person on the totem pole!"

"I would also like to have seen questions asked on ethics—what moral imperatives have we laid on ourselves, and which seem valid? Like male intellectuals taught me it was immoral to tease, so I didn't neck or anything unless I went to bed with someone—a good and bad thing that worked more to men's advantage than mine, I feel now. Because marriage is so difficult, I will never complicate it by having anything to do with a married man, but people all around me are adulterizing. Sometimes I feel, 'the hell with their marriage, I need somebody to love too!' "

"At fifty, I have come not to look or hope for an ideal. I think I have poor judgment in men, and besides, no man has seriously approached me in years. Well, none that I would consider. I want to do a lot of things, and I have to get to them before it's too late. Men take up a lot of time—at least the men I choose. I am tired of helping them get their Ph.D.'s, write their books, learn to love, raise their children, and learn to let women achieve. I cannot bring myself to have a homosexual relationship—I just don't feel that way. I can stand it without sex and I don't want any relationship now except friendship, which I find vital. I need to talk, have reactions, brainstorm, laugh, get moral support, inspire others, trade, get help and give it. My ideal relationships now are friendships with achieving women. (Sometimes I still get a brief yen for a man, but then I wonder who?—not him, not him either.) But I still hope I haven't slept with my last person."

"I am sure I have loved. I am not sure they were healthy relationships, but I don't know any that are. The couples who looked best to me are all divorcing now. But that's not the test, is it? I loved the woman in *Sexual Honesty* who said that she had just completed her third successful marriage."

Some older women had lovers.

First, one long answer:

"This is the first chance I have had to let anyone know what and how my life has changed in the last eight years. I have one very close female friend who knows of my lover but besides that it is untold, as it should be for the sake of his wife and my husband. I do not feel guilty about this because I feel that I have been more understanding of my husband and his needs since my coming of age.

"I am now fifty-one, and my first orgasm was at the age of forty-four during intercourse with my lover. At about seven I made a feeble attempt at masturbation, at which I was caught by my mother, who gave me a very long lecture on how this would cause me to become insane. This was my last attempt at masturbation until seven years ago.

"There are many men whom I think it would be enjoyable to have sex with, but so far I have only had sex with my husband and my lover. With my husband I have always just given as he demanded to keep him in a good mood. He has always been very quick in having an orgasm and then going to sleep—often leaving me in a state of tears (in my early years of marriage) and now just in a state of sexual excitement. With my lover it has always been a mutual need and he has never left me unfulfilled. With my husband there is never time for myself. It seems that my lover always thinks of me first. Maybe that is why I have continued this affair so long. Seven years. Taking the long slow time to be aroused is the thing that my lover seems to be glad to do. My husband only takes about five or six minutes.

"I think my husband was as uninformed as I was when we were married and has not bothered to learn anything more. My lover is the one who taught me how to be sexual and how I was a complete woman who was not frigid and unfeeling. Now I am able to ask him for anything that is stimulating and he responds, and he also asks me for things that he likes. We have become very free with each other, and I am not ashamed at all. In fact, I am proud."

"I'm forty-eight years old, and I have never been more optimistic and hopeful. I do not have the sexual satisfaction I need yet, but with three new lovers in the wings and two current ones, I should do well. My sex life has left much to be desired, but my *love life* has almost always been rich and full, and right now is no exception. I am married, second time, eleven years. I hate being married but I try not to let it affect my disposition. It has been nonsexual for five and a half years (my choice)—sexual incompatibility. I have had about ten affairs, ranging from one to five years in length. The effect on me has been to make me blissfully happy (especially the last seven years or so). With my marriage, infidelity has allowed it to endure, both for our child's sake and for convenience. Open marriage may be okay for some, but it would not work for us; it seems important to us to keep up appearances."

"I am, as I stated, fifty-one and have been married to one man for thirty-three years. We have four very lovely children, who are married, happily, and have nine grandchildren. I did not finish high school until after my fourth child was born; at that time I finished my last year of high school and went on to college, and since then I have become a teacher. I have for the last twenty years worked at a school for the physically handicapped. My husband has a high school education and has worked at many different things. He has been disabled for the last two years after having several strokes. Eight years ago I met and fell madly in love with a man who is ten years my junior. I kept my distance, for I felt that this was very foolish of me and I was sure that he would think of me as an old woman. He made the first approach and I made sure that he knew that I was married and how old I was. From there he became my teacher and lover and still is. He is also married and has four children. He is good to his wife and children and I would not want to at any time break up his marriage. I just revel in what I have learned from him, that sex is good and that I am attractive and sexual and wanted. If I never was able from this day on to have sex with anyone I would not mind too, for I have had seven years of sexual relationship that cannot be put aside, for through that relationship I have learned that I am a real woman. I was an only child brought up by a very strict mother who has during her lifetime been married four times. I never knew my father, only stepfathers. Her attitude toward sex was, I am sure, part of my problem and the fact that my husband was not too interested in my part in the sex act. There had been much petting before marriage but I had always held back because 'good girls' didn't go all the way. After marriage I wanted to let go but because he was so quick it was not long before I was just enduring sex because he demanded. It is difficult to tell you what my lover has done for me—I dress differently, I think differently, I see myself as a rather attractive person now where before I felt that I was just a middle-aged woman getting more so each day."

"I am forty-three years old. I've been married for twenty-five of those years. I have a twenty-five-year-old daughter; yes I married because I was seventeen and pregnant and desperate, and I also have a twenty-three-year-old daughter, to whom I still owe much in the way of truth-telling. We are either of lower middle class or upper working class background—take your choice. I think it was unfortunate that I married so young and was then so unsure of myself that I was willing to accept my husband's values as the only 'right' sexual morality. I accepted and, for twenty-five years, tried to live up to his ideal of exclusive, possessive sexual love. This was totally contrary to my nature, for I know now that the more I love, the more I can love. I am incapable of selective inhibition. The one experience which has drastically affected my sexual life was the occasion of my taking a lover after twenty-five years of marital fidelity. I was a 'frigid wife' and became one as a result of the necessity of faking orgasm for the sake of preserving love. This was not because of my own attitude toward the function of sex, but rather in a futile attempt to subordinate my own natural feelings to my husband's social conditioning. The end result of my effort to control my 'anti-social' sex drive was to totally repress all possibility of spontaneous response. The first time I went to my lover I was terrified that I would be unable to feel anything with him either. But he was so patient and skillful that I was able to rediscover what I had known so long before. He reawoke what I had wasted so many years trying to deny. He was twenty years my junior, but I am infinitely and forever grateful to him and so should my husband be, for he also enjoys my sexual revitalization."

Some older women had begun to relate sexually to other women.

"I have had many sexual experiences with men, and found them satisfying. However, eighteen years ago (I am sixty-six now) I met Sarah, for whom I had great admiration and respect. When she announced she loved me and proceeded to demonstrate it, there was no further need for men. I feel my sex life is as complete now as it ever was. I haven't had any sexual relationships with other women. For me at this point it would be impossible. I feel my life is more complete and happier than if I were formally married. Ours is no 'male-female' relationship but a sharing of everything with mutual respect."

This reply was *signed*—by a woman who obviously had very few fears about life.

Other women enjoyed sex with younger men.

"I think that sex is better in my forties than ever before. I feel in my prime and at my peak. I have never felt better or looked better. I feel good about myself—my body and mind. I have found a very satisfying relationship with a man twelve years my junior and we are compatible. There will be a time for it to end and I think we will know it, but I really feel that will be just the beginning of a new phase of my life. I wish all women could find what I have found."

"My marriage was the deepest relationship I ever had, I suppose, and the longest lasting (thirty-five years). We had a wonderful mental thing going, and a serviceable physical relationship that was rarely great. We fucked okay, but he never really made love to me—was very unaffectionate and unsensual. After a number of years, I began to have affairs outside the marriage and that was when my real sex life started. Now, since the marriage ended, I had one big love affair with a much younger man, which was very high both physically and mentally. It was probably the best physical match I have had, in many ways—but that was because of psychological factors, more than anything else. Probably the best sex I've had in the last four years has been with younger men, come to think of it."

"I had a wonderful experience two weeks after my divorce. I was asked by a man twenty years younger than I to meet him the next day for an assignation. We both knew it would probably be a one-time thing, as we might never see each other again, and we had practically nothing in common except that we were both very horny. I had time to think it over, so I wasn't rushed into anything, wasn't in love, had no obligation whatever, to him or anyone else—for the first time in my life I was free to make a decision concerning my sex life, without worry about the consequence. We spent a wonderful afternoon doing all the things we both enjoyed, and both of us were completely satisfied and happy. He was wonderful to talk to, and was the first person I ever talked to about other women. That was the first time I knew that other women couldn't come without clitoral manipulation, like me. I have had many other wonderful experiences, some much better sexually, due to the cumulative experience of several years, and the tenderness and love I feel for my partner, but that one stands out for many reasons. For one thing, to learn that age makes no real difference in sex, that I was attractive to him, was wonderful for my ego, especially so soon after my divorce. Another thing was the twenty-four hours of anticipation, knowing I could change my mind."

However, quite a few women were disappointed and bitter about their sexual experiences.

The following three women explained at length:

"Sex isn't important to me. I am fifty-eight years old, married to the same man and faithful thirty-five years. Lots of rough years. We've raised two fine children, a dentist and a lawyer—have four darling grandchildren. About five years ago, my husband at about fifty-two started drinking every night—knocked me around. I've never heard a word of praise except while having intercourse, and I keep wondering how in hell I could enjoy that when I'm so poor in every other way!

"I only have orgasms occasionally in dreams—about strangers. Kissing the back of my neck is most important to me to have an orgasm. I told him that for years but he never does it. I do not like oral or rectal sex but both have been forced on me. I can be feeling pretty mellow with vaginal intercourse and when he mentions oral or rectal, I go on with the act but the glow is gone; I hope he gets his fun just talking about it.

"I've tried masturbation and get *nothing* from it . . ."

"In the early years I initiated sex several times but it never got anywhere—it has to be his idea. Sex is bound to be good if you are 'friends' with your partner—guess you can tell I'm pretty bitter. I went to a marriage counselor two years ago—I'm immature—my husband hates all women, starting with his mother—he sends me roses —buys me gifts and tells me how stupid I am."

"Yes I fake orgasms—nearly every time—which is nearly every night, sometimes twice."

"Now I'm very upset because he wants to sell our house (thirty-two years) and move to a small town—he handed me this questionnaire and said it could tell me why I'm nervous. I'm definitely not 'with it'—I'd settle for a few kind words."

"My current sexual life is zero. It has been zero for twenty-one years. That is, I have been celibate for over twenty-one years. I am sixty-two, and have been married twenty-five years (in my present marriage). I am married to a typical male boor, selfish and insensitive, also alcoholic, but I stay here because I am aging, I have no skills, and I have cardiac problems.

"Masturbation has been important to me because I cannot seek sex outside of marriage, rotten as it is. So, masturbation is a release, but I do not practice it intensely because of religious and parental taboos left over from childhood. I feel guilty. However, since the women's movement and succeeding literature I am trying to modify my views. I enjoy masturbating 'during,' but later feel guilty and then try to rationalize. It usually happens during sleep. I have a dream where I awaken sexually aroused. I spread my legs, then go ahead and manipulate my clitoris or caress my vaginal area until orgasm.

"With my husband, I only sometimes had orgasms. He was more interested in his own wants than mine. Also, nobody ever gave me any information about sex—with parents and teachers, my God, you never *dared* ask! The first time I had sex, I had no knowledge of what to expect, and my husband was a crass pig—he said, 'Go clean yourself up.' No sensitivity, no anything! I was an object, a convenience. But I married him to escape home, so I did the best I could. Anyway, romance is really a laugh, just a bill of goods sold us by parents, the media, and the makers of products. From pregnancy to the grave, we are brainwashed on Romance.

"Since I have been asexual for all these years now and will remain so, I have adjusted to it. It gives me a sense of freedom; I don't have to play stupid games or use sex for bargaining or manipulation as I did in the past. I am sorry I am not one of today's young women—they are their own persons, can be free to choose a career, their own life style, and be independent. Many older women like myself have only known marriage and family—their own life was submerged into service for others. They are losers. Ask them!

"My sexual feelings have been repressed simply because of the situation, not because of my age. If one had a loving partner, why should feelings decrease? Age would not enter into it, except if your partner was ill, or etc. I had a radical hysterectomy and I still have sexual feelings. But since I have no actual contact with my partner, I can't say about the physical part of it. The hysterectomy threw me into a deep depression (five months ago) and I am now in therapy because of that problem—and of course the support at home is not so good, so I am glad for the therapy.

"I answered this because if in any way another woman can identify with my one little statistic and know she is not alone—fine! I am stuck in a small bigoted Southern town where women keep quiet and rarely rock the boat and men beat hell out of them. You never saw such ignorance, but we are (a handful of us) trying! Good luck to you."

"I am now fifty-six, mostly a housewife but I work off and on. I never worked when the children were small. Actually I never had worked and had no confidence in myself. My husband used to give me the impression that I couldn't do anything anyhow that anyone would pay for. I know now that we both had a king-sized, low, sense of self-esteem. Mine is better now than it was but he won't even admit that there is such a thing! At various times I've boarded children, been a sales clerk, been a receptionist, a file clerk, done indexing, and lately I've been paid for interior decorating! I'm a high school graduate.

"I was a virgin when I married at twenty and was so hung up. I did what I thought I was supposed to; never looked at another man (I mean that I would avert my eyes)! I didn't know about orgasms. Also, now I know my husband never did know what he was doing. I just knew it mostly was disappointing. I loved the foreplay and (to be honest) the feeling of power over him that the whole schmeer gave me. I could turn him on like a light switch.

"I thought I was in love with my husband; now I think I just wanted to be and it took me years and years to realize that he just wasn't the man I idealized him into. He was a good guy, kind to me (but wanted to control me completely), but now I know he's a bundle of nerves (he denies it) and has more hangups than I do! He denies all problems! Also he was a virgin. I naively thought all men had experience but he didn't. My husband and I went together for five years. He was seventeen and I was fifteen when we met, so after about a year we started heavy petting. We never went all the way but we did finger fucking and oral. He did, that is; I had never heard of it before but I loved it. We were really hot—all I had to do was talk to him and I got all wet. I loved sex so much it frightened me. I'm not sure about orgasm, though.

"To make a long story short, after thirty years or so of marriage we got bored, started talking about swinging, then, when we finally went through with it I became so *sick* over the fact that my husband, my lover, was much less than ideal! I wanted him to be a good lover and earn a good living, be a good father and so proud of our marriage that he wouldn't want another man to touch me! Ha ha. He was a terrible lover— earned a mediocre living, was never ambitious. He was a so-so father—alienated the oldest almost completely and was not a strong personality as a father and also I felt he had no real respect for me or our marriage so I thought, 'What the hell!' If he doesn't care I might as well pick my *own* man. Besides by then I was on the hormones, had lost fifty pounds, and had become very active nights with community improvement group (lots of nice men). So I started meeting one guy two years older than my husband. We'd been flirting at parties etc. for years. So I said casually, 'We could have fun without hurting anyone,' and he jumped at it. He was *great* and I found out what sex was all about. That's when I learned about the orgasms. He was a passionate, tender lover. I enjoyed him about fifteen or sixteen times. I wasn't in love with him but it was good."

"I've been twice to a county type family counseling because I was desperate and unhappy. I was helped; now I know that I can cope. I value my marriage for its own sake. I no longer am 'in love' with my husband but he is very good to me and we need each other. We share many interests and I feel that although I'd love to try living alone a while with all the freedom it would bring I'm not sure I'm brave enough and I'm mostly dependent on my husband for support."

But some women were finding new experiences:

"I have been thirty-six years with the same man. I have not had extramarital experiences. I do not approve of my partner or myself having extramarital experiences, because we are happily married and sex is no barrier with us. As far as I am concerned, age (I am fifty-eight) only improves sex under the right conditions, as I am blessed with at this time: my husband and I have retired from employment, as of June last year, and due to freedom of mind, plenty of time and relaxation, find sex is a hundred percent better, because now we have no kids around the house, no relatives and time is our own. We fuck whenever we feel like it, many times during the day and night, anyway we wish it; we walk around the house in the nude and take air baths and exercises—take 'golden baths'— all of which makes us appreciate each other's bodies. In other words 'sexual freedom'—free from the old barriers based on sexual taboos. I am fifty-eight years old, my husband is fifty-seven; we have had two male children during our thirty-six years of marriage. Now I always come first in any sexual activity and my mate orgasms later, as he believes passion originates in the female. Always, he loves me for hours and stimulates me first, him second. I thought Masters and Johnson were okay but my husband and I could have written the book; they are amateurs!"

"I was seventy-five this September. I am a singer. Though I had an excellent voice once, my career was spoiled through enormous emotional and other experiences. I was married three times but had relations with many, probably twenty, maybe more. I was easily sexually aroused, went high—but had no release, most of the time. It drove me up the wall. I hope to make a comeback as a singer. Vocally I am not deteriorated, hope that feminism will help me to develop my personality, which it still needs much.

"Yes, I have had orgasms but in my rather long life, too few. Now I suddenly enjoy sex again. That is, masturbating, which I do now almost every night. Sometimes during the day. Since I began masturbating voluntarily and very strongly, not just playing around a bit, I must say it makes me quite happy—yet I think I am most of the time happy. I feel it frees me—or liberates me more. I am generally frightfully shy, can become stiff and unpleasant. I am now more friendly and easygoing. Sex without orgasm made me extremely nervous and upset. I believed it was my fault. The harder I tried the less it worked. With my previous two husbands I had only vaginal intercourse. I liked it, was aroused, but that was all.

"Once I began to use a vibrator, which made me feel as if I was torn apart. Very strongly. The pain I felt was wonderful. I always thought dying must be like this. Like blasting into outer space. I had an extremely strong orgasm, feeling like flying over the highest mountain. Maybe two or three weeks ago I did not even like to think on masturbating. Now, since I began to understand feminism, I *love* to do it. Unfortunately I need too many hours—mostly from three to six hours—by hand.

"I was married three times but I had no relations with men for maybe ten years now. I did not want anything more to do with sex with men. I wondered if I am or became a lesbian; I love warm-hearted, interesting women, but never felt sexually aroused. I live alone since my husband died. Found it wonderful, but now I'm aware this isolation went too far. I had very seldom if ever discussions about sex. Did not dare. Now I love and need it. As I come just out of isolation (mentioned above) I love my children again much, see once in a while friends, most of the time they bore me. Music was always a wonderful surrogate.

"In my life I just fell deeply in love for no reason. I was more than once in love. It seems to me I was emotionally immature, desiring to lose myself. I don't think I could feel now the same. I don't like to say I feel superior to man, I don't find a better word. Man's relationship with me was too one-sided—only material and mechanical. I was extremely happy when my children were babies. I wanted at least twelve, but stopped after six, which seemed to be necessary.

"Now I have deep relations with my music teacher. He helps me tremendously in my technique and expression. But he does not arouse me. No man did this for more than ten years. If a man would like to play and arouse me sexually till I have orgasm I might do it. Yet it does not seem to be possible nor would I ask for it.

"I like my vagina and genitals. Smell good. I like my body. When I am slim, my body looks still good, but through losing weight once too often, my skin is now too loose which I don't like. Therefore I don't feel comfortable.

"I like now tremendously to talk about sex and to learn a lot more about it. I like these questions very much. Filling them out I got the desire to know you in person and continue our questions and answers, especially now where I begin to see all about sexuality from a new angle. I was always for many years and am convinced women have to play an enormous new role, not to destroy men but to improve this world. It seems to me feminism is a bottomless entity to discover incredible treasures, none of us may be aware of now. It is really for this task I am living and fighting."

TOWARD
A NEW FEMALE
SEXUALITY

REDEFINING SEX

Our definition of sex belongs to a world view that is past—or passing. Sexuality, and sexual relations, no longer define the important property right they once did; children are no longer central to the power either of the state or the individual. Although all of our social institutions are still totally based on hierarchical and patriarchal forms, patriarchy as a form is really dead, as is the sexuality that defined it. We are currently in a period of transition, although it is unclear as yet to what. The challenge for us now is to devise a more humane society, one that will implement the best of the old values, like kindness and understanding, cooperation, equality, and justice throughout *every* layer of public and private life—a metamorphosis to a more personal and humanized society.

Specifically, in sexual relations—which we should perhaps begin calling simply physical relations—we can again reopen many options. All the kinds of physical intimacy that were channeled into our one mechanical definition of sex can now be reallowed, and rediffused throughout our lives, including simple forms of touching and warm body contact. There need not be a sharp distinction between sexual touching and friendship. Just as women described "arousal" as one of the best parts of sex, and just as they described closeness as the most pleasurable aspect of intercourse, so intense physical intimacy can be one of the most satisfying activities possible—in and of itself.

Although we tend to think of "sex" as one set pattern, one group of activities (in essence, reproductive activity), there is no need to limit ourselves in this way.

There is no reason why physical intimacy with men, for example, should always consist of "foreplay" followed by intercourse and male orgasm;* and there is no reason why intercourse must always be a part of heterosexual sex. Sex is intimate physical contact for pleasure, to share pleasure with another person (or just alone). You can have sex to orgasm, or not to orgasm, genital sex, or just physical intimacy—whatever seems right to you. There is never any reason to think the "goal" must be intercourse, and to try to make what you feel fit into that context. There is no standard of sexual performance "out there," against which you must measure yourself; you aren't ruled by "hormones" or "biology." You are free to explore and discover your own sexuality, to learn or unlearn anything you want, and to make physical relations with other people, of either sex, anything you like.

* This will be discussed from men's point of view in the analysis of the replies received to the questionnaire for men, to be published in the future.

THE FUTURE OF INTERCOURSE

SEX AS USUAL?

It must have been clear throughout this book how tired women are of the old mechanical pattern of sexual relations, which revolves around male erection, male penetration, and male orgasm. As one woman said, "Cutting an orgasm short doesn't leave me frustrated if I'm masturbating, but I am becoming more and more short-tempered about cutting sex with my husband short just because he is satisfied. Continuing along the same unsatisfying sexual patterns expresses to me a lack of care and concern for me that I am finding unacceptable. It isn't so much cutting an orgasm short and the biological tension that results that hurts—it is an emotional hurt that frustrates me."

In answers to many different questions women mentioned their frustration and annoyance with this pattern, and many wished for something different.

"What would you like to do more often? How would you like to see the usual 'bedroom scene' changed?"
The following types of answers came up over and over again.

"I wish men would be more sensitive rather than acting like a big penis, having an orgasm and that's all. I would say that seventy-five percent of the men I have known knew nothing about a woman except that they had an orgasm and that should be a big treat to me."

"I'd like to change the whole kiss—feel—eat—eat me—fuck routine."

"I would like more love and gentleness instead of bare sexual stimulation—more emotion and communication, rather than sex along the lines of expectation and demand and then routine follow-up."

"I wish it were easier to start sex play and see where it goes, rather than knowing this kiss will lead to touching each other's genitals, and then intercourse."

"I'm sick of focusing on cocks and cunts. I hate the feeling that I can't hug my partner without 'taking him all the way'—that means I must hold back lots of good feelings just because I'm not in the mood for intercourse. I also like getting into the sexual experience as much as possible and feel terribly frustrated when we don't because he has an orgasm and falls asleep. I would like to have an orgasm, yes, but then continue lovemaking and not make that the end!"

"More kisses, more time, more tenderness. Why don't men like to be touched in other parts of their bodies? I do. I would like to see more men with more imagination."

"I'd like to kiss mouth to mouth more often. I'd like my husband to act less controlled, less in control. I would like to be aroused to the point of complete abandonment. This I have never known."

"Men should stay awake longer afterwards. They should *never* get out of bed right after sex, or clean themselves off!!!"

"I would like to be able to sustain sexual activity indefinitely. I find a man's exhaustion after orgasm disappointing."

"I've never been able to say, 'Yes, that's all I could have asked for, there's nothing more I want.' I've always felt that my sexual encounters have been only beginnings; they've never been even nearly carried as far as I would like them to be."

"To me, sexuality should not be contrived, expected, or routinized. I feel sex should be an exciting, spontaneous thing—not a package you 'buy' with a marriage certificate. Since sex has not yet happened to me 'spontaneously,' I do not feel that I ever truly felt sex as I feel it should be."

"I'd like to see spontaneous *passion*. No contrived situations, like the lights *have* to be off, we *have* to be in bed, we have to wipe away the sperm, we have to be polite, modest—shit."

"More passion. Often he is in too much of a hurry and he pays too much attention to my vagina and not enough or *any* to my sensitive area near my clitoris. I would like petting-type genital manipulation, with clothes on, pushing up dress, pushing aside underpants, that sort of sexy thing. I would eventually like to be free enough to do anything and everything without embarrassment, with complete abandon."

Many women were also tired of men's preoccupation with mechanical perfection in performance, and lack of interest in general body feelings.

"Many men are not as free to be sensual over-all or give as much to the partner as women are. They are almost always genitally focused."

"Men seem to be inhibited, in a way, and even show fear of my body and any 'surprise reactions' it might have—and they are especially preoccupied with their own pricks."

"Many men think sex is just fucking, or something to do with hands, mouth, and cock but not the rest of the body. Men don't feel that their whole bodies are beautiful or that the touch of thigh and thigh is a caress as much as a touch with the hand."

"I would like to have leisurely sex with a man more often, talking and fooling around and entertaining each other. Feeling relaxed. My doctor tells me men don't like this."

"No matter what I do or say, most men simply won't believe that having my ears and the back of my neck kissed is really important. I like playing with their bodies, but it seems that, except for fellatio and fondling of their penis, they don't get much enjoyment out of it. I remain confused as to whether they really have so few erogenous zones or whether they are afraid to feel sexy in 'non-sexual' parts of their bodies."

"Until I lived with gay men I never realized that a

man could actually get intense pleasure out of sex; in my experience women and gay men let themselves be responsive whereas heterosexual men have to sort of grit their teeth and concentrate really hard on keeping it up long enough to come; I have kind of an image of stright guys ardently pursuing It but not really enjoying it once they get it; I always felt rather badly for my lover because it seemed that for him it was like scratching an itch—relieving himself of something negative—where for me it was absolute bliss."

"If only people would let down their fake fronts and be honest. Men are totally dishonest. Nobody will ever admit to his own inner feelings—they all act the way Hugh Hefner tells them to. There's more to sex than crawling on and off."

"Do you feel most men get more pleasure from intercourse than from sexual play?"

Yes	388
No	115
Not my partner	6
Not necessarily	47
	556

"Yes, men think of the preliminaries as an unnecessary delay. I feel during foreplay like I'm being condescended to, dealt with, like he's going through a necessary inconvenience for a long-run benefit."

"The foremost and principal male interest is ejaculation—unhappily the sooner the better. I learned long ago the essentiality of holding off their gratification until I'm ready."

"Yes, most men just want to have an orgasm, and sex play is their 'contribution' to my enjoyment."

"I think my present partner feels that any lingering by the way, or anything besides quick hit-and-run genital sex is unmanly. Macho shit—too bad!"

"He thinks foreplay is a favor, like opening a door."

"It's a big bore for most of them, just a necessity for the Big Entry."

"Yes, they like intercourse best, but fellatio is a close second."

"Yes, but even *they* like sex play if they're the center of attention!!"

"He enjoys a quickie more than I do—but he also seems to enjoy *his* orgasm more if I play with him a long time before intercourse."

"They like sex play about as much, as long as *they* are the ones being played with."

Many women felt that this mechanical approach on the part of most men reflected not only a general lack of feeling for them, but also a lack of development of the man's own sensuality and ability to enjoy his own body.

"Yes, they enjoy intercourse more, but I think that's conditioning, because men feel that sex play is undignified and revealing. Actually, they can enjoy it as much as we do."

"If a man feels that way, I think of him as childish and undeveloped—he doesn't appreciate the subtleties of sex."

"Yes, men often don't know how to get into play, or just touching, and get hung up on orgasm. But they can learn."

"Yes, they don't know how to enjoy it. Many men have a completely genital approach to sex. Sex play is not play to them, but a series of mechanical maneuvers needed to get the woman ready for what they really want. I try to teach them otherwise."

"Yes. They're so hopelessly confused it's not worth bothering with them. Men who do not like to 'neck' are usually bad lovers. Pacing is important in bed, and if a man is too impatient to get there he will probably be too impatient once he is there. He won't know how to enjoy it."

"No, not if he is sexually mature—a sensitive, alive person. My husband says that's a male myth that men enjoy intercourse more."

One woman explained in a long answer how disappointed she was in her husband's lack of interest in anything but intercourse.

"I have viewed married love as a growing together in the ability to express love and pleasure, but I haven't seen this growth in my marriage. My husband really doesn't seem to enjoy anything besides intercourse, and that very briefly, and I don't know what to do to change him. I've tried hard.

"Masturbation is very important for me and I am really sorry I didn't know about it a lot sooner. (I started doing it less than a year ago, at the age of twenty-seven.) I was interested in my sexuality, but my husband wasn't, so I decided to do something about it. Three years ago I came across the idea of masturbation for adult women in *The Sensuous Woman*. I cried and cried and cried because I had this romantic idea of having my husband care about and develop my sexuality— a feat for which I would be forever grateful and therefore endeared and close to him. (I had never had sex until marriage.) This was really important to me, so for the next two years I hinted and openly expressed my desire to have good sex and to develop my sensuality. Nothing much happened. So I finally said, well, if you don't care about my sexuality, I do! Then I asked him what he thought about masturbation. I found, to my surprise, that he did it! And that he thought it would be great if I did it! It relieves him of that responsibility(?) of having to touch, caress, and learn about my genitals(?) Now, I have learned to masturbate, and I do enjoy masturbating, but I feel sad that I can't develop my sexuality with my husband. For many women, sex is a union with another person and the cosmic universe. It is a leaving of the body and a dissolution of the self—so that isolation can end. Somehow I can't help but feel that my aloneness is intensified by the fact that my sexual partner hasn't shown the care of my sexuality. In that sense I really wish that I had learned about my own sexuality on my own a lot—being a teenager and learning about your body is different from being a married adult woman who is learning about her body because her mate isn't interested.

"I have accepted monogamy for seven years because I have felt a deep commitment to and a love for my husband. This is the only sexual relationship I have ever had. I do not think I am the kind of person who could jump in bed with just anyone—yet I have a certain admiration and envy of the woman who can jump into bed with anyone and have a great time. But I love my husband very much. I am very much attracted to him, and I care about him. I want to be close to him. I think that he is a wonderful person in so many ways. But I am also terribly disappointed in and hurt by our sex life. I haven't seen any growth in our ability to love each other well.

"I have been thinking about this questionnaire a lot, and through my responses I am seeing my husband as something of a prude and perhaps threatened or scared of my sexuality. All he ever wants is intercourse. I have been hurt by his refusals and by his lack of reciprocation. I don't feel my husband is emotionally involved during sex. I don't feel he finds me delicious—as it is, he doesn't caress me much. When he does, it is awkward, for the most part. I do most of the caressing. When I am caressed, I feel like it's stilted, not enraptured. Thus, instead of getting involved in the good feelings, I feel like I am on exhibit. Now I try to be aggressive and experimental, but the times when I only follow my husband's lead it is dull, insipid, uninspired! We end up just going to sleep after his orgasm and a brief intercourse. Perhaps this lack of excitement and involvement partially explain why I'm nonorgasmic with him.

"He forgets half the things I tell him that turn me on or off. At first telling him things like that was embarrassing because I would have preferred that he would have asked me if and what I liked. He didn't, so I began to volunteer information—at first very delicately. Later more blatantly. I easily accepted his ignorance at first. No problem. We had a chance to grow together sex-

ually. But after six years of marriage, I see his ignorance as evidence of not caring, and it really hurts.

"He still sees my clitoris as something that is secretive, hidden by hair (the first time he came down on me
he came up spitting out hair. Now, when he goes down
on me, he very meticulously pulls the hair aside). It is
inconvenient to him. But his penis he sees as very convenient and available—although he feels compelled to
jump up and wash it right after intercourse. I am coming to the conclusion that what I need is a more experimental, spontaneous, and uninhibited partner, who has
a real sense of joy in sex and lovemaking."

DO WOMEN ALWAYS WANT
INTERCOURSE?

Not only were women tired of the old mechanical
pattern of "foreplay," penetration, intercourse, and ejaculation, but many also found that *always* having to
have intercourse, *knowing* you will have intercourse as
a foregone conclusion, is mechanical and boring. If you
know in advance that intercourse has to be a part of
every heterosexual sexual encounter, there is almost no
way the old mechanical pattern of sexual relations can
be avoided, since intercourse usually leads to male orgasm, which usually signals the end of "sex." (It would
be very interesting to explore whether this needs to be
so.) If heterosexual relations are to be deinstitutional-
ized, intercourse must not be a foregone conclusion, or
male orgasm during intercourse as the conclusion of
"sex" must not be a foregone conclusion. Women must
claim the right *not* to have intercourse, *unless they want
it*, even when having physical relations with a man.
After all, why is it "natural" for a man to expect intercourse to orgasm with or without clitoral stimulation,
but treasonable for a woman to expect clitoral stimulation to orgasm without intercourse?

In addition, the kind of change we are talking about
in this book is much deeper than just the idea that "a
woman needs an orgasm too." It is not a question of the

woman having an orgasm, and then the man having his, or vice versa. Fixing on orgasm as a goal also keeps physical relations focused on a mechanical pattern. In fact, sex need not always be directed at orgasm, or even at genital stimulation. There are many other ways to relate physically to another person. Male sexuality too must be expanded to include many more options, without the almost hysterical emotional fixation on intercourse and orgasm currently prevalent. What is really needed is a total redefinition, or that is, an *un*-definition, of sexuality, and an expansion of our idea of physical relations to another level of awareness.

Would women still want to have intercourse at all, since it does not usually bring them to orgasm, if they were not pressured to have it?

When asked "If you had to choose between intercourse and clitoral stimulation, which would you choose?" most women perceived their choice as being between intercourse and masturbation—not even considering clitoral stimulation by a partner as a possibility!

In their answers, most women showed mixed feelings.

"Which would I choose? I don't know—on the one hand, I wouldn't like intercourse at all probably if I didn't love him. By itself, intercourse is really nothing, but with him on the other end, it's dynamite. However, I only have orgasms through masturbation. I have never had an orgasm with my lover, although god knows we've tried. And having orgasms is extremely important to me. When my lover has one and I am left to fall asleep wishing I could have one, I could cry (and I often have cried myself to sleep). Still, I enjoy sex—obviously, or else I wouldn't be sleeping with him. But it would be much better if I had orgasms. (Maybe part of the problem is that I happen to masturbate in a very unusual way; I have to be leaning against something, like a chair, and rotating.) I guess if I didn't love him, I might not want intercourse so often, but I'm not quite sure what I would want."

"If I had to choose between having either intercourse or clitoral stimulation, I'd pick clitoral stimulation. I— I've thought about it more and I don't know. I imagine good sex to be an experience where both people sincerely want the other person to feel good, be satisfied, be pleasured as intensely as possible—not just a deal where your partner's satisfaction is the coin you use to buy your own satisfaction. I was going to blithely choose clitoral stimulation because I enjoy this and would be getting what I want, but perhaps that's unrealistic—search for balance."

"I used to like penetration a lot, but lately I wouldn't miss it if we left it out. Physically, it doesn't really stimulate me (except for deep, deep penetration). Psychologically, I love the feeling of closeness, but it still isn't all that important to me. However, it is for my lover. Since he is concerned about my satisfaction, I am equally concerned about his. Therefore, I would not be able to choose either without the other."

"Intercourse is something in itself which will never make me come, however exciting and treasured an experience it *can* be for other reasons. When the contractions seem about to begin and the final drive to orgasm is on, they seem to be stopped by the resistance of the penis itself. It seems to be a 'no-win' situation—at least by the terms of conventional intercourse success. I would solve it by making my orgasm a nonintercourse matter. Then I could entirely let myself go and enjoy bodily and spiritually the trance-like state and the special male-female chemistry characteristic of good intercourse."

"I guess it wouldn't be necessary to choose if I would masturbate while intercourse is going on, although men resent this. But strangely my clitoris sort of blanks out as the movement of intercourse continues. Although it is exciting in itself, I can't come during intercourse and even if I masturbate after intercourse (I have only done it secretly), I have a hard time getting the clitoral feeling back again. Perhaps good intercourse in relationships has not occurred a sufficient number of times for me to learn how to deal with it. Maybe if I persuade men (and myself psychologically) to let me stimulate my clitoris during or after intercourse, and just me enjoy intercourse undisturbed, we can have both without choosing."

"I have always felt that accepting a penis in my vagina was an act of pleasing the man. At first I super got off on my new ability to please and give pleasure. It made me really happy. I liked it a whole lot; it felt really good to be able to please someone I loved so much so directly, so specially. And I liked it because he loved me and was trying to please me too and I liked being petted and touched and getting a lot of attention and earning my man's love in a deeper way. I was eighteen and I wanted to be a woman, and in my mind I needed to have a man to be a woman and all in all it seemed like a real good deal. I was getting a lot of things I wanted: love, physical affection, attention, protection, and a role to play to make me seem real, grown up, realized. But as we lived together longer, grew out of our Acute Romantic Phase, we were no longer the total energy center for the other—life went on—my lover was very busy, working long hours, going to meetings at night, teaching on weekends, etc. He began to do the wham, bang, thank you ma'am routine and I felt cheated, used, and rejected. I tried to forget about it. The good woman's role is not to question her man. By the time I brought myself to speak with him about it I had a lot of anger. I'd begun to question what do *I* want and what makes *me* feel good. It's never since been joy enough just to please my man. This began a time of painful and good search and questioning which has lasted four years (with the same man—I like him) and isn't ended yet—with long cop-out periods of copping out wanting so bad to return to our first blissful months together, when I could follow his lead, think only of him and feel very, very happy and good. Now I'd have to have something more than intercourse, but I still would enjoy intercourse sometimes."

"I like intercourse in some ways. I like the feeling of having the man's penis inside me. What I don't like is the psychological feeling of pressure to 'come,' to perform. If the man comes too fast, it feels like I haven't been part of it at all, and if it takes him a long time, I feel inadequate, like I'm doing something wrong, or not doing something that I should be doing. I like just lying together with the man's penis inside me, and being close, but when the man starts thrusting, I often feel detached, passive, like an object, with no real part in what is happening. It doesn't feel like we're together."

A few women did choose clitoral stimulation.

"When I was freshly in love with my husband, I wanted to be fucked by him all day and all night. This lasted a long time, but gradually grew into the need for less fucking. Now I wouldn't like to choose, but if I had to, I'd pick clitoral stimulation."

"Vaginal penetration is more psychologically than physically satisfying to me. Sometimes I find it boring and would like to leave it out entirely. I don't like the idea of feeling determined for intercourse after foreplay, like something inevitable. I'd like it to be more flexible and optional instead of it being the regular or main course of action. There is a certain form of unity in intercourse which is beautiful, but during other forms of sex, when we do things to please each other, there is still a distinct sense of unity there also. I would definitely choose clitoral stimulation. I find it much more exciting, delicate, loving, and fulfilling."

And some women chose intercourse.

"I would choose intercourse. I feel very close and content then, and it makes my partner very happy."

"Although I feel very physically satisfied after masturbation, I miss the sharing I feel during lovemaking. Sometimes I also feel puzzled, or even guilty at the thought that I am often more satisfied after masturbation than I am after intercourse. I love my husband and the union of our bodies is a beautiful experience to me. However, I feel more fulfilled when I have an orgasm, and that only happens during masturbation. There are times with my husband when I just don't seem to get excited, and I have to psyche myself up for intercourse.

But over all I like it best when my husband is just so sexy that I can't resist him and I just let myself move to his movements and let myself go. That is the best for me, and also I would not choose to do without sharing his orgasm."

"I would always want to have intercourse because it makes me feel good to cause so much exultation in my husband."

"It is easier to orgasm by clitoral stimulation without intercourse, but I would prefer intercourse because it is a fuller, more total experience and I feel as though *sharing* penetration is a much happier experience."

"I think I may put too high a value on penetration, tending to discount other kinds of sex as not 'really' being sex. But I really do like the feeling of a man's penis inside of me, and those moments seem much less detached, less controlled, much less contrived, less like people 'operating on' each other than the others. I would choose intercourse, but maybe I can only say that because penetration really does bring me to orgasm."

Quite a few women mentioned having had stronger sexual feelings as a teenager during "necking" or "making out," before sex had always included having intercourse.

"My best experiences were some sexual encounters (not intercourse) when I was a teenager. In those days, sex seemed like a powerful force that could overcome all kinds of conventions and inhibitions. Whereas today, as a woman of thirty, it seems that it is a much more mechanical routine which actually works as a barrier to keep me and the man from actually experiencing each other. But in those days, it was like some powerful force would just drive us together and we would find ourselves making out."

"My best sexual experiences were all the heavy petting I did before I had intercourse at about nineteen. I used to do that for hours on end and fantasize afterwards for hours. It was the most beautiful, pleasureful thing in my life—especially with one guy I loved and went with for two years."

"My body responses are the same now except I think

I was more easily stimulated when I was a virgin and always reached orgasm even with my clothes on. Maybe it was just the excitement of knowing I wouldn't have intercourse."

"I worry about the loss of sexual feeling from what I had back in college before I was introduced to orgasms and intercourse. I feel my responses have become dulled since then in all areas."

"I was in those back seats in the late fifties, caught in the double bind of having to put out something in order to get dates, but not allowed to fuck. I had innumerable orgasms without penetration. When penetration came along, it wasn't as good."

"I had been masturbating since I was twelve years old on a regular basis (reaching climaxes), but somehow the penis penetration of my first intercourse did not arouse the same feelings in me at all. I vaguely thought (from his urgings) that I had reached a climax when we made love, but it was completely different from masturbation and in my vague innocence I didn't connect the two. The next person I made love with I went with for two years and lived with for one. We petted for three months before I broke down and went on the pill. Our petting was ecstasy and I felt higher on sex than ever before in my life. Then when I was safe on the pill, we made love at a crowded parking place under the steering wheel. He came instantly (shocking after the hours of our petting, when I wasn't safe). It was very disappointing for both of us and our sex life was very poor for the next two years. Foreplay was very poor (I could never get used to that after the hours of passionate petting earlier) and sometimes he took forever to come and just couldn't. It was then I started realizing that Steve was never touching my clitoris and I was very aware of the intense feelings touching it could give me (reinforced by my own masturbation). I tried to show him gently and he got furious, saying wasn't he a good enough lover for me, etc. I was crushed and after a few more half-hearted attempts to show him, I gave up."

"I would like more kissing, more stroking, more slow

sensuality to lovemaking. Perhaps, then, I would get that marvelous feeling back of 'butterflies in the stomach' that I would feel for *hours* when I was fifteen and endlessly petting and having neither intercourse nor orgasm."

"What my generation called 'petting' was very exciting. We were demi-virgins,' which meant *anything* as long as the hymen remained intact. Although actual genital sex is enjoyable, it never reaches the heights of virginal necking."

And one teenaged woman said:

"It is strange, but being tickled on my back gives me a great deal of pleasure, and I don't insist on it, though often I indicate that I really like it and would enjoy having it done. As things stand, I much prefer having my back tickled to having intercourse, but so far I haven't said this to a man. But I think I will pretty soon just to see what will happen. I am tired of being so secretive, and I would rather be called weird and 'not a real woman' to having all these withholds and secrets."

But some women thought intercourse felt good even though it did not culminate in having an orgasm.

"The feeling of penetration, especially if the penis is large enough, is fantastic to me. I sometimes just like to hold it inside me—not moving at all. I love the feelings of different positions, each one seems like a whole new sensation. I like deep, hard thrusting, although most men don't seem to be able to do deep or hard enough (some have been able to, so I know what I like). I also love the feeling of it sliding in and out and love to be teased by taking it all the way out and begging for him to put it back in. It never leads to orgasm for me."

"To be filled is a great body pleasure. There are nights when I want just *everything* in me—including in my mouth, my ears, my vagina, and my rectum—wow."

"Sometimes, if my lover slowly penetrates very, very deeply—and then doesn't move, I get these ecstatic flows and ripples all through my lower abdomen, inside

and out. It's not exactly a climax—I'm not exactly sur
what to label it—but when my lover lets me fully enjo
his penis, with no direct motion on his part, the feelin
is glorious."

**And, finally, as observed earlier in the book, man
women liked to give a man they loved pleasure, and t
feel his body experiencing it.**

"Intercourse doesn't give me an intense clitoral kin
of orgasm but I still get very carried away. Most of th
excitement is about holding and being held, and espe
cially having him come, which both of us can feel in
tensely—which is very satisfying to me."

Finally, to answer the question of whether wome
would still want intercourse if they didn't feel obligate
to have it, the point is not whether women in *genero*
would still want to have intercourse, but that it woul
become a choice, an option, for each *individue*
woman. Whether she wanted to have intercourse or nc
would become her own *choice*, not something she ha
to do to have physical relations with a man.

Intercourse, as a pleasurable form of physical con
tact, will always be one of the ways people choose t
relate. However, it will not continue to be the *only* way
It will become deemphasized, one of many alternativ
possibilities in a whole spectrum of possible physical re
lations. Heterosexual intercourse is too narrow
definition to remain the only definition of sex for mos
people most of the time.

Of course, it can only be surmised at this time ho
much of what we feel now during intercourse is rea
physical pleasure and how much is a product of th
glorification of intercourse. Most women would prob
ably still want intercourse sometimes—especially witl
men for whom they had strong feelings. Some womer
might like intercourse almost always, while other
would almost never want it. Perhaps it could be sai
that many women might be rather indifferent to inter
course if it were not for feelings toward a particula
man.

Three women had stopped having intercourse, but continued sleeping with their partners, with varied reasons and results.

"I used to like intercourse but my lovers' insistence on the pattern foreplay/fuck/sleep turned me off to intercourse. I always felt/feel pressured to fuck (are you ready yet?). I started to resent it and now I don't like fucking and I've fucked only once or twice in the past year. I like putting my foot down and trying new ways to get what I want from my lover, but it's created another block, because I've had to stop fucking out of stubborness and not anything cooperative and mutual, and it seems like communication around this is hard for both of us. However, since I've stopped letting myself be fucked, it's been hard for my lover to ignore my sexual dissatisfaction—which was real easy for him to ignore as long as he was happy. At least now he's started to look for solutions too."

"With my boyfriend of four years, we pretty much stopped fucking, because it just wasn't worth it for me, and he doesn't want me to do it if I don't like it. What with the problems of contraception and no orgasms, it's a waste. We fucked about twice in the past four months. I feel a little guilty about not fucking my boyfriend, but I know I'm right. He still comes, and I do too, and I don't have to worry about pregnancy. It's good this way. I get mad if we fuck and I don't come (and I never have)—I feel 'frigid' and 'out of it' when my partner is ecstatic. I feel silly. I feel like a punching bag."

"I've just come home from vacation all geared up and enthusiastic about being sexually honest, and I ran into a difficulty with my boyfriend. He's been pressing me to go and get a diaphragm, and I have some kind of stigma about it. I thought it over and decided that I didn't want to make an 'official' promotion of sexual intercourse by getting something to make it always possible because I really don't *like* sexual intercourse. I told this to my boyfriend and he felt very highly insulted and made a scene and told me we'd discuss it later. We haven't discussed it yet (two days later) but I have the feeling that in order to continue seeing him there is a prerequisite that I have to have intercourse with him. This is terribly upsetting to me."

TOWARD A NEW KIND OF INTERCOURSE

Not only are intercourse and male orgasm not necessary in every heterosexual contact, but, in addition, the manner in which intercourse is practiced can change to become more mutual and more varied. It is not necessary for intercourse to be a "male dominant" activity. Intercourse can become a varied and individual practice, which can be done in any way you might create. For example, there are many ways of joining and having intercourse besides male "penetration" and "thrusting." Remember the answers women gave in the intercourse chapter explaining how they had orgasms during intercourse? Much of this intercourse did not involve any in and out movement, but more a kind of pressing together (with the penis inside) so the clitoris could get the kind of continuous stimulation necessary for orgasm.* Intercourse need not be as gymnastic as we have usually thought, and it is probable that what we think of as the "natural," physical, movements of intercourse are nothing more than "learned" responses. Isn't it possible that men have been told that "mounting and thrusting" is the "right" thing to do, but that they too, if allowed to experiment, would find many other ways they liked to have intercourse?

Although the most common position used for intercourse is the man-above-woman position, there is no physical reason why it should be better for men. As a matter of fact, Masters and Johnson have pointed out that if a man is on the bottom, he can receive more orgasmic pleasure, since he is not at the same time in-

---

* Whereas male stimulation for orgasm can be discontinuous, female stimulation, due to differences in anatomy, must be *continuous* for orgasm to occur.

volved in physically supporting his body, etc. Further-more, to call male "mounting and thrusting" natural and "instinctive" is highly questionable. After all, most men masturbate *not* by thrusting but by moving their hands on their penises; women with Type III masturbation always thrust. What is natural?

In fact, a few women felt the man-on-top position was more political than natural, as evidenced by their replies to "Do you feel that having sex is in any way political?"

"Yes! Who gets the top?!!! Everyone knows that a woman is more likely to have an orgasm on top, since you have more control. On the bottom, you must more or less just cooperate with the one on top—sort of like having a man 'take care of you,' like you're a baby almost."

"Yes, it is political in every way. Men are demand-ing, women are meant to please. Men are on top in a traditional sense—in society and in conventional inter-course. Men do the action, women are meant as the ori-fice to be used. I'm *tired* of being on the receiving end!"

However, once again, the point is not to "reverse" the situation but to expand our ideas of what physical relations can be; there is no reason to believe that being on the top is always better than being on the bottom for all women. Many women did enjoy the bottom position sometimes, mainly because it is good to just lie with an-other person's body and the bed completely surrounding and enfolding you.

"I like being on the bottom. I feel closer and more connected then."

"I like the bottom. I am shy about being on top, and I miss being held in that position."

"Being on top is most stimulating when I feel there might be a chance of orgasm. On the bottom is most comfortable, cozy, and loving in terms of being freer to embrace."

In the same way, a passionate desire to be "taken" or "possessed" by someone during sex is not automatically a sign of victimization, as long as it is not the only feeling you ever have. The desires to be "taken" or to "possess" someone, to "take" *them*, are merely part of the natural spectrum of feelings that can be experienced by either men or women at times of great intensity.

Intercourse can also become more androgynous.

"I'm inclined, at this point, to try and describe the situation with my current lover. T. is ten years younger than I, and was a virgin when we became lovers. Although I had had a good deal of previous sexual experiences, I can hardly say I taught him all he knew: his openness and wonderful curiosity have taken me into explorations I'd hardly dreamed of, in a forthright and fearless fashion. We've also struggled a lot with the differences between our sexualities, especially men's limited ability to have orgasms. We have evolved a way of making love that accommodates both our needs, or tries to: usually starting with long slow kisses and caresses, than mutual manual and sometimes oral stimulation. As I get more aroused I have a hard time paying attention to what I'm doing to him and eventually stop, letting him work me into several orgasms. Then he enters me—positions vary—and continues to stimulate me for as long as he can. I usually climax several times, sometimes with a frightening emotional intensity. Just before he's going to ejaculate, we switch positions so that he can lie down and I sit on him, penis inside me. I move up and down, my vagina tight around him, and usually insert a finger in his anus and play with his nipples. He gets to be passive, just lies there and *feels* the full intensity of his coming. Yes, it does give me a sense of power, and also a lot of joy in being able to return the pleasure he gives me fullfold. The feelings are very strong and loving. I get a little of the same feeling sticking a finger in his anus—it feels very good to him and I like being able to penetrate him, not having it only go the other way."

"I reached the point several times with both men and women of being very excited when on top, feeling I had, or wanted to have, a penis and penetrate them. Other times I have thought it would be fun to trade bodies with and find out what it feels like for a man to make love. To identify with his penis, and his whole body, and the emotions behind his desire. . . . "

Suppose men won't cooperate in redefining intercourse, or in leaving it out sometimes? What if they still try to follow the same old mechanical pattern of sexual relations? There is no reason why women must help men during intercourse. The fact is, we usually cooperate quite extensively during intercourse in order for the man to be able to orgasm. We move along with his rhythm, keep our legs apart and our bodies in positions that make penetration and thrusting possible, and almost never stop intercourse in midstream unless the man has had his orgasm. We do not *have* to cooperate in these ways with a man if he will not cooperate with us.

Although we do not *have* to, we are taught that if we are anything but helpful (or at least noninterfering) during intercourse, it is tantamount to castrating the man. This is nonsense. Our noncooperation with men in sex is no worse than their noncooperation with us—for example, their using clitoral stimulation as a "foreplay" technique, and withdrawing the stimulation just before orgasm. It is perfectly all right for us to follow the example of one woman who said, "I feel quite confident about ending sexual activity in midstream if it is not working out, or if I begin to drift or feel disinterested." As another woman advised, "Try to get what *you* want and do what *you* feel. (Don't be afraid to act on your most basic, secret, and ultra-secret desires.) If you are not enjoying it in the midst of sex, *say* so. Ladies, you don't have to do anything you don't feel like doing!"

And another women: "I spent most of my adult life doing what I 'ought'—and having an awful time. It was only when I broke out of that, fairly recently, that sex began to mean anything to me, or feel like anything. And I got no help from the popular culture, or from psychoanalysis, or indeed from anything except something a friend chanced to say, and the women's movement. I would advise women to look to their *own* hearts and bodies, and follow them wherever *they* lead."

DO MEN NEED INTERCOURSE?

Before we automatically react to the previous section with: "Well, what about men? Don't they *need* intercourse? Won't less intercourse mean less pleasure for men?"—let's reexamine briefly what little we know about male sexuality. There is no basis for saying that men are getting the greatest pleasure they can get from our current model of physical relations, although they are at least having orgasm. Isn't it possible that male sexuality is capable of more, and more in the way of individual variety, than men's sex magazines would have us believe? Are we sure we know what male sexuality is? Books and articles by men have started to appear that question these old sterotypes, and many men—thought far too few at present—are beginning to take a fresh look at what they are getting out of their sexual relationships.

Rollo May and Marc Feigen Fasteau, among others, have written that they feel men, by concentrating on achieving orgasm and the *satisfaction* of desire, are in a way missing the whole point of sexual pleasure—which is to *prolong* the pleasure and the feeling of desire, to build it higher and higher. This is what women were talking about in the chapter on orgasm when they described the heightened feelings of arousal they felt before orgasm. Rollo May:

> The pleasure in sex is described by Freud and others as the reduction of tension; in eros, on the contrary, we wish not to be released from the excitement but rather to hang onto it, to bask in it, and even to increase it.[1]

If the importance of female orgasm has been underemphasized, to say the very least the importance of male orgasm has been greatly overexaggerated. Although or-

gasm is wonderful, a very large part of the pleasure is
building up to the orgasm, as Fasteau wrote:

> What the masculine disdain for feeling makes it
> hard for men to grasp is that the state of desire . . .
> is one of the best, perhaps *the* best, part of the experi-
> ence of love.²

A woman in this study said something similar to this:
"My sexuality has more to do with the desire than with
satisfaction. I am not interested in 'satisfaction.' I don't
know what it is or why it is considered valuable. I like
to be hungry for a person, to desire intimacy and understanding, to be inspired to be loving and to find reciprocation." The real pleasure of sexual relations, in this
sense, then, is the prolonging and increasing of desire,
not ending it or getting released from it as quickly as
possible.

It was recommended in ancient Sanskirt and Hindu
literature (and was actually practiced in the New York
Oneida Colony, in the nineteenth century) that men
could achieve the greatest pleasure by the continual
maintenance of high levels of arousal, by refraining
from orgasm for long periods of time:

> In this technique it is common for the individual to
> experience as many as a dozen or twenty peaks of re-
> sponse which, while closely approaching the sexual
> climax, deliberately avoid what we should interpret as
> actual orgasm. Persons who practice such techniques
> commonly insist that they experience orgasm at each
> and every peak even though each is held to something
> below full response and . . . ejaculation is avoided.³

This concept is again being tried at present by some
groups of men living in various experimental communi-
ties.

There is no reason why the reintegration of intercourse into the whole spectrum of physical relations
should threaten men. Men too can profit by opening up
and reexaming their conception of what sexuality is.

The association of intercourse with masculinity is at least as much cultural as it is physical, and hopefully male sexuality will also undergo an individualizing and expansive process. Men who would like to contribute their information and feelings by answering the questionnaire for men can write me c/o Box 5282, F.D.R. Post Office, NY, NY 10022.

TOUCHING
IS SEX TOO

Feelings About Physical Closeness

Besides changing the inevitability and manner of intercourse, what other changes did women emphasize they would like to see in physical relations? One of the most basic changes involves valuing touching and closeness just for their own sakes—rather than only as a prelude to intercourse or orgasm.

"In the best of all possible worlds, sex would be a way of being close, of communing with another person. This would not necessarily mean that we would all have sexual experiences with more people or that I, for example, would be running around bedding down with all our male acquaintances. It might even make it possible for me to have the closeness and affection I need *without* having it lead, inevitably, to sexual intercourse. Perhaps if we all had more people we related to with physical affection and touching, we'd have a generally more loving atmosphere in which to dwell; we wouldn't necessarily feel that every contact points in the direction of intercourse . . . a warning and yet somehow commanding finger . . . so that you don't feel free to take Step A unless you are willing to take Step B, C, D, etc."

"Does having good sex have anything to do with having orgasms?"

Women often said, in answer to this and to many other questions, how much more important body contact and closeness were to them than orgasms per se in sex with a partner. This *could* be accepted purely at face value; however, since women do masturbate for orgasms it is clear that orgasms are also very important to

women. The truth is that both orgasms *and* close bo
contact or touching are extremely important
women,* but they have often been forced to get them
separate ways. The important point to realize in readi
the answers below is how important touching and bo
contact are and how undervalued they have been in o
model of physical relations.

"Orgasms are important but being close and loving
as important. My husband, knowing I have multiple
gasms, feels the more I have that the better sex is. Th
is not true—my orgasms are purely physical and can
arrived at without much foreplay. I do not feel it
'making love' just because you have an orgasm. It c
still be just as quick 'screw.'"

"I have intense orgasms during masturbation, but i
tercourse involves a sort of emotional as well as phy
cal satisfaction being with the man I love. Just from t
point of view of having an orgasm, masturbation can
just as satisfying, but the rest of my body isn't alwa
satisfied. I still want the rest of my body to be touch
and kissed and to feel a warm man next to me."

"Closeness with another person is more important
me than orgasm (which I can have by myself, if nece
sary). If I had to *choose* between the two, I'd choo
touching. I really dig kissing, hugging, fondling, looki
at, and feeling the other person. I feel like I'm shari
more if we don't get into genital stimulation, especia
when first getting to know each other, because sexu
arousal and orgasm takes a sort of concentration

---

* (See appendix for statistical breakdown.) Many other a
swers to this question did reflect a militancy about getti
orgasm, not represented in these quotes. For example:
"If I could not orgasm with a partner, I would look f
another. If a woman has *never* had an orgasm, she might thi
she's having good sex without them, but I never could. You
not really experiencing sex without orgasms."
"Having fabulously outrageous sex has to do with havi
orgasms for me. I *can* have a wonderful sexual experien
without orgasm if I am very high emotionally. But sooner
later I feel that I am missing out unless my partner learns
bring me to orgasm."

myself, so I feel more alone when I'm into that—although it can be shared, too."

"Good sex, for me, is much more than genital. It involves two whole bodies and two whole souls, exploring each other, sensitizing and being sensitive to each other, holding, caring for, being gentle with each other, being very aware of each other and working into a oneness that is neither and both persons. Orgasm can be the peak of that process, but it's only one (and not necessarily the best) point in a complex process."

"Too much pressure to have orgasm makes sex goal-and-success-oriented and misses the whole point. Trying to make women have 'just as good orgasms as men' is male-oriented and not the right direction at all. Sex should be sheer luxuriating in pleasure, being close to the other person, enveloped in warmth and touching all over—not a race for orgasm."

"I think the emphasis on orgasm, the separation of orgasm from general sensuality, from warmth and openness and love, is unfortunate. I have the feeling that women's sexuality is emulating the orgasm-oriented, mechanistic male style in this. Good sex, for me at least, has much more to do with a sense of real communication and closeness, and a kind of passionate nuzzling."

"I do think you emphasize orgasm excessively. There is, it seems to me, an erotic continuum, of which orgasm is merely one point, one period, more intense, but qualitatively not different from the experience preceding and following. I often wonder if questionnaires like this and all the how-to-do-it books aren't a bit like the college co-eds who keep their orgasm average. Since it's been proven scientifically that women have orgasms, therefore if you don't have them every minute there's something wrong with you. The kissing, touching, talk, and tenderness that happens when two people like and enjoy each other is much more important than orgasm. The understanding of each other's sensuality and the appreciation of physical togetherness is what sex is. It is a kind of intensified aesthetic experience—experiencing with all of one's senses the complete beauty of another person."

"Do You Enjoy Touching?"

"Touching is the most important part of sex, part of a natural eroticism, being in physical touch with my body and others' bodies."

"Long, gentle passionate encounters, with much touching and enthusiasm, give me a feeling of being loved all over and are all I need most of the time."

"I love making out fully clothed—just kissing and *very* lightly petting—all clothes on and all buttons buttoned, touching and talking. I would rather make out than screw. And it's not the same if it's just a prelude to screwing. A lot of times I screw when I'd rather just make out. I guess I don't think of it as a choice I have."

"General body touching is more important to me than orgasms. A good kiss, to touch each other in the middle of the night, to listen to breathing and heartbeats, smiles, eyes (for sure eyes), the open talks that occur in bed after making love, all of these make sex extra extra special and cannot be filled by masturbation or orgasm. A good hug—an I-love-you-and-always-will-and-care-so-much-for-you-and-here-is-my-heart-and-soul-and-I-am-taking-you hug is worth the world. It is so much more than words. A really good hug will take over an orgasm any day."

"You can't love sex without loving to touch and be touched. It's the very physical closeness of sex that is the main pleasure. With my present lover we spend anywhere from two to six hours caressing, touching, cuddling and hugging, kissing, and just resting against one another. It feels marvelous!"

"I am a snuggler and a toucher. Now that I am single, this has had to be suppressed. I had been in the habit of sitting close, sleeping snuggled up, holding hands. The death of my husband ended that abruptly. But now I try to continue this 'touching pattern' when I get a chance with my lovers."

"Hugging is really important to me. I also like kissing and caressing all parts of the body. I like a lot of eye contact, and I like to be touched on my face and head. It depends on my partner and my mood whether talking is important. I enjoy these activities as much, if not more, than regular genital sex, because it is very communicative, and very personal. I like a man to say my name. I really enjoy just holding each other."

"Best are the long tender hours of stimulating each other and relaxing before orgasm, then starting again, talking, petting. It is extremely important to me to have this much body contact, and I also like sensual touch games—wrestling is great, and dancing nude and sexy, and also just 'immature cuddling.' A previous lover told me I'd taught him lovemaking was seventy-five percent touching and twenty-five percent intercourse."

"I like to neck on the floor, fully clothed, to music— and play silly games pretending this and that, feeling utterly abandoned!"

"There's something very warm and intimate and very beautiful about lying in the dark with someone, holding them close and talking softly. Frankly, I enjoy it more right now than genital sex, but that could be due to my rather limited experience."

"Sex itself is not terribly important to me, but physical contact in the form of touching, hugs, embraces, caresses, etc. is most important. I am more interested in having that kind of physical contact than I am in having sex. Sex doesn't play that big a part in my life. If I have the above-mentioned physical contact with the person and I really like it and the person doing it, then I may have sex—not always, though."

"I like the intimateness of lovemaking almost as much as the sex itself. Hugging and kissing and caressing someone is more loving than sex, and is very important. I also love the way people talk and smile and giggle when they make love. People after sex tend to become very silly, and sharing that is really important to feel loved. If you want a good orgasm, you can masturbate. The whole reason you make love with someone is to share the closeness and warmth of making love, of giving pleasure, of appreciating each other's bodies, of saying things you would never say elsewhere, of being very loving without feeling silly or foolish—anything is okay to say in bed."

"I *do* feel very strongly that keeping in physical, real physical *touch,* flesh to flesh, with another, or with other human beings, is absolutely necessary to keeping healthy: sane. I *know* that for me it is. That's why I do feel that 'there's more to sex than that,' only nobody's found ways (no biological stain, or recording device) yet to *see* what the effects are of sex, mating, fucking touching, all that physical stuff—on the people who do it together. I feel that there may be subtle neural and chemical interactions set in motion in each partner' body by direct physical contact with the other partner.'

The overwhelming number of answers received to this question were just like these; desire for more touch ing and body contact was more or less universal.

Sometimes it has been implied that petting is "imma ture"—something people do only when they aren't able to "go all the way." This is not true. Petting has been a major form of sexuality from time immemorial, but once again, it was condemned in the Judeo-Christian codes unless it was an adjunct to intercourse, and con tinues in this status up to the present.

Other mammals also engage in a lot of petting and "making out," as Kinsey pointed out:

> Among most species of mammals there is, in actual ity, a great deal of sex play which never leads to coi tus. Most mammals, when sexually aroused, crowd to gether and nuzzle and explore with their noses mouths, and feet over each other's bodies. They make lip-to-lip contacts and tongue-to-tongue contacts, and use their mouths to manipulate every part of the com panion's body, including the genitalia. . . . The stu dent of mammalian mating behavior, interested in ob serving coitus in his animal stocks, sometimes may have to wait through hours and days of sex play be fore he has an opportunity to observe actual coitus, if indeed, the animals do not finally separate without ever attempting a genital union.[4]

There is no reason why we should not create as many different degrees and kinds of sex as we want—whether or not they lead to orgasm, and whether or not they are genital. If the definition of sexual pleasure is sustaining desire and building arousal higher and higher—not ending it—many possibilities for physical pleasure and for exciting another person open up. The truth is that "sex" is bigger than orgasm, and involves any kind of deep physical intimacy one shares with another person. Intense physical contact is one of the most satisfying activities possible—in and of itself.

However, in reply to questions about their desire for physical affection and touching, many women said that men usually did not like to touch except during sex.

"Touching is very important, but I don't do it as much at all as I would like. Men never want to touch and kiss without fucking."

"Touching is very important and meaningful, but doesn't happen often because men most generally have but one end in mind when they touch you. Although I have discussed this with my husband, he ignores me. And he insists *he* knows I *really* want 'it.' "

"I really enjoy it, but I find that some men do not understand this and so become aroused and want to have sex. Yet I just wanted closeness and affection. So at times, in order to get this, I have ended up having sex, which is not what I started off wanting."

"I have had sex just to be close and touch a man, but not often any more because I get the orgasm off by myself and the hugging satisfied to a large extent from my daughter."

"Very important. I only wish men could do this without it always and only being a lead-in to sex. I don't think I would feel as used and frustrated all the time if there were any playing around, or signs of affection without it being in bed."

"After sex it is very depressing for me if there is no hugging and kissing. I feel like a discarded shoe. But most men don't like to do this."

"I feel affection is very important. How nice it is to know someone is hugging you, because they really care about you as a person, instead of a cunt. If a partner is not very physically affectionate at times when sex is not involved, I resent being touched later just to prime me for sex. Too many men act this way."

"Extremely important. I love touching, physical demonstrations of affection and all that. Right now I am able to do as much as I like and receive as much too, due to relating exclusively to women. It was difficult to get enough and give enough with men."

"I feel physical affection and touching are much more important than all sex and orgasms, but I am somewhat deprived because my boyfriend feels that a need for such contact involves neurotic insecurity."

"I have become very much aware (since my divorce and subsequent cut-off from easy contact with another person) of the importance to me of touching others. I long to embrace and be embraced; just to stretch out next to a man and feel the contours of his body. I certainly do not do as much of this as I would like to, because it would only be accepted as part of sex and I really am not ready for that yet."

"I crave physical affection. I don't get it at home, and have gone out and taken a lover because he will hug me. I require hugs and in exchange give sex. This is all right with me because I enjoy sex; however, I want to stress that often all I really am seeking is for a man to touch me."

"Touching is as important or more, to me, than having sex, and is my main motivation for sex, with intercourse itself sometimes an unwanted intrusion."

"I used to be starved for physical affection and so got into sexual relationships with men looking not for sexual satisfaction (I could please myself more easily) but for physical contact and tenderness, which is what I want most out of lovemaking. Now I get a great deal of it from my husband, but formerly that was probably about the only reason I went to bed with anyone."

"With my husband, physical touching always leads to sex, which inhibits me from being affectionate when I just feel like cuddling and not making love."

"Physical affection is tremendously important to me. Often I resent the fact that my husband limits most of his kissing to sex-resulting situations. I like being held and kissed spontaneously, and playing around—but he doesn't."

"Physical affection and touching for its own sake is so devalued and devoid in my life I could cry. I don't dare do it without really thinking first, but sometimes I sacrifice myself to a man just to get it."

"Physical affection and touching are extremely important to me, and a large part of the pleasure of sex, as far as I'm concerned. However, this is a part of my marital relationship that is lacking. A caress or a kiss can feel great, but not the dead fish type of kiss that seems to come about after a few years of marriage."

"I have learned within the last few years to be unafraid of open expressions of feelings, including hugging and kissing people of all ages and sexes, whom I feel good with. One of the problems I had when I was married (1938–48) was that touching was only a prelude to sex, and I resented it tremendously."

"*Very.* But touching and holding like I want makes men tire of me. I can never hug or hold onto a man like I want. Sometimes I feel cheap."

"Essential. In the background of my alienation from my husband is his dislike for touching and demonstrativeness in general. He is not able to give affection and touching freely and easily to anyone at all (it isn't just me)."

"I love physical affection and touching but find that this inevitably leads to sexual desire on the part of men. Therefore I refrain from physical affection even with men I like unless I am willing to have intercourse with them."

"I've learned that unless a female wants sex, it is wise not to touch a man *too* much. Most men interpret my caress as sex-inspiring when all I was doing was trying to relax. It pisses me off because most men can't accept it and make me feel like I'm 'leading them on' unless I sleep with them. Phooey."

"I usually don't touch as much as I'd like because girls think I'm queer and guys think I want to be raped. Once I was touching this guy, just to make us both feel good, and he said, 'Why are you making me hot?' and I said, 'Am I?' "

"I like touching very much, but with my husband a touch is all he needs to think it's time to hop into bed. *All* of our marriage (two years) he touches me *all* the time and never gives me a chance to touch him—and then he claims I'm not affectionate. But *his* affectionate moves drown mine! It's all a vicious circle."

"Hugging and kissing are *so* important. Odor is great too. I love to stop and just smell each other. I don't get enough of hugging and kissing though. My lover is a fantastic person, but his level of affection can be very low. He has sometimes rolled over and gone to sleep after we've had sex. I can't blame him, I guess—he's not much good when he's dead tired. I just wish he could hold me while we fell asleep. He will if I ask him, but it won't last for long. Once he's asleep he's untouchable and needs a lot of room. I have very mixed feelings about this. I *need* a lot of hugging and kissing. One time we had sex without kissing each other at all and I felt really terrible."

Lesbian sexuality, as seen in Chapter 5, is quite different and does often involve this kind of extended intimate physical contact. Since one orgasm does not automatically mean the end of sex for most women, whether or not the focus of sex is orgasm, touching and kissing can be continued almost indefinitely.

There were a few exceptional men.

"My long relationship with John had a lot of touching and petting. It was such a super relaxer after my awful job—it connected me with him and humanity again. He would pet me into a blissful haze on many a night. What a doll."

"I've just met a man who loves all kinds of touching—we shower or bathe together, we often sit and simply snuggle, we go to sleep entwined. At odd moments he simply reaches out to take my hand. Sometimes the closeness becomes blissfully erotic and sometimes it's calming beyond belief. His delight in it all tells me volumes about his generous look on life."

In reality, it is likely that men do like physical intimacy and affectionate contact as much as women do, but are afraid to express these feelings.

Not only is touching men outside of sex generally impossible, but touching other women in friendship is not generally acceptable either.

"Sometimes I get so angry at this society for being so cold. There are so many times I would like to kiss a girl friend or hug her or even put my arm around her but I can't because she would be horrified, and think I was a lesbian. Damn, that makes me angry."

"I would like to touch some people, but hesitate because they are aware of my 'sexual preference,' and this makes me and them uncomfortable. It's awfully hard to explain to an old friend that I only want to hug her because she is an old friend and not a potential bed partner."

"I enjoy touching other women, but most of the times you are allowed to do this, like with hello's and good-bye's, the hugs lose most of their sexuality and become just reassuring routines, and as far as I'm concerned don't serve any purpose at all."

"There are occasions I'll look at a friend—someone I've been close to for years—and see them as very beautiful, and I'll wish we could be very close. I've always been too frozen in the safe patterns of friendship to reach out to a friend when I feel sensually and sexually attracted to them. I would like to be able to do this, to see what happens, and take these feelings out of the realm of my mind even if it's only to say to the man or woman, 'You're looking really *good* to me right now!' "

Aside from touching one's partner during sex, it only seems possible to touch children and animals.

"Right now touching is mostly reserved either for parent–baby relationships or sexual relationships. Outside of this it is often construed as sexual even when it isn't. I touch my friends, my dogs, my cats, soft things, myself, and children. Actually, my daughter is about my favorite person to touch."

"Until recently, I satisfied most of my need for touching and physical affection with my young children, including breast feeding."

"I am in conservation service in wildlife and it is amazing how much a homo sapien can relate to other species (all wild) through touch and speech. It means a great deal to me."

"In regards to touching and kissing—I enjoy kissing a cat. It is a pleasant sensation for me to put my lips against a cat's soft warm body. Also, I love to feel the vibrations produced by a cat's purring. Needless to say, this is not sexual—certainly not!"

"I only touched my beloved kittens and cats when I was growing up. People have never measured up since. I love touching children and men I love, and I would doubtless love much more general touching if it were allowed and cultivated."

But even parent–child touching is curtailed, lest there be the slightest "sexual" (genital) overtones!

"My mother and I used to hug a lot when I was young. But as I got older she sort of weaned me away from that, fearing I might turn into a lesbian. As a result, it's just in the last couple of years I am beginning to feel comfortable in kissing or touching relations."

"I sometimes felt that my son derived sexual pleasure from my touching him (say, while giving him a bath). He was about four or five then. It was very confusing and embarrassing to me; I also felt guilty—clearly if I'd been a better mother this wouldn't have happened. I knew that guilt and evasiveness made everything worse, but I simply didn't know how to deal with it."

"Sometimes I feel turned on embracing my little sister, who I'm fond of. Yet I cannot imagine actually 'doing anything' with her—the thought horrifies me. I've heard that one often feels warmth and contentment in a seemingly sexual way because emotion does register in the genital area, as well as actual excitement. But I don't embrace her as often as I would like, since I am afraid it might look funny."

"I touch my children a lot hoping they will grow up more attuned to it. I was raised in the 'cry it out' school of child psychology by a very well-meaning but frustrated mother. Now she touches my kids a lot too."

"Both my sons wanted to sleep with me when they were little, but I never permitted it or had sexual desires toward them. I told them that big boys didn't sleep with their mothers; they had their own beds—but that I was very near and if they needed me for anything, they could call me and I'd come."

"Once in a while I look at my big six-foot fifteen-year-old son, nude—and think—wouldn't it be nice if part of 'parenting' was to teach one's children (male or female) loving sex techniques; instead I bought him *The Joy of Sex,* which he seems to peruse occasionally, as well as *Playboy,* I regret to say. I also used to have sexually stimulated feelings when nursing him and I liked it."

"There was a time (around age nine I'd say) when I liked to play a game with my mother: I was the princess and she was the prince. I would wear a long nightgown, and I wanted my mother to take off her dress—her stockings and garters made her look more 'like a prince' to me. She didn't like the game at all, and would only play it reluctantly, usually not in the 'costume' I wanted."

However, one woman said:

"I think perhaps I have had sexual feelings toward family members but they are hard to acknowledge usually. Like last night when my daughter was cutting my hair and her breasts and body were close to mine— it was a nice feeling—and after she was through with the haircut she bent down and kissed me—this doesn't mean we want to jump into bed together—but I think it is sexual and good and not to be feared."

Most women felt they would like to be much freer to touch others.

"I would just like it to be normal to touch the body, not necessarily to further sexual contact, of anyone I felt close to. Especially I wish I could be more comfortable in touching my friends."

"There are so many people I would like to touch, but being a part of a 'no touch' society, it is either misinterpreted or taboo to touch anyone else in a friendly gesture or even one of deeper commitment. I hate when people pull away from my touch."

"Physical affection and touching are so important it's beyond belief. So many people (including me) are suffering from lack of it that if we could get rid of our social hangup about it, half the psychiatrists in this country would be out of business. But people tend to shy away from you if you touch them anywhere on their body. I think we are becoming a country of 'touch me nots,' lest they feel an emotion arousing in them."

"I think all people of both sexes could use more physical touching and massaging for the sense of real human contact and relaxation that it gives. None of us ever get as much of that as we can use. I don't do as much as I would like because I feel inhibited socially and hold back touching friends, because I do not think they would be accepting. I guess we have all had sex just to be close to someone and be touched when all we ever wanted was to be loved."

"My sexual life is very separate from the rest of my life. I wish I could be more open, loving, and physical with children. Perhaps I wouldn't feel such a strain in my relationship with my husband if I also had some other outlets for the love, openness, joy, and affection I feel and want so much to express."

"Touch brings feelings of warmth, security, comfort, and tenderness. It makes me feel more human, and gives me a sense of kinship, belonging, and acceptance. Besides, it feels good! But where are all these people that let you touch them like that?!!"

"In the best of all possible worlds, what would sexuality be like?"

"Sexuality would become just a simple joy and recognition of one's sexual feelings and from there letting all humans define their sexuality as is most comfortable for them at any given time, in any given situation. 'Sexuality' would become an intergral part of being, greatly varied and personalized, part of life as a *whole*."

"Sex would be more nourishing. Self to self, self to others—lots of warmth and involvement and love and touching on all possible levels as a natural expression of body and emotions. Babies, children, pets, old, young, everyone would be cuddled and fondled, touched and encouraged to do so to and for each other and themselves. There would be public rejoicing in the pleasure of affection and the human body."

What kinds of touching do women like?

Sleeping together.

"My lover and I are very physical with each other although we don't have sex very often. We sleep naked and intertwined together every night, we shower together and kiss and hug, pat and touch, bite, etc. all the time."

"I really like touching, sleeping next to, and waking up the next morning with the person still there. Holding them. I have slept with two of my close friends like this, and it was wonderful."

"Touching is very important. I sleep cuddled up with my best friend and have for six years, although we do not participate in sexual behavior. (That is her decision, not mine.)"

"I love to embrace and touch completely. I love to curl up back to front together in bed. I intensely enjoy sleeping with my little girl, cuddling with her, stroking her back or her mine."

Pressing together.

"Lying pressed together is a wonderful feeling—a kind of body to body embrace. I like to lie in this position, bodies touching all around, kind of mushing."

"My favorite: deep kissing and pressing of bodies together full length with arms holding tight. Opening my whole mouth to the other person and vice versa."

"I get this kind of swelling feeling in my chest, a feeling like I will burst with emotion and feeling—and a desire to press them to me and myself to them so tightly—"

"I love it when my husband presses me up against him *real tight,* squeezing me all against him. I like to wrap him up in my body, bury my nose in him, wrestle, kiss, and fuck."

"Until a few years ago, I experienced desire separate from sexual desire: it was an intolerable buring sensation in my chest rather than in my genitals."

"What is most stimulating to me is the closeness of the entire other person. If I can feel any separateness or separation of us, it reduces the excitement. Pressure is the single most important arousal element—generalized, dull (i.e., not sharp), rhythmic pressure. This gets me really excited, and my nipples, clitoris, and genital area go crazy for it. If it keeps up like that, I will have an orgasm."

"Merely lying on top of a desired person will bring me extremely close to orgasm. The only thing required is body movement."

"I like the total immersion of body and mind—if it were possible for the entire surface of my body to be simultaneously very lightly stroked, slow probing kisses all over, tender yet firm—hugging our bodies together and rubbing."

"I like to get in bed and hold each other, flesh to flesh, warm and tight."

"The embrace, which involves the whole body, is important to me. Having my naked body lying against the naked body of my partner—especially my full front touching my partner's full front."

"Two naked bodies together just feels good—complete head to toe contact!"

"My best sexual experience was a long embrace with a boy my age (age sixteen)—full of warmth. It was not so much sexual as something from a sense of happiness."

"I often feel this urge to squeeze people very hard."

"I'd like to examine another body closely, press it to me maybe, or press myself against it!"

"I think of myself as flat (stretched out) to their flat—front—arms stretched out, spread, pressed flat and symmetrically together—close and kissing."

"I would like to be naked and have my girlfriend naked too. We would face each other and press ourselves against each other."

"Pleasure for me is wanting to give and being hungry to take—kissing, embracing with all of the body, lying on top of, being lain on—occasionally intercourse and cunnilingus. Rejoicing in desire for the other person."

Kissing.

"Tons of kissing is what I relish."

"A lot of kissing and eye-to-eye, face-to-face contact. A lot of stroking, caressing all over—sides, back, stomach, legs, vulva, vagina and clitoris. Verbal communication."

"Kissing is *very* important to me. I can sometimes almost orgasm from kissing."

"Gentle and passionate kissing especially on my neck—ahhhh . . ."

"I could kiss with a good kisser for hours!"

"I love an excellent kisser. It is also important to enjoy it without always having to have intercourse after."

"When my lover hungrily kisses my mouth and eyes and whole body—wow!!"

"I love kissing, especially when some of the fleshy, inside parts of the lips touch."

"We used to walk in the woods together, talk, take off our clothes, and just look at each other. Sometimes we would walk around completely or partly nude. And we would talk and kiss and touch, usually kissing with me kneeling over him and him lying on his back. I loved to watch his mouth, the way it would quiver after each kiss. It almost made me feel dizzy, the feeling was so intense. We used to stay that way and look into one another's eyes for a long time."

"Once my lover said he wanted to spend a whole day doing everything for me that I would normally do for myself—from the minute I got up until the time I went to bed. He started with brushing my teeth and washing my face, then brushing my hair and dressing me. It was so wonderful, I'll never forget it my whole life long. It was the most intimate I've ever been with anybody, and we're still together. We put our fingers and tongues inside every place of the other one's body, and try to be as totally close physically as possible. He is beautiful."

"My best life experiences were sexual, I suppose, erotic experiences; but not genital—most of them an instant of exchanged glances, secret, instant, 'cosmic' understanding, with the few people I have loved. . . . "

APPENDICES

QUESTIONNAIRES: VERSIONS I, II, AND III

The purpose of the questionnaire is to try to understand ourselves better, both collectively and individually. On the one hand, asking yourself these questions is a good way to get further acquainted with your sexual feelings, and on the other hand, it is wonderful to hear what other women are thinking and feeling about the same things—especially since we never talk about them. The results will be published as a general discussion of what was said, with a few statistics, and a lot of quotes, like a giant "rap session" on paper.

The questionnaire is anonymous, so don't sign it: if any questions do not apply to you, just write "nonapplicable." Please use a separate sheet of paper and number your answers accordingly. **Don't feel that you have to answer every single question** (although we would really like it if you did). You can just skip around and answer the ones that interest you—Just let us hear from you!!!*

Questionnaire I

September 1972

NATIONAL ORGANIZATION FOR WOMEN, N.Y.C.
CHAPTER
47 EAST 19 ST., N.Y.C. 10003

1. Is having orgasms important to you, or would you

---

* This introduction or one similar appeared on each questionnaire.

enjoy sex just as much without ever having an orgasm? Is having sex important to you? Why?

2. Could you describe what an orgasm feels like to you?

3. When do you usually have orgasms? During intercourse? Masturbation? Clitoral stimulation? Other sexual activities? How often?

4. Supposing all the psychlological factors were right, what physical stimuli would cause you to have an orgasm?

5. In other words, if "a man has an orgasm when there is up-and-down friction on his penis, a woman has an orgasm when . . . " Fill in the blank.

6. Are your techniques for reaching orgasm the same in intercourse (vaginal penetration) as in masturbation?

7. Please give a graphic description or a drawing of how your body could be best stimulated to orgasm.

8. Do you usually have orgasm during intercourse? Never? Sometimes? Rarely?

9. What positions are best for having orgasm during intercourse? Do you like to be on top or on the bottom, or sideways, backwards, etc.?

10. Do penis size and shape make a difference to you? What shape and size do you find are most compatible with your body—long and fat, short and fat, thin and short, etc.?

11. Describe which techniques of vaginal penetration or intercourse would be most stimulating for you— softer or harder, with pressure to the back or front or neither, complete or partial penetration, etc.

12. Where (at what physical area) does the sensation of orgasm occur when you have it during vaginal penetration?

13. Is it easier for you to have an orgasm when intercourse is not in progress? In other words, do you have orgasms more frequently by more direct stimulation of the clitoral area?

14. Are these orgasms different from orgasms during intercourse? Which is stronger? Which is "better?" How?

15. What positions are best for having an orgasm during this direct (clitoral) stimulation? Does it matter if your legs are together, or can they be apart? Do you move very much, etc.?

16. What kind of stimulation of this general clitoral area do you prefer? Do you like a hard, medium, or soft massage? Do you like rhythmic movements? Do you like the position varied or remaining constant?

17. Please explain ways you and your partner practice this direct stimulation.

18. Do you have orgasms during cunnilingus? Do you have them during oral/clitoral contact or both? Explain how it should be done to suit you.

19. Do you use a vibrator to have orgasms? Where do you use it (what body area)? Is it used by you or your partner? During intercourse?

20. What physical preliminaries are important to you for reaching orgasm?

21. Do you like intercourse? Physically? Psychologically? Why? Do you ever have any physical discomfort?

22. Do you feel free to do all the things you would like, or do you think the other person(s) would be shocked?

23. Do you enjoy masturbation? Physically? Psychologically? Is it more intense with or without a partner?

24. How do you masturbate? Please explain with a drawing or detailed description. For example, what do you use for stimulation—your fingers or hand or a vibrator, etc.? What kinds of motions do you like—circular, patting, up and down, etc.? Do you use two hands, or if not, what do you do with the other hand? Are your legs together or apart? Where do you touch yourself? Etc.

25. What is the sequence of physical events that occurs when you masturbate? For example, one person might put her legs together, then massage the clitoral area with her hand, while pushing the lips together rhythmically between her legs, with the pelvis also moving slightly, etc.

26. Do you enjoy rectal contact? What kind? Do you enjoy penetration? How often are you requested to do this and how often do you do it?

27. What other sexual activities cause you to have orgasm?

28. Is the time of the month important? Do you have intercourse during your period?

29. What do you think about during sex? Do you have fantasies? What about?

30. Are sounds and words important to you? What sex words and phrases and sounds do you find stimulating? Dislike?

31. Does pornography stimulate you? What kinds, what actions?

32. What do you think of sado-masochism (domination-submission)?

33. What would you like to try that you never have? What would you like to do more often? What would you like to see incorporated into the usual bedroom scene? How would you like to see that scene changed?

34. What were your best sex experiences? Please explain.

35. How important are orgasms to you? Do you like them? Do they ever bore you? Is it more fun getting there or having the orgasm?

36. Do you think you look ugly or beautiful when you are having an orgasm?

37. How often do you desire sex? Do you actively seek it?

38. Is one orgasm sexually satisfying to you? If not, how many?

39. Do you go for long periods without sex? Does it bother you? Do you feel you are missing something when you are not sleeping with a partner?

40. If you almost never or never have orgasms, what factors do you think would contribute to your having them?

41. Do you prefer sex with men, women, either, or yourself?

42. Do you think men are uninformed about your sexual desires and your body? Do you think women are?

43. Do you like objects in bed with you? That is, do you like to use objects in lovemaking?

44. Do you ever fake orgasms? How often? Why? Under what conditions?

45. Do you feel you must have a climax to "perform" for your partner, because otherwise you are not normal, not a "real woman"? Do you feel that you should have an orgasm because it would be good for you, or a "fun expereince"?

46. Is having an orgasm somewhat of a concentrated effort?

47. Are you shy about having an orgasm with a partner? Why? With only new partners or with everyone?

48. Do you feel embarrassed asking for clitoral manipulation? Do you feel your partner is sacrificing to give it to you?

49. What is it about sex that gives you the greatest pleasure?

50. Do you feel most men get more pleasure from intercourse than from sexual play? Do you feel guilty about taking time for yourself in sexual play which is perhaps not that stimulating to your partner?

51. Does your partner realize you come when you come? Do you show any particular signs? What are they?

52. Describe how most men have had sex with you (if there are any standard practices, etc.).

53. Please describe how most women have had sex with you.

54. Do(es) your partner(s) masturbate you? Without being asked? For how long? Do they practice cunnilingus? Without being asked?

55. Is there anything, any sexual practice, which you enjoy that you would like to share with or recommend to other women?

56. Do you ever find it necessary to masturbate to achieve orgasm after "making love"?

57. Which would cause you to become more excited, physical teasing or direct genital manipulation? Psychological teasing? Describe how you would like to be teased.

58. Would you free-associate sex with childbearing, going to the bathroom, pleasure, or love? Other?

59. Have your opinions about all of this changed over

a period of time? Do you feel your body responses and interests have changed?

60. Do you feel that having sex is in any way political?

61. Have you read Masters and Johnson's recent scientific studies on human sexual response, or articles discussing their work? What did you think of them? Of Kinsey? Any other writers?

62. What things were not covered in this questionnaire that you wanted to say?

63. How did you like the questionnaire?

Questionnaire II

January 1973

NATIONAL ORGANIZATION FOR WOMEN, N.Y.C. CHAPTER
47 EAST 19 ST., N.Y.C. 10003

1. Is having sex important to you? What part does it play in your life?

2. Do you have orgasms? When do you usually have them? During masturbation? Intercourse? Clitoral stimulation? Other sexual activity? How often?

3. Is having orgasms important to you? Do you like them? Do they ever bore you? Would you enjoy sex just as much without ever having them? Does having good sex have anything to do with having orgasms?

4. If you almost never or never have orgasms, are you interested in having them? Why or why not? If you are interested, what do you think would contribute to your having them? Did you ever have them?

5. Could you describe what an orgasm feels like to you? Where do you feel it, and how does your body feel during orgasm?

6. Is having orgasms somewhat of a concentrated effort? Do you feel one has to learn how to have orgasms?

7. Is one orgasm sexually satisfying to you? If not, how many? How many orgasms are you capable of? How many do you usually want during masturbation? During clitoral stimulation with a partner? During intercourse?

8. Please give a graphic description or drawing of how your body could best be stimulated to orgasm.

9. Do you enjoy arousal? For its own sake—that is, as an extended state of heightened sensitivity not necessarily leading to orgasm? What does it feel like?

10. Do you like to remain in a state of arousal for indefinite or long periods of time? Or do you prefer to have arousal and orgasm in a relatively short period of time?

11. Do you ever go for long periods without sex? (Does this include masturbation or do you have no sex at all?) Does it bother you or do you like it?

12. How often do you desire sex? Do you actively seek it? Is the time of the month important? Do you experience an increase in sexual desire at certain times of the month?

13. Do you enjoy masturbation? Physically? Psychologically? How often? Does it lead to orgasm usually, sometimes, rarely, or never? Is it more intense with someone or alone? How many orgasms do you usually have?

14. What do you think is the importance of masturbation? Did you ever see anyone else masturbating? Can you imagine women you admire masturbating?

15. How do you masturbate? What is the sequence of physical events which occur? Please give a detailed description. For example, what do you use for stim-

ulation—your fingers or hand or a vibrator, etc.? What kinds of motions do you make—circular, patting, up and down, etc.? Do you use two hands, or if not, what do you do with the other hand(s)? Where do you touch yourself? Does it matter if your legs are together or apart? Do you move very much? etc.

16. What positions and movements are best for stimulating yourself clitorally with a partner? Do you have orgasms this way usually, sometimes, rarely, or never? Please explain ways you and your partner(s) practice clitoral stimulation.

17. What other sexual play do you enjoy? Is it important for reaching orgasm? How important is kissing (mouth stimulation), breast stimulation, caressing of hips and thighs, general body touching, etc.?

18. Do you like vaginal penetration/intercourse? Physically? Psychologically? Why? Does it lead to orgasm usually, sometimes, rarely, or never? How long does it take? Do you ever have any physical discomfort? Do you usually have adequate lubrication? Do you ever have a decrease in vaginal—genital feeling the longer intercourse continues?

19. What kinds of movements do you find most stimulating during penetration—soft, hard, pressure to the back or front or neither, complete or partial penetration, etc? Which positions do you find stimulating? Does the size and shape of the penis or penetrating "object" matter to you?

20. Do you have intercourse during your period? Oral sex?

21. Is it easier for you to have an orgasm when intercourse is not in progress? In other words, do you have orgasms more easily by clitoral stimulation than intercourse? Are the orgasms different? How?

22. Do you enjoy cunnilingus? Do you have orgasms during cunnilingus usually, sometimes, rarely, or

never? Do you have them during oral/clitoral or oral/vaginal contact or both? Explain what you like or dislike about it.

23. Do you use a vibrator to have orgasms? What kind of vibrator is it? At which body area(s) do you use it? Do you use it during masturbation or sexual play or intercourse or at other times?

24. Do you enjoy rectal contact? What kind? Rectal penetration?

25. What do you think about during sex? Do you fantasize? What about?

26. Does pornography stimulate you? What kinds? Which actions?

27. What do you think of sado-masochism? Of domination-submission? What do you think is their significance?

28. Do you prefer to do things to others or have things done to you, or neither?

29. Which would cause you to become more excited—physical teasing, direct genital stimulation, or psychological "foreplay"?

30. Who sets the pace and style of sex—you or your partner? Who decides when it's over? What happens if your partner usually wants to have sex more often than you do? What happens if you want to have sex more often than your partner?

31. Do you usually have sex with the people you want to have sex with? Who usually initiates sex or a sexual advance—you or the other person?

32. Describe how most men and women have had sex with you (if there are any patterns, etc.).

33. Do most of your partners seem to be well informed about your sexual desires and your body? Are they sensitive to the stimulation you want? If not, do

you ask for it or act yourself to get it? Is this embarrassing?

34. Do you feel guilty about taking time for yourself in sexual play which may not be specifically stimulating to your partner? Which activities are you including in your answer?

35. Are you shy about having orgasms with a partner? With only new partners or with everyone? Why?

36. Do you think your vagina and genital area are ugly or beautiful? Do you feel that they smell good?

37. Do you ever find it necessary to masturbate to achieve orgasm after "making love"?

38. How long does sex usually last?

39. Do you ever fake orgasms? During which sexual activities? How often? Under what conditions?

40. What would you like to try that you never have? What would you like to do more often? What changes would you like to make in the usual "bedroom" scene?

41. What were your best sex experiences?

42. How old were you when you had your first sexual experiences? With yourself? With another person? What were they? How old were you when you had your first orgasm? During what activity? At what age did you first look carefully at your vagina and genitals?

43. What is it about sex that gives you the greatest pleasure? Displeasure?

44. What can you imagine you would like to do to another person's body? How would you like to relate physically to other bodies?

45. Do you enjoy touching? Whom do you touch—men, women, friends, relatives, children, yourself,

animals, pets, etc? Does this have anything to do
with sex?

46. How important are physical affection and touching
for their own sakes (not leading to sex)? Do you
do as much of them as you would like? Do you
ever have sex with someone mainly to touch and be
touched and be close to them? How often?

47. Do you ever touch someone for purposes of sensual
arousal but not "real" sex? Please explain. (If desired, refer to question #9).

48. Is there a difference between sex and touching? If
so, what is that difference?

49. In the best of all possible worlds, what would sexuality be like?

50. Do you think your age and background make any
difference as far as your sex life is concerned?
What is your age and background—education, upbringing, occupation, race, economic status, etc.?

51. Do you usually prefer sex with men, women, either,
yourself, or not at all? Which have you had experience with and how much?

52. What do you think of the "sexual revolution"?

53. How does or did contraception affect your sexual
life? Which methods have you used? Did you ever
take birth control pills?

54. Do you feel that having sex is in any way political?

55. Have you read Masters and Johnson's recent scientific studies on sexuality? Kinsey's? Others'? What
did you think of them?

56. Please add anything you would like to say that was
not mentioned in this questionnaire.

57. How did you like the questionnaire?

Questionnaire III

June 1973

NATIONAL ORGANIZATION FOR WOMEN, N.Y.C.
CHAPTER
47 EAST 19 ST., N. Y. C. 10003

1. Is having sex important to you? What part does it play in your life, and what does it mean to you?

2. Do you have orgasms? If not, what do you think would contribute to your having them?

3. Is having orgasms important to you? Would you enjoy sex just as much without having them? Does having good sex have anything to do with having orgasms?

4. In most of your sexual encounters, does your orgasm(s) usually occur during cunnilingus, manual clitoral stimulation, intercourse, or other activity? Which of these activities usually lead to orgasm? How often?

5. Could you describe what an orgasm feels like to you during the build-up? Just before the orgasm? During the climax? After?

6. Is having orgasms somewhat of a concentrated effort? Did you have to learn how to have orgasms? Did they become better or easier for you with practice?

7. Is one orgasm sexually satisfying to you? If not, how many? How many orgasms are you capable of, and how many do you usually want during masturbation? Intercourse? Clitoral stimulation with a partner? Cunnilingus?

8. Do your thoughts and emotions affect your desire for orgasms? How?

9. If you are just about to have an orgasm and then don't because of withdrawal of stimulation or some similar reason, do you feel frustrated? How do you feel? When does this tend to happen?

10. How often do you desire sex? Do you actively seek it?

11. How important are physical affection and touching for their own sakes (not leading to orgasm, or even necessarily to sex)? Do you do as much of them as you would like?

12. What do you think is the importance of masturbation? Did you ever see anyone else masturbating? How did they look? Can you imagine women you admire masturbating?

13. Do you enjoy masturbating? Physically? Psychologically? How often? Does it lead to orgasm usually, sometimes, rarely, or never? How long does it take? Do you prefer masturbating or the same activity with a partner?

14. How do you masturbate? Please give a detailed description. For example, what do you use for stimulation—your fingers or hand or a vibrator or sheets, etc.? What kinds of motions do you make— circular or up and down, etc? Where do you touch or rub yourself? Does it matter if your legs are together or apart? Do you move very much? Etc.

15. Do you practice clitoral stimulation with your partner(s)? How? Does it lead to orgasm usually, sometimes, rarely, or never?

16. Do you enjoy cunnilingus (oral sex)? Is it oral— clitoral or oral–vaginal or both? Does it lead to orgasm usually, sometimes, rarely, or never? What do you like or dislike about cunnilingus?

17. Do you like vaginal penetration/intercourse? Physically? Psychologically? Does it lead to orgasm usually, sometimes, rarely, or never? Did you have

to learn to have orgasms during intercourse, or did you always have them?

18. If you have orgasms during vaginal penetration/intercourse, how long does it usually take? Do you prefer the penetrating "object," or penis, to be holding still or moving? Is any accompanying stimulus necessary to reach orgasm? What is it and how do you achieve it?

19. Which kinds of movements do you like to make during penetration to increase your stimulation—soft or hard, pressing to the back or front, using complete or partial penetration, or any other technique? Which positions do you find stimulating? Does the size or shape of the penis or penetrating "object" matter to you? Do you use vaginal or other muscles to help achieve orgasm?

20. Do you ever have any physical discomfort during intercourse? Do you usually have adequate lubrication? Do you sometimes feel less excited the longer intercourse continues?

21. Is the emotional and psychological relationship more important during penetration than other forms of sex? What is your emotional reaction to penetration?

22. Is it easier for you to have an orgasm by clitoral stimulation when intercourse is not in progress? If you had to choose between intercourse and clitoral stimulation by your partner, which would you pick? Why? Do orgasms with penetration feel different from orgasms without penetration? How?

23. How important is what you do to the other person for your own stimulation?

24. Do you fantasize during sex? If so, is it to help bring on an orgasm, or just in general? Exactly what fantasies do you have? What activities are involved?

25. Does erotic art or pornography stimulate you? Which kinds, with what activities? Would you prefer some other kind of erotica than you have seen?

26. Do you ever have a feeling of power during sex? When? How does it feel? Is it exciting or frightening, or what? What are your feelings toward your partner and yourself at such times? Do you ever want to attack or hurt or rape your partner?

27. Do you ever have a feeling of powerlessness or submission, or wanting to be "taken" during sex? When? How does it feel? Do you enjoy it, and what are your feelings at this time?

28. What part do your emotions and relationships play in sex in general? Do you like unemotional, "casual" sexual encounters? Do most of your sexual relationships start out being basically physical or basically emotional? Is it different with men and women?

29. Do you often feel your partner is not emotionally involved during sex? Or, what emotional responses do you most often feel from your partner? Are these usually different with men and with women?

30. What type of person usually attracts you? Are there certain physical or personality traits you often find attractive?

31. What have your deepest relationships been like, with both women and men? How were they satisfying or unsatisfying, both emotionally and physically?

32. Ideally, what kind of relationship would you like to have with a sexual partner?

33. If you have ever experienced something you called "love," which emotions were involved? Was it, or were they, a healthy or unhealthy relationship? How did these relationships affect sex?

34. How often do you desire sex? Do you actively seek it?

35. What is it about sex that gives you the greatest pleasure? Displeasure?

36. Are most of your partners sensitive to the stimulation you want? If not, do you ask for it or act yourself to get it? Is this embarrassing?

37. Do you ever find it necessary to masturbate to achieve orgasm after "making love"?

38. Have you ever been afraid to say "no" to someone for fear of "turning them off"? If so, how did you feel during sex? Afterwards?

39. Do you ever fake orgasms? During which sexual activities? How often? Under what conditions?

40. Do you think your vagina and genital area are ugly or beautiful? What other parts of your body do you like or dislike? Are you comfortable naked with another person? Do you worry about how your body looks?

41. What would you like to try that you never have? What would you like to do more often?

42. Describe how most men and women have had sex with you.

43. How have these experiences influenced your current thinking or sexual behavior? Did you have any one experience which drastically affected your sexual life?

44. How old were you when you had your first sexual experiences? What were they? With yourself? With another person? How old were you when you had your first orgasm? During what activity? At what age did you first look carefully at your vagina and genitals?

45. What is your age and background—occupation, education, upbringing, race? Do you usually live

alone or with someone you have sex with? Where did you obtain the questionnaire?

46. Do you usually prefer sex with men, women, either, yourself, or not at all? Why? Which have you had experience with and how much? Was it mostly long- or short-term relationships?

47. What do you think of the "sexual revolution"?

48. Do you feel that sex is in any way political?

49. Do you think "sex," as we usually define it, is a conditioned response? That is, do we act in ways that, had we not been taught them since childhood, we would not consider "natural"?

50. What changes would you see as leading to a better sexuality or physical expression? In other words, in the best of all possible worlds, what would sexuality be like?

51. Have you read Masters and Johnson's recent studies on sexuality? Kinsey's? Others'? What did you think of them?

52. Please add anything you would like to say that was not mentioned.

53. Why did you answer this questionniare (thank you), and how did you like it?

STATISTICAL BREAKDOWN OF FINDINGS

MASTURBATION

How many women in the study* masturbate

	TOTAL POPULATION	DO MASTURBATE	DIDN'T ANSWER (MAY OR MAY NOT MASTURBATE)	DON'T MASTURBATE
Q.I :	690	562 (81%)	23 (4%)	106 (15%)
Q.II :	919	743 (81%)	31 (3%)	145 (16%)
Q.III:	235	200 (85%)	11 (5%)	24 (10%)
	1844	1505 (82%)	64 (3%)	275 (15%)

* Only replies to questionnaires I, II, and III were analyzed statistically (1844 women total), although quotes from the replies to questionnaire IV are also included in the text, making a total of three thousand women. Questionnaire IV was distributed while tabulation of the results was already in progress. In addition, replies from women who had read *Sexual Honesty* were not included in the statistics, since they might have been influenced by what the other women had said, but quotes from these replies were at times included in the text.

How many women orgasm during masturbation

	DO ORGASM DURING MASTURBATION	DIDN'T ORGASM DURING MASTURBATION	DIDN'T ANSWER IF ORGASM DURING MASTURBATION	TOTAL POPULATION WHO DOES MASTURBATE
Q.I	542	1	19	562
Q.I	714	5	24	743
Q.III	193	2	5	200
totals	1449	8	48	1505

Breakdown of frequency of orgasm during masturbation

	Q.I	Q.II	Q.III
"yes"	298	124	29
always*	79	339	88
usually	143	215	66
sometimes	10	27	8
rarely	2	9	2
	542	714	193

* In Questionnaire I the question was phrased, "Do you usually orgasm during masturbation?" In Questionnaire II the question was worded, "Does masturbation lead to orgasm usually, sometimes, rarely, or never?" In Questionnaire III "always" was added as a choice, since so many women gave this as their answer in Questionnaires I and II.

Percentage who answered "yes," "always," or "usually" to the question, "How often do you orgasm during masturbation?" (see above)

Q.I	530
Q.II	678
Q.III	183

*	1391	96% of women who do orgasm at any time and who do masturbate orgasm regularly during masturbation.

How do you masturbate?

TOTAL POPULA-TION	DID MASTUR-BATE AND DID SAY HOW	DID MASTUR-BATE BUT DIDN'T SAY HOW	DIDN'T ANSWER WHETHER OR NOT THEY MASTUR-BATE	DIDN'T MASTURBATE
1844	1391	114	64	275

Breakdown by Type of Masturbation

Type I : 1015
Type II : 76
Type III : 53
Type IV : 46
Type V : 31
Type VI : 21
Women who masturbate in more than one way : 149

total : 1391

Breakdown of Types

IA : 657   47%
IA$_1$: 67   5%
IA$_2$: 70   5%
IA$_3$: 12   1%
IA$_4$: 11   1%
IA$_5$: 20   1%
IA-direct : 56   4%

893

IB : 96
IB$_1$: 17

IB$_2$	:	8
IB$_5$	:	1
		122

IIA	:	44 (+ 18 in combination with other types)
IIA$_1$	:	4 (+ 2 in combination with other types)
IIA$_2$	:	4 (+ 2 in combination with other types)
IIA$_5$	:	0 (+ 1 in combination with other types)
IIA$_3$	:	1 (+ 3 in combination with other types)
IIA$_4$	:	3 (+ 2 in combination with other types)
IIB	:	15 (+ 8 in combination with other types)
IIB$_1$	:	3 (+ 0)
IIB$_2$	:	2 (+ 1 in combination with other types)
total type II	:	76 (+ 37 in combination with other types)
III	:	40 (+ 28 in combination with other types)
III$_1$	:	6
III$_2$	:	1 (+ 1 in combination with other types)
unusual III	:	6
total type III	:	53 (+ 29 in combination with other types) (includes 11 who also held cloth between their legs simultaneously)
IV	:	36 (+ 20 in combination with other types)
IV$_1$	:	6 (+ 1 in combination with other types)

IV₂	:	4 (+ 1 in combination with other types)

total type IV : 46 (+ 22 in combination with other types)
(includes 25 who held a pillow or towel between their legs simultaneously)

V-tub faucet 17 (+ 33 in combination with other types)

V-shower 6 (+ 9 in combination with other types)

V-shower hose with head removed 1 (+ 2 in combination with other types)

V-tub faucet or shower hose 1 (+ 2 in combination with other types)

V-hose spray attached to tub faucet 3 (+ 6 in combination with other types)

V-exact method not given 3 (+ 1 in combination with other types)

total type V : 31 (+ 53 in combination with other types)

VI : 21 (+ 10 in combination with other types)

total type VI : 21 (+ 10 in combination with other types)
(includes 17 who use clitoral stimulation before entry)

*Combinations of masturbation types (women who ma
turbate in more than one way)*

IA and IB	5	IA_3 and II	2	II and V	
IA and III	10	IA_3 and V	6	II and VI	
IA and II	9	IA_3 and III	2	II and IV	
IA and IV	6	IA_4 and II	1		
IA and V	26	IA_4 and VI	1		
IA and VI	2	IA_5 and III	2		
		IA_5 and IV	2	III and IV	
		IA_5 and VI	1	III and VI	
IA_1 and II	3	IA_5 and II	1	III and V	
IA_1 and IA_4	1	——		III and II	
IA_1 and IB	1		101		
IA_1 and III	1				
IA_1 and V	4				
IA_1 and VI	2	IB and IA_5	1	IA and II and III	
		IB and III	1	IA and II and V	
		IB and IV	3	IA_1 and II and V	
IA_2 and VI	1	IB and V	5	IA and III and IV	
IA_2 and III	2	IB and VI	1	IA and IV and VI	
IA_2 and IV	2	IB and II	2	IA_2 and II and III	
IA_2 and IB	1	IB_2 and III	1	IB and III and VI	
IA_2 and IA_3	1	IB_2 and VI	1	IA_3 and I and V	
IA_2 and II	1	IB_4 and II	1	II and III and V	
IA_2 and V	5	—			
			16		

Total: 149

Breakdown of type of insertion for masturbation type

OBJECT INSERTED

	vibrator	one finger	fingers	"one hand"	wide object	narro objec
A_1 and B_1	10	30	28	10	9	9
A_2 and B_2	11	31	35	16	17	12

MOTION

	in and out	stationary
A_1 and B_1	10	36
A_2 and B_2	41	23

Most finger/fingers fell into the in-and-out category, especially moving in and out near the opening of the vagina, while objects tended to fall into the stationary category. All type III and IV inserts were stationary.

Out of *all* the type I's, figures were:

in-and-out	stationary	occasional entry for lubrication
56	78	22

LEG POSITION

apart: 90   together: 31   slightly apart: 6
apart, then together: 13   together, then apart: 2
alternating: 14

Breakdown of leg position for type II masturbation

legs apart:	17	legs together: 30
legs slightly apart:	5	legs together at orgasm: 4
with a pillow be-tween legs:	7	scissor movement (butterfly): 3

What kind of motion was involved in manual stimulation during masturbation?

Descriptions such as these were given: "My fingers play gently with myself," "I gently squeeze, rub, and pat the area," "I caress myself with a circular, up and down motion, sometimes pulling up toward the navel," "I rub lightly, almost shaking the whole area," "I keep my body fairly still, while I have a gentle and quick massage with a piece of clothing," "I press on the whole area, from clitoris to vagina, with my whole hand, heel on clitoris, fingers near vagina—press and release, press and release," "I rhythmically push some clitoral flesh into the lower fleshy folds of my vulva," "I move my finger on the area just below the clitoris, back and forth, sliding to below the vaginal opening, pausing slightly then back up, then down, etc., pressing in just a little at the lowest point," "I squeeze my clitoris between my labia, pushing the lips together rhythmically, using my fingers in a scissor-like motion," and "I tickle the clitoris softly, then stroke back and forth."

All these motions, though remaining soft and light, became faster, sometimes with pressure slightly increased. Actually, some women believe that speed and circumference of rotation are not as important as the amount and *constancy* (reliability/predictability) of pressure and rhythm. It is true that, basically, any kind of gentle constant motion will enable you to begin feeling the exact spot that is sensitive to stimulation at any given time, and focusing on it.

Then, for orgasm, a very rapid agitation of the area is usually necessary—not large strokes, just rapid, in effect simulating a vibrator as closely as possible:

"I jiggle skin over the whole area with a vibrating motion of my hand and arm."

"I make my whole body vibrate by tensing my arm and moving back and forth as fast as possible."

"At the end, I rub from left to right in one-inch sweeps over my clitoral shaft as fast as possible."

"I just rub the sponge as fast as I can."

"Increasing the tempo, the stroking becomes almost a vibration or rapid agitation."

"Press—exert pressure then release very quickly. The effect is like a vibrator."

Other than fingers, sponges, pieces of clothing or bedding, washclothes and vibrators were used. Another way of making sure the clitoral stimulation is not too direct, sometimes referred to, is using your vulval lips as a covering of flesh for your clitoris—they form a perfect cushion to rub and massage through:

"I usually masturbate by rubbing the folds of skin that cover my clitoris; I don't usually touch my clitoris directly because that's usually uncomfortable."

"My fantasies go to work while I lightly and slowly fondle my clitoris. That is, I don't touch it directly. I cover it with some of the skin around it."

Using the surrounding skin, or labia, or some cloth to

make a sort of covering, pressing the labia against the clitoris, and massaging that way, or putting a piece of soft cloth or a pillow or washcloth between fingers and clitoris can feel good, as can wearing clothes or underpants. One woman said, "Through pants is better because the material spreads the vibrations over a greater area, whereas rubbing the clitoris itself is just annoying."

Of course, types III and IV use no fingers, instead pressing the area against something soft, or between their own inner thighs, but the same kind of focusing of sensation is involved.

ORGASM

Arousal

What did women say when asked, "Do you enjoy arousal? For its own sake—that is, as an extended state of heightened sensitivity not necessarily leading to orgasm?"

Seven hundred and thirty-five women out of 919 in Questionnaire II said they enjoyed arousal; 11 said they did not enjoy it, and 2 said they enjoyed it with a partner but not during masturbation; 15 enjoyed it "sometimes"; 156 did not answer.

But as to whether or not they would enjoy it for its own sake, "not necessarily leading to orgasm," only 266 answered yes, while 260 answered no. Thirty-six said they would enjoy arousal for its own sake "sometimes," and 2 said it had been "okay as a teenager." Ten said orgasm always happened anyway, so that they really weren't able to say. Within the "yes" answers, some said it was okay for a short time, but not a long time, or that if involved in *direct* sexual activities, it was *not* enjoyable without orgasm. Three hundred and forty-five women did not address themselves to this part of the question.

When the same group of 919 women were asked, "Do you like to remain in a state of arousal for indefinite or long periods of time? Or do you prefer to have arousal and orgasm in a relatively short period of time?" the answers were:

349—long amount of time
36—medium amount of time
198—short amount of time
91—variable, depending on partner, mood, and time
13—short amount during masturbation, but long with a partner
35—both ways are good
22—since orgasm did not end arousal or "sex," the question was inappropriate; these women preferred to keep having orgasms every so often, "never really coming down off them."
18—"a few hours of the day in bed"

---

762   (out of 817 women who do orgasm in Q.II)*

* Throughout this appendix, the difference between totals given and the total number of women involved in the study represent the number who did not answer the question, unless otherwise stated.

Replies to this later question contained many complaints that long arousal was impossible with men because they would not leave things at that point for long without going on to intercourse and orgasm. Also, included in the above "long" answers were twenty who said the reason they liked long arousal was that the longer the arousal, the better the orgasm. Six other "longs" mentioned that it was especially enjoyable with a loved one. And two women who answered "short" declared that too long a state of arousal made orgasm impossible.

"When you are about to have an orgasm and then don't because of withdrawal of stimulation or some similar reason, do you feel frustrated? When does this tend to happen?"

39—angry, furious and outraged

      4—terrible
  109—frustrated
      4—tense
      2—incomplete
      6—don't feel frustrated
      6—cheated
      5—let down, disappointed
      5—emotionally hurt and rejected
      3—depressed
      1—resigned
      4—sometimes frustrated
      4—I cry
      2—defeated and cheated, "ripped off"
      1—in pain
    10—never happened

  205   (out of 205 women who do orgasm in Q.III)

It seemed from the reaction to the question that this had happened to most women many times, although many women did not answer the second half of the question, "When does this happen?"

  35—when he comes before I do/during intercourse
        (a few of these mentioned "premature ejacula-
        tion")
  19—phone rings, family interruptions, baby cries
    5—partner is stoned, drunk, or tired
    4—I lose concentration or interest
    2—I'm tired
    3—during intercourse when I am not getting any
        clitoral stimulation
    6—when he changes position
    7—when my partner stops stimulating my clitoris
    1—it never happens any more since I've taken over
        responsibility for my own stimulation
    3—when I don't tell my partner what feels good
    8—with incompetent and inexperienced partners
    8—with an insensitive partner

The seeming discrepancy between most women saying arousal without orgasm is "bad" here, and only approximately half saying "bad" in the preceding section, "Do you like long arousal?", is probably best interpreted to mean most women agree that not having an orgasm when you are on the verge is dreadful, but that just coasting along feeling aroused and sensual is great.

Is one orgasm sexually satisfying to you? If not, how many?

	Q. I	Q. II
yes, one	258	370
1–2	31	52
1–3	12	24
2–3	41	27
2	15	17
2–4		1
2–5	8	2
1–4		4
3–4	24	15
3–5	3	6
1–6	1	6
3–6	3	2
3	9	10
4–5	5	6
6–8	5	1
7–10	4	2
5–6	4	2
6		1
8–10	1	1
2–20		1
18–19		1
15–25		3
one BIG one	12	10
one "vaginal" or several "clitoral"		18
what is important is satisfaction, not numbers		35
one is satisfying but prefer more		36
the limit is fatigue, nothing else	9	4

one "big" one, or several small ones	9	
one is okay sometimes	30	26
multiple	4	6
no, one is not satisfying	24	19
one is okay, but usually have more		11
the more the better (as many as possible)		30

total

513	749
(out of 608 women who do orgasm)	(out of 817 women who do orgasm)

How many women in the study orgasm

TOTAL POPULATION	DO ORGASM	DON'T ORGASM
Q. I : 690	608 (88%)	82 (12%)
Q. II : 919	817 (89%)	102 (11%)
Q. III : 235	205 (87%)	30 (13%)
1844	1630 (88%)	214 (11.6%)

How many women who never orgasm do masturbate? Don't masturbate?

	WOMEN WHO NEVER ORGASM	DO MASTUR-BATE	DON'T MASTUR-BATE	DIDN'T ANSWER
Q. I:	82	36	43	3
Q. II:	102	33	57	12
Q. III:	30	14	8	8
	214	83	108	23

Type of masturbation of women who never orgasm but who do masturbate

IA	37
IA_1	3
IA_2	4
IB	8
IB_1	2
IB_2	1
IA_3	1
IA_4	3
IA_5	1
IIA	1
IIB	1
III	1
IV	1
V	3
VI	12
didn't say how	4
	83

Ages of women in Questionnaires II and III who never orgasm

AGE	NUMBER OF WOMEN	AGE	NUMBER OF WOMEN
18	4	41	0
19	4	42	1
20	6	43	0
21	6	44	2
22	3	45	1
23	6	46	2
24	8	47	2
25	10	48	1
26	2	49	1
27	3	50	2
28	1	51	1
29	3	52	1

30	1	53	3
31	5	54	1
32	4	55	0
33	2	56	1
34	2	57	0
35	6	58	0
36	3	59	0
37	4	60	1
38	0	61	1
39	1	77	1
40	6	total:	112

Phrases most frequently used to describe orgasm

Arousal
  intense tingling
  tickling
  buildup of tension
  pressure
  whole body a delicious aching
  rising from level to level, shifting gears
  filling up, swelling
  rhythmic moving or touching
  gradual buildup of tingling tension, body tenses
  will explode
  heat
  heightened sensuality/sensual ecstasy
  intense buildup (gradual)

Peak
  reach peak
  explode
  sudden
  release of tension
  tense, rigid
  intense electric shock
  can't speak
  pressure, overflow
  body forgotten, only think of genitals
  mainly in genitals but also whole body

Contractions
- rolling pulses
- throbbing
- waves
- spasms
- vaginal contractions
- vibrations
- pulsating
- shuddering
- uterine contractions
- starts in genitals and spreads from feet up
- waves of heat up through body

Aftermath
- relaxation
- alive
- peaceful
- free
- elation
- relief of tension
- euphoria

What is the difference in feeling between orgasm with penetration and without?

Questionnaire I: Are these orgasms (from clitoral stimulation) different from orgasms during intercourse? Which is stronger? Which is "better"? How?

Questionnaire II: Do you have orgasms more easily by clitoral stimulation than intercourse? Are the orgasms different? How? Questionnaire III: Do orgasms with penetration feel different from orgasms without penetration? How?

	Q. I	Q. II	Q. III
clitoral orgasm is stronger	86	4	19
clitoral is better	36	9	
stronger in masturbation	25		
stronger in intercourse	42		
intercourse more intense	8	23	3

clitoral more intense	18	88	30
clitoral more defined	2	1	2
intercourse is better	55	12	
intercourse because muscles hold tight to penis	3	3	11
intercourse is more satisfying, more "complete"	6	19	
clitoral more satisfying	2	5	
clitoral more localized, intense; intercourse more diffused, whole body	21	46	24
vice versa	1	3	
yes, they are different	20	23	10
no difference	42	80	14
intercourse is psychologically/ emotionally better	19	22	14
clitoral is psychologically better		5	
intercourse better because shared	12	8	5
intercourse more internal, deeper, stronger	1	18	
Total	425	351	94

In Questionnaires II and III, only the answers of those women who did orgasm both during intercourse,* and during masturbation and/or clitoral stimulation by a partner were counted.

Comparison of leg position and number of orgasms desired

	Q. I	Q. II	Q. III	TOTAL
Legs together				
one orgasm	58	57	10	125
more	51	68	21	140
Legs apart				
one orgasm	102	110	17	239
more	91	80	44	215

* With or without simultaneous manual clitoral stimulation.

Leg position
    not specified
        one orgasm   80   99   15   194
        more   62   89   36   187

Although these figures are not large (since so many
women did not give their leg position), they do indicate
a tendency for women who prefer their legs together to
desire more orgasms.

*Comparsion between preferred leg position for orgasm,
and whether orgasm is considered stronger with
or without intercourse*

(This chart does not include those who do not have orgasms during intercourse. Questionnaire II and III figures include those
who orgasm via simultaneous manual clitoral stimulation during
intercourse; Questionnaire I give these figures separately.)

	Q. I		Q. II	Q. III	TOTAL
	ORGASM W/SIMUL-TANEOUS MANUAL CLITORAL STIMU-LATION	ORGASM DURING INTER-COURSE			
Legs apart:					
stronger with intercourse	6	11	11	8	= 36
stronger without intercourse	4	30	27	15	= 76
Legs together:					
stronger with intercourse	4	12	3	0	= 19
stronger without intercourse	8	22	23	10	= 63
Leg position not given:					
stronger with intercourse	7	9	15	4	= 35
stronger without					

intercourse	12	25	32	14 = 83
	41	109	111	51

total stronger with intercourse: 90
total stronger without intercourse: 222

Most of the remaining women answered only in psychological terms, the majority saying that intercourse was better emotionally.

INTERCOURSE

Questionable Orgasm Definition Group

In a few cases it was difficult to know with certainty from a woman's answers if she was actually having an orgasm. In most cases, by listening to other answers a decision could be arrived at. However, there were a few women whose answers were unclear, and these answers formed the "questionable orgasm definition" group listed separately in the statistics. Although the answers of this group were followed throughout the analyses of all the questions, it was found in the end that their numbers did not affect any of the over-all results significantly, their answers usually being well distributed throughout the complete range of answers to any given question. They were not listed separately in any of the other chapters, to avoid overcomplicating the figures. They were presented to provide the most complete and detailed breakdown possible. Examples of answers falling into this category are:

"I can have a constant orgasm for as long as he wants me to. He trained me that way."

"When I have an orgasm, I don't completely lose contact with what's happening around me but it's such a total feeling of pleasure. I become very content and receive this desire to be enveloped in something warm. I feel it in the lower part of my body and usually it goes up my back."

"I get *real* wet; my partner can tell, too. Then I start

getting dry and if my partner isn't close to finishing, an artificial lubricant (whether spit or corn oil) *must* be used. Whereas *occasionally* I feel slightly unhappy or cheated after sex, if the above happens I always feel tired, relaxed, content. That's why I figure it's an orgasm. But there's no extra body or emotional feeling when it happens."

"I feel a sense of physical ecstasy, heat, and I tingle all over, especially my toes."

"I feel lost and floating and not in control of myself and slightly delirious."

"Turning inside out of my body, merging with another or my own mind, falling *up*, about to pass out, then release and relief."

"Very sensitive all over, totally shook."

"Feelings vary from gentle floating to complete release from my genitals to my head. It starts in my genitals and streams all over my body. If it's great, it goes up through my head."

"It starts at my toes and sweeps over my body."

"High like floating."

"Orgasms are mind trips with feelings of floating, being separated from all corporal things."

"Other memorable occasions caused a great physical awareness to flood over my body, so that motions became the pleasure. I had a tingling sensation from my toes to my fingertips and a very aroused feeling of lightness and movement."

"I can't answer whether I have orgasms or not. A large part of the problem is semantic—the word is rarely defined and often seems to be an imitation of how men describe orgasms. Maybe I've never had an orgasm. With me it's a gradual sensory buildup that I feel all over. I've never experienced them as 'them's'—there's really no takeoff point or cutoff point. Something like 'total sensory experience' is my best verbal attempt—sorry."

The last quote is reminiscent of a remark Sherfey made:

Many women seem innocently vague and uncertain when we ask them to describe the nature of their sexual sensations, or they sound like a marriage-manual recitation on the nature of the orgasm. One wonders if this well-known difficulty women have in reporting their sexual sensations does not stem from the fact that they deceive themselves and us about the nature of these feelings—because they are afraid that what they *do* feel is not what they *should* feel.[1]

The general criterion adopted for orgasm description in this study was similar to that chosen most frequently by the women in Fisher's study: "Excitement mounts to a high tension followed by sudden release." Indeed, this was the most frequent common denominator of all the descriptions given in this study. It would be interesting to further investigate whether there are any correlations between a woman's description of her orgasm and the type of stimulation she prefers, or the activity during which she orgasms.

In addition, there were a handful of women who referred to orgasm in terms of levitation, rising in the air, or the head being separated from the body:

"It feels like levitation. Waves of heat go up through my body to my head."

"I once thought convulsions and tightenings all over my body were the signs of orgasm. But I was thoroughly shocked once when my head and whole body seemed to be ecstatically removed."

"I feel the top of my head is coming off, and am unaware of what's happening."

"My head is separate from my body, lost to consciousness. It is always diffuse and I am not keenly aware of what my body feels like. Once my lover and I looked deeply into each other's eyes and felt a slow, sweet intense pleasure that was more mental love."

"High up in my vagina, there is a pleasurable sensation which becomes stronger until it is almost unbearable. Suddenly there is a break and the sensation decreases accompanied by contractions which seem to spread all over the body. With this goes a sensation of rising in the air.*

"At orgasm my head separates from my body at a higher elevation."

How was the 30% figure for orgasm from intercourse arrived at?

Women who said they only orgasmed "sometimes" or "rarely" during intercourse were not counted in the final over-all percentage of 30 percent. The "questionable orgasm-definition" population *was* counted. In other words, this percentage is based on all women who answered "yes," "always," or "usually" to the question, including those whose definition of orgasm was questionable.

Since the questionable-definition group contains almost as many women as the "sometimes-rarely" group, the percentage could also be seen as reflecting half of both the "sometimes-rarely" group and the questionable-definition group.

This percentage may be slightly high, due to the inclusion of the questionable-definition group, and also because women are under such great pressure to have orgasm during intercourse, both from others and from themselves, that in cases of doubt they may very well have said yes, not wanting to think too carefully about the possibility of being "frigid." This brings to mind one woman who, worried about not having orgasms during intercourse, discussed the problem with her analyst. He assured her that she could say she had "climaxes" during intercourse, since she did reach a peak of feeling— even though she didn't really "orgasm."

Other women said they had orgasm during intercourse, but meant by "intercourse" *all* the physical activities with another person: "It seems that you take intercourse to mean penis in vagina, wheras I mean by intercourse all that happens from the time we start until the time we're done. So, if that's how you're using it,

---

* This woman was not included in the questionable-definition population.

then I've never had an orgasm strictly through 'intercourse.' I always require some manual stimulation of my clitoris. Whew! Maybe I've been getting my terminology confused for a long time, but by your usage, I guess I've never had an orgasm during intercourse except by the incidental manual stimulation."

In conclusion, all of these factors may have slightly inflated the percentage arrived at in this chapter.

Frequency of orgasm from intercourse

	Q. I	Q. II	Q. III
"Yes"	30	47	5
(questionable definition)	18	16	7
Always	17	15	2
q.d.	14	11	1
Usually	81	88	23
q.d.	40	55	17
Sometimes	65	86	27
q.d.	15	26	3
Rarely	29	54	16
q.d.	0	6	1
	222+87 (q.d.)	290+114 (q.d.)	78+29 (q.d.)

Do you ever have any physical discomfort during intercourse?

	Q. I	Q. II	Q. III
Yes	19	48	13
(no orgasm during intercourse)	8	45	28
Sometimes	73	69	12
(no orgasm during intercourse)	17	46	22
No	115	97	25
(no orgasm during intercourse)	26	48	44
Yes if: too long or too frequent	22	4	2

(no orgasm during intercourse)	8	2	1
not arroused/no lubrication	46	5	6
(no orgasm during intercourse)	13	2	13
thrusts too deep	29	6	3
(no orgasm during intercourse)	7	7	3
always with the first few thrusts	6	9	0
(no orgasm during intercourse)	1	9	2
too large penis	24	10	5
(no orgasm during intercourse)	10	2	3
yes, due to yeast infection	12	8	4
(no orgasm during intercourse)	4	3	1
	440	420	187

"If the man is larger than average, there is some pain—sometimes too much to have orgasm, and I spend all my time trying to keep him from penetrating too deeply."

"I avoid positions that allow his penis to hit my uterus (like being on the bottom with my legs up). In other positions I can avoid his penis hitting my uterus by tightening the muscles in my vagina or by shifting my hips."

"I think my cervix is in an unnatural position because I often experience a sharp pain when the penis is thrust in me at certain angles. I can usually lie in a position that enables painless penetration."

"Occasionally I have a sharp pain with deep penetration. At one time I bled profusely after rough intercourse. Had a minor operation that ended the problem. My uterus is tipped backwards and my doctor attributes the discomfort to this. Sometimes discomfort is due to my diaphragm."

"Sometimes it hurts when he gets carried away with deep hard thrusts when he comes. I get a stomach ache, feel battered, and urination becomes painful."

"Sometimes it feels as though the man's penis is poking too hard against another more sensitive internal organ. It gives me a sharp pain."

"I'm easily hurt by too deep penetration or too vigorous thrusting, but adjusting my position to limit penetration usually takes care of it."

"The discomfort I experience during intercourse is because I have an extremely retroflexed uterus that gets 'banged' into sometimes, which hurts."

"Wow, I'm really glad to see this question. I thought I was weird like that—yeah, sometimes I sure do get sore, although my partner can't believe it. I don't know why. I used to think we didn't 'do it right' but after a few other guys that doesn't seem possible."

"I love intercourse, but I've had a lot of pain in the past, especially when I had severe vaginal infections where I thought I'd die from the pain. After the infection was supposedly cleared up, I probably carried psychological thoughts of the pain with me and that made it linger on. Nowadays I never have pain except if I'm dry (unusual) or the guy lasts longer than fifteen minutes—in which case I tend to swell up quite a bit and have trouble sitting down."

"When I have a fungus it causes burning especially after intercourse. I have also heard that the pill can make intercourse painful—more burning. But then the pill also makes you more prone to fungus. Maybe they're connected."

"Sometimes the first penetration hurts because some men don't realize the importance of going in slowly. Also, sometimes an IUD can get poked the wrong way."

"During penetration, I seem to wait, expecting pain. Then when I find it's in and okay, I relax."

"Sometimes it burns if my pubic hair is pulled by my being dry, or him being large, or penetration too sudden or deep. It hurts in another way not to come after a long time, with aching and tightness."

"The only time it is uncomfortable is when I am not ready for it and that is simply rape. If fucking is uncomfortable, then it is just that. That's when it's time to resort to some other kind of negotiation, and maybe that should involve, just possibly, parting the bastard's hair with a frying pan. Think about it."

Of women who don't masturbate, how many do and do not orgasm during intercourse?
(not including women who never orgasm in any way)

	DON'T MASTUR-BATE	HAD NOT HAD INTER-COURSE	DON'T ORGASM DURING INTER-COURSE	DO ORGASM DURING INTER-COURSE (REGU-LARLY)	SOME-TIMES, RARE-LY	UN-CLEAR HOW OF-TEN	ONLY WITH SIMUL-TAN-EOUS MAN-UAL CLI-TORAL STIMU-LATION
Q. I :	67 =	1	7	23	15	12	9
Q. II :	87 =	6	16	27	14	12	12
Q. III:	13 =	1	4	1	4	0	3
	167 =	8	27	51	33	24	24

Of those who orgasmed regularly during intercourse, by what method did they do it? (The second number given refers to women in the "questionable-orgasm definition" group.) Since this question was not specifically asked in the questionnaires, some women did not give this information.

	"YES"	"ALWAYS"	"US-UALLY"
Questionnaire I:			
1. Did not describe how	9–12	7– 9	36–27
2. Woman on top	8– 5	6– 3	16– 2
3. Grinding of pubic areas together	1– 0	1– 0	6– 0
4. Touching of pubic bones together during inter-course	8– 0	0– 1	11– 2
5. Partial holding of the			

penis inside the vagina,
allowing clitoral contact

6. Frequent re-entry of the
penis into the vagina,
stimulating the lips   1– 0   3– 0

7. After the first orgasm, one
of the methods listed here
is possible   0– 2

8. Extended "be-fore play"   3– 1   2– 0   6– 5

9. With one partner only;
no explanation   1– 1   2– 0

                              30–18   17–14   81–38

Questionnaire II:

1.	18–14	8– 7	40–40
2.	13– 1	3– 2	20– 7
3.	1– 0		3– 1
4.	6– 0	0– 1	11– 0
5.	1– 0		1– 0
6.		3– 0	1– 0
7.	2– 0	1– 0	1– 1
8.	2– 0		9– 5
9.	2– 1	2– 1	1– 0
	45–16	17–11	87–54

Questionnaire III:

1.	2– 6	1– 1	10–13
2.			4– 1
3.			1– 0
4.	2– 1		2– 2
5.			3– 0
6.			
7.			
8.		1– 0	3– 0
9.		1– 1	0– 1
	4– 7	3– 2	23–17

Frequency of orgasm during intercourse by simultaneous manual clitoral stimulation

	Q.I	Q.II	Q.III
"Yes"	25	67	20
"Always"	11	5	3
"Usually"	33	42	12
"Sometimes"	24	9	5
"Rarely"	10	10	3
	103	133	43 = 15% of total population

CLITORAL STIMULATION

Other types of stimulation to orgasm

	Q. I	Q. II	Q. III
tribadism	15	28	4
penis stimulation of clitoris	54	46	
leg or body stimulation of clitoris	11	42	
other types:			
dreams	21	14	
breast stimulation	18	9	7
nursing	1		
mental stimulation (fantasies, etc., usually during other activities)	19	2	
horseback riding	3		
dancing	1		

Do you enjoy rectal contact? What kind?

	Q. I	Q. II
Yes	211	230
Sometimes	58	78
No	268	363
Don't know	80	106

Type enjoyed, of those who answered yes or sometimes

Touching	63	142
Penetration by penis	83	63
Penetration by finger	77	70

Do you think your vagina and genital area are ugly or beautiful?

	Q. II	Q. III
Beautiful, I like them	245	71
Fascinating	23	8
Ugly	116	28
Average/Okay	90	24
Neither: neutral	192	30
Part of the whole, natural, functional and utilitarian	53	18
Varies, mixed feelings	17	4
Strange	8	5
	744	188

Do they smell good or bad? (Q. II)

good	206	neither	8
great	18	bad	114
good if clean	141	sometimes good, sometimes bad	62
okay	75		
earthy	5	funky	2
interesting	8	bad after intercourse	7
unusual	10	bad with discharge	2
sexy	25	odor with fungus	19
natural	21	yummy	4
exciting and stimulating	16		
desirable	1	Total	744

Are men uninformed about your sexual desires and your body? (Q. I)

yes	334
no	87
varies	49
men are not uninformed, they just don't care	10
I inform them	35
in general most men are uninformed, but my partner is informed	71
	586

SEXUAL SLAVERY

"Do you like vaginal penetration/intercourse?"

	Q. I	Q. II	Q. III
Yes	539	693	186
It's okay	12	23	6
Sometimes	21	38	8
Depends on the partner	18	13	6
No	27	41	6
Total	617	808	212

Since it has become general knowledge that the interior walls of the vagina are more or less insensitive physically, some sex researchers now talk about "proprioceptive feeling"—the sensations caused by the distention of the vagina by the penis rather than friction on the vaginal lining itself. Only a few women mentioned feelings that might come under this heading—that is, pleasurable *physical* feelings not connected to orgasm:

"Just the feeling of having a penis in my vagina can feel good, and has nothing to do with having an orgasm. It just satisfies a need to be touched internally."

"I like vaginal penetration both physically and psychologically. Physically, it feels good to have the whole area moved around the way penetration does. It feels 'full.' That's probably psychological. Anyway, I like it a lot."

"I like being filled up. Love to eat. Before I stopped, I used to smoke and fill my lungs and found it very satisfying. Being penetrated is a nice feeling, not necessarily even sexual!"

"Physically it feels good to have the whole vaginal-clitoral area moved around the way penetration does—it feels full."

"Intercourse has never led to orgasm but I enjoy the bulk and the movements inside of me, and the enveloping feeling."

"Yes, it feels close and I feel filled, supported and moved about by the genital region. I think it derives from being lifted and carried as a baby. Horseback riding is also good this way."

There were several reasons given by those women who didn't like intercourse.

"I don't enjoy intercourse because it's a bore and I never come."

"Penetration is frustrating and boring because it doesn't excite me. Also I do not like being laid, come in, getting slightly excited and then being deserted."

"Having a sweaty jumpy body on top of me is physically uncomfortable."

"I like intercourse when it feels good physically—which is only during the first penetration. After that it gets boring and pointless, and feels like you're being pounded."

"Intercourse is the least pleasurable to me of all the sex acts, particularly if it lasts too long. I don't find it repulsive or painful, just fatiguing and boring."

"Physically it is slightly pleasant, but boring, as it takes so long and never brings me to orgasm."

"Not really—because it's dreary and boring. There was a time when I did it a lot, hoping it would get better. It's okay, but I feel there must be something more."

"It's great with a musical and sensitive person—like dancing. But most often I find it boring and psychologically oppressive."

"Physically, I can take it or leave it. Psychologically, it's pleasant but not necessary—except for him. Penetration itself never leads to orgasm for me. I find that penetration has the effect of separating my partner from me. It becomes an act unto itself, and its necessarily increased motion (thrusting, etc.) is all well and good if it helps him, but it strikes me as unconnected with any concept of 'love' and therefore inappropriate and humorous. I don't get the suggestion of brutality or selfishness on his part—it's just that all that bouncy activity strikes me more as genital gymnastics or as 'making sex' than as 'making love.' It's close to masturbation in communication value—you wind up talking to yourself."

"It's grossly built up into something it's not. It's just a thing you have to do because guys expect it. You really have to talk to yourself into it."

"Physically it doesn't matter unless it's too rough or painful. Psychologically, I hate it. I didn't always. But now I feel assaulted, skewered, and I feel like the penis is a club or blunt instrument."

"Intercourse has always felt like rape to me, for a host of reasons: like, my partner is insensitive to my feelings, my partner is coercive, he does not treat me as an equal, he treats me like an object, and I could go on . . . "

"As of late, I just feel used and abused, and can't help having the feeling that he uses me because I'm convenient and won't say no. Of course even if I do say no, it doesn't matter and we do it anyway."

Other women had more mixed feelings.

"Not as much as I used to—I learned that it wasn't as much as I once thought it would be, and I don't need it to have an orgasm. Once in a while it feels sort of nice. I like to hold someone I care for closely."

"I don't miss it when I don't have it. Sometimes I enjoy it while it's happening. Usually during intercourse

I think about whether I am, in reality, aroused, or am I pretending and just caught up in the movements and making the man believe I am truly enjoying it?"

"I've only had intercourse ten times in the last year and a half. My favorite time is immediately after my orgasm because it feels good that way. It's not something I think of as the only way to have sex with a man . . . it's sort of something I do when I'm too lazy to satisfy a male partner. I guess I like it sometimes but not as something important in lovemaking."

"I like intercourse: it's a moving experience to be naked and together and warm and moving together— unique and tender. But sometimes I'm not in the mood, and I get tired of having to go wash my vagina (otherwise it sticks together) and sometimes I'm swollen."

"I like the moment of penetration, but intercourse is often disappointing. As things stand, I prefer having my back tickled to having intercourse, but so far I haven't said this to a man."

"So far I haven't enjoyed it, per se, all that much— maybe because it hasn't been with the right person. I really prefer the warm affectionate touching, feeling, kissing, and being together, and hugging."

"I like the moment of penetration, sometimes best of all (and I've had male partners who agree with me). But the pain and discomfort of having my legs spread so far apart and a heavy body on top are distracting, and I find it hard to concentrate on the build-up of sexual feeling under those circumstances. I enjoy the feeling anyway, for a while, and I like to feel that the man is experiencing deep pleasure. If I really love him, I don't feel any resentment even if I'm uncomfortable; in fact his ecstasy is arousing to me. Sometimes the feeling comes and goes in 'spurts,' so that I vacillate between arousal and pain (and boredom) until either he comes or I come or (five times in my life) we both come at the same time."

"How I feel about it is inseparable from my mood and attitudes about my husband. I resent being used as a security blanket, i.e., when under tension, he increases his sexual demands for intercourse. I can only enjoy intercourse if I feel good about our relationship at the moment."

"Intercourse with a man without orgasms for this woman falls into one or another of the following categories . . . an accomodation of his needs experience, a nurturing parenting type thing, plain submission, a martyrdom or self-hate thing, or an extreme loneliness and just glad-for-the-company type thing."

"It's physically okay—rarely exciting, usually boring. Psychologically the most I get out of it is pleasing someone else. I love feeling close to someone but you don't need a penis to feel close!"

Some women didn't like intercourse for the reason mentioned earlier that watching the man have an orgasm when you don't can be maddening.

"My husband is brash and too fast for me. I require direct stimulation, and feeling loved, which he usually doesn't give me, to have an orgasm. I'm usually not enjoying intercourse, although I pretend to. God! If he only knew!"

"I don't like intercourse so much because men get so aggressive and intense then, and I need slower gentler movements to have an orgasm."

"Usually I like intercourse, but sometimes I feel it isn't fair I don't experience orgasm too and so when I am penetrated I tense up and it isn't enjoyable. Men expect intercourse to satisfy me, and just refuse to understand that it doesn't."

"I could live without intercourse. If we are having sex, and by the time of intercourse I have not had an orgasm, I feel like it's all over, that my stimulation is now ended. I feel disappointment and anger maybe sometimes that I have to do it. Pissed off."

"I only like intercourse after I have orgasmed through another method, so I know that the anxiety about orgasm will not be there."

"I wish I had orgasms during intercourse. When I have had them during intercourse (rarely) it has made intercourse more satisfying. When I don't, it seems unbalanced—like the man got more pleasure out of it than I did. Also, I've been conditioned to think it's more 'normal' during intercourse."

"I feel psychological ambivalent about intercourse. Sometimes I feel good about myself, I feel I've willingly chosen it as a means of mutual pleasure. Other times I feel my pleasure is not important to my partner, that I'm merely a receptacle, and that virtually anyone or anything could be equally satisfying to him."

"It depends on the other person. The kind that just want their own release and don't give me enough time—I am usually thinking about that, and how I am aware that I am just beginning to relax or something and they are panting away and all done, ready to go to sleep—then I think about how it wasn't even worth getting into and starting myself up just to be frustrated cause I usually don't dig that faking . . . if they live with me I could cry, silently, later cause I love them so much and they don't know how to appreciate me so I can give them more of my love and they're cheating themselves and I think about whether this can go on or how I can resolve it."

"I have made it my motto for the past year that no man will lie back relaxed after intercourse if I haven't come. Why should he come if I don't? Equal orgasms!!"

THE SEXUAL REVOLUTION

How often do you desire sex?

	Q. I	Q. II
More than once a day	72	64
Daily	124	139
One–two times per week	80	122
Two–three times per week	84	128
Three–five times per week	106	105
"Often"	44	43
One–two times per month	20	19
Three–four times per month	4	7
Varies	32	80
Infrequently	13	13
Never	3	9
Total	582	727

In fact, the figures for "How often do you desire sex?" are somewhat misleading, in that they were usually given by the women as averages, with the complete answers indicating a much more sporadic interest in sex.

For the majority of women, the desire for sex fluctuated according to desire for a certain person.

"How much sex I want really depends on the partner—the more attracted I am, the more I want. When I am interested in someone, several times a week is good. But since I don't have someone around permanently, sex usually consists of making love two or three times each night when I am with someone, and then doing without for days."

"I rarely desire sex without desiring some one person in particular. My husband has refused me so many times that I now get nothing out of sex with him and do not really desire it. But during the six months when I had a lover, I desired him at least one time every day."

"I only want sex if I am deeply attracted to another person, for the most part. For example, I used to want sex two or three times a week when my marriage was good, but then I lost interest as we grew apart. Now, with my current lover, I want it constantly again—just the sound of his beautiful voice turns me on."

"When I love someone very much, my desire is high every day, sometimes days and nights on end. It's like craving physical closeness, out of which sexual desire emerges."

"The sexual passion between my husband and myself has fluctuated greatly. The early feelings I had for him (rushes of emotional and sexual feelings) are much less frequent now, but I am much more sexually satisfied than I was three or four years ago. It seems like when you get to know a person, that special excitement dies down after a while—but it doesn't mean that I don't love him as much; I love him *more*."

"In a long relationship, my interest in sex settles down to about two times a week. But in a new relationship, I want it daily at least. And some people make me more horny than others. On the other hand, when I'm alone, I almost forget about sex. Intense sexual activity, followed by periods of near celibacy, has been my pattern for so long I no longer know if it's imposed or chosen."

Some women mentioned that unhappy experiences or periods of depression can cut down or end entirely their interest in sex.

"I usually want it all the time, until I have it with someone who ends up fucking me over."

"If I am troubled, I have no, or very little, desire for sex. After the death of my son, two and a half years ago, I lost all desire for almost two years. I did not even wish to masturbate, and may have had three 'wet dreams' during these two years. Under normal conditions, I find I am stimulated by my partner if I feel affecionate toward him, and if he is 'giving' to me in other ways."

"The better I feel about myself and my life, the better my sexual activity. When I am depressed I have less or no desire. Also, I have discovered myself feeling sexy after a big fight with my husband where I have strongly asserted myself."

Other women feel that sex is addictive: the more you have it, the more you want it, and the less you have it, the less you want it.

"My sexual desire seems to decrease without heavy sexual activity. Going without only bothers me after I've just had it and my body and emotions are used to sex and affection."

"If I go without sex for one month, then going six months is easy."

"After the initial month or two, I got used to not having sex and didn't miss it."

"Soon after my ex-lover and I split up, I ached for it, but as the separation became wider the aches became less."

"It is definitely habit-forming for me. Right now, since I haven't had it in so long, I don't desire it quite so much."

"Although I'm glad to have discovered my own sexuality and it is important to me, if I had to I think I could live very happily without sex, as I did for many years. I think if you have it, you want it regularly; if you don't have it regularly, the need decreases. Right now I am off cigarettes; I hope I shall never smoke another cigarette again in my life; I know that in some ways I shall always desire to smoke a cigarette, but it is not an all-consuming need for me now because I haven't had one for three years. I think people's need for sex is very similar, except of course there is no reason for people to have to go off the joy of sex."

Quite a few women didn't know for sure how often they would want it, since they were having it more often than they wanted.

"I want it one or two times a week, I think, but I have it five or six times a week. I think I'd enjoy it more if I had it less."

"We usually have sex about four or five times a month. Of course, being married and having access to sex any time, or giving it to him any time he wants it, I don't know how I would be if I could set my own desires."

"I really can't say. I can say that I have sex a lot when I don't desire it, due to my partner's desires."

"Before I was married I thought it was wrong for a girl to have any big desire for sex. I never did have any big desire for it. Occasionally I felt like masturbating. Now my husband wants sex so often that I haven't had any big length of time to build up a big desire for it."

Is the time of the month important? Do you notice an increase in sexual desire at certain times of the month?
(Questionnaire I)

Yes, before and during menstruation	320
During and after menstruation	24
After menstruation	30
During ovulation	62
"Yes" (did not say when)	99
Total	571

It is interesting to notice that women are generally more interested in sex during times of the month when they are not fertile. This agrees with findings of other sex researchers. Kinsey found that approximately 90 percent of his sample preferred sex during the pre-menstrual phase, and Masters and Johnson have shown that women produce more lubrication at this time.

TOWARD A NEW FEMALE SEXUALITY

What is it about sex that gives you the greatest pleasure?

	Q. I	Q. III
Orgasm	71	42
Touching, sensuality, body contact	60	43
Emotional intimacy, tenderness, a closeness, sharing deep feelings with a loved one	86	47
Pleasing him/giving	37	7
A partner I like	13	2
Giving and receiving pleasure	13	8
His orgasm	16	2
Intercourse	17	5
Clitoral massages	5	2
Good cunnilingus	8	3
Foreplay	13	2
The sexiness of it	14	
Release and relaxation	15	
Intercourse with a loved one	6	
The "entry," penetration	12	1
Fellatio	4	
Being together after; the feeling after	13	1
General good feelings	5	3
The excitement just before orgasm—the passion and losing control	19	4
Fantastic physical sensations	5	4
	432*	176

* 103 women in Questionnaire I were not asked this question, due to substitution of an alternate question.

The greatest displeasure?

Sexist men who demand to get laid, don't respect you, etc.; power trips, used as a sex object, conquered, exploitative sex	18
Insensitive partner	5
Selfish partner	7
Harsh and rough or abrupt treatment	3
Neurotic partner	3
Casual sex with no emotions, impersonal sex	8
No orgasm	12
Lack of passion, sex with no arousal	7
Not being into it but trapped anyway	7
(Marital) duty	3
Any form of forcing	1
Messiness after: changing sheets, diaphragm or condom, etc.	4
Only having intercourse	4
No displeasure	14
Vaginal infections	1
Jealousy	1
Penetration when not ready	1
Pain from sudden thrusting in intercourse	2
Exhaustion	2
Lack of feeling	1
Anal sex	1
Fellatio	1
No after-time together	1
Total	107

"Is having orgasms important to you?" (Most women answered this question in terms of sex with a partner.)

Q. I

26—I would not enjoy sex without orgasm; I would feel frustrated.

157—I would not enjoy sex *as much* without orgasm.

115—Sex is okay *sometimes* without orgasm.

31—Orgasm is important but I can enjoy sex without it.

4—Orgasm is important, but over-all pleasure is more important (like kissing, talking, and tenderness).

7—Orgasm is important but not always with one you love.

16—It depends on mood, partner, degree of arousal, etc.

43—Orgasm is not important; I would enjoy sex as much without it as long as there is closeness and a feeling of oneness.

15—Orgasm is not necessary, but it is pleasant.

203—Yes, orgasms are important.

---

617   Total

"How important are orgasms to you?"

Q. I

473—Very important

24—Not always necessary

8—Not important

4—Okay

33—Not really important

---

542   Total

"Is having orgasms important to you? Would you enjoy sex just as much without ever having them? Does having good sex have anything to do with having orgasms?" (answered as one question):

Q.II	Q.III	
9		Having orgasms is not important.
71	4	Having orgasms is important.
152	45	Orgasm is important, but sex is sometimes okay without.
13		Yes, but closeness is more important.
14	6	Orgasm is not necessary but pleasant.
325	54	I would not enjoy sex as much; good sex involves orgasm.
60	29	I would not enjoy sex without orgasm.
15	7	It depends on the mood, partner, etc.; sometimes closeness is enough.
16		Sex can be okay without orgasm, but orgasm is necessary for good sex.
50	23	Sex is only okay without orgasm if there is love and affection, emotion, and tenderness present.
9	33	Good sex leads to orgasm.
26	21	Orgasm is important, but not all there is to good sex, which involves affection, love, and sharing.
51	13	Sex is fine with no orgasm; good sex has nothing to do with orgasm.
811	235	

QUESTIONNAIRE FOR WOMEN
WHO READ THIS BOOK

This questionnaire is anonymous, so do not sign it. Please use as much extra paper as you need, or answer on a tape cassette. Don't feel that you have to answer every single question; you can skip around and answer those that interest you the most. If you begin your reply, but do not complete it due to lack of time, please send it in anyway. Just let us hear from you!

Please mail answers to Shere Hite, c/o Hite Research, P.O. Box 5282, F.D.R. Station, New York, New York 10021.

1. Have you read *The Hite Report*? Which issues or chapters do you most agree with? Disagree? Which parts were most important for you? Least? Most emotional?

2. Has your sexuality changed very much in the last few years? In what way? What were the reasons?

3. Which is the easiest way for you to orgasm: Through masturbation? Clitoral stimulation from

your partner? By hand? By cunnilingus? Through intercourse/coitus? With a vibrator?

4. Do you orgasm from intercourse/coitus? If so, exactly how do you do it?
   (a) By added clitoral stimulation from your partner? Please explain.
   (b) By your own clitoral stimulation/masturbation during intercourse?
   (c) By rubbing of pubic bones together?
   (d) Other? (Please describe.)

5. When did you first orgasm:
   (a) During masturbation? (Did you discover it on your own, or did you read about it? How did you feel? Did your mother or family know about it? Your friends?)
   (b) With a partner? (How did it first happen [During which activity]? How long had you been having a sex life apart from masturbation?)

6. Have you told a man you do not (if you don't) orgasm from intercourse? What did he say? Did you tell him most women don't? How did you feel?

7. Have you masturbated with a partner? During intercourse? During general caressing? Was it hard to do the first time? How did you feel about it? What was his/her reaction?

8. Have you told another woman you don't orgasm from intercourse? Explained your sex life to her? What did you say? How did she react?

9. Have you talked with other women or your mother, sisters, or daughters about some of the issues in *The Hite Report*? Do they know if you masturbate? Do you know if they do? What else have you talked about? What would you like to talk about?

WHO ARE YOU?

10. Who are you? What is your own description of yourself?

11. Are you in love?

12. Are you happy?

13. What makes you happiest in your life? Your work? Your love relationship? A hobby or side career? Music? Going places (travel, concerts, or dinner with friends)? Your children? Family?

14. What do you want most from life?

15. Will you be able to get it?

16. What was your greatest achievement personally in your life to date?

17. What was the biggest emotional upset or disturbance that ever happened to you—the greatest crisis, the thing you needed the most courage to get through?

18. Who is the person you are closest to? A woman lover? A woman friend? Husband? Boyfriend? Relative?

19. Do you spend much time enjoying yourself by yourself—reading, taking baths, lounging around, listening to music, etc.?

20. If you are "young," how do you feel about getting "older"? Or if you are "older," what is it like to find yourself growing older?

21. What makes you maddest?

22. What is your biggest problem?

23. What is your favorite way to "waste time"?

GROWING UP FEMALE

24. Growing up, were you close to your parents? Your mother? Father? What did you like most and least about them? Did you parents love you? In what way? What did you think of them?

25. What was your relationship with your mother like? Were you close? What is/was she like? What do you think of her? Do/did you like to spend time with her? Were you physically close growing up? Was she affectionate?

26. Were you close to your father? In what way? Was he affectionate? Did he talk to you? Do/did you like him? Fear him? Respect him?

27. What did you learn from your father was the proper attitude toward your mother? What did you learn from your mother was the proper atti-

tude toward your father? Were they affectionate in front of you?

28. Were there ways in which your mother showed you how to be "feminine"—how to act like a girl or a "lady"? Did you and your mother do things your brothers (if any) were not expected (or invited) to do?

29. Were you ever a tomboy? What was it like?

30. Do you remember being warned against becoming a "tomboy," or doing too many "boyish" activities, not acting "ladylike" enough? Can you remember any specific incident?

31. Did your father tell you to be a "good girl"? Your mother? What did they mean?

32. What kinds of things/behavior did your father give you approval for? Your mother?

33. Did you have a pet as a child?

34. Was there great pressure to conform—be like the other girls—in grade school or high school? To dress like the other girls? Be popular?

35. Were you ever refused admission to a club or sorority you wanted to join? How did you feel about it? Did you like high school? What did you like and dislike about it?

36. Did you masturbate as a child? How old were you? Did your parents know?

37. Did your parents discuss menstruation with you?
    Your mother? Your father? Were you prepared for
    it when it started?

38. Was there an age at which you began to want to,
    or to feel pressured to, date boys? How old were
    you? How did you feel about this?

39. What was your mother's attitude when you started
    dating? Your father's? How did you feel? Did you
    discuss with your parents what happened when you
    went out on dates?

40. When was the first time you said, "I love you"?
    Held hands with someone? Kissed? Made out?

41. What was this early relationship like? Did it last
    long? Was it close or distant? Was it pleasurable
    or not? Did you tell your friends about it? How
    did it end?

42. Was it difficult leaving home? Declaring your inde-
    pendence?

43. Were you happiest as a child, a teen-ager, or are
    you happiest now?

44. If you are still living at home with parents or fam-
    ily, what rules are there concerning your sexual
    and dating activities?

45. If you have had a sexual relationship, do your
    parents know? If so, how did they react?

46. Are parents and relatives willing to discuss sex

realistically with you? Friends? Teachers? Is getting information a problem?

FALLING IN LOVE

47. Describe the time you fell the most deeply in love. How did it feel? What was the person like? Did the relationship last? What happened?

48. Did you ever cry yourself to sleep because of problems with someone you loved? Contemplate suicide? Why?

49. What was the happiest you ever were with someone? The closest? When were you the loneliest?

50. Do you/did you like being in love? Is being in love a condition of pleasure or pain? Learning? Enlightenment? Ambivalent feelings? Frustration? Joy?

51. How do your friendships compare with your love relationships? Which are closer? More rewarding? More enduring? Have love relationships followed any particular patterns that you can see?

52. Do you think falling in love is important?

53. What is your favorite fictional love story—the greatest love story you have ever seen or heard? Was it a book or a movie? What was the story about?

54. Have you found what you are looking for in love, or is your greatest love yet to come?

YOUR CURRENT RELATIONSHIP

55. Are you in a relationship now? If so, whom is it
with and how long have you been together? Do you
live together? Do you have children?

56. What is the basis of this relationship? Is it love,
passion, sexual intimacy, economics, daily companionship, or the long-term importance of children and family? Other?

57. What is the best, most rewarding aspect of this
relationship? The worst or most difficult aspect?
Are you happy?

58. Are you "in love" with the person you are with?
Or do you "love" them more than being "in love"
with them? In what way do you love them?

59. Do you love your husband/lover as much as
he/she loves you? More? Does he/she love you
enough, or too much? Does one of you need the
other more? Is one of you more dependent? Is the
way your partner loves you satisfying to you? Do
you feel loved?

60. Do you agree or disagree with the following statement?: "It is quite possible to be in a heavy emotional relationship with someone you are *not* in
love with, or don't love—it's just a kind of famili-
arity or friendship."

61. What is the biggest problem in your current rela-

tionship? How would you like to change the relationship? How could it be better?

62. What do you enjoy doing together most? Talking? Having sex? Being affectionate? Daily life together? Sharing children? Hobbies? Going out? Other? Nothing?

63. Do you like the way he/she treats you? Are you usually treated with respect and affection? Or are you sometimes made to feel silly or childish or stupid? Is he/she usually emotionally supportive when you need it, or frequently challenging?

64. How does he or she act toward you in intimate moments? Does your partner tell you he/she loves you? That you are wonderful or beautiful? That you make him/her want sex with you? Other things? Talk tenderly to you? How do you feel at these times?

65. What is the worst thing your partner has ever done to you?

66. What are the negative things your partner says to you? Most often criticizes about you?

67. Is it easy to talk? About everything? Would you like more intimate talk—about feelings, reactions, and problems?

68. Do you generally know what is going on in the relationship, or do you sometimes feel out of touch and out of control?

69. Does your partner look at pornography? How do you feel about this?

70. What is the most important thing you get out of the relationship?

71. Does the relationship fill your deepest needs for closeness with another person? Or are there some parts of yourself that you can't share? That aren't accepted or understood? How well do you think your husband or lover knows you? Or do you prefer not to share every part of yourself?

72. Is the kind of love you have received/are receiving now the kind of love you would most like to have? Have you seen a type of love in a friend's relationship or in a film or novel that you would like to have? How was that love better than your relationship?

73. Is your lover and your relationship with your lover the center of your life? How important is the relationship to your life? More important than work? Children?

74. What is the best way you have found to make a love relationship work? How did the most successful relationships you have seen/been in work? What were the inner dynamics?

75. If you are married, how many years have you been married? Do you like it? What is the best part of being married? The worst? Before you got married, did you think it would be different than it is?

Do you like or dislike the term "wife"? Do you like using your husband's name (if you do)?

76. What were your reasons for getting married originally? Were they romantic? Social? Economic? Sexual? Would you do it over again? Do you plan to stay married?

77. If you have children, do you like having them? How did you feel when you first knew you were going to have a baby? Did you have to give up some things in order to be married and/or have children? How would your life have been different? What did you gain?

78. Did having children change your relationship with your husband? How?

79. What are the practical arrangements? Who does the dishes? Makes the beds? Does the cooking? Takes care of the children? What is daily life like?

80. How do you share the money? Who controls the money? Do you both work outside the home? Who pays the rent or the mortgage? Buys the groceries? What is your financial arrangement? How do you feel about it? Do you feel it affects the relationship?

81. Do you believe in monogamy? Why or why not? Are you monogamous? Have you had/are you having sex outside of the relationship, or "extramarital" affairs? If so, how many and for how long? What was the reason (if there was one)?

What is/was the effect on you as an individual and on your relationship or marriage? Did/does your partner know about them?

82. What is/was the affair like? Is/was it serious? How did you feel about your lover? What did you, or are you, getting out of it?

83. Has your partner been "faithful" to you? How do you feel about this? Do you want your partner to be monogamous?

84. Have you ever (as a single person), or are you now, going with a married man? What is it like?

85. What part does sex play in your current relationship? Would the relationship end if you did not have sex?

86. What is sex with men or the man you have sex with (if you do) usually like? Do you like sex with him? Do you usually orgasm? During which activity? Does he know how you masturbate? What is the worst thing about sex with him? The best?

87. How often do you like to have sex? Do you think sex is important, or is it overemphasized?

88. Which is your most frequent source of orgasm—masturbation, or sex with a partner? Is there any particular way in which your sex life has changed over the last few years?

89. Does sex with the same partner change—and if so,

for better or worse—over a long period of time?
Does it become boring or more pleasurable?

90. Do you feel a choice has to be made between a
passionate relationship and a more stable relationship? Is there a contradiction between passion and
a long-term relationship? Do the daily details of
living and working at a relationship conflict with
or make impossible feelings of passion? Cool them?

91. Describe the biggest (or most recent) fight you had
with your husband or lover—no matter whether
the fight was over something trivial or important.

92. How do you feel about fighting? What do you
most frequently fight about? Who usually wins (if
anybody)? How do you feel during? After? Can
you function when you are fighting?

93. What does your lover do that makes you the
maddest?

94. How do conflicts or arguments usually get resolved—or at least ended? Who usually says
they're sorry first after a fight? Who usually initiates talking over the problem? Making up?

95. How do you feel about the following statement?:
"You don't try hard enough to find out what is
inside of me."

96. Do you agree or disagree with the following statement?: "Maintaining love over a long period of

time is for me less a case of 'working at it' than being careful not to kill it. Love does not remain over a period of time without much attention."

97. If you are in a very long relationship or marriage, have you found that certain disagreements or conflicts continue to be present over the years, or do old ones gradually get resolved and new ones take their place? Did you argue more or less at any particular periods you can remember? Have you found that the same problems keep cropping back up, even after you have talked about them, or thought you had worked them out? Have you learned to live with them, or do they still bother you?

BEING "SINGLE"

98. Have you ever gone for long periods of time (as an "adult") without a sexual relationship? How did you feel about it? Do you like being "single," or do you prefer to be in an intimate relationship with someone, to be part of a couple?

99. What are the advantages of being "single"? Disadvantages? Do you enjoy/feel comfortable going out alone (to a party, restaurant, shopping, etc.)? Do you ever get the impression people think there is something "wrong with you" when you are not in a relationship? That no one loves you, or that you are unlovable?

100. Do you think of being "single" as a temporary or permanent way of life?

101. What is your sex life like? Do you enjoy "dating"?

102. If you are currently uninterested in a relationship (sexual) with anyone, how does this feel? Do you enjoy periods of celibacy (no sex with a partner)?

103. Is it easy or difficult to find or meet someone you like and are attracted to and have respect for?

104. Do you feel there is pressure to choose between being married and having children, or having a career or full-time job working outside the home? Which is more important—love, family, or career? Which would you give up for the other?

BREAKING UP, OR GETTING A DIVORCE

105. If you have ever broken up with someone who was important in your life, or gotten divorced, what was it like? Were you glad or did you have regrets? Who wanted to break up or get the divorce, you or the other person? Why? How did you feel about it?

106. How did you get over it? How long did it take you?

107. Did your mother or friends encourage you to stay in the relationship when you were having difficulties? Support you in leaving it? Or were they no help at all? Did you tell them about your feelings?

108. What does rejection feel like? Did you ever love someone who didn't love you (or at least not as much)? Did you ever want to marry or live with someone who didn't return your feelings? What did you do? How did you feel?

109. How do you feel if a man is very emotionally dependent on you in a relationship? Loves you more than you love him? Complains that you do not love him enough?

110. Did you ever feel like a "clinging vine"? Feel you were too emotionally dependent? What was it like?

111. Have you ever felt that you were "owned" in a relationship so that you wanted out?

112. When you broke up or divorced, did you feel free or like a failure? Hate the other person? Cry a lot? Talk to friends? Hide from them? Work harder? Feel happier? How did you finally feel about the experience?

113. After breaking up, would you look for a new love to replace the old, or tend to shy away from love altogether for a while?

114. During times of turbulence in your life, like breaking up or getting a divorce, what did you feel was the most permanent, solid thing in your life? Your relationship with your children? Your work? Your parents or relatives? Friends? Yourself?

115. Was there a time at which you gave up on love relationships as not being as important as you once had thought? Decided to give less time and importance to them? Or do you basically think that a rewarding life comes mainly by working through a love relationship and developing it over time?

SPECIAL PROBLEMS IN RELATIONSHIPS WITH MEN

The following are random questions that have been suggested by women. There is no particular order and no attempt to imply any particular point of view. The questions are just a way of opening the subject up for discussion. Answer only the questions you want, or add your own.

116. What do you like best about men? Least? What qualities do you admire in men? Dislike?

117. What do women need from men, if anything? Is there something you get/want from men that you can't get from women? From women that you don't/can't get from men?

118. Do you think men take love and falling in love with a woman seriously? What part does it play in their lives?

119. Were you ever financially dependent on a man you lived with? Was this a problem? How did

you feel about it? Did/does it affect your relationship?

120. How do you think men feel about women working outside the home? If you work, and are married or living with someone, how does he feel about it?

121. Does your husband/lover see you as an equal? Or are there times and ways when he seems to treat you as an inferior? Leave you out of decisions? Acts superior?

122. How do most men you know feel about the women's movement? How does your husband/lover feel about it?

123. Have you ever been deeply hurt by a love relationship? How? What happened?

124. Did you ever enter therapy to try to solve personal problems related to your love relationships? What were they?

125. Did therapy help? What were your conclusions?

126. Did you ever think of killing yourself?

127. If you had one overall grievance about your relationship(s) with the man/men you have loved, what would it be?

128. Do you have a comment on the following statement: "I would like a study of the emotional trips

a woman goes through in a sexual relationship with a man."

129. Do you think you pick the "wrong" men? What kinds of men do you pick?

130. Do love relationships in general make you feel good?

131. Do you ever feel your loved ones are suffocating you? Holding you down?

132. Are you jealous? Of friendships? Career? Other men or women?

133. Did you ever grow to hate a lover? Did you act violently toward them? Scream at them? Hit them?

134. Describe the man you hated the most. Why did you hate him? Did you do anything about it? Did you remain angry or become depressed? Did you tell your friends? How did they react?

135. Is there any way you have hurt a man in the past, for which you are now sorry? Or gotten revenge— for which you were *not* sorry?

136. Did someone you loved deeply ever grow to despise you?

137. Did a lover ever strike you or beat you up? How did you feel?

138. Did you ever have a sense of having to work to

keep someone with you? Keep the relationship together? Did you have a fear of his leaving you? Losing his love? That he would grow tired of you? Do you feel a lover usually becomes less attentive over a period of time? Loves you less?

139. Are you honest with men, or do you find it necessary to manipulate them to get what you want?

140. Do you have a nagging fear of being deserted by your lover or husband? Are you afraid he will stop loving you? Why? Because you are getting older? For reasons you don't understand?

141. Who usually breaks up the relationship first—you or the other person?

142. When someone broke up with you (rejected you first), how did you feel? Ashamed? Disgraced? Did you hide your feelings in front of your friends? Have you ever gone away to hide/recover?

143. Did you have long periods of depression after the breakup with an important lover in your life? Did you think of suicide? How did you manage?

144. When you broke up, did you feel shame because your relationship was not "successful"? Or because he had left you, didn't want or love you anymore? Did you feel used or exploited? Relieved? Free?

145. Are you willing to experience misery if you love someone? Have you ever loved someone who hurt you in spite of what had happened? Can you stop yourself from loving someone?

146. Do you sometimes feel at the mercy of the other person to either accept you or reject you?

147. Does it help to keep them by being beautiful or seductive? To be better than other women in some way?

148. How do you feel about the following quote?: "She was afraid that if she showed a man she loved him, he would consider her inferior and leave her."

149. Have you ever pretended to a man you cared less than you did? That he was less important than he was? Put up a front? Why? How did you feel about it?

150. Do you find you have to employ "a streak of manipulative coldness" to keep your distance, keep things "cool"?

151. Do you often feel you are more loving toward the other person than he is toward you?

152. Do you ever feel you have "unhealthy" needs and cravings for love, or dependency? As one woman put it, "My love has usually been too blind, too desperate." Do you ever feel you have an "excessive" need for affection?

153. Do you feel more insecure and self-doubtful when you are in love?

154. Do women need love more than men do? Do women need affection more than men do?

155. Do you feel as strong as the person you are in a relationship with emotionally? Intellectually?

156. Does loving someone, or being loved, give you greater pleasure?

157. Do you think love is a problem for most women? If so, why?

158. Are you afraid of clinging to a man? Making him feel tied down? Unfree?

159. Does the following quote mean anything to you?: "Scratch *his* love and you'll find *your* fear."

160. What is the closest you have even been/can conceive of being to another person? Do you feel that the individual is always, in the last analysis, alone? Who do you turn to in time of trouble (if anyone)?

FRIENDSHIPS BETWEEN WOMEN

161. What was your most important relationship with a woman in your life?

162. Describe your closest woman friend. What does

she look like? How much time do you spend together? What do you do together? How do you feel after you see her? When you see her? What do you like best about her? Least? Has she helped you through difficult times in your life?

163. Describe the woman you loved the most. Hated the most.

164. Were you close to your mother? Physically? Emotionally? Are you now? What was she like? Did she work outside the home, or was she a full-time mother and "housewife"? What did you think of her? What is she like now, and what do you think of her today?

165. Are you like her?

166. Were there other women in your family you were/are close to, or particularly liked or admired? A grandmother? An aunt? Do/did you have a sister(s)? What was your relationship like? Do/did you like her (or them)?

167. What things about women in general do you admire? Dislike? What do women contribute to society?

168. Do relationships with women tend to have the same dynamics as relationships with men? Is love between women different?

169. How do you feel about this statement?: "My relationships with women are not sexual but are

emotionally more deep and sincere than with most men."

170. Would you like to fall in love with another woman (if you have not)?

171. What do you think of the role of being a mother (whether or not you are a mother)?

172. What do you think of women's liberation? Do you consider yourself a feminist or in favor of the women's movement?

173. Have your feelings about the women's movement and its ideas affected your life? Your relationships with women? With men?

CONCLUSION

174. Looking back, who is the person you have loved most in your life? What is the most you have ever loved someone—man, woman, child, friend, pet, parents, or lover—who was it?

175. Who made you feel the most alive, the most *you*, in your life? The most excited? The most loved? Happiest?

176. How would you define love? Is love the thing you work at in a relationship over a long period of time, or is it the strong feeling you feel for someone right from the beginning, for no known reason?

177. Why did you answer this questionnaire, and how did you feel about it?

178. Was there anything you would like to say but didn't? That you would like to add now?

Thank You!

NOTES

Masturbation

1. Dodson, Betty, "Liberating Masturbation," distributed by Betty Dodson, Box 1933, New York, N.Y. 10001; Eve's Garden, 119 W. 57th St., New York, N.Y. 10019; 1972, p. 18.

Orgasm

1. Sherfey, Mary Jane, *The Nature and Evolution of Female Sexuality* (New York: Vintage Books, 1973), pp. 93–4.

2. Ibid., pp. 104–5.

3. Ibid., p. 112.

4. Ibid., pp. 134–35.

5. Kaplan, Helen Singer, *The New Sex Therapy* (New York: Brunner/Mazel, 1974), p. 31.

6. Sherfey, op. cit., p. 116.

7. Herschberger, Ruth, *Adam's Rib* (New York: Har/Row Books, 1970), p. 72.

8. Brecher, Edward M., *The Sex Researchers* (New York: Signet Books, 1969), pp. 220–21.

9. Kaplan, op. cit., p. 29.

10. Singer, Josephine, and Irving Singer, "Types of Female Orgasm," The Journal of Sex Research, Vol. 8, No. 4, pp. 255–67, November 1972.

11. Brecher, op. cit., pp. 214–15.

Intercourse

1. Brecher, Edward M., *The Sex Researchers* (New York: Signet Books, 1969), p. 156.

2. Kaplan, Helen Singer, *The New Sex Therapy* (New York: Brunner/Mazel, 1974), pp. 340–41.

3. Masters, William, and Virginia Johnson, *Human Sexual Inadequacy* (Boston: Little, Brown and Company, 1970), p. 218.

4. Sherfey, Mary Jane, *The Nature and Evolution of Female Sexuality* (New York: Vintage Books, 1973), p. 80.

5. Ibid., p. 90.

6. Marval, Nancy, "The Case for Feminist Celibacy," New York: The Feminists, 1971 (pamphlet).

7. Kinsey, Alfred C., et al., *Sexual Behavior in the Human Female* (New York: Pocket Books, 1965), p. 322.

8. Marval, op. cit.

9. Fisher, Seymour, *Understanding the Female Orgasm* (New York: Bantam Books, 1973), pp. 113–14.

10. Ibid., pp. 213–14.

11. Ibid., pp. 106–107.

12. Ibid., pp. 219–20.

13. Sherfey, op. cit., pp. 27–28.

14. Fisher, op. cit., p. 238.

15. Koedt, Ann, *The Myth of the Vaginal Orgasm* (Boston: New England Free Press, 1970).

16. Masters, William, and Virginia Johnson, *Human Sexual Response* (Boston: Little, Brown and Company, 1966), p. 59.

17. Sherfey, op. cit., p. 177.

18. Ibid., p. 111.

19. Shulman, Alix, "Organs and Orgasms," *Women in Sexist Society: Studies in Power and Powerlessness,* ed. by Vivian Gornick and Barbara K. Moran (New York: Signet Books, 1972), p. 296.

20. Sherfey, op. cit., p. 122.

Clitoral Stimulation

1. Sherfey, Mary Jane, *The Nature and Evolution of Female Sexuality* (New York: Vintage Books, 1973), p. 168.

Lesbianism

Kinsey, et al., *Sexual Behavior in the Human*